we are on a funeral march. We accept divine forgiveness but deny it to everybody else, from Communists to homosexuals to criminals to the person in the pew next to us.

"We think the world will come beating a path to our doors because we look so... What? Pious? Holy? Sanctimonious? There's a path to our doors all right, but that's because many with integrity are heading in the opposite direction."

"Andy," Gary said, "you sound so cynical! What's happening to you?"

* * * * *

When Andy Norton joins an evangelism team headed for West Berlin during the height of the Vietnam War, he thinks he has all the answers. Little does he realize the experience will become a crucible that forces him to re-evaluate virtually everything he believes. In the spirit of the best coming-of-age tales, *Chrysalis Crucible* takes Andy—and the reader—on a journey of discovery, transformation, and rebirth.

"An absorbing and passionately written novel… The book is a challenge to the evangelical community and should be read by them."

—Clark Pinnock, Professor Emeritus of Systematic Theology at McMaster Divinity College and author of *Most Moved Mover: A Theology of God's Openness*

"The *Colloquies of Erasmus* spoke the depth and breadth of the Christian prophetic vision to his time. Wayne Northey's novel, threaded together like an Erasminian Colloquy, does much the same thing for the Evangelical ethos today."

—Ron Dart, Professor of Religious Studies, Philosophy, and Political Science at University College of the Fraser Valley and author of *The Red Tory Tradition: Ancient Roots, New Routes*

"The read dances to and fro on the journey toward 'pure heart' and 'true faith.' What do love of God, love of neighbor, and love of enemy mean for belief and behavior in the context of unconscionable killing and suffering inflicted by Americans—even Christians—in WWII and Vietnam? Stock Evangelical arguments, with opposing perspectives, are there to hear and see. What really is the gospel we proclaim?"

—Willard Swartley, Professor Emeritus of New Testament at Associated Mennonite Biblical Seminary and author of *Covenant of Peace: The Missing Peace in New Testament Theology and Ethics.*

CHRYSALIS CRUCIBLE

A NOVEL

WAYNE NORTHEY

FRESH WIND PRESS

Copyright © 2007 by Wayne Northey. All rights reserved.

All rights reserved, including the right to reproduce this book or portions thereof in any form whatsoever. For information, contact Fresh Wind Press at freshwind@shaw.ca.

Printed in Canada by D.W. Friesen and Sons Ltd.

Cover image and design: Photoshop by Brad Jersak from two photo images:

http://commons.wikimedia.org/wiki/Image:Streichholz.jpg
http://en.wikipedia.org/wiki/Image:Chrysalis_by_Kaliyoda.jpg

Library and Archives Canada Cataloguing in Publication
Northey, Wayne, 1948-
Chrysalis crucible / Wayne Northey.
ISBN 978-0-9780174-5-3
I. Title.
PS8627.O79C47 2007   C813'.6   C2007-901532-8

Fresh Wind Press
2170 Maywood Ct.
Abbotsford, BC, Canada V2S 4Z1
freshwind@shaw.ca

For Joe and Tom who know

I want to see what happens in that chrysalis. It's the only part of the transformation to which I'm not privy. I can watch the caterpillar chomp on milkweed. I can watch it shed its outer layers of skin. I can watch it weave a connection to a flat surface and hang in a "J," waiting to change. I can even watch the caterpillar begin to shed that last layer and become a chrysalis. But then... I can no longer see anything. I wait. The most amazing transformations are happening at that point in the process. What was once a caterpillar mouth with jaws and "teeth" in the chrysalis becomes a butterfly's tongue, no chewing leaves, only an apparatus for sucking nectar from flowers. Legs turn to wings. Thick and pudgy turns into light and free. But in the meantime, from the outside all there is to see is an emerald green sack dotted with shimmering gold "buttons." No movement. No changes. I have no window to peek in. No matter how long I stare, or how many different angles I look from, or how many different people I get to check the chrysalis... I can see nothing happening. Even the 12 days of a caterpillar melting in a chrysalis crucible are too sacred for us to know.

I wait.

From the Blog, "Promise of Paradox" by Alethea, http://www.promiseofparadox.blogspot.com, *Sacred Silence,* Tuesday, September 05, 2006.

Dear Professor Norton:

Well, do you have all the answers yet?

Strange to be writing to a future, imagined self twice my age—let's say turning 50! Like a relative I've never met. Okay, this presumes that you actually survived that long!

I like that verse in Proverbs 16:9, "A man's heart deviseth his way: but the LORD directeth his steps." Man proposes. God disposes. Man denkt. Gott lenkt. *I wonder how many languages that proverb is in? A kind of Christian fatalism when you think of it. Only, as Uncle Joe keeps saying, God makes no mistakes. Just men do. So, in spite of God's "disposing," who knows where you are at 50 except you?*

I hope you enjoy looking back, as much as I like the anticipation of this exercise I hope to keep up. It seems appropriate to have begun this correspondence with my future self while on the verge of the first major transition in my life.

For as you well know, your previous self is about to embark upon a two-year short-term missionary experience in West Berlin, beginning with six months of advance training. You know it well, because you will have been shaped by it. Will the memories still be vivid twenty-five years later or will they have receded along with that hairline? I'm willing to bet on the contrary that this experience will be a kind of watershed or at least significantly transformative.

Notice I have written "Professor." I can well imagine that you taught high school a few years then went for your Ph.D. in something—likely literature or languages-related. That's sure a break from the norm at Carriage Street Gospel Chapel. Good on you. And you have had an interesting career, I'm sure. Have you navigated the "publish or perish" syndrome? Are you still in the faith? I'm sure you are, if I know you at all…

There's so much else to catch up on but I must run. Take care. Don't worry about writing. I'll keep you posted…

Sincerely,

Andy

1

Lorraine Takahashi was what Andy's high school friend Chris would call a "stunner." It was an original, used only by him and Andy. Andy found it worked for an elite few girls he had met. Andy himself possessed a tall lithe frame and sturdy looks.

Lorraine was one of only two girls with whom Andy had ever pursued more than a platonic relationship. The first was not a stunner. Lorraine decidedly was.

She was a psychology major, one year behind Andy when he first met her at Inter-Varsity. A Canadian-born Japanese, she was gorgeous in an understated way. She wore mostly unremarkable clothes and rarely wore make-up. That didn't matter. She was… simply stunning. Beauty may be in the "eye of the beholder," but in this case, it was the "bull's eye."

Andy had begun his fourth year with a firm, almost penitent, resolve to steer clear of girls after initiating a break-up with a girlfriend in his third year. But in his fourth year, he had plugged into Inter-Varsity Christian Fellowship for the first time, and there she was...

Through the first semester, he watched her longingly from afar. In the New Year, she and Andy served together on the Outreach Committee. He began looking for opportunities to be alone with her: offering her rides home in his dad's car after meetings, volunteering on the same special projects, and so on. All of this in spite of himself. With no apparent reciprocation. And with virtually no success. He gathered that there had been some other guy in the recent past. (Surprise!) But he was fading, so Andy perceived, thank the good Lord. The intense yearning built to near crescendo over the year. Yet, by year's end, he had not talked to her alone for any sustained time.

After thinking he'd never see her again, at the last minute she joined an IVCF-related Christian commune forming for part of the summer in Kitchener. Andy had already reached a similar decision and was euphoric when he heard the news. He doubted she knew of his secret infatuation, so he formed no illusions.

They were only into the second week of the commune experiment when there were some plumbing problems at the expansive rented house. The plumbing crisis was perhaps premonition of not a few plugged relationships yet to develop that summer. A ditch had been partially dug around one side of the yard. Right after supper, Andy went out to investigate. Moments later, the screen door swung open, and there she was coming toward him.

Andy's mind churned furiously as he nonchalantly (he hoped) said hello.

"I thought I'd look at the scar too," Lorraine said. "What are they doing, Andy?"

Ask Andy about plumbing? Or anything else mechanical?

"Apparently the 'snake' they use to clean out the… um… Guck in the toilet just didn't cut through the… um the…"

"Shit, Andy! Go ahead, you can say it!" Lorraine supplied mockingly.

"Wash your mouth out with soap and water!" Andy shot back, smiling. Where did that come from? Why was he suddenly so at ease?

He looked at her up close and gulped. She had changed into more casual clothes since her job searching that day. A tight white T-shirt accentuated her full bosom. Denims flaring into bell-bottoms completed the pose. Could anyone look more…? Words failed.

"Did your mom do that?" She asked.

"Uh, what Lorraine?" He racked his brains for the antecedent.

"Wash your mouth out with soap."

"Oh! No. Never had to. But my sister got it once. Just once!"

Andy turned to look back at the ditch. His train of thought kept derailing. She'd either put on more perfume or an earlier application remained potent. What had they been talking about? Ah yes… ummm… He couldn't even say the word to himself.

"So," Andy soldiered on, "they suspected a broken pipe or something, as Jim explained to me. They'll finish everything tomorrow." He hoped she wouldn't ask for anything more technical than that. He'd just shot his entire wad.

He waited. So did she.

Crows shrieked in the backyard chestnut tree. A kid next door screamed, "You're it!" A squirrel chattered furiously, possibly at those same kids playing tag. Then the whole world grew silent.

He was on a cliff of dizzying heights now. He had to jump or perish. "Lorraine," he began, "*Lawrence of Arabia* is showing right now. If I were to ask you to go see it sometime, would you consider it? It's on for a couple of weeks apparently. You may have seen it before. And I can go with someone else. Jim, for instance, really wants to see it..."

His life played out before him as he waited for her to answer.

"I'd love to, Andy. It's likely too late this evening. How about tomorrow night?" Her smile was pure enchantment.

Had it really been just that easy? He pinched

himself on the way back inside.

The next night, they walked the several blocks to the theatre. They cut through Victoria Park, always peaceful and beautiful on a warm summer evening. Older ornate houses, meticulously kept lawns, and towering trees presented agreeably in all directions. Andy offered to carry Lorraine's jacket. ("Because of the air conditioning," she explained.) A gaggle of geese scurried into the huge pond people skated on in winter. Majestic white swans floated effortlessly. Cumulus clouds billowed. The sun still shone brightly. Squirrels and pigeons abounded, beneficiaries of many willing feeders.

Andy studiously kept his hands in his pockets, even though carrying Lorraine's jacket. How could he break the ice as they set out in silence?

"Years ago, we used to have a whole family of squirrels we taught to feed from us," he began. "Then one day, my brother actually got one to come through the back door into the kitchen. Before the summer was over, we had all of them actually coming to get peanuts from us through the kitchen, down the hall, all the way to the couch in our living room. It was quite amazing that these creatures would trust us enough to come right into our house repeatedly.

"I wonder sometimes how we build trust with people. One simple thing learned from the squirrels: Never betray it. Another: Have something they want, then give it freely."

Silence.

He continued: "We never had a crop of peanuts in our yard from that summer. Not for trying by those squirrels. Dad dug them up by accident in the garden several times. And we found them tucked under grass tufts, fallen bark, you name it."

CHRYSALIS CRUCIBLE 13

"Andy," Lorraine said, "I'm glad we're doing this. I was so shocked to hear you were staying at the commune, too. I wondered what kind of summer I was going to have... Whatever happened to your thoughts of working in London at Kellogg's?"

She remembered? She had paid him some attention after all?

"My uncle works there, and he got me to put in an application. So far, no bites," Andy replied. "But I'm pretty committed to staying here for the summer, *now*..."

The intonation came from nowhere.

"Today I got a phone call from St. Matthew's Parish. They're starting a summer Day Camp in two weeks and still need workers. Someone at IVCF had told them I'd worked the last several summers as a camp counsellor. They have some government grants, so the pay is not that bad. It lasts until the last week of August. Interested?"

He barely hoped.

"Are you?" Lorraine asked.

"I said I'd drop by to pick up an application form tomorrow. One for you, too?"

"Yes. One for me, too, Andy," she said as she brushed against him lightly. He caught another scent of her delectable perfume.

"So, what did you think?" Andy asked upon rejoining her in the lobby after the film. He had just returned from the bathroom. On the way over, he saw some guys looking her over. She's mine tonight; he almost swaggered, and then chided himself immediately.

"Awfully violent, Andy! But I liked it. Shows some really interesting history I knew nothing about. Did the British ever live up to Lawrence's ideals?"

"Is the pope Protestant?" Andy heard himself say.

"I read a long review about the historical background. The British weren't very nice in the end. Suffice it to say. What empire ever is?"

The evening was still quite warm, though Lorraine kept her jacket on. The streetlights exuded a soft glow as they headed home. Once away from the theatre, there was virtually no traffic. Horns honked in the distance. Leaves stirred gently. The moon, almost full, was rising. Andy's hands were not in his pockets.

Andy continued: "But that's the stuff of history. Really. I remember once my second year French professor said 'Civilization, in fact, *has never been!*' To quote Mahatma Gandhi's answer to the question, 'What do you think of Western civilization?' he said, 'I think it would be a great idea.' Or something like that."

"What do you suppose he meant, exactly?" Lorraine sounded intrigued.

"I guess every empire but Christ's gives way to greed and violence in the end," Andy said. He was surprised at this observation. Maybe his French prof's numerous digressions had worked the ground more than he realized. "My prof even called the United States an expansionist empire like the Soviets and warned that Nixon's election would be a move toward fascism, which he claimed was a mirror image of Communism." Andy had always been fairly clueless, even less interested, about world events, but some of this was coming back.

They strolled a while in silence.

As they went to cross a street, a car seemed to come out of nowhere. Instinctively, Andy grabbed Lorraine's hand and pulled her back.

"Trying to get us killed?," he asked in mock remonstrance. They proceeded across the street, hands still clasped.

Then suddenly, self-consciously, "I never asked..."

"Yes," came the dreamy reply. "I like that you ask."

The moon shimmered off Victoria Park pond now. There seemed to be no one around as they cut across toward 101 David Street.

"Andy," Lorraine spoke suddenly, "I love staring at the moon. Can we sit and watch it for a while?"

Did the moon brighten noticeably?

A breeze ruffled the water. She snuggled close. "Aren't you cold, Andy?"

"Not anymore," he said boldly. He moved his arm to scratch his leg.

"Yes," she answered again.

His arm slid around her shoulder.

"Andy," Lorraine spoke softly after several minutes' silence, "don't you wish the whole world could be like this and stay that way? Everything so deliciously peaceful you can taste it. I love it! I just wish..." The thought hung fire.

Andy had no idea what to say, afraid to break the spell with words. Her comments could remain rhetorical.

A man out walking his dog finally interrupted their reverie. The playful Sheltie ran right up to them before the owner knew anyone was there.

"I'm sorry, I had no idea," he said as he chased the canine to their park bench. "C'mon Mikki," he called, and the dog bolted away again.

"Well," Andy said, "two nights ago I'd never in my wildest dreams..."

"Me neither, Andy. Let's just say you weren't the only one 'noticing' last year..."

Andy was blown away. "Did you?"

"No, I had no idea you would be in Kitchener this

summer, let alone join this commune. I thought with luck I might bump into you sometime, that's all…"

He was staring into her eyes. She reciprocated.

"Yes," she answered once more. They kissed silently.

"Wow!" was all the vocabulary Andy could muster as they climbed the porch stairs at last. Then, "Thank you."

"*Wow!*" was all Andy entered into his diary later that night. Except to add: "*More later*."

"How was the movie, you guys?" Jim greeted them gleefully as they entered the house. "You'll take me the next time, Andy—though I grant I'm a poor second choice!" His countenance laughed. Jim was married and acted as commune leader.

"Care to come upstairs for some cookies and coffee to discuss it?" he asked. Andy looked at Lorraine, and they agreed.

They entered Jim and Marcia's apartment to strains of the *Love Story* theme so popular that year. Who orchestrates this stuff? Andy wondered.

Later that night, Andy could not get the song out of his head.

2

It turned out Lorraine had also been a counsellor for two summers at a Baptist camp near Toronto. She proved to be a talented pianist as well, constantly surprising Andy with her abilities. The camp board was equally impressed and asked her to co-direct the camp with Andy. He could never have planned something so perfect. And the pay, for university students, was not all that bad.

Needless to say, Andy's relationship with Lorraine took off. So much so that a few days later, Jim suggested very gently that they allot a prescribed amount of time with each other and stick to it. He said they should do this not only for their own sakes but also for others at the commune who were observing. There was more, Andy sensed, but Jim did not say.

Walking home from the Anglican church with Lorraine the following week, Andy felt emboldened to suggest a "one-kiss-a-night" policy. From previous experience, he wanted to savour this relationship, not swamp it.

"I want to get to know you, Lorraine, for all the wonderful *you,* you are!" he said as they waited for a stoplight to turn green. He added recklessly, "But I don't mean in the *biblical* way... Yet! So I won't be asking for any more 'yeses,' I think you agree?" He felt his face tingle. Where had that come? She certainly elicited boldness.

The light changed, and they started across. "Yes," Lorraine answered. Nothing more. Her purposeful irony was not lost on Andy. But what else was her face saying? He looked intently, nearly tripping on the curb as he did so. Then she added: "No Dustin Hoffman stunts either, Andy," which was utterly lost on him. He said as much.

"I'll remind you after *Little Big Man*, or maybe you'll remember yourself," was all she'd say.

Andy told his parents he would not be attending their home assembly on Sundays. He would attend the Anglican church that was running the day camp instead. He knew they would not be pleased. After all, brethren followed the "New Testament pattern." Some of the first brethren in mid-1800s Plymouth, England were disgruntled Anglican priests who had left the "dead formalism" of Anglicanism to join this new exciting "restorationist" movement of God's Spirit. Why would Andy go back to the dead formalism?

He was polite but firm, citing practical considerations such as the lack of good bus service on Sundays and the fact that he didn't own a car.

When he found out his sister Susan was coming home the last weekend of July—in part to see the commune "and your new girl," she said—Andy decided he would bring Lorraine along to meet the family. Susan would stay at their commune Saturday night then drive them all to Carriage Street Gospel Chapel the next morning.

Susan, a recently employed nurse at the Toronto General Hospital, worked until early evening. She barely made it in time to watch *Little Big Man* with them. She'd raved about it after seeing it in Toronto and suggested watching it again with them when Andy had asked for ideas on what to do. This was no small step for Andy. The first movie he'd ever seen was *The Sound of Music*, only in the past year, and that with a group of Christian friends. Cinema was "of the devil" in brethren circles. Though Billy Graham's Christian movies were exceptions…

"You must be Susan from Andy's description," Lorraine said. She was sitting on the front porch as Susan roared up in her used yellow Mustang, for which she could barely maintain the payments. She was late, and Andy was impatient. He had just stepped inside but came back out as soon as he heard the car.

Susan, two years Andy's senior, was much taller than her mom, over whom Andy towered. Andy would never think of her as a "stunner" (He was her brother!) but for years, the guys had called her a real "looker." That's about all they got, a look, at least all through high school.

Susan had auburn hair, cheekbones that accentuated playful brown eyes, and a trim figure maintained through regular athletics. She was the family jock. She especially shone at racket sports. She played circles around Andy in tennis and badminton, which used to bug him. Whenever Andy thought of her, he thought of fun. Susan loved having fun.

"And you're *definitely* Lorraine!" Susan responded. "I know *that* from Andy's description, too. Though he hardly mentioned you were Oriental," she added impishly. Lorraine did not blush, though Andy did. Both girls saw it and laughed.

"My brother always claimed he had a good eye," Susan said gaily. "But I thought he meant in target practice."

"So you're suggesting that Andy was stalking me, like big game!" Lorraine spoke with an affected Japanese accent, something she could summon on command. "For how long?" She was so quick-witted, too. Then Andy thought he saw a fleeting facial shadow.

"C'mon the two of you!" It was Andy's turn to display feigned hurt. "Besides, if we don't get going, we'll miss the previews. I like those, too. And we're walking, Susie Q. Let's go!"

The movie was quite violent once again with what looked like very realistic blood and gore in the shooting scenes. For Andy, the film's "raw" sex scenes were also not a little shocking. Then he remembered Lorraine's comment. No Dustin Hoffman stunts indeed, Lorraine, we're trying to be Christian here! He caught himself. Why in this context did that suddenly seem a tad judgmental?

"Doesn't the violence bug you, Susan?" Andy asked. They were at *The Merry Malt* ice cream parlour, which was adjacent to the theatre. It was Susan's treat. She and Lorraine had been chatting up Toronto for some time. Susan had landed a job there about eight months prior and was still on her honeymoon with the city. Lorraine was second generation Torontonian and knew the city well. Andy was gratified and not surprised they were hitting it off. Both had similar mettle. Maybe that's why I like Lorraine, he thought…

Finally, they said something about Dustin Hoffman in another role, which allowed Andy to manoeuvre the conversation back to *Little Big Man.* He wondered whether—hoped—Lorraine would say something again.

"Not really, Andy. It's part of life, and fitted naturally into the movie," came Susan's reply. She looked at Lorraine for affirmation. There was none. Lorraine may have missed the cue.

"Well, just don't mention to Mom and Dad that we saw it. Mom can hardly handle swearing, okay Susan?"

CHRYSALIS CRUCIBLE 21

Andy knew Susan did not mind shocking her parents.

Lorraine still made no comment.

Their time together went quickly. "Oh my gosh!" Susan exclaimed suddenly. "It's past eleven o' clock! If I don't get some sleep now, I will fall asleep you know where. Even worse than swearing would be snoring during morning meeting.

"Church and me are a sore point with Mom and Dad right now as it is. Though I must say, sitting through two church services tomorrow is going to be no small shock to my system. But I guess we're into keeping Mom and Dad happy, aren't we?" She spoke with not a little chagrin.

The next morning, they barely left in time. Arriving late for service was another major offence. Susan commented, "Better I get a speeding ticket than make it late to Breaking of Bread. There are so many 'dos' and 'don'ts' around church." Then self-consciously, "Lorraine, Mom and Dad are truly wonderful, don't get me wrong. They're just picky about some things, I guess. So be on your best behaviour."

Was that a nervous laugh, Andy wondered as Susan ran a yellow light? It was almost as if she were going to her first job interview.

Thankfully, Susan had brought a second head covering for Lorraine. Lorraine had been briefed about the need to "cover up," as though her gorgeous jet-black hair on its own was indecent at church. They also warned her she would be grilled at the front door about her faith. One didn't just show up unannounced at the most sacred hour of the brethren week. It was a privilege of immense proportions. If someone was visiting, there was due protocol of (ideally) a letter of commendation to present from one's home fellowship.

But since that practice was unknown in other traditions (That being the very point, his cousins' grandpa would say disdainfully, "They are *mere traditions of men!*"), there was some allowance, though little margin, for visitors.

The church building was hardly recognizable as such. It was plain on the outside, simple brick, no slanting roof and spire. This was intentional. "Reminds me of our doctor's office," Lorraine whispered to Andy as they went up the steps.

Andy's dad was greeting at the front door. "Dad, I'd like to introduce Lorraine *Takahashi* to you," Andy said, then immediately spelled the name.

Andy's dad was not a big man, over six inches shorter than Andy and an inch ("and a half," his mom would add sometimes) shorter than his wife, who was a tall woman. Mr. Norton possessed a handsome face and a ruddy complexion that only deepened throughout the summer from long hours in the garden. His nostrils flared as he jotted down her name. Andy had neglected to mention Lorraine's surname or ethnicity to him before.

Andy could tell this had been a mistake. In that initial wordless response, his dad had taken, if not given, offence. But what? She was appropriately dressed, sported the requisite head covering, held out her hand demurely. "Very pleased to meet you, sir," was all she said with a (knock-out) smile.

Susan stepped up and gave her dad a hug and kiss. Diversion tactic, whatever else. Thank you, sis!

How was Lorraine handling it?

Andy's mind exploded like a Fourth of July sky. As he moved down the aisle with Lorraine, she whispered, "Andy, your dad didn't ask me a thing about my faith journey like you warned me. Do we have to go back?"

CHRYSALIS CRUCIBLE

"No, he knew that from me already, and I guess it was enough," Andy replied, covering up. He'd only told his dad she was a Christian he'd met at IVCF. Andy was at a loss. His dad's behaviour was so inexplicable. Unless… Surely not.

The inside of the church was as unadorned as women were supposed to be. Several matching plaques on the wall sported scriptures, such as: "For whosoever shall call upon the name of the Lord shall be saved," "Behold, now is the day of salvation," and "But of the times and the seasons, brethren, ye have no need that I write unto you. For yourselves know perfectly that the day of the Lord so cometh as a thief in the night," all with chapter and verse. The front of the chapel boldly if unimaginatively declared in Gothic script, "WE PREACH JESUS CHRIST CRUCIFIED, RISEN, AND COMING AGAIN. MIGHTY TO SAVE; ABLE TO KEEP."

There was a pulpit, an organ to the right, piano on the left (all deliberately silent in the Morning Meeting). A baptismal tank was built into the front wall with Sunday school rooms beyond.

They sat down directly behind Andy's mom. She turned, smiled, and held out a hand to Lorraine. It was quite a concession for her, Andy realized, who was so religiously "collected" before the service began, head bowed and covered. He watched for a reaction, his antennae now probing everything. Her face remained inscrutable. Years of practice at these services, he knew.

His mom also had a very pretty face. One of her first jobs as a teenager was sitting as a live model in a department store window. The manager had hired her on the spot. She worked there until her strict Baptist dad heard about it and forced her to quit the next day.

Andy's Uncle Joe told him that story. Thirty years later she still turned heads, though she never wore a hint of make-up. When he was young, Andy believed she had been a movie star—until she had gotten saved, of course.

Susan followed Andy after he had directed Lorraine to sit down first. "Andy, didn't dad fly missions over Japan with the RCAF?" Susan whispered very quietly into his ear. "Wow, Susan. Wow!" Andy whispered back. Then again, "Wow!"

"And I'd like to welcome back our daughter, Susan, and Andy's friend Lorraine *Takahashi*, if I pronounced that right," his dad said, part of the ritual to get the meeting underway. What was not right was nothing more was said about her. Was Andy alone holding his breath?

Whatever Lorraine, his sister, mom and dad got out of the service, Andy was far, far away, sometimes over the skies of 1940s Japan. His dad had never talked about the War years. Not once. So maybe his sister was wrong. Wasn't Japan an American theatre of war? If so, why would the RCAF fly there? His dad had not been a pilot. He read instruments or something. He knew that much from his mom, who told him so when he was doing a school project on the War.

Andy knew the Japanese had done some pretty horrific things in the War. He also knew the Canadian government had forcefully relocated lots of Japanese living on the West Coast, which was not so nice either.

His mind turned to Lorraine. How had she taken this (to him) diplomatic disaster of first encounter of his parents, mediated in a church setting? It would have been better to have just taken her over one night for a visit. Then again, what if his dad had been even more embarrassing in private? At least this service provided a buffer.

"Please turn in your hymnals to…"

Andy obeyed mechanically. Likewise, he opened his Bible several times when asked, bowed in prayer, turned to more hymns, even tried singing them—but with no zest. All the time trying to help Lorraine get through the service.

The moment things reverted to silence, which was mercifully often in brethren worship, his mind revisited the debacle. At one point, he found himself seething with anger. In church of all places! But there it was. The anger tasted good, sweeter, he had to admit, than the bread or wine that morning…

Andy felt mad at the world for its enormous prejudices and wars. It wasn't his fault he'd fallen for a Japanese girl whose kin his dad could have bombed during the War. So why this apparent visitation of the "sins of the fathers"?

He retraced all the coaching he and Susan had done for Lorraine the night before. He remembered one of his sister's harsh warnings: "Whatever you do, Lorraine, don't convert to brethrenism the way my mom did from your same faith group, the Baptists! Mom looks on this as her 'new freedom.' We kids—Right Andy?—felt it was more like *bondage*…"

She went on to describe the rules laid on to the rules already accepted by the Baptists and other fundamentalists about no smoking, no drinking, no swearing, no going to movies, no playing cards. "In addition, there is," her voice reached a crescendo, "no talking in church (for women), no uncovered hair for us either, no truck with Christians of other stripes, and certainly no concourse with the world; in sum, no tolerance." She paused a moment, then added: "Capping it all, there was one Supreme Rule of brethrenism: NO FUN!" Then she lightened up, smiling wryly, "But they did allow sex, if only 'the missionary position,' or by now, plain and simple, they would have to face the inevitable: No brethren! Right, Andy?"

The kitchen clock had a loud tick to it. Andy heard several seconds click by…

He turned to Lorraine and forced a smile. "My sister is a bit battle-scarred from church, I'm afraid. I don't quite see it that way. Then again, she came first and maybe blunted a few edges, at least with Mom and Dad." He wondered again at her bitterness. Otherwise, she seemed so carefree.

He rehashed Lorraine's response: "Strange that something Christians talk about all the time in terms of freedom should turn out to be such a terrible burden!" Andy didn't feel up to responding, though his mind tried. He just turned off the ignition.

Tabula rasa. That was the safest state for his overheated mind at present. What to do though after the engine cooled down? Abandon the vehicle altogether? What would that mean? Then he realized his mind was still sputtering, like those engines that run on even after turned off. Please!

Brother Swanson gave out a closing hymn. Had things really gone by so quickly? Relief again. But this wasn't exactly how morning worship was supposed to be. Self-recrimination. A quick prayer for forgiveness.

Roast beef dinner at the Norton's was about as revered a tradition as the Morning Meeting itself. His favourite meat, his favourite (done-around-the-roast) potatoes, his favourite vegetable (corn), his favourite dessert (apple pie), and his favourite anticipation afterwards: the proverbial Sunday afternoon nap. He'd forego that last this time, however. His mind gladly turned aside to such anticipation.

Susan broke the ice. She had noticed, she indicated, one change to the front of the church—new curtains on the baptismal tank—and immediately set to talking about them. How long had they taken to decide? What colours were considered? Why did they choose the ones they did? Who did the work?

They survived the ordeal! By mid-afternoon, with naps beckoning his parents, Andy, Susan, and Lorraine took their leave. Susan had Monday off and had promised to help her mom with some canning. So she'd be back after the evening service, she'd said emphatically, to spend the night.

"Well, Lorraine, you did it!" Susan said once they had pulled out of the driveway.

"Did what?" Lorraine asked.

"Created a great impression on Mom and Dad. No small feat. I know, I've been trying for years." Susan's laugh, which accompanied the comment, did not quite come off.

"I really liked them both, I can honestly say," Lorraine responded. "I noticed your dad listening intently when I mentioned part of our family was originally from Tokyo. He seemed a little familiar with that part of the world. Has he traveled there?"

"Apparently," was all Andy said. "We don't know much about Dad's past," he added. Susan was silent.

They spent the rest of the afternoon driving around old haunts: the elementary and high schools Susan and Andy attended, Susan's nursing school, and the university. It was all great reminiscing. In many ways, they'd had an idyllic childhood, both Susan and Andy expressed. Lorraine seemed near tears in response. Andy was nonplussed.

No one had felt like eating supper, so they ended up in the park sipping tea and just talking until it was time for Susan to leave. She seemed loath to go. "I've had such a good day," she repeated once more as she stepped into her car.

Lorraine and Andy had some preparation to do for camp the next day. About an hour later, they emerged for their nightly walk. Victoria Park had become a familiar site by then. They went almost immediately to their favourite bench.

The moon was advancing toward full, though still more crescent than orb. They wore jackets since the air was a touch cool. The bench was off the main pathway, right at water's edge. People rarely "happened" by them. Just dogs. That entire summer, no one was ever at "their spot" when they wanted it.

"Andy," Lorraine began, "I need to tell you more about myself. To begin with, have you wondered why I don't offer to take you to meet my mom and dad?" Her voice cracked, and suddenly, she was engulfed in tears.

Andy was at a loss.

3

The next morning, waking up was as intolerable for Andy as sleep had been the night before.

"The morning after," indeed, but there had not been delirious joy the night before. Her story invaded every self-conscious moment like shards of glass. It was an all-pervasive London smog. Where had he heard, "If something's too good to be true, it likely is"? There had not even been a perfunctory peck from him as they separated to their rooms. How could there have been? He just wanted to scream and scream, or retch and retch, or… His mind revolted in pure disgust. And she said she'd spared him most of the details!

Visit her parents? I guess not. Her dad, God bless those Baptist deacons, had started the touching when she was about five. Sometimes right after church when she'd go down for a nap. But usually at night when he'd go in to settle her. She was sure her mom and brothers knew nothing about it for years. Then there was denial.

She had tried to make herself invulnerable. To shield herself. Even to crawl into a crack in the wall beside her bed, she imagined, whenever he'd come in. It was their "special secret," he'd say. No one ever need know. It only stopped when she came to Kitchener to study. At last!

"Intercourse is dirty and sin," he'd say. But everything else was fair game. Afterwards she'd wash and wash her hands like they had been rummaging through putrid garbage.

Relationship with a guy? Revolting. When she hit puberty, he began to label her "dirty."

"He said no boy would ever… would ever…" she couldn't complete the sentence at first. "He said," sonorous sobs, "he said no boy would ever… want me… when he found out… the things I did… he made me do!" She screamed at the end.

Andy had no categories for this. He was at a complete loss. Where was this in the Bible? What would Uncle Joe have said? What would he have done? What might Francis Schaeffer have advised? How would Jim have responded? Above all, he had wished his sister, that great fun-loving, maddening cynic, could have been there. She'd have known what to do. Instead, he had been it. The man of the hour. Ha! The Knight in Shining Armour…

At last, the thought came: What would Jesus do? He put his arm around her.

How long could anyone sob? How many tears do our bodies contain? He held on. He did not know what else to do…

On their way to camp that morning, Andy said, "Lorraine, I just need some space, I…" He had no more words. The walk home was also silent. Andy did not make eye contact the whole day. Even some of the kids noticed.

He excused himself before the communal supper, saying he was not hungry, and went out for a long walk.

There was a message for him to call his sister when he returned. Lorraine was nowhere to be seen. Just as well. He was in an angry reckless mood. Susan's message read, "Urgent."

His sister's voice began, "Andy, I'll be blunt. I found out from Mom that Dad is really upset about you and Lorraine. He said nothing at suppertime, but loads to Mom before I got there. Mom kept saying to me, 'It'd be their kids, Susan. Can you imagine?'

"But Dad was harsher. The RCAF didn't bomb Japan, but they did bomb Germany. Dad was part of the Dresden bombing, Mom told me, a month before they hit Tokyo. At the time, they used to chant, 'The only good Nazi is a dead one. The only good Jap is a fried one. A roasted Wop is the pope's nose,' or something like that. You get the idea. Germans, Japanese, and Italians were viciously hated.

"Then Mom said, 'At least if she was an Italian or German it wouldn't show…' Apparently Mrs. Swanson had a few words for Mom on the phone yesterday, though Mom didn't say, exactly what.

"A question, Andy: Do any Japanese families live in Kitchener? I honestly have to admit I don't know of any. I told Mom this was a different world. I know we had a few Orientals in nursing. And I work with quite a few foreigners right here at the Toronto General."

Andy was listening more intently than she knew.

"I guess the short of it," she summed up, "is you've got two very upset parents. Sheesh, Andy, I thought *I* was the troublemaker!"

The phone was in a hallway on the second floor. There was another one downstairs in the kitchen. Andy could hear people in the living room downstairs. He wasn't sure who might be on his floor. The single girls' bedrooms were on the third floor. Was Lorraine in hers?

"Sis, I need to talk with you more. I can't say a lot now. Any chance of you driving out here again in the next few days? I know that's asking a lot."

They hit upon Friday night. It would have to do. She was done another shift rotation and off the next day so didn't mind being up late. Andy had a bright idea. Why didn't he catch a bus to Toronto and have her pick him up? He could stay the night and return the next day. "It's about time I saw your digs anyway," he added. "And you wouldn't have to do so much driving."

"What about Lorraine?" Susan responded.

"We need a break anyway," Andy responded.

After hanging up, Andy wandered downstairs for a cup of tea and a snack.

One of the other commune members, Paul, a recently graduated law student who was articling that summer, wandered through. "Hi Andy. Thought you and Lorraine would be doing your evening stroll by now. About that time, isn't it?"

The phone rang just as Andy opened his mouth to respond. Paul, who was standing right by it, picked up the receiver then promptly handed it to Andy. "It's for you. See you around." He wandered out of the kitchen.

It was Andy's Uncle Reg. Turns out the job at Kellogg's had come through. Uncle Reg had worked at Kellogg's in London for ever. He'd gotten his dad his first job there years ago when they were fishing buddies. At that time, Andy's dad met Reg's sister, and the rest was history. He told Andy they'd be calling him tomorrow, sight unseen, though he'd put in an application. It helped that Uncle Reg worked in Personnel.

"Oh man, Uncle Reg! That's mighty tempting, and a lot more than I'm making now. Thanks so much. I'll be around at this time tomorrow night to give you my answer. Hey, thanks a lot!"

Andy hung up and promptly dialed Susan collect. She was surprised and a little chagrined. "Andy, I'm not made of money, you know…"

CHRYSALIS CRUCIBLE 33

Andy interjected. "Susie. There's a pay phone in Victoria Park. I'm sure there's a number there. Can I call you collect from there once more, give you the number, and you phone me there? I *really* need to talk to you right now!"

Andy looked at his watch. It was just after 9:00. For the last three weeks, at this hour, Lorraine and Andy would be normally on their walk. It felt strange. He wondered again where she could be. He also hadn't seen Jim and Marcia all evening.

The phone booth did have a number, sure enough. Andy told Susan his story. Last night at this time, he suddenly realized, Lorraine was recounting hers. Was it really only 24 hours ago? And was it less than a month ago they'd first sat together in Victoria Park under an enchanted moon?

There was a long pause after Andy's rendition was over.

"Andy," came Susan's measured response at the other end, "I think you're still the praying sort. I hope you're praying. And I really liked her. Add that to what Mom and Dad already said, and you're up against a… I don't know. You're up against it, that's all!"

As if Andy did not know.

The darkened sky was not unlike the night before, except Andy could not see the moon from where he stood. He wished he could sit down. He had to go to the bathroom. In his haste, he had not taken his jacket, and the air was cool.

"Susan, I should let you go. Here's what I think: Lorraine and I need space from each other. Kellogg's pays really well. Uncle Reg thinks I can likely stay on into the fall. He's even offered me his downstairs room for free. I can find someone to replace me here for the summer. I think I should go for it.

"It's just that… I mean, wouldn't this really hurt you if I suddenly ducked out of your life as a boyfriend when I, I mean, when you needed me perhaps the most?"

"Andy," came Susan's reply, "Lorraine needs a *lot* more than you can offer right now. Sure, she needs you to care for her. And it would be nice if you could care, like a nurse or something. But I can tell you right now; this could easily be the first time she's ever talked to anyone about this stuff. You're not a therapist. It's way over your head. Bowing out right now may be the kindest thing you can do, even if she can't see it. I don't know…"

Euphoric heights, abject depths, all inside a month. What had just happened to Andy's safe little world?

"I think I'll phone Mom and Dad, Susan—not to talk about Lorraine. They don't dare, I don't think, at least on the phone, and neither do I. I'll see in general what they think of me moving to London and working at Kellogg's. They might jump at it, without saying so, as a way of nipping my love for a 'strange woman' in the bud."

Was there not some bitterness to his tone?

When Andy contacted his parents, nothing was said about Lorraine, though Andy knew he did a bit of dancing around that topic when asked how "it would impact things there" were he to move suddenly to London.

"You could be a good witness to Uncle Reg and Aunt Marion even," said his mom.

"And to your cousins," his dad chimed in, "And be a reason for us to visit more often."

His cousins had not been raised in the church. His uncle and aunt had walked away from it in their teens—she a former Catholic, he a Baptist.

CHRYSALIS CRUCIBLE

Periodically, Andy's mom tried to get Uncle Reg to attend evangelistic crusades in London. Once, she phoned him and pleaded with him to attend a Billy Graham crusade in Toronto. He steadfastly refused. "If he could just come under the sound of the Gospel once more," she'd say wistfully. She desperately wanted to ensure her brother's safe passage to eternity.

They said and asked nothing about Lorraine.

"Son, I popped some literature from Gospel Outreach into the mail for you today. You might find it interesting. They're organizing a team next year to evangelize in Germany. With your language skills, you'd be a shoe-in."

"Thanks, Dad," came Andy's nonchalant reply. "I'll definitely have a look at it. Oh, and Susie Q sends greetings. I talked to her earlier tonight. Gotta go—in more ways than one! Bye."

4

Lorraine made the first move. Literally.

There was a quiet knock at Andy's bedroom door not much after six the next morning. It opened uninvited, and Jim walked in.

"Andy," Jim whispered, "can you get dressed and come down to our apartment?" Andy was in the bottom bunk of a three-person bedroom. Five minutes later he stole out of his room down to the only first floor apartment.

Both Jim and Marcia were up with the coffee on. Jim was bookish. He was finishing off a Ph.D. dissertation in philosophy and had been a leader at IVCF for some years. Andy always felt a little intimidated by Jim. He seemed to have read everything Andy had—and so much more.

Marcia was warm and exuded caring. She was obviously in the right line of study, completing her Masters in counselling psychology that year. She was amply built, had medium length brown hair, and wore large-rimmed glasses.

"Care for some coffee, Andy?" She asked.

Andy felt wary. What was going on?

Homemade muffins were passed to him.

"Marcia and I just got back from Toronto a couple of hours ago, Andy. So forgive us if we look a little baggy under the eyes. We took Lorraine to stay at her aunt's."

Lorraine, back to Toronto? He remembered a slight commotion on the stairwell during the night. The steps squeaked no matter how softly descended.

"We really tried to talk her out of it," Marcia said.

CHRYSALIS CRUCIBLE 37

"I didn't see Lorraine all last night. Nor you guys…"

"Lorraine took me aside right after supper—which you skipped—and asked to talk to us in private," Jim began. "So we headed off to the university. Marcia has an office in the psych department.

"She told us her story, Andy, the one she had just told you the night before. She'd never told anyone before, Andy, you have no idea…" Jim did not complete the sentence.

"I think you have a very good idea, Andy," Marcia interjected, "of what Lorraine might be going through." She paused. "I wonder how you're doing…"

"I'm at an utter loss!" Andy responded. "What should I do? What would you do?" his voice turned plaintive.

"We'll pray, for starters," Jim piped up. "I will in a moment. But Andy, can you run the Day Camp on your own today? Lorraine thinks she has simply abandoned you. And if you leave at the end of this week, too, our poor priest! I guess that's why they pay him the big bucks."

Jim prayed for them all. Then, "Andy, one last thing, from Lorraine…" He handed Andy an envelope. "I know you'll want to read it right away. Only she knows what's in it. Hope we've left you enough time to get to Day Camp."

"Thanks," Andy said. Where did the tears come from? He averted his head and walked through the door. Marcia squeezed his hand as he did, and said, "Good on you!" Moments later, Andy read the letter in his room.

My dearest Andy:

You're owed an explanation. Where do I begin? I feel so fucked up right now!

Andy recoiled as though he'd fired a shotgun.

There. I said it! Didn't know I could. "Nice Christians" don't talk that way, do they Andy? Well, like my dad always said, "You're not a nice Christian girl, Lorrie dear." (Not like those other pristine pure Sunday school girls.) That's right, he had a few pet names for me, like I was his little puppy or something. Doesn't Hugh Hefner have little puppies, too? I mean "bunnies," right? You know why I know? Because I used to look through my dad's Playboy's *he kept stashed in a secret place I saw him go to once.*

Well, fuck Hugh Hefner and all his goddamned little bunnies! And fuck my dad—'cause he sure FUCKED ME UP BIG TIME!!! (Though never intercourse. No, no, that was "sin." Besides, I wonder now, there could have been evidence. I might have gotten pregnant!) But he, but he... Ah shit! Andy, I'll spare you the details.

Maybe if your mom reads this she'll want to clean my mouth out with soap. That's not fair, Andy. Sorry. I like your mom. Not mine, though. In the end, Andy, she knew. She had to! And she did nothing, nothing, NOTHING to protect me! That's not right! Moms nurture and protect, not propagate to let dads copulate. (Funny saying, eh?)

AND I HATE, I HATE, I HATE MY DAD!!! I can never tire of writing that.

That's not right either, eh, Andy? Children are supposed to "honour and obey." Dad quoted that repeatedly as I began to find out this wasn't normal.

CHRYSALIS CRUCIBLE   39

But I let him keep his little secret, didn't I? Way too long! So I'm just as bad as he is. No, worse, 'cause Eve tempted Adam, after all. We're the seductresses, Andy.

I could have undressed right in front of you that first night on the park bench, Andy. At least enough to make your blood boil to fever pitch! I saw it happen with my dad enough times! (Only I never agreed! He always had to force me!) Then I could have dragged you off into the bushes and made you do it! You'd have been out of control by that point, Andy. I don't care how much Bible is stuffed into your brain! And you'd have been under my control, my spell, my power!

I came to that, finally! Hey, I realized, I'm really the one in control here. With all the power, I'd mock my dad 'til he'd turn red in the face (funny colour for us Japanese). I started to threaten, right at the very end before I moved to university, about telling the secret. He got so angry, Andy, it was delicious! He dared not hit me though. "Evidence" again, I suspect.

Then suddenly I was gone! I had scholarships the first year so I didn't need his money. And I came into a small inheritance the next year from an uncle's estate. It was in my name and my dad couldn't touch it.

I never go back home, though I really miss my brothers. Then I imagine sometimes they're turning out just like him! My widow aunt stays in touch regularly. She's really nice, like a real mother to me. She really loves me. I've never told her my story. She's also a good Christian, a really good one. Doesn't say much, just does. I'll be at her place when you read this letter.

Until Sunday night, I'd never told my story to anyone! "It" always told me not to. I can see why now, though for different reasons.

For four years at university, I prayed that God would help me understand. I took psychology for that reason. I understand lots now, but I still don't know how one human can treat another like that. And my own dad!

Well, "it" had so brainwashed me, I thought no one would ever pay attention to me unless to undress me with their eyes and worse. I heard again and again I was no good for anyone! That made it easy to stay clear of guys.

But I came into my fourth year thinking, okay; maybe I'll say yes just once to try it out. Then we ended up together on the outreach committee in the New Year. I loved something about your hands right off. I could never imagine them doing... I fell in love with those hands, Andy. That's why I said "Yes" twice, before you really even asked. And I knew that maybe someday, maybe... I'm glad you didn't ask for another "Yes." On the contrary! That's what really told me about your hands, Andy. Then I knew for sure. I knew. Imagine! A man's hands that were safe like that crack in the wall I always imagined crawling into... How can I expect you to get that? Can you? I guess I can only write it and pray you do. It's all the difference, all the difference in the world.

What I liked next, how can I put it, was your "innocence." Not that you were just naïve (you are!), but innocently so. How can I explain? You didn't have to be suave, or something. I noticed you noticing me, Andy. In my abnormal psych course they say some victims react by making themselves ugly. I didn't. I couldn't. I mean (sounds like I'm bragging), I wouldn't. Some victims (surprise!) end up hating the opposite sex with a passion. Funny, I never did. It took me four years to let out enough poison to say I'm maybe ready. And there you were... And you never undressed me with your eyes, Andy. So I knew you wouldn't do so without

CHRYSALIS CRUCIBLE

my permission with your hands. (Back to those hands—and maybe the same thing said a different way.) See what I mean by "innocence"? It's everything, Andy!

I guess where I miscalculated was thinking it safe to tell you my story. I couldn't lead you on any further, Andy! It was tell or break things off. That simple. Turned out the same thing anyhow.

I'm sorry. I'll be all right. I've survived this far. My aunt said I can stay as long as I need. I guess I'll finally tell her what happened.

I'll find work in Toronto. Always have. Could have been a great summer. It had been... My best ever... MY BEST EVER!!! You need to know that, Andy.

I'm really sorry.

Take care, Andy. I can't say, "I love you," because I can't say that! How can I ever? But I would, Andy, if I could. Maybe some day...

Lorraine

P. S. Andy, I still really love those hands!

5

"Hello," Andy said simply at their first meeting in the Gospel Outreach (GO) parking lot. "I'm Andy. Can I help you with any of your things?"

He felt mesmerized. Auburn blonde hair long to the shoulders, features that converged like some well-executed dance. Her eyes veritably sparkled, invited, tantalized. She simply replied, "Yes, thank you. My name's Fiona."

South Carolina? South Dakota?

"No, Texas," she said and laughed.

"I'm from Canada myself," he replied. "We don't have states but—"

"Provinces," she chimed in. "I know. I've been boning up on my Canadian geography since I knew I was coming here. The closest I ever got to Canada until now was having a pen pal from Guelph. Ever heard of it?"

He nodded. "Just a stone's throw away from Kitchener, which, interestingly, was called 'Berlin' until the First World War."

"I remember the name," she drawled back. "But that was ten years ago."

All the right vocabulary, Andy mused, only the tape had been slowed down.

"Ever seen a hockey game on TV?" Andy asked. "Almost every pro player is Canadian, even if most of the teams are not."

"Really?" Her perfect teeth sparkled a smile.

Wow.

She was used to guys, Andy was certain. Probably had been dating the last several years. Maybe had a

CHRYSALIS CRUCIBLE

steady in Bible School preparing for full-time ministry. And she was off to serve the Lord with Gospel Outreach for the same two years. Perhaps they were engaged. (Andy had not yet learned the trick of looking at the ring-finger; he who with all his 22 years had with two exceptions only noticed girls from afar.)

His diary entry that night was cryptic:

I met Fiona today. What can I say? Infatuation at first sight. She's gorgeous. Do I think she noticed me? Hope springs eternal...

At his official send-off the weekend before, Andy's Uncle Joe, like everyone else at Carriage Street Gospel Chapel in Kitchener, wished him well. Andy had grown up in that church, had been saved at four, and had basically done all the right things ever since—short of getting married. But he did not feel a sense of urgency just yet. The Lord would supply the right girl in his own time.

A new graduate of the University of Waterloo, Andy was proud of his Honours French and German degree and had been impatient to put his language skills to practical use. What better way than to serve the Lord in Germany with Gospel Outreach, founded by George Elwin Moore, one of Andy's faith heroes?

"G. E." as George Elwin Moore was known affectionately, had come up through the ranks of the brethren, Andy's denomination. Born in Scotland (impeccable pedigree), upon his emigration to America he had become a noted youth leader for several churches in the Chicago area. From there, he studied at Emmaus Bible School and subsequently headed up its worldwide Bible correspondence course program for two years.

Then he spent a year on an Operation Mobilization evangelistic team in India. There had begun the stirrings. As he recounted often and warmly to each successive wave of GO recruits, it was on the streets of Calcutta that the vision for GO had come. While slipping tracts under the gutter dying—in the event they might roll over, read, and be saved—he conceived the vision of the future of brethren missions. *New Wineskins* (as one of his later books was entitled) would be needed to contain the new waves of dedicated brethren youth. Just give them a taste of short-term missions and not only would a majority return full-time (70 percent or better the statistics proved to be), but it would be a great shot-in-the-arm to local churches as well.

Andy came to wonder how many of those Indian beggars dying on the streets ever did enter heaven, perhaps clutching the tract like some theatre ticket, dutifully collected by St. Peter at the pearly gates. Visions of Mother Teresa's House of the Dying invariably accompanied this imagining, a strange juxtaposition. Perhaps for some, her house proved to be heaven enough....

"I'm so honoured to meet you," Andy said while sitting in G. E.'s spacious office during his first week of studies. His eyes took in the collected works of C. H. Spurgeon on an ornate bookshelf. It was accompanied by a systematic theology by Lewis Sperry Shaffer, several works of apologetics (including some by Francis Schaeffer, which made Andy's heart leap), and what looked to be shelves and shelves on Christian mission. Wow, this guy reads, Andy thought enviously.

G. E. had invited Andy in because of his dad, Andy was sure, who was a noted brethren leader in Ontario. So G. E. was also a good strategist, came the cynical thought, though Andy revelled in the attention.

G. E. shook his hand warmly, even clasping a second over the first to underscore his pleasure. He maintained that posture while sizing Andy up.

"A strapping, good-looking young man!" G. E. said at last. "Just to look at you does your father proud." He held Andy's hand a bit longer then released it at last and, slapping him on the back, directed him to a chair.

"It's such a pleasure to meet you—though not for the first time. I remember well ten years ago a seemingly shy youngster with his dad at Guelph Bible Conference Grounds, right? It was just after I had given a talk on prophecy, and your dad wanted to meet me. I remember you were a great fan of A. J. Boswell and proudly displayed a brand new *Scofield Reference Bible*. Well, I'm one of his fans, too. I understand he's from your home assembly, though you obviously don't see him much."

Andy remembered the meeting well. "What I liked about that lecture, sir, was how you made such a compelling case for the identification of the Antichrist 'system' with Communism. I've read lots since about Communist Europe. It looks like some of that reading might pay off in West Berlin."

"I think, Andy, you and I will hit it off just fine. I saw you take in my library. These hold pride of place, though my study at home is bulging, too. I understand you're quite a scholar in your own right, both from the degree you just completed, and your transcripts."

Andy blushed slightly.

"Now, how is your dad? The last time I heard he was embroiled in that inerrancy controversy in Windsor. But more importantly, I presume he'll visit us at last now that his son is here!"

"Between regular work, a heavy preaching schedule, and some writing projects, he's not too likely to come until Easter," came Andy's reply. "At least, that's what Dad told me."

G. E. seemed pleased at the prospect. "Then we shall wait until then to roll out the Red Carpet."

At that, the phone rang. Andy waited politely as G. E. was caught up immediately in the conversation. Andy still waited. Had G. E. forgotten him already? Andy stood up to scan the bookshelves more closely.

With that, G. E. put his hand over the receiver. "Andy, I'm sorry. It was great to share. There will be lots more occasions, I trust. This is long distance, and I should attend to it."

Suddenly, Andy was in the hallway outside G. E.'s closed door. He remembered a professor who encouraged students to take all the time with him they wanted. Remarkably, no student ever needed more than five minutes.

G. E.'s vision for GO had expanded to three overseas teams in training that year: a France team, a Spain team, and a German team. Students converged on the GO Center on that Labour Day weekend of September 1971. They were mainly from the States, but several, like Andy, came from central Ontario. The multicolour brochures highlighting each projected team location—Nîce, Madrid, and West Berlin—might have been created by each city's chamber of commerce, they were so attractively produced. The glamour was interwoven with soundings on the countless lost in each metropolis, the great need, the shortage of labourers.

The West Berlin intonation ran like this, "See the Brandenburg Gate through which Napoleon and Hitler marched their triumphant armies. Take up the challenge to recruit a different kind of army for Christ!" It went on to explain that with West Berlin's two universities and an exemption from military service included for students there, the city teemed with young people desperately in need of the Good News but tragically more likely to hear only the Bad News of Marx and Lenin.

The Jesus Movement was at its zenith that year, with *Time, Newsweek,* and *Life* all doing feature articles on it. Whether largely a media event or a bona fide groundswell of youth getting high on Jesus with staying power, the word was out. As one book put it, *The Jesus People Are Coming!* Presumably, out in front was Jesus himself, trumpets blaring. Then, depending on one's eschatology but certainly according to theirs, all hell would break loose.

The GO students that year were high on the wave themselves, index finger recurrently jutting skyward and responding endlessly to the "Let's-hear-it-for-Jesus!" cheerleaders. The challenge was to take this great outpouring of God's Spirit to the uttermost corners of the earth. Presumably, the target cities—or at least their satanic minions—were bracing for the onslaught.

There was some haphazardness to the layout of the GO headquarters. A wealthy couple had bequeathed the grounds in trust to their home assembly, Oak Street Gospel Chapel in Arlington Heights, Illinois. They were to be used for the Lord's work. The buildings more or less sprawled out at will, with only the six missionary ("mish") houses built in line with the preceding. The Admin Building, the shed, and the cafeteria seemed to have simply sprouted unaccountably.

G. E. had returned from his year's evangelistic work with O. M. afire with his new vision for brethren youth. The elders at Oak Street had been praying during the preceding year about what to do with the beautiful estate, and the conviction had grown that their title and Moore's vision were in sync. So it happened that G. E., invariably beaming with bright ideas, was presented with the option of using the land. After due exercise before the Lord, Gospel Outreach was born. G. E. was thirty-five then. Twelve years later, he and GO were still glowing brightly.

Twenty-one young people had come to the first GO training course. The men were all whiskerless and sported those short-cropped brush-cuts. The women had spiral hairdos like Dairy Queen ice-cream cones. Their group picture proudly occupied a central place in the "rogues' gallery" of GO teams. Beneath it in beautiful Gothic text was the KJV version of Matthew 28:19: "Go ye therefore, and teach all nations, baptizing them in the name of the Father, and of the Son, and of the Holy Ghost."

And gone they had! Back to Calcutta's teeming throngs. And whether only two years after G. E.'s initial time there they rolled any of the same beggars or passed some of the same tracts, no one knew.

Andy met Janys the first day of classes, her name spelled, she was quietly emphatic, with a "y." On the surface, it was perhaps the most arresting feature of Janys Thane ("Plain Thane," as her school friends and enemies called her, much to her endless childhood chagrin). He met her at the cafeteria over lunch. Virtually all weekday and weekend lunches were taken there, although each "mish" house had a full kitchen.

Janys' physical presence was undistinguished. She had a face that was not unpleasant but which made Andy wonder at how unremarkable one could actually be when all the same elements—eyes, nose, throat, skin—were common to all. Perhaps he had too

CHRYSALIS CRUCIBLE 49

much Lorraine as comparison in mind. She had a small figure that came off similarly: like a pitcher who threw imperfect curves, though the loose clothes she wore probably did not help.

She laughed as they shared a little of growing up in Ontario. She was easy with guys, too. "I've always been a Tomboy," Janys told him that first day. "Clothes, make-up, manicures, all that girly stuff were of no interest to me. I guess I'm still somewhat that way."

Also on the debit side was dark brown hair she had curled into a bun, likely still respectful of the brethren rule about women not cutting their hair, though lots did. She sported large, dark-rimmed glasses that were a little too overbearing for her petite face. Bottom line, apparently she did not care too much about how she looked. Her personality at first blush also seemed so mild as to hardly register. However, that perception quickly changed.

At least she was *safe,* Andy thought that first day. For other reasons, too, she became Andy's best friend those first weeks at the Centre. He knew right away she had the smarts.

It was the second week of September, with a touch of fall in the warm air. Janys suggested they go outside. A sudden gust teased her hair, threatening to unmoor it. That's sexy, Andy thought in spite of himself. Wonder whether she's ever done anything except wear her hair tied up? They sat under a chestnut tree on a bench.

"We might get beaned," Andy warned. "We used to collect these by the thousands every fall. We'd carve 'em, throw 'em, save 'em, trade 'em. Auburn gold." He unshelled a few that had fallen.

"I don't really know why I'm here," Janys began. She was answering a question Andy had put to her earlier. "I'd like to think it was the Lord's will, but it was as much my dad's as God's, I'm sure. I also have an older brother preparing for the mission field, so, all in all, it seemed the thing to do when I graduated this spring."

"How do you know if it was the Lord's will?" Andy quizzed, wincing as one of the spiked shells pierced his skin.

"Doesn't Paul Little say somewhere that God's will boils down to two commands in the Bible: 'Love God and love your neighbour'?" came her response. "So I guess you get on with it and muddle through what you don't know in life, which is just about everything.

"Besides, I've decided to do my own little research project on how missionaries *really* act far away from home. My working hypothesis is: the nearer home, the more effusive the God-talk. The farther away, it's just the inverse—except in prayer letters asking for support. So you seven, well, I'll throw myself in—we eight—are my guinea pigs. Every time I hear you pray, I'll be peeking to see what's really going on just beneath."

She flashed an impish grin. Andy liked that. Had she ever done anything to her face, he wondered. There was general brethren prohibition against "self-adornment."

"I thought you were supposed to 'judge not,'" Andy replied, feigning shock.

"You stick to your agenda, I'll stick to mine," came her quick response.

A jet streamed by overhead. Another impish grin flashed. Andy did not want the lunch break to end.

"So what are we all about coming here, Janys?" Andy launched in a different direction, eyebrows arched.

"Andy, if we all just did a tenth of what we claim as Christians, the world would be truly turned upside down! For instance, I see huge hype right now about the Jesus People." Her nose wrinkled, one hand flung back a strand of hair. "My brother Ted says religion's up in America, morality's down, and I agree."

"What do you mean?" Andy retorted, his voice surprisingly loud.

"Ted was telling me about a book on missions by Stephen Neill that he'd read. It alludes to that kind of reality in North American Christianity. It seems that the more religious America becomes, the less evident is its *charity*—'love of neighbour and enemy' in the biblical sense. He says to look at the Bible Belt, for example. It's perhaps the most religious place per square inch on the planet, next to a mosque. Yet some of the worst racism, nepotistic patriotism, and self-serving religiosity fester there. Go figure.

"Or take the Vietnam War. What Evangelical do you know of who even raises a question about the righteousness of that cause? As if napalm, bombies, and civilian casualties are part of God's will to rid the world of Communism. Billy Graham totally supports the war, and we all love Billy. So Ted has his doubts about a lot of the Jesus People enthusiasm. He says to give it a few years to see if anything but froth is left."

Such a critique was new to Andy. He'd seen some of the protesters at university but had steered clear. Like most of his church peers, he was largely unaware of world events.

"Just what are 'napalm' and 'bombies'?" He asked.

Janys explained patiently: "Napalm creates a holocaust when dropped by bombers. In Dresden and Tokyo, for instance, during the last year of World War Two napalm bombs burned to death more than 100,000 civilians. Dresden was chock-a-block full of refugees at the time, so no one really knows how many died. For the thousands who were scorched but who survived, the dead were the lucky ones."

"I thought they just bombed military and industrial targets," Andy said.

"Afraid not," Janys replied, her face contorted. "Do you know that the general in charge of the bombing over Japan, a French name... LeMay, said after the war that it was a good thing their side won or he'd have been tried as a war criminal like the Nazis at Nuremberg. They used napalm on dozens of other Japanese cities after Tokyo, killing or wounding about a million civilians."

"Really?" Andy whistled his incredulity. "How do you know this?"

"You didn't take that in History 101, Andy? Not likely," Janys responded. "We did, thanks to a prof my last year, who was a Vietnam War draft dodger."

"Then he was obviously totally biased, Janys," Andy pounced on the insight. "Though granted, in my second year, I had a Texan draft dodger for a prof. He was the straight goods."

"Hey, I thought you just said, 'Judge not,'" Janys came back in feigned offence. "The historical documentation isn't the problem, just who admits to it and denounces it—or does not. Ted says hardly anyone in the Evangelical world at the time did—or has done since. At the beginning of the war, President Roosevelt called civilian bombings an 'inhuman barbarity' unbecoming modern civilized nations. No one of course wants to admit we're *barbarians* and *savages*. So we don't. You've heard of the Nazi Holocaust deniers? There are also Allied Holocaust deniers—that's most of us in the West."

Andy's gut wrenched.

"And bombies?" he felt compelled to ask.

"Little, brightly painted balls that look like they might be fun to play with. They have detonators guaranteed to kill kids outright and maim or even kill adults. Millions are being dropped in Vietnam right now."

Suddenly, Andy felt like throwing up. Where had the gorgeous fall afternoon gone?

He asked more about her brother Ted. He had to change the subject. Janys respected him deeply, but Andy failed to share her enthusiasm. It was a new idea to think that Evangelicals could be *wrong* about something, rather like Catholics doubting papal infallibility. Ted also seemed not a little intimidating.

"Janys, why is Ted so cynical? Isn't love supposed to 'believe all things'? Why should he be so questioning of Evangelical ways? I remember Dwight Moody's come-back to the guy who didn't like the way he did evangelism: 'I like better the way I'm doing *something* than the way you're doing *nothing*!' Well, maybe that response was judgmental, too. Still, the other guy started it.

"When I see Jesus People on fire for the Lord, going out everywhere, preaching the Gospel, aren't they getting it right about their faith? I hope I have half the zeal they have by the time I leave here. I think Ted should cut them a little slack."

Why was Andy's heart pounding?

Janys said no more.

6

The first three years, GO had run only two months of training before the teams did a year's service. Things had evolved since. Their training was now one school year long, followed by a two-year overseas stint.

The minimum eligible age was 18. Of the twenty-five trainees that year, about half were fresh out of high school. The other half were couples, some with young kids. Many of these had been out in the work force for a few years. The remaining older singles had either completed Bible school or university or had been working a few years. There seemed to be some unwritten rule that over-40's were not welcome on teams, though a smattering helped out at the Centre, not least of whom was G. E. himself, who was 47 that year.

Most instructors were missionaries on furlough or on loan from nearby Emmaus Bible School, Inter-Varsity Christian Fellowship, area brethren assemblies, and the like. There was a basic course on biblical doctrine à la Lewis Sperry Shaffer, a course on personal evangelism taught by affable Paul Little, and several mini-courses on various missionary survival tactics.

Language study was one of their major time commitments. There was a German teacher and another who was fluent in both French and Spanish. The latter, Linda Darnell, had grown up in South America, but her French had been school-learned in southern France. The German instructor, Joanne Schwartz, was doing post-graduate work on some aspect of Thomas Mann's writings. Her parents were German, but Joanne had never visited home turf. This was set to change, however, with an imminent marriage. The groom-to-be was Hans Beutler, a German exchange student who had studied two years at Wheaton College. They had met during that time.

Andy was in the unique position of being familiar with all three languages, having just picked up two years of Spanish en route to his double major. He didn't mind the obvious admiration this elicited.

For instance, after the trainees were introduced to the local congregations on their third Sunday morning at the Centre, Joanne had the bright idea to have Andy do a brief testimony about why they were there. He was to begin each statement in each of the three Centre languages, and then translate. It was meant as a light touch, but several seemed awestruck at his linguistic facility, especially when they discovered English was his native tongue.

Classes lasted only half the weekday and were certainly not heavy, apart from language study, which was source of anguish for most. But not Andy. With typical arrogance, he treated them all as *bird* courses, letting others know his attitude freely.

One day, Joanne approached Andy as he exited the Admin Building. A zephyr breeze tossed a few fallen leaves into swirling eddies. He kicked at them aimlessly as they walked across the yard toward Andy's mish house. Birds were everywhere, not least the bright red cardinals, which Andy especially loved.

"Have you ever considered grad school?" Joanne asked.

Andy shook his head. "By the time I was done my BA, I was so burned-out there was no way I could have gone for my Masters. But maybe when these two years are up..."

Joanne nodded emphatically: "I would, Andy. You

owe it to yourself with your flare for languages and your obvious intellectual gifts."

Andy protested mildly. "They're not all that unique, I don't think."

"Andy, you're the academic type. I could tell that the first day in class. You don't almost win the German prize in your last year without demonstrating that gifting. No, you've got to consider further studies after this."

Andy smiled inwardly. He had sounded for a compliment, and had gotten one. He thanked Joanne for her encouragement then entered his mish house and napped until lunchtime.

Apart from classes, the other half of the normal weekday was physical. It involved rotating chores of maintenance, meal preparation, and practical evangelism. While these activities rounded out the eight-hour day, it was expected that voluntary service would fill up evenings as well. It did for most. It was one of those subtle expectations one dared not buck. All veritably leaped at the opportunity to prove to G. E. the other staff, and God, ultimately, that they meant business for the Lord. "If He's not Lord of all, He's not Lord at all," was the motto on a beautiful plaque in the dining room. It served as an ongoing spur to participate in Boys' and Girls' clubs, Sunday school classes, Bible studies, the Friday evening Root Cellar coffeehouse, and so forth. "Only one life, 'twill soon be past. What's done for Christ alone will last." Another of those Christian workaholic aphorisms on the "Joyful Wall," this time in the Admin Building, written by an outgoing missionary.

Apparently, G. E. had never heard about the "God rested" part of the creation ethic. He constantly burned the midnight oil for the Lord, apparently singeing one family member along the way, as Andy came to discover when he met Dan, G. E.'s 22-year old son….

Andy wondered how many real estate agents cringed the day GO took over that property in the middle-to-upper crust section of Arlington Heights. It was at least a workable theory that the annual concentrated waves of eager youths knocking on doors, taking religious surveys, inviting people to religious movies, prophecy lectures, and the like, and generally excavating for convertible pay dirt would be enough to encourage even the most ensconced to uproot and move on. Unless, of course, they were won for the Lord.

All twenty-five recruits fanned out during those six months in ever-widening circles as they attacked the doors. The strategy that year was to have each pair tackle a specific geographic area each month. The population densities of each section were supposedly equally proportioned, a guessing game once they went further afield to multiunit housing. If a given area was covered before the month was up, a new bailiwick was assigned. This became quite a contest. Some couples on the France team moved at an astonishing rate, knocking on thousands of doors.

G. E. personally intervened; reminding all that this was serious spiritual warfare, not an evangelistic board game. But even that didn't squelch it altogether. In spite of G. E.'s warnings, some form of records was still kept. Besides, GO readily modeled such numbers games, tossing out figures in the thousands on much of its promotional materials.

Usually, a multi-coloured brochure, together with an invitation to a special lecture or film were left at each door. They were to try and make personal contact twice over two successive days then leave the literature if that was not possible. Also included was an invitation to the Root Cellar for kids ages 15 and up, and to church services on Sunday mornings in the brand new Admin Building auditorium.

If personal contact was made, then it was out with the survey and a disarming, "Hello, as part of a study course, we're conducting a religious survey of the area and wondered if you could take a few minutes to respond." The survey was designed as sure as an electronic tracking device to lock the unsuspecting dupe into a presentation of the *Four Spiritual Laws*, Campus Crusade's all-season, all-time bestseller which deftly laid out God's wonderful plan for each human being and other choice secrets of the universe in a few broad strokes. However, G. E., always innovative, had his own version available for use by the New Year, entitled *God's Plan, Man's Choice*. It was slicker and more colourful than the plain yellow prototype. He held, too, that it was more balanced, coming down strongly on the new convert's discipleship call, especially to do evangelism.

The idea was to pair people off according to their prospective target countries so that team relationships might begin to gel. Married couples were kept intact, since, it was argued, wives invariably did less of this work on the field, seeing as they were given to domestic duties and caring for children. This would afford them a real taste—in case their home assembly had failed to arrange this—of the husband's spiritual authority. Otherwise, the idea was to rotate the pairings each month.

There could be rebuff. Once, an overweight middle-aged man came to the door. When Andy began with his canned line, the guy said, "That's what you said last year! And I just had a Mormon here last week pushing his stuff. Why don't you just take that goddamned religion of yours and stuff it up your ass?" An explosion of expletives followed this. Andy and Janys, his first partner, beat a hasty retreat, not particularly up for persecution that day.

Usually, however, there was a firm, "We're not interested." Then, when someone did actually bite, whatever rejoicing in heaven, it was a great psychological lift for the fishers of men. Some even got reeled into the church and made commitments. Others were saved at various outreach events, including the Root Cellar. Everyone was caught up in fervent prayer, even more than Andy had experienced his previous year's work at the Hobbit House run by IVCF and the Missing Peace coffeehouse at his summer commune.

G. E. was also the author of the attractively done piece of literature they invariably tried to leave behind. Though the content changed, G. E.'s two main themes were prophecy (à la Hal Lindsay and "pre-trib" dispensationalists) and worldwide revival. For him, the Jesus People movement heralded a great awakening of God's Spirit. He was at maximum wattage when writing and speaking about this. They passed out several other pieces of literature over the next six months, each stamped with the GO emblem, which, for the life of Andy, evoked the image of those American Army recruiting posters. Only this was not saying: "Uncle Sam Needs You!" Rather, a side profile of a stylized Jesus pointed to a wheat field, declaring: "The fields are white already unto harvest... Therefore GO YE!"

It was easy for Andy to take the lead on the doors, easy for Janys to say nothing, which Andy would chide her about from time to time. But the alternative for him was hardly bearable: actually letting *her* speak first. Not that he was more chauvinistic than the next brethren guy. He just found that when she did say something at the doors, her voice turned uncertain, cranked up to a falsetto beyond her usual high pitch. He fairly expected it to run off the scale some day, like a cassette tape chattering feverishly seconds before becoming hopelessly tangled.

Yet she had so much to say, Andy knew. And he knew she did not fear speaking her mind. So why the hang-up?

Finally, they hit upon a successful arrangement: If Andy managed to get the person at the door through the *Four Spiritual Laws*, Janys would pipe up with an invitation to the next church service and lecture while simultaneously handing over the literature. It was like a decoy manoeuvre to make her forget it was she who was talking, like those prenatal exercises designed to take one's mind off the pain. There *was* pain nonetheless, for her and for him. Invariably, they both breathed easier—perhaps finally took a breath—at their first step away from the door. Only to go through the same ordeal the next time someone else got hooked by the religious survey. Had it not been for their obligation to win souls, the repeated ordeal that first month would have been enough to put them both off door-to-door evangelism for good.

While walking past a park on their second day of this exercise, Andy commented on how impressed he was by the expectation of zeal to be about the Lord's business.

Janys quipped, "Christ, yes. But what about the neighbour?"

Andy arched his brow.

But instead of explaining, she continued, "And what about just enjoying yourself? Non-self-consciously, non-religiously, just plain humanly?"

The park was rolling with closely cropped, luscious

green grass. Huge maples lined the walkway, along with towering oak and many other varieties. Sunlight splintered variegated patterns through the trees. Birds and butterflies twittered and fluttered. A squirrel ran right up to them as they paused to talk.

"Janys, I don't get it," Andy said, his face tightening, "How come you question missions so much when that's what we're here for?"

"Do you mean on earth, Andy?" she asked undeterred, "or here in Arlington Heights at a missions training centre?"

"What difference does it make?"

"Because I'd say you aren't supposed to act any other way here than at any other time in your life. If God called everything good, then *everything* is good, not just missions or religious activities."

"And what about evil? Everything isn't good, Janys, and evil is what our mission is supposed to overcome."

"With 'good' that God declared creation to be in the first place. And aren't lots of missions evil?"

"Like when?" Andy felt his throat constrict. The squirrel darted away onto the road, barely missing certain death under a car's wheels. It shot back into the park.

"Like the Crusades a thousand years ago, for starters—maybe even today's crusades," she added with a look of mirth in her eyes that distressed Andy.

They had come to the end of the park. Andy noticed a bench and suggested they sit down. He needed to cool down before approaching another door.

"Janys, you're confusing me. I thought we came—rephrase that—I know I came to do missions pretty single-mindedly. What did you come to do?" He locked her gaze.

"Andy, lighten up. I came to do missions, too. But surely that means having some fun at the same time. And if you're not having fun, then you're probably not doing missions. How's that?"

Andy closed his eyes, his face contorted, and suggested they head back.

Before entering her mish house, Janys stopped and turned to Andy: "Don't take me too seriously on this stuff, Andy. I try not to."

She slipped inside before he could respond.

7

Janys was from a small assembly in Sudbury, Ontario, that atrociously raped nickel capital. The local lake was a victim of acid rain pollution, and Sudbury was a veritable eyesore en route to enchanting northern Ontario. While she didn't initially volunteer it, it was only logical to ask, Andy finally clued in, if she was any relation to the Thane's of the first GO team.

"I'm right there," she said, pointing to a photo in the Admin Building's auditorium, location of GO's Rogues' Gallery and Joyful Wall. They were taking a brief break before afternoon chores, which meant bathroom detail for Andy.

"So I guess my becoming a missionary could be called *predestination*," she commented playfully.

Andy's forehead furled. "Why always so sacrilegious, Janys?"

She raised her eyebrows.

"I mean, 'predestination' is one of those amazingly laden theological terms that means so much in our understanding of God's way with man. Paul develops the theme grandly, and the whole Bible pulsates with it. It's all about God's *choice* of us, we who were sometimes far off from God's grace."

Pause and silence.

Andy continued undaunted. "So I believe you really were predestined. First to accept Jesus as Saviour and Lord. Then you had a calling to become a missionary. It was not 'in the stars,' a pagan notion, nor 'in the cards,' up to fate. It was God's choice followed by your response.

"On one of Francis Schaeffer's tapes, he calls

predestination a 'non-negotiable true truth.' You can't fight it. You can't deny it. He also says, ominously, that there is a double predestination: some toward eternal Glory, others toward everlasting Damnation."

Pause and silence.

Andy resumed his lecture. "As I see it, it all hangs on God's choice before creation began. Imagine that. God figuring out my little life before he even set the galaxies spinning. I don't understand it, but I do accept it by faith. It is not to be made light of…"

He stopped talking and looked at Janys. Sometimes one had to dig for her thoughts, like eating a pomegranate. In this way, she and Andy couldn't have been more opposite. At times, especially when upset, she was as tight-lipped as a taciturn oracle. Meanwhile, he was so ready to spout verbiage, multilingual even, that for some it was an elaborate manoeuvre to cap the word-burst once the drill had struck—so great were the willing reservoirs within. One friend had once caught Andy up short that very summer, exclaiming, "Congratulations, Andy, you've just said the same thing five different ways!" And that was only in English.

At times, Andy thought Janys was like the Dead Sea Scrolls. There was a lot in there if one could break the code. He was a colloquial Bible paraphrase. Was he also as superficial?

Nonetheless, they hit it off well as friends. *Just* friends. He didn't even have to think about that consciously. How could it be otherwise given his self-serving predilection toward "stunners"?

They had much in common: both from Ontario, the same age, and university graduates (her B.A. was in sociology with a minor in history.) Andy loved northern Ontario, as did she. He had even camped two summers previously at Killarney Provincial Park near Sudbury. They even discovered early on that Andy had met her brother Ted at a Christmas holiday retreat in Belleville. He stood out then as a real thinker. Her father, like Andy's, was a businessman *cum* preacher/teacher/writer/elder in the assembly.

During a table tennis game one evening in the Games Room of the Admin Building, during which Janys was surprisingly holding her own through a maddening defensive strategy, Andy asked about her brother Ted.

"Didn't Ted have great dreams of missionary service in South America? Is he still headed for that?" Andy queried as he served. "I remember that he had even taken Spanish in high school and was intending to major in that at university."

"He did," Janys responded as she smacked the ball back at him. "And he had a real flair for it. He went on a GO summer team after Grade 13 and came back speaking a passable Spanish. I remember that because a Peruvian family in our assembly used to remark on how excellent it was."

"What's he doing now?" Andy asked, diving to return her volley.

"He's in his first year of a Master of Christian Studies program at Regent College in Vancouver," came the reply. Her return was weak.

"Never heard of it," Andy shot back as he spiked the ball.

Janys bent down to recover it. "It just started with a full-time enrolment. It's an Evangelical college on the UBC campus. What's interesting is, it was begun by some brethren from England and by some assemblies people in Vancouver. Dad raised a lot of questions when Ted first thought of going. He was especially concerned that they taught amillenialism."

Andy failed to let on that the term was at best vague to him. "'Some even hold,' Dad used to tell Ted, 'to a progressive evolution view of Creation, albeit with God superintending the process.'"

"Did your dad really advise against Ted going there?"

"He'd never quite say as much, but yes."

"Pretty brave of your brother then," Andy said, trying to imagine how his dad might have reacted in a similar situation. He had a fairly good notion. "What does that give him again?"

"His Master of Christian Studies. It will take him two years and then some, seeing as he has to write a thesis."

"On what?" Andy questioned, suddenly feeling jealous of her brother for doing advanced studies.

"He hasn't decided yet, so far as I know. But maybe he should do it on the history of GO, with an eye to the dynamic impact of G. E. on the revitalization of brethren (lower case) assemblies in North America and beyond toward world missionary enterprises."

Janys' eyes held a slight moistness. Andy came to identify her humour by just such a faint glistening. *He* might have said such a thing seriously, but not Janys. Why not? It bugged him.

She said more than once in those early weeks that she found it surprisingly easy to talk with Andy—more than with most people. Perhaps all his loquaciousness cascading over her primed the pump. He was not vain enough to guess at other, more hidden reasons for freeing up Janys' tongue.

As for Andy, he liked Janys' *smarts*. This was invariably a plus for Andy in sizing anyone up, due as much to his own arrogance as to any resonance with his intellectual capacities, which were quite average after all, he feared. He learned quickly that Janys was a shrewd analyst of human behaviour. She sized up many of the "problem" people early on that fall before anything showed obviously. She might have done so of Andy, maybe even had…

Instead of returning to the Centre for break on the Thursday afternoon of their last week together on the doors, Andy suggested an ice cream cone at *Take Your Licks in Style*; a retro ice cream parlour located a few blocks from the Centre.

The overstuffed booths were ornate. A jukebox was belting out *Yes! We Have No Bananas*, and the walls displayed a colourful array of *Coca-Cola* advertisements, "Uncle Sam Needs You!" World War Two recruitment posters, and an array of other period memorabilia.

"This one's on me," Andy said. Everyone usually went Dutch treat. Janys said nothing.

"Andy," Janys queried, "have you spent any time with Ken Kincaide?"

"Not yet," Andy said, "but I have loved his piano-playing. No doubt I'll get around to it. Why do you ask?"

"Because I think he's very lonely," she returned. "And I think he needs a friend."

"I think he's already got one. Or haven't you noticed that he spends a lot of time with the receptionist?" Andy returned.

"I mean," she persisted, "that he needs someone in whom he can confide, not someone to whom he's attracted. I think you should befriend him."

Just then, the jukebox began belting out a garbled Frank Sinatra piece. The manager hurried to turn down the volume control. "Next time, don't kick the machine," he muttered. Andy and Janys smirked. Ken Kincaide was forgotten for the moment. Their ice cream came, and they ate in silence for a while.

"Janys," Andy began, remembering Joanne's talk with him, "have you ever considered advanced studies like your brother?"

Janys laughed after a cold, wincing swallow. "Not likely. A brethren girl going off to seminary? A woman getting theological education in Jesus' day? Things haven't changed much in two thousand intervening years—at least in our circles!"

"But Jesus changed that!" Andy blurted out. "I mean, the reason Martha got upset with her sister was she was discussing theology with the Master like a learned Rabbi—or like the pre-teen Jesus in the Temple—instead of doing 'women's work' as Martha understood it."

Wow. Andy thought. Wow.

"I know Francis Schaeffer holds to a traditional role for women, but—"

"Francis Schaeffer?" Janys almost spat his name. "Why are you always quoting him, Andy? I don't mean to be too bold, but Ted says he doesn't hold a candle…"

She hesitated at Andy's blanched face. "Let's just say there are lots of contemporary and past thinkers you should read, too, Andy." Her voice trailed to a subdued whisper.

Andy looked the other way. It irked him to hear that Ted took exception to Francis Schaeffer's apologetics approach. Andy was already gaining the nickname "Francis" at the Centre, Schaeffer being only next to the Bible in authority for Andy. Andy fancied himself well read and had been especially taken with historical and philosophical apologetics since his second year at university, mediated through popularizers such as Schaeffer and John Warwick Montgomery. He never had been one for going to primary sources. Ted was intimidating all right, but gratefully 3,000 miles away. Andy knew he wasn't angry toward Janys but rather her brother. But he couldn't quite say so. Why?

"We better get back to do our chores, Janys. You still on food prep? I'll just call you Martha…"

Janys looked at him and smiled. She *really* had a nice smile, he noted again.

During those walks to and from the appointed outreach sites, and sometimes through getting together to talk over strategy, Janys became, next to Andy's diary, his closest confidant—with some exceptions of course, in particular, his infatuation with Fiona.

He also never shared about Lorraine Takahashi.

8

"Girl problems?" Jack jolted Andy from his reverie, a page of neatly inscribed copy on slightly scented notepaper in his hands. Andy's look of consternation had obviously given him away. Lorraine's first communication, to put it mildly, had blown him away! Thankfully, he'd just read it through for the first time as Jack came in.

Jack Dumont was from New Orleans. He didn't know more than *oui* and *non*, but who knows, perhaps he was from French aristocratic heritage generations earlier. "Jacques Louis" was on his birth certificate. Apparently, there had been another with that namesake who had distinguished himself in the Civil War. For the Confederates, was Andy's hunch, feeling vague on his American geography despite having learned every state and capital in public school. Jack stood six feet, four inches in his socks and weighed about 210 pounds. Handsome and lithe. Worst luck, he was also happy-go-lucky, self-assured, and unassuming. An all-around nice guy. He was also Andy's roommate for the six months of training.

"I've had them, too!" Jack continued. Then with a raucous laugh: "Golly have I had them! My only trouble is, I like too many of 'em. Just friendly, you know. But they all take it so seriously. The way I got it figured, there's about one guy sold out to the Lord for every ten committed girls. No wonder we're in such a high demand! But gee! I'm not ready to settle down yet!" So much of Jack's talk was exclamatory.

They were into their second week of classes, and Andy was beginning to feel his way with Jack. He lacked all the northern, certainly Canadian, reserve, plunging headlong into any subject like a surfer into a wave. He especially enjoyed the topic of girls, and they had many a free-flowing session about them. Andy was entirely protective of the Lorraine saga, revealing only vaguely that there had been a summer romance. But Jack had an endless repertoire. They discussed the pros and cons of everything about women, from celibacy to free love, from dating to casual group encounters, petting to sleeping together—the gamut. Jack's enthusiasm never waned. Andy was beginning to feel normal again.

What had made Andy decide against moving to London was the material from GO that arrived the day after Lorraine left. Had it been the week before, in light of his whirlwind romance, he'd have dismissed the possibility out of hand. If ever there had been a leading from the Lord in his life, Andy sensed, this was it. (Okay, he'd also felt that throughout a recently failed romance, but Andy wasn't arguing.) His dad wasn't thrilled with GO, yet was encouraging him to go, even if for questionable motives. Things moved quickly. He was accepted by GO in early August and on his way there Labour Day Weekend.

Andy had no way of reaching Lorraine, and she never phoned. He asked Susan to look up "Takahashi" in the phone book. He didn't dare call all the listings randomly. Who knows what he might have stirred up? The trail had gone absolutely cold. He never had the nerve to ask Jim and Marcia to direct even his sister to Lorraine's aunt's place. Marcia confirmed his intuition inadvertently by saying once, "Andy, pursuing her would be another violation. She has to take the first step. No matter how hard this is for you." That comment clinched it.

And yet, he felt really angry! He only talked about it to his sister, whom he visited two weekends later. (Did he half hope to bump in to Lorraine by happenstance?) Susan, ever practical, said finally: "Andy, you've got to move on."

It had been Susan whom Lorraine had finally phoned in early September. Hence her getting Andy's address, and his sitting not a little stunned in their upstairs bedroom as Jack came in. Susan had promised Lorraine she'd let the letter be a surprise.

Lorraine's letter was enigmatic. She talked only briefly about herself, still looking for work, but a few good possibilities, especially now that university students were back to classes. How strange it felt to be in Toronto and not a student. How good her aunt continued to be.

"You'll be happy to know I'm going with her to church. They love my aunt, and she loves them! So I guess they've accepted me, no questions asked. I keep expecting someone to see my horns or something..."

Nothing else about her family. She expressed surprise at Andy's sudden turn. *"Off as a missionary. Imagine."* But she placed no value on it.

Lorraine apologized for the swearing in the last letter. *"I'm not like that most of the time, Andy. Really! I was venting big time, and to be honest cannot remember exactly what I said. I was so rushed and upset! I hope you can forgive me. Please forgive me!"*

Her letter ended with: *"When I start making money, I'm going for therapy. I've known for a long time I should be doing that. Otherwise I'm not much good to anyone in a relationship of any kind, Andy."*

Andy put Lorraine's letter aside for several days. Was he putting the relationship behind him just as easily? What did that say about him? About Lorraine?

CHRYSALIS CRUCIBLE 73

About life? Why was he endlessly asking questions?

The unlikely roommates began calling their long discussions the *Jack and Andy Show*. They weren't restricted (topically or otherwise) to just girls. They ranged far and wide, late into the night, entirely stream-of-consciousness. Except, in Andy's case, for Lorraine. He made no further mention. He had, had he understood it, begun to cauterize that wound.

Andy's relationship with Jack had developed alongside that of Janys. Janys by day, Jack by night. Janys was clearly more Andy's style, but Jack's rough and readiness, his non-intellectual practicality and zany zest for life endeared him to everyone, not least to Andy.

They became something of a phenomenon. Jack was robust, aggressively athletic, brimming over; Andy was intellectual, reserved, though decidedly argumentative. Someone dubbed them the *Dynamic Duo,* and it stuck. Such notoriety was garnered from his link-up with Jack, Andy surmised, that he found himself the object of attention from the opposite sex, as he had never experienced before.

Jack typically took the adulation in stride. A veteran of two years of Bible school, he knew the familiar paths. Hang loose, be cool, play the field. And even if you do start betting on one horse for a while, don't fail to watch the rest of the race. It all was so natural to him.

But Andy was encountering a new phenomenon and was unsure of himself in this novel role. He didn't know how to interpret his own, he suspected, derivative powers of attraction. He could see it well enough in Jack and appreciated his unruffled response. Jack laughed a lot about it but admitted to only one or two he was keeping an eye on. For the most part, their interests were widely divergent.

One night, two months or so into the program, just as Andy's consciousness was sinking beneath the sheets, Jack queried: "What do you think of Fiona, Andy?" Andy wouldn't have known until that moment that he had even thought of her at all. But in a split second, an adrenalin rush brought his consciousness to blazing noon. He suddenly knew exactly what he thought of Fiona, and, as instantly, that big Jack Dumont and he were rivals. He became guilt-ridden.

His response, however, was a well-controlled, drowsy, nonchalant "Jack-I'm-tired-and-almost-asleep-let's-talk-about-it-some-other-time" production, eliciting a "sure-thing-good-night" response. But Andy lay awake a long time savouring a new bittersweet emotion, wondering, doubting, dreading, remembering. Did he have the heart for this?

9

The first week of October occasioned a shift in door-to-door work. Andy and Jack switched partners. Janys looked diminutive enough beside Andy as they walked together, but she was positively tiny alongside Jack, who was a good three inches taller than Andy. The four headed out together partway and laughed when Fiona pointed out the "Mutt and Jeff" effect to Jack and Janys.

At their first experience together on doors, Andy was surprised then relieved that Fiona spoke first. He hadn't even thought to strategize on that with her. When he mentioned it after their first encounter, Fiona said she and Jack took turns. It made sense, Andy realized, though it was not Janys' inclination. Nor had it been the Centre's intention. Theoretically, the men were supposed to be developing "spiritual authority" during these outings.

Fiona was an elementary school teacher, Andy had found out that first month, and had already taught for two years. It had been a major decision to leave that behind.

"It's a bit of a story, Andy," she replied when he asked her why she did it. "I'll tell you when we're done today. Remind me."

Andy had relished the change of partners—with some guilt. Fiona Sanchez was blonde. Her golden tresses sparkled that afternoon in the autumn sunlight, dazzling the eyes. Her brown eyes tantalized in tandem with her entrancing smile, which was ready and unaffected. A perfectly bronzed facial complexion played off her matching body. Andy could only imagine (suppressed immediately) what she looked like on the tennis court or at the beach. Beyond that was strictly *verboten.* How could any guy resist who might venture to the door? Few had—on Jack's authority.

She laughed at Andy's next question. "Yes, there is some Mexican in the name! The ancestry can be traced back at least to the mid-1800s. I don't know how much you know of Texan history," she began "but six weeks after the..."

"Battle of the Alamo, Texas became a state," Andy interjected. "You knew about Canadian provinces. I know a bit about Texan history. Davy Crockett was a childhood hero," he added, breaking out into song, "Davy, Davy Crockett, king of the wild frontier!"

She laughed, and the world tilted.

"Anyway," she continued, "Texas was part of Mexico until then. Our family name comes from that time. I'm sixth generation American—and Texan! So no, Mr. Linguist, I don't speak any Spanish beyond '*Si*' and '*No*,' and I'm only just barely learning German."

"German with a Texan accent," was Andy's comeback. "Don't know if it's possible!"

"C'mon, Andy!" She shoved him playfully.

"Hey!" He pushed back. "What will the neighbours think? We're on a mission, don't forget…"

She promptly began beating him about the head with some of their promotional literature as he affected self-defence.

"They'll think we're having fun, Andy!" She shouted "And maybe that's a better message than G. E.'s in here!" She whacked him resoundingly on the head.

"Ouch! No fair! I'm not allowed to fight back!"

"Oh yeah?" She rained down another series of blows. "Jack always does, and you are the 'Dynamic

Duo,' right? Show your stuff!"

This was new territory. It felt good. Something released inside.

"Okay, lady! You asked for it!" Andy leaped into the air as if to fly over her then deftly sidestepped and pinned her arms to her sides from behind. He hoisted her up from the ground then back down in determined grip, her hair deliciously careening across his face. Literature spilled everywhere.

"I give! I give!" She cried.

And she did. Beyond imagining. Andy could have held on forever. He stood transfixed by sheer sensual proximity that only moments before had seemed a galaxy away, time-frozen forever in a Kitchener park. The associations engulfed. He delayed just beyond appropriate, then let her go. She wasn't his.

Just then, he noticed a dark car drive past.

"Andy, look what you've done!" she exclaimed in mock schoolteacher tone. "How will you ever explain?"

"Explain nothing!" he shot back.

They laughed. Something inside took wings. He felt it but sternly forbade question or comment. They still had doors to do.

Andy liked the Arlington Heights neighbourhood. It could easily have been a Toronto or Kitchener suburb. The economy was good by the looks of the wealth reflected in houses, yards, and cars.

The leaves were just starting to turn. Andy especially loved the deep red Maples. But that was yet a few weeks to come. When the breeze picked up however, autumn's encroachment was evident.

On the return walk, Andy reminded Fiona about her story.

"I guess I was a typical teenage American girl,"

she began, "into guys and how to attract them. Our youth group was huge, so I had no want of… Andy, I'm not bragging. Boyfriends. They do say 'blondes have more fun.'"

Andy watched her face. She sounded so matter-of-fact, eyebrows knitted in concentration. She flicked her hair back as a snatch of wind tussled it. They walked deliberately, she the pacesetter.

"I had an older brother, Tim, whom I idolized. We had a fantastic relationship growing up. He was…" She hesitated. "Like Jack in a lot of ways. Tall, handsome, really athletic! Incredibly fun-loving too. He was youth leader when I first joined Youth Group. He always talked about pursuing some kind of ministry. He'd done lots at camp, etc., for years.

"Then he had the opportunity of a lifetime: to learn to fly while being put through university by the Air Force. When Timmy joined (I never stopped calling him that), the Vietnam War was just beginning. He was thrilled at the prospect of serving God and country. Soon, he became an officer. He was such a natural leader. And he passed flying school with 'flying' colours, like everything else he attempted in life.

"He started to get trained on fighter jets. He was in heaven, Andy, I can get through this," she interrupted herself. Andy realized she was close to tears. "And then his trainer jet crashed, killing him and his instructor…"

Andy was in shock. "I'm really sorry..." Ever so awkwardly, he put an arm around her shoulder. There was no triumph.

"There was an investigation," Fiona said, recovering. Andy removed his arm reluctantly. "Mechanical failure was the cause. It was very technical. Timmy had been at the main controls with the second set for the instructor, a veteran pilot with over twenty years' experience flying fighter jets. It was nobody's fault, not even the maintenance team, who had all done the right things, too...."

A jet streamed overhead. No sound. Only Andy was looking up. They were nearing the Centre. Their pace slackened.

"I was devastated," Fiona continued. "We all were. It rocked our family, our church, our town, even our state, since the Governor mentioned the instructor and Timmy in tribute during his speech at the Republican convention that fall."

"Wow," Andy said, impressed. Then remembered the last time he'd said that to a beautiful woman.

"To make a long story short," Fiona said as they neared the Centre's front gate, "I made a vow that I'd serve the Lord as a missionary in tribute to Timmy. Timmy's death gave me a direction and a purpose I had not had before. A speaker from GO was at our youth rally not long afterwards. I talked to him, and, two years later, here I am at last."

She looked at him, holding his eyes. What was she asking? The signal was powerful...

"Fiona, I..."

"Hi Fiona and Andy!" A familiar voice boomed from down the street. All Andy could do was slip through a "Thanks!"

From Fiona: "Jack, Janys. Hi! So how'd it go?"

Jack's face was beaming, every fibre brimming with earnest enthusiasm. How could one compete with that?

10

The next morning, there was a note in Andy's mailbox from G. E. asking if they could meet in G. E.'s office right after classes.

Andy's heart pounded slightly as he approached the door to G. E.'s office later that morning. This was only his second visit with his childhood hero.

"Hi Andy," G. E.'s voice said, "come on in."

For the first time, Andy noticed the bay window with padded bench and reading lamp. From that vantage point, Andy guessed G. E. could just about see the entire GO campus. Three books lay on the bench, pencils nearby. Andy bet G. E. spent hours in that spot. He felt envious. A fireplace and mantelpiece were tucked into a squared corner. *Gemütlich* was the German word: cozy. A warm comfortableness pervaded. And yet, the office had a feeling of organized busyness. It made Andy feel lazy just standing there.

"Andy," G. E. began, "I wanted to talk to you a bit about how things are going at the Centre. I trust you've settled in pretty well by now?"

As in his first meeting with G. E., Andy, felt like he was being "sized up." Something about how his eyes moved. Andy nodded. "I've loved the first month, Mr. Moore!" Buoyed with the day's experience, a little of Jack's exuberance came out in his reply.

"My son's music has not been too loud?" G. E. asked.

Andy noted a family photo on G. E.'s desk. He recognized G. E.'s son Dan, GO's groundskeeper, handyman, and housemate to Jack and Andy. "If he's listening to music, Mr. Moore, it must be through ear phones. I haven't heard a note."

"Oh, he listens to music all right." G. E.'s comment went no further. "I trust you're getting along fine?"

"If you mean with Dan and Jack, yes sir! For that matter, with everyone else in our house, and at the Centre."

"How about with Fiona?" The question hit Andy like a sucker punch. He was instantly wary. Then he remembered: the car!

There was again a searching. Andy distinctly disliked G. E.'s probing eyes, this fattening up for the kill.

"I hardly know her. But she's my new doors partner. I like her," was Andy's straightforward response.

"Andy, sometimes I drive around to see you guys in action. I saw you and Fiona 'in action' all right, but it wasn't exactly what I'd expected…"

Those eyes, what was it? Andy hadn't noticed the clock on the mantelpiece before. But in the silence, it seemed to keep time with each of Andy's thoughts, turning over deliberately like a slot machine. Something tugged at his memory. Of course!

He had been a camp counsellor at Forest Cliff Camp on Lake Huron the first summer of university. A very attractive teacher, at least five years Andy's senior, had come to counsel for part of the summer as well. They took a liking to each other, but neither had to say "only as friends." Andy was certain that her friends would have said she was robbing the cradle.

Innocently enough, one day she was driving into town during a few hours off and asked Andy if he wanted to come along. He needed a haircut, so he said sure. They phoned to let "Sparky," the camp director, know. (They all had camp names. Andy's was "Chips.") His wife took the message and said she would inform him.

They were just heading to the car when the cook came running from the kitchen. "Andy, Sparky wants to talk to you."

"Andy," Sparky began in agitated tones, "I cannot permit you to go with Raven into town." Raven's hair was long and black. "I'm sorry."

"Why?" Andy responded, incredulous.

"Because of how it would look… to the kids."

"Okay," was all Andy could muster, with attitude.

When Andy let Raven know he would not be joining her and why, she laughed and said, "Heck, Andy. You are good-looking!" Her face reddened.

In disgust, Andy crawled into his bed back at the cabin for a nap. There was a light tapping on the door just as Andy was going under. It was Sparky. He wanted to talk. They headed toward the lake.

"To let you know how seriously I take this, Andy," Sparky began, "I want to tell you that even my wife and I do not hold hands in front of these kids for fear they will get the wrong idea."

Andy could only say, "And the wrong idea being…"

Sparky was instantly red-faced. Whether due to anger or embarrassment or both, it amounted to the same thing. He told Andy with the strictest warning that he was never to be seen around Raven except when others were present. Sparky would be watching personally. He would also be writing a letter to Andy's elders. Andy didn't tell him his dad was the head elder.

Andy recalled Raven's response to this exchange. "How will they ever explain to their kids how they got there? Or maybe the parents don't know themselves." Then she added, "Makes you want to break the rules just

CHRYSALIS CRUCIBLE 83

for the heck of it, right, Andy?" She was a free spirit.

Here he was on the carpet again. Would G. E. be as stern an inquisitor?

"Andy, what do you have to say for yourself? I hold you personally responsible."

"With due respect, sir, for what?" Andy said evenly.

G. E.'s eyes flashed anger. "Are you denying that you and Fiona were embracing in plain view today?"

"Mr. Moore, like I said, I hardly know Fiona! We've not talked to each other much since I arrived. Like everybody, I find her... really attractive. And today, well, we were just fooling around. She was kidding me about something, and I took it upon myself to put a stop to it. It lasted all of a minute. Honestly, that's all there was to it. You can ask her."

G. E. paused to collect his thoughts. "Andy, we have to be so pure here. You know the warning about the devil going about like a roaring lion. You'll never see my wife and I even holding hands on campus for the same reason."

The *déjà vu* almost rocked Andy back on his feet. They had three kids after all...

"So I implore you as a Christian brother, but then command you as one responsible for your soul, you must not touch people of the opposite sex here at GO. Period!"

Andy knew he had not read that in any of GO's promotional literature or seen it in any of the fine print. Yet here it was by overt oral fiat. What to say? He thought of Jack, how this would totally curb his style.

"Mr. Moore, I came to GO with every intention of obeying the rules. I honestly did not know yesterday that I was breaking them. I take full responsibility for what happened. I'm sorry, and I can assure you it will not happen again. I came here to serve the Lord, not just my whims."

Again those uncomfortable eyes.

"Andy, it's not easy sitting where I do. I take personal responsibility for the care of your souls. I sit here every morning, overlooking the grounds, and pray for you all by name.

"Sex is one of those things that can waylay us so easily. That's why I'm so cautious. Fiona's a seductress just by how she looks. You know that already, don't you Andy?"

Andy did not want to answer, but G. E. was insistent. "Sir, she's very good-looking. But so is that sports car I see our theology teacher, Mr. Campbell, drive around. I've seen lots of guys—and girls—admire it.

"So, isn't the problem how we respond to beauty? If I covet it, 'lust' Jesus called it, then I'm its slave…"

G. E.'s response was sharp. "Andy, don't minimize sexual lusting!"

"I'm not, sir, I'm…" G. E.'s eyes were so offensive.

It would be lunch soon. Andy could hear people congregating outside the cafeteria below. This conversation felt surreal. He thought how anyone from university who listened in might take it. He almost laughed at the thought, just as he and Raven had about poor Sparky and his sexual hang-ups. But G. E.'s face was too sobering. This was surely not the respected G. E. he had admired and read about over the years.

"Andy, that's all for now. I'll be before the Lord on this. I may even phone your dad. Whatever else, I expect there will be no more shenanigans from you. We simply have no room for such moral lapses at GO."

CHRYSALIS CRUCIBLE

His tone was ominous.

Andy didn't go for lunch. He was too upset. Some of it was guilt, though he was trying hard to understand why. He'd let G. E. down big time, obviously. That rankled. But he couldn't agree with G. E.'s assessment of his actions. That bugged him even more.

He walked aimlessly over the deserted grounds until he ran into Dan. "Hey, big guy, looks like you've seen a ghost," Dan said.

Andy recovered enough to smile.

"So why aren't you at lunch with the rest of the good missionaries?" Dan queried with a touch of sarcasm.

"Do you really want to know?"

"Of course."

Andy led Dan to a sunny spot beneath the campus maples. A warm, Indian Summer breeze stirred the leaves like a master organist filled cathedral pipes. Andy was grateful he could not see G. E.'s office window from where they sat. Then, feeling angry and reckless, Andy told Dan his story, vaguely aware that it might not be the best idea.

Dan was an eager listener.

11

Dan Moore lived by himself in the room opposite Jack and Andy's. There were five in the mish house: Dan, Gary and Sharon, Jack, and Andy. Dan was the only one not heading overseas—or, ostensibly, anywhere else for that matter. He projected to others that the only thing in life he wanted was *not* to be like his father.

He had bushy eyebrows and shoulder-length hair (quite common since the Beatles phenomenon) that he kept in a ponytail when working. He was of average height and build and hid well what was going on behind the scenes with a pair of sunglasses he might even have worn to bed. He'd taken them off to talk with Andy, thankfully.

"Sounds just like my dad all right," Dan commented at the end of Andy's tale. "Then he told you he'd pray for you, right?"

"Something like that. What makes your dad tick anyway, Dan? I even wondered the other day whether your dad got one of those mail-in degrees," Andy responded.

"Why?" Dan asked.

"Today in apologetics class, your dad told us the story of Voltaire, the atheist, who used to go around on horseback collecting huge audiences so he could defy God to let loose a thunderbolt.

"According to your dad, Voltaire would pull out his watch and dare God to strike him dead within the next five minutes. When nothing happened, Voltaire railed against puerile Christian belief."

"Yeah," Dan replied, "I've heard dad tell that story

before. He's a collector of that kind of hagiography—or anti-hagiography. Then he would also tell us that Voltaire also used to say that some Christian contemporary, who was also a scientist, claimed that the Bible speaks of man travelling in some kind of machine at a speed exceeding that of a horse. Voltaire would hold this scientist's credulity up to scorn, that a man should ever achieve such speed and withstand the shock to the system."

"You've got the story down, all right," Andy said and smiled. "Your dad's punch line, of course, is how history has demonstrated the correct biblical view of that scientist, while Voltaire, though not having succumbed to a lightning bolt, nonetheless deserved it, since the last laugh was on him."

"Right," Dan said. "And there is always the line about how Voltaire used to predict Christianity's demise in just a few more years, retreating before the inevitable advance of the great Enlightenment."

"Your dad used all those stories in his lecture today. The only problem is, he nailed the wrong guy—at least in part. First off, Voltaire was not an atheist but a deist. He believed in God as the Original Clockmaker who wound up everything then left it all to unfold according to natural laws. So he had little use for the endless sects of Christians, or even the varieties of belief in God amongst the world religions. But he hardly went around doing what your dad said.

"He is obviously confusing Voltaire with Ingersoll, an American atheist in the last century. It's always bugged me to see how irresponsibly this kind of—as you say—anti-hagiography gets hold. Anyone who's in the know obviously discredits not only the story but the teller and the purpose of the story."

Dan seemed to like that, said he'd challenge his

dad on it. Andy sported a smug smile.

"So what do I do, Dan?" Andy felt strange asking Dan for advice, not sure even if he was in the faith.

"Watch my dad closely, too, Andy! He makes slips. You can always go tit for tat with him. That's how I've handled him. I can get him so riled he'll go apoplectic on me. Then I quote Scripture: 'Be angry and sin not.' That knocks the wind out for a time. Like us all, he's a complex man, Andy. Give him enough rope…"

Dan checked his watch. "Well, lunch break's up for me. Here's a thought before I go though: Switch."

"Switch?"

"Yeah, switch partners on the doors! Then there can't be any more complaints. Unless… She's a looker way out in front this year! Missionaries shouldn't come looking so good, Andy," he deadpanned.

"Thanks for the compliment, *guy*!" Andy used the arm's length term that could do service even as expletive.

Dan smiled and bowed. "At your service, Mr. Missionary." Then he started walking toward the storage shed. Andy was thankful they had developed an understanding.

The next morning there was another note from G. E. in Andy's mailbox.

Greetings in the name of the Lord:

After prayerful deliberation today, and in consultation with your dad, I have decided to have you work again with Janys for the rest of your doors training.

While I really need not explain more—your breach with Fiona already being adequate cause—after asking explicitly (your dad made sure I'd let you know how this happened), I learned of your relationship this summer in Kitchener and its abrupt end, as I understand it, at the girl's initiative. Whenever I hear of such things, flags go up. You may have seen The Way of a Man With a Maid *in our library or elsewhere, Andy. If not, I encourage you to read it. Though dated and a little quaint, it is still some of the finest writing I know regarding appropriate Christian relationships between men and women. A lot of these newer books on the market do not hold a candle to it!*

What am I saying? You and Fiona obviously have some growing up to do in your relationships with the opposite sex.

I was tempted to put you and Jack together on the doors, but this is not safe in the long run here or in Germany. Janys is pretty levelheaded, so I'm sure things will go fine as they did last month.

I have no business speculating on your part in the failed relationship. Only this: It is not wise to start another on the rebound.

I have instructed Fiona about this as well. My wishes are simple: I want no interaction between you and Fiona for the entire month of October, other than what might be deemed "natural," such as greetings at classes and meals. This is to begin immediately. I informed Fiona, briefly, of your summer romance. She has a right to be on her guard.

Further, I do not want this to hit the rumour mill. Therefore, I forbid you and Fiona to talk about it together, unless I say otherwise. I also forbid you to talk this over with anyone else, including Jack.

If I or our Leadership Team (with whom I am sharing this) hear about or if any of us discovers you and Fiona together this month, it will be grounds for dismissal.

I will review all this with you at the end of the month, as with Fiona.

Andy, I know this may seem drastic. Purity always is. And God's work will be in order at GO. It is with that, that the Lord has charged me.

I see in you so much leadership potential! May you take this month as a chastening from the Lord, as learning to accept His discipline channelled through His chain of command. If so, I predict a joyous term, not only here at GO but also in your future service to His glory.

Finally, I am asking you to report to me once a week for the rest of the month. It will be a time of counsel and mutual edification. We'll pray, meditate together on God's Word, and trust God for His way in your life. This will be at 4:30 p.m. sharp each Friday afternoon for one hour.

Joyfully in Christ,

G. E. Moore

Andy ran to the bathroom and promptly threw up. He had no choice but to go into Doctrines class late. As he entered, Fiona looked up at him. He made no gesture. He learned little that session.

At the end of class, he moved quickly to exit alongside Fiona. "I'm so sorry, Fiona!"

She whispered back, "Andy, I got us into this!" Pause. Then she laughed and spoke in normal tones. "And I'd do it again!"

12

Andy did not know for certain who was on the GO Leadership Team. Suddenly, he feared spies everywhere. His heart ached.

Andy was not looking forward to his appointments with G. E. He debated about calling his dad but decided against it. He was still angry about his dad's rejection of Lorraine. He didn't need him to reject another woman Andy had barely gotten to know.

G. E. was not an accusing taskmaster, as Andy first anticipated. He came across instead as rather caring and nurturing. He welcomed Andy to each meeting with a warm smile, even put an arm around him the first time to accompany him to a chair at the bay window. He asked after Andy's internal thoughts regularly. He did not mention the episode with Fiona directly again. He bent over backwards to show understanding. By the second encounter, it reminded Andy of the studies he used to do with his Uncle Joe. They had always been uplifting.

But Andy was confused. He'd smarted under the unfair censure, especially the fact that G. E. told Fiona about Lorraine. Then again, he knew Fiona had had lots of "boyfriends," her mention. Maybe it only mattered that Andy had not told Fiona about Lorraine first. Though he never would have done so. That subject was taboo with everyone.

At their last session, G. E. grew more intense. "Andy, I feel the Lord directing me in this. If you are to fully cleanse your mind and heart, it might be helpful to reveal to another some of what needs cleansing. The Catholics have a confessional. Paul enjoins us to,

'Confess your sins one to another.' For this last session, I want you to think about any sins of commission or omission you may have committed in the sexual realm. This may be uncomfortable, but I trust cathartic, too. What in your past relationships, with the woman in Kitchener, perhaps, Fiona maybe, in your fantasies, do you need to bring before the Lord? It's just you and me, Andy. This is totally confidential. No one will ever know."

It was the last comment that did it. Andy remembered Lorraine saying her father said something almost identical to her. Well forget it, Mr. Moore, Andy thought. You aren't getting any secrets out of me for anyone else to guard over. Funny. Andy and Jack had covered identical territory already. But that had been fun and free. This felt totally different.

"Mr. Moore," Andy began, "I'll be honest. I don't really have much to say. Though my friends did, I never looked more than a few times at *Playboy* or any of the other magazines. They grossed me out. As kids, we experimented, but that was pure curiosity and harmless. No need to talk about it.

"Before I knew what it was, I masturbated a bit. But I don't do it much. What's the word, 'libido,' I think. I guess I have a pretty low one. Though, like everyone, I can have my fantasies.

"Funny, the whole time of my involvement in Kitchener, I made a conscious choice not to even let my mind go there. Sure, I want it someday. But I never cared to unwrap Christmas presents either, not even to peek, until December 25th."

It was the end of October, and daylight was already receding significantly at 5:30 in the afternoon. There was only the soft glow of two lamps in the office. Andy was tired of these *tête-à-têtes*. He was hoping to hear some kind of absolution, not more inquisition. He'd toed the line. He was hoping for the chance to talk to Fiona again. He felt he'd done some internal soul-searching and cleansing, and he wanted to move on.

G. E.'s eyes probed again, uncomfortably long this time. Supper was at 6:00. So far no one had noticed he'd been "serving detention" with G. E. He didn't want to be exiting the office upstairs as everyone came in for supper. He shifted his weight.

G. E. spoke at last. "Andy, I've decided to put you and Fiona on probation. I want you to continue limiting how much time you spend with each other. I want your relationship with her to be strictly brotherly. You're here as soldiers of Christ. This is not Bible school but a training ground for battle. I wish you two were not going to the same assignment, but Fiona's language study is well underway, and I understand German is stronger for you than Spanish. So for now, we'll leave things as they are. But we will be watching—And praying!—As we are admonished."

G. E. reached over to pat Andy on the shoulder. Then he took both of Andy's hands in his and prayed a long concluding prayer.

Andy slipped downstairs unnoticed.

13

On the Friday after Veterans Day, G. E. came to the Doctrines class along with George Myers, his second in command. The regular lecturer had told them the day before that he'd not be in. During the first two weeks of November, G. E. and Mr. Myers had interviewed every trainee. Andy could not help wondering what their interview with Fiona was like.

G. E. began: "The staff have all been feeling a special burden for each one of you these past few weeks. Mr. Myers and I have felt a particularly strong satanic attack during the past week, and we have both experienced a sense of near exhaustion as we have struggled, prayed, and agonized over each one of you.

"We finally felt led of the Lord to do something unprecedented in our training sessions of bygone years. We have undertaken to draw up a list of those we consider *on the right track*, exempt, as it were, from the need of further examination by ourselves, provided the same course is maintained.

"But we exhort those not on the list to take seriously, as from the Lord, the admonitions, counsel, and encouragement we gave in the interviews. Even more importantly, listen to the voice of the Spirit as he speaks to each one of you in the inner chamber of your hearts. Furthermore, those not on the list must be re-examined just prior to the Christmas break."

Fleetingly, Andy imagined a funeral-like procession at G. E.'s office door, awaiting the private word from his lips. But such a sombre rite was not to be. Instead, incredibly, G. E. proceeded to read the list of *acceptables* in full hearing of everyone, like an Inquisition judge, leaving the rest to sweat it out until their names had been decidedly passed by on the alphabetical roster.

As name after name became horribly conspicuous by its non-mention, sharp looks and gasps were exchanged. Some excused themselves, scarcely suppressing sonorous sobs.

Andy fixed an intense look on G. E.'s expressionless face as his equally monotone voice skipped name after name. He did not miss Andrew Norton, however, nor, shortly thereafter, Fiona Sanchez.

G. E. concluded the unfathomable ordeal thusly: "We have decided to give you the rest of the morning off from classes. We request that you all return to your individual rooms and spend time alone before God, reflecting, meditating, and beseeching God to make you empty vessels for his use. Please, no horsing around or indiscreet behaviour. We want you to take this time to mean business with God."

Even Jack was uncharacteristically subdued, although he was amongst the acceptables. Neither he nor Andy said anything the rest of the morning, except for Jack's, "Well, this oughta produce some spiritual housecleaning!" Andy read the Bible, prayed, and continued devouring *True Spirituality*, Francis Schaeffer's latest. Andy's "Schaefferisms" were increasing.

Recently, he had even argued openly with his Doctrines professor, based on Schaeffer's sharp disconnect between the "true truth" of the Bible, and neo-orthodoxy's seeming embrace of a Bible "true" in doctrine and spirituality but not in science and nature. Mediated through Schaeffer, Andy disputed Karl Barth's "strange new world of the Bible," saying it was strange and new, as Schaeffer claimed, only because he did not take it totally at face value.

"As Francis Schaeffer puts it," Andy intoned, "if one had been in the Garden of Eden when Adam and Eve were looking at the forbidden fruit, between the time of contemplating and eating it, one could have looked at one's watch ticking away the seconds."

The Doctrines professor, a bit of a free spirit who loved his sports car, quipped, "And that should have been the *only* thing anyone there at the time had his or her eyes on!" Andy had to laugh, too.

With the doors campaign completed, studies intensified. The leadership team wisely replaced the two hours on doors with study time, though for some, including Andy, it could have been dubbed "nap time." The two hours were expected to be a quiet time overall with little movement, unless to the library and back.

Right after lunch on the Monday following G. E.'s pronouncement, Janys asked if she and Andy could talk. They sat on a bench under a tree between the two mish houses. The wind could still tug at oak leaves, which were amongst the last to fall. But most of the other trees had shut down for winter.

Andy knew he might have been one of the blacklisted, so understood the hurt and anxiety the leadership team's action had created for the "unchosen." He felt the alienation of the "inner circle syndrome." The thought occurred: "How could a loving God engage in similar behaviour, only with cosmic, irreversible ramifications?"

"Whatever do you suppose led up to such action?" Andy queried.

"I think G. E. feels a real weight of responsibility for the group this year," Janys replied.

As he looked at Janys, he caught sight of a cat chasing a squirrel. The cat was no match. "But why this year? They've never done such a thing before."

"Maybe it's not all bad, Andy. I mean, there has been a lot of fooling around. And I've even heard rumours that a few people were caught pubbing in another town. Imagine!"

Andy noticed a flock of geese high overhead. He had a new sense of G. E. burdened with so many behaviour issues from his disparate flock. His anger receded a bit. "Maybe they were just contextualizing themselves," he said wryly. "After all, everyone will have to get used to booze overseas."

"I doubt it. Sometimes I wonder..." Janys was past master of the verbal trail-off. Just as one thought the wind was up and the sails billowing, all would suddenly go still. No amount of coaxing, cajoling or the like could get the wind up again. He had learned from two months on the doors that simple, quiet patience was the best manoeuvre. Only he rarely had the fortitude or consistency to pursue that tactic. Whatever else, Janys was proving to be one complex being. Perhaps it was the vicissitudes of Janys' moods themselves that militated against his ability to follow through consistently. But he was to be spared that afternoon.

"Sometimes I wonder why some have come to the Centre. I fear it is for every reason *but* to train as a missionary."

"Such as...."

"Such as to get a boyfriend or a girlfriend. Or perhaps because of lack of anything better to do. Or in order to appease the wishes of parents or elders at home. I really question the motivation of some people in coming."

"Rule out the boyfriend/girlfriend thing right off, Janys. At least, if they came with that in mind, it'll be nipped in the bud, or haven't you noticed?"

Was he playing with her? "What was yours?" Andy asked, knowing that Janys had already admitted to not quite knowing all the reasons. He rarely played devil's advocate with her, usually impressed with the inexorable logic of her views.

"*Touchée*, Andy," she said and laughed. "But I at least know..." Silence again. This time definite. That line of thought, wherever headed, had been halted abruptly.

A small plane droned overhead. He saw another flock flying in a V pattern. It was feeling chilly.

"G. E. had his reasons, I'm sure," Janys said, standing up. "But even my dad, a great supporter of G. E. from his time in Calcutta, in possibly one of his more unguarded comments, said that G. E. likes to make it known who's in charge."

They parted ways after that, but not before Janys thanked Andy. Andy thanked her as well. She was so easy to talk *to*, if not always *with*, he thought.

If nothing else, G. E.'s manoeuvre had made everyone all the more dependent on his benevolence. Everyone wanted to please G. E. with the exception of his eldest son.

Dan's response to Andy's description of the morning's proceedings was limited to one word: "Typical!" Then he slipped on headphones and closed his door. Yet, Andy conjectured, was he not also controlled by his dad, driven to defiance by G. E.'s own intransigence? Boy, things sure were complicated.

Andy's diary for that date yielded the following:

G. E. is a man of God. I have to conclude that, residual anger notwithstanding. God is using him to encourage new missions initiatives amongst the assemblies. In many ways, I wish I could have his prestige. But his behaviour in this instance is reprehensible.

How God will use this incident, only he in his infinite wisdom can know. But as Paul says, "Forgetting what lies behind..." And Francis Schaeffer, on one of his tapes, says, "When the personal-infinite God of the universe begins taking charge in one's life, watch it, the sparks fly!" So praise God anyway. It is 12:06 a.m. Goodnight.

At times, Andy fantasized about his diaries being discovered and quoted some day, so he would wax flowery à la Jim Elliot ("He is no fool who gives what he cannot keep to gain what he cannot lose.") for the sake of his imagined future readership.

Andy thought of a scripture in Jeremiah: "For this is what the LORD says: 'I will make you a terror to yourself and to all your friends...'" G. E. had certainly achieved that at GO!

It had never occurred to Andy before to think about religious "terror." He well remembered summer camp, when every visiting preacher threatened terror in various ways if the children did not accept Jesus as their personal Lord and Saviour. "If your mom and dad, brothers and sisters are Christians," various ones intoned, "where would you be the moment after Christ returned—in heaven with your family or in hell, forever lost because you did not decide for Christ tonight?"

Isolated from the moment, for the first time Andy felt shocked at how abusive such tactics seemed. Yet, Andy knew, he had gone forward (more than once, just to be sure) to "pluck a brand from the fire," with giant tongs and place it into a smaller adjacent fire. "This signifies," explained the camp director each year, "that you have opted to choose against the fires of hell and join a new community of faith that glows with a holy passion for other lost souls."

Most camp kids, from Christian and non-Christian homes alike, responded. It took some fortitude, some Daniel-like audacity (they often sang, "Dare to be a Daniel/Dare to stand alone") *not* to go forward at such emotional times. Ironic, Andy thought, that the "world" to be resisted and chosen against back home should be so on the defensive at Christian camp. Then again, maybe not, he realized. But it took guts to stand up against religious conversion at a Christian camp, or in church. It was not unlike that called for by evangelists in choosing to become a Christian "against the world."

Andy wondered about Christian conversion. In the end, was it simply an exchange of prejudices? If so, how did one escape such inevitable bias? How could he step outside himself—and the culture that shaped him—and really be objectively "free" of faith or worldview predisposition? Whether the most ranting atheist or the most tolerant modernist or the most ardent religious convert, prior faith choices mainly outside "reason" informed rational thinking and action on these issues. How could it be other? How could one, like the illusory positivist quest, find an objective standard against which to be sure of one's own rational choices? Impossible, Andy realized, with a finality that surprised and somewhat terrified him.

Then how could one ever be certain about Jesus? Then again, how could one be certain *against* Jesus—or any other religious belief? There was no objective measure of rationality outside a community of belief, Andy realized. Only from within a prior faith choice of the "right" community of dialogue could one ever be "certain" about anything. There was no such thing as "the logic of faith," Andy intuited with sudden clarity. Only a prior faith choice of a community of belief that one then works out logically from that point on, or not. Francis Schaeffer once wrote demeaningly of Karl Barth that, in response to a student's question about "reason" in Christianity, he said sharply, "I use it!" Schaeffer faulted Barth for his extra-biblical rationality. Could Schaeffer have misunderstood? That was troubling.

Andy thought of Pascal's famous wager in his unedited *Pensées,* which was meant as *apologia* for his Christian faith over against "Christianity's cultured despisers." Pascal, whom Albert Einstein had dubbed the greatest mathematical mind of the previous millennium, freely allowed that Christian belief was a faith choice whose "logic" was only self-evident from within that choice. Andy knew all faith, therefore, to be unprovable on principle. *Credo ut intelligam* "I believe in order to understand." But wasn't that how all scientific inquiry started out as well? Or, "I intuit, therefore, I seek understanding." But Pascal, possessor of that brilliant logical mind, could also write: *"Le coeur a ses raisons que la raison ne connaît pas,* "The heart has its reasons that reason does not know." Andy wondered about G. E. in this light. He also wondered about everyone's heart in the prior faith choices they make just to continue on in an incredibly unyielding universe.

The next day, Andy caught Dan at an early breakfast before he had headed out for work. Andy launched forth. "Why would your dad, who knows well the feeling of 'outsider,' have done what he did, Dan?"

"You've got to understand, the paradox of G. E. to understand that, Andy, but it's a simple human paradox. Think of the Jews devastated as a people by the Holocaust, who then turn around and do exactly the same to the Palestinians. Think of the colonial pre-Americans who flee to the new land for freedom and to escape tyranny, then promulgate identically vile state laws against fellow Americans, not to mention founding the modern 'penitentiary,' an American invention of terror now tragically imitated around the world. Or think of the decimation of Mexicans in Texas before statehood, of Indians across the nation, and of blacks and slavery, just some of the atrocities committed by Americans in the 'land of the free,' legitimated and celebrated by the state.

"So my dad is a walking paradox. Welcome to the human race! Welcome to our own lives full of paradoxes. Ever know of a Tibetan monk that didn't step on ants? Ever imagine upholding our laws without, as a state, doing what any individual citizen could never do—killing others? Isn't it grandly ironic that America, the most 'freedom-loving' country in the world by its own mythology, should be so oppressive toward others the world over? Isn't it strange that in past societies, the king was best defined by his exclusive right to do violence and kill, just as the State is today? Isn't it utterly paradoxical that America, in its desire to be 'free' and 'legal' should slaughter enemies, beginning with the British, continuing on with the Indians, the Mexicans, the Blacks, the Filipinos, the Viet Cong… Well, you get the idea.

"So my dad is really a paradox like all of us. I find his kind of religious inconsistency utterly frustrating at times, yet fascinating as well. I know my dad's anger toward me, yet I also feel his love—if I admit it, which I don't care to do very much these days…" Dan's voice trailed off.

Andy was at a loss. His mind was going every which way just trying to keep up.

"Andy, face it. Nothing in life is straightforward, uncomplicated or self-evident, least of all Christian faith. If you haven't realized that already, you'll see."

With that, Dan headed outside to mow the lawns.

Dear Professor Norton:

Sorry not to have written for a while. A lot has happened since I last wrote! Explain to me, dear Professor, one small request, the mysteries of life. You've lived twice as much now. You must know. Okay, Uncle! I get it! I'm asking twice as many questions now as at twelve-years-old! Does it just pick up? Are the questions cascading over you at twice the rate now? When does it end?

What's that quip by the black gang leader turned evangelist out of New York? "If Christ is the answer, what are the questions?"

Over here! Here! I've got my hand up! Ask me! Only, the questions will fill up the universe as surely as those books about Jesus would, as John says in his gospel.

I came to the Centre with immense respect for G. E., as you know. Well, that's wilted a bit. Not, as I think about it, primarily because of my experience of him, though there have been moments—not least this "who's in, who's out charade" he just pulled off!

Rather, it's Dan. He's a whole universe of questions in his own right. But something's not right, and it is not just Dan, I fear. I think his dad is Dan's biggest question, enigma. Find that answer and…

I'll finish off with one more: Janys. She pays me mind, and already more than she knows, shares her skills, keeps me on track more than anyone I've known. That says a lot. She's not Lorraine. She's not Fiona. She's… Janys, quirky spelling and all. I hope you haven't lost touch…

Time to go! Toilet detail this week. Thanks as always. Write sometime!

Andy

14

The best ideas are stolen, so the saying goes, and GO cashed in on its share of *pop-evangelica*. If Inter-Varsity could hold a triennial missions conference at Urbana, why couldn't the brethren do likewise at Wheaton College, Billy Graham's famed alma mater? So the interval between G. E.'s bombshell and the Christmas break was astir with preparations for the fourth triennial *GO YE* ("Gospel Outreach Youth Evangelism") Congress for brethren young people from across Canada and the United States.

Adding insult to injury, or certainly in perpetuation of that inner circle motif, the *chosen* were assigned the task of organizing a four-day workshop for the Congress, entitled *Care to GO?* The *hoi polloi* were assigned the more menial tasks of constructing booth dividers, folding thousands of leaflets and schedules, and helping with mailings. Work assignments from mid-November until Christmas break became almost exclusively related to the Great Event. G. E. became simply inaccessible, likewise Mr. Myers. Support staff showed the strain, and "voluntary" overtime for everyone became routine.

Mr. Myers asked Gary and Andy to lead the GO workshop team. For Andy, this came as exoneration, though nothing was said about his relationship with Fiona. For almost two months, they had hardly talked to each other. With what had they threatened her? Whatever it was, she steered clear, and Andy reciprocated. He could almost be philosophical about it. He was not "burning," as Paul put it. He was on a mission for God. Obviously, a relationship would be a serious distraction. Then he'd catch sight of Fiona across the cafeteria and wince. How had Dan put it? "Way out in front!" Jack never talked about her. Andy presumed she was keeping Jack at arm's length too.

Gary and Andy's preparation for the seminar was to be completed in five afternoon planning sessions. Gary and Sharon Collins had become newlyweds at Emmaus Bible School the previous summer. Gary was bright, a quick learner, and innovative. He was also a gifted guitarist with a powerful tenor voice. He and Sharon became a veteran duet in church circles while at Emmaus. It was not surprising they consequently tied the knot.

Sharon was pretty and vivacious, redheaded, with a singing voice that soared. She loved teasing, though had an almost wooden Christian ethic around sex. She could be enormously naïve. Once, in a Doctrines class of all places, she opined that abstinence in marriage was a great source of spiritual edification! Poor Gary crumpled into his seat, not a little red-faced. Everyone knew they'd been married only a few months…

Gary and Andy did some initial planning right before supper one night at their mish house. They got talking about Francis Schaeffer. Gary told Andy he had finally read Schaeffer's first major book, *The God Who is There,* which had created quite a stir in Evangelical circles. What had Andy thought of it?

"In my third year," Andy responded, "I was studying Gotthold Ephraim Lessing, an 18th century German intellectual and literary critic. He was drinking at the wells of an incipient Enlightenment understanding of reality that is, of course, the air we breathe today. He ended up taking on a Christian pastor who took strong exception to Enlightenment thinking in a public exchange of letters. Lessing is credited in this exchange with having written the unofficial motto of the Enlightenment, in response to Orthodox Christian belief: 'There is an ugly broad ditch between the accidental truths of history and the necessary truths of reason.'"

Dan came in and sat down, immediately perking up at the discussion.

"So Lessing was saying," Gary paraphrased his statement into a question, "that historical events so claimed by Christians, such as the Crucifixion and Resurrection, are not in themselves self-evident 'truths,' compared to the 'necessary truths of reason' held universally by the clear-minded, such as the belief that the earth is flat, which was once held universally as an axiomatic truth?"

"Gary, that's brilliant!" Andy responded, glancing at Dan. "Kant called such things 'categorical imperatives.' And your Declaration of Independence starts out, doesn't it, in classic Enlightenment fashion, 'We hold these truths to be self-evident…'

"Schaeffer and others have helped me see the fallacy in such thinking. I ended up doing a major essay on Lessing's 'ugly broad ditch' critique of Christianity. Luckily, I was reading Schaeffer, Colin Brown, John Warwick Montgomery, Norman Anderson, and others at the time. My essay got an A-plus from a surprised German prof who doubted initially that I should take on such a great thinker…

"And," Gary prodded.

"Well," Andy replied, "there was a 'self-evident' truth Lessing himself was overlooking. The truth is, 'truth'—even the 'necessary truths of reason'—are not so obviously 'true' or 'necessary' after all."

Dan could not hold back. "The great Michael

Polanyi objection, precisely! Had Mr. Lessing been able to transport himself magically and linguistically to the headhunters roaming around New Guinea at the time, he'd have quickly found out how *non*-universally-self-evident were his 'necessary truths' after all, perhaps only moments before falling prey to their 'necessary truth,' namely, *outsiders were best in the cooking pot, and his sun-shrunken head pride-of-place charm above the chief's doorway.*

"Such counter-cultural 'truth' to Lessing's might have been just the corrective needed to have nipped in the bud the overweening arrogance of the emerging new orthodoxy called 'Enlightenment,' which quickly displaced Christianity amongst the educated elite. At the very least, it might have lopped off Lessing's own smug rationality by turning it into an emaciated piece of door decoration. The Enlightenment myth of necessary truths of reason is precisely that: *a myth,* about as compelling as a wrinkled prune—or a shrunken head."

Andy's face turned wide-eyed. The image was evocative. This was the Great Cynic himself defending, it sounded like, Christianity, or clearing the way for it…

"Truth is," Dan continued, eyebrows arched, face fully animated, "those early Enlightenment intellectuals, like their heirs today, took up their own pick and shovel and dug themselves that 'ugly broad ditch,' which they discovered they could not cross over. There is a Latin term for the phenomenon: *petitio principii* or 'begging the question': you start out with the beliefs and disbeliefs (usually called 'presuppositions,' less kindly, 'prejudices' or 'superstitions') you end up with. Otherwise known simply as circular reasoning. If I start out telling you, like the famed atheist Albert Camus, that I will accept answers to the riddles of the universe *only if* they eschew Transcendence, then, golly gee, I'll end up an atheist at the end of the day, just the way I began. But I ask, who was the ditch-digger in that case?"

Andy heard Sharon rustling about in the kitchen. Gary had leaned forward and was listening intently. Andy sat back and took it all in.

"Fact of the matter is," continued Dan, "there are no necessary truths outside prior faith commitments. The issue then becomes openness or tolerance. *Credo ut intelligam,* 'I believe in order to understand.' That is as true of Christian understanding as it is of all science, which invariably has its origins in irrationality and intuition, or if you like, non-rational prior faith commitments."

Gary let out a low whistle. "And you figure all this out on that ride-on lawnmower of yours, Dan?"

Andy looked up as Sharon stepped into the doorway. She loved to cook. Better yet, her mom was German, so Sharon was beginning to try out some amazing German recipes on her willing guinea pigs. "I'm sorry to bring you all back down to more simple self-evident truths," she began, "where the men were invariably hunters and we women folk dressed whatever meat you dragged in! Well, good hunters all, let's set that heady stuff aside for a while and do what the good Lord truthfully and self-evidently made you to do: appreciate the woman's homemade cooking! Can someone please call the others?" Their intense meeting broke up with a laugh. As Andy bounded upstairs to call down the others, he still couldn't get over Dan.

After supper clean up, Andy and Gary settled in at the dining-room table. Fifty or more participants were anticipated at the *GO YE* workshop. Included in the offerings were target projections of trainees for the next two years. One of Gary and Andy's tasks was to concoct imaginative ways of inducing enlistment.

G. E.'s pride and joy was also to be presented at the Congress: a new Ken Anderson film entitled *Who Will GO?* It was to be premiered on the first evening for the entire assemblage then shown again during Andy and Gary's workshop. Gary and Andy first viewed the film in George Myers's office. It was impressive, a globe-trotting extravaganza that encompassed all seven continents, saturated the viewer's conscious and subconscious mind with myriad images and facts, and had strains of *So Send I You* reprised throughout. The effect, at least on Andy, was a sense of needs overkill. It evoked longings to transform his own puny mission endeavours and life into some kind of earthshaking, cosmic initiative—as if he should replicate somehow the 2,000-year impact of the Incarnation itself. He felt exhausted as the last credit faded, giving in to a wave of deep intimidation. He was so horribly inadequate, so unprepared, so uncommitted! He felt morose, identifying with the "such a worm as I" of the hymn writer. Yet G. E. had spoken in the film of God's "call of the small," even if his examples of such appeared as giants of the faith to Andy. Andy's respect for G. E. went way up once again.

A specific plug for GO would have appeared presumptuous or even anti-climactic in the body of the film, so it was worked into the introduction and end credits. GO's headquarters and emblem were also highlighted at one point when the film spotlighted some of the recent burgeoning youth missions.

Mr. Myers was nearly euphoric in anticipation of the film's impact for *GO YE '71* and countless other occasions of expected showings. There was talk of having it distributed worldwide through Billy Graham Evangelistic Films.

CHRYSALIS CRUCIBLE

The next day, Gary and Andy viewed it again together with the "Eighteen Club" or "The Chosen," as Dan called them. The effect was immediate: a McLuhanesque illustration of "hot communication" par excellence. It was so inspiring that their first organizational meeting was ablaze with a kind of holy delight. Prayers expressed a profound sense that the Holy Spirit would surely use that film and the workshop to reach countless youth with the missionary challenge. A near mini-revival attended the unusually long prayer time. All were loath to bring the session to an end.

A Priorities Questionnaire was to be developed for the first session, designed to facilitate reflection on where each participant stood in response to the film's message. The questions were to prick already tenderized consciences...

During the last planning session, Mr. Myers was so impressed he called G. E. in on the spot.

"Well done, well done!" G. E. enthused. "I think you've done the film justice, and *GO YE '71* a great service! Furthermore, you've demonstrated a real grasp of missions principles." Then, after a brief word of prayer with the group, he disappeared once again behind his heavy office door.

Just like his son, the observation leapt into Andy's consciousness as he turned to observe the near beatific appearance of Mr. Myers' countenance.

A memo in their respective mailboxes greeted Gary and Andy the following day:

You have both shown creative leadership. I like how you have worked together. I am thinking of having you jointly head up the West Berlin team, though traditionally team leaders have been married. Please be praying.

Triumphantly in Christ,

G. E.

P. S. Please, no word of this to anyone else.

P. P. S. for Andy: I sense in you a cleansing work of God's Spirit, not only in relation to Fiona but hopefully to women in general, and also in accepting authority—something seriously missing in today's young adults. Can you please book an appointment with Jean before Christmas? We're both very busy, I know, but I'd like to share personally with you again before Christmas break.

The effect of G. E.'s memo on Andy was allegiance: like the eager pup delighted by pats and goodies. Andy sensed this made him somewhat traitor to Dan's unvoiced cause. But he wanted what G. E. could give, what G. E. was way too much…

The month of December, while milder overall than in Kitchener-Waterloo, was nonetheless adequate to awaken in Andy a recurrently joyous anticipation of Christmas. If April was the cruellest month for T. S. Eliot, December, for Andy, was the most magical. Myriad recollections fuelled his thrill at the season's advance: endless hours of backyard hockey rink-building with games played throughout the day and under night illumination, with indoor breaks only to get the rink flooded. These breaks were also filled with indoor games in Andy's basement. There was also the early childhood thrill of Santa—who was permitted to delight them in contradistinction to other church families bent on precluding any possibility of Christ enduring a rival—as well as relatives, friends, food, gifts, games, and kaleidoscopic images all in colourful abundance.

And there was the celebration of Christ's birth itself, which struck deep, resonant chords in the centre of Andy's being. He had only recently discovered J. R. R. Tolkien's masterful description of the Nativity as the *eucatastrophe* of human history—the pivotal point of all humanity's strivings, of which the Resurrection was the eucatastrophe in turn. The Christmas season evoked the deep wistfulness of a better place, a different world, the *Sehnsucht* of which Tolkien's contemporary and erstwhile friend, C. S. Lewis wrote. At times during Christmas, the longing inside Andy could grow into an excruciating ache, so intensely charged was that time of the year. The expectant mood in anticipation of *GO YE '71* only enhanced his personal euphoria. Yes, his dad had anticipated aright the Lord's call to this place…

A mini-renewal movement swept through the Centre the first week of December. Spontaneous prayer meetings erupted regularly. *GO YE '71* was upheld in a concert of petitions lasting through the night at times. It was perhaps the closest any anti-Pentecostal brethren group dared get to a charismatic experience, though such terminology was anachronistic to most then.

On the second Friday night in December, Andy was called to the phone in the Admin Building after 11:00. Luckily, some were still playing ping-pong at that hour. It was Lorraine. Susan must have given her the number…

More than a third of a year had passed since their last talk on a magical bench in Victoria Park. Andy imagined that bench now, likely covered with snow, the pond frozen. He wondered if people were skating on it already. He pictured their relationship similarly frozen.

"Lorraine?" Andy spoke into the phone.

There was a long silence though palpable presence at the other end. Andy imagined every particle of her face. His entire body sagged onto the hard wooden chair. He closed the phone booth's door tightly.

He heard soft sobbing, but there was no supple body to encircle, however awkwardly. Every fibre wanted to protect her, to reach out, to nurture, to caress, to make it to never have happened, to fast forward hers, his, everyone's, the universe's, narrative to that part in the fairy tale where it was eucatastrophe, where "they lived happily ever after." He was delirious with it, with her, with aching longing. Remembered enthrallment cascaded like a zephyr waft of pollen-engorged summer breeze. He had feelings all right!

Through her tears, "It's really you, Andy?"

"Yes," he said just above a whisper.

"I've fantasized about this moment for weeks, just to hear your voice…"

"How are you doing, Lorraine?" Such flaccid words!

"I'm all right. I have a job, in a day care. My aunt's been great. I'm starting therapy in the New Year. I miss you!"

Andy paused a long time. "Me too, Lorraine. Me too."

Long silence.

"When are you coming home for the holidays, Andy? Can I see you?"

Andy had wondered about this a thousand times. Would she want to? How to fit it in? And where? His parents… He hated the thought. "Lorraine, we'll work something out. I know we will. We have to!

"I'm literally making a flying stop home for Christmas. Don't know yet how I'll even get there. But I have to be back right after Christmas for this huge congress. And I have to spend time at home... It'll be tight, Lorraine. But we'll make it happen."

Several sobs ensued. "Andy, I have to go. Call me about Christmas. Here's the number..." She gave it and was gone. Andy couldn't even repeat it to her.

Frost was crisp underfoot, the air biting, and the stars magnificent at quick glance as he headed back to his mish house. He also felt frosty and biting, hardly magnificent. But she had phoned!

I am so confused, he confessed to his diary that night. *Where is all this heading? Can't someone tell me? O, wretched man that I am!*

Praise the Lord. In him is the victory!

It is 12:36 a.m. Good night.

Depression was his mood upon awakening. Even a friendly tussle with Jack didn't shake it. Why couldn't he rewrite the summer to turn out right? He wouldn't even be at GO in that case. So was it God's severe mercy? Or should he remove Lorraine from his memory, like expunging an act in a play, as if she had never been a part of the script in the first place? She walked out on him after all. She also walked in, for that matter, laden with baggage she had not warned him about. The mood persisted all day. He was not good company for anyone.

The next week, Tuesday, December 21st, the snow came at last. Just in the nick of time. Two vanloads were leaving for O'Hara Airport the next afternoon. The snow had started after midnight and was still dropping copiously the next morning as people streamed out of the mish houses in exuberant response to the white magnificence. For many, snow had been known only from photos. Expressions of wild delight punctuated the snow-charged air. Classes were cancelled since some teachers could not make it in.

Snowballs began to fly, texture just right. Novices quickly learned that it was a stinging business with bare hands and retreated inside to emerge with new winter gloves. Snow forts began to pile up, from which sallies were made against other bastions, with loyalties falling roughly along team lines. The French team succeeded early on in demolishing the Spaniards' stronghold, only to lose theirs to the Germans while gloating over their victory. In turn, Andy and others suddenly were the recipients of a full-scale onslaught from all available recruits; quickly leaving only crumbled snowy debris and chaotically arranged body parts as a sign of the short-lived building-spree.

Out of that wreckage emerged snowmen-making initiatives, some of the creations towering over their fashioners. The Spaniards tackled one of them, cascading down in another mass of arms, legs, and whitish morass. Soon thereafter, all others lay in ruins as well.

"Let's head over to G. E.'s!" someone shouted, "where the snow is all fresh." Twenty or so were off, hooting and volleying snowballs back and forth over the two blocks' distance G. E. lived from the Centre in a spacious ranch-style home.

Some organizing quickly transpired en route, resulting in a massive snowman quietly and efficiently being erected in G. E.'s front yard. Finishing touches were needed on top, and suddenly there was Jack hoisting Fiona onto his broad shoulders, eliciting a gleeful hoot, which enabled her to position a hat, a big stick for a pipe, and some rocks for eyes. "Like this Andy?" she caught his eye. "I've never done this before! Isn't this absolutely grand?" A nose was missing until Jack reached up his black comb.

"Jack! I'm falling!" Fiona's frantic scream pierced the whitewashed tranquility. Andy lunged to break Fiona's fall, caught her desperately around the waist, then lost his footing and careened backwards with Fiona crashing down on top of him, her snow-laced hair splashing over his face. He held on for dear life. Memory flashed a similar embrace on a warm fall afternoon, car disappearing around the corner. Again his hold lingered. Fiona made no move. The world stood still in its white magic grip.

Then she exploded from on top of Andy, and, with a squeal, picked up a great scoop of snow and promptly washed his face in it. Then she did the same to Jack, who was still lying prone. "You both deserve it!" She cried fiercely as the front door opened and G. E. stepped out onto the front porch.

Everyone erupted as planned into *I'm Dreaming of a White Christmas*. G. E.'s wife, Dan (surprise!), and sister also stepped out. Andy, Fiona, and Jack scrambled to their feet, looking a mess. It took several gulps of frosty air before they could join in.

The merriment subsided only long enough for them to cajole G. E. and his family into joining an uproarious snowball fight that saw the snowman toppled and the large front yard churned into snowy cheese. Dan got into the fray fully. It occurred to Andy that he saw him laugh out loud—and repeatedly—for the very first time.

Andy couldn't help but notice (Or was it his imagination?) that Fiona stayed near Jack—or was it the other way around? Then, just as he was on the verge of feeling sorry for himself, she flew at him with all her might, tumbling him wildly backwards. She pinned his arms to the ground and sat fully astride his chest. She swooped her head low, brushing his face with more than hair, and whispered triumphantly in his ear, "I don't care who's noticing!" Then, just as abruptly, she was up and gone. Andy was too stunned to give chase.

He looked around, but G. E. was not in sight. Then he scooped up a snowball to hurl at Janys, who had just turned his way. She ran, and he pursued.

The action streamed on to the Myers' a few blocks away for a more or less repeat performance, then finally dispersed.

Dan invited Andy to the Jack in the Box for lunch, a rather slushy affair. They continued a conversation in his room afterwards. It was Andy's first time to see Dan's set-up. Books were everywhere. There was also an expensive sound system in one corner.

The walls had two posters, each a surprise. One was of Martin Luther King, Jr. "Yeah," Dan explained. "That was the night he started out, 'I Have a Dream.'" Andy had not heard of that speech, or much of King himself, so he said nothing. The other poster was of a seated, elderly woman framed by torsos of two policemen with billy clubs and guns. She wore a sun hat and was looking up at them with smiling determination.

"Dorothy Day, ever heard of her?" Dan asked.

Andy had not.

"She founded something called *The Catholic Worker*. She took a stand against war when it was totally unpopular with her Catholic peers, claiming Jesus as her reason. She also founded all these community houses that cared for poor and marginalized people."

"Was she a Communist?" Andy asked.

"Not sure," came the reply. "Why?"

"Sounds like it," Andy returned. "I noticed you were home last night, Dan."

Dan's mouth could twitch sometimes. He explained that he had spent the night with his family—a periodic occurrence—and had felt frustrated again. "I just don't understand Dad. He can't unwind or something. We're watching TV all together, and the next thing I hear, Dad's on the phone to someone. Not because they called but because he called them! That's always been Dad's way. He never seems to sit still. Always preoccupied, so driven. It's impossible to even try a card game with Dad.

"And I can't get very far discussing anything with him, except on his terms. He invariably turns around and lays another heavy on me about my Christian walk. As if he doesn't know *he's* the greatest stumbling block to it!"

Dan's last sentence jolted Andy from his own reveries, preoccupied with snowflakes and Fiona. Andy asked Dan for the first time whether he had problems with Christian belief. He had, after all, been reading great thinkers who were not by any means Christian. "But I also heard what you said at supper the other day about presuppositions and such."

"Andy, I won't be one of your converts—nor anyone else's! The question itself makes me nervous, like the *shibboleth* the ancient Hebrews used to determine who was in, who was out. I know you wish I'd just come out cleanly for the Lord. I have been around enough other waves of Dad's recruits over the years, after all. But I won't play that game. Though I know Dad and Mom wish your influence would really rub off one day."

Dan continued. "After everyone went to bed last night, I watched TV for a while. There was this evangelist on, the kind that makes my blood boil. Just as I flipped to that station, he was interviewing some famous football player out of Texas I'd never heard of. The gist was, believe like this guy, and you can become great, too. Shit, Andy. That's the great American con game, selling everything from snake oil to Jesus!

"'Losing in the great game of life?' they all intone," Dan's nostrils flared as his voice switched to falsetto pitch, "'Swallow the Jesus pill, or use Brylcream, no difference. Sign on the dotted line, and you'll be a winner, too. Look at this guy or gorgeous female…' And if you swallow that bait, you're hooked all right, though hardly a winner."

He turned to face Andy. "So how do *you* avoid it?"

"Avoid what?" Andy asked.

"Being a con man for Jesus. I mean, isn't that what you're all here for? To move product à la Adam Smith and *laissez-faire* capitalism, this one labelled 'Jesus'?"

Dan connected dots often that Andy hadn't a clue about.

"So what do you say," Dan asked, "to those who claim Christianity will make you a winner? What about all the football and basketball games that start with prayer in the dressing room?

"Like all the wars that start with the chaplains praying down God's victory on both sides? In a word, Andy, *Bullshit!*"

Dan's vocabulary was nothing if not pointed. But Andy had to agree with him on some points. He had also grown leery of the "celebrity Gospel" that seemed to be all about inner and outer circles. "Follow Christ and be as famous/beautiful/talented/rich/successful as So-and-So." What had Dietrich Bonhoeffer written? "When Jesus calls a man to follow, he bids him come and die." Just how did the celebrity Gospel fit into that?

Andy used to think there was only one Gospel. He was discovering there were many. The trick, he realized, was to choose the right one. Something like discerning the spirits, he mused. The trick further was to choose without self-indulgence yet, paradoxically he knew, with passionate engagement.

"So, Dan," Andy asked, "the same question. Are you a Christian?" Even he couldn't believe his persistence.

Dan smiled. "Guess!"

Andy went next door for a nap.

15

Classes ended Wednesday morning, December 22nd. GO was squeezing the most out of its trainees, "redeeming the time." That same afternoon, two vanloads of trainees left for the airport, amongst them, Fiona.

Just as the driver of Fiona's van called for everyone to hop in, she beckoned to Andy, who was standing with a few others on the periphery. He stepped toward her. "Hope you have a great Christmas, Andy. Doing anything special other than with family?"

Was she fishing for something?

He said simply, "Mainly with family." Close enough to the truth.

"Pray for me," she said. "This is only our third Christmas without Timmy." Her eyes welled with tears. She hugged him quickly, told him to take care, then stepped into the van. He went back to his mish house to pack, overwhelmed.

At 4:30, Andy headed for the requested meeting with G. E. He shook Andy's hand warmly, placing an arm around him until he sat down. There were two desk lamps lit. It was completely dark outside.

"Andy," G. E. began, "I believe we have come a long way since our talk in early October."

Andy wondered at his use of the term "we."

"If you mean, sir, that I have gone through some changes since coming here, there is no doubt about it," Andy said tactfully.

"That's good to hear, son. Good to hear…" Another of G. E.'s long, probing pauses. "I see that you and Dan have been spending some time together."

How had he known?

"I hope you take what he says with a grain of salt…"

Andy glanced out the bay window. Someone was walking toward the Admin Building. A dog barked in the distance. The office had less the feel of bustle than ever before. Just then, Andy noticed soft Christmas music playing from a tape deck.

His mind drifted to his anticipated trip home. One of the trainees from Colorado was flying home, determining the long drive over treacherous passes in the winter was too dangerous, especially in a VW Bug. He'd offered it to Andy after hearing that he and Janys, who would be travelling with him, would have to take a long series of buses home, and spend forever getting there. Andy's dad had not been pleased about the VW but agreed the alternative cut too much into his time at home.

So it was set. Andy and Janys would be heading out together in the wee hours of the morning and would drive straight to an uncle and aunt Janys had in Toronto. Her dad and Ted would be waiting there to drive her north to Sudbury. That was two days before Christmas. Andy would stay the night at Susan's then drive with her Christmas Eve morning to Kitchener. She had been having a few car problems anyway, and had to be back to work on the 28th. So it was perfect. On December 27th, they would reverse the process. There was so little time.

What was not shared with anyone but Susan was that Andy would get together with Lorraine the night they arrived in Toronto. They would have supper at Susan's if Andy made it in time. Then Susan was going out with friends, leaving her delightful apartment available to Andy and Lorraine for a visit. Andy couldn't wait.

A question from G. E. penetrated Andy's wayward thoughts. "…been hard to avoid girls this fall, Andy?"

"Pardon, sir?" came Andy's self-conscious reply. What else had G. E. been saying to him while his mind took in his reunion with Lorraine?

"How has the Lord worked in your heart this fall about your relationship to girls?"

He wanted to give G. E. something to chew on, but he really had no bone to throw.

"Well, sir… I guess I've learned to be patient." He had to be honest. This was a bit of a dance.

"Andy, God has the right person for you, to be sure. But, I mean, are you still feeling the urge to… Experiment, shall we say?"

"Sir?"

"Andy, you told me you masturbated sometimes. Do you think about any of the girls you've dated or anyone else you've known, when you do? I mean, to experiment in any way?" G. E. closed in.

"Sir, I've never 'experimented' with any girl I've been in a relationship with," Andy said back, a hot tingling rising at the nape of his neck. Was it showing in front, too? He hoped not. "If you mean sexually."

There was a long silence. The probing eyes.

"Andy, all men struggle with lust. Plain and simple," G. E.'s voice hissed on the word. "You know Jesus' words about 'lusting after a woman' being the same as fornicating with her. It's the purity of your soul at issue, Andy. That's what I'm after."

Strange, the thought occurred, in all his sessions with Uncle Joe—who could sometimes tell stories you'd only hear in a bar—Andy had never felt a hint of questioning from him sexually. Maybe it was his sister's modelling, but he honestly had no great interest in "experimenting" or fooling around. His sister once called it boring with reference to a friend who bed-hopped.

"You've seen one, you've seen 'em all, Andy!" She'd say with a laugh. It was true, Andy thought. She'd seen enough for sure from her nurse's training and hospital work. "Besides," she said, ever playfully, "who wants to keep cleaning up the sticky mess all over you know where?" He'd asked her once if she ever would do it before marriage. She wouldn't say but clearly hadn't, Andy was sure. For his part, he doubted he'd ever tire of seeing nude women. It had just always been a conscious choice not to go there.

"Mr. Moore, I've got some packing to do. Dan and I were going to take in a movie, and it's almost supper, which I told Dan I'd help with." Andy knew movies were accepted in the States for brethren youth to watch. "I know I'm not clean sexually. I do have lustful thoughts. But like Mrs. Graham once said of her famous husband regarding doubts, I don't entertain them. I think I fairly successfully 'flee youthful lusts' as Paul wrote Titus. Though were a nude nubile woman to walk into the office right now, I'd likely take a second look in spite of myself, even though that was David's problem with Bathsheba, not the first look but the second…"

G. E. stood up in some fluster. "Andy, you don't get it! You can't even talk like that! It betrays a lustful heart! And there is no place on the mission field for such!

"I cannot possibly place you into a role of leadership with those kinds of thoughts coursing through your mind! I believe this is an area of unconfessed sin, Andy. I implore you, seek God on this, as David prayed after Bathsheba, and see if there be a wicked way in you. Let God show you, Andy. That is my charge to you over Christmas."

Andy wanted to help Dan with dinner, and he really did not want to go to the late showing of the movie. Didn't G. E. have to get home, too? He could hear no movement now in the whole building. He caught the clock on the mantle from the corner of his eye, but could not see the time on it in the darkened light.

"I hope there will be nothing going on over Christmas with that girl in Kitchener, Andy." At that moment, Andy could have screamed at his dad for ever having talked to G. E. about Lorraine. It felt like a violation.

"Andy?" G. E. repeated imperiously.

All Andy wanted to do was bolt. "Mr. Moore, there will be nothing whatsoever 'going on' with 'that girl from Kitchener,' I assure you," he said evenly, like a cat backed into a corner. There was a tone in Andy's voice that even he had not known before.

G. E. hesitated. "Andy, I can see we're going to have to keep these counselling sessions up in the New Year. I'll be instructing you about that once you return.

"We'll go ahead with your co-leadership of the seminar at the Congress. Everything is in place for it now, and last-minute changes would be impossible. But I'm putting on hold any thought of your leadership on the Berlin Team. That will be the focus of our times together in January.

He took Andy's hands. "God can do great things through you, through us all. But we must be totally clean vessels for God to declare us 'a man after God's own heart,' as it says in Hebrews. I've wrestled mightily for you at the Throne of Grace in prayer already. I assure you, that will continue. You have great gifts, Andy. You're bright, talented, 'tall, dark, and handsome,' a natural leader. Don't squander it all for a mess of pottage, my son. Don't throw it all away for a woman! Let's pray."

He launched into a fervent prayer for God's special portion to be on Andy and travelling mercies for their journey the next day. He gave Andy an extra squeeze of the hands, a reassuring pat on his back, and sent him on his way.

As Andy descended the staircase, he thought that the "man after God's own heart," according to Hebrews, was the sex addict David with hundreds of wives and concubines, who'd set up Bathsheba's husband to be killed in battle so he could have Bathsheba all for himself and to cover up the fact he'd already got her pregnant while her husband was on the front lines. A "man after God's own heart," indeed he snorted derisively. Then he caught himself. He was beginning to sound too much like Dan, he self-scolded.

His mind was racing, seething. He thought of the *Eighteen Club*. The sequel to the whole caper had been anticlimactic. In the mailbox of the entire blacklisted group, the Friday before Christmas break, was a terse memo from G. E. personalized only by his signature: "You have shown progress. Keep up the good work. You're off probation."

Everyone had received an identical memo, it turned out. There were no further interviews. Except Ken Kincaide. Andy had heard from him on Monday. Ken had not received that note. He had also been scheduled for a series of interviews with G. E. in the New Year. Poor Ken! Andy had already agreed to get together with Ken in the New Year to talk about it, but without relish. Ken was strange by all accounts, not least of which his roommate's.

Had the blacklisting all been a holy ploy? Andy

wondered. And where was G. E. getting off with him? Andy would see it through, he knew. He was committed to GO . He thought of Dan. In response, Fiona flitted across his mind, chased away immediately by G. E.'s stern censure. Maybe I am fickle more than I admit, Andy thought.

Whatever else, he realized as he dashed across the yard toward their mish house, he was coming to dread crossing the threshold of G. E.'s office. Dan had warned him.

G. E. was complex… Indeed.

16

Early the next morning, while the sky was still a black dome of stars, Andy walked over to Janys's mish house to get her bags. Jack had already flown home, and Dan had moved home for the holidays, so no one was around to see them off.

They set out at about 4:00 a.m., praising the Lord for such excellent weather and road conditions. But not far into Canada, it began to snow. Andy chuckled at that, mentioning to Janys how most Americans in the southern states believe that, summer and winter, snow is actually piled up in huge drifts along the border, acting as a natural demarcation of the 49th parallel. He included the story he had heard several times from his mom about Americans arriving in Kitchener during a July heat wave, skis atop their car and obviously packed for winter weather.

"Voltaire wrote, in *Candide*, I think, of Canada as *quelques arpents de neige*—a few acres of snow. Though I doubt many Americans have ever read Voltaire, I reckon they have about the same notion," Andy chortled.

Janys chided Andy for having translated *quelques arpents de neige.*

Conditions worsened rapidly. The thermometer plummeted, and it soon became apparent that a Great Lakes blizzard was brewing. The radio broadcast storm warnings and notices of extreme caution to motorists.

By the late afternoon, traffic had slowed considerably. They passed several stalls. Even with the additional defroster at full blast, the front windshield scarcely allowed a view through it. Suddenly, a fierce gust of wind whipped snow directly under the rear of the car. The motor sputtered and died. Andy was barely able to coast to the side of the highway.

Andy had looked at car engines about long enough to verify his suspected intense disinterest in—even passionate dislike for—the intimidating pile of metal and hose. He had not even obtained his driver's license until he began to date at the age of twenty when his erstwhile girlfriend had suggested it might be a nice thing to have. It was also she who had suggested it might be nice for Andy to have feelings, he remembered with a pang. So it was purely male ego show that induced him to get out and look at the engine this time. Thankfully, the owner of the car had pointed out that the engine was in the rear. He'd really have looked the fool otherwise.

Andy actually breathed a sigh of relief upon discovering that the motor was sufficiently whitewashed with snow, such that little could be seen of anything. It looked far better that way, he thought.

He tapped on the passenger window, and over the raging wind told Janys to climb into the driver's seat to get ready to try starting the car. "Perhaps," Andy ventured, mustering up all the authority his voice could pretend, "if I clear some of this snow away we can make her turn over." That sounded fairly authentic, he thought. Snow had packed in amazingly solidly under that small lid. He cursed Hitler, who had originated the idea of a little "People's Car," for putting a motor in the rear. "Probably would never have happened had the motor been in the front," he muttered to no one in particular. The wind blew his words right back.

As it turned out, in Andy's vigorous snow-removal activity, he had inadvertently pulled a spark plug wire. Had he noticed, he would have wondered where it came from and what to do with it. Within minutes of that mishap, a clear diagnosis of the problem emerged: a dead battery. Janys actually volunteered that information just ahead of Andy's observation, which left him a little nonplussed.

It was late afternoon. The wind was wild, the snow horizontal, and the thermometer hovering at about zero degrees Fahrenheit or lower. Daylight was fast retreating. They couldn't even get the news on the radio as they huddled inside under blankets mercifully kept in the front with just such emergencies in mind. Andy had tried for a few minutes to flag down passing motorists. But either they did not see him or feared stopping and getting stuck themselves. He hoped that someone would at least report them. As he retreated beneath the blankets, he wondered why could this not be with Fiona. The thought sprang forth before he could stuff it back down. Why couldn't his mind give it a break?

"Why don't you pray, Andy?" Janys suggested, deferring naturally to his male presence.

Pray? How incongruous, even absurd, it seemed suddenly. To pray! As if his prayer would somehow instantly stop the storm, like Jesus on the Sea of Galilee. Impossible. Then what use prayer? Andy's mind panted furiously. What is prayer? Had he ever uttered an authentic prayer, one that could move a few drifts of snow or make a car motor come back to life? Had prayer ever been more than a rote exercise, like rhyming off poetry or reciting a creed? Had he ever known any answers to prayer beyond the endless rationalizations of ostensibly unanswered petitions?

All this processed through his consciousness in seconds. Evoking a cough as a kind of prelude, Andy proceeded to beseech the Almighty. He felt his reputation was at stake, even more so than when he had looked at the dead motor. But he was no *thaumaturge*—nor wired to one. Did he really know anything more about God *experientially* than he did about reviving a car motor? Or was he content to be a mere passenger in the Christian enterprise without really looking into the motor itself—the reality, or otherwise, of a God who somehow acted into history or did not?

These questions flooded his mind in the extended silence after his rather perfunctory prayer until Janys broke into his brooding with a spontaneous, passionate plea to God to watch over them and remove them from danger. Thank God women were allowed to pray at GO with men around (brethren assemblies forbade it). Andy couldn't help but laugh inwardly. At least her prayer had a chance of getting above the wild blizzard. He thought he'd heard his bounce off the car roof.

Andy's mood darkened with the sky, leaving an uneasy aftertaste of uncertainty, like the acrid smell of burnt hair. It was tinged with an undefined sense of fear, not so much about the real predicament they were in as that this little experiment might elicit an unwelcome hypothesis, namely that God was just a product of one's religious upbringing cum wish fulfillment. Could he honestly face that possibility? And why could he not have prayed like Janys? Was this his "ugly broad ditch"?

The snow, caught intermittently in the headlights of passing cars, continued to blow mercilessly.

After some discussion of various courses of action, they fell silent, nursing their own fears, having decided that it was best to do nothing except wait. *Waiting for Godot* was culled up from Andy's memory. He recollected the hopeless absurdity of the Samuel Beckett play. It was, after all, in the "theatre of the absurd" genre.

Godot was obviously Beckett's variation of God—perhaps meaning a little, ineffectual, and ultimately unreal god. The play had been as bleak as Sartre's *La Nausée*. Andy remembered that often Beckett would not get out of bed until well into the morning or even into the afternoon, so fatigued was he with life. None of the brave staring down of evil urged by Sartre and other popularizing existentialists. Just the absurd routine of day-to-day living, relieved perhaps only by his creative instinct, like a full bladder was relieved by a satisfying urination, with perhaps no more appreciation of the act or the outcome.

"And if he comes, this little, useless god," asks Estragon stupidly. "Why, we'll be saved," Vladimir assures him as blankly. Otherwise we'll hang ourselves tomorrow. Why not? After all, what is the difference, if only in the state of consciousness, unless Godot comes? Unless Godot comes...

Suddenly, there was a loud banging on the roof, followed by faint yells over the wind. With great difficulty, Andy pushed open the driver's side door. He was also amazed at how high the snow had piled in such a relatively short space of time.

A large snowmobile had come up behind them. Andy was amazed they had neither heard the motor nor noticed its light.

"There's simply no way, lady!" the driver responded tersely to Janys's question about loading their luggage. "Don't even bother locking the doors! No fool thief will venture out in this weather, and you can come back in the morning when this blows itself out."

As it turned out, there was a motel a couple miles further down the road. The snowmobile driver, together with his brother, had been delivering people from other stalled vehicles for the last hour or so.

When Andy and Janys got there, several people were crowded into the foyer waiting to hear about a room, using the pay phone or simply warming themselves in front of a huge fireplace.

When it was their turn, Janys phoned her aunt first and asked them to contact Susan, who would then let Andy's parents know. Andy wondered if Lorraine was already at Susan's. They should be able to complete their journey the next day, Janys' aunt had said, given the weather forecast of a clear and cold Christmas Eve. Provided they could get their car started, Andy worried.

"One party to a room," the hotel proprietor explained to everyone. "Don't matter how many or who. Just be thankful you've got a warm place at all! Before the night's over, we might be sleeping six deep!"

Thankfully, it didn't turn out to be quite that crowded, but there was some doubling up of strangers. For their part, the two would-be-missionaries were assigned a small one-bed room. "Mr. and Mrs…?" she had asked, and Andy had deadpanned "Norton," before Janys could say anything. Why even bother explaining? They scanned the room briefly—there was only one bed—and then returned to the fireplace where they waited for supper.

Food was in good supply, though there was a hint of rationing certain items such as bread and butter. "Has to last to breakfast," the proprietor explained, "and God only knows how many more will be arriving."

Supper was sumptuous. Someone there knew how to cook! Amazingly, everyone fit into the dining room. All the tables were crowded with extra chairs scrounged from throughout the motel, but no one minded—on the contrary! The sense of warm, spontaneous community among this group of strangers was palpable. There was excited chatter and loud laughter throughout the supper hour. When had Andy last felt that at church?

Everyone at Andy and Janys' table had harrowing tales to tell, and all expressed immense gratitude. A minister was asked by the owner to say a prayer for the food. It was heartfelt, accompanied by several equally animated "Amen's."

"No atheists in fox holes I guess," Andy could hear Dan say cynically.

"I just hope the car isn't buried under a mountain of snow," Andy said to Janys during a rare lull in the conversation. "Or maybe the plow'll just run right over the little bug! I remember seeing a picture in the *Record* once of just that: a parked car in London had been squashed by an army vehicle doing emergency snow removal. Apparently the driver didn't even know until he'd rolled over it what had happened!"

Janys was not amused. "Just remember it's your stuff in there, too!" she said. Andy heard one of their rescuers report that they had checked every car on both sides of the highway in both directions until the next county, and that all traffic had ceased. Sure enough, guests stopped arriving by the time supper was over.

Afterwards, a spontaneous singsong erupted. Thanks to Eaton's carol sheets, almost all the verses of all the carols were sung, together with a good many of the more secularized kind that were not on the sheets.

Midway through the singsong, the motel plunged into darkness. A voice rang out saying there were lots of candles! Just be patient. Sure enough, soon candles were being lit and distributed for each table.

"My insurance is paid up," the proprietor said, "but please, be extra cautious. No one wants to stand around a bonfire tonight!" There was loud laughter. She had a spirited sense of humour just right for the occasion. "And can I ask just one thing? PLEASE DON'T FLUSH THE TOILETS UNTIL THE LIGHTS COME ON AGAIN! We'll hope everything doesn't freeze solid in the meantime! Now, let's have some more singing!"

The singing went on for a while longer. Then people began to drift off to their rooms. A final carol was suggested. Someone *had* to call out the all-time favourite, "I'm Dreaming of a White Christmas!" The room exploded in guffaws then erupted into a glorious rendition of same.

The landlady wrapped things up. "Goodnight to all, and don't hesitate to ask for anything. It's going to be a long night. More candles are on the table up here. Just remember to blow them out! Extra blankets are piled in the lobby. Please take just one per room, and cuddle up with your honey tonight."

With nothing left to do except go to bed, Andy and Janys picked up their duly assigned blanket and headed back to their room.

Awkwardness. It was unthinkable for Andy to sleep in the same bed with Janys. But where else? The floor was hard linoleum. There was no extra mattress. The rooms weren't the cleanest. Who knew what might be crawling around? And they'd need all the covers on the bed, and possibly still then some. If the power didn't come back on, it would be mighty cold by morning.

Janys read Andy's mind. "Andy, when we were kids, we'd sleep three and four to a bed sometimes, boys and girls. I think we have no choice tonight. We are, after all, 'Mr. and Mrs. Norton,'" she added flatly, her smile—Was it red-tinged?—expansive. Then impishly, "But we'll keep our clothes on. It's gonna

CHRYSALIS CRUCIBLE

be cold tonight!"

Andy laughed. That smile.

He recalled the Morrisons, former family friends that used to visit the Nortons for a few summers after they'd moved to Michigan. The whole family would move in for a week or so, including three sisters, all around the same age as Susan and Andy. They always pitched their tent in the backyard. One night, a huge thunderstorm streamed water through the floor, and everything was a soggy mess that took two days to dry out.

The night after the storm, the parents all went off to a church meeting, leaving the kids with a babysitter. Two sisters were to sleep with Susan in her bed, but there was not enough room for the third, so she was settled with Andy. They were all of seven or eight years old.

Not long after the sitter told them goodnight, Andy went to his dresser in the dark and, after some discussion with Carolyn, pulled out a pen flashlight he'd won for reciting verses at Sunday School and told her she could go first. Under the covers that night, abetted by the tiny flashlight, they both had repeated hands-on lessons in human anatomy.

Andy wondered about a repeat performance, but he knew candles caught fire under bed covers. He really had no interest in exploring Janys sexually that night. He was a committed Christian. Janys had not attracted him particularly, except her smile. He'd really come to like her smile. What was it he saw? He pushed all further thinking below his consciousness and rubbed his hands together. Already, the wind-battered room felt chilled.

"Well, okay, no toothbrush, Janys. I guess I'm about ready to crawl under," Andy said, after they'd tucked in the extra blanket at the end of the bed. "Do you want to use the bathroom first? Remember, there's no flushing…"

"No," she said calmly, "you go first."

"Coast is clear," he chimed afterwards, "Although a word of warning: The lock on the door is broken."

He climbed into bed, feeling a little more sexually charged than he'd thought.

"Good thing you have a sister!" Janys said as she stepped into the washroom.

"And you a brother," he fired back.

They laughed. Was it nervously?

Andy lay wide awake. He was feeling aroused. Yes. That was *le mot juste*, remembering the quip in *My Fair Lady*, "The French don't care what they do actually, as long as they pronounce it correctly—or have the 'right word.'" He did have the right word, but he also cared what he did.

It had been a long day. He'd done all the driving, the last two hours or so with taut nerves that still had not relaxed. The room, in candlelight glow, was simply appointed. It had a washroom with sink and shower, a bed, a desk, and a single easy chair he could have otherwise somewhat slept on. He thought of Lorraine. And Fiona. And his mom and dad. Susan! He could just imagine her mocking! Dan. G. E…. Groan, this last was the corker.

Janys came out at last. Andy was surprised to see her hair cascade almost to her waist. When she took off her glasses, he thought, wow, she should wear contacts. Then he thought he'd best stop using the word "wow." Then he thought he'd best stop thinking. But could not. She blew out the candle and climbed into bed. Two bodies in a single bed. Good thing she was petite and he slim. This was really weird.

CHRYSALIS CRUCIBLE   **139**

Though the storm raged furiously outside, Andy was already feeling cozy warm, almost euphoric in the darkness.

"Janys," Andy began, "have you already thought of this? What will people say if they know we literally 'slept together'?"

Janys giggled. "There was a Christian sect in medieval France called the Cathars that used to believe sleeping together without 'doing it' was a powerful spiritual exercise. I think we should see how much more spiritual we are in the morning, Andy, then maybe suggest this as a way to jack up the flagging spirituality of some at the Centre that G. E. is so exercised about."

Andy could sense her grinning in the dark. He felt a tad mortified.

"Seriously," Andy pursued with a tinge of recrimination, "can we agree we just won't talk about… this part of the journey?" He felt a slight tingle.

"Okay, my dear," she said playfully, "if you insist. There won't be too many asking the details anyway, and mum's the word! Now, are you going to say a goodnight prayer or shall I?"

This was really no big deal to her at all. Had she been through this before? Andy couldn't imagine.

"You can do the honours, Janys," he replied. "But before you do, can I ask one thing? Why don't you ever wear your hair down?" Where had that come from? His boldness tingled, again.

Janys was quiet for a time. Maybe he'd gone too far.

"Maybe I will sometime, Andy. Okay, I'll gladly pray." And she did, thanking God above all for shelter and warmth.

"Goodnight, Andy," she said at the end.

"Sleep tight, Janys," he said back. And they each turned sideways, backs to each other.

Not long afterwards, Andy heard a patterned breathing beside him. It sounded a minor key to the furious lament outside. And she could fall asleep just like that, he thought. For his part, he was reviewing every discussion he'd ever had with Jack, G. E., Lorraine, his sister, and much, much more. Throughout it all, Janys slept on peacefully. Well, Andy thought, at least she doesn't snore….

Minutes later—Or was it hours?—Andy awoke from a dream. His mind reached for it, but it slipped beyond recall. He noticed the wind had stopped. Light from an engorged moon streamed through the window. He had to go to the bathroom. What time was it? He slipped out of bed. The heat must be back on, he thought, uncomprehending. He tiptoed to the washroom door, and without thinking, flicked on the light switch. Light blazed. His eyes blinked, dazzled.

That shock paled before what his blinking eyes suddenly took in: Janys at the sink, in bra and panties only, blouse held in her hands, an utterly startled look emblazoned across her face.

He gaped. She gasped.

"Andy, the light! Turn off the light!" She thrust her arms upwards to spread the blouse across her bosom.

Andy floundered a minute then finally found the switch. Glorious moonlight alone bathed the scene. A shaft fully spotlighted Janys. She stepped sideways instinctively and banged into the sink. "Ouch!"

"I'm so sorry, Janys! Whatever are you doing?" Eyes averted, Andy beat a hasty retreat.

The door shut tightly behind him. Silence. Wow! And again, wow! He didn't care now. His mind started doing an instant replay. There was a close-up of her bra, her bare skin, her…

"Andy," from inside the bathroom, "do you need to use the toilet? I'm done now."

She stepped out, bath towel draped over her body. He stepped in.

He had to sit down to go pee. Only then did he realize he'd wet his pants. How embarrassing!

Her blouse and sweater were hanging over the towel rack directly above an electric heater, which belted out hot air. The bathroom felt invitingly cozy. Whatever had happened? Andy was still uncomprehending. He took off his pants and wet underpants, quickly ran some water in the sink, and soaked and squeezed them several times. Then he pulled on his pants, very careful of the zipper. He hung his briefs on the same rack. Hopefully they'd be dry by morning. He looked at his watch in the moonlight. It was 3:00 a.m.

Andy crawled back into bed as quietly as he could, trying desperately to take measured breaths. His heart took even longer to slow down.

Janys shifted her weight toward him. "Andy, I'm sorry."

"No, Janys, *I'm* sorry!"

Deep breath. "In case you haven't figured it out, it's my period. I had no tampons. They're frozen solid back in the car. I should have at least tried to get those out, but that snowmobile driver was not waiting for anything. Besides, I thought I could get some at the motel. Wrong. They were all out. So she gave me… Andy, is this grossing you out?"

"I do have a sister, Janys, remember?" Andy said evenly.

"So," she went on, "the lady obligingly gave me a wad of paper towels. Now this gets even more embarrassing. Do you really want to hear? But I've gone this far…"

Andy said nothing. The moonlight outlined everything in the room, including Janys' face. It gave her a pleasant, appealing, soft glow.

"I woke up to go pee and discovered nature had taken its course a bit more than I'd expected. Thankfully, she'd given me lots of those towels. But my panties, and the bottom of my blouse and sweater were… I'll spare you further details. So I poured water into the sink to rinse everything out. I was almost finished when you stumbled in.

A pause, then, "Andy, the look on your face was worth a million bucks!"

Andy said nothing. Outside was utterly, eerily still. The moonscape must be glorious, he imagined. A faint snoring came through the walls.

Ever practical, Andy asked, "So, do you have enough…"

"Paper towels?" Janys completed the query. "I hope so. And yes, before you ask, I had to put those well squeezed wet underwear back on, too. They're feeling a little uncomfortable right now. But they'll dry out by morning I'm sure. Pretty light material, and nice and warm under the covers."

She grinned at the ceiling. "I think you're right though. I won't be talking to anyone about this. 'Mr. and Mrs. Norton' indeed." She chuckled. "If only some of my girlfriends could see me now. Goodnight again, Andy."

He debated about offering to spend the rest of the night in the chair. He was very conscious she was wearing only her underwear beside him. He saw her bosom again in his mind's eye, full light blazing, and then fleetingly in the moonlight. But they had come this far without mishap. He knew he'd do quite fine until morning. She certainly would. Probably be asleep in just a few minutes. He fell asleep thinking about the Cathars.

Morning sunlight blazed through the frosted window. Andy sat up and rubbed his eyes. Just then, Janys stepped out of the bathroom fully clothed, hairbrush in hand.

"Good morning, sleepy head. Found this under the bed. After I'd cleaned out the hair, the brush works fine." She stepped back into the washroom. "Oh, and I guess you'll be wanting these." She threw Andy his underpants. "They're dry. So were my clothes." She laughed at his look of embarrassment. "Thought we got over that last night... I can guess what happened... No need to explain."

He didn't.

"Look out the window, Andy."

He gasped. As fearsome as the storm had been as dazzling was its morning afterglow. If the scene was a painted landscape, the sun was the virtuoso artist, enlivening every square inch with a textured grace that was irresistibly exquisite. Each point of sight was a-shimmer.

"Wow," Andy said simply, surprised he still found the word usable. He noted her long hair glistening in the dancing sunshine as she looked out the window beside him. Moments later, they headed downstairs to the dining area. All the way, her hair swooshed seductively across her back.

After breakfast, they connected with a tow-truck driver, and Andy accompanied him to their stranded car. The after-glory of the storm evoked associations of a desert traveller's first happening upon an oasis or the sudden turn in the fairly tale (Tolkien's eucatastrophe) with the sure knowledge that good would ultimately triumph. It was the apotheosis of Bing Crosby's *I'm Dreaming of a White Christmas* sung so lustily the night before. If only the world could stay this white, he thought. A sense of deep tranquility settled over him as he praised God inwardly for this glorious Christmas Eve. Surely this must be a taste of heaven, even if there would be no snow up there.

"A mother and her two children are dead, after failing to be rescued last night from their stalled car," the newscaster announced over the truck's radio, "and President Nixon vows more troops for South Vietnam. But first, these messages from our sponsors."

Andy's reverie ended abruptly as his mind turned to the awful tragedy of the night before. How could such radiant whiteness have occasioned such stark misfortune? On Christmas Eve no less? How could anyone near that family sing "Joy To the World!" ever again? Why? Andy's mind spun at the sheer gratuitousness of such evil.

It was not even man-made. Not like Vietnam, he thought further. He remembered Voltaire savaging any Leibnitzian notion of living in the "best of all possible worlds," given the earthquake in Voltaire's lifetime that had killed thousands. How to explain a good God in the face of such a happening? And if there is an omniscient God, mustn't his switchboard be besieged daily by similar events? Yet he failed to lift a finger to prevent even the natural disasters—quite apart from man's inhumanity to man!

An acquaintance had loaned Andy a copy of Bertrand Russell's *Why I Am Not a Christian* while he was in university. Andy read it dutifully. He remembered how airily he had dismissed Russell's entire thesis since he only treated of philosophical objections. "The Christian faith is not primarily a philosophy but a fact of human history—rooted in the space-time continuum we daily encounter," he had urged upon his friend. No "accidental truths of history" either, he'd argued forcefully. There had ensued a hot debate, which was halted abruptly by his opponent's searing words. "If God is so good, damn it, why is my sister, who believes in God, dying of leukemia right now?"

In the face of such raw emotion, Andy had fallen silent. He never discussed faith matters with that person again. He tasted the guilt of his failure once more. He had no answer then and still felt at a loss as he watched the tow-truck driver hitch up the VW, which, thankfully, had neither been buried nor run over by a snowplough.

The driver laughed when he found the loose spark plug wire. "If only all car problems were this simple!"

With the plug in place and the car jump-started, Andy and Janys finally completed their journey. Hasty phone calls arranged for Janys's brother and dad to pick her up at the Nortons'. Susan would drive to Kitchener, hoping for the best from her Mustang.

Before twilight eased into clear stellar night, they arrived safely in Kitchener. As they neared Andy's home, he noticed Janys putting her hair up again but said nothing. He really liked it down and made a mental note to tell her that again sometime.

"So good to have met you," Janys said to Andy's parents upon departing. Then to Andy: "Yesterday and last night will remain unforgettable!" Right in front of everyone. Andy felt a red rush. But nothing was said, perhaps Janys's very intention. Though Susan did look at him strangely. With that, Andy finally entered into the warmth and joy of Christmas Eve celebrations at home, feeling suddenly exhausted...

At the first opportunity, he and Susan slipped into her bedroom, and Andy asked about Lorraine. "Sounds more like I ought to be quizzing you about Janys, Andy," she said, eyeing him sharply.

Andy lay back on Susan's bed and took in the familiar surroundings. Her bedroom was just as she'd left it, including the *Beatles* posters on the wall that her mother had asked her repeatedly to take down, with not a few arguments over such "godless music." Susan had painted the room herself. It was compact, but it had "Susan" written all over it.

"So what happened last night with you guys?" Andy maintained a poker face that amazed him. How could last night seem "normal"? But that's exactly how it felt. Objectively, to sleep in the same bed with a half-naked woman and for nothing to have happened, well… His head cross-examined his heart, and the testimony held with not even an "Objection, your Honour."

"Susan, I really do like Janys. But what happened 'happened.' Pure and simple. Nothing else. Nothing new. Nothing to tell. No regrets but the obvious: *I missed Lorraine!* Now what to do?"

Susan appeared to accept the finality of Andy's tone, dropping her probable temptation to cross-examine. "I told her you'd call as soon as you could. But she knew this would show on the phone bill. Instead, she's agreed to call at eleven tonight, sharp! You or I will grab the phone first, wherever we're at in celebrations. Hopefully we're done and mom and dad are already tucked into bed. In that case, you take the kitchen phone into your bedroom. I will discreetly close the hallway door. And keep your conversation short. The only possibility for a rendezvous is late

Boxing Day evening.

"I ended up taking the bus to Kitchener today. My car was so jittery Dad suggested it. I can now say I have to get back to Toronto a day earlier, and you can drive me, stay the night, and pick up Janys at her relatives' really early. Then you can drive here, exchange cars, and be on your way.

"This all seems so ridiculously tight, I realize, though I don't mind cutting out early after you've left. It'll be a bit rough around here with Mom anyway. Can't you delay returning by one day? It'd be so much better, Andy."

"Can't," Andy said resolutely. He thought that's all G. E. would have to catch wind of, Congress '71 exchanged in part for Lorraine. "I *have* to be back. There's no give."

"Okay kiddo! What a sister won't do for her kid brother."

"Oh, give me a break," Andy came back, catching the mirth at the corners of her eyes. She'd proven it more than once: She'd do *lots* for her kid brother, Andy felt so lucky and proud to have her for a sister.

At eleven sharp, the phone rang. His parents in bed, Andy snatched up the receiver. He thrilled at the sound of her voice. Although the Christmas tree was surrounded by gifts, Andy already knew this was going to be the best one.

17

Christmas Day at the Norton house was the usual mixture of gifts, gastronomy, games, and gaiety. All were conscious that this would be Andy's last Christmas at home for the next two years. It showed especially in Andy's mother. He sensed her trying to retard time's advance, like pushing the slow motion mode on a Super 8 camera, as she savoured each bittersweet passing moment. But time was no one's servant, least of all his mom's on that day. Andy shared in his mother's melancholy mood somewhat. Between him and Susan, he shared more of her personality traits. He *loved* Christmas, but he could hardly wait for the next evening!

Thankfully, Boxing Day, not Christmas, fell on a Sunday that year. In Andy's childhood, it had been pure agony to have to wait an additional day to open presents whenever Christmas was the Lord's Day. Every other kid in the neighbourhood except the Norton's would have a twenty-four-hour head start on playing with their presents. About the only consolation was that some toys thereby lasted twenty-four hours longer than his friends'.

It was agreed that Andy's mom would nap right after lunch while he and his dad met. Then she and Andy would launch into their dictation/typing routine until 4:00, when his Uncle Joe would come visit for an hour. His mom was okay with this arrangement. It was her way of having some concentrated time with Andy before he left with Susan right after an early supper. If she had not quite finished typing the essay by then, his mom would finish it after the evening service. Not even Boxing Day displaced the Gospel Service.

At Carriage Street Gospel Chapel, the Breaking of Bread began at 9:30, Family Bible Hour at 11:00, and the Gospel Service at 7:00. Such had been the schedule since time immemorial—ever since Christ, as Andy had once believed and some let on. The Norton's attended all three services as surely as the earth revolved about the sun.

After all, the *plymouth brethren* (to be *in*, emphatically small *p*, small *b*) were, over against all other denominations, most faithful to the New Testament pattern of meeting and doing. They were not actually a denomination, only reluctantly allowing themselves, for governmental and others' convenience to be called such. They were rather the prototype itself, most true to original standards. While every local assembly was autonomous, directly under the Holy Spirit's leading, each stood as evident proof that the Spirit was not the author of confusion. For there was a monolithic quality to brethrenism equal to the most rigid ritual of any mainline church, despite the total absence of a written creed or liturgy. From one end of the land to the other, throughout North America, encircling the planet, an *open brethren* assembly had nearly identical body life. It was, after all, the New Testament pattern, and the Holy Spirit was globally in charge.

Neither the Christian nor secular calendar affected the central brethren worship experience: the weekly Breaking of Bread. The theme was ever the death of the Lord Jesus Christ and entering into that through the bread and the wine. The ritual was as binding as a Latin mass. Upon entering the building, a funeral parlour hush prevailed, punctuated only by the loud whispers of children or seniors. The proceedings, lacking orchestration by any human agent, were filled lacking orchestration by any human agent, were filled with prayers and hymns. Several might make up any morning meeting fare, reflective silences ensuing between each.

Women's heads were fully covered, their lips sealed, except to sing the hymns and—at GO at least—to share, a disturbing aberration. Otherwise, they were as silent as the soundless piano and organ, unless to discipline an unruly child. Meditative countenances masked all that entered their consciousnesses—whether pious thoughts on the morning's emerging theme or stewing about the pre-service mad rush to get to the meeting on time, the visiting preacher's joining the family for dinner or simply gratefully experiencing an hour's peaceful blankness in the midst of life's worries.

For the most part, the hymns were colourless relics of bygone anti-sacramental fashion; languorous tunes as joyless as the lugubrious texts themselves. Ironically, the central motif was a throwback to essential Catholic piety, forever preoccupied with a Jesus languishing on the Cross. Yet for plymouth brethren folk, Roman Catholicism was *anathema*.

The morning meeting was a grand Scrabble game: everything was built on the preceding moves. That morning, Brother Price rose first to give a word, unmercifully long as usual. Andy remembered timing him for thirty-five minutes once. Andy's dad followed, keeping with the general drift of the former. Then a hymn was suggested, which uncannily matched the first two speakers' themes. This was truly a sign of the Holy Spirit's leadership of the meeting. Andy contributed a tributary thought, first through a Scripture reading then adding a few comments of his own. In his earlier years, these were always somewhat tentative;

nonetheless they invariably emptied into the grander theme of Christ's death. As the service progressed, one brother continued to build upon another's meditation, intuiting a connection here or arbitrarily establishing one through direct commentary. When such a silver thread was perceived to emerge, uniting all the various inputs—hymns, prayers, and messages—it was a sure sign of the Lord's blessing. Eventually, Andy wondered how it could be otherwise, given there was only one legitimate theme: *Christ's death*. Still, he had come to appreciate the nuances.

Unperceived by outsiders, the service's climax was reached with the breaking of bread and the passing of the wine. On one occasion, Mr. Pelusso—former Catholic and new convert—"accidentally" left a wad of chewing gum on the inside lip of the cup. Just why no one ventured to remove it during its slow, silent advance toward the front of the church remained a mystery. But it arrived in just such a state at the front pew where the Norton's sat. It almost put Andy off from getting baptized and partaking of the ritual himself, which was to happen right after the chewing gum caper unfolded. Strangely enough, Mr. Pelusso and family eventually "fell away" from their newfound faith, possibly drifting back to Catholicism or, who knew, perhaps finding more acceptance amongst the Jehovah's Witnesses or Mormons...

Prayer was given before each of the emblems was offered, an act that could turn into a sermon itself at times. Then the loaf was broken silently, a rite performed spontaneously by brother Swanson each week unless he was away. It passed slowly from hand to hand. Subdued restlessness passed amongst the children like dominoes falling as pent-up energy knew some minor relief in conjunction with the slight commotion, mitigating an otherwise incredibly straight-jacketed worship time.

The cup was likewise passed thereafter, preceded, of course, by a prayer.

Then a protracted silence ensued. Brother McInnes suggested a hymn then decided to read out all seven verses first. Andy noticed the kids beginning to show more impatience as the seventh verse was finally sung. Things hung in the balance for a moment. Andy could almost hear the bated breath of the kids, reflecting back on his own agonizing over the years at this most dangerous juncture of the service. And then…

"I just want to share a few simple and humble words and thoughts with you on the glorious and infernally most lovely truths and realities revealed in the wondrously profound verses recorded for us by direct and infelicitous inspiration of God, the Holy Spirit, for our edification and nourishment, as found in the fifty-third chapter of Isaiah, beginning, for sake of context and in order to understand the setting, with chapter fifty-two, verse thirteen, which passage immediately precedes the most wondrous words recorded for us by direct inspiration of the Holy Spirit, who even centuries before the exceedingly woeful events of Calvary, knew whereof to write, in glorious anticipation of the Incarnation, indeed, birth, death, and triumphant Resurrection of our Lord and Saviour Jesus Christ, whom we remember as believers this morning, for as Brother Boswell often reminds us, 'to you who believe, He is precious,' and isn't the crucified and risen Saviour wondrously precious to each and every one of us this morning, who have had the opportunity, and have taken the initiative and incentive to respond to this so great offer of salvation, which it behoves each one of us here this morning not to neglect, or at least if we have, and especially you dear young people, whom the Lord so truly loves, and for whom Christ died that most agonizing death on the cross as a sweet savour up to heaven, we beseech you, in the Lord, to 'choose now this day whom you will serve,' for 'today is the day of salvation,' choose Christ today, I implore you, whom to know is life eternal, and everlasting joy and contentment, secure and steadfast in the knowledge that we are our Beloved's, and 'He is mine....'," Brother McCandless began.

Andy was sure only one other outdid Mr. McCandless in breathless loquacity: Karl Barth, master of the ultimate theological German run-on sentence. They could go on literally for pages in his famous *Church Dogmatics*. Even so, Barth had been awarded a prize for excellence in academic prose. Not likely Mr. McCandless, who had doubtless never heard of Barth, let alone read him. John McCandless was the all-time windbag in brethren circles. He had the most incredible capacity for piling up adjectives, nouns, verbs, and phrases, like ice formations on the St. Lawrence River, and could likely win hands-down the title of *Mr. Royal Redundancy* and *Mr. Magnificent Malaprop* against all rivals.

Isaiah 53 was the all-time favourite meditative piece during a brethren morning meeting. Most knew the passage by heart. Nonetheless, those "few words" burgeoned into a mini-sermon of some twenty minutes' duration. Toward the end, people began to squirm. In particular, it was the Sunday school drivers who simply had to get going to pick up children from around the neighbourhood so they could be back in time for the 11:00 service.

Andy remembered one occasion when Mr. Swanson, whose impatience was as great as his deafness, let out a thunderous sneeze several minutes into one of John McCandless' verbose disquisitions, which so distracted him that he rather abruptly brought his talk to an end. Andy subsequently detected no cold in Mr. Swanson, something he specifically took note of that evening after the service when the Swansons came over for a visit. He also doubted it had been allergies. He knew, in fact quite envied, that their son, and Andy's best friend, Doug could as readily produce reverberating burps on demand.

When the service finally concluded, Andy knew nothing had changed. As if he could really have hoped a tape sent to the elders in November enthusiastically describing the unusual freedom of worship at GO might have produced any new procedures in such a short space of time. "Over the long haul," had been G. E.'s words. The Sunday morning services at the GO headquarters had dramatically broken with the hoary ritualism of the brethren standard, Andy opined, allowing for genuine not pre-cast Spirit-led spontaneity.

Andy was eager to pass on these newfound experiences to his dad and Uncle Joe. He settled in right after lunch with his dad.

Discussing differences with Andy's father always presupposed patience and tact. Andy lacked both that afternoon, and his dad exhibited less (so Andy thought). By the session's end, Andy's father was so worked up that he talked of phoning G. E. immediately to "set some things straight." In the end, he determined to write him a letter. He said nothing, wisely and thankfully, about G. E.'s pastoral concerns for Andy.

Andy's father, Samuel Edwin Norton, had been a convert to brethrenism after having "come out" with his mom from worshipping with the Fellowship Baptists. He had learned to know Christ from the

the "assemblies" ("brethrenspeak" for churches). The latter seemed of even greater importance. He had a zealous loyalty to everything brethren, a trait that Andy had admired and imitated until quite recently.

It was Andy's Uncle Joe who had caused some of the disillusionment. Late in high school, Andy had recruited his uncle for a weekly Bible study at 7:30 on Saturday mornings. It took place at the chapel and was missed only when Uncle Joe was preaching or visiting out of town.

Uncle Joe had a quick wit, a vast store of jokes and stories, and had been brought up within the brethren fold. He had also served the Lord for twenty years in Angola and had learned to appreciate a practical ecumenism far ahead of anything obtaining in Canada during the same years—especially within the brethren. He even numbered an Anglican bishop amongst his circle of cherished co-workers in Angola.

But Uncle Joe did not readily reveal the extent of his *glasnost*, and Andy was one of the few who caught glimpses of his uncle's broadmindedness from time to time. On one occasion, he stated wryly that brethrenism was more tradition-bound than most denominations, chiefly because of their vehement disavowal of same.

"The gentleman doth protest too much, methinks," he said one Saturday morning of a current article in the well-known brethren publication *Interest*, which argued for the distinct nondenominational character of the brethren. Andy had read it and wondered about his uncle's response, which he asked about the next Saturday morning.

"Russell was one of those notoriously closed missionaries," he said, referring to the writer of the article, who had recently published his memoirs on brethren missionary endeavours in Angola, entitled brethren missionary endeavours in Angola, entitled *Angola with Love*. "He wrote another article a few years back arguing that the use of 'Thees,' 'Thys,' and 'Thous' in prayer was God's will and clearly a more respectful and biblical procedure. Incredible, given that in Portuguese, we use the personal pronoun in our worship of God, which, in King James' day, is reflected equally in the Thees, Thys and Thous. But little kids are also addressed by the same pronouns, as are lovers. It is the language of familiarity, as in 'Abba Father,' far more than some stuffy idea of extra respect and holiness being central in our addressing the Deity! To insist upon that usage today, when such words are only fossils, is as ludicrous as urging use of only horse and buggy like the Old Order Mennonites.

"If the Gospel is to be relevant to all cultures," he added, "it must be heard in the contemporary idiom and accent of each language and society. And if the New Testament could be written in the rough, unsophisticated language of *koine* Greek—where grammatical errors abound in comparison to classical style—then I suspect we can speak of God in today's normal English.

"As for brethren non-denominationalism, that disappeared when the brethren stopped welcoming everyone to the Lord's Table regardless of denominational background—as they did in the first enthusiastic flush of the movement—and began accepting only those who held to the principle of a weekly practice of breaking bread. Such is the way of all renewal movements. They begin with a desire to draw a circle large enough to fit in every stripe of Bible-believing Christian, and end with excluding everyone but their own kind."

Uncle Joe could be hilarious as well. Andy roared

told of a riverside baptismal candidate in Angola. He had just gone through the waters of baptism and was changing into dry clothes behind the makeshift curtain when the next candidate slipped while being led into the water, grabbed onto the nearest object for balance—which happened to be the pole holding up the curtain—and caused the whole apparatus to come crashing down, leaving the brother behind the curtain as exposed as a newborn baby. He reconnoitred the situation for one terrified second then did the only honourable thing and dove straight into the water for a second dunking!

"Twice as holy he re-emerged," was the added comment once Andy's laughter had subsided.

So it was that Uncle Joe offered a sympathetic ear that afternoon, both in response to Andy's excitement about GO's innovations and to his more immediate frustrations with the earlier afternoon conversation with his dad. More than he had done with anyone else, Andy revealed his feelings and struggles over the fall, explaining his misgivings about, yet strong magnetic attraction toward, G. E. But once again, he avoided the specifics of G. E.'s counselling sessions.

Fiona also received no mention. Neither did Lorraine, since Andy did not know how to interpret these phenomena, let alone defuse the emotions sufficiently for someone else.

Andy left the talk encouraged, as he usually did. There was a certain buoyant quality about Uncle Joe's far less dogmatic faith that was attractive and reassuring. His uncle always exhibited qualities of integrity and authenticity, characteristics more elusive amongst Uncle Joe's less tolerant counterparts.

Strange, Andy thought after his uncle had left despite being invited to stay for leftovers, but he felt despite being invited to stay for leftovers, but he felt so strengthened in the faith despite his uncle's lack of dogmatism. He thought of Uncle Joe's repeated joke about the places in the preacher's sermon notes where the comment was inserted: "Weak point. Tap on pulpit extra loud!"

In his diary that night, Andy reflected,

'The gentleman doth protest too much, methinks' is perhaps an apt quote for so many zealous dogmatists I know—not least myself!

18

It worked out as Susan suggested.

That evening, for the first time since the summer, Lorraine and Andy met in a coffee shop near Susan's. Lorraine knew the city, and took a bus to the rendezvous.

It felt absolutely tense to Andy. Where to begin? Lorraine would not.

"Lorraine…" Andy said after they'd each ordered a steaming hot chocolate with whipped cream. But he couldn't continue.

Lorraine for her part seemed far away, though so invitingly close. She said nothing.

Andy said nothing further. They sipped their hot chocolate in silence.

He finally ventured: "This is the hardest conversation–non-conversation–in my life. Lorraine, I don't know where to begin?"

She looked at him but said nothing. He looked back, and said no more.

Hot chocolates done, Andy had to say at least something more. "Lorraine, this obviously is too soon. I don't know what has to happen, but…"

She looked at him again and said, "Andy, I'm going home." She put on her coat and headed out the door.

Andy sat a long time, left a tip, paid for the drinks and walked slowly back to Susan's.

19

At 4:00 a.m. the following morning, this time at Janys's uncle and aunt's in Toronto, Andy deposited her bag in the trunk. As he did so, he added officiously, "Or shall I place it in the back seat, ma'am, for greater accessibility?"

Janys laughed and replied just as formally: "'Twill not be necessary, sir. I'm over that. Period!"

A nimble mind for such a brittle early morning.

Her hair must be half her height, Andy thought as she flung it forward to take off her heavy winter jacket.

They exchanged cars and switched over bags an hour later in Kitchener. Andy's parents came out to wave them off. His dad had let the VW warm up a half hour or so beforehand. It felt almost toasty inside.

Andy's departure was hardest on his mom, even though she knew they'd visit at Easter and he'd be home a week or two at the end of training. The flights overseas were being booked to depart from Toronto. He stepped out once more to hug her. She'd want that, he knew. And then they were off.

The trip was enjoyable though uneventful by their previous trip's standards. There was an almost intimate comfort level between Andy and Janys that made the time fly by. They talked as freely as Jack and Andy, though sex and dating were studiously avoided. Janys had offered to drive some of the time, during which Andy napped. The car performed well. There was no hint of a storm brewing the entire distance. They arrived in time to put some things away at the Centre, change, repack, and then scoot out to the beginning of Congress '71.

The theme of the Congress that year was: *The King is Coming: Therefore, GO YE!* The auditorium was packed the first night. The film premier proved stunning. In the holy-hush aftermath, G. E. called for a profound recommitment of all gathered to the Lord's service, which they could indicate by standing when he gave the signal.

"Who is on the Lord's side?" he intoned. "Who will choose this night whom he will serve? Don't stand if you don't mean business with God. This is a holy moment. God is stirring our hearts to hear his call.

"I sense that hearts are responding all over this auditorium. Please, in a moment when I say the word, stand, if you rededicate all that you are, all that you have, to serve the Lord. Let this be your moment of decision. All of us at the Centre are praying..."

A pregnant pause, then: "All right, please take your stand *now!*"

It was truly electrifying. Almost in total unison, like a grand orchestra under the sway of the Maestro's wand, the great assemblage rose. The few pockets of resistance quickly capitulated, and, from his vantage point at the back of the auditorium, Andy was sure that no one remained seated. Certainly not Andy. In spite of his misgivings. In spite of his doubts, in spite of his shallowness, in spite of his conflictedness and unworthiness, in spite of his frustrations with G. E. he knew he wanted God's will for his life, whatever that entailed. So he stood. As did Janys. Low sobs were heard throughout the building.

G. E. Andy sensed, was at maximum wattage.

Andy's roommate for Congress beamed afterwards as well. He was from California, and was afire with reports of the Jesus Movement, mass baptisms in the ocean, the ubiquitous street witnessing, the myriad Jesus People bumper stickers, and the sheer euphoria of it all.

"The Spirit is moving!" he kept saying that night. Andy suspected he spoke in tongues but didn't ask him. He was too tired to engage in any such discussion. It came out the next day, however; so irrepressible was its newfound thrill.

"Never in my home assembly though," he said. "Perish the thought. My parents would be aghast!" He chortled as he recounted the feeling of incredible ecstasy such utterances delivered. Why didn't Andy try it? *Like any other drug in Haight Ashbury?* Andy thought. Like the "Jesus pill" Dan spoke of people swallowing?

The format of the succeeding four days was plenary sessions in the mornings, workshops in the afternoons, and a major rally (thrown open to the surrounding community) in the evening. There was also much encouragement during the breaks to seek out counsel from the star-studded cast, which included missionaries, Bible teachers, full-time workers, and the Centre staff. Attendees could also peruse dozens of displays from other missionary agencies, Bible schools, and seminaries. One especially colourful set-up was staffed by members of a local Jesus People commune called *House of the Eternal Son*.

Andy was never quite sure whether their presence had been authorized, but it was innocuous enough. Besides some literature on the commune itself and a locally produced Jesus People rag they were promoting, (every issue of which they claimed was prayed through letter-by-letter—like the Bible itself—by the editorial staff), they handed out a vast number of Jack Chick publications, the grossest presentation of Christian beliefs Andy had ever seen. Grotesque images and characters abounded when resistance to Christ was the theme. Violent come-uppance on all unbelievers was depicted with vengeful glee worthy of the vilest Crusaders of a bygone era, such as those who would maraud a whole village of infidels and roast their children on spits for supper.

But for some (to Andy) unfathomable reason, G. E. seemed to be taken with the Chick materials and ordered hundreds of the booklets for their coffeehouse during the fall. The lines of demarcation, not to mention the gargoyle comic characters, were stark, uncompromising, and grotesquely frightening.

Andy met several past acquaintances and friends at the Congress that first night, encountered through previous involvements with Christian camps and conferences. He loved it.

The next afternoon, Andy spotted Fiona across the cavernous gymnasium that housed the displays. His pace quickened. Then a tall frame stepped from behind a booth, blocking her from view momentarily. It was Jack! Andy watched her face light up. The two talked animatedly while others milled about. Andy wasn't going to crash the party, though he hadn't yet seen Jack either. He reversed directions, certain neither she nor Jack had seen him.

That evening, he scanned the vast auditorium for her face. He finally ended up sitting with Ken Kincaide, not the highest priority on his list. He hadn't seen Janys all day either. Then he saw them both, way across the room, backs toward him, but he was sure it was them from their hair—Janys' dark brown and flowing, Fiona's shorter and golden hued. And there was Jack. It was unmistakable when they stood to sing. Andy's lips pursed as he joined with the throng in singing, *He is Lord*.

Throughout the talk that night, Andy observed Ken scribbling furiously. Andy, by way of contrast, didn't even have notepaper. Afterwards, Ken tried to get Andy talking. But Andy was determined to be by the exit Janys, Jack, and Fiona had to come through. Ken tagged along.

"Hi!" Andy said over the heads streaming from the auditorium. Jack heard him, whooped, and came right over. Janys and Fiona followed. Jack gave Andy an enormous hug. "Golly! I missed my roommate already!" He thought Fiona might have given a similar embrace, even Janys, but there was Ken, obviously with Andy. Their greetings were more distant.

"Great Congress so far," Andy mustered. He so wanted to talk to Fiona alone, but that was *verboten*. He asked, if mainly Fiona, "So how was Christmas for everybody?" His eyes caught Fiona's. Inward catch of breath. A "stunner" all right, he remembered.

This was not how it should have been. Drat Ken! Drat Jack! Even drat Janys… Andy didn't like what his mind was doing, didn't feel the Christmas spirit at all. Janys deserved better. So did Jack. Even Ken.

Everybody said a little about their Christmas.

"And you, Andy?" Fiona asked. "Nothing too eventful?"

Janys told about their trip home, the storm, the stalled car, the motel, the spontaneous carol sing, the arrival the next day in Toronto, her getting to Sudbury finally late Christmas eve.

It was Jack who asked the obvious: "Did they have rooms for everybody?"

Janys was quick. "You took whatever they assigned. There was some doubling up of strangers.

Andy and I were lucky. We got a single room. He slept in the bathtub, and I slept on the comfortable bed. Only I had a bursting bladder in the morning!"

Had she rehearsed this or was she that adept spontaneously? Andy could believe the latter. Whatever, it forestalled any more detailed questions. Relief.

As the conversation continued, Andy's spirits fell. What should have been a joyous reunion with Fiona (which he did not realize he had been anticipating so eagerly) was going sideways. He watched but could not extend a hand to stop it. He had imagined they would all go off for a coffee or something. That anticipation quickly deflated and scudded across the floor.

Suddenly, Jack charged into his thoughts. "Andy, got to talk to you! You wouldn't believe the discussion I had with a former classmate of mine I bumped into just before Christmas. He's a real intellectual just like you. Gotta talk to you. Got some time now?"

Ken perked up and said he'd love to join in. Andy could tell he was lonely. Why was that also Andy's mood?

Fiona said, "Fine. You guys go and talk your intellectual theology. Janys and I are going to be sensible and catch some sleep. Right, Janys? These Congresses are marathons! I remember from the one before. And we have to last until Thursday afternoon! Good night, guys."

Did she especially look at Jack? Andy wondered as he watched the girls head off together.

Andy did not spend any more time with Janys or Fiona the rest of the Congress. But he saw Jack and Fiona together several times. He started to wonder if Fiona was trying to avoid him. Maybe she thought the same of him. But she didn't see Andy hanging around with Janys every time she turned around, Andy thought angrily. Maybe it was just chance… Andy knew G. E. had told her some things. He also knew Jack liked her, despite the fact he had never admitted as much. Then again, Andy had never made mention of his own feelings either…

The workshop Andy and the other *acceptables* had worked on was packed out each day. About fifty eager potential GOer's participated in each session to see what might be in store for them. Thankfully, Andy and the crew were well prepared. There was a real sense of accomplishment as they wound down the last meeting. G. E. even appeared, by request, during the final minutes of the last day and shared excitedly about how God would be using GO during the next few years. The challenge was for each one to see if they fit into the picture, as doubtless some did.

Upon leaving the workshop, G. E. took Andy aside to inform there was a letter for him in his mailbox back at the centre. No "How was your Christmas?" or "Trust you had an uneventful trip?" Andy was thankful, for then he didn't have to reply, "Well, actually, Mr. Moore, the first night Janys and I were caught in a snowstorm and we ended up in bed together after she stripped half naked and I took my pants off..." It was G. E.'s fault for not asking. Then Andy berated his insolence.

Each evening, Mr. Myers did a fifteen-minute presentation on the theme "The King is coming!" The song by that title was sung majestically at the end of each talk. There was a sameness to his addresses. One stood out in particular, however, though not for content but dramatics. George Myers came clothed like Amos straight out of the Old Testament. Slides flashed on the screen in step with his talk. The thrust was to highlight

CHRYSALIS CRUCIBLE

the way the world was wallowing in wars, poverty, and strife, all in delicious anticipation of the finale, namely, "But praise God, fellow Christians! This can only mean that Jesus is coming sooner than we hope! As the world scene grows darker, the Light shines correspondingly brighter. So lift up your eyes! And quicken your readiness. Let's bring in a mighty harvest of souls for God before the End!"

The music rolled then, and the evening concluded with G. E.'s keynote address.

For the first time that week, it struck Andy as strangely incongruous, this rampant gloating over the world's ills, a gleeful delight at their increase, as this must surely expedite the Second Coming. The great 19th-century evangelist D. L. Moody used to say, "When the boat is sinking, one ought not waste time polishing the brass, rather be about rescuing the perishing." Andy thought with sudden blazing insight that surely one could at least take a stab at plugging the leaks.

His diary for that night read,

Sharp at midnight, suddenly the magnificent strains of Händel's Messiah *burst forth upon the entire expectant hearers. It was glorious! And like that first night with G. E. we all leapt from our seats, to remain standing 'til its conclusion.*

How anyone can listen to that music and appreciate only the medium and not the message escapes me entirely. Is there anything more thrilling in the entire world? Can the angels even outdo such inspired brilliance?

The entire Congress was outstanding. Even thrilling! Glad our part's over, too.

G. E. was impressed and told Gary and me as much this afternoon.

God is great!

It is 1:10 a.m.

Good night!

P. S. I know I have feelings, because they're confused right now.

By Friday morning, Congress '71 was history. All returned to the Centre in a euphoric mood. They had just been part of something *big*. God was doing a mighty work, and they were right in the midst of it. Andy could not imagine a place on earth he would rather be. Except in Toronto. He still had not processed his last night with Lorraine, though he had written the Professor about it. He loved her. But… That three-letter word contained a universe.

Andy took the note from G. E. back to his room. Jack was not there, so he sat down at his desk and opened it.

December 30, 1971

Dearest Andy:

We still have some more work to do, my brother. I have a busy travel schedule for the next two months. So I am booking the last Friday of January and February at 4:30 p.m. in my office for our times together.

Meanwhile, I continue to prohibit any times together between you and Fiona. It is enough that you are simply civil to her. You do not know all that is going on with her (her burden is not light). She only knows from me in a general way that I have concerns about you and relationships with the opposite sex. It is you who must exercise the discipline of abstinence. You are training as a soldier for Christ. There are hardships to endure, disciplines to develop, and eventually victories to win.

If you are to serve as the Lord's foot soldier in West Berlin alongside Fiona and the others, you must have well-developed habits of single-mindedness. I use that word ever so deliberately. Andy, you must learn to keep your eyes on Christ during the rest of this training and throughout your two years overseas. Otherwise, I fear disaster. I have seen it in others before with singular gifts. I need not supply details of past trainee failures to remind you that the devil goes about as a roaring lion. I want you to last on the mission field, Andy. Your fellow soldiers need you. God needs you! Don't throw away this calling from God for a mess of pottage.

I believe you can gain victory, Andy, for God's glory. I'm praying for it fervently. You need not give in to Eve's temptations. You can do it! You will overcome.

Triumphantly in Christ

G. E. Moore

Andy went through the letter three times. If G. E. only knew... He was relieved though. He had expected worse: weekly appointments. He could weather two more. He believed in the mission. Even still in G. E. He sensed greatness. Something real was stirring. He marked the dates on his calendar and tucked the note into the back of his diary.

20

Term papers were returned the first day of classes. Andy felt keen disappointment that his had produced no greater stir than, "Well done! You'll need this kind of ammunition in Germany!" from George Myers. There was no grade.

That first week back, the thermometer plummeted. Winter waxed wanton.

There was still some snow around from before New Year's. Snow had also fallen during the Congress. It was quite enough for Andy to recruit several for an undertaking dear to his heart: the building of a skating rink on the Centre's garden surface. The first evening some fifteen people responded to his invitation to join in the fun. Dan even fixed up the little lawn mower cum snowplough to help out.

Andy knew from experience that there was a knack to making an ice rink from scratch, especially over a frozen garden with a dip toward one corner. Above and beyond the creativity called for, Andy knew that sheer persistence was what counted. The initial fruits for backbreaking work in the first few sessions were paltry indeed.

First, the snow on the potential rink surface had to be packed down methodically by foot. Shovels of snow were mobilized wherever the earth reared its ugly head, like an erupting pimple. Then, with the garden hose on a light sprinkle, he laid down a glaze over the entire surface. This process took hours for a moderately sized rink. During this time, everyone else—including Dan and the mini-tractor, were assigned the task of garnering great volumes of the white stuff from the surrounding area. This snow was deposited at garden's edge by buckets and wheelbarrows. As the water seeped into the frozen underlay of dirt, snow had to be added and packed down until all holes were plugged.

That first night, the men were separated from the boys. By the next evening, only five recruits besides Andy reported for action: Dan, Jack, Janys, Fiona, and Ken. The undertaking was new to all but Janys. The same process ensued until most of the GO acreage looked like a giant snow-eating slug had slithered everywhere in an insatiable bid to gobble up all remnants of snow.

Then, the next day, it thawed! What remained of the snow turned to green/brown again, and all the ice puddled at the low end of the garden. That day, even Andy's faithful five lost heart.

The next night, winter rallied with a vengeance. The thermometer plummeted precipitously. The following afternoon, Andy spent his work time systematically repositioning the sprinkler all over the garden surface. By nightfall, his efforts had begun to pay off. An ice-film was discernible everywhere the sprinkler cast its watery net. And the weatherman predicted a low of minus ten degrees. Andy was ecstatic. It was a Friday night, and he knew that one all-night stand would abet the undertaking immeasurably. Mr. Myers had given the nod in G. E.'s absence. Andy said nothing about Fiona's involvement, and Mr. Myers did not ask.

The "Faithful Five" (Dan's dubbing) did duty until about 5:30 a.m., with the first shift beginning after 10:00 p.m.

Fiona commented wryly that they might need the skill to evangelize in Berlin. She was taken by the snow. She would have loved that Christmas trip home, Andy thought. Two figures not made of wax slipping together under bed covers, the world without ablaze in white, presented behind mind's curtain up. Yes, inner eye lingered.

The arrangement was for one person at a time to do the unenviable task of flooding the surface for a half-hour period. There had to be a continuous flow, since the hose could not be stationary for long without freezing. Besides, the rink needed great washes of water, even if the surface never completely set before the next layer was applied.

Everyone congregated in the Admin Building basement. Ken, who played the piano beautifully and sang well, began the evening by treating everyone to an impromptu performance. Someone jokingly asked for the "Hallelujah Chorus" while Ken got up for a quick drink of juice.

"Sorry, I don't have the music for that in my head," he replied.

They all laughed. Then Janys said, "Fiona…" Did she know something they didn't?

The surprise of the night came at that point. Fiona stepped to the piano deliberately, paused, and then launched into a flawless flowing rendition of that magnificent piece. As ever since its first public performance, the little crowd leapt immediately to its feet. The room pulsated with its joyous throb. They went wild with cheers and congratulations when the last notes sounded and held.

Andy was blown away. "Why?" he managed to say.

"It was a promise I made to myself." She said no more. Except, "And I do not want it known around the Centre. So please, nothing said by anyone. Okay?" She looked around as though in a conspiracy. Heads nodded in agreement. No one pursued the why, given the finality of the request. What else lay hidden? Andy wondered.

Recovered, Andy said, "Let's get started. It's going to be a long night." Andy started by showing everyone how to work the hose (unnecessarily detailed, opined Jack with a guffaw), then stayed out to take the first shift. By the time he came in, replaced by Dan, Ken was winding down a second concert and seemed to be in a reflective mood.

Ken's blonde hair was about as long as Fiona's, though he usually kept it tied back in a ponytail. It was also a distinctly lighter hue. Long hair for men was another concession at GO, discordant with dominant brethren mores. Ken also had intense grey eyes and a generally "artsy" (Dan's word) persona. Apparently, he had won numerous piano competitions and was considered performance material. But he had felt the call to GO, and at that point walked away from it all. Strange, Andy thought. He doubted he would have done the same.

Andy had spent little time with Ken that fall. He had sized him up to be a strange bird, an observation that was borne out enthusiastically by occasional remonstrations from Sam Kolowski, Ken's roommate. Presumably out of sensitivity to Dan, Ken waited until his departure before asking rather abruptly:

"Andy, do you believe this whole mission is being conducted in a biblical way?"

Andy glanced around. Fiona had dozed off on the couch. It thrilled Andy just to be in the same room with her. Jack and Janys turned an inquisitive ear. The games room had two ping-pong tables, three foosball tables, and several tables and chairs. There were also comfortable couches at one end, on which they sat.

"Why do you ask, Ken?" Andy parried.

"Take this whole concept of the 'short-term missionary,'" Ken responded eagerly. "I am increasingly convinced that it is simply not biblical. Can you imagine Paul saying he'll try it out for a few years to see if he likes it? Paul was called of God with no ifs, ands, or buts, and he became unequivocally an apostle, a 'sent-one.'"

"Hey, Ken, what's 'unequivocally'?" Jack chimed in. Ken hardly heard as he continued intently. "Another thing, what about all this study we're doing—or that students are doing at Emmaus? Where is there warrant for that in the Bible?

"'Study to show thyself approved,'" Andy said, quoting Scripture. He was greeted with an approving nod from Jack. "And don't forget, it seems Paul seldom spent more than two years in one location—what we're about to do—before he declared the job done and moved on."

"But that's just it," Ken replied, "Study what? All these manmade books of theology? To paraphrase Paul, 'I'd sooner read one verse from the Bible than ten thousand words from some Bible commentator!'

"What is it Paul meant for us to study? God's Word, of course! Not mere cacophony of men's words."

Jack opened his mouth with another question but must have thought better of it.

"Ever listen to sermons, Ken?" Janys smiled.

Ken's eyes flashed. His answer was obvious. Though Andy could agree with Ken's use of the word "cacophony" (and worse) as he did a quick review of the many sermons he'd heard throughout his life.

"I see what you're getting at, Ken," Andy began, a tad more diplomatically, "but surely God has given us lots of teachers from whom we can benefit? And to repeat, Paul was the original 'short-term missionary,' since he spent only a brief time in any locality, got a few converts, passed on some kind of 'apostolic succession,' oversaw a few pieces of Scripture translated into the local dialect, a few indigenous hymns written perhaps, then packed it all in, saying the job was done. Where do you see that kind of mission anywhere in the world today? Except with us, YWAM, GLO…" Evangelical missions had a penchant for catchy acronyms, Andy's internal commentary overlaid. YWAM, "Youth With a Mission," GLO "Gospel Light Overseas," and GO. Where did this stuff come from? Andy came up with one of his own: GAIN: "Goofy Acronyms of Inane Nincompoops."

"You know what I think?" Ken continued, still not really acknowledging the responses. "I think that every Bible school should begin by making each student do nothing for the first year but read the Bible and make notes. By that time, they would know the Word inside out. Then let them read other commentaries during the second year and following. I think we ought to do a scaled-down version of that here, too."

Jack began to fade, having leaned back on the couch at the beginning of the discussion. In no time, he was emitting a sound like that of a slowly pulled zipper, slightly amplified. Andy noticed Fiona's face, placid and still against the couch. Her allurement was only magnified by such pure irenic composure. How possible? He thought of Janys and him, then Fiona and him, in bed together on a long winter night. He looked at Janys, whose head was drooping, too, acceding to a "not fair" recrimination. Then back at Fiona, and knew what exponentially enhanced her beauty: a gently rising and falling bosom. He felt the responsive stirrings.

"So, what do you say, Andy?" Ken's challenge

invaded his yearnings.

Andy squirmed under Ken's direct gaze. He had never come close to reading the Bible right through, though he knew of such reading guides and had even begun one once. He also knew all too well of his own heavy dependence on second-hand sources for much of his knowledge, biblical or otherwise. Thankfully, Ken barely needed more than the perception of a listening ear so intent was he on pursuing a particular line of thought regardless of any real kind of feedback or response.

"Take G. E. for instance. He's working on his doctorate in 'Missiology.' That isn't even a biblical word! No doubt, he has to read all kinds of books, write papers, and attend lectures and seminars. But I'll bet he's not really digging into the Word itself.

"That's why I entitled my paper, 'The Word of God, and the words of men.' I purposely did not capitalize 'words of men.' I knew I had to tie it in to Spain somehow but didn't really manage to do so. I just felt I had to look at this whole problem of man's wisdom versus God's."

Andy observed Ken's intensity. His eyebrows arched as he spoke. There was a conspicuous effort of concentration in his choice of words.

Andy was at a loss for words, himself, searching inwardly for what Schaeffer might say. He was relieved when Fiona awoke with a start and asking, of all things, if the stars were out. Andy wondered what she had been dreaming about to prompt such a thing. Then he assured her the stars were out in full brilliance. She indicated a desire to observe them, and Andy seized upon the excuse to accompany her. The prospect of a plummeting thermometer with Fiona was hands-down preferable to the hot ambience created by

CHRYSALIS CRUCIBLE 177

Ken. Ken demurred at the thought of going out any sooner than was his turn.

"They're… Magnificent!" Fiona's exclamation strafed the stillness, evoking a wave from Dan, who was swooshing faithfully.

"Ten more minutes!" Andy called out cheerily, to which Dan saluted. Andy made as though he would walk toward the rink when Fiona took his hand, pulling him in the other direction. She leaned in close and spoke softly. "Andy, look at the moon riding high over the trees now, ominous and silent." His whole body arced. Their hands held fast. "I've *never* seen the moon so 'wintry winsome' (Robert Frost, I think) in all my life!"

He'd never held hands so "wintry winsome" in all his life either.

Andy's first date at age thirteen was Coral, a cute brunette he'd grown up with in church. Together with his friend Dale Burkholder and a girl named Renate, whom Dale was sweet on, they had gone skating to the local arena on a frigid January afternoon. Memories flooded of the thrill in skating round and round, hand in hand, pop tunes blaring. He could have skated for hours. He loved the dashing joy of cold steel slicing effortlessly across the glistening surface.

He remembered Coral. He thought of Lorraine. But he held hands with Fiona. She wasn't letting go. Neither was he.

"The moon, silent silvery portent of dawning dapper day," she recited somnolently. Who? Andy's mind raced: Gerard Manley Hopkins? She did not say. Their hands held fast like winter's grip. The steady motion of Dan's hose moving back and forth like the conductor's baton rendered the stillness symphonic.

The Admin Building door slammed. Hands dropped, heads turned. Jack was heading toward Dan. Ten minutes had gone by in what seemed like seconds. Jack looked their way, two figures doubtless silhouetted against a "silvery moon." They were not in a wax museum.

"There you are!" He cried. "I thought our fearless leader might have gone off to bed, abandoning ship."

"Hi Jack," Fiona called out. "We just stepped out for some fresh air. Isn't this absolutely grand?" Andy noticed that the moon shimmered off the rink's surface, making the slight mist dance.

"Golly!" Jack exclaimed. "I've never been out in such cold weather in all my life." Strange. Andy was feeling wondrously warm all over.

"Jack, how could you even feel the cold with all those clothes on—hat, scarf, ear-muffs, mitts, long underwear (Admit it!), heavy socks, boots, and winter coat?" He and Fiona strode toward him while Dan handed the hose off to Jack and beat a hasty retreat back inside.

This evoked a consternated cry of foul. "Just because your Canadian blood only freezes at minus 40!" Jack shot back, smiling.

Despite her ample winter clothing, Andy could sense Fiona shivering beside him. The night was doubtless at its absolute coldest. There was the loud and music-to-Andy's-ears pop of ice congealing in response to the relentless hosing. Another portent no less welcome to Andy.

"Fiona," Andy turned to her, "Why don't you go off to bed? I appreciate the willingness to help, but I think if you don't, you'll turn into an icicle. Besides, after a half hour out here, you might wish you had some of Jack's get-up on top of yours. Then you wouldn't be able to move anyway." Jack guffawed. Andy continued, "I'll do another shift after Jack. I'm used to it, true enough. And so is Janys. And Ken at least grew up in Seattle where they get snow. I think we'll be fine." There was more to say, but not with an audience. Andy was not even wearing a toque. He never did, even when their youth group went tobogganing all night New Year's Eve in similar temperatures.

It took no time for Fiona to gratefully acquiesce. "Say goodnight to Janys, Ken, and Dan," she requested.

When Andy went back inside, Ken was sitting by himself meditating on Scripture. Janys was still sleeping soundly. She could fall asleep through anything, Andy thought, remembering their night in bed together.

Thirty minutes later, Jack was quite ready for Andy as replacement. "Even with all this stuff on, I can still feel it!" He expostulated.

When Ken went out for his turn, Janys awakened. She, Andy, and Jack got going on a game of Rook, or "Gospel Chapel Euchre," as it used to get called, since it was the only kosher card game plymouth brethren youth played—with *ersatz* playing cards.

All but Andy turned in by about 4:30 a.m. He decided to do one more flood under a falling moon.

There were two notes in his mail slot the next day. One read, "Mr. Norton: Sorry to let you down in the rink-flooding department. 'The spirit was *very* willing' indeed, but... I have never seen the moon as I did last night. Then again, I don't usually go flooding rinks under a romantic moon in Texas. Definitely a new experience. Our nocturnal tryst was pure serendipity—and delight. Do you read much poetry?

Thanks for having facilitated the experience. Fiona."

The other note was terser: "Andy, I'd like to talk with you more. After last night's discussion, and from other indications, I sense a spiritual kinship. Please consider this. Your brother, Ken."

Andy relived the warm glow from Fiona's note. G. E. hadn't prohibited writing to each other, he thought with some triumph.

Ken's was much more problematic.

21

Whatever else the previous night had precipitated, Andy was delighted to discover the rink had fared well. From the moment he awoke Saturday morning after a short sleep, Andy started flooding. They were in a serious cold snap. The thermometer barely rose above zero all day. This meant the flooding could start at the top end of the rink as soon as the lower half was completed. There was some consequent "shaling" when air pockets prohibited a solid freeze, but overall the surface was sound. The Faithful Five applied dozens of layers throughout the day, to the point that Dan commented on the impending spike in their water bill.

Andy had just returned from another round of flooding when Fiona walked into the Games Room. They were alone—at last, Andy couldn't help but think.

"Fiona," Andy began, "thanks for your note. To answer your question, no I haven't, except for volumes in French and German literature, and English for that matter. But I don't usually just sit down and pick up a book of poetry. I probably should.

"My favourite German poem though is by Johannes Goethe, found in his hunting lodge after he died. It's called *Mailied*. Can you translate that?"

Fiona was at a loss.

"How about trying to repeat a few lines after me?" Andy suggested. "It goes, *Wie herrlich leuchtet Mir die Natur! Wie glänzt die Sonne! Wie lacht die Flur!*"

Each line came back sounding like southern expletives spoken in a drawl. Andy howled. Fiona scowled.

"Okay, buddy! How many years have you been studying this darndest language?"

A *Jackism* to be sure, Andy recognized.

"Seven? And how many *weeks* have I been studying it? So what does it translate as, anyway?"

Andy loved her accent, suddenly realizing how little he had ever talked with Fiona. He could listen tirelessly to her mellifluous voice while gazing into her eyes at close quarters. This was real, he was doing it, and he was shooting for the moon, "silvery portent" *indeed* "of dapper day." How could the same set of items common to all humanity—eyes, nose, ears, and throat—be so differently arranged? In some instances, enthralling, in others, he refused to supply a name, just *plain Jane*. (He did it anyway.) Andy barely acknowledged the fundamental injustice. He was not noticing much else either.

"*May Song.*" He remembered the question with effort, giving the translation, and continued, "'How beautiful Nature shines to me. How the sun dazzles! How the meadow laughs!'" Andy went on for a few more stanzas in German without translation. "Can you just hear the lilt and thrill of the author in the very cadence even if you don't understand a word, Fiona? Goethe sets words spinning like so many tops that dance and leap across the page. A verbal hologram, if you will. I love it! But like I said, I don't read enough myself." Andy's face was flushed with sheer passion.

He became very self-conscious suddenly. Every fibre screamed for what the movies endlessly provided next. "Fiona," he knew any word would instantly dissipate like dancing faeries vanishing in pre-dawn mist at sun's first shafts. "I can't. I want to. I… G. E…"

Their lips drew close.

CHRYSALIS CRUCIBLE   183

A commotion at the door. Fiona jolted back, as did Andy.

Dan burst inside calling for Andy. Then, "Well, excuse me," he stuttered and promptly exited, saying he must have gotten the wrong door.

Fiona turned back to Andy. "Well, I guess that's that!" Then, "By golly!" And like the first day of snow at G. E.'s, she lurched forward, threw her arms around his neck, and kissed him ferociously on the lips, pausing only to say, "And I don't care *who's* noticing!" Suddenly, neither did Andy. Delight billowed. He had noticed another *Jackism* but did not care.

"Is the coast clear?" Dan said from around the corner.

"Yes!" Andy and Fiona chimed in unison. Dan sauntered in, insolent grin all over. "Geez," he said, "I never knew rink-making could get so *hot!*"

Andy's neck tingled warmth. Fiona eyed Dan accusingly. "You won't tell your *dad*, will you?" She asked in mock trepidation. She had picked up Dan's vibes.

"*Mum's* the word!" All three of them laughed. The tension was over.

"Yes, Dan?" Andy said. Dan looked at him blankly. "Remember? You had something to ask me?"

"Oh yes. About the rink. You remember, Andy? We're building a rink?" He laughed at his cleverness. "I came in with a question Jack and me were discussing. How do you know when the rink is ready to skate on? How thick does the ice have to get? We're figuring it must be getting there already."

Andy replied, though he had trouble focusing. "Think of a hockey player with all his gear on, weighing in at over two hundred pounds. His legs churn furiously as he flies around, flashing steel and slicing ice every which way. Add five more guys like that, and you have just one team, though the goalie stays put most of the time. Multiply times two, plus however long the game is (sixty minutes for the pros), throw in a few refs, and you get the idea. The ice, even with flooding between periods, has to be pretty doggone thick to withstand all that sustained abuse.

"So, granted. We're not making a hockey rink. But every layer of water laid down makes things stronger and smoother. At the rate we're going, if we can keep it up and the snow doesn't come, I'm thinking by tomorrow sometime." Andy was feeling optimistic, but had to admit he'd never made a rink in such ideal conditions with only grown adults. A group of neighbourhood kids during his growing-up years was no match for the team he had assembled at GO. One whole hockey team, he smiled at the realization. He imagined Jack and Fiona playing hockey for the first time, neither of whom had ever strapped on a pair of skates. Funny, associating Jack and Fiona together no longer seemed to bother him.

"Andy, just one more thing, then I've got to go relieve Jack. At Emmaus Bible School, they have the 'six-inch' rule. Ever heard about it? Here it's the same, just unwritten. I could swear I just caught you guys in contravention of same, though I tried, ahem, not to look. Now, I don't want the sky. Just, next time at the Jack in the Box, treat's on you, Andy boy. Otherwise," and he couldn't resist, "'*Dad's* the word!" Then he beat a hasty retreat.

Andy turned to Fiona and opened his mouth to speak when the door opened violently and a voice cried out, "Golly! I think every finger and toe on my body has frostbite and the rest of me feels like an iceberg!"

A second later, Jack lumbered down the hallway

into the Games Room. Fiona, eyes flaring, caught Andy in a tight gaze then released him after several seconds.

"Hey Jack, maybe you could borrow Andy's jacket and gloves, too. They say Canadians' blood runs white in the winter anyway. Next thing you know, Mr. Eskimo here will be stripping down to go for a splash in the Garden Pool then crawling into his igloo for an afternoon nap."

"Very funny, Miss All-Texas Wimp," Andy shot back, and barely missed being clobbered by a flying table tennis paddle.

Fiona and Andy had no time alone the rest of the day or evening. If by "civil" G. E. meant being *obliging* toward Fiona, Andy rationalized that he had fulfilled his duty. Even with the delightful turn that afternoon, Andy was committed to obeying the *letter* of the law, being a bit more liberal, he knew, on the *spirit* than G. E. intended. He'd feel his way on that.

When Andy got to his house that evening shortly after 9:00, the phone was ringing. It was Ken. "Andy, I saw you out just now flooding the rink. I know you're not out again until midnight. Could I come over for a while?"

"Sure," came Andy's leaden reply.

When Ken arrived at Andy's door, Andy told him straight-off he wanted to have a nap before midnight, because he hoped to do a couple of floodings after everyone else had gone to bed. Then he looked at Ken's hands. He was holding a seventy-page copy of his paper. He wanted Andy to read it. As Andy glanced through it before setting it aside, he noticed over two pages of handwritten comments by Mr. Myers.

"Did he write you an essay back?" Andy joked.

Ken remained serious, and Andy realized he could

not treat Ken's earnestness lightly. But to Andy's relief, his main purpose in visiting was actually to ask him to read his paper as soon as possible, that very night if he would, so that they might subsequently discuss it. Within fifteen minutes, Ken was headed back home. What a relief. Andy decided to nap first then get up and read the paper. He awoke refreshed and plunged right into Ken's *magnum opus*.

The paper was a thorough scouring of Scripture in the interests of mustering every possible text that might show the absolute gulf between man's reasoning and God's Word. It was completely devastating to all human pretension to explain God's ways or even understand life in any meaningful way. It was utterly disparaging of man's attempt to discover truth outside of biblical revelation. And it was shot through with scriptural quotations culled from every corner of the Bible. If the Bible was a huge jigsaw puzzle, Ken demonstrated a phenomenal ability to cobble together at least a few thousand of those pieces into a bizarrely coherent picture.

Andy held to a belief in the verbal inspiration and inerrancy of Scripture. He also believed in its perspicuity. But whether or not clothes could ever be rendered "whiter than white" by whatever new laundry product on TV, Andy had encountered someone more "inerrantist" than the Bible and more committed to it than the ultimate bibliolater. Ken's fervour simply knew no bounds. Andy felt awestruck upon reading the paper, though not warmed, like meeting some alien from outer space about whom there was a deep sense of uneasiness mixed with ineluctable fascination.

Mr. Myers praised the incredible biblical work undertaken then commented on Ken's excessive rejection of the discoverability of "truth" outside of the

Bible. He pointed out how utterly untenable that was in terms of myriad mundane realities of life about which we know, quite independent of biblical revelation. But he also alluded to the Reformers' notion that "all truth was God's truth," regardless of where or how or by whom it was detected. He stressed that the Bible was the ultimate yardstick of truth, not its sole fount. His concluding comments were: "You obviously are a gifted biblical expositor. Keep up the good work! But you also spent far and away too much time on this paper. From what I hear, you invested endless late night hours on this. That is excessive and obsessive. You must learn to work co-operatively with others. Team life will otherwise be far too difficult for you. Though I daresay, it may also be very good medicine. Finally, you failed to do the actual assignment. You did not connect this to the Spain team enterprise. Thanks for your paper. I value it highly."

Andy read the paper twice, once before he went out to do a double flooding, the second quicker perusal after 1:00, since he was still wide awake. Jack did not mind the study light on while he was sleeping, he always claimed.

Throughout the readings, Andy thought a lot about Fiona. He crawled into bed toward 2:00, barely able to put a notation into his diary—still nothing about Fiona though.

He woke up to snow falling furiously. The campus' entire giant slug slithering was completely replenished. It was still below freezing, so Andy knew the texture of the snow would not readily yield to shaping into snowballs or forts, though he saw a few outside trying just the same. No flooding for the time being. He wasn't sure if Mr. Myers would have permitted it on a Sunday anyway and was grateful he had snuck in two floodings after midnight.

The snow had still not let up after church. It was a phenomenal dump. Dan, who typically did not attend church, met Jack and Andy at their mish house entrance. He was donning winter boots and muttering, "Man! Yesterday I work all day on an infernal rink, and today, snow removal! 'No rest for the wicked,' as they say. Guess I should have gone to church with you guys. So much for trying to keep the Lord's Day holy," he said in mock anguish.

"Andy and I are game to help, right Andy?" Jack responded immediately.

Dan laughed. "You're on! Doesn't know what he's in for, 'eh, Andy'?" He inserted a mock Canadianism. "They say the only dispute between the Americans and the Canadians since the War of 1812 has been which way to pile the snow along the 49th parallel."

"You've got the easy part, Dan," Andy responded, "riding that garden tractor with the plough. Jack and I'll be doing the heavy slugging. Meet you at the shed in a few minutes." They went inside to change.

Upstairs, Jack surveyed the scene out their window. "Boy, Andy, I can see why you could fall in love with this kind of scenery. Kansas wheat fields have their own beauty, too. But this is, I don't know. You're the one with words. How would you describe it?"

Andy thought of his night with Janys and the sensuousness of the post-blizzard snowscape that sparkled from infinite points of light, the engorged moon…

"'Whitewashed munificence,' Jack. Not just 'a few measly acres of snow,' as Voltaire wrote about Canada. But an entire panoply of pristine purity the way all creation should be."

In spite of himself, Andy thought of the mother

CHRYSALIS CRUCIBLE

and two children, Christmas Eve victims of that pre-emptive prurient purging. Nothing is straightforward in Christianity—or life—Andy was now adding. Dan had warned, "You'll see, you'll see."

"Yeah," said Jack. Then, "What was that again?"

After the snow-shovelling bee—which devolved into a wrestling match between Jack, Andy, Dan, and Gary (while Peter Oosten looked on), Andy hurried back to his mish house for his 3:00 meeting with Ken.

Andy was flattered by Ken's offer of friendship, but he was also intimidated at the likelihood of letting him down. If Andy counted himself a perfectionist, Ken was that raised to the *nth* power. Compared to him, Andy was a small photographic slide, whereas Ken was the magnified projection of said image. Perhaps that was the difference between them, thought Andy. Andy was content to do his own thing quietly, whereas Ken needed to project, to make waves, to be encountered grandly.

Andy gathered that Ken came from a small home assembly in Washington. As the "prize" young person, full sway was granted him in his many church involvements. His awesome energies and talents enabled him to wield wide influence in the larger assemblies network, a kind of brethren prodigy. Like a wild mountain torrent, he cascaded precipitously, establishing numerous ministries that he expected others to perpetuate. But in G. E., he had encountered for the first time a sand-bagging dynamic that was intent at channelling, if not damming up, his rushing torrent of will, ideas, emotions, talents, and the like.

Ken had not been amongst the *chosen* on the pre-Christmas "Doomsday Roster," which had occasioned a crashing halt to the fury of Ken's piety against G. E.'s impervious dyke. Since then, Ken had avidly sought circumvention, if not breaching. Andy regarded himself as a bare trickle in comparison, but he did not dispute some feeling of solidarity with Ken.

Matters were coming to a head Ken explained when he arrived. Response to his paper was an example. It was a massive combing of Scripture for a doctrine of inspiration and inerrancy, real or imagined. It was all original research, if one discounted use of *Strong's Exhaustive Concordance* and the translated KJV text of Scripture, itself (which presupposed massive scholarship by vast numbers of academics in a wide array of fields as diverse as anthropology and archaeology). But it did not remotely meet the requirements laid down, as Mr. Myers noted. Ken's rewording (Andy was amazed at his taking such liberties) of Jude 3, "Beloved, when I gave all diligence to write unto you of the mission field, it was needful for me to write unto you, and exhort you that ye should earnestly contend for the doctrine of the verbal inspiration and inerrancy of Scripture," in his introductory comments simply did not wash with G. E. Like Cain, Ken was insisting upon the appropriateness of his offering, but G. E. had already given the non-negotiable prescription.

It seemed this was Ken's way in other areas as well. If his work assignment called for potato peeling and Ken felt the need to minister to someone on floor-scrubbing detail, then scrub floors he would. This led to the cook's near declaration of holy war on Ken for the next week. Irma Bauman was a large woman not to be "taken lightly," and it was she who had been left with the pile of potatoes to peel. Ken worked compulsively, but it was entirely to the beat of his own drum.

Andy knew from Sam, Ken's roommate, that he slept little and hovered hours on end over his portable typewriter. He reformulated reams of notes from class presentations, engaged in personal Bible study, and corresponded voluminously. When a curfew was finally imposed upon everyone, Ken interpreted this to mean he had to stay in his room after 11:00 but not necessarily in bed. So Sam eventually purchased earplugs and eyeshades, thus enduring Ken's nocturnal obsessions until G. E. discovered this, too, and squelched it.

"Thank you so much for meeting with me," Ken said at session's end. "It's a tremendous relief to talk to someone about all this. I hope we can do it again soon."

Andy felt exhausted and yearned for a nap as he showed Ken to the door. He registered mainly great perplexity, sensing in Ken a kind of mirror-image, but one of such gargantuan proportions that it evoked a sense of dread he knew only in nightmares.

By Ken's evaluation, he and Andy "hit it off" those first few weeks after the New Year. But Andy could not shake his personal disinclination, mixed, however, with a compelling fascination. Ken would often remark to Andy: "I can at least *talk* to you!" Which he did, unusually for Andy, more than *vice versa*. So the relationship was somehow nurtured along. Ken was in need of an ally, and Andy, perhaps in an undefined way, found out more about himself, albeit writ large and grotesque in the intense, exaggerated personality of Ken. Andy further thought he might somehow *help* Ken: though to do what he was unsure. Buck the system? Find himself? Find God?

Ken never did ultimately inscribe anything on the *Joyful Wall*, which all team members wrote on before heading for their overseas assignments. Andy often surmised that had he, he might have quoted Luther's famous words before the Diet of Worms: "Here I stand. I can do no other." But there really was no place for that on the *Joyful Wall*, Andy was discovering, because only one man at the Centre could be allowed to hold to that, and he was already in charge.

Following Andy and Ken's meeting was an event at the Admin Building, during which area churches received a report on *GO YE '71* and got a chance to see the film that had been premiered there. G. E. was still away, so George Myers, dressed again as Amos at one point, took charge. Andy noted his style was less aggressive than G. E.'s.

By the time Andy and the rest of the Germany team were cleaning up after coffee, tea, and desserts it was nearly 11:30 p.m. The snow had long since stopped. The moon was fuller than a few nights ago. It was perfectly still, and very cold.

As the group headed back toward their mish houses, Sharon Collins kidded Andy about his great skating rink buried under a foot of snow. "I know, Sharon! Tomorrow after supper, you'll see!"

Once inside, Andy told Jack he was going back out to check the rink, just to see how it looked. Jack was too wiped to join him and asked Andy to tiptoe when he came back in. He was going straight to bed.

Andy grabbed a shovel from outside Dan's shed and began by clearing a path from the Games Room door to the rink. Then he stepped onto the rink and just about wiped out! He carefully cleared away one corner of the rink, with mounting excitement. The ice was perfectly smooth, and, Andy knew, eminently skateable. He almost lost his footing again as he scampered to the edge. Then he stabbed the shovel into the snow and dashed down the well-cleared sidewalk back to his house.

He re-emerged moments later, skates slung about his neck and carrying a wooden chair. At rink's edge, he sat on the chair, removed his boots, and laced up his skates. Then he plucked the shovel from its snowy sheath, pushed off from the edge, and ploughed through the powdery whiteness. This was the very best kind of snow to remove from the rink, Andy knew. It was fluffy, fine, and did not stick to the surface. The ice below was smooth and firm. Andy was thrilled.

Back and forth, Andy pushed the shovel up and down the full length of the rink for the next half hour or so. At one point, he noticed that the hallway light in the Admin Building had gone on. Someone after a late night snack, he guessed, there being a vending machine at the end of the hallway.

Andy could have kept on for hours. The ice had frozen perfectly below. He did not slice through to the garden at any point. Though it would be important to keep up daily floodings, in forty-eight hours they had achieved critical thickness and more. The progress had exceeded his greatest expectations, especially the rink's glassy surface. Skating party at the Centre tomorrow night, he knew! Wow! They'd done it!

After rounding up the last bits of errant snow, Andy slammed the shovel into a three-foot high snow bank. It was time.

Andy had been skating since his dad first built a backyard rink when Andy was only four. It was barely half as large as what he had just built at the Centre. He had played endless hours of hockey ("fastest kid on skates," he'd been dubbed as he grew into the longest legs) on that same backyard terrain winter after winter until well into his teens. He was also a fancy stick-handler.

Andy remembered well the first time they had a

"January Thaw" during, of all times, the week before Christmas! It was unheard of, unthinkable. A green Christmas Eve and raining? Andy and his friends were devastated at not being able to use the rink throughout the holidays that year.

Andy swooshed and pirouetted before an imagined audience of thousands in a stellar Gold Medal performance. He cut this way and that in long flowing glides, reversing to furious backward leg action, he the sole defenseman before the onslaught of Maurice Richard and Jean Belliveau, who bore down on him in the dying moments of game seven of the Stanley Cup Playoffs between the Maple Leafs and Montréal Canadiens. The Leafs were ahead by one goal, and this was the Canadiens' last shot at tying the game and precipitating sudden death overtime. His fantasy morphed into the finale of a glorious figure skating routine, performed to the strains of the *Love Story* theme song in consort with his fellow Gold Medalist, Lorraine Takahashi, in response to which the crowds break out in rapturous applause.

Andy's fantasy was shattered by just such a sound from the direction of the Admin Building. One solitary set of hands clapped furiously as he turned effortlessly while maintaining the momentum of his glide.

"Well, I'll be jiggered," Andy said in perfect *Jackism* tone. "Fiona, what in the world are you doing?" His voice trailed off as she sat on the wooden chair, legs crossed, white figure skates mounted, long laces dangling. "Wherever in the world?" But again he did not complete the question. "It's way after midnight, and you should have long since...." He wasn't getting through anything.

"Janys already told me I could share her skates, since we're the same size. When I saw you out the window, I decided, why not?"

Andy watched the moonlight dance across her face. He flashed back to a shimmering body that quickly sidestepped the moon.

Fiona stood shakily to her feet. "Andy," she said huskily, "I want you to teach me to skate."

G. E.'s office directly overlooked "Norton's Notion," as Dan had dubbed the rink. But G. E. was far away. In fact, he was at Fiona's home assembly as part of his travels. The rest of GO lay still.

Andy still hesitated. Send Fiona home to bed? Not even a Cathar would do that. Was she an evil seductress, a roaring lion in disguise, a fowler with a trip wire, he the unwary prey? Was he betraying any commitment? During their last time together, Lorraine had told him she had no right to a hold on him. Did anyone have a hold on him outside of God? Did G. E.? And still he remained immobile. Had he pursued Fiona in any way? Had he set up any of these encounters? Had he initiated anything? Had he asked Fiona for this?

"Andy, will you teach me?" Her voice came again softly, like a sigh.

"Let me start by tightening your skates and tying back your laces," Andy said. He dropped to his knees and nestled her skates between his legs. The laces encircled her ankles twice before Andy tied them off in a double knot. "There, stand up and tell me how it feels."

She stepped out, and instantly lost her footing. Andy caught her in full embrace. "Steady, Fiona." He scarcely believed what he was holding. What giddy scent was she wearing? "Skating is just plain counter-intuitive at first. If you really want to get the feel of it, here, I'll get behind you like this." He put his arms around Fiona and instructed her to lean back against him as he propelled her forward.

"Andy, I *love* the feel already, and we haven't even started!" Her slow syllables syncopated each stride.

They skated and skated, leisurely at first, a Texas drawl. Up to the far end, turn, and back down again. She squealed with delight. "Sshhh, Fiona," Andy said looking around warily. "You'll wake up the whole compound. Steady. You're getting it. Now we'll go backwards. Faster now, we'll pick up speed. Great. Now, lean to your left as we take that corner, the other way. When you're skating, you just *flow*."

They did. Soundlessly. Back and forth. Around and around. Up and down. The moon was their spotlight, they the stars, celestial counterparts a-twinkle. To Andy, the rink's surface shifted suddenly and took wings. On magic ice, they were the world's prima donnas in effortless thrust and counter-thrust, pirouetting, gliding, tirelessly, timelessly, and in perfect unison. On and on and on, no horizon.

Finally, Fiona pushed against his arms. He released her. She launched. A deafening scream as she freewheeled precipitously, he in desperate pursuit, both exploding into a recently neatly piled snow bank, body parts flailing in snowy disarray.

"Oh, I loved it! I loved it! I love..." There, straddling a white snow stallion, atop the world, encircling the earth, they kissed. Again. Lips on lips, blue ice fire.

"Encore, Andy, encore!" When she came up for air.

He leapt up, strong arms lifting her high above the surface then setting her down again, brushing away scattered white feta. The encore began: glide and thrust, lift and bend, soar and sail, around, around, around, world without end.

CHRYSALIS CRUCIBLE   197

"This is the only way I ever want to skate, Andy."

"Then I haven't done my job, Fiona," Andy whispered back. "You asked me to teach you how to skate. We haven't gotten past the warm-up yet."

"We got past that, Andy. We got past that."

They glided back toward the chair. Andy quickly took off his skates then helped Fiona untie hers.

"I can't walk barefoot. This isn't Texas sand exactly that warms between the toes," she protested.

"Hang on," Andy instructed, hoisting her high in one motion. He carried her toward the Admin Building directly below G. E.'s darkened sentinel.

"Fiona," Andy was already thinking strategically, "you'd better go back alone. If anyone in our mish houses happens to see the two of us walking together at this hour…"

"Oh, Andy, I was hoping for a moonlit handheld stroll to my doorstep. 'Here we are together in the middle of the night. This is no time for a chat!'" She sang softly, adding, "or a cool head."

"Come again?"

"*My Fair Lady*, Andy. It's Elisa singing to Freddy, or was it Fiona to Andy?"

"Whatever," Andy retorted. "We both got cool heads in that snow bank. And *I* say, 'Let cool heads prevail.'"

"Okay." She pouted delectably. Then her face brightened. "But first, *encore*, Andy." She pulled his head low.

Of one thing Andy was certain, though he had never acted on G. E.'s recommendation and looked up *The Way of a Man With a Maid* in the library. The guy's supposed to take the lead in these things. It was the brethren way. Except in Texas, apparently.

"Goodnight, Andy. That was some first lesson. I

think I'll be back for more." With that, she was out the door toward her house.

Andy mopped up the drippings from their skates and galoshes in the hallway then walked home under the watchful moon. He left the chair and shovel at rink side.

As he slipped under his covers, he knew he had pushed the spirit of the law to the breaking point. He hadn't come to GO looking for such a development, and yet it had happened. He finally knew what it felt like to bite into the Delicious Apple called Fiona. He consoled himself with the reminder that it was unnamed fruit in the primordial garden anyway. Then he slipped into blissful unconsciousness.

22

The next night was indeed a glorious inaugural skating party on Norton's Notion. Andy was amazed at how many pairs of skates—ancient, new, and everything in between—came out of the woodwork.

The girls from the Nîce team cooked up a great cauldron of hot chocolate, which made French the language of choice for the evening. Everyone learned to say *Oui, Non, Merci,* and *Encore, s'il vous plaît.* Andy was quite amused. Then he thought of Fiona's French *encore* the night before. But no French kisses, he thought, before deciding it was best to abandon that line of thinking.

Dan rigged up an impromptu lighting system using Christmas lights that added a quaint festive accent and emboldened the novices to give it a try. The northerners were the default teachers. Several expressed absolute delight that Norton's Notion had turned into reality, given much initial scepticism. All were aware that, like Frosty in the Christmas song, the rink's days were numbered.

Andy stood out more than Jack for once. All Jack could do was totter around the rink while leaning heavily on Janys, who was instructing him. It didn't help that he had to literally cram his feet into Andy's skates, which were one full size too small. He returned them gratefully to Andy after ploughing into a snow bank.

As Andy laced up his skates once again, Fiona sidled up to him and asked for "Lesson Number Two." Andy smiled obligingly, emitting a *"Oui,"* then said, "But not like last night." A torrent of pleasure washed over him. "You're basically on your own tonight, lady, after I get you started."

Unlike Jack, at least she did not land in the snow bank, though she did her own version of his inelegant totter.

By this time, someone had plugged in a tape recorder, adding music to the frivolity.

"This ice rink certainly separates the men from the boys," Dan said as Andy glided Fiona to a chair, where she unlaced her skates and returned them to Janys.

As Janys put her skates back on, a chant emerged, eventually taken up by everyone: "Janys and Andy a skate! Janys and Andy a skate!" They were definitely the undisputed stars of the evening.

Realizing the crowd wouldn't take no for an answer, Andy turned to Janys, who was ruddy-cheeked. "Game?"

"Sure."

"What about your hair?" Andy noted she had mostly worn it down since Christmas.

"I think I'll just leave it, Andy. Isn't that how you like it?"

Andy blushed slightly. Had Fiona heard?

While everyone cleared off the ice, Andy turned to Janys. "You're the figure skater. I'll follow your lead and just kind of skate around. You do the fancy stuff, and I'll take the bows with you."

"Okay," Janys said, smiling. As Andy had watched her skate, he knew she'd had training all right.

"I've got just the tape for the occasion," Gary called out. "Wait until I put it in."

There was a hush, and then the music began. Gary had chosen the theme song for *Love Story*, and Andy's mind flooded with wincing memories of Lorraine.

Janys moved gracefully, with Andy more like a

hockey player following in tandem. He mainly skated around and accented her moves. It seemed to be working, if no gold medal performance.

At the pulsating height of the song, Andy picked Janys up—to his and her total surprise! He deposited her onto the rink seconds later with a flowing glide, which drove the crowd wild. It also verified to him that his flash picture of a month earlier had indeed snapped an ample bosom. Her flying hair had almost blinded him.

As they glided to a stop somewhat in sync with the closing bars of the song, wild cheers accompanied them. Not a few tried out their newfound French language skills with cries of "*Encore! Encore!*" But Andy and Janys merely bowed and skated hand-in-hand to the side to catch their breath.

"Andy," Janys said between breaths, "what was that move all about? I thought *I* was taking the lead." Her eyes smiled. "Thank you," she added simply.

"But I should thank *you*—and do," Andy replied.

The party began to wind down after that. It had been a roaring success. Fiona came over to congratulate them. "Wow," she said to Janys, "I sure wish I could skate like that. I guess that's one difference between growing up in Ontario and Texas! And you, Mr. Dynamic Skater, outdid yourself," she said, turning to Andy. "You learned all that from hockey?"

But it was Dan, following on the heels of Fiona's comment, who dubbed Andy and Janys "The Skating Sensations," a name that stuck with them for the rest of their time at the Centre. Dan seemed to come up with fitting names for everything, like a primordial and possibly similarly errant Adam.

The rink lasted just over two weeks. Andy, Janys,

Fiona, and Jack skated on it every day, with the latter two displaying marked improvement before the inevitable thaw set in. There were, however, no more nocturnal trysts.

Andy reluctantly bid *adieu* to the rink as if to an old friend. Would anyone carry on the tradition of "Norton's Notion" next year at the Centre? Andy had heard of the Paul Newman movie *Sometimes a Great Notion*. Sometimes, indeed. But all notions, too, pass. What had the Great Apostle written? *Whether there be notions, they shall vanish away* (slight paraphrase).

G. E. imposed a curfew upon his return in late January. Lights out by 11:00 was the ruling, the spirit and letter of which was adhered to by most, however much it cramped some persons' styles. It had nothing directly to do with Ken or Andy's nocturnal habits but with too many heading too often to Burger King, Jack in the Box, and the exotic ice cream parlour Take Your Licks in Style!

Andy felt especially sheepish one night when returning with an uproarious group from Take Your Licks, only to encounter G. E. and Ken sitting in a car in the parking lot. Obviously, an impromptu emotionally charged counselling session was going on in this most unlikely of places. How inappropriate their hilarity seemed compared to the sobering spiritual skirmish of the moment. All turned homeward in a subdued mood, like dogs with their tails between legs.

The curfew took effect the week prior to the Bill Gothard Seminar. This much anticipated event at the Centre had all the trappings of a papal visitation, so revered was Gothard by most there. Few had ever attended a Gothard seminar, but his mystique had permeated most evangelical churches. Mr. Myers, who had attended once before, said repeatedly that it was the most enjoyable week of his life. Upon hearing that line, Dan quipped, "Must have been an abstaining honeymoon they had!"

Andy wondered what Dan's most important week might have been, then thought about his own, then forgot the whole thing over a round of ping pong with Gary, who demanded every ounce of concentration.

Ken had also been through a "Basic Youth Conflicts" seminar and was nearly ecstatic as the week approached. He should have been called "Bill" as surely as Andy's nickname of "Francis" had taken hold, a result of Andy's frequent use of such Schaefferisms as "personal-infinite God," "honest answers to honest questions," and "true truth," in addition to regular quotation of or allusion to Schaeffer's writings and tapes. At the time, Schaeffer's publications appeared regularly, with orders at the Christian bookstore immediately upon Andy's learning of them.

In usual Kincadian fashion, however, Ken was a *total* devotee of Gothard and his seven principles for successful living: 1) self-acceptance, 2) a clear conscience, 3) being under authority, 4) suffering, 5) surrendering ownership, 6) embracing freedom, and 7) discovering consequently true success in life. Ken's rationale was simple: Gothard hardly said anything without scriptural proof texts, and he did so effortlessly, as if the Bible were made to fit Gothard's very thought patterns and ideas.

Ken showed Andy the huge binder he had from the seminar he had attended the previous year in Seattle. The binder bulged with Ken's personal interaction, as did his favourite study Bible. Strange that Ken should so oppose commentaries yet veritably inundate the field with his own, Andy mused. His devotion to

Gothard was likewise paradoxical, who seemed a close second in authority to the Bible itself.

Much to Andy's chagrin (and in a way relief), Ken did not permit him to crack open the binder. "You must experience the seminar before you can grasp the text," Ken explained, aping, of course, Gothard himself.

Andy was wary of such hype. Such was his attitude as he traveled to the first evening's "performance." The trainees and support staff rode on a chartered bus each evening with G. E and Mr. Myers. The seminar ran for six days, including all day Friday and Saturday. The pace was gruelling.

Inside the huge auditorium, diminutive Bill stood in front of an overhead projector, his neatly typed transparencies projected onto a giant screen, and talked. Simply. No particular rhetoric, resonance or even emotion attended his delivery. It was a monologue bordering on the monotonous. Non-charismatic by religious and secular definitions, even his face looked expressionless from where Andy sat.

And yet, from his small beginnings as a part-time instructor at Wheaton College, Bill Gothard had achieved Evangelical guru status. Thousands packed out stadiums and auditoriums throughout North America to hear him or to watch videos of his seminar. He possessed an undoubted mystique, which he turned to God's glory.

Night after night throughout the week, the GO crowd streamed into the huge stadium on Chicago's south side in step with multitudes that hovered near ten thousand, total attendance duly noted in Gothard's deadpan each session. Though Andy lived under a prohibition, Jack did not, which was quite obvious in the noted frequency of Jack's proximity to Fiona on bus rides and in the auditorium. Why, presumably, was Jack not being reined in? Why was Andy the only target? Who was the real "lady's man" anyway?

Gothard repeatedly warned his audience not to circulate any of the handouts or his bindered notes, since others should *experience* the seminar first. One was not to regurgitate or discuss Gothard, Andy learned, but rather imbibe and flesh out in one's own context the inviolable truths disseminated. This was not a marketing ploy; Andy was convinced, though Gothard's "Institute," if not the man himself, quickly became a multimillionaire. But it certainly controlled who might evaluate the material. Alumni were permitted to attend free and repeatedly in order to have their batteries recharged. Millions did so. Recurring rumours circulated that Gothard had recently married or was about to marry. They were untrue, but they certainly added to the Gothard aura.

Though vigilant, Andy was taken in by Gothard's ability to organize Scripture around uncomplicated, straightforward insights. If there was a personal problem or conflict, there was invariably a surface manifestation, a subsurface contributor, and finally a root source. This ultimate cause invariably had a simple scripture attached, culled from any part of the Bible on a flat plane of interpretation. It mattered not the historical or cultural context, what literary genre the text was in, what portion of the Old or New Testament or anything else on an exegetical checklist. All biblical material was neatly reduced to bite-sized proof texts. Everything was made to fit the Procrustean bed of Gothard's "root causes."

Many themes resonated with evangelical proclivities, not least Gothard's strict chain-of-command hierarchy, which was urged on all as *foundational* to a Christian walk and utterly at odds with contemporary youth culture, which was in the midst of ubiquitously casting off authority. Gothard insisted that all Christians needed an "umbrella of protection" and were constrained to get "under the protection of authority," such that "God could get his directions to us through those he has placed over us." He was such a person in his own organization. Andy wondered eventually who was Bill's "umbrella," since it was widely known that in his organization he was an authority unto himself. Brethren elders and evangelical church leaders in general loved Gothard for it. Doubtless, G. E. aspired to the same status at GO.

Janys once told Andy that her brother Ted had recently heard a sermon on the "tripartite being of man." It was a brilliant presentation, full of superbly organized proof texts. He said it unfolded like a puzzle, all the pieces fitting together into a coherent whole. "The only problem is," Ted commented, "that picture did not even remotely match the one on the biblical box cover!" Gothard, Janys implied, was in a similar league.

The wizardry of Gothard's handling of Scripture eventually left Andy with a feeling that something was strangely, alarmingly, suspect. Clearly, however, his was a minority opinion. Throughout the auditorium, pens scribbled furiously, like so many violinists responding to the Maestro's slightest gesture. Ken alone produced subsequently about 100 pages of typewritten notes.

At one point in the seminar, the trainees and all attendees responsively wrote their parents, expressing undying appreciation for them and asking them to continue God's established role as primary authority in their lives. Many other letters were sent at Gothard's direction, imploring forgiveness, expressing guilt for

CHRYSALIS CRUCIBLE

sins committed, and so forth. Gothard stressed that this was only second best to a face-to-face personal encounter. Andy imagined Lorraine doing that with her dad and wanted to vomit or throw a grenade. Why was he so violently angry all of a sudden?

It was an overwhelming week. By the end, most showed signs of physical and emotional exhaustion, intertwined with heights of spiritual exhilaration.

Andy had not sat with Fiona on the bus ride once. It was not possible under G. E.'s watchful eye. On the final bus ride home that Saturday he sat beside Gary. Sharon and Jean were behind them, and Jack and Janys slid in front.

"You know," Gary launched in, "our head elder says there is no one in America that God is using more than Bill Gothard! He's been to a seminar five times and is endlessly recruiting our youth, friends, family, and a listening audience on a local radio station to attend. You'd almost think he works for the organization; he's so fired about him. Despite all that, this is the first time Sharon and I could attend. And now I can see what we've been missing all along."

Andy remained silent.

Jack turned around excitedly. "Man! Enough stuff got shared this week to last a whole lifetime of working out! It was... Andy, help me out, you and your way with words."

"'Truly astounding,' Jack," Andy could hear the irritation in his voice, but surely it was G. E. with whom he was arguing.

Jack continued undaunted. "I just wish I could get some of our elders hooked the way yours are, Gary. But how do you do that when you can't show them anything and really can't say much?"

"It has to *show* in you first, Jack," Sharon piped up,

"not saying it doesn't. But that's what Mr. Gothard's been saying all week."

Still no comment from Andy, Janys or Jean.

Andy had turned around to hear Sharon and caught sight of Fiona toward the back, not far from G. E. He didn't dare attempt eye contact. His mind was churning about the "umbrella of authority," with which they had been bombarded all week. He knew Paul talked of being a "slave of Christ," so patterned one was to be after his way. And he knew, paradoxically, this meant (claimed) "freedom" beyond belief. So where was the rub?

"I think what Bill Gothard gave me was a kind of blueprint," Gary said. "I want to go over all of his notes and mine, adding more, no doubt. I get a sense that one can follow this way and just not go wrong. Like there is a scriptural principle for everything in life, every decision and eventuality. Gothard's given us a pile from the Bible already. With those examples to build on, I think we can just about guarantee not going wrong if we stay true. That's so liberating! I do have a question though: anyone else heard rumours about his brother Steve?"

"What do you mean, Gary?" Jack's quick question.

"We have," Jean spoke up for the first time.

"And..." Gary prompted.

"Our teaching elder thought they were likely the same as those about Gothard's wife, widespread but false."

"Fill us in," Jack pleaded.

"That he'd been sexually inappropriate with some of the women working at their headquarters," Gary supplied.

"But don't you think that's the work of the devil?" Jack responded. "Though I can see why G. E.'s so protective around here. I mean, wouldn't the devil just love to undo Mr. Gothard's effectiveness by spreading rumours and lies about him and his family? That's just Satan's way." He seemed unduly steamed about it.

Janys turned back to face Gary. "Don't you think if you asked Jesus today how many barns you could build, keep or had to tear down, he'd look at you funny, and just, well, walk away?"

Gary's eyebrows rose as his mouth fell open. "What are you saying, Janys?"

She paused for a moment to formulate her thoughts. "If we had our whole lives more or less sewed up so we always knew at the outset what to do or say, just consult the manual with chapter and verse, then wouldn't we be more Pharisee than Christian, and wouldn't Jesus be saying to us, 'Woe to you'? And wouldn't we be more Catholic than Protestant, with all their 'canon law,' like the Galatian Judaizers who got Paul so riled he said he wished the knife would slip when they did their circumcisions?"

Where did Janys get this stuff? Andy looked at Gary.

"Well I..." Gary began, "Are you saying Janys, that Bill Gothard is more Mosaic legalist than Christian, more law than grace, more form than freedom? That's amazing. I've never heard that before. But you know, you might be on to something."

"What?" Jack asked, his nose scrunched, eyes slits.

The group sank into a pensive silence the rest of the way home.

23

January had gone by quickly. Andy's next session with G. E. was upon him. He had had no times alone with Fiona since the unexpected pre-season opening of Norton's Notion. Eye contact and body-language communication do not a relationship make. But that wasn't the point of the training, Andy kept reminding himself. Did his dad have any idea of the vicissitudes of the unknown or the perplexities he was experiencing? How would he?

For all his intelligence, Andy's dad was really quite uncomplicated. Or at least his world was. Not unlike Bill Gothard, Andy thought. Andy's universe, on the other hand, though just next door was not at all straightforward. Or at least it was becoming less so. It had been otherwise. Even through university, he had thought much like his dad, like millions of evangelicals throughout history, the "great cloud of witnesses." Or had they? Had he? He had known lots of questions, then lots of answers through his university years. He'd finished a B.A. with faith intact. Everything he'd done since was in a Christian ministry context. Yet he seemed to be having more questions now than he had then.

G. E. was one of them, a walking question mark for Andy. When he thought of G. E., he oscillated between attraction and repulsion. He loved his prophecy lectures and enthusiastic teaching in general as well as his passion for missions. Yet he was so frustrated with his ethics *à la Gothard*. And yet Andy liked Gothard, too, Janys notwithstanding.

So intent was Andy as he passed by the now

sagging Norton's Notion that he almost collided with Fiona, who approached hastily from the opposite direction. She laughed. He languished.

"Have you seen a ghost, Andy? Or is it just me?"

Andy snapped to attention, casting a quick glance up at G. E.'s window. "Fiona, you're an armful, a sigh, and lips full of irrefutable proof you're no *Gespenst*. Quick, what's the German translation?"

"Ghost!"

"Right," Andy replied. "See? You do speak German. And there is nothing 'just me' about you, Fiona Sanchez, no matter from what angle. All my circuits bar none go off every time I see you. Only, like the elusive trillium, I may not reach out and pluck, or something dies. Do you know trilliums in Texas?"

He was conscious of where he was headed, of whom he was talking to, of his gut aching, of time standing still. No casual encounter was ever possible with Fiona, his heart trumpeted.

Fiona shook her head, smiling.

Dare he? Andy took her right hand in his left—low, furtively—and squeezed. "Trilliums," he said, "are of rarest forest beauty that unfold only once every seven years. In native Huron culture, they are a symbol of unparalleled purity. When plucked, you have to wait seven long years for the next bloom, Fiona. *Seven long years*."

He unsheathed her hand, her eyes, and walked on, not looking back. Had the sentinel been watching? He did not care. He knocked on the office door sharp at 4:30 p.m.

Warm smile and welcome again, arm around Andy until he sat down.

"We've hardly talked, son. I trust you had a good Christmas with the folks?"

"Yes," Andy said simply. He could have asked at Congress. But that was not his agenda then. So did he really want to know?

G. E. held up a letter. "I'm not sure exactly how to react to this," G. E. said, getting straight to the point. "But I want you to read it and come back tomorrow to discuss it."

Andy groaned inwardly.

"You have a good pedigree, Andy. I feel I know your dad quite well, actually, despite how little we've talked. We've 'stayed in touch' over the years, shall we say, through articles in *Interest*, attending the same conferences, and so on."

Andy's dad had contributed several articles to *Interest,* the chief magazine amongst the North American brethren, in the past; primarily extolling established brethren polity and theology. Andy's dad and G. E., for G. E.'s conciliatory words, were at opposite ends of the "progressive/reactionary" scale.

G. E.'s usually darting eyes suddenly locked with Andy's, projecting a hint of fear. "He wouldn't really cause GO trouble, would he?"

Andy took a breath. "I haven't read the letter. But it was dad who urged me to come to the Centre this year. True, though, dad is like a dedicated hunter. Once the scent is up, he's indefatigable."

"For instance?"

"You remember the Peterborough case?"

"Your dad had something to do with that?"

"His name never appeared on the excommunication letter. But behind the scenes, he was the prime motivator."

Andy reflected on church discipline. It had always been closely watched in brethren circles. When Andy was nine, the first major occurrence of it in his memory rocked Carriage Street Gospel Chapel. Don Brooks was leadership material all the way: affable, bright, musically gifted, good-looking, etc. He had been dating one of the Penner sisters, Mennonites-turned-brethren in the Wallenstein assembly. Don and Anita seemed destined for full-time ministry.

Then one Sunday morning there was much discussion in hushed tones amongst the adults. That evening, Andy's dad went off to a hastily called elders meeting. The following Sunday, the children were sent downstairs at the end of a record short morning meeting. Andy's dad, the head elder, read some appropriate scripture. Then Don and Anita were "read out" of the assembly. A stern warning was extended to all others. With that, the ceremony was over.

The procedure was repeated when Andy was a teenager. Andy was present this time. Once again, his dad presided. Coral, Andy's one-time pre-teen girlfriend, had gone off to another university and "got in trouble" with a guy.

To his dad's credit, on both occasions he cried privately—or so Andy's mom explained. He had done what he felt he had to do by biblical prescription, but he took no relish in it.

As it turned out, neither of them ever darkened the door of Carriage Street Gospel Chapel again. Both subsequently married the other party and "went on for the Lord," having repented of their premarital adventures. Still, they had to be excommunicated to be an example "so that many may hear and fear" the scripture was adduced.

Sex, Andy knew, was the ultimate bugaboo in assembly circles. Unlike the French of *My Fair Lady*, the accent was nothing, the act everything. Other kinds of transgressions, from spiritual or emotional violence against spouse and child to avaricious business practices, were ignored or at least not singled out.

The response to sexual indiscretions was not designed to reform offenders but rather to teach the faithful a lesson and to bring judgment upon the wrongdoers. "For the time is come that judgment must begin at the house of God," Andy had heard the Apostle Peter's words many times with concomitant warning: "And if it first begin at us, what shall the end be of them that obey not the gospel of God?"

Andy learned the name for this phenomenon during his first year sociology class: *scapegoating*. It was the ancient "ban" by which unanimity was achieved, minus one, the all against one. It had always troubled him.

G. E. asked Andy the details of the Peterborough case. Andy knew some of the children of the people involved, and if he had learned anything from that incident, it was that there was only one thing worse than sexual misconduct: *doctrinal impurity.*

As it turned out, for a few years some brethren businessmen had produced an underground publication entitled *Open and Loose*, picking up on the in-house designation of the brand of brethrenism with which they identified. Only they proved to be *too* open and *too* loose doctrinally, pursuing a policy of welcoming contributions on any subject, with any content, provided the writers appealed to *sola scriptura*. Presumably, opinions of people like Jehovah's Witnesses could even be printed as long as they quoted the Bible.

The businessmen who edited the publication did so anonymously, and many contributors—depending on how controversial the piece—used pseudonyms such as "Theophilus" or merely initials. The perpetrators were eventually flushed and then kicked out, with

Andy's dad serving as the Chief Inquisitor.

"Don't get me wrong," Andy ended off, "Dad is very loving overall and a wonderful father. But he burns with a red-hot zeal for the 'Lord's House,' as he puts it."

In the soft glow of the two desk lamps, G. E. pursed and licked his lips. His eyes darted. "Andy, let's change the subject. Our time is short. I want to know whether you visited the girl from Kitchener over Christmas."

Out of the blue. From nowhere. Wham!

Andy was so tempted to say "no," because, technically speaking, she had visited him. Instead he said, "Yes, we saw each other at my sister's place."

G. E. let out a low whistle. "Did you not, Andy, commit *not* to visit her over Christmas? I thought we had established that."

"Mr. Moore, I did not make such a promise."

"But you knew it was against my better judgment," G. E. bore down. "That God had given me your care while here, that, from all our talks, it was not healthy for you or her."

Andy said nothing. He looked out the window. Everything outside was too dark.

"Did your parents know?" G. E. queried.

Once again, a lie would have been so easy.

"No, I did not tell them about seeing her." Andy still refused to speak Lorraine's name, not wanting to supply G. E. with further ammunition. "My dad, my dad had issues…" Did he even want to reveal she was non-white? Quick inventory: There was one non-Caucasian at the Centre that year, a Guatemalan named Carlos. "My dad has issues with dating other races." He vowed to explain nothing more. He didn't care what G. E. asked.

A long silence. At last, "Andy, I have decided not

to put you down as co-leader with Gary. Peter will do that, though please wait until we have talked before telling him.

"What I am about to instruct I do for your soul, Andy. I am asking that there be no form of communication, written or spoken, between you and Fiona without a third-party present. That means no little notes under the table, as it were. And certainly no other communication. I am instructing Fiona the same.

"If you chance to meet alone while walking the campus, in the cafeteria or somewhere else, you are to be friendly but not to carry on unless with others. I likewise forbid this with what's-her-name from Kitchener."

G. E. paused. Andy did not take the hint. G. E. did not push it.

"Jean looks after the mail and will take note."

I thought they just did that in prisons, Andy remonstrated inwardly.

The clock on the mantel moved with agonizing slowness. The room really was not *gemütlich*—a wonderful German word for everything congenial and cozy. It was actually rather menacing. Andy did not even want to look around. But where else? Beyond was a disappearing rink, and memories with it? He was being forbidden a woman he hardly knew, whatever the deep resonance, and a woman whose name G. E. didn't even know.

"May I leave now, sir?"

"Andy, that sounds like insolence. I will not abide it! You know God's call is upon you. I saw that in the excellent paper you did about Germany. You have a heart for the lost, Andy. You have heard Jesus' call. Listen to his words again now." He picked up an open

Bible: "'Verily, verily, I say unto you, Except a corn of wheat fall into the ground and die, it abideth alone: but if it die, it bringeth forth much fruit. He that loveth his life shall lose it; and he that hateth his life in this world shall keep it unto life eternal.'

"Andy, this has been hard enough. We were not finished though. What I am about to say is the hardest of all. *I am extending this for the entire two years you are in Germany.* There is to be no private communication with Fiona of any kind, written or otherwise. I will be instructing Gary and Peter on this matter. I cannot do the same about the Kitchener girl. I can only hope that you're mature enough to know how wrong carrying on that relationship is while on missions in West Berlin. Earthly soldiers on the battlefield endure overwhelming privation. How much more heavenly forces for Christ, Andy?

"You are one such. I, by the authority of the Lord (which Bill Gothard makes crystal clear), am your Commissioning Officer. I have given you your marching orders, Andy. I appeal to you, stand up, stand up for Jesus! Andy..."

He grasped Andy's hands in utter earnestness. There was a long silence. His hands were dry ice that burned. Could Andy stand it? Stand up? "Andy... Lord, we pray this afternoon for our dear, dear child of Yours, Andrew Norton, son of Samuel Norton, both beloved servants of the Cross..." The prayer was powerful, passionate, pleading, and very long.

"You can do what's best, Andy. I know you can. Want to. Will." Embrace, and Andy was out the door.

Before returning the letter the next day, which he went home and read that evening, Andy photocopied it and stuck it into the back of his diary. It read:

Dear Brother Moore:

I have laboured much in prayer before the Lord before addressing this letter to you.

Over Christmas, my son Andrew and I had a long discussion about GO. I had reservations about his attending the Training Centre in the first place, though I was also the one to encourage him. I was convinced enough that it was committed to assembly principles, so I gave Andrew my blessing.

But I have become deeply disturbed since our Christmas conversation about the following:

1. Andrew informs me that neighbourhood women attending your "informal" meetings at the Centre do not wear head coverings even during the breaking of bread service. And upon further questioning, I discovered that some of the students have adopted this anti-biblical activity as well!

As you should know, 1 Corinthians 11 is explicit about the head coverings. This has been one of the marks of our own unique faithfulness to the New Testament Pattern. This is one of the reasons it is a privilege to fellowship with those known as "plymouth brethren."

2. As I understand it, you have replaced the Spirit-blessed Believers' Hymnbook *almost entirely with the latest pop songs of the ephemeral Jesus People Movement. This is a travesty of the worship time.*

I have always taken pride that wherever I have travelled in the English-speaking world, I can fellowship with my Bible and Believers' Hymnbook *faithfully at hand. Surely this is one of the great signs of the unity of the Spirit amongst us. It seems, though, that I could not do so at your local assembly. Do you mean to discard so casually what God has used for decades to grace our breaking of bread services?*

Further, I know that some "modern" assemblies, much to their discredit, have imposed a piano or organ onto the quiet waiting before the Lord each time a hymn is given out. But you have gone even further and are using guitars! Where is the holy order of which Paul speaks in 1 Corinthians 14?

God has clearly revealed a New Testament Pattern, which, thanks be to God, our forebears have faithfully discovered and passed on. Frankly speaking, your tinkering is like some upstart mechanic fresh out of apprenticeship trying to improve on the Rolls Royce engine! Only it's that and more. For, my dear brother, you are tinkering with the very Counsel of Holy God.

Paul rebuked Peter to his face, but at this time, I am unable to do the same. Meanwhile, I would ask you to consider prayerfully these matters and to respond. I will accept nothing less than a full biblical accounting! I am accountable here in this part of the vineyard God has vouchsafed to my care.

God willing, we plan a visit at Easter. I would enjoy fellowshipping with you and your elders.

In Christ,

Samuel Edwin Norton

Would dad write a letter to *Interest*? Andy wondered. Yes, he knew quickly, but not before making a firsthand visit and hearing G. E. out. His dad was principled, if narrow.

Dear Professor Norton:

I wish we could talk. You know me the best of everyone, yet we can't sit down in front of the fire and chat. I'd drop over in a flash if we could.

Life, which is often enough weird, just got more bizarre. Remember?

So what is faith to you, Professor? "Substance of things hoped for"? To be sure. "Evidence of things not seen"? No argument. I think faith is like a miner staking his claim. No prior reason for choosing "this spot" except intuition. And he drives in the stakes. Now he's committed. Of all the places at that river, in this territory, within the province, country, continent, world, universe, galaxy, cosmos—he chose there. Or maybe it chose him? Diviner rod dipping right "here." Then he works the claim ever after, always hoping he'll succeed, always striving toward striking it rich. Loving every minute of it! Loving, at least. "Faith, hope, and love," the enduring metals, mettle, of eternity. Pascal's famous Pari, *right? The Cosmic Wager that our French prof said Pascal never knew. Oh, he "knew" all right, "Fire! Fire! Fire!" he wrote and sewed into the tunic of his coat, discovered only after his death. He knew. That's faith to me, Professor. That's faith.*

And if that's faith, everybody has it, is doing it—staking a claim against life's ineffable mysteries, working it, hoping to strike it rich. And I say more power to the whole world for doing it. There's room enough for everyone. 'Cause truth is, wherever the stake is put down, there's gold! Just how things were made. Yet still precious. Never not rare and beyond price.

So what am I saying? I'm saying, Professor, I staked my claim in coming here to the Centre to embark on a mission. And I'm sticking with it. Though the universe tilts and shifts and everything familiar goes sideways and my feet go out from under me. "Though the fig trees do not blossom..." The stakes are down, Professor. The stakes are high, too. G. E.—God bless him! (Could have said the opposite, too.)

There. I'm better already for writing you. I wasn't sure if I could. But I did, and I'm right. And have you struck it rich yet Herr Professor? Or are you collecting by the installment plan like Pascal's Wager?

Write when you get the chance. *(Ha!)*

Andy

24

"Let's hear it for Jesus!" Gary yelled out. Some 200 index fingers jutted skyward immediately as the large upstairs auditorium reverberated three times with "Hip, Hip, Hooray!" The Jesus People Cheer had become one of many trademarks of the Jesus Movement. Another was the protruding index finger. Both gestures had become popular at the Centre that year.

The occasion was the first of a series of three successive Sunday praise nights, Gary Collins's idea conceived the last night of *GO YE '71* as the majestic Hallelujah chorus broke over the electrified throng.

Invitations were prepared and slipped into all door-to-door literature. They were also mailed to area assemblies, including some in southern Chicago. All evangelical churches and several communes received mailings, too.

One of the Christian music groups that had come several times to the Friday and Saturday night Root Cellar coffeehouse led worship that first evening. They were called the "High on Jesus Troupe," and they produced an overwhelming sound.

Gary performed superbly as emcee. Everyone at the Centre was up for the occasion, and the evenings were colourful in every way. Shouts of "Praise Jesus!" abounded, upraised index fingers equally erupted frequently, and arms stretched out throughout the worship songs. It bore no resemblance whatever to the very staid worship service back home at Carriage Street Gospel Chapel. None at all.

Andy headed for the bathroom mid-way through the first service and discovered Dan listening at the bottom of the stairs. Dan never attended religious functions at the Centre, about which family and trainees alike offered much prayer.

"What are you doing here?" Andy asked.

"Aw, I came over for a Coke from the machine, that's all," came the response.

"How long have you been here?"

"About a half hour."

"Well, what do you think?" Andy was careful not to push anything.

"About what?" Dan was serious for a moment before he broke into a grin. "Care for a Jack in the Box?"

"Sure!" Andy responded, "Just let me hit the john first."

Light reflected off "Norton's Puddle," which, sadly, was what the rink had become. Had there been a similar relational meltdown with Fiona? Andy had no way of knowing.

Dan was his usual monosyllabic self, muttering only "Cold" as he scudded a chunk of ice across the parking lot.

They ordered at the drive-through, still such a novelty, and pulled into the parking lot to eat.

"So what did you think?" Andy asked again, not anticipating a ready answer. The silence lasted long enough that Andy suspected Dan had ignored the question entirely. Then Dan ventured a response.

"Andy, you at least do some thinking," he began.

"Gee, thanks!"

Dan snorted. "No, I mean you haven't just bought the whole bag of tricks, right? I mean, you couldn't have done four years at a secular university and never questioned the faith."

"I had my doubts, true enough!"

"But that's the very thing. How did you handle them? I mean, don't you find they come bubbling up from every fissure, like some ubiquitous toxic gas?"

Sure, Andy thought. He remembered working on an essay one night when doubt so overwhelmed him that he was forced to stop his work. That night, he imagined himself like a caterpillar in a chrysalis, just waiting for the moment to emerge into the glorious sunshine of freedom from religion! The confining cocoon of faith would be discarded like a straightjacket, and he would finally reach out for the magnificent throb of life itself in one tremendous leap into the invigorating sunshine. More recently, he had encountered doubts during his interactions with G. E. But Andy was wary around Dan, knowing his duty to "win him for the Lord." Old habits died hard indeed. So Andy decided to play down his recent experiences.

"I guess you could say I turn them over to Jesus. Ruth Graham, I read somewhere, said that Billy had his doubts, too, but he didn't entertain them. For me, the certainty of the personal-infinite God in light of the historical evidence about Jesus outweighs the puny doubts that come my way." Why did this Schaefferism ring hollow as he spoke? Andy suspected he was so eager to win Dan over that he affirmed by sheer bravado what was at best a thin experiential reality.

Dan fell silent again. The silence lasted so long that Andy guessed he'd turned him off. The windows were steamed up. Cars proceeded through the drive-though and out onto the roadway. Cold seeped upwards from the vinyl seats.

"Look," Dan said finally, "I've just finished reading Engels's antireligious writings. I've also read a lot of Marx's critique and Russell's *Why I Am Not a Christian*. I've read most of the existentialist writings of Sartre and Camus."

Andy appeared surprised, which must have communicated.

"Yeah, I read a lot of that kind of stuff, Andy. I spend hours in my room listening to hard rock and reading. Most books I check out from the library. I buy some. But they're the frontal attacks," he continued. "You expect it and find them strangely shallow or beside the point. Most I mentioned fit that. It's the non-direct, fifth-columnist stuff that really gets to me."

"Like?"

"This showy emotionalism of the Jesus People Movement. Or the frothiness of GO and my dad's world-conquering dreams. The bickering and infighting amongst the brethren. The sheer banality. I once read a book on church history, and it was enough to make me sick. The writer seemed to find God in it all. I saw mainly ugly warts."

It was Andy's turn to fall silent. Then he took the offensive. "Dan, where is your own personal faith at? You never go to church, and it's obvious you have real differences with your dad. So where are you at?" Andy's response got him out of a tight corner, diverting the conversation.

"You're lucky you still have faith and hope."

"You can have it, too!"

"No I can't."

The conversation ended there. Andy felt intimidated by Dan's doubts, by his fierce searching, by his own spiritual impotence, the sheer mystery of life.

"Hey, isn't that..." Andy began as Dan started the car.

"Jack and Fiona," Dan agreed. "Two-timing, Andy?"

Andy said nothing, but slunk low in his seat. Dan said no more.

"O wretched man that I am," Andy wrote in his diary that night. *"Some wrestling after a talk with Dan at the Jack in the Box. All right, doubts, but also Fiona… 'Nough said. She owes me nothing. But I…*

The Praise Night also felt unsettling, though I don't know why. Glad to have left a bit early with Dan.

It is 11:36 p.m.

Good night.

It was well after 11:36 p.m. that Jack tiptoed into the room, and undressed quietly in the dark. They must have parked the car on the street, he concluded.

It was also well after Jack's breathing turned deep and steady that Andy, himself, succumbed. He felt of all men most miserable.

25

Coffee houses were a common evangelistic tool. Andy had helped run one called Café Pensée, sponsored by Inter-Varsity, in his fourth year at university. It had echoes of the brilliant mathematician and apologist Blaise Pascal. At the summer commune, they had called theirs The Missing Peace, with a jigsaw puzzle piece framing a stylized Jesus painted on the sign. The Centre's Root Cellar was in the basement of an older house on the property and given over to imaginative wall decorations and paintings, including a few upthrust index fingers.

Andy had volunteered to serve on the coffeehouse committee. He was a natural conversationalist and a self-consciously well-informed apologist for the faith—although he was no mathematician.

The Root Cellar was open on Friday and Saturday evenings. Christian youth were encouraged to attend only with non-Christian friends.

Many local music groups were featured, including Gary and Sharon several times. There was a simple fare of pop and munchies available for reasonable prices. Lights were low, furnishings sparse, lots of short-legged tables and cushions. Candles burned at each table. Some got saved there and were discipled by the trainees. Several even began attending church.

Kim Sutton was one of them. He was a basketball jock and had come to the Lord through Janys and Andy one night. They met weekly with him after that, usually at the Centre. He helped influence several others to come to the coffeehouse at least.

An unusually heated discussion was in progress with some of Kim's friends one night when Ken forged through the din to whisper in Andy's ear, "Andy, I've got to talk to you!" One look showed he was very distressed.

The interruption, however, seemed somewhat diabolical. Andy had been waxing eloquent, drawing on his second-hand apologetics, much, he hoped, to the approbation of Janys, who was also at that table but saying little. "Not 'til after the Root Cellar!" Andy whispered viciously. Ken withdrew meekly, saying he'd wait up.

Andy had forgotten the incident and was headed for bed after a short post-coffeehouse debriefing and prayer time. As he stepped through the mish house door, there was Ken waiting for him. "Andy, let's go to the Games Room. I doubt anyone else is there." Regrettably for Andy, curfew didn't apply Friday or Saturday nights, so he was caught.

The Games Room was indeed in the dark. Ken went to turn on the reading lamp so they wouldn't attract attention, but Andy would have none of it and switched on the main lights.

When agitated, Ken's eyebrows looked like McDonald's arches. His hair was even somewhat golden. As Ken shared, Andy wondered if his eyebrows could somehow be worked into a McDonald's ad, beginning with a close-up of them and moving to a mouth munching on a big hamburger...

Ken also had penetrating dark eyes when uptight, which he certainly was that night.

"Andy," Ken began, "I think I'm through!" With what, Andy's mind flashed. Everyone knew Ken spent a lot of time with Jean, the secretary. Or maybe he had just completed some major Bible compendium of irrefutables to use against J. W.'s, or to prove verbal inspiration, or... The definitive *apologia* of Bill Gothard. Andy waited. Silence.

His mind drifted to Heinrich Böll's *Doktor Murkes Gesammeltes Schweigen*—"Doctor Murke's Collected Silence," they had studied in Grade 13. One story in the book told of a World War Two radio technician, Dr. Murke. In a dialogue with his boss, Murke admitted to collecting the silences in various speeches he edited. He spliced them all together, then listened to them in the privacy of his home. He explained, *"Es ist noch nicht viel, ich habe erst drei Minuten, aber es wird ja auch nicht viel geschwiegen."* He didn't yet have a lot, only three minutes' worth, but there really hadn't been lots of silence. His boss for his part told him about once editing a four-hour talk by Hitler, out of which he had to remove three minutes to fit it into a radio broadcast. *"Als ich anfing, das Band zum erstenmal zu hören, war ich noch ein Nazi, aber als ich die Rede zum drittenmal durch hatte, war ich kein Nazi mehr..."* When he began the editing, he was still a Nazi. After the third time through the speech, he was a Nazi no more...

Perhaps all of life's significant truths are the "in-between" pauses, Andy thought suddenly. He felt a quick injection of guilt, knowing how few "in-betweens" he'd ever allowed in his own talk. In between time and eternity, life and death, heaven and hell, God and the devil, the endless enigmatic dichotomies.

"I met with G. E. tonight," Ken continued finally, "for two solid hours, no less! It was hell, Andy."

"What happened?"

"'Things have come to a head with Jean,' G. E. began. I was accused of leading her on, what with borrowing her car sometimes, etc. I've had a strong relationship with a girl back home. I expect I'll marry her when I finish on the team. G. E. knows that.

"Jean's just been a friend, that's all, Andy! Sure, I've spent lots of time with her. But that's it. I'm not a two-timer.

"Anyway, according to G. E., that was really only the last straw. The big thing is, by his observation, I've been disruptive to the Centre since my arrival here."

"In what ways?" Andy asked, perplexed.

"Lots of examples were given. They boil down to this: If G. E. said step to the right, he perceived me stepping left. If he said to stand, I sat. That's his idea of me, anyway.

"And then this thing with Jean. G. E. takes her aside today and tells her all about Cheryl, my girl back home. Jean leaves G. E. in tears. G. E. summons me tonight. He says I'm not to see Jean alone again. And then he tells me I'm to leave the Centre by next weekend! It's like, it's like he has something personal against my even talking to members of the opposite sex!"

Andy sat back, stunned. The great blacklisting again! His dad reading miscreants out of the church. The Peterborough assembly heretics. The consignment of the goats to hell. He hated it!

"What will you do?"

"I don't know, Andy, I don't know." Ken's body shuddered with deep sobs.

Andy was as ineffectual as ever before raw emotion. Perhaps, he considered, his whole life was only a reel of silences, whose voluminous words were a cover-up for a profound lack of anything truthful or significant to say.

When Ken collected himself again, Andy suggested they pray. Dark hollow invocation to a silent Deity—

as silent as Dr. Murke's collection—like a psalm with only *Selah's*. Andy's mind mocked him throughout his prayer.

Andy could suggest nothing more, only that they would remain in touch (however much he did not want to be continuously reminded of such an enlarged self.)

Ken left two days later. It was a great surprise to everyone. The rumour mill churned.

Later that afternoon, Andy talked with Janys about the whole matter as they wandered aimlessly toward Norton's Puddle. Ken's departure coincided with a definitive warm spell that totally melted the remainder of the rink.

"You had become good friends?" Janys asked.

"I guess so."

"I know he looked up to you," Janys continued, sensing his ambivalence.

"How come?" Andy asked, hoping for a compliment.

"He just said you understood him."

Dan Moore had a compelling way of exhaling through his nostrils like some Spanish bull before a red flag, such that one instantly interpreted it as a "cynical guffaw." Andy wondered if he practised the gesture before a mirror, so accomplished was the execution.

Andy might have given a similar response to Janys's comment, had he possessed Dan's integrity, but, typically, he did so only inwardly. "Let no unseemly word proceed from thy mouth," the Scripture said, perhaps including nonverbal nostril flaring. But to be on the safe side, and in the interests of well-nurtured piety, Andy remained silent. Yet, like Sarah's laugh, it seemed someone overheard.

"Why do you have so little faith in yourself, Andy?" Janys asked.

Andy was amazed. What had he said? What had he not said?

Then, perhaps caught off-guard by her own insightfulness, she added, "I mean, you really do have more of an effect on people than I sense you allow. I know people around here look up to you." A long silence followed. Was Janys blushing?

"I had a good talk with Jean, anyway," Andy continued, "She told me she really had built up unwarranted expectations, and it was her own fault for getting carried away. I sensed she has learned a lot through this."

"What will Ken do?"

"I suppose he'll enrol in Bible school now, become a full-time worker, get engaged."

Andy's prediction proved true—at least about the marriage. Two summers later, Andy received a two-hour tape of the proceedings at their outdoor wedding. Nearly half of that was taken up with the vows Ken said to his bride. Yet, in Dr. Murkean fashion, all Andy remembered years later were the silences: the twitter of birds, the droning of bees, an airplane high overhead, far-off traffic sounds.

Deep down, Andy was relieved to see Ken gone. Andy was not used to looking into such a large, distorted mirror. He wondered what that said about himself. Then he purposely forgot about it.

26

"Golly! You fight like a wildcat!" Jack expostulated that night after supper. There he was in their living room, rolling over and over with Fiona.

"Oh yeah!" She shrieked defiantly, "I've taken on guys just as big, too!" She straddled his chest, momentarily pinning both arms. "Say Uncle?" she taunted.

Andy's mish house had caught wind that liver was to be served for supper. Gary and Dan loved liver while Fiona and Janys next door abhorred it. Jack liked it well enough, but he *loved* pizza. So all the liver-lubbers were offered two servings that night while Jack and Andy conspired with the adjacent mish house to avoid eating the unsavoury fare.

The mood at Andy's house was festive, like an unplanned party had erupted. An extra edge to the celebratory feeling was the awareness of having put one over Irma, the cook. While not disliked, her rigid ways and meticulous standards of cleanliness and imperious insistence that her menus were not to be tampered with fairly invited a mini-rebellion, if not outright mutiny. Tonight was it.

And Jack, ever so physical, could only last so long with a "no-touch" rule where girls were concerned. So another taboo was shattered that night, with Sharon, Andy, and Janys cheering Fiona vigorously from the sidelines.

"I'll take you all on!" Jack yelled, then grabbed Sharon's leg and dragged her into the fray. "I don't see any 'knight in shining armour' here to protect you!" He lunged for Janys next, momentarily releasing the other two, and snatched a piece of her long hair. She shrieked like Fiona.

Andy launched out of his chair, totally catching Jack off-guard. The vehemence of his sortie surprised Andy, too, who sent Jack sprawling, thereby enabling all three girls to scramble to the safety of the sidelines. Jack was literally stunned into a prone position, panting. Then, with enormous vengeance he hurled himself at Andy, the two men, one built like an anvil, convulsed on the floor, sending lamps flying and the couch skidding across the floor. Nonetheless, it was over almost as quickly as it began.

"Say it! Say it!" Jack bellowed as if he'd bagged an elephant.

"Uncle!" Andy could barely get the word out; so little air was left in his chest. Andy remembered then why tackle football had not been his game of choice, though he could outrun just about everyone. Then again, most of his opponents would be no match for Jack. But who was? Who was a match for Jack? The thought lingered.

At Andy's surrender, Jack leapt up and did a war dance right in the living room while Andy fought to catch his breath.

Just then, the doorbell rang. "The pizza!" Sharon exclaimed. "Quick, who's got some money?" It was Jack who saved the day, bounding up the stairs three at a time like an energized Tigger, despite the fact he'd just taken on the entire assemblage. Sharon, who was the most presentable, opened the front door.

Everyone else got up to quickly rearrange themselves and the furniture, since the front door opened right into the living room. Just what had the pizza delivery boy heard from outside a staid missionary residence where trainees prepared to

CHRYSALIS CRUCIBLE 235

spread the Gospel "to the ends of the earth," including, presumably, Pizza Hut?

As Fiona helped Andy slide the couch back into place, she whispered sharply, "I noticed you finally came to the rescue, Andy, when *Janys* got pulled into the fray. But what about me?" Her eyes darted, but not with mirth.

Andy was stunned. What did she expect? That he'd take on G. E. somehow? Might as well flail against a brick wall, tilt at a windmill, mission doomed from outset. Buck G. E.? How? With what? *I can only build rinks,* he thought silently, still breathing heavily, face flushed, feeling now the distinct effects of rug burn. *And they don't go over well in Texas.*

The pizza was delicious, devoured in derisive juxtaposition to the liver next door. During the meal, Fiona and Jack got talking about her cousin, who drove a big sixteen-wheeler across the state.

"Man, would I ever like to meet him sometime!" Jack enthused.

"You've got to come for a visit, Jack," Fiona said with matching zest. She was animated, her hair lilting luminous, pushing her consummate countenance off the charts. Andy remained silent. Was she rubbing it in? Janys and Sharon got talking about German recipes.

Irma the Irate heard about the party. Nothing food-wise happened at GO without catching her ear. She was not amused. Next week there was to be a royal visitation by the "Queen of Chefdom" herself. And everyone living in Andy's house was a guaranteed guest at the dinner table with three additional invitees, two of whom were Janys and Fiona. Queen Irma took it upon herself to prepare the evening meal, imperiously, and ever so methodically. There was no escaping it. There was also no pre-meal hanky-panky. The third invited guest, besides Irma, was His Royal Highness George Elwin Moore, who loved liver.

The liver-haters more or less gagged through it, which was its own art form, Andy knew, from years of forced feeds growing up. Dan and Gary were delighted to have liver for two nights running, and extra portions the first time!

Irma had prepared the liver in an unusual way. There was an abundance of sauce that was entirely unrelated to a typical liver meal. Dan and Gary both commented on it. Then the truth came out: Irma hated liver!

"Last laugh's on me, I know," she chuckled. "But I declare," stern soliloquy: "The next time anyone skips one of my menus—I don't care if it's raw tongue—will not only eat double portions but will have to cook it themselves, even if it is raw!" There was a punch to her joviality. For the rest of that term at least, no one bucked her royal decrees again.

It was strange to see someone upstage G. E. Irma was a *presence* all right. Or was Dan's presence the stopper? Was G. E. afraid of opening his mouth for fear of getting more than liver down it? Whatever the accounting, G. E. mainly kept his comments to requests for things to be passed, and how delicious the sauce was, strange to him, too, until Irma's confession.

After supper, G. E. asked, "Is this a free night for most?" It was, except for Andy and Janys, who had to go to the Root Cellar at 8:00.

"Well then, if you're game," G. E. said, brightening, "let's see if Peter and Jean can join us, and we'll hold an impromptu Germany team meeting. I have one main issue to raise that I thought I'd call you all together about next week anyway. And a few minor points. We're moving toward countdown, guys! And you may

CHRYSALIS CRUCIBLE   237

have some agenda items, too. We'll get done in time for Janys and Andy to help at the coffee house."

With that, G. E. took charge again. Andy saw Dan's nostrils flare but heard no snort.

Irma said, "Dan and I will do the clean-up, won't we Dan?" Andy would not have dared such bold recruitment.

"Of course," Dan said, looking straight at his dad. Irma was a presence, Andy reminded himself, and then remembered it had been his turn on dishes.

The team met in the living room of Andy's house for about an hour. The main agenda G. E. raised was leadership. "The key to making your work overseas a success is spiritual leadership. At GO, we pray over every one of you even before you arrive in September. And we watch, as the Bible admonishes.

"After much discernment and discussion before the Lord, it should come as no surprise that we have decided to award joint leadership to Peter and to Gary, with their wives as willing helpmeets."

"Hurray, Peter and Gary!" Jack said. Everyone else chimed in congratulations.

"Dear young people," G. E. continued, "this is an awesome responsibility, one that will often weigh them down like Moses' arms at the battle of Ai. But through your prayers and ours, they will persevere.

"We will hold a commissioning service at the end of term. Specifically, the mantle of our spiritual authority will be extended to them. Bill Gothard has taught the biblical pattern in this: We are all expected to live out our Christian lives 'under the umbrella of authority.' This is the ultimate counter-cultural expression of the Gospel, so at odds with the youth counter-culture exploding around us today."

Andy found G. E. ever lucid and pointed. Though

he chafed under G. E.'s spiritual authority, his call to be disciplined and shaped by it was undeniably compelling, charged with inherent biblical logic. He intuitively resisted the anti-authority ethos of his peers. Had he been raised Catholic, he'd have doubtless resisted Vatican II. He liked authority and tradition, even the brethren "non-tradition." They were comforting and secure in a crazy world beyond ken. Above all though, what mattered most to Andy was that they were so deeply *biblical*.

Without moving his head, Andy scanned each attentive face taking in G. E.'s talk. Andy respected everyone in that room and saw great promise in each. He was proud to be here at GO in training to make a difference in a world that was largely indifferent to Jesus. All his life had been honed toward mission, had *been* mission. Where else did he want to be? What else did he want to do? Nothing. This was it. He sighed with contented pride.

He could lose Lorraine. He could lose… Fiona. He could. Catholic nuns talked of their celibate vows as "marriage to Christ." He got it just then. All their emotional, psychological, intellectual, spiritual *and* sexual energy was channelled toward Jesus. Somehow the alchemy worked, or it did not. He knew there were many shipwrecks littered across the annals of church history. How many dozens of kids did some of those popes and bishops sire? Or Catholic sisters produce maybe (and get kicked out)?

But he knew if it worked, *it worked!* How had Jesus put it? Some were born; others made (*Castratos!*). Still others *have* made themselves *eunuchs for the kingdom of heaven's sake*.

The penny dropped. This is what G. E. had been urging upon him since his first "public" embrace of

Fiona: *Be a eunuch for the Kingdom, Andy!* At least a temporary one. Be Christ's foot soldier for two years. Discipline. Self-denial. Death to self. Channel all that sexual *élan vital*, *libido*, sheer animal energy, toward Christ, transposing by a kind of spiritual alchemy from something *base* like a metal, though part of God's good creation still, transposing it into a spiritual love affair with Christ, so much higher a service.

Don't *repress it*; redirect it. (He'd taken Psychology 101.) Let all that glorious God-shaped sexuality channel first to God as offering. Then let him give it back as gift. How had C. S. Lewis put it? Something like: "Aim at heaven, and you will get earth thrown in. Aim at earth and you get neither." He liked that. He could do that. Not Fiona the temptress, the eternally seductive *Eve*. No, Fiona the wonderful person also made in God's image who did not need to serve his needs these next two years. Nor he hers.

Andy was onto something. It sifted through his brain like a saltshaker. He wanted to write the Professor immediately. Did *he* get it still? Was this not *liberating?*

"... questions. What about you, Andy? You're usually good for some." Andy realized G. E. was looking straight at him.

"No sir," he responded immediately, hoping no one had noticed his mental drift. "I'm good with the set-up under Gary and Peter. I'm prepared to accept their *authority*. No questions, Mr. Moore." The word had taken on a new sweetness.

When Andy looked at Fiona, he saw her in a new light—though to look at her was no less breathtaking. He didn't *need* her for fulfillment these next two years. *Needing* was tantamount to *using*. He could focus rather on "things above," to use quaint biblical language. He could live with G. E.'s prohibition and let God give her back as gift, if He so chose. It was all so crystal clear.

"Well then," G. E. concluded, "if there are no questions, then I just have a few more housekeeping issues…"

When Andy and Janys headed across to the Root Cellar later that evening, Andy felt he could take on a few lions.

Before climbing into bed, Andy plunged further into *True Spirituality* by Francis Schaeffer, his latest. He even savoured the jacket covers of Schaeffer's books. Jack was still out, maybe with Fiona? Andy told himself that didn't bother him now. He read until his eyes drooped, hoping to find an echo of what he'd been discovering…

"I have to admit that I am kind of jealous," Andy's diary said toward the end that night. He had already explained as best he could his new insight. Though it sounded flatter, writing it down. *"But I respect Jack and Fiona, so can't legitimately be down on them. 'But I seek to rise in the arms of faith and be closer drawn to Thee.'"*

It is 11:48 p.m.

Good night.
(P. S. Jack still hasn't come back in.)

27

"Well, I'll be jiggered!" Jack exploded. It was early Friday morning, the last of February. The sun was strident, spring stirring. Norton's Notion had long since turned into "Norton's Mud Puddle," shortened by some to "Norton's Muddle." Crocuses thrust upwards, and daffodils danced after winter's nap. Robins had returned the past few weeks, indisputable portents of spring.

Jack and Andy were in the midst of an impromptu inventory of their wardrobes. Almost every shirt proved partially unbuttonable, zippers unpullable; underpants unopenable, and all their shoelaces were in knots. "Even our boxers!" Jack feigned utter scandal. "They really did a number on us, those rotters! And to think we were right in the house the whole time! Doggonit!"

The previous night, Andy, Jack, and Gary had been downstairs talking with two Jehovah's Witnesses. Turns out the GOers were not the only people working the neighbourhood. Others stalked the same prey. The J. W.'s were generally fairly direct, the Mormons slyer. Unashamedly, GOers collected the "enemy's" literature from any of the houses' mailboxes and threw it into the garbage bin back at the Centre. "Almost as good as winning a soul," Dan once commented wryly.

One night, Jack had answered the doorbell and got talking. Andy happened along, and the conversation heated up. It seemed a kind of Paul-Timothy situation with the J. W.'s: one older (German-born) and well versed, the other obviously a novice with little proselytizing experience.

The conversation wound down a half hour later, but another appointment was set for the following week. Jack and Andy, fresh from some classes on the cults, established the agenda: a discussion of the deity of Christ.

An assignment for the Cults class dovetailed nicely with the Duo's boning up on some of the evangelical mainstays: *Chaos of the Cults, The Kingdom of the Cults,* and *The Four Major Cults*. Gary wanted to meet them, too, so all interchanged books and ideas. Not at all indifferent to Ken's observations, Andy also did some word studies based on *Strong's Exhaustive Concordance*.

The three strategized about who would speak to what kind of statements or questions. All three had some experience with the ubiquitous Kingdom Hallers.

For two hours on the scheduled night, the GOers locked horns with the J. W.'s around the thorny issue of Christ's identity. Prayers had been intense just prior to the battle. Sharon, Jean, Janys, and Fiona had promised to pray faithfully during the engagement. They were all in an upstairs alcove with knitting needles and crocheting hooks. Andy had run to his room for a book in the middle of the tense discussion and saw them doing their thing. When asked how it was going, he urged them to keep praying.

The hope and strategy was to plant sufficient seeds of doubt at least in the younger cultist's mind to make him reconsider his decision to become a J. W.

The three defenders of the "faith once delivered" held their own, outnumbering their opponents in any event. But if it could be termed a victory, it was at best pyrrhic by Andy's estimation. If they had "won," it was not because the enemy had capitulated. There

CHRYSALIS CRUCIBLE

was no hint from them of wanting to reengage, as Gary suggested. That felt sweet. But there was also no sense of really meeting as full-blooded people, interested in one another for any number of reasons, including "things spiritual." There was such a feeling of the *artificial* to it all. No one suggested, for instance, "Meet you at the Jack in the Box sometime."

Andy felt keenly aware that they had met only on one level—the abstract/doctrinal/intellectual—and there was really no further incentive for meeting again once a kind of stalemate was acknowledged.

Andy remembered C. S. Lewis alluding to the psychological letdown predisposing him to great doubts about the faith *just after* he had most virulently, publicly defended the same. A kind of Elijah or Jonah syndrome. It was cold coffee, flat pop, dust in the mouth, rejection at the first attempted date.

The expected high from witnessing so valiantly turned into a low of wondering whether anything had been accomplished. Some of the arguing around Christ's deity was hairsplitting at best, far removed from what Andy thought of as *the essence of Christianity*.

Now Andy and Jack had discovered that the four self-appointed "prayer warriors" had been in their bedroom wielding tiny silver swords unrelated to those of the Spirit. If they had played the "Aaron at Ai" role at all, it came secondary to their busily stitching together shirts, underwear, trousers, and shoelaces. This, in spite of the open request in class that day for prayer and their solemn commitment to the same. Andy recalled it had been awfully quiet upstairs throughout the long discussion. The "Dynamic Duo" had been reduced to the "Defenceless Duo."

Andy was indignant. "Not even the spirit was willing, Jack."

"Aw, c'mon Andy, surely there's room for a bit of fun, even on the battlefield?"

Andy's face was a dagger. "Jack, this *is* the battlefield! We're fighting for people's souls! And all those girls can think of is… Is guys' underwear! I hope they got their jollies feeling all through it.

"Jack, can't you take something serious for once? We're soldiers, Jack! In a war, on a mission. Even on leave, we sleep with our guns loaded, our eyes half open. Ever alert. We're not a bunch of 'teeny-boppers' hanging out at the Jack in the Box like there's no tomorrow playing around with 'Miss Texas'!"

Jack's faced turned thunderous. He strode over toward Andy and cuffed him hard on the chest. Andy lost balance and crashed backwards onto his bed. Jack was upon him, dragging him away from the bed, pinning him fast to the floor. "Don't you ever speak disrespectfully of Fiona again!" His face was molten. Then Jack pulled up and stormed out of the room.

Andy was a leaden weight on the floor.

28

Andy left the bedroom shortly afterwards, and he didn't show up for classes that morning. Instead, he ensconced himself in a library nook. He didn't even take *True Spirituality* with him.

Janys discovered him there just before lunch. She asked him where he and Jack had been.

"Jack didn't show up either?" Andy asked absently.

"What happened, Andy?"

"We had a difference. He knocked me backwards. I ended up here."

Finally, "Andy, I can go…"

"Aw Janys, it's not right taking it out on you. I just can't say much more. That's all."

"I'm sorry, Andy." She got up and walked away.

Andy skipped lunch, too. He went downstairs and shut himself into the phone booth in the Admin Building. "Reverse the charges, please." He hoped she would accept.

"Susan?"

"Andy?"

She heard him out, and at the end couldn't resist saying, "Let brotherly love continue." She said no more. Strange, Andy thought, hearing her quote scripture.

Eventually, she suggested it would be still nice to make a car payment this month. He apologized. She laughed. They hung up. But not before he said simply, "Susan, thanks."

He didn't ask after Lorraine. He was grateful Susan had not volunteered any information. Still, she must have wondered why he had not.

Andy walked out of the Admin Building, and there was Jack. Talking to Janys. Now or never. Andy walked right up to them. "Jack, I'm sorry for what I said. It was wrong."

Jack's tense face showed relief. "I'm sorry for what I did, big guy." Brief hesitation. Then Jack gave him an enormous bear hug until Andy wanly said, "Uncle."

When Jack released him, Janys was nowhere to be seen.

Fiona was nowhere to be discussed. It was an unspoken truce.

As sure sign of their reconciliation, that night Andy and Jack planned their revenge. Jack owned a small portable tape recorder and timer used to play wake-up music. The next morning before breakfast, they recorded some acid rock, readily supplied by Dan. That afternoon during work detail Jack, at some risk, smuggled the recorder and timer into Janys and Fiona's bedroom closet.

The timer was set for 2:00 a.m. Jack and Andy set their alarms for ten minutes earlier. They had a good view of the girls' bedroom window. They wouldn't hear anything, but they expected to be treated to a dazzling light show.

Right on cue, the girls' bedroom lights flared. They stayed on for at least five minutes. Jack and Andy laughed until their sides split, treating each other to lurid conjectures of the pandemonium next door.

"Hi Fiona, have a good night's sleep?" Jack asked her rather audibly before Doctrines class later that morning. Andy smirked at his side.

"Yes, thanks for the concern," came the icy response.

"And yours, Jack?" She parried.

"Great! Great!" he said nonchalantly.

"Right through the night?" She persisted.

"Pretty much," came the reply.

Apart from their having witnessed the lights go on and Fiona's withering replies, they would never have known the retaliatory trick had worked except for two additional indicators: The first was Jack's timer and tape recorder. The next time he snuck a look for them, as expected, they were nowhere to be found. It rather cramped the Duo's style for the next few weeks. Jack's abrasive alarm clock had to be reinstated, and neither was able to send home any cassette tape letters. Jack did finally sneak in for a more thorough search. He found the items stuffed into one of Fiona's shoeboxes with a little note: "If you find these, you're trespassing! And the recorder will self-destruct in ten seconds. Watch out! Fiona and Janys."

The other indicator was an immediate tip-off from Peter van Oosten. Just before supper at the Admin Building, Peter took Jack and Andy aside. "I know it was you two who did that trick last night. Why did you do that?"

Although Peter's English was fluent, he still had a trace of a Dutch accent. The word syncopation was like a northern Ontario lake during a storm, Andy thought, a little choppy. Peter was tall and lean. A receding hairline bore witness to previous fuller plumage. While his face was not arresting, it was handsome, accented by a well-shaven complexion. A smile was seldom readily on his lips, but there was an air of dignified reserve not unlike contentment. He did not signal pleasure at that moment, however.

Jack responded first with feigned ignorance. "Trick, Peter? What trick?" But he saw the face contort and knew he had better 'fess up. "They raided us first!

I still haven't freed up the zippers on all my flies and underwear!" He said in mock indignation.

Peter clearly liked Jack, but his tone remained serious: "I don't understand why you North Americans carry on so. Back in Holland, we'd be totally embarrassed at sewing flies and underpants. Christians wouldn't do such tricks—at least not real Christians.

"Then your trick! I laid awake for a full hour after all that terrible music and commotion in Fiona and Janys' room."

Jack's face grew serious. "I guess we weren't really thinking about you and Jean."

"Those girls listen to the most awful music sometimes. When I first woke up, I thought they had just accidentally turned the volume up loud. Then I saw what time it was, so I went out to investigate.

"They were laughing and giggling. I told them through the door what time it was and asked what they were doing.

"Through their giggles, they told me, and I told them I couldn't see the joke."

"We promise you, Peter," Jack responded, "that if we ever do any kind of stunt like that again, it will only affect those for whom it was intended!"

"Wouldn't it be even better simply to do no more tricks?" Peter replied. "That would be surely more honouring to the Lord?" Peter left the question hanging and walked away.

"We really had them going, Andy!" Jack nearly shouted in glee after Peter left. He went on to comment on Peter's words, not putting him down, but simply reaffirming the legitimacy of their good clean fun.

Andy couldn't help but feel resentment toward both Peter *and* Jack. He lacked Peter's serious piety and Jack's carefree spontaneity. He was neither hot nor cold, he suddenly felt, or at least somehow not quite authentic. Then he tried to forget about it. Rather like stuffing the clown back into a Jack in the Box. Then, with smarting pain, he remembered Jack's recent nocturnal visits with Fiona to the Jack in the Box and thought in juxtaposition it should be "Andy-in-the-Box." He felt woefully cornered. *Huis Clos*, title of a Jean Paul Sartre novel, "No Exit." The walls felt they were closing in. Then he *really* did try to stuff Clown Andy down somewhere where he'd just not keep popping up.

29

Three weeks later, it was Easter weekend. Suddenly, the family visit was upon him. Andy hardly had time it seemed to brace himself.

He had sailed through the end-of-month encounters with G. E. The third was on Maundy Thursday. Andy took the initiative to assure G. E. that it was "All Quiet on the Norton Front." He detailed enough to assure G. E. that he had neither met with Fiona nor read secret letters from Lorraine. Was he intent on seeing Lorraine before going to Germany? Andy could honestly say he had made no plans. G. E. responded like a little child about to open his Christmas gifts. "Well done, Andy! Good and faithful servant. Remember, in enthrallment to Christ, freedom. I am privileged to be a mere conduit of Christ's authority vouchsafed through me to you, his liege. In your utter devotion, may you discover joy forever more."

The rest of the interview, significantly shorter than all previous, was devoted to discussing the impending visit from Andy's dad. G. E. quizzed Andy sharply and at length. G. E. was clearly apprehensive, but apart from asking Andy to pray, he shared none of his misgivings. G. E. was truly a loner who, with rare exceptions, took none other than his own counsel. In the spirit of rugged individualism, G. E. was a quintessential pioneer. He performed best when surrounded by "yes-men," Dan intoned more than once. On one occasion, Dan even parodied Mr. Myers' relationship to G. E. by doing a perfectly inflected, "Yes Mastuh, yes Mastuh" routine. Yet, the amazing quality exhibited by G. E. was his ability to inspire this kind of puppy-like devotion.

Surely that was the sign of a born leader, Andy thought, knowing its elicitation in him as well.

"Son," G. E. said at the end, "there is no further need for these interviews—though I've personally delighted in them. Thanks for holding in there, Andy. And remember, the door is always open." With that, Andy was free, like a parolee first stepping beyond the prison gate, so Andy imagined.

Andy's dad had requested a session with G. E. Saturday morning. They were driving down the next day, Good Friday, and returning Easter Monday. It was to be a flying trip.

Maybe they'll both end up blacklisting the other, Andy thought, and use *Interest* magazine for their battlefield.

The whole Norton family arrived just after supper on Good Friday. A sure indication Andy's father's desire to meet G. E. was his decision to drive up on that day. It would be the first time in years his dad would miss the Easter conference held annually at Guelph Bible Conference grounds.

There was, nonetheless a local brethren Easter conference in progress, and Andy encouraged them to arrive in time for the evening service, which they did, barely. Only Andy and his dad attended. The others felt too beat from the long day's drive. Andy made sure they were well set up in the guesthouse before he and his dad headed off.

Andy felt relieved that this was his dad's first exposure to area brethrenism before he encountered the more radical ways at the Centre. Furthermore, G. E. was one of the slated speakers, and he was definitely gifted. He also would not appear "different" from any typical conference speakers, and this would also be a good first exposure for his dad.

"We should have him up next year," Andy's dad said on the way back. "The man clearly knows the Word, and expounds it admirably."

Andy never did hear the details of their two-hour discussion the next morning. Whether G. E. clamped down more on head coverings afterwards, Andy also never knew, since he left two weekends later. And whether the *Believers' Hymnbook* was subsequently at least somewhat reintroduced, Andy likewise did not know.

What was evident, however, was that his dad had been satisfied that G. E. was committed to assembly principles and that his apprehensions had been largely amiss. There was significant rapprochement.

Andy was impressed. Whether prayers had helped or not, G. E. had a clear mastery in the art of pleasing. His dad was a significant challenge for G. E., but the latter had emerged undimmed, with Andy's dad an enthusiastic GO -supporter after that. Amazing! Just in time, too. Beyond expectation, possibly even beyond Andy's unconscious wishes, his dad and G. E. had made their peace.

The family spent the afternoon and evening in Chicago, Andy's first and only visit to the famed metropolis. His impressions from that visit were vague—as indistinct and grey as the Chicago skyline that time of year.

They also made time to drive out to Emmaus Bible School, most famed of brethren institutions, and tour around Wheaton College, Billy Graham's *alma mater*. Though Andy's dad was a Bill Gothard fan, they were out of time to visit that third holy shrine, the Institute's luxurious Oak Brook headquarters.

The whole family attended the next day's communion service. Andy's dad even shared a word in it. He said nothing afterwards about the numerous uncovered heads of female visitors. They had a light lunch at the Moore's, which went well. Andy's dad engaged freely in a wide range of discussion, he and G. E. clearly the focal point. Dan was on his best behaviour.

Supper was at Andy's mish house with the Germany team in the Norton's honour. Sharon had outdone herself with *Rouladen*, boiled potatoes prepared in sauce, and red cabbage sauerkraut. Andy's dad, whose mom had been German, raved about the sauerkraut—the best he'd had in years! Susan chimed in, "Of course Dad. Mom never cooks the stuff, and when you do from the can, it stinks up the entire house." Then, "No offence of course meant for what's here tonight. My vote's with Dad!"

"Thanks for the compliment, Susan—I think!" Sharon said, laughing. "Mr. Norton, my mom's German too. That's where the recipes came from tonight."

Afterwards, they took coffee and dessert—*Schwarzwälderkirschtorte*, an absolutely decadent cherry cake with real *kirsch* liqueur flavouring—in the living room. Everyone raved.

Later, Andy thanked Sharon profusely. "Fit for a king!" He exclaimed.

"Anything for 'King and Queen Norton,'" she replied with a grin.

Andy's mom capped off the evening for Andy with a comment to everyone during dessert. "Well, Andy, I can rest assured now that you're in good hands. I can at last picture you over there eating with this wonderful group of young people. Just like a mom, eh?" After the laughter died down, she continued. "And Sharon, I'll book you anytime at our house to cook!" To which Andy's dad fired back with great gusto, "Amen!"

Susan hit it off well with Jack throughout their time together. And why not? Andy did not think Susan was Jack's type. He was almost three years younger. But Jack was a hunk and all-around nice guy, even if he was on an entirely different trajectory from Susan's at that juncture. And Susan was a stunner, after all. She was one way of taking Jack out of commission, Andy thought wryly, then chided himself. If you can't beat 'em, recruit 'em. His mind was inexorable. Andy clamped it shut.

30

The next two weeks were full of practical arrangements. Each team had to organize shipment of their goods overseas, finalize their flights, and make contact with local people in each city. When all was set, the trainees were to spend two weeks at home before flying out.

An atmosphere of great anticipation charged everyone that final week after Easter. As the various missionary endeavours on the home field wound down—the coffeehouse, Bible studies, Boys' and Girls' Clubs—there was a heightened sense of expectancy about what glorious things God would do through them in their new fields.

Friday night, April 7th, was a formal commissioning service. It began with a candlelight meal, for which all dressed in their finest. Fiona was beyond words. All eight Germany team members sat together at a round table. Andy sat directly opposite Fiona and could not; despite immense will, keep his eyes off her. Janys' hair had been "permed," Sharon, who was seated beside Andy, commented in a whisper. Then added, "Isn't she a knock-out?" A first? Andy wondered. Sharon whispered again: "Now, if she'd just get contacts." *Sharon, would you get your mind off this?* Andy pleaded.

In the auditorium after the meal, the Leadership Team put on an outstanding commissioning service. It was profoundly moving, a foretaste of saints gathered about "The Great White Throne," Andy commented to Gary afterwards.

When G. E. got up to speak, the anticipation was

electric. "In just a few weeks," he began, "you will all be scattered to vastly different mission fields, following in the paths of other GOers 'to the ends of the earth.' Then, for two years, you will labour to bring in a mighty harvest of souls for God.

"You are the vanguard of future assembly missionaries. Many of you will stay or soon return to the mission field after these two years—some seventy percent or better, according to the statistics. Most of you will cherish the next two years as *the most significantly life changing of your entire life*.

"There will be times of great testing. The lion is roaring, seeking whom he may devour. You are invading enemy bastions. You all still have a lot of growing pains, as we discovered together this year.

"But above all, God will work through you for his greater glory. We know. We have watched wave upon wave of you pass through these splendid gates to great spiritual exploits beyond. Our hearts are brimming with humble pride at our privilege to have had a part in your preparation to do the greatest mission there is on earth: rescue the perishing, care for the dying, and cause the angels in heaven to rejoice over each soul plucked from the burning.

"We live in tumultuous times. Satan's forces are aligned against the Church as never before. But God is also mightily at work, bringing revival worldwide. It is a wonderful privilege to be in the front ranks of what he is doing. 'And the gates of hell shall not prevail against his Church,' we have it on the highest authority in heaven and on earth. Jesus Christ himself, praised be his blessed name forever.

"For many of you, going to the mission field at this time has meant forfeiting an educational degree for the time being. For others, missing two years of valuable professional work experience. For others, it means postponing marriage prospects. God will reward you, however, multifold, pressed down, and overflowing. In the words of our Lord: 'Give, and it shall be given unto you; good measure, pressed down, and shaken together, and running over, shall men give into your bosom. For with the same measure that ye mete withal it shall be measured to you again.'

"You have given sacrificially and joyfully. You will receive back beyond measure. As Jesus said again: 'And every one that hath forsaken houses, or brethren, or sisters, or father, or mother, or wife, or children, or lands, for my name's sake, shall receive an hundredfold, and shall inherit everlasting life.'

"GO is above all a family. It is hard for us back home to see you leave. We have come to love each and every one of you. But we would not have it any other way than to see our beloved family go off joyfully to the fields white unto harvest.

"We expect each of you to visit us upon your return to North America. After that, we will do our part to keep you on our alumni mailing list as you continue to serve the great God and Jesus Christ throughout the rest of your lives. We hope that you will always remember your service with us and see this training, this commissioning, as significant lodestar for the rest of your spiritual journeys home.

"We consider it a great privilege that you report to us about your triumphs—and yes, your sorrows. Just like Jesus' disciples came back to him after they were sent out two-by-two. We anticipate in the next two years many joyous times of sharing God's work on planet Earth through you..."

G. E. went on to talk about the "umbrella of authority" he had specifically prayed for each one of them. First to fall under the respective team leaders, second toward GO's Leadership Team, third subservient to their home assemblies, and finally, mutually toward one another. These lines of authority were of the essence, he urged, quoting Gothard at some length.

Finally, he prayed, and the service was over. For a few moments there was a kind of holy hush as people processed G. E.'s words. Then all moved quietly out into the foyer toward the Joyous Wall.

One section of whitewashed wall alongside the auditorium was kept for each group of trainees to sign after their commissioning. It would take at least a hundred years for the Wall to fill up. Andy watched the eager hands pen pious verse that night: Scripture quotations and other sayings together with their signatures. His was one of those eager hands. With a shock, there came to him the image of wave upon wave of World War I soldiers going over the top to sure carnage. Onward Christian soldiers indeed...

There were no misgivings that night. Or if there were, they were buried deep. In due course, Andy wrote: "Andrew Joseph Norton: *Mein Äußerstes für sein Höchstes!*" It was the German title of Oswald Chamber's *My Utmost for His Highest*, a devotional classic. Andy had been reading through the book in German, ever since Joanne, the German instructor, had loaned it to him. She told Andy to ignore the underlining. But Andy was a great underliner himself and always liked to see the work of others.

So Andy's signing was not original. But it was unique in that only he and Gary wrote a saying in German. There had been no previous German team at GO.

Lots of cameras flashed during the signings.

Gradually, the mood became festive. Dozens of group pictures of every configuration followed. Celebrations continued laced with lots to eat and drink for the next two hours. A dam of collective energy burst that night as people buzzed about garnering autographs, chattering away, and savouring their last moments together, *ever*. Except in the *forever*, Andy thought. Never again, though, would this group be together like this in one place. Never. This was sheer gratuity. Andy wondered at the chance congruence of people and events. He thought also how saying goodbyes was so gut wrenching.

It was well after midnight that Jack and Andy returned to their house. They had stayed behind to stack all the chairs so that the auditorium could be thoroughly cleaned the next day. As usual, their course took them underneath the girls' upstairs window, when suddenly there was a magnificent splash as a direct hit of ice-cold water cascaded over them. Loud laughter erupted overhead.

The adrenalin peaked in the Dynamic Duo. They looked at each other, dripping wet. Peter or no Peter, their honour was at stake. In the following fifteen furious minutes, Jack and Andy inflicted terrible retribution upon the perpetrators. Mercifully, Peter and Jean returned only at the tail end. Peter appeared shocked but said nothing.

By the end, the girls were dripping wet and Fiona's bed was unusable. She and Janys would have to share Janys' bed that night, their last at the Centre. Andy could not help but think again of him and Janys snuggling in together under a howling moon.

Colleen, a Centre staff person from Toronto, drove Janys and Andy home early the next morning. There was not a hint of snow.

31

Susan had booked off the first weekend Andy was home, including two days into the next week. Andy was delighted. He wasn't sure yet what to do about Lorraine.

Susan finally protested over the prohibition against Lorraine. She was aghast that such a thing could still be imposed in this day and age. It was late. Their parents had gone to bed, and Andy and Susan were sitting at the kitchen table sipping coffee.

"Susie, *in this day and age*, people do tell others what to do all the time. Your boss, for instance. Another obvious one is the military with its chain of command. Agreed?

"So what you're objecting to is not that. It's the idea that Prime Minister Trudeau popularized: 'The State has no business in the bedrooms of the nation.' Neither does the Church nor anybody else. Your boss may tell you what to do in the workplace, but please, no other authority, and nowhere else. Especially in the bedroom.

"Now, when you think that through, you have to ask why. If it is okay for people to tell you, to tell me, what to do sometimes and in some places, why is it not at other times and places?

"Once you ask that question, my dear sister, you find pretty quickly you're up against something called 'religious prejudice.' Fact is no one wants the Church to tell us what to do *in this day and age*. Or the Bible. Bosses yes, but not Bibles or Bishops (or brethren).

"So I ask, if it is not an airtight 'given' across the board that everyone just *knows,* if it is not simply self-evident that no one should *ever* tell us what to do, is it not at least a little suspect when people get so incensed at the Church for telling people what to do? Then the problem is not the *telling* but *who* does the telling. 'In this day and age,' the boss (at least) is *in*, but the Church is *out*. I have a simple question: Why?"

Susan opened her mouth to respond, and then closed it. "Andy, Mom always said you should have been a lawyer! I don't know the answer to your question. I just know it ticks me royally to see the Church bossing people around.

"*Bossing*, sis?" Andy cut in.

"Oh Andy! You can get a person so riled, and you've just been home a few hours!" She whacked him hard. "Anyway. I hope you plan to see her. That's all. You *have* to see her, Andy. My place is always available."

"I'll think about it," he said.

The next morning, Andy took part in the Breaking of Bread Service. He also shared for about fifteen minutes after the Evening Service. He had been asked to tell about his training experience and anticipated ministry in West Berlin. He recounted his excitement at the prospect of serving the Lord in West Berlin, at learning how to evangelize at GO, and his keen desire to win many to the Lord. He closed off with a poem he had written for a class at GO (his mom's idea), which eventually found its way into the monthly publication *The Scatterers*.

Even Susan came along, since it was Andy's send-off. How it affected her, she did not let on. But several others commented very favourably about Andy's sharing, especially the poem.

At the tea and lunch afterwards, there was a special

presentation of a Globetrotter luggage set, a cheque for $500 from the assembly, and a commitment of support for $50 a month for two years. Andy was very moved.

Furthermore, Mr. Langdon, long revered for his ministry amongst area assemblies, had composed a poem for Andy. It was called "The Commissioning," and it read:

> *With fasting and prayer the early church there*
> *At Jerusalem prayed from the heart.*
> *They sought to be led and the Holy Ghost said,*
> *'Saul and Barnabas, set them apart,*
> *To a great special task I have summoned these two.*
> *Send them forth with your blessing to the work they must do,*
> *And with prayer you must follow them all the way through.'*
> *The Holy Ghost still summons those whom He will—To service just where He may please.*
> *He must find it dandy that our young brother Andy Goes soon to serve overseas.*
> *Thank God he is willing God's word to obey,*
> *We are sending him forth with our blessing today.*
> *May God guide him through all life's troublesome way.*
>
> *Dear Andy, we would say, as you go forth today—*
> *He who called you is faithful and true.*
> *Many trials you will face, but he giveth more grace*
> *To those who His purpose will do.*
> *You are going to battle with evil and sin,*
> *You will meet storms and sorrow without and within,*

CHRYSALIS CRUCIBLE 263

But with Christ in the vessel you surely must win.
We Christians all know there's a cruel bitter foe;
How he hindered God's servants of old.
He hates what is right, and it's no easy fight;
He is subtle, deceptive and bold.
Your recourse is in prayer in temptation's dark hour.
Through Christ more than conquerors we know that His power
Will strengthen our souls and refresh like a shower.

In the Bible we're told about Aaron of old;
When his hands dropped, the enemy won.
We at home here must plead with our God for your need—
Every day 'til the race has been run.
May we pray for you always in morning's first light,
Thrice daily like Daniel amid noonday bright.
May we intercede also in watches of night.

And some day, God knows, perhaps among those
You work with we hope you will find
A companion in life to share joys and strife —
A partner of much the same mind.
When we follow God's guidance, our way will be blest.
When we leave things to God it is there we can rest,
Knowing always His choice will be ever the best.

And in the glad home when the Saviour shall come,
May you win a reward, a bright crown.

We know that we all at His feet will then fall,
And our trophies before Him lay down.
Blessed Jesus our Lord we shall worship and praise;
We shall look back and thank Him for troublesome ways;
We shall love and adore Him throughout endless days.

Dear old Mr. Langdon, Andy reminisced. Two summers previously, Andy and his cousin Rod were up in arms with Mr. Langdon and the entire Forest Cliff Camp board for accusing them of living "high on the hog" while preparing the grounds for summer camp. They had volunteered to go up early to cut lawns, lay out soccer fields, baseball diamonds, and prepare the cabins. They asked for no pay, just their keep, which they could charge at Loblaws in Forest, the nearby town.

Loblaws must have wondered what two youths were doing so early at the camp, racking up a grocery bill. They phoned a board member, and the next thing, there was an investigation and accusations of wasteful spending.

Andy and Rod had bought supplies for the next two weeks or so, and the bill seemed rather high. There was such a "to-do" about it that the cousins returned home in a huff, leaving most projects barely begun. Ironically, the previous year, they had done the same work so well that one board member had commented he had not seen the grounds looking so good in twenty years. Now their integrity was being impugned.

Mr. Langdon, who was one of the board members, tried to talk it over with Andy and Rod, but he proved unbending in asserting it was they who must back down and apologize. Neither did, nor did they ever return to the camp. "The umbrella of authority," Andy knew, was weighted toward those already in power, certainly not toward youth even mildly—and justifiably—challenging such authority.

Mr. Langdon had lost his revered status with Andy ever since. But at least his poem seemed to betray no continuing hard feelings. While he appreciated the sentiments, something nonetheless rankled.

Early the next morning, Susan and Andy headed off to go fishing, a sport Andy relished. They rented a boat at Fanshawe Lake outside London where the Thames River had been dammed up. Andy and his dad had caught a lot of bass there two summers previous.

Soon, they were nudging into some distant coves, far from where most people boated or sailed. It was early April, and though the sun shone, it was hardly spring yet. So there were relatively few others on the water.

Susan and Andy were not disappointed. Andy hooked into a nice silver bass, something of a rarity. Susan was especially delighted. "Supper tonight!" Soon afterwards, they pulled into shore for lunch.

"Andy, what *really* motivates you to head off as a *missionary?*" Susan asked, her mouth half full of egg salad sandwich (prepared by their mother the night before). Whether intentional or not, the last word came out sounding like an expletive, and was followed by a small eruption of egg, Miracle Whip, and partially chewed bread.

Stock answers darted into Andy's mind like fish rising to the bait. "I feel God's call." "Necessity is laid upon me." "The fields are white unto harvest." Or Jack's good-natured and scatological, "If you gotta go, GO!" Andy smiled inwardly at Jack's proposal that the saying should be GO's unofficial motto. But Andy was talking to Susan, who eschewed stock answers or clichés. He told himself to concentrate. He was about to step into a serious spiritual battleground. He said a brief prayer.

"I told you already how it all happened, Susan. It was a combination of a friend suggesting I do some traveling and apply my language skills and Dad sending me the GO brochure about a week later. I just put two-and-two together.

"Okay, I've heard that before," Susan replied. "That's what got your mind going on doing something other than a Master's degree. The 'Lord's leading,' if you like."

Susan had a way of expressing distasteful matters as if she had just bitten into a rotten piece of fruit and was spitting it out.

"But I mean, what keeps you *determined* to go? It's not been easy there, right?"

Andy mused. Could he really say he knew for certain it was God's will? By no normally objective means of attaining "certainty" or knowledge. So to say he knew it was God's will was not really honest. Then why else? Adventure? For sure. Excitement? Of course. But these were rather sub-pious if not impious reasons.

"I guess when I really think about it, Susan, it's for a variety of motives. One might be as simple as, once on the escalator, it's harder to get off than keep going. Who knows why else? I do want to serve the Lord. I want to go to Germany. I believe in soul-winning. So I'm heading off."

"Andy, what if the whole thing's a big scam? A farce? A blind alley? I mean, look at Carriage Street.

If it's really true that this great relationship with Jesus brings so much joy, why all the uptightness and 'unfreedom' of just about everyone there?

"And if love is really what all Christians have, why all the backbiting, why the judgementalism and bigotry toward everyone else—from unsaved so-and-so to fallen-away Mr. & Mrs. Wilson, the Pelusso's, the J. W.'s, and even the Baptists for not wearing head-coverings *for Chri... for kripe's sake?*"

Andy was shocked that Susan almost used Christ's name in vain, but he was more shocked at how much feeling was packed into it, like a four-inch firecracker.

"You know how it's been in our family. All the Christian cousins we know well. The rest? I bet you couldn't remotely say all the names, or put many names to faces, Andy."

"Nor you, Susan," he replied.

"Why though? I guess I've felt cheated. Did you know that Leanne has won some ballet awards and might be signed with the Winnipeg Ballet? Mom and Dad wouldn't even go to a big performance she starred in, because 'dancing wasn't Christian'! And who knows," she suddenly pirouetted, "I might have become a star, too—but couldn't even take the first lesson."

Just then, there was an enormous "zing" on Susan's line. While sitting there, Andy had left their lines in the water with bobbers and slugs he'd found under a rock. If not a snapping turtle, it had to be a nice bass. The next several minutes were taken with landing it successfully. Susan performed admirably, with lots of coaching from Andy. "And that's supper tomorrow night," Andy said. He took it to water's edge, gutted and cleaned it, and laid it on ice in their cooler. "We never did teach you how to clean a fish, did we?" He said as he cleaned his knife in the lake. "Should be a rule: 'No clean; no eat.'"

"Sure," Susan shot back. "After the first rule: 'No cook. No eat.'"

"Touché," Andy said, smiling. He couldn't imagine a better sister. Except her hang-up about church. He picked up with their dancing cousin Leanne. "Uncle Sam and Aunt Yvonne didn't come to that Christian Brigade's night when we all won a bunch of medals, remember? Or to our baptisms or much other church stuff. They never heard us recite at a single Christmas pageant. I could go on, but I think you get the point."

"Fair enough. I know it cuts both ways. But we're supposed to be Christians! I heard that Mom once asked for juice in her small wine glass at a niece's wedding. I'm sure it made a far greater deal of it than if she had just sipped a bit or even faked it during the toasts. But that wouldn't have been a *witness*."

Another of those expletives from Susan.

"Like I said, I feel cheated. You remember those notes saying we were excused from dancing in gym class for religious reasons? Not that we minded then, but we were already marked as a little weird. You remember that Sunday the huge natural rink froze over in our playground? We go over, fairly drooling to join in the fun. But no, it's the *Lord's Day!*"

The French turn all their holy words into curses, too, Andy thought wryly.

"And so on all through school. No dances, no movies, no drama clubs, no to just about everything else that might be classified as 'worldly.' 'Ye are a *holy* people,' the Bible says. *Weird* might just as easily have been the word!

"Yet along comes a 'world war.' How *worldly* can you get with the name right in it? And Dad goes off to fight like every other Canadian pagan in the land. So much for 'love your enemies.' I see *that* in the Bible lots, but nothing against dancing. King David danced before the Lord so wildly that his wife despised him, right? When I challenged Dad on that once, he told me that was a different 'dispensation.' I suggested that so was fighting in war, which is about all King David did, the 'man after God's own heart,' and everyone else in the Old Testament. Dad didn't take too kindly to that. Well, I'm in a different dispensation, too.

"I find it a wonder that Christians ever produce kids! Though even there, I remember a long discussion with Mom about voluntary abstention. It sounded horrid. And I remember reading a *Power* magazine story about this couple that prayed before they had sex—probably all three times, one for each kid! I figure if they'd just taken off their clothes, there'd have been no need for prayer." Susan chuckled.

"What do you suggest as an alternative?" Andy replied rather weakly.

"I don't know, Andy. I really don't know. Anything but that!"

"You mean you'd choose instead all the messed-up families, all the crime, all the wars, all the narcissism?" Andy had looked up that last word in one of Schaeffer's books.

"No, but also not ever the bland, repulsive, repugnant, judgmental, intolerant *Pukeianity* that's been pushed on me all my life!" Susan's face contorted. Andy could imagine her stomach having spasms, too. It scared him.

"So, Andy, no one at church knows this, but I've done a few of those 'taboos' myself the last while. I've grown to like beer. Some friends at Nurses College first got me going to the pub. I've even gone alone sometimes. Just sipped it and sat around. Mom would be horror-struck, what with her pious prayers for me and all. I'm tempted to tell her sometime, just to see her reaction. I know that cousin Rod has been doing similar things and has told Aunt Sarah."

Rod had returned with his family from the mission field very needy. Andy knew he'd struggled a lot in his faith. Aunt Sarah wept when she first saw Rod and his sister enjoying TV serials like *Combat!* and *The Fugitive*. Andy could only imagine her reaction to Rod's revelations. Aunt Sarah, by admission, was "super-pious." Just the opposite of her husband, Uncle Joe. *Did she love her enemies?* Andy wondered.

"I'd like to try dancing," Susan continued, "but I'll need lessons first. Most normal people have done it since childhood. Just not us oddballs. I'm a crack poker player, though. Everyone in our class played."

"Well, did you feel anything?" Andy asked. The question hit him out of the blue.

"What do you mean?" She squinted at him.

"Well, if conversion's supposed to get you all charged up, I suppose your 'unconversion' must have given you some good tugs, too."

Susan fell silent for a while, obviously thinking about the question. There had been no further action on the lines. Fishing was a patience game at the best of times. Still, early in the season, two nice bass was not bad. He thought of his dad's preferred "fishing for men," of the hooks and bait they'd use in West Berlin.

"I guess I didn't feel/don't feel guilty for any of it anymore," Susan said finally, "Though it took a while to get the guilt out of my system. But I must admit I don't feel any freer for doing those things either. I just needed to do them, that's all. And you're right, Andy, reaction isn't freedom."

Susan had always been transparently honest, Andy reflected. It wasn't just that she told the truth; she exuded a kind of integrity that made her be what she let on. What you saw was what you got. Strange (Or perhaps not?) that such a quality had led her *away* from the Church when Jesus had said 'you shall know the truth and the truth shall set you *free.*' Free from what, church? Andy didn't like his question and sent it away.

By contrast, Andy always felt he was putting on an act. His whole religious upbringing predisposed him to a certain style, a way of being noticed, a kind of posing, which somehow was beyond personal experience, however sincerely aspired to. Something like operating on a deficit budget, Andy thought, or more accurately, like printing more and more paper money without the gold in reserve. Wily Coyote running on thin air. For how long? Could he dismiss all his questions?

"You know," he heard Susan continue, "Sometimes I think Christianity is more addictive than alcohol. You remember that skit we did at camp about a border crossing? The guy comes to the crossing repeatedly with his wheelbarrow full of wares. Though meticulously inspected, he was never found to be smuggling anything, despite strong suspicions every time by the same guard. The final scene shows the wheelbarrow owner letting the audience in on the secret: He had been smuggling wheelbarrows!

"Maybe our church has been so concerned about addictions to alcohol or card-playing and all the other "don'ts" that it's missed the most obvious one of all: addiction to church! Or religiosity or piety or whatever. *Maybe that's the deadliest addiction of them all, and the most to be abstained from!"* She almost hissed the last sentence.

Andy felt the bite. He glanced at the bobbers. They floated peacefully, though little ripples set them in motion at times.

Susan was relentless. "Didn't Jesus even talk about the religious addicts of his day going across the ocean to proselytize, to get their big fix—sorry, Andy—only to make their converts 'twice the sons of hell' for their efforts? Maybe that's all evangelists, including you guys at GO, are doing. I've often heard the addictive craving for 'souls.' Maybe that's the ultimate substance abuse."

Andy's mind processed reams of apologetic arguments at computer speed, right up to Schaeffer's latest book. Nothing. His own non-intellectual sister stumping him? Then what did he have to offer in Germany? He felt the sucker punch. He was defenceless.

Susan's face lit up. "I get it! I think the Church is right after all. Abstinence *is* the only cure—something I've been trying to get into Mom and Dad's heads for the past two years about me and church! Who knows? Maybe I can come back some day, a recovered *church*aholic."

Andy's mind raced. It latched onto a stock Mormon and J. W. answer. (He'd had it used on him.) "Well, Susan, I hear what you're saying about Carriage Street and all that. But I have found new joy in Christ. And I have learned to love as I've never known before. And I believe, Susan, however trite it sometimes sounds, that *only Christ is the answer.*"

Andy wanted to believe his words, did in some sense. He also knew that they rang hollow somehow. Unlike famed evangelist John Wesley, his heart felt "strangely cornered," not "warmed." He looked at the water. Still nothing biting.

"I guess I wish I had some of that, Andy. I really do," was Susan's response. It was preceded with a slight questioning cock of the head. Had there been a nibble? Susan could have responded cynically, "If Christ is the answer, Andy, what is the question?" But she was not just being cynical, Andy knew. She was being real. What was he? Could he ever fish again with artificial bait? Is that all he had to offer the world, West Berlin, he, aspiring "fisher of men"?

They decided to pack up and get into the boat again for a little more fishing. They had no further success. Andy had lost his zest for fish anyway.

As they sat there in silence, Andy's mind drifted to another fishing scene where they had had no luck all night until Jesus came along and told them to try again, only in a most unlikely place. Suddenly, they were swamped. It was just after that when Jesus said he'd make them "fishers of men." Andy wished for such a clear word from Jesus now. To dispel all his doubts. To make it crystal clear to himself and Susan—and anyone else—that he was a *bona fide* commissioned fisher of men, "under the umbrella of the Highest Authority," no mere proselytizer. That he had direct orders to throw his net on the other side of the ocean in a city known as West Berlin.

Fried bass for supper that evening elicited appreciative comments. Andy's mind felt fried, too. Susan never discussed the topic again before Andy left for Germany.

That night, Andy mused on how he and Susan had turned out so differently on matters of faith. He knew his sister's dislike for church had been building for years. He witnessed her reaction to their mom's piety several times. "She just wants to be Aunt Sarah!" Susan had said once. Andy did not like the comment and defended their mom, if not Aunt Sarah, vehemently.

Susan had always been like that. A free thinker and a straight shooter. Far more religiously precocious than Andy on the questioning side, she posed all kinds of questions about God, evil, and the Bible while Andy was quiescently reading C. S. Lewis then Francis Schaeffer, *et al.*

Susan had always remonstrated against the violence of the Old Testament. Especially the animal sacrifices. She had been an animal lover from Day One, an assortment of strays cared for over the years from dogs to cats, to squirrels, to birds, positive proof. She just could not figure out why God ordered so much bloodshed.

Then she read some church history, innocently enough. She had a school project in grade twelve about the Crusades. It fascinated her at first, all those knights going off to fight for Christ. She was still a strongly committed Christian then. But she couldn't get over the wanton destruction the Crusaders left in their path: sacking Constantinople just because it was in their way, raping and pillaging thousands; the *coup de grace* being the cannibalism practised by the "Lord's avengers," even of little children.

Andy recalled a long discussion between Susan and their dad. He summarily discounted the Crusades because they were by Roman Catholics and hence not "real Christians." But one night Susan asked a simple question: "And what about the military crusade you participated in, Dad?"

They were sitting around the kitchen table snacking. Andy's mom had already gone off to bed, unable to handle even a whiff of controversy.

"There is no moral equivalency whatsoever!" Mr.

CHRYSALIS CRUCIBLE   **275**

Norton shot back. "Romans thirteen tells us to obey the government and to follow our leaders in wielding the sword. That is our God-given duty, no questions asked."

"Then what about Uncle Joe?" Was Susan's quick rejoinder. "Why did he choose the Medical Service and refuse to bear arms?"

Mr. Norton bristled. "If Uncle Joe would stop reading only the New Testament, he'd know God supports 'just war' everywhere in the Old Testament. Hitler was far worse than King Agag in First Samuel fifteen, whom the prophet Samuel in his zeal 'put to death before the Lord.' And Samuel said in that same passage, 'Behold, to obey is better than sacrifice, and to hearken than the fat of rams.'"

So that's where that verse comes from, Andy reflected, one of his dad's most-quoted Scriptures.

"The point is, Susan, God says in his Word we are to obey the authorities over us, since they are God-ordained. If Samuel could kill the King of the Amalekites for his wickedness, we may rightly kill Hitler and his henchmen for theirs. It's a simple case of obedience to the Word of God."

Susan was not impressed. She picked up a Bible. "First Samuel Chapter fifteen, you say?"

Her dad nodded.

There was a silence for several minutes as Susan read the chapter.

"Dad," she suddenly expostulated, "this chapter is crazy! Have you ever read it, I mean in its entirety? I can't believe it!"

"Of course I've read it, many times!" came their dad's chafing response.

"Well, this verse about obedience to the Lord no matter what has a very interesting setting. First,

Samuel, on the Lord's behalf, tells Saul, now get this: 'Thus saith the LORD of hosts, I remember that which Amalek did to Israel, how he laid wait for him in the way, when he came up from Egypt. Now go and smite Amalek, and utterly destroy all that they have, and spare them not; but slay both man and woman, infant and suckling, ox and sheep, camel and ass.'

"A couple of things. Dad: How long before King Saul had the Israelites come out of Egypt? Centuries before, right? So the Amalekites in Saul's day were descendants of many generations. It would be perhaps like remembering today what Christopher Columbus did to the natives (if he ever did anything). There was no connection whatsoever, since centuries later descendants are involved…

"Anyway, the *Lord* tells Samuel to tell Saul its open season on the Amalekites, scorched earth policy and all. Genocide. Even the tiny infants are to get wasted. Dad, this is brutal. And this is what God tells the Israelites to do?"

Her dad opened his mouth, but Susan continued before he could get a word in. "So Saul goes off and does the deed. You gotta give him credit. He spares the Kenites, because they'd been nice to the Israelites centuries before. Only not quite. He returns with his men after the terror and the horror, and Samuel meets him.

"'Uh, buddy,' Samuel says, 'you didn't quite do what the Lord commanded. 'But we did, Samuel!' 'Then why this bleating and lowing?' And Saul says they were brought back to do sacrifices to God—as if all the slaughter was not already a massive human sacrifice to the LORD already.

"King Saul repents, but Samuel does not listen. And right on the spot, Samuel declares that Saul and his entire line have lost the kingship forever, just after that favourite verse of yours, Dad.

"Then Samuel turns to King Agag. Now listen to this, straight from the Bible: 'Then said Samuel, Bring ye hither to me Agag the king of the Amalekites. And Agag came unto him delicately. And Agag said, "Surely the bitterness of death is past." And Samuel said, "As thy sword hath made women childless, so shall thy mother be childless among women." And Samuel hewed Agag in pieces before the Lord in Gilgal.'

"'King Agag looked for mercy,' the text says (Doesn't Jesus say somewhere that he wants mercy, not sacrifice?) and Samuel 'before the LORD' (I take it that means with the Lord's instructions and full approval) carries out this incredible act of religious revenge—Sacrifice!—and hacks the king into little pieces on the spot! Can you imagine the bloody horror of that scene?

"And you, Dad, take passages like this as support for going to war and claim only the evil Catholic Crusaders were un-Christian? Really? And how many times did the Israelites do the same thing to their enemies? Isn't the Old Testament—you know, you've read it through enough times—full of similar blood and gore? And you base your ethical decisions on that horror?"

Andy couldn't believe his dad did not fly into a rage or something worse. He'd seen it before when his dad's religious zeal was aroused. Instead, quietly and firmly, he said: "This discussion is over, Susan. When I know I'm talking to someone seriously looking into the things of the Lord, I will continue it."

He picked up the Bible Susan had just been using as if to underscore his disapproval and walked out of the room. Was he "shaking the dust from off his feet"?

Andy and Susan sat nonplussed.

"What was that all about?" Susan muttered finally. Then she went outside and stayed there. Andy did not follow.

32

The evening after fishing, Andy and Susan went out for coffee near Victoria Park. Later, they strolled around the park itself. It was Andy's first time back.

They passed by 101 David Street, site of last year's commune. Jim and Marci had moved away, he knew. Was anyone else living there from last summer? He saw some kids' bikes in the driveway. Guess not. "The old order changeth," a line from *La Morte D'Arthur*. Yes, Andy acknowledged. Nothing in the universe stands still. Isn't that Einstein's great insight? Everything to the smallest atom is in a grand cosmic dance of perpetual transformation. But this was not grounds for applause. Andy wished *something* in the world had constancy. "For I am the Lord, I change not," he heard it intoned, and "Jesus Christ the same yesterday, and today, and forever." Right then, that sounded awfully religious.

"So are you still a Christian, Susan?" Andy asked as they walked by his and Lorraine's bench from last summer. He'd asked Dan the same question. Persistently to his own surprise. Andy was still guessing.

"I really don't know what to think. I believe it's true, I guess. But somehow it's just never 'taken.' Reading the Bible for me is too often like eating sand—or what dogs do in sand when it comes to those nasty parts in the Old Testament. I get a lot more out of a good novel. I don't let mom and dad know my thoughts though."

"But Susie," Andy responded, "if it really doesn't mean a lot to you, what does? I mean, what about the big questions of life? Where we came from? What's it all about? What ought we to be doing? Do any of those grab you at all?"

"You've always been the philosophical one, Andy, the dreamer. I guess there are 'religious types' and there aren't. Like I said. I know it's all true. I really do. But I'm just more down to earth or something. I'm not that pious, I guess. I'm happy enough to have been exposed to it all, but I've got a good job, a car, and I want to live a little. Eventually, it may mean something more. I don't know.

"Whatever way, I'll never turn into one of those pious ladies who is cluck-clucking about every little sin and afraid of her own shadow! There is a lot more stuff we can do that isn't wrong. And 'worldly' is usually just tradition. Why should going to movies be worldlier than watching TV? Sure, there are bad movies you avoid. Why should using a real deck of cards be any different from playing Rook? Why should going to dances be wrong but not a youth group volleyball game at the beach with lots of skin showing and more bouncing around to catch guys' eyes than just the ball? Oops! Excuse me, Andy. Somewhere someone decided those things were wrong, and they spread to become a big tradition in our kind of churches and some others. Christian Talmud or something, Andy.

"You told me yourself that brethren young people in Germany drink and smoke. And so do many in the Christian Reformed churches. And most assembly kids in the US go to movies. So much for all these things being self-evidently right or wrong. How do you know? Not from Jesus' teachings at least. And wasn't he the one who complained about the religious police of his day piling heavy burdens on those under their authority but not lifting a finger to help?"

"What do you think are the main rights and wrongs,

Susie?" Andy asked, trying to divert her.

"I attended First Reformed with Bonnie, one of the nurses. The preacher there got talking about politics and how the faith was supposed to shape our ideas. That was all brand new to me. But I remember being really struck by his emphasis on Jesus' teachings about rights and wrongs. He said Jesus' teaching boiled down to two things: love God and love neighbour. He said less than that was *for sure* not Christian. But he warned that more than that was as bad—human tradition and anti-Christian. Like the Pharisees.

"I concluded that in our assemblies we sometimes have less, sometimes have more. He quoted James about the difference between showing faith by what we say versus what we do. And he quoted somewhere else about how we can't even claim we love God if we do not love our neighbour.

"Think of Mrs. Stark all those years bringing those people to church from the mental asylum. I remember how much Mom didn't like it. I don't remember anyone ever inviting those people to their homes after church or being particularly friendly to them. 'Get them saved!' may have been their wish. Sure, bring them under the 'sound' of the Gospel. But what about the 'feel' of the Gospel? I'll bet the only feeling those people had at our church, much like elsewhere, was rejection."

Andy knew that too much of what his sister was saying was true. How can you attract others to the faith when it never hits the road except at prayer meeting, in church services, and evangelizing? Was that really hitting the road? Where had he seen real care and love shown to outsiders by the home assembly people?

"Objection, your Honour."

"Over-ruled."

Then I can bury it. He did again.

Susan broke into his brief reverie. "Andy, what are you supposed to be doing in West Berlin? Just 'preach' the Gospel? Or are you supposed to do practical things too, like, well, I don't know. I've never seen a church do much practical."

"We're there mainly to do evangelism. We'll go door-to-door for sure. That's one of G. E.'s favourites. And we'll do Bible studies, kids' clubs, a coffeehouse, stuff like that. It'll depend upon the local churches and what we come up with ourselves."

They were walking around the park like he'd done so many times with Lorraine last summer. It had a ubiquitous magic hue then. There was no magic today.

"What do you want to do most over there, Andy?"

Good question. Learn German? Of course. Experience a different culture? Yes. Serve God? Without question. Hide in a crevice somewhere to reconnoitre while the rest of the world went on spinning? Perhaps.

"I guess when I think of it, I just most want to learn to be *me*!" From where that arose, Andy was not sure.

"And who *are* you?" Susie asked after a long pause.

Andy had no response. Susan laughed. She may have posed the question in spite of herself, not knowing its origin either. It wasn't like her to delve into philosophical things. Still, she seemed to be waiting as she headed closer to the swans and *their* bench! Andy followed the lead. No one was there.

"I don't really know," came his answer at last.

"That's okay," Susan responded immediately, "because I do. You're my younger brother. You're the winner of the Grade thirteen history prize at Sir John A. Macdonald and one of three to carry off top marks that same year—and lots of other prizes over the years including at university. You're also the guy who waltzed into several high school track and field meets in your two last years without any training, without any school support, just raw, and won repeatedly. You finally shot up past me in height, though it took you until grade eleven—and you tower over all the family now. Then you dropped your track the first year in university and never went back. You're the guy who got twice the mark I got in the same subject the first year you took French. You're the guy some of my friends called the 'silent type,' thinking you were cute and mysterious. Of course, I knew you were just a plain brown nose square who never had any fun. What else? Lots. You're my favourite kid brother—Okay, my only brother. I could go on…"

Non-philosophical indeed, Andy thought.

"Anyway, I do hope to get over next year for a visit. I should have the car paid off in about six months. Then I'll start saving like mad, God willing."

"God willing, Susie?" Andy couldn't help himself.

"Yes, Andy, you caught me. Make you happy?"

They returned to the car.

"Above all, Andy" she said, as they climbed in, "*Be yourself.* I guess that's the one thing I find about Christians. I don't know who the *hell* they are!"

33

Andy finally decided to see Lorraine. How, in good conscience, could he not, soldier of Christ notwithstanding? This was not for him, of course, but for her. They would meet at Susan's again, setting aside Thursday evening and all day Friday. As far as Andy's parents were concerned, he was going there to spend one last bit of time with his sister and to meet a bunch of her friends Friday night for supper at her place. He had obeyed the Great Prohibition while at the Centre. He was about to disobey it now, but he saw no inconsistency.

Toronto was a city Andy was always happy to leave. It seemed to have all the negatives of a big city with few redeeming positives. He had developed a phobia of megalopolises, he knew, and wondered at times how he'd handle a city entirely hemmed in by a wall. In all fairness, he also barely knew Toronto.

Susan picked him up as arranged at the bus depot and drove him to her apartment. As they drew nearer, Andy felt like he was on his way to the dentist. If Susan sensed it, she said nothing.

"Lorraine was already over by mid-afternoon, Andy. We had a really good visit. I hadn't seen her for quite some time. Boy, I like her! Her honesty, mostly. Though we talked mainly about our jobs.

"Her aunt dropped her off, and she was carrying a clothes bag with her. She's obviously dressing up tonight, Andy." Susan looked at the suit-bag Andy was carrying. "So are you, obviously. I made the reservations for six thirty sharp. That doesn't give you a lot of time to change and get there. Here's the route.

They said not to be late."

She pulled up in front of her apartment building and gave Andy the keys. "I'm getting a ride back with one of my friends, so don't worry about me. Lorraine has a key to the apartment. Stay out all night as far as I'm concerned. Except when you come in, tiptoe, since I get up early to go to work.

"And just so you know, you're welcome to bring Lorraine back to the apartment whenever."

She headed off for the bus stop with a final, "Have a fabulous time, Andy!"

"Thanks!" He called after her.

Andy walked up the several flights to Susan's apartment and tapped lightly on the door. When Lorraine opened it, Andy's breath caught. She wore a full-length velvet dress cut perfectly to her figure. He could scarcely focus on her face initially, gorgeous as it was.

"Hi Andy. Come on in," she said simply and turned her deliciously bare back toward him as she preceded him inside. Andy made a mental note to ask Susan about the mechanics of a strapless bra. They did not embrace, but her quick movements and welcoming words broke the ice.

"Before I forget, here are the apartment keys," she said, then dropped them as she extended her hand. When she stooped to pick them up, Andy's eyes were riveted. He had never seen her in more alluring attire. Andy winced at a sharp crotch-level stirring.

"Thanks, Lorraine." He cleared his throat. "I'd best get changed. It's so *great* to see you!" *But no touching.* He had already pre-determined that. They could not just pick up where they had left off on a park bench nine long months ago. He didn't know who she was. He didn't even know who *he* was. How could there be other than violation if there was touch beyond the perfunctory. This was *not* G. E.'s prohibition, it was his own.

Lorraine's choice of the revolving restaurant atop the CN Tower was priced well above anything Andy had previously experienced. But Lorraine had insisted that this was her treat. She was a working girl, he a poor missionary.

The CN Tower was within walking distance of Susan's. The night was warm. As they set out, Lorraine handed him her shawl. Andy remembered a similar gesture with a jacket their first night. They proceeded along scented sidewalks. It was surreal. No plan. No anticipation. He… was… G. E.'s… soldier, intoxicating induction of amnesia notwithstanding.

High above Toronto, high above expectations, Lorraine talked Andy into trying a bit of wine for the first time. She positively giggled at his inexperience after the waiter handed him the cork. "What does it smell like, Andy?" He took the hint, further cued by previous TV viewing. He performed appropriately, though slightly spluttered at the quick bite of the unaccustomed liquid. Lorraine's eyes laughed.

When Lorraine shifted forwards, Andy dared not gaze at her directly, nor could he quite glance fully away. Did he catch her eyes laughing at his sudden intake of breath? Was she having fun at his expense, consciously tantalizing? He hadn't expected this. Lorraine was so relaxed, so… Was she doing a command performance, Andy the enchanted, or *vice versa*, he star performer, responsive to the slightest twitch of her voluptuous marionette strings?

Andy commented on her dress at one point, something to the effect that it must have been new since last summer. It was lame, but it pleased her. "There have been other things new, Andy," she said mysteriously, no elaboration. Neither talked about the abuse, as if it had never happened, nor about the sudden break-up it had occasioned. A kind of undeclared truce.

The Toronto skyline was vivacious. The evening felt similar. They did not talk much, and yet they communicated freely. Time flew by. Paradoxes were palpable. Soon, it was approaching midnight.

Lorraine suggested a walk to a green space near Susan's apartment. They stopped by Susan's place first, and Lorraine ran in to replace her shawl with a jacket. Andy looked up at the sky as he waited. It was not quite a full moon. The air was calm and warm for an early spring evening.

Their hands joined en route to the park.

He knew that Lorraine pressed close as they sat down. He also knew that it was not just a sudden cooling of the night air that induced him to slip his arm obligingly around her shoulder.

They sat silently for several minutes. Pulsating pleasure entertained unlike doubts at the Centre. She was not Potiphar's wife. He was not Joseph.

"Andy," Lorraine said huskily, "I'm different from a year ago."

He looked down at her, theology, philosophy, psychology, and G. E. deliriously upstaged.

Lorraine shivered. He pulled her gently closer, at the same time watching his left hand migrate toward the top of her bosom. "Do you mind?" he asked, to which came the silky reply, "No." He watched his hand, utter fascination as if another's, slowly move to nearly encircle her right breast. His mind was exploding.

Suddenly, he jerked his arm back as if from a hot burner.

"Lorraine, I'm *really* sorry! I didn't intend this.

It just..."

Lorraine laughed, remained nestled at his side, and said dreamily: "It was all right, Andy. It was in no way indecent. I liked the feel of your hand."

She was breathing quickly, not lost on Andy looking down. Further explosions.

The evening was over. It *had* to end. As graciously as he could, Andy returned Lorraine to her aunt's apartment, car ride there largely silent. He gave her a brief hug and a kiss outside, saying all in a rush at the end he had never seen her look so desirable, that he would be around toward 10:00 in the morning, but that she'd better… cover up tomorrow. As he turned for the car, he said again, "Lorraine, I really went too far. I apologize. That was not fair to you for all kinds of reasons."

Lorraine sighed. "Andy it was *okay*."

"But I know no other guy has ever done that to you, except..." her dad materialized just beyond words.

She responded softly, looking up into Andy's eyes, though he felt overwhelmingly tempted to look elsewhere once more. "I've never *wanted* any other guy to do that to me."

34

The next morning, Andy found a note on the table from Susan saying she had once more freed up her car and taken the subway.

Andy determined to focus on enjoying the day with Lorraine, letting her "lead" and just be along for the skate. He thought of Janys. He thought of a fierce blizzard. His hand thought of its first taste of bare boob.

Lorraine and Andy spent most of the morning and early afternoon at Casa Loma, "house on the hill." It was a rich man's dream to build a castle fit for visits by royalty in the environs of Toronto. Sir Henry Pellat certainly had his fantasies and his misfortunes. Eventually, he went bankrupt, and the $3.5 million castle was taken over by the city and turned into a tourist attraction.

By mid-afternoon, they were starving. So they left and headed for the waterfront and picked up fish and chips wrapped in newspaper, the English way.

"I sure hope that I'm hungry at supper or Susan will kill me. She's put in a roast beef with the oven timer. My favourite, as you recall," Andy commented, reminded of Lorraine's visit to their church and parents.

They walked hand-in-hand for a while along the lakeshore. The wind was cool, making them both zipper up their jackets tightly. Lorraine's snugly fitting T-shirt also precluded any revealing glances. But her dazzling figure was not lost on Andy. Nor, Andy suspected, was her effect on him lost on her.

As they headed back to the car, Lorraine ventured

a question that had probably been on her mind all day. "Andy, do you have any second thoughts about going?"

"Second thoughts, yes," he shot back piously, "but first thoughts, no." That really didn't make other than "religious" sense, he realized immediately. He knew Susan and Dan would both have snorted had they been there.

"But what is going to happen to us?" She persisted.

"Lorraine, I think the question is, what first is going to happen to you? I don't know much about this stuff. You tell me."

Lorraine said nothing more. The drive to Lorraine's was in total silence. He'd ask Susan to explain to Lorraine about not writing to him in West Berlin. She could always give it to Susan to send, he realized.

They both knew Lorraine could not see him off at the airport. This was it. Her parting words, she taking the lead as always, were, "There is a Japanese saying that 'love called forth can never die.' I love you, Andy. I always will."

He heard himself say, "So do I." Then they embraced, and he was gone.

Andy was thankful for the supper at Susan's that evening. It took his mind off Lorraine and showed Susan in a different light. Three of her nursing friends were there as well as an intern, Thomas. He was clearly interested in Susan, an interest that was somewhat reciprocated, and a really nice guy. They kept Andy in stitches describing some of their antics during nurse's training and since.

At one point, Thomas turned to Andy. "So what exactly will you be doing in West Berlin?" Obviously Susan had not been too explicit on the matter. Suddenly,

CHRYSALIS CRUCIBLE

Andy found himself the man of the hour, in the hot seat, star witness. He opened his mouth then shut it again. What would make sense? *I'm actually a soldier for Christ out to recruit other soldiers so we can fight against the Devil and all his strongholds?* That was the talk he had heard his entire life. But now he heard it through Thomas' presumably pagan ears, and he might as well have responded in German or Latin. In fact, he thought, *Quidquid recipitur per modum recipientis recipitur,* "Whatever is received is received according to the capacity of the one receiving it." Was it Schaeffer quoting St. Thomas Aquinas? No, Schaeffer did not know other languages. Some other apologist then. And it made sense. Now how could Andy say something so that Thomas would say, "Cool." Andy wanted him to, if not for his own acceptance, at least for Susan's.

Was he just imagining that everyone was holding their breath, not least Susan?

"I'm going with a group of young adults to work with churches in West Berlin to bring a little bit of... love—God's love hopefully—over there."

"What exactly will you be doing?"

Andy wasn't going to get off that easily.

"I'm not sure really. We'll be feeling our way as we get to know the people. Some teaching, a coffeehouse, looking after people in need." This was not sounding very intelligent. Andy was an intellectual. Why could he not just out and say something profound that would wow them and get him off the hot seat?

"Do you have a job over there or what?"

It was unrelenting.

"We're sort of structured like the Jesus People communes you read about. We hold things in common and work on joint tasks once we're there. Kind of like, well, the Peace Corps or CUSO here in Canada. Only it's under the churches, that's all."

The thought of proselytizing at that juncture never seemed so unappealing. But Susan came to Andy's aid with a light-hearted quip about "saving all the heathen savages, too," and the moment finally passed. Both Andy's evangelistic zeal and his defensiveness had been aroused, however. The rest of the evening he felt a little on edge, but he kept up a good front.

Why was it so uncomfortable to be a Christian? The religious response was that the Church was ever under attack from Satan's minions. But a more immediate and obvious answer, he knew, was, *because the Church is so in disrepute*. Because there seems to be such a gulf between what it claims and what it does. At least he knew his home church was that way. For a church that sang so much about joy and a Bible that talked so much about service, it was hard for Andy to understand why, as Freud had observed, Christians seemed so joyless, so unredeemed, why they didn't look *erlöster*. And clearly his church was not engaged in sacrificial living toward the poor or anyone else. Mrs. Stark came to mind again. The mentally ill simply were not welcome at Carriage Street Gospel Chapel, *period*.

Going door-to-door to get the local people "saved," that was a worthy activity. Going door-to-door because people had needs, or better yet, establishing some things in the community such as daycare, this seemed foreign to his church. He knew instantly what showed greater integrity and authenticity and why the discomfort.

Susan and Andy had a good discussion after her friends left. He complimented her on her choice of friends, questioning in a roundabout way if any of them might be Christians. She either knew what he was getting at and ignored it or simply didn't catch on. He couldn't quite bring himself to ask her directly.

"How was it with you and Lorraine?" Susan asked.

"She told me she loved me."

"And what did you say, brother dearest?"

"I said I did, too," was Andy's phlegmatic reply. He could have been describing a slightly irritating skin rash.

"Andy, c'mon! In the movies when the stars say that, the rest of the firmament blinks its approval to the swelling cords of the *Love Story* theme!"

Andy took evasive action. "I notice that Thomas was signalling not a little approval your way, Susie Q. Or was I imagining something?"

Andy Norton had actually succeeded in making his sister turn red in the face. He bore down. "Tell me about him, Susan. I really like him—even though he gave me the third degree."

It worked. He actually got over the hump. It *was* interesting hearing about Thomas, when his sister had finished, punctuated by several prompting questions from Andy.

A little later while hovering over his diary, he felt guilty implying it was largely Lorraine's "fault" that he had come up with a handful of boob the night before. He knew it wasn't fair. But somehow he let float that way a trial balloon, implicit "tall tale" as well.

Andy could say nothing to Susan about Fiona, just as he could never tell his parents about Lorraine. Could he even tell himself what that made him: a shallow two-timer? And he could tell no one at all about Janys in bed—yet. In baseball, that was "three strikes and you're out."

He decided against asking Susan about Lorraine's dress and the mechanics of a strapless bra. He daren't return to that subject with Susan, only in mind's enraptured eye. Another uneasy truce. He wondered if Susan wondered about it at all, if she even knew of the dress Lorraine had worn. Would Susan dress up like that, he wondered further, risk possible chance encounter with Thomas' migrating hand? Was his sister "like that"? Was Lorraine? Was he? How could a man not "look on a woman and lust after her," he asked Jesus silently, prayer sent aloft like an S.O.S.

Mercifully, Susan had not mocked him for some of his obvious pieties that rang not a little hollow. How could he know that and still act so "religious"? Why was he 'doing life' that way? Why, when part of him was so aware of how phoney it was?

Dear Professor Norton:

I'll get straight to the point! So what's the big deal about sex? When I analyze it coldly, all that turns me on is arranged clumps of flesh, like clay figurines shaped by a skilful sculptor. And I'm sure even my desire for the kind of form that most turns me on is induced in turn by imitation of others' desire before me. Pleasantly plump brunette 'beauties' do not turn Andy on. Because socialization has taught me to prefer the svelte blonde. Though in this case Lorraine has straight jet-black hair, proverbial rule-proving exception. But her body arc is about a perfect ten from all I have seen so far, from one serendipitous feel.

So what's the big deal? Why, upon seeing a sexy woman, does my penis jump to attention like a trumpeter snapping his instrument skyward to play morning taps? Could I not just as readily have been programmed to similarly salivate in front of a delicious beef stake? Like Pavlov's dogs. Yet as C. S. Lewis points out, he knows of no club the world over that climaxes in a suddenly revealed gorgeous slab of roast beef! Worst luck.

So, Professor Norton again: What's the big deal? I presume that by now you're an old pro! Let's say you finally married at thirty and remained so. That would be about twenty years of regular sex. If you are normal and sustain about three sexual encounters with your wife per week, then you should have notched about 3,000 scores by the time you get this! Does that skilfully arranged clump of flesh look any more or less attractive than the first feel you had under Lorraine's strapless bra (How do they do that?)? Even if it is a different woman?

And just what is it exactly that keeps you coming

back for more? Knowing you as I do, you will not be into kinky sex. Nor will you be into extra-marital adventures. You will still be doing more or less the same kind of sex now with the same partner as when you first began. So just what is it that keeps you going these three thousand some odd times, Professor Stud?

I guess it has to be more than the physical, right? I mean, after 3,000 times, with the same woman, surely the novelty has worn off!

What then, romance? Wouldn't that have worn off by now, too, or at least have come and gone lots? I mean, there are doubtless kids around, and maybe many years where the romance is at least seriously syncopated, if you get my meaning. I guess then, it comes down to commitment, does it not? What else could it be?

But what then about sex per se? Is it not a great chimera when considered conduit to ultimate joy or pleasure? I suspect it is nothing of the sort! Yet why does this particular appetite, the sexual, so dominate species homo sapiens? *Is it primarily cultural, or is it more congenitally human? Whichever way, the genitals play a big part indeed! But in the end, sex itself,* qua *sex, is really rather immaterial to the human condition, other than for procreation. For that it has been crucial until very recently. But test tube babies, I've read, and a plethora of reproductive innovations, are about upon us. Then what? At the least, the sex act will be cut from procreational human necessity.*

Will the issue then strictly be pleasure? And if so, why? Why the overweening dominance of sex in comparison to, say, eating? And why this consistency throughout human history?

Maybe, Professor Norton, your specialty should have been sexology. (Did I just make up that word?) There should indeed be such a specialty, if not in existence.

What about the whole Christian side of things? Nothing gets Christians more heated than matters sexual. People get read out of churches for that reason, and the Anita Bryants of the world lead national campaigns against homosexuals. Taboos swirl in Bible-believing churches. Don't dare even name certain body parts or risk being labelled salacious and pornographic.

I'm sure you've studied the issue at far greater length by now. But perhaps you can at least help me out on one straightforward observation: Jesus hardly ever mentioned sex or sexuality compared to other issues. Then why has the Church made sex into the unpardonable sin? Why is it we learned about the "Birds and the Bees" not from our parents but from our school friends and health classes? Why couldn't our parents have been more straightforward with us?

I presume it'll take twenty-five years for a response from you to some of these questions. How long does this incubation process last before one "arrives"? I just wish I could know more about this one now!

Of course, in general, Professor Norton, you have also worked out so much more about faith and life. The bafflements on that one are endless. Maybe the next time I write I'll go into them more—the bewilderments of a faith commitment I mean.

But I have things to do now. So, 'til next time.

Sincerely,

Andy

35

The three Canadians were to leave Toronto on Tuesday, April 18th. The intervening week and a half proved to be busy with shopping and visiting family and friends.

As at Christmas, Andy had two separate visits, one with his dad, the other with Uncle Joe. Uncle Joe was mainly concerned about the "missionary agency" status of GO , an idea quite foreign to brethren circles and considered less, therefore, than a "faith mission." But both sessions were essentially positive.

Andy had one good long talk with his mom Wednesday night. She could not quite discuss what it would mean for him to be gone two years. Instead, they talked a little about Susan and what they would do in Germany. A note written right after that discussion was included with a farewell gift from his mom and dad. In it his mom expressed what she could not say face-to-face. An excerpt:

If I really said half of what is in my heart, you'd probably feel as badly as I do. Even now, I can't think of you without the tears flowing, and I'm sure there will be more before the two years are over. Yet, I want you to know that the life into which the Lord has led you is the one we would choose for both of our precious children. When I think of so many broken-hearted parents whose children have gone after the bubbles of this world, I can truly rejoice in what the Lord has done in your life and pray He will continue to do.

Others have seen their sons go off to war not knowing if they'd ever return. Still others have had them run away from home. So I remind myself how very much I have to praise the Lord for—and I really do. I'm thrilled that you will be with fellow trainees who you have come to love in the Lord. This is so much nicer, humanly speaking, than seeing you go off alone.

So Andy dear, know that you will never be long out of our thoughts and prayers. May God bless you and keep you and use you, as I know you desire above all else.

Included in the note was a poem his dad had found in a Christian magazine, apparently adapted (by his dad?) from the hymn-writer Thomas Kelly.

Speed Thy servants, Saviour speed them!
Thou art Lord of wind and waves,
They were bound but Thou hast freed them;
Now they go to free the slaves:
Be Thou with them,
'Tis Thine arm alone that saves.

Friends and home, and all forsaking
Lord they go at Thy command.
As their stay Thy promise taking
While they traverse sea and land.
Oh! be with them,
Lead them safely by the hand.

When no fruit appears to cheer them,
And they seem to toil in vain,
Then in mercy, Lord, draw near them,
Then their sinking hopes sustain;
Thus supported,
Let their zeal revive again.

In the midst of opposition
Let them trust O Lord in Thee:
When success attends their mission
Let Thy servants humble be:
Never leave them
Till Thy face in heaven they see.

There to reap in joy forever,
Fruit that grows from seed here sown:
There to be with Him who never
Ceases to preserve His own.
And with triumph
Sing a Saviour's grace alone!

Gerard Manley Hopkins it was not, Andy mused. In fact, he had seldom seen any evangelical verse rise above the sappy mediocre. He wondered at that. Was the entire tradition so stultifying or were those with such talents so preoccupied with the missionary task that they never got around to setting their creativity to writing? Was it a case of not just refusing to polish the brass *à la* D. L. Moody, but a downright commitment to polish nothing but soul-winning techniques? Were evangelicals so frozen in "rescue-the-perishing" mode that they could never get on with life? Then what about the repeatedly promised "abundant life"?

He thought of Ken Kincaide, Bill Gothard, Aunt Sarah, his own mom, Joyful Wall signers, and the myriad "cloud of witnesses." The "Grand Evangelical Vision of Life" seemed for them—for too many—one long breath-intake while traversing T. S. Eliot's wanton "wasteland" world of woes without end and soaring stentorian stench. All life offered these "pilgrims in a strange land" was concomitant gargantuan gasp or ferocious fart at the end of it all. Until Glory. Ah, then

THE BIG PAYOFF. What we've all been waiting for. Andy just knew: Life does not work that way. Nor eternity. What is Here and Now determines, predisposes, There and Then, positively locks it in as inexorably as death and taxes, as the saying goes, world without end.

Lorraine phoned late the night before Andy's departure. She had arranged it through Susan that he catch the phone before his parents picked up. The conversation quickly turned sour.

"So what if it's the Lord's will?" Lorraine exclaimed at one point. "What about my will, and yours Andy? Don't they count for anything? Is the Lord some kind of Cosmic Tyrant delighting in riding roughshod over our feelings?"

Andy was at a loss for words but used what he could not find anyway. "I think God's will sometimes so transcends ours that we often fail to understand it. I'm a fallible human, Lorraine. I don't pretend to know everything. How can I know that my choices are best for me or anyone else if I don't seek God's will in it? How can I hope to get it right?"

"Well, just maybe God leaves it up to us to muddle through. Or just maybe God doesn't even care. Or possibly God isn't really there like you think, despite what Francis Schaeffer claims." Long pause. "When my dad was doing his thing, Andy, *God was not there! Either that or he was deafeningly silent!*"

Andy didn't know how to respond. He had read Schaeffer's books *The God Who Is There* and *He is There and He is Not Silent.* He knew it was true. He just *knew!* Not Pascal's wager in the negative only— that one would collect at the moment of death. No, the text indicated clearly that one collects on *this side* of the grave if one is patient, if one is willing to *see* and *hear*. Was he? Was she? Andy felt the abandonment of Jesus on the cross.

"Lorraine, I can't talk any longer. I'll write or send a tape soon. I just know this is right for me to do *now*, and I'm doing it. God comes first, that's the bottom line. And I know God is there."

Lorraine wished him well through quiet tears then hung up.

Andy and his parents arrived at the Toronto airport with his two new *Globetrotter* suitcases and a carry-on gym bag in tow. They met up with the Thanes, including Janys's parents, her younger sister Mary, and Ted.

"Hi Andy." Andy knew the voice, but the face!

"Janys! Where are your glasses?" He thought of Sharon Collins then answered his own question. "Contacts?"

She smiled and nodded. Her long auburn hair was still permed. Was there a touch of lipstick and eye shadow? Perfume? What had her parents thought? Said? She was, Andy admitted, striking.

Andy felt a little wary around Ted, but he was friendly enough. "Take care of my little sister, Andy," he said. "In case you don't know, there's more going on under that frizzy mop than all the uncovered heads at our assembly combined."

Intimidated, yes. But Andy decided he really liked him.

Andy and Janys checked in amidst tearful goodbyes from parents and siblings. Susan turned away sobbing after she gave Andy an enormous hug, whispering, "Part of this is from Lorraine. Next year in Berlin!"

CHRYSALIS CRUCIBLE

As they walked toward their gate, Janys was visibly upset. Andy's anguish did not show openly. They were finally going. Though dreamlike, the reality was unmistakable.

They boarded the plane after what seemed like hours of waiting. Then, there was regal rush of Rolls Royce engines, and the jet catapulted into the sky. They exchanged excited glances. This was the first flight overseas for both of them.

Andy took the aisle seat so he could stretch his long legs. Janys sat next to him.

"Mr. and Mrs...?" The man across the aisle queried. Andy laughed. "No, we're not married." He briefly explained who they were and where they were going. The man was intrigued upon learning of their "job" in West Berlin.

"A lot of pagans in that city," he commented knowingly. He lived near Frankfurt and claimed he was not religious though "open-minded." He had been in Canada on a business trip. He even gave Andy a card.

"You know," he continued, with an unmistakable German accent, though his command of English was superb, "these jets are great for this kind of flying. To get you from point A to point B. But it's nothing like gliding—without a motor, under bright sunny sky. That, my son, gets you from Point A to Glory, if ever there is one. And that's heaven enough for me." Andy thought of the poor beggars at Mother Teresa's House of the Dying, which he had read about recently.

The German traveller continued on for quite some time, talking about the gliding club to which he belonged, how many hundreds of flights he had taken, the record for glider distance, the unsurpassed beauty of Alpine vistas. He was utterly captivating.

Andy thought that he would seldom be allowed to

go on similarly about his Christian faith. Why was this man allowed to discuss his passion in polite company but Andy was not allowed to discuss his spirituality, something much deeper and more meaningful?

At one point Janys whispered to Andy that the German gentleman could talk circles around him—even in his non-mother tongue. And that was no small feat. But he was fascinating. Andy weathered the brunt of his enthusiastic conversing. Janys was only drawn in occasionally.

Eventually, sleep proved to be the polite way to break off the ultimately tiring monologue. They would need the rest. It was already 1:00 a.m. in Frankfurt. They knew Wednesday would be a big day with further travel to Berlin and lots of moving-in work.

"There they go again. Andy and Janys sleeping together!" Janys said playfully as she pulled an Air Canada-issue blanket over her and positioned her pillow.

"Pardon?" Mr. Glider asked from across the aisle, "was the young lady speaking to me?"

"I don't think so," Andy replied, casting a frown and then a grin at Janys.

As Andy nodded off, it drifted through his mind that he had heard many stories of people being gloriously saved on such trips. Somehow the person would be attracted by the Christian's smile or sense of peace or the Lord's presence or whatever godly otherworldly aura. Then, sooner than later, *The Four Spiritual Laws* would be drawn out, and by the end of the flight, angels were rejoicing once more in heaven over a new soul in the kingdom.

But Andy didn't quite know how to get started after the initial mention of their mission did not elicit further inquiry. He felt mildly a failure. He also felt a real fear that somehow this worldly-wise, very successful, apparently well-adjusted German professional might make his faith appear simply irrelevant, like most uninterested fellow university students. Was this what he would encounter in Berlin? The thought proved uncomfortable and precluded sleep for a time, even though his eyes remained shut.

36

They touched down right on time in Frankfurt. They were on German soil! Their luggage had been booked through to Berlin, and they had three hours free before connecting to Berlin. So Hans and Joanne, who met them at the airport, arranged a bus tour of Frankfurt. It was Andy and Janys' first chance to use German on native turf. Andy found it exhilarating.

Hans Beutler proved to be an affable graduate from Wheaton College, where he had studied *cum laude* the previous year before returning to Germany to continue medical studies. He was able to take one week off from a very busy practicum in Bonn to help the team get settled. His English skills were excellent, and he was native German.

A good-looking man in his mid-twenties, Hans had a bushy head of hair, tiny glasses, and a classic "German look" reminiscent of photos Andy had seen of Dietrich Bonhoeffer, famed theologian of the "Confessing Church" who was executed in retaliation for an attempt on Hitler's life.

Joanne was Canadian. She had medium dark hair and wore stylish glasses. She and Hans had met at Wheaton. She had German in her blood but, like Andy, had learned the language only through school. Unlike Andy, she had spent her fourth year of German studies in Bonn, where she had been immersed in the language. She was completing her Masters in German literature, working through a thesis project that looked at "desire" in the writings of Thomas Mann. Andy had read Mann's *Tod in Venedig*, "Death in Venice," and had found it hauntingly beautiful in style but troubling in content, the story of an older man's homosexual preoccupation with a younger boy.

In no time, all four were lifting off for West Berlin on a smaller jet. During the flight, Janys read aloud to Andy from an in-flight magazine:

"West Berlin is nothing if not gargantuan—with the largest land-area of almost any city in the world. If one can imagine a Wall surrounding 900 square miles of island city, one has some picture of the reality known as West Berlin. Amazingly, two-thirds of West Berlin is green, with 63 lakes, miles of beaches, woods, and nature trails. There are more boat owners per capita in West Berlin than throughout the rest of West Germany. Of a Sunday, Berliners also turn out by the thousands to go for walks around the lakes, through the wooded trails, etc, and in the winter, even at times on the frozen lakes.

"There are at least twenty theatres, fifty convention halls, sixteen museums, 35,000 students in two large universities, and 100 professional schools. There are nine daily newspapers, 200 publishing houses, 450 bookstores, 106 libraries, and over 400 hotels and motels."

"Wow," was all Andy could say when she was finished. His mind went on about the sheer magnitude of West Berlin on every level. Were they not guilty of rather incalculable overweening gall in their "Berlin-for-Christ" intentions? The task was so massive, their preparedness so minuscule to the off-the-charts reality, their cultural sensitivity utterly nonexistent. Just what did they think they were doing there anyway? And what of G. E.'s "world-conquering" (Dan's expression) ambitions, or any other evangelist's, for that matter? Did they really have a clue?

They arrived at Berlin's Tempelhof Airport, scene of the famous post-War *Luftbrücke* (Airlift) that forever made America, especially J. F. Kennedy, West Berlin's friend. *Ich bin ein Berliner*, he had said. "I am a Berliner."

After they landed, the group took a taxi to the girls' apartment. It was in an older pre-War structure. As Andy entered, he was taken by the cavernous sweep of high ceilings and ornate light fixtures. A bedroom to the left was already well appointed, home of Peter and Jean for almost two weeks. Janys and Fiona's bedroom overlooked the street, *Günzelstraße*. Beyond their bedroom, also overlooking the street, was a living room area, what was to become the scene of all team meetings.

Immediately off that room was an enormous dining room. Peter and Jean had already secured a large table for it. They had also located beds, chairs, and couches. Jack and Gary moved them all in upon their arrival, together with Peter.

The kitchen was also large, but it contained only a matchbox refrigerator and stove. For the rest of their stay in Germany, they drank room-temperature pop, no room in the fridge!

"And there's even an alcove off the kitchen large enough for a washer and a dryer," Peter explained excitedly. He was so proud of both apartments they had found for the team. Temporarily, Hans was to sleep in that alcove on a mattress, Joanne in the girls' room, Gary and Sharon in the living room, and Jack and Andy on couches in the dining room. There was only one bathroom.

After a short visit, they toured the guys' apartment. Andy was excited about their accommodations. All was completely brand new, if unfurnished. When it was all set up, Peter and Jean would stay with the girls. Gary and Sharon with the guys.

The team had a good visit over a supper prepared by Peter and Jean. A brief prayer meeting and planning session followed. Then they went for a walk around the neighbourhood, mainly along the *Kurfürstendamm* (or *Ku'damm*), the most famous street in Germany. There, they met up with some Bread of Life people who were selling books. Andy bought *Jesus unser Schicksal* by Wilhelm Busch, noted evangelist of a bygone generation. He was glad to have already made a contact.

West Berlin immediately felt an extraordinary city. By far the most historic in Germany, seven centuries old, Andy had read it ceased being capital of West Germany at the end of the Second World War because of its location inside East Germany. East Berlin was, however, East Germany's capital.

By the time he got back, Andy was feeling quite disoriented and, as he later told his diary, "peculiarly attacked by Satan. But my hope and trust are in God."

Andy awoke to the sound of chiming church bells. In the kitchen, Peter and Jean were preparing a continental breakfast, the staple of which *Schrippen*— the unique Berliner term for *Brötchen* or fresh-baked rolls—was still warm. Andy pinched himself to be sure he was actually on a couch in an old apartment in West Berlin. This was his first full day there. Breakfast was sumptuous. Fresh cheese, jams, meat, and fruit accompanied the rolls. The newcomers raved.

A few hours later, he was delighted to be praising God in his first ever German worship service. It was Sunday, April 23rd. Only Fiona was absent as they walked the few blocks from the girls' apartment to Wilmersdorf Church. (She would not arrive for another two days.) Both apartments and the church were located in the Wilmersdorf *Bezirk* or district; hence the name, *Wilmersdorfer Gemeinde*. Peter and Jean had not yet attended that assembly. They had gone the previous Sunday to *Lichterfelde Gemeinde*.

Peter's everyday German was better and more practised than Andy's literary German. Peter had picked it up in his younger years and had gained a fair degree of fluency through use in a department store near the German border. However, Andy was the first to enter church that morning and introduce the team to Arthur Knecht, the elder who greeted them at the door. Herr Knecht looked a typical prosperous middle-aged businessman, which he was. He wore a dark suit, matching tie, and a somewhat stern countenance. Andy noticed a momentary shift of composure when he mentioned they were a missionary team from North America there to do evangelism. Something clouded. Was it even dismay?

But it passed quickly, and he offered an appropriate smile and greeting. He did not ask for "Letters of Commendation," but Andy nonetheless produced one from the Centre, duly translated by Hans, who with Joanne had headed off on their own for the day. It explained briefly the team's purpose, that various team members would eventually be worshipping in each of Berlin's five assemblies, and that they would be focusing on youth and children's work. Andy expected Herr Knecht to read it at the appropriate moment before the gathered assembly, but when that time came, he merely supplied a curt *précis* of the information, adding, strangely Andy thought, mention of the connection of the team with *Schwester Boswell*. Some gave knowing nods. That was reassuring. Sister Boswell had been the contact person for G. E. Andy understood that it was through her that the Berlin assemblies had invited them. They would meet with her for the first time in the coming week.

Andy recorded nothing in his diary about the first church service. Nothing memorable really happened. Other than the language difference and a few cultural distinctives, they might have attended the same kind of service anywhere in Ontario and probably anywhere in the world. The brethren were right about the universality of the phenomenon. For some, this was proof positive of the divine inspiration of the Spirit upon their order of worship.

A more likely explanation, Andy had long since concluded, was brethren were more tradition-bound than most denominations, though they vehemently resisted any notion of following "customs of men" and refused the designation of "denomination." The all-time classic was A. P. Gibbs' *Why I Meet With the People Known as the 'plymouth brethren,'* one of the most denominationally exclusive, tradition-oriented pieces he had ever seen. A. P. Gibbs ("A Perfect Gentleman") was his mother's favourite preacher.

Over the next few days, the team accomplished much. They bought furniture and curtains, transformers for small appliances, bicycles, pots and pans, and all of the other basic necessities they would need over the next two years. A long list was being checked off slowly. They also made application for permission to sell books on the *Ku'damm* and registered their presence in West Berlin, something all but temporary visitors were obliged to do.

Early into their second week, the guys' apartment began to take shape, proceedings watched over carefully by Sharon. She had a decidedly artistic eye, and it showed at both apartments as she took charge of all aspects of interior decorating.

Hans only stayed the first week. Joanne would stay for two entire months to conduct intensive language training. She also was pursuing her thesis project, with two university libraries available to her. Classes were from 9:00-12:00 daily throughout the week. On the weekends, there was invariably a written assignment that required the team to field-test their expanding language skills.

Both Peter and Andy were exempt from classes, but they had to do a five-page written essay each week about life in Berlin. Joanne was a stern taskmaster, fair and fun.

Andy sucked in his breath as Fiona emerged from customs at the Tempelhof Airport, waving excitedly and beaming when she caught sight of them. He thought how little he had seen Lorraine even smile.

"Where's the rest of the team?" she inquired in her captivating southern drawl after she had extended hugs to them both.

"Joanne's already got them slugging away at German," Andy returned. "How was your flight? Fiona, it's so *great* to see you!"

"It's so good to see you—and Peter, too. Can't wait to see everyone, Andy. I've been practising. *Guten Tag. Ick heisse Fiona. Wie heissen Sie?*"

Andy laughed. "Now, can you say that again but not in Texan? And to answer your question, *Ich heiße Andreas*," he replied in perfect High German accent.

As she turned toward the luggage carousel Andy's gaze lingered.

On the taxi ride back to the girls' apartment, Andy and Peter filled in a lot of the team's doings. Fiona's exuberance was entrancing, as ever.

Hugs and excited chatter marked their reunion back at the apartment. The team was complete at last—even though Fiona's actual advent had not matched any of Andy's fantasies.

37

The big news during Andy's second week in West Berlin was purchase of a little Renault *Deux Chevaux*, which was to service the team throughout their stay.

The car's first non-team passenger was "*Schwester* Boswell." The entire team was to meet her Thursday evening at the girls' apartment. She was joining them for supper and a team meeting afterwards. Peter and Jean had visited with her a few times previously. There was keen anticipation.

Beatrice Boswell was one of those amazing brethren missionary women whose dogged stick-to-itiveness and indefatigability were a matter of unceasing wonder. Andy felt sure psychologists could do fascinating case studies on the motivations, aspirations, inspirations, and machinations of such determined women. They seemed to be everywhere on the mission field, in far greater abundance than their male counterparts. They flogged it alone, year after year, until they died on the field or returned to their homeland, usually forgotten and relegated to minor roles in the church. Either that or they did the "women's meeting" circuit, if brethren. Most remained "eunuchs for the kingdom." As Andy saw the car pull up with Beatrice inside, he wondered if women like her were the original "Women's Libbers" in Western culture.

The whole group assembled at the apartment doorway to welcome Beatrice. Surprisingly, she did not have long hair, and she was quick of movement as she stepped through the door in front of Peter. She was average height, robustly built, and in her late forties, they guessed afterwards. "Probably G. E.'s age," Jack opined.

She had dark brown eyes that matched her countenance; a plain though preoccupied face, and stern demeanour. Even her smiles were wan, like facial muscles forever in a tug of war between warmth and serious spiritual solicitation, "Her Father's business," she was tirelessly about. The etchings of that battleground were readily evident on a composure of chiselled granite. She took each proffered hand and returned the name spoken. She never miscued afterwards.

A *presence* entered into their lives that afternoon, Andy sensed it as surely as Banquo's ghost began haunting Macbeth, combination perhaps of Irma Bauman and Ken Kincaide, who would pursue spiritual perfection, "that good part," Jesus had told Martha, like and until there was no tomorrow. They ushered her in to supper right away.

After supper, with the team ensconced in the living room, Gary asked Beatrice the question uppermost on their minds. "Beatrice," he began (she had insisted on their using her first name), "how do you see connecting to us? As I understand it, you have worked for several years in the city to get brethren involved in evangelism. We're here now, a whole team committed to it. What do you hope from us?"

She responded by first speaking warmly of the team's being there; that this was an unbelievable answer to her prayers of several years. She spoke rapidly almost in staccatos, as if afraid each breath might be her last. There was a pleading earnestness in every word. Andy noted that she maintained a greater Scottish accent than did G. E., but her German was pronunciation-perfect, facility in it enviable. Andy knew immediately there was indeed hope for Fiona.

"When Brother Moore first corresponded with me, I had no idea *this* would be the outcome," she began, arms spread out to take in the whole team. Her eyes glistened. She composed herself after several minutes.

"To see a whole team of young Christians eager to serve the Lord here in this city for two years is beyond my wildest dreams. G. E. had been to Germany to scout out possibilities for a team during the Munich Olympics. And as you know, for a variety of reasons the Munich Team option transformed into the Berlin Team project, into you dear young people here today. I still cannot believe it!" She choked up again, her eyes moistening, and pulled out a Kleenex.

Peter interjected into the awkward silence, "So Beatrice, what have you and G. E. talked about with reference to us? What understanding did you arrive at?"

Beatrice was uncomprehending for a moment, as if the questions had been in Dutch. "Well, G. E. agreed with my proposal, once it was clear you would be coming to West Berlin."

"Your proposal, Beatrice?" Gary asked this time.

She looked at Gary strangely. Then at Peter. Then she seemed to stare blankly, or perhaps was taking in the entire team at a glazed glance. "Well, as I proposed," came her slow, very slow for her, response. "for these next two years you work with me and the *Lichterfelde* eldership in strategizing to evangelize West Berlin." She pressed on quickly, as if afraid to let even herself interrupt. "I know there will have to be planning times together with myself, Peter, and Gary. And no doubt at times we'll hold joint team meetings to work out details.

"I think, for instance, we need to start right away with location. It only makes sense that we start around the assembly in *Lichterfelde*. The elders are ready. Well, I'll be honest, a few need coaching still. But the

CHRYSALIS CRUCIBLE   317

youth are certainly with us.

"You know that biblical pattern of beginning in Jerusalem, and spreading to the ends of the earth? Though we can always work with, say, *Wilmersdorf* if they give us the invitation. My hope is to so awaken the other five assemblies by our example that we'll start a mighty work of God that will just go on and on for years to come, even after you are gone." Beatrice was animated. She had a torrent of vision for what was going to happen now that, at long last, the "dream team" had arrived at her doorstep.

"I ran this by Peter the other day. He said to bring it up at our first team meeting. And, by the way, I'm more than willing to attend all your meetings once you establish a schedule. You could even meet at my apartment, if you like. Perhaps alternate between locations.

"Anyway, here is the brochure just waiting to be printed. I described it already to Peter over the phone. I'll show it to you then help some of you with the German. We have a fine artistic youth named Sieglinde. She did up the design for me, which we can have reproduced at the printer's tomorrow. We'll just have to decide how many. I'm just so excited about what the Lord is going to do in our city through all of us for his glory these next two years."

She possessed an amazing capacity to speak beyond the apparent limit of her lungs. Such was her immense intensity. Andy thought again of Ken Kincaide.

Beatrice laid out the brochure on the floor. It invited all and sundry to an *Evangelisation* at *Lichterfelde* assembly May 19th and 20th. Horst Paetkau of the assembly was to present on the topic "*Was Kommt auf uns Zu?*" a lecture about biblical prophecy in light of momentous world events. Then, there it was, in bold print, translated: MUSIC TO BE SUPPLIED BY THE AMERICAN SINGING GROUP! An adjacent stylized eagle merged into a cross, with the biblical passage quoted from Isaiah that promised one would mount up on wings as eagles if one trusted in the Lord.

Sharon liked the dignified artwork. "That name 'Sieglinde,'" she said, hesitating at the name, "almost sings, doesn't it? That Sieglinde is good!"

Jack was excited, too. "Wow, our first chance to evangelize and try out our German so soon. This is great! We'll barely have been here a month!"

Bolstered, Beatrice began anew, "Surely some experience witnessing from the very start will not hurt. And, in spite of the Vietnam War, the young people really are so taken with American—North American—culture. You wouldn't even have to sing in German at all..." Beatrice's explanations flooded out. She knew that the team was musical.

Suddenly, Beatrice looked at her watch. "I asked for an hour with the team, and I will stay within that. Thanks so much for this evening and for the good news about the *Evangelisation*. We'll work out more details about our team arrangement later. Can we just close with a word of prayer? Peter, perhaps you could lead us?"

Afterwards, Beatrice shook hands with everyone again, calling each by name, thanked Sharon and Jean for the delicious meal, and was shown to the door by Peter and Jean.

"Golly!" Jack exclaimed seconds after the door closed. "She's sure a ball of fire!"

In a few minutes, Peter and Gary re-entered. "It's late," Peter began, "but I thought we should discuss Beatrice's work with us for a few minutes then quickly do the rounds for any concerns. Is that okay with everyone?" Peter's pattern was to second-guess any decision with a solicited approbation.

"I'm all for her!" Jack shot through the starting gate. "She'll light a fire under us and knows the scene here. How can we go wrong? I think she should come to all our team meetings. We'd get a huge jump-start on our campaign ministry, that's for sure! And we've already got one outreach ready-made landing on our laps, just like that. What a gift!"

Most were of similar impression. Janys remained quiet though, and Andy alone expressed real misgiving. "Didn't she seem a bit presumptuous?" He asked.

Peter came to her defence. "She's just very focused. I think she is a Godsend that God prepared for us. Already Jean and I are really taken. We're going to start attending *Lichterfelde* because of her. Probably Gary and Sharon should, too, so we can have the leadership working closely with her from the start."

"I don't know," said Andy, "She could at least have asked us first about this *Evangelisation*."

"She did, Andy," Jack chided. "Tonight."

A week later, Andy received an invitation from Beatrice to join a youth Bible study she conducted at *Lichterfelde*. He felt flattered, though it must have been Peter who suggested his language skills were sufficiently up to speed. The Bible study happened once a month on a Friday evening. The other Friday nights were regular youth activities like bowling and movies. Beatrice invited Andy over for supper to discuss the proposal.

She lived in an apartment building in the same district as the church. What struck Andy upon entering was how tiny it was compared to the girls' place. The second impression was the wealth of reading material.

She had books, magazines, papers, and shelves in organized disarray everywhere. Whatever else she was, Beatrice Boswell was *informed*. Andy had this enormous urge to start going through her "library" like a long lost museum piece.

There was something delicious-smelling in the kitchen. Soon, it was on the small dining room table and they were bowing their heads in thanks. Andy did the honours.

As they ate, Andy asked Beatrice how she had come to be a commended worker in West Berlin versus, say Angola, where he was used to hearing of committed single missionaries.

"I was twelve when the War ended," she responded, "and for the first time that year, when I moved into what would be like your high school, they offered German studies. All that had been suspended during the War years."

Andy quickly did the math. They had all been wrong. She was in about ten years younger than G. E., just under forty. Andy was surprised. She would have been eligible for a GO team after all.

She continued. "My dad was good at languages, and he encouraged me to take German. I took to it like a duck to water. Eight years later, a friend and I visited West Berlin. We had both studied German for all those years and were keen to put it to use.

"West Berlin was at the height of the Marshall Plan, by which billions of Marks were funnelled toward the reconstruction of Germany. In fact, the summer we visited was when some of the last trees were planted in the *Tiergarten*, trees shipped from countries around the world as gestures of goodwill toward a hopeful future. They're mature trees today. You'll see them when you visit there.

"During my stay, I became so intrigued with the language and culture that I returned with my friend for another visit the next summer, only to return on my own early the next year to look for a job. They were abundant in those days, and I found one working with The Marshall Plan *Tiergarten* Restoration Project. The rest, as they say, is history. I've lived here since 1955. Seventeen years now. Hard to believe."

As Beatrice spoke, Andy looked at the reading lamp at the opposite end of the table, together with an assortment of papers. Must be her desk when she isn't entertaining, Andy thought. He decided he would feel quite claustrophobic living in Beatrice's space. His mind idly played with the metaphor.

"When that job came to an end, I had also become quite involved in one of the local assemblies. I was running lots of kids' programs, and my German was coming along so well it was arranged for me to continue this as a ministry, provided I could also receive support from my home assembly in Scotland. It was a bit unusual, to be sure.

"I received the support, however, and I've been doing missionary work here ever since. I work part-time in a dental office to supplement the home assembly money. I'm a certified dental hygienist. Ten years ago *The Missionary Handbook* 'discovered' me. So now I get money, channelled through my home assembly, literally from around the world. It enables me to carry on quite well."

Andy wondered at the German term for "dental hygienist," as he was doing for hundreds of other words and expressions. Languages were enormous cultural vaults, words and idioms so many tumblers which, spun with the appropriate ear, unlocked rare treasures indeed.

He noticed some pictures. Her parents? Were there siblings? Who were some of the others? Friends? Her girlfriend who had first come over with her to Germany? There was a good-looking, even dapper, man in two photos. Her brother?

Andy felt suddenly emboldened by a hunch.

"Beatrice, somewhere in there was romance I'll bet, and not just with culture and language!"

He watched her face carefully. He was not prepared for the initial flash of dark anger. Pain? Hurt? He couldn't read the smudged etching. It lasted momentarily, so in control was she. Rigidly, thought Andy.

"Andy," she replied firmly, "you hardly know me, and *vice versa*. I like you. But that comment was impertinent at best! But I will respond. Yes. There was a man. I'll say nothing more. It didn't work out, it didn't work out..." She repeated in spite of herself. Her eyes scanned an interior landscape. He wanted to ask if he was Scottish or German. Did she stay in West Berlin to run away from pain and hurt or to embrace hoped-for joy? How had Robbie Burns put it?

> *The best-laid schemes o Mice an' Men,*
> *Gang aft agley,*
> *An' lea'e us nought but grief an' pain,*
> *For promis'd joy!*

She would know him, Scotland's poet laureate, rake, and heretic. Who had written the novel *Of Mice and Men*? Andy tried to remember. John Steinbeck. Were those themes in it? If not, what else? Isn't that the *very stuff* of life, and thus of novels?

He found his mind imagining Beatrice in a relationship with a man. It was hard. What would a guy see in her? Fiona overlaid that visage, her figure. He would not have looked twice, or would he? Maybe she's changed for the worse. His mind was vicious. Why did looks and body contour dominate his initial, sometimes only, assessment of a woman? Was it overweening arrogance that saw himself Lady Killer *par excellence*, a business card he might hand out to every woman who would look at him twice? Did he *only* look on women and lust—at least undress? He was too hard on himself. He thought of Susan. He thought of Janys half-undressed indeed! He thought of Lorraine and Fiona, whom he had looked beyond far more than at mere, though granted initial, "skin-deep."

What would attract Beatrice to a guy? She who was so... Pious, holy, otherworldly. He thought of his Aunt Sarah saying the Lord had called her to Africa and his Uncle Joe could do with that as he pleased. So they both responded to the call for Africa and were married there. Ever after, his uncle quipped about holding the record for travelling the farthest in the world for a first date. Andy had often wondered about the romance in that relationship and, if truth be known, about the sex. The "missionary position" took on concrete imagination when he thought of Uncle Joe and Aunt Sarah. But they had sired twins. So they must have taken that position at least once. And now Beatrice?

Eunuchs for the Kingdom, almost. Except to fulfill the creation mandate. And not a tad—tit—more. But could he imagine Aunt Sarah, Beatrice, his mom actually engaging in sexual pleasure? No, to be honest. He felt guilty for asking, then answering, the question. Nor, for that matter, could he imagine anyone wanting to have either as playmate. Would his mind let up? But he knew self-critically he'd always had a Venus goddess fetish, more a function of his own arrogance and inflated sense of self than any real life experience of having attracted such. Well, Lorraine, and (Still?) Fiona… And years ago, Coral. Not bad, in spite of himself. Andy the Dandy.

He might have continued in such a vein (Vain!) indefinitely had it not been for Beatrice's intrusion. "Andy, don't go talking about this with your team mates. I've probably given away more than enough already!"

How long had their separate reveries lasted? Had her countenance changed? Did she not look even angry now, layered atop the hurt?

"No," Andy replied, "your secrets are safe with me."

He thought she was inclined to say more, might have given the right nudge. But her jaws set firmly at last. Some things one just *knows*, Andy thought. And faith? What "Certainty Meter" did that engage? But didn't John say one "knows" somehow by faith, too? And certainly knew the guy who wrote Hebrews claimed as much.

Andy thought of the title of an InterVarsity lecture he had once seen but never attended: "Certainty in a Post-Modern World." Would faith be any different in a "modern" world? A pre-modern world? A medieval one? His mind stretched back rapidly across expanses of history of which he had only vague intimations. What would doing evangelism in the heart of the "Mother of Western Civilization" have looked like during the Black Plague? It was impossible to scratch that itch with any historical tool he possessed. He placed it firmly beyond conscious reach at least for the moment.

Perhaps the first thousand years of heaven would involve receiving patient answers to all the unanswered questions stored just beyond memory's reach in a cosmic vault, to which God alone held the key. But there was no reassurance in that. Was heaven, in that case, *Ultimate Language,* a grammar already to be grasped and wrestled with by finite minds as surely as German nouns, verbs, adjectives, and adverbs?

They barely had time to clean up and get to the church. From her flustered behaviour, it was obvious to Andy that Beatrice was not used to being late for anything. They arrived on time, however, and the study went well. Andy fell in love with the language even more.

The team talked by phone with Beatrice almost daily, benefiting from her German fluency and extensive knowledge of the city. Even Joanne was impressed by her verbal skills.

Beatrice began to impress in other ways, too. After attending their first two team meetings, she had to skip the third, because she was ensconced at home in some project. Jack had gone outside to the nearby phone booth to phone her for information on something. The others waited patiently for him to return. It took some time.

"Beatrice is a bear!" Jack said upon entering the living room. This was somewhat different tune for Jack.

"Beatrice Bear!" Fiona mimicked. "B. B.!" And hence a nickname was born.

This led to quite a discussion of B. B., with joking at supper finally about whether or not, come May 19th and 20th, Joanne couldn't extend her school hours to Friday evening and Saturday morning. She insisted she needed her time off, too, playing right along with them.

Some cracks were appearing already, Andy thought, his smile fading.

38

The schedule that evolved over the next few days, and which more or less obtained the first two months, was German classes in the morning for all but Peter and Andy, a noon break of two hours, two hours of language study, and one hour of mission-related work before supper preparations began at 5:00. Evenings were free.

For the first month, Peter and Andy stayed busy easily with setting-up errands. Into the second month, time began to hang heavily for Andy. He had already bought enough German Christian books to keep him going indefinitely, but he wanted breaks from these at times.

Andy filled in the daytime hours rather haphazardly once errands-related activities had fairly much ceased. He wrote, read, and helped the others with their German exercises. It was sloppy, however, and not clearly structured. It left him ill at ease.

Andy expressed his frustration at their next team meeting. Leadership was not proving to be Peter's *forte*, though Andy had supported putting Peter into that role together with Gary even though it was unthinkable that someone younger than he should be placed into a leadership role just because he was married.

For his part, Gary was unsure about asserting himself around someone almost twice his age. So he deferred to Peter, who felt in turn insecure about making decisions.

Andy proved to be the most forthright at times. But Fiona held very strong opinions, too. At first, perhaps being a woman, she was reluctant to speak her mind. Not for long. Whether elicited by the same spirit of independence that B. B. showed, just frustrated at times, or tainted by a fierce Texan arrogance epitomized in the Alamo mythology, she spoke up increasingly. Andy reflected often on this last dynamic, the overweening haughtiness of inhabitants of the "Lone-star" state.

As in the Alamo story, Andy thought, at times Fiona demonstrated a stubborn single-mindedness unworthy of all but the real hero. Andy had never told her that he had done a major historiography project on the Alamo in second-year history under the tutelage of a graduate student Texan draft dodger. He was anti-American foreign policy and anti-Vietnam War to the core. In the Alamo myth, there was one man who refused to cross the line to "defend" to the death the Alamo. In Andy's guided research project, this "traitor" to Texan orthodoxy in fact gave the lie to the "righteousness" of the rampant rapacity and butchery of those pre-state Texan "authorities," brutal terrorists all toward the Mexicans and Indians in wresting their land from them.

Andy first heard from him the term "Identity Christians" with reference to those convinced of white American Manifest Destiny supremacy over every inch of "America." The "intrepid Texas Rangers," Andy discovered were anything but. They were rather originally a group of thugs and thieves who slaughtered and extorted at will, not unlike other westward advancing Americans or the Spanish *Conquistadores* to the south.

"Perspective," his prof used to intone, "history's all about perspective. In the broadest strokes, it makes all the difference whether one looks at it from underdog or top dog vantage point. Americans, such as they even care about world history or that of the first Americans, only see history from top dog perspective.

They follow a 'Might is Right' doctrine of Manifest Destiny stretching all the way back to a Babylonian creation myth about human origins, bathed endlessly in conquerors' blood-letting. This is true bottom-line American civil religion." Then he would add, "Though hardly 'civil.'" He claimed that the ancient creation myth was the true "old-time religion," good enough for every American, whose ultimate God-given constitutional right was the pointed barrel of a gun. The Ultimate, not just the Second, American Constitutional Amendment, was the right to blow the "enemy" (anyone in the way) to Kingdom Come. This was American civil religion evangelism that "invited" to Kingdom Come all right! This was for him the only "true home-grown American religion."

He claimed that more surely than religion informed by the biblical "creation myth," the "Promised Land myth," or the "Jesus myth," all of which for him were just as shamelessly violent anyway, the Babylonian creation myth underwrote American Manifest Destiny doctrine.

It always bugged Andy that he would never budge from holding out the Gospel Story as sometimes quaint but indisputable mythology designed to mollify quiescent adherents with the promise of "pie in the sky when you die." Andy wondered about Mr. Matheson's own perspective when he revealed one day he had been raised fundamentalist Christian. "Perspective" indeed, Mr. Matheson! Andy thought more than once. He had read recently of an outspoken American Episcopalian priest and childhood fundamentalist whose name appropriately rhymed with "wrong"—Spong—who sounded much the same toward evangelicals. He thought of René Girard's claim, encountered in an anthropology class, that the Jesus Story was Ultimate

Demythologizer of all cultural founding myths of murder and expulsion.

In short, Andy found annoying at times the astounding insularity of Miss Texas, Mr. Matheson's take, and his essay now remembered.

By the second month, staff meetings settled into a Monday afternoon regularity. They began to discuss a potential emerging issue: American soldiers who had "discovered" the Berlin team. It happened quite simply. Fiona and Janys were walking along the *Ku'damm* on their own when two Americans called to them from an ice cream kiosk to ask where they were from. The girls almost did not stop. But, as Fiona said, it was nice to hear an American accent, albeit not Texan. Andy knew there was not a healthy American male alive who would not try his best to be noticed by Fiona.

A conversation was struck amongst the four. When Fiona mentioned they were there to work with some churches, the guys were quite taken. They were part of a Bible study group at the base, they said excitedly. Furthermore, Christianity was breaking out everywhere in the Army, they explained. Fiona was thrilled. The guys told them they really wanted to stay in touch, thinking it great that the team would be witnessing in West Berlin. "A pretty pagan city," said one. Andy remembered the knowing irony in "Mr. Glider" on the plane trip over. The girls did not feel comfortable giving their address. Phone hook-ups for the apartments were months away. But the guys gave theirs, strongly urging more contact.

Fiona enthused about this encounter at the staff meeting. Janys was silent, however. What did Andy read in her expression? He thought of a nightstand face, glasses set aside, hair cascading. Not Fiona, not

Lorraine, but… She had her own distinctive *persona* all wrapped up in arresting looks.

"Fiona," Andy began, knowing he was treading on dangerous ground, "I think it's really neat that you met these guys. I'm glad you didn't give them your address, too. And I think we need to think very carefully about phoning them. For starters, how will our language skills improve if we talk to Americans a lot? We'll have that problem amongst ourselves enough.

"More, Fiona, you're blonde and beautiful." He blushed, definitely involuntarily. How else could he say it without excluding Janys? "What guy wouldn't want to see you again? I guess I'm questioning motivation here. Maybe even their sincerity about faith." He did not look at Janys, could not look at Fiona.

Her eyes flashed. The implication she was naïve was unmistakable. Was there something more? Andy asked it of himself. Was it bad enough "sharing" Fiona with Jack, his mind blurted out? Now he would have to expand to who knows how many soldiers at the American Army base. Was it, Andy forced himself to admit to the question, rank jealousy?

Jack jumped in. "Of course a full-blooded American guy is going to notice you both. I know. I'm one of those. So Andy's right. And who knows how sincere their faith is? They could just be lonely guys taking advantage of what guys do every day in America to attractive females that come into range. Maybe it was just 'target practice' for them, and they bagged some game when you stopped to talk. Then again, maybe not. And if there's revival going on at the base, maybe we should plug in to let it flow into our work. So I think Andy is right to question what to do about these guys. I know I need all the practice I can get in German! And guaranteed I won't get it at the Army Base!"

Andy had a mental image of a gigantic crane scooping up Main Street America, and plunking the deposit down on army bases all over the world, hundreds of them so that everything is carbon copy of back home. Little America dotting the worldscape like Disneyland Main Street.

Heaven on an Army Base was every American cultural icon preserved, from Dr. Pepper in pop machines to the latest Hollywood blockbuster at the cinema to American spoken in the far reaches of the globe. *Pure Americana* preserved at all cost, expense without limit. Heaven not only of American spoken as Ultimate Language but "American heaven" imposed ubiquitously in a grand global melting pot. Andy knew as sudden revelation that such a vision of *pax Americana* bore all the markings of hell.

Fiona said she would gladly let the team feel its way on this and not push an agenda of evangelizing or fellowshipping at the American army base.

Jack proved more than once modifying influence on Fiona.

The next day, the team booked a break from studies to go on a bus tour of West Berlin. They had loads of fun, and it was rather reassuring about their team life as a whole and what they were supposed to be doing.

They had all expected somehow to move into mission-related activities fairly quickly. There had been notions at the Centre of being invited by the local assemblies within a short time to join with them in some of their ministries. Strangely, none of that had happened. On the contrary, the team noticed a definite coolness toward them from the assemblies.

Andy planned to continue attending the Bible studies at *Lichterfelde* assembly. Only a few youth came regularly, but they were keen to learn. B. B. was a good Bible expositor, Andy discovered. She seemed especially keen on helping her students discover the beauty of the truth of Christianity. Her favourite verse was John 8:32 in the King James: "And ye shall know the truth, and the truth shall make you free." Truth was a jailbreak.

She also had the smarts around apologetics and could almost be funny. This last was somewhat of a shock, given such dour demeanour upon first impression. She had a subtle sense of humour bordering on the sarcastic. During one study, someone expressed a belief in the relativity of all ethics. At least that was what his teacher was expressing in mandatory Religion class. B. B. shot back that he should take and serve tea at the next class. When the student looked lost, B. B. said, "Simple Jörg. Go up to the teacher, pot of freshly boiled tea in your hand, and offer him some. At the same time, ask him about the relativity of all ethical systems. When he is expressing that, you say, 'Well then, I guess it really doesn't matter whether I pour this into your cup or over your head!' Then sit down." Andy liked that kind of implicit put-down.

Andy noted she seldom shared of herself. All her relationships were externalized with no reciprocal invitation. Was this a defence mechanism after the mysterious failed romantic relationship in her life, or was it just B. B.?

Andy's first prayer letter to supporters read:

Some of you will be surprised, some disappointed, but this is officially known as a "prayer letter," and it is my first stab at this literary genre. Just before sitting down to write this, I went over the list of names to whom it is being sent. To say the least, there is a great variety in those receiving it. Some are just kids (forgive me for calling you that, Brian) and some are octogenarians (in the dictionary under 'o'). Some are Christians, some are not, and some are on their way from the latter to the former position (though hopefully not vice versa). Whoever you are, please do not feel obliged to read these letters as they come, hopefully about every six weeks. If you do though, I hope that you'll find them interesting and informative, and that naturally if you're a person who has a genuine relationship with Jesus Christ, you will pray for the things mentioned below. So here we go...

Berlin is truly a beautiful city, and we are pretty well in its centre, not too far from the Kurfürstendamm (Ku'damm for short), its main street.

Immediately, all kinds of differences can be noted: stick door handles instead of circular ones, sand-paper toilet paper with no perforated divisions, no closets, many houses have no telephones and you must wait months for one to be installed, no big fridges since you go grocery shopping every day, delicious rolls instead of emaciated white bread, all kinds of meats, pornography on every street corner and at the news stands so that you hardly know where to look when buying a newspaper, different traffic signs (hardly any "Stop" signs and no speed limit signs), busy streets all the time with maniacal drivers and lots of bicycles, plus many more I can't think of right now—not to mention the foreigners all over the place speaking some crazy language!

Since my arrival, we have done nothing but run around getting things for our apartments, having classes and meetings, and generally going about the business of settling down in a strange city with weird customs and strange surroundings.

Though exhausting and very frustrating at times it has been a lot of fun and quite exciting. It's suggested, rather strongly, that we keep these prayer letters as short as possible, and I think I have already passed the limit. But unfortunately, I always did have the gift of gab, so must add a little more—after all, it is my first prayer letter. I'll call it "gabber's license."

Why did I come to Germany? That simple question doesn't really have a simple answer, except in the most important sense: I came because I felt that God said, "Go!" Many other things could be included in that statement, but they would be superfluous. Seen from God's perspective, the whole world is the mission field, and if God wants to spend a few thousand of His dollars to send me a quarter of the way around the world, that's His prerogative. I must merely be willing to go wherever He says.

The prayer requests I'm about to mention are given because I ask that you pray to the God who really exists and who really specifically answers prayer in specific ways. I must admit that my experience in this area is quite limited, though not totally absent. But on the authority of Jesus and God's Word (and why should that authority not be taken literally?) I know that God answers prayer. So please pray that:

- We will stick at our language study

- Our team of eight young Christians might so grow and work together that our little world about us here in West Berlin might know that the great God who made us wants to share His life with us.

I'd love to hear from any and all of you and will try to answer all who write. Please forgive my tardy letter writing. I must say this in advance.

Andy

Andy and Gary were walking together on the *Ku'damm* one evening during the first month talking intently about Francis Schaeffer's differentiation between people who believe in the Bible as true *Historie*, such that, had one been observer at the Tree in antiquity when Adam and Eve were hesitating, one could have heard the clock ticking. This over against those like neo-orthodox Karl Barth who believed that the biblical story of the Garden was mere *saga*, lost to any historical verification in antiquity and not true "stopwatch history." It was *Geschichte*—religious history to be sure, and to be taken seriously even, but not as literal happening. Andy was explaining to Gary that this would be a major battleground in Germany. It was straight out of his apologetics paper. They needed to hold out for *true* truth (Schaefferism), namely, that everything in the Bible fitted into the phenomenological world as surely as an itchy leg.

Suddenly, a young woman accosted them, with a thick German accent. "Hey, you *Amerikaner* like some more of *this*?" She wore high leather boots, skimpy mini-skirt, and imitation leather vest. She flashed open her vest to reveal a skimpy bra with bulging bosom. Just as quickly, the show was over. "There's lots more of *vher* that came from over there." She pointed toward a street-level doorway with a similarly fleshy prostitute standing outside, face painted, smile pasted, invitation proffered.

"*Danke nein*," Andy said curtly, prepared to move on.

Gary, however, responded with "*Moment mal*," and went on to ask her in halting German if she had ever met Jesus. She responded with surprise to his German, complimenting him on it and saying most *Amerikaner* knew only a few body parts. Her eyes dipped to her chest, and Andy and Gary's followed obediently. Were they both hoping for the curtains to open again? She had met all kinds of guys, and at least a few of them were called *Jesus*—though she allowed she did not always get their names.

"No," Gary responded, "I mean Jesus *Christ*."

"Are you Jesus People?" she asked.

"Yes, and you can become one, too," Gary responded. He looked at Andy to say more. Andy spoke haltingly, not because of inhibitions about speaking in German but because of wondering how Jesus was someone on whose name she, like anyone else, could call to be saved. She seemed to listen, and he tried to lock eyes with her like the Mormons at the Centre had. It was safest that way, too. To tell the truth, he felt more grossed out than aroused, mixing in a memory of Janys. No comparison, he reported in spite of himself.

He looked at Gary and caught something in his eyes he didn't understand. He *was* staring intently.

"Look it," she cut in, "If you're not buying, I'm moving on. Someone can be watching. I can't speak long. I've got work to do!"

She turned and walked toward the doorway with the other woman. Andy watched Gary's eyes follow. "Well, that was sure a great evangelistic foray," Andy said.

"You never know, Andy. She could have been ripe for the picking. I figured it was worth a try. I was watching while you talked. She was paying attention. Maybe you planted a seed."

Andy snorted. "She's interested in planting seeds all right, but not with Gospel words." He looked over at the doorway. The same smile was pasted on the same face at the door, like a kids' plastic sticker. He remembered the expression "happy hooker" and wondered at the oxymoron. *Happy hooker*. He thought of Canadian writer Pierre Berton, who lost his virginity at the hands of an assembly line whore who kept crying, "Next!" Gross! Andy couldn't imagine anything more opposite to being human. Is that all men were destined to do, pass through life looking for places in which to insert themselves? Andy felt unnerved, not by the failure of their evangelistic venture but by the sheer ugliness of life that would have people plying the oldest trade known to humanity. We're a sick bunch, he concluded. Then he forgot about it. He couldn't read Gary, and soon afterwards picked right up again on Francis Schaeffer and the Garden of Eden.

Apart from Andy and Peter and Jean, no one on the team had written a prayer letter from West Berlin. So at the next staff meeting in mid-May, Andy offered to read his out loud. Fiona asked why. A tad perturbed, Andy said maybe it could serve as incentive, even a model, for others. There was an awkward silence. It was not the obvious good thing Andy had expected. He suddenly felt angry.

"What's the matter with everyone?" He asked, looking around. "It's a simple suggestion. I was only going to read a part of it, anyway. I thought we were a team, that we would share things we'd written or read. The early Christians 'held everything in common,' it says in the book of Acts. I sometimes wonder about us!"

Fiona replied evenly. "I think it's too long a meeting anyway, from the looks of Peter's agenda—and you get a lot of air time already, Andy…"

Andy quietly put his letter away and said little throughout the rest of the meeting. Had he been honest, he'd have acknowledged its consequent greater brevity.

There were times he knew he could have added a piece of information, an observation, a suggestion, but he held back, smugly for some reason, satisfied that the meeting's obvious (to Andy) lack of sparkle was causally linked to his sullenness. These emotions felt new, unwelcome. What was happening to him? Them? Fiona? And him?

39

Much of May was spent preparing for their first *Einsatz* with B. B. at *Lichterfelde* on May 19-20. Thankfully, Joanne could advise them on some contemporary German songs to use. Gary was an excellent guitar player with an appealing singing voice. Sharon also had a beautiful voice and was quite a vivacious presence. Everyone else on the team could at least carry a tune, and thus added significant volume and no lack of enthusiasm. They sang some songs together, including a few secular ones by *Peter, Paul and Mary.* As expected, these songs went over really well. Peter gave a brief testimony. Andy talked a little about what they were doing in Germany. Joanne read a Bible passage.

The elders did not frown obviously on a woman speaking at an *Evangelisation*, for it was B. B. who introduced the team initially. *Lichterfelde*, Andy noted, seemed at a stage where it readily enough accorded B. B. leadership in the whole area of evangelism. Clearly she was at least doing something! Andy remembered D. L. Moody's quip to a detractor he had heard from Paul Little: "Well, sir, I like better the way I am doing *something* than the way you are doing *nothing*!" She also obviously had a certain way with young people, surprising considering her outward school marm, stiff-upper-lip appearance. The *Lichterfelde* youth enthusiastically joined in with the North Americans in the evening's events, as they did in Saturday's literature distribution.

It was only several months later that the team learned that B. B. had problems previously at one of the other assemblies and had moved on to *Lichterfelde* at about the time of G. E.'s visit to her. They began to wonder how long she would last at *Lichterfelde*.

Horst Paetkau, the preacher, did not lack in enthusiasm though his message failed to be very relevant. He was about Andy's age and had spent two years at *Wiedenest*, an assembly-based Bible school in southern Germany.

Horst expressed excitement about the team's presence in Berlin, indicating high expectations about how God would use "Beatrice's team." The designation was not lost on anyone, even in German.

Joanne was very positive about the team's participation. "I only noticed a few mistakes, Peter and Andy," she said, meaning it as a compliment but not specifying further. "And the rest of you looked like seasoned performers! Obviously you knew your songs well. And it really went over."

They returned *en masse* that Sunday morning to *Lichterfelde* for church services. Andy was taken by the surprising beauty of the four-part harmony sung with each hymn. No one led or gave instructions. No organ or other musical instrument accompanied them. This proved to be distinctive only to that assembly, and it was delightful.

A medical doctor preached that morning. He was Horst's father. After the service, they spent a little more time with the church youth. Horst's sister, Sieglinde, stood out as an especially attractive person with a dazzling smile. "There you go, Andy," Sharon said on the subway back. "Get to know her, and your German can only markedly improve, if you listen as much as talk. Marry her, settle in as a teacher, and soon they'll think you were born here. Not a bad idea?"

Andy smiled, but inwardly he thought he didn't

need any other woman to catch his attention just then. Juggling two—at least in terms of his personal feelings—was quite enough.

Peter and Jean became regular attendees at the fellowship. It was definitely "older style," which fitted Peter's proclivities, if not Jean's. The team had decided to strategically fan out to all but one of the assemblies. *Wilmersdorf* was to be attended regularly by Gary and Sharon, Fiona and Jack would attend *Hohenstauffenstraße* assembly, and Andy and Janys would begin taking the subway, then bus, then short walk, to *Mariendorf*. The fifth smaller assembly received scant attention. It was tiny with no young people's group at all.

Despite the team's initiatives, there seemed to be no counterpoint initiative from the leadership in any of the churches. Jack raised the issue during a team meeting after the *Lichterfelde* success. B. B. was not in attendance. "I just don't get it!" Jack began. "Here we've come all this way to serve the churches, and it's as if they're saying, 'Yankee go home,' or something! Sorry, you Canadians. Seems they're saying, 'Canucks, go home,' too. I would've thought G. E. would have had far more set up for us here. You know how much he stresses getting your home assembly support, not striking out on your own. But over here, it's like we landed in alien territory even amongst the churches, not to mention all these German heathen!"

The discussion continued for some time. It was Peter who expressed concern about Beatrice. "From the first time I met her, in light of our misgivings, I felt she was hungry to have us serving her. There was a kind of eagerness about our presence here that left me a little uneasy, I'll confess. In our first week, she pressured us many times to choose apartments near hers. I kept saying that G. E. told us to find some near the *Ku'damm*. But she expressed impatience with G. E., saying, 'What does he know about West Berlin? He only visited here once, and that only overnight!'

"I think now that, if you women will pardon me saying so, B. B. is acting like a typical woman given a little bit of power. It goes to her head. No doubt that's why God put men in charge and gave women-folk a head covering in the churches to show it."

"And that's perhaps why the Church has been in such a mess ever since?" Janys shot back, her face reddening.

Andy remembered his mom had once said to him conspiratorially, "Andy, we know how to get our men-folk to do our bidding." As proof, the women got their way with a new convection oven installed that very fall. He thought of how powerful an influence his mom was on his dad.

Joanne offered to raise the concern with G. E. upon her return to America.

"But do you think he will really listen?" Janys asked. It was the stopper. G. E. the visionary, the indefatigable founder of GO, noted evangelist and leader. But G. E. the listener?

"I have my doubts," Andy commented.

"Why?" Came Peter's pointed query.

"Because he doesn't even listen to his own son," Andy returned, in spite of himself. Then he explained a little of his discussions with Dan to illustrate the point. He was careful not to betray any trust, he hoped.

Joanne excused herself suddenly, saying she'd promised to go to the phone booth to call Hans sharp at 10:00 a.m. She returned in a few minutes, beaming. "Hans is coming this weekend! He got a three-day pass and is borrowing his dad's car to drive out on Friday. I'm so excited!"

Andy had tried several times to engage Joanne in conversation. She was intelligent, had overlapping interest in literature, and yet was quieter than Janys with her opinions. On a few occasions, she had made comments like, "You should hear Hans on that." Or, "I think Hans and I would have a fairly different take." But she would never elaborate. Was it a latent brethren reserve that kept women silent and inhibited no matter how bright or capable? Andy thought about Jesus' offer of abundant life and wondered again about how, in brethren circles at least, that "abundance" had to be held in constantly. Then he thought of himself as much the same, only less blatant. Muted Andy. Mutant Andy? The thought was novel that faith might distort growth rather than nurture it. Faith as a disease rather than the "balm of Gilead." He thought of how Jesus treated women. Like people.

His mind was on a roll. Why did church invariably suppress abundance rather than liberate it to limitless heights? What was it about church that made it a major inhibitor to life? Was this what Christ intended for his followers, to constantly repress themselves at every turn, not least sexually? What if he had turned the other way toward Janys the night of the Big Howl? What if his hands had reached out to, he might have hoped, a yielding response? He pushed the image down, wary, fearful of when it might pop up next. Yet Jesus had said, "Fear not!" The truth would set one free.

"I think we need to stop right now and pray," Peter brought Andy's reverie to a grateful conclusion. "The Lord promised that where two or three ask anything in his name, he will supply it."

Their prayers were pointed and in Jesus' name, and yet Andy felt that nagging sense of *Godot* about the good of such an exercise. He thought again of the

Big Howl, in spite of his suppression. Why should God move heaven and earth for them, he wondered? Why did his piety keep leaking?

The team began to develop a bit of a siege mentality after that. There grew a sense that they were an island of would-be evangelists plunked down amidst the greater sea of unwelcoming West Berliners, including the churches. Not unlike "Little America" everywhere in the world, Andy ruminated. No physical walls shut off the team from their immediate environs, yet something "Berlin Wall-like" was emerging regardless. The team came to see itself blockaded, cordoned off from numerous meaningful lifeline connections. With no airlift. They had already undergone such separations from family, friends, and everything familiar. Who would have guessed that such feelings would arise from West Berlin itself so soon? Andy reflected back on the contrast between this reality and their euphoric days back at the Centre when the prospect of the grand missionary enterprise so fired his imagination.

One reaction to the sense of isolation was the new contacts made with the American Army base. There were about 5,000 servicemen posted there, a permanent fixture since World War Two's end. This relationship was helped along by the fact that Jack discovered a friend's uncle, a pilot, was at the base.

Few American servicemen ever learned much about German culture, let alone Germany. What was said of the English at the height of the British Raj was as true of the Americans in Europe: *You can tell an Englishman anywhere, but you can't tell him anything!* There was only one culture of interest or worth in the universe, right? *And they were it!* They were picked out consequently everywhere, even in civvies, on the streets. For that matter, so were the team members similarly pegged.

American soldiers began to drop by the team apartments. They were all Christians, of course, and were quite attracted to seeing single American women around rather than servicemen's wives. They were also lonely. Andy noticed the attention even Janys was getting. He acknowledged a contextual reassessment.

During the soldiers' third visit on Friday night, a soldier named Brian Barrington and Andy got into a discussion about the Vietnam War. Brian was affable and bright. (His service would end up paying his way through college, something his parents could not afford.) He'd been raised a Christian, and to him, godliness included unquestionably swearing allegiance to the flag and following the government's directives according to Romans 13.

Andy had been fairly oblivious of what was happening in Vietnam before arriving in Berlin. But on the third Saturday afternoon of his sojourn, an anti-war rally took place around the corner on the *Ku'damm.* Placards against Nixon, the Vietnam war, and the American presence in West Berlin were displayed everywhere.

"Why are you fighting the North Vietnamese?" Andy asked.

The answer was unadorned. "Because they are godless Communists." Brian went on to explain his understanding of the origins of the conflict and of America's increased involvement.

A new thought then occurred to Andy. "Brian, Jesus taught, 'Love your enemies.' The Communists are clearly your enemies. How can you love them and kill them at the same time?"

Brian was taken aback, apparent from his knitted brow. "Jesus really said, 'Love your enemies'?"

"It's right in Luke's gospel. Just a minute." Andy grabbed a concordance from the bookshelf and found the reference. "There, Luke 6:36."

Brian read silently for a few minutes. "I don't know about this," he began, "but certainly the Jews didn't love their enemies in the Old Testament."

Janys, who had been listening in, spoke up. "Maybe that's why it's *old* and this is *new*. Maybe one of Jesus' new things was precisely that. In fact," she took a Bible and flipped to a passage in Matthew, "Jesus even says in Matthew five, 'You have heard that it was said, "Love your neighbour and hate your enemy." But I tell you: Love your enemies and pray for those who persecute you.' There you have it: the old, and the new!

"I've heard my brother Ted on this. He points out an obvious point: Jesus taught that 'all the Law and the Prophets'—that is, the entire Old Testament—hang on two commandments: love of God and love of neighbour, enemy included. Ted says that whatever else, Jesus leaves no room for violence by Christians."

Brian shifted in his chair. "That sounds *communist* to me. I mean, surely Jesus must mean some kind of exception. Just look at all the enemies God's people slaughtered in the Old Testament. Or think of all the wars Christians have fought in since Christ. Jesus just couldn't have meant what he said..." As he said it, his face looked more troubled. "At least…" He reached out for Janys's Bible.

"Wait a minute, Brian," Andy said. "The Communists killed millions in Russia before the War. That hardly sounds like what Janys is saying."

Janys continued, Andy surprised at her boldness. "My brother, who reads a lot about these things, tells me that the Americans have been using napalm against the Viet Cong. You know what napalm does? It burns flesh right through to the bone. Whole villages get napalmed, I've heard. Of course, they firebombed hundreds of cities in Germany and Japan, too, killing hundreds of thousands of innocent civilians.

"I've also heard about the 'bombies' dropped by the millions in Vietnam—and some say secretly in Cambodia and Laos, too. They dig under the soil so that when a person steps on one or hits it with a hoe even years or decades later, their leg gets blown off— if they're lucky. Of course, if it's a child, he or she invariably dies.

"The victims are indiscriminate. They may be the Viet Cong, but just as likely they are non-combatant men, women, and children. I've heard that over eighty percent of all modern aerial warfare casualties are non-combatants. And there will probably be thousands more years after the war is over. That's called, 'loving your enemies?'"

Brian squirmed. One of the other servicemen, Gerald Johnson, had overheard and waded in. "Look, the Communists are godless and deserve to die, as do their children. They're like the Amalekites in First Samuel, where even the babies deserved death. If they didn't, our President wouldn't be telling us to fight them. We've got to make the world safe for democracy."

"Or safe for American business?" Janys asked, her eyes on fire. "Who appointed you the world's policemen? God?"

"In a way, yes," Gerald responded, unperturbed by her obvious anger. "We're the richest, most powerful nation on the face of the earth, probably that ever was. God has blessed America. There are more Christians per capita in America than in any other country.

'Righteousness exalteth a nation,' and many believe that is why America is so great.

"President Nixon is an honourable man, some, like Billy Graham, who is a personal friend, compare him to Abraham Lincoln. Others believe he's a Christian, as many of our presidents have been. President Truman was a Sunday school teacher, and he authorized the first A-bomb dropped over Hiroshima, and the second in Nagasaki, saying the atomic bomb was the greatest thing in history. If killing Japs or Communists was wrong, our Christian leaders in America would have told us so."

"Over 120,000 innocent civilians were incinerated on President Truman's orders," Janys said quietly. "And some Christian leaders *are* telling you that is wrong, that this war—all war—is wrong! Jesus did, too. Did you ever hear of Reverend Martin Luther King, Junior, who said your country was 'the greatest purveyor of violence on the planet'?"

"Yeah, but they're all Communists and Liberals themselves!"

Andy was frankly perplexed. His dad had fought in the Second World War but his uncle had not. He had known that but had never talked to either about their differences. He had just assumed that killing civilians was a necessary, dirty part of any war effort. Would he feel that way if some of the victims were his own family? Susan? His dad? His mom? With a start, he thought that some of Lorraine's family must have been slaughtered if they were from Tokyo.

Love your enemies; kill their civilians. The juxtaposition was stark. Maybe there was a kind of tit for tat formula. So many in retaliation for so many. Or a percentage of for a percentage of. The numbers would come out differently depending upon population density. More certainly allowed to be slaughtered in Tokyo than, say, in Kitchener. It didn't work.

The cold calculus offended everything Andy knew, not least of Jesus. *Whom would Jesus kill or bomb?* He wondered. The answer was patent the moment the question posed itself. Yet why had Christians killed nonetheless throughout the centuries in reckless disregard of Jesus? This was not comfortable. His mind needed a straightjacket. Then he realized that's precisely what the Church had been all these years—a straightjacket! This was shocking. He refused to go there and shut the production down.

"I've been reading through the book of Second Corinthians in my devotionals," Andy said. "The other day, I came across this passage in chapter ten, verse three: 'For though we live in the world, we do not wage war as the world does. The weapons we fight with are not the weapons of the world.' What do you suppose Paul means in this passage? You guys believe in the verbal inspiration and perspicuity of Scripture, don't you?"

Everyone laughed, including Brian. Andy explained that "perspicuity" meant that Scripture interpreted itself. He continued, "Is there some kind of meaning other than the obvious one here? And don't forget the Ephesians six passage that talks about a totally different armour for Christians from what you guys are trained to use."

Brian looked at his watch. Gerald looked at Brian looking at his watch. The third serviceman, Randy, looked up, saying, "We have to get going. But it's obvious whatever else those verses are saying; we have a God-given right to kill the Communists! All Christians all through church history have believed it's right to kill their enemies. If people didn't do that, just imagine what kind of world it would be. We'd fall hopelessly into violent anarchy."

"And what kind of world is it now—in your ghettos and cities, and many international spots of American influence, including Vietnam?," Janys asked, again very quietly. "And if *everyone* stopped killing enemies, wouldn't killing just… Stop?" Andy looked over at Fiona. She remained quiet, her face inscrutable.

Randy opened his mouth to respond just as the dining room clock chimed out the hour: 10:00. It broke the spell, and he and his companions quickly went home. As it turned out, that was the last time American servicemen visited the team.

40

Hans arrived, as planned, the following Friday in time for supper. Together with Sharon, Joanne prepared a repeat of the meal she had set for Andy's parents' visit, *Rouladen*, *Rotkohl*, and *Schwarzwälderkirschtorte*. Such a spread was now right up there with roast beef for Andy.

After supper, Joanne suggested an evening of games. She said Hans' family never played games, that sitting around their table was like being at a funeral wake, so serious were they all in discussing "issues." Hans' dad was also a physician, his mom a college professor.

Hans was completing his practicum as a doctor and would begin working in a hospital in mid-October. He and Joanne were also to be married at the end of September. They would spend their *Flitterwochen* in northern Ontario. Janys and Andy had promised to give them some good tips for the trip.

At the end of the meal, the conversation turned to biblical infallibility. Andy was remonstrating about the difficulty of getting Germans even to understand what was at stake. Hans' response was mild enough: "When I arrived at Wheaton, I wasn't even sure what the term meant. It's not anywhere in the Bible, of course."

"Neither is the word 'Trinity,'" Andy replied quickly.

Hans continued undaunted. "But as I discovered, it has a long and revered history in North American churches, particularly because of an interesting experience of a major 'fundamentalist-modernist' controversy earlier this century."

Andy was very sketchy on recent—for that matter, most—church history, so he remained silent.

"How I have come to understand it from my studies in the States, it seeks to affirm that the Bible, in its original manuscripts, is equally accurate in all areas it touches upon: theology, science, history, anthropology, etc.

"The first question that arises, of course, is about manuscripts. There are no originals in *existenz*, not even fragments."

Occasionally Hans' pronunciation took on a German colouring—not unsurprisingly. However, his vocabulary was even better than his usually excellent pronunciation. Andy felt jealous. He realized his eyebrows were knitted in intense concentration and tried to relax them.

"This doctrine always claims infallibility to be true in 'the original manuscripts.' But if 'the original manuscripts' have long since been lost to history, it's rather empty to claim anything about something likely forever disappeared. Like the Angel Moroni's magic glasses and manuscript from which the Mormons got their *Book of Mormon*.

"Second, to say something is true in history is at best only talking probabilities. You weigh many conflicting theories and opt for what seems most probable. Now, to say, for example, that the creation story is 'true history' raises problems immediately. Francis Schaeffer claims you could hear a clock ticking in the Genesis story of Adam and Eve. But the story really takes place in the era of pre-history. It was only written down centuries after the purported events, and only after a long process of oral transmission. So there are no comparative records to glean from—except other entirely fanciful accounts of the origins of creation found in most cultures throughout the world. So to say the creation story is true is really to say, 'I believe, for this and that theological reason, it is true, though no scientific/historical research can ever touch the issue, and fair enough.'"

"That sounds very neo-orthodox to me, Hans," Andy chimed in.

"What do you mean by that term, Andy?"

"Francis Schaeffer says neo-orthodox theologians like Karl Barth fall into the Hegelian synthesis by seeking to have the best of both worlds: a religiously true Bible in the area of *Geschichte*, salvation history, but a higher critical view of the Bible in the area of *Historie*, what really happened, which allows for the Bible to have mistakes. That is really schizophrenic thinking, however, and the dilemma of modern man is that the Bible always stands for the *antithesis*: there is no 'leap-of-faith' truth in the religious realm that is not true in the phenomenological world.

"But," and he pushed his point hard, "there has never been one proven error in the Bible. Many apparent discrepancies have been dealt with through further diligent research, and those which have not been will no doubt be explained in time. That is why infallibility is so meaningful to me. As I mentioned already, the word 'Trinity' is not in the Bible either. But the New Testament reflects the concept everywhere. Likewise, whenever the New Testament touches down on Scripture, it implies the concept of infallibility.

"Perhaps the only uniqueness of finding it mainly in North America is that is where the doctrine has been especially developed in response to certain historical circumstances. Just as, so I understand, the two-nature aspect of Christ at Chalcedon was developed in response to certain specific circumstances. That makes it no less biblically valid."

Andy felt fairly satisfied with his response to Hans. He thought he had done with Schaeffer's material what Bill Gothard encouraged people to do with his *Basic Youth Conflict Seminars*: so imbibe the teaching that it becomes one's own. What had been purely theoretical to Andy back in North America had been experienced in Germany. Andy had begun to suspect that behind every thinking German Christian was a Hegelian mindset. He sensed a need to challenge this wherever he met it. He even felt compelled to elicit it, where it perhaps lurked just beneath the surface.

Hans, however, did not look all that impressed. The others listened to the conversation politely but rather blankly, too. Andy wondered why, not once thinking how esoteric it all sounded to "non-intellectual" ears. There was some uncomfortable movement at the table. Was Joanne about to say something?

"Have you ever read Karl Barth?" Hans asked Andy. Andy had to admit he had not. "Do you know that Dr. Barth has *written* far more theology in his lifetime than most Christians *read* in a lifetime? That he is considered the greatest theologian since Thomas Aquinas, a kind of theological Mount Everest?"

It was Andy's turn to be unimpressed. So what if it is all error? Why scale a manmade mountain like the one at Disneyland? Why read manmade theology? Ken Kincaide's point. Hans did not press for a response.

The discussion with Hans would have ended then had not Gary, who was not put off by the rarefied tenor of the conversation, asked Hans to state his own view of Scripture. Andy thought Joanne was about to interject again. She was keen on a games night, he knew. He looked at her. Was there a slightly deflated countenance?

"Like all youth in Germany who reached the draft age, I knew I would have to do service soon in the army," Hans said, oblivious to Joanne's discomfort. "I had been a fairly nominal Lutheran until then. But someone had given me a small book entitled *Militia Christi* by Adolf von Harnack, a German theologian. I became intrigued by his discovery that early Christians opposed war and that the war imagery of the New Testament had to do with spiritual, not earthly, matters.

"This New Testament understanding is summed up in Paul's words in Second Corinthians chapter ten, verses three and following. Please hand me that Bible. 'For though we walk in the flesh, we do not war after the flesh. For the weapons of our warfare are not carnal, but mighty through God to the pulling down of strong holds.' I think that sounds too old-fashioned. Any modern translation around?"

Peter went to his room and returned with J.B. Phillips' paraphrase. Andy was amazed to hear the Scripture he had just discussed with the Americans.

"Here: 'The truth is that, although of course we lead normal human lives, the battle we are fighting is on the spiritual level. The very weapons we use *are not those of human warfare* but powerful in God's warfare for the destruction of the enemy's strongholds.' This is why Ephesians 6:12 and following says our 'whole armour' is for fighting spiritual battles.

"And by the way, early Christians understood Ephesians six to be *the* passage concerned with the State, not Romans thirteen where exactly the same Greek for 'authorities' appears. From Ephesians six, it is clear that the authorities are part of the spiritual enemies of Christ and his church and not a benign, or, since Constantine, benevolent State that

Christians should obey uncritically and benefit from its wielding the sword. This view of the benevolent State is especially demonstrated by Reinhold Niebuhr, a great twentieth century American political ethicist and advisor to presidents, since democracy for him is nearly Kingdom Come. Interesting that Niebuhr, who *genuinely* did not take Scripture normatively and was truly 'neo-orthodox,' should articulate by far the dominant North American *Evangelical* position on such a crucial matter as the State. Ironically, and I argue in line with John Howard Yoder, this position is profoundly unbiblical."

Andy felt the point was somewhat arcane. "Do you mean," he asked, "that God did not ordain the State, let's say especially one with Western-style democracy like the United States and Canada, as a 'good' by virtue of its being a constituted State?"

"Exactly," Hans said. "And incidentally, the violence of the State, claimed as divine right and mandate in the 'sword' language of verse four, is only extended—by interpreters ever since Saint Augustine—to the nation state but never to revolutionaries or other kinds of 'Robin Hood-style' do-gooders, which are likewise 'constituted authorities.' The text never mentions 'state' as the only kind of legitimate authority. Revolutionaries are self-appointed, but such is the history of all royalty—and through invariable vanquishing violence.

Often, as in South America, revolutionaries' causes may be vastly more righteous than the State they are subverting or overthrowing. For that matter, the United States was born of a revolution deposing Britain's power in the New World—for very questionable 'righteous' reasons. For all intents, the War of Independence was a mutiny against the legitimate (according to most interpretations of Romans thirteen) prerogatives of the then God-ordained 'authority' in North America, the British Crown. George Washington, John Adams, and their supporters were, by Evangelicals' account of Romans thirteen, 'pirates' deserving the very sword they used to overthrow British rule!

"Ironically again, most American Evangelicals indulge in hagiography about the great Christian 'founding fathers' of America. Most were deists, in fact. And George Washington, amongst others, was indeed 'father' of the nation in ways generally disapproved of by Evangelicals today."

Andy was shocked by these assertions. He fully expected an outburst from Fiona, maybe even from Jack or the Collins', but it never came. Joanne, however, finally butted in. "I was really hoping we could play some games tonight. Anyone else *game?*" All but Andy, Janys, Gary, and Hans put up hands.

Gary piped up, "I really want to hear Hans out some more. But if some of you want to clear the table at least, that will get us started."

Peter and Jean volunteered immediately. Joanne might have, Andy wondered, but stayed perhaps to watch over what Hans would say next. Andy looked at his watch. It was only a little after 7:00. What was the big rush?

"Continue, Hans," Gary said. "Though I have some real questions about your interpretation of American founding history. And I have one clarification question: What is a deist?"

"At the time of the founding of the United States," Hans explained, "many of the intellectual elite imbued with the Enlightenment spirit of scepticism toward the truth claims of Christianity turned to deism as a kind of way station en route to atheism or secularism.

Deism purports a Clockmaker for the universe; one who wound it all up 'in the beginning' then let it all slowly unwind without interfering. No Revelation. No Incarnation. No Resurrection. God as Ultimate Non-Interventionist."

Peter and Jean finished clearing the table. Would they come back to hear more? Andy heard water running in the kitchen. Not likely.

Hans continued by saying he went through a re-conversion, ended up joining the SMD, then applied for alternative military service. He was accepted at Wheaton College. While there, the major project to which he devoted himself was a research essay on the Early Church period and its applicability to the Church today.

"Through authors such as Jean-Michel Hornus, C .J. Cadoux, Jean Lasserre, and others—not to mention the church Fathers themselves—I concluded that the early church was mainly pacifist.

"There was, further, a new theological study about to be published by Eerdmans called *The Politics of Jesus*, which developed this theme extensively from Luke's Gospel. A Mennonite theologian, John Howard Yoder, wrote it. I also read other writings by him, including one on the State. He had studied under Karl Barth, and, like Barth, was a committed Biblicist.

"It seems that the early church underwent a 'Great Reversal' at the time of Emperor Constantine more far-reaching, arguably, than the negative effects of the Enlightenment and modernity. The so-called 'Great Reversal' was a triumph of an alien non-Christian ethical ideology.

"You want to know why the Muslim world cannot see a *loving* Jesus to this day? Because they see the sword of the Crusaders ever in Jesus' hand. They only hear the words of Constantine's vision: *In hoc signo vinces,* 'In this sign you will conquer.' The sign of the *labarum*—for all intents, the sword. They know that they were direct targets of that vision. Incidentally, how Billy Graham can continue to use the term "crusade" for his rallies astounds me. There could not be a more offensive term imaginable for the Muslim. It totally drives them away from Christ. Is that what he, what America, wants? To declare war on Islam? One wonders that when considering the near universal American Christian support for Israel…"

Andy looked over at Fiona. Her face was clouded. Sharon's nose was wrinkled in concentration. Jack appeared to be taking it all in. Janys was inscrutable. Did Hans remind her of her brother? Gary seemed right on the edge of more questions. And Andy? Frankly, he was confused. He suspected Hans would have facts and figures to support his interpretations. Why then were they so at variance with American Evangelicals? There must be underlying ideology at work. Could one look at anything without that sieve? Lessing's "necessary truths of reason" given the prior ideological set of coloured glasses. Put on a different pair, and Kant's "categorical imperatives" were suddenly less of the essence, perhaps even to the contrary.

Hans was on a roll. "You want to know why I believe Europe secularized so quickly and is so incredibly resistant to the Gospel today? It's not all that unlike the Muslims. You North Americans are so hung up about the Enlightenment and its disparagement of the foolishness of the Gospel. But you fail to understand that Western Europe simply became sick of the endless and horrendous bloodshed blessed or instigated by the Church. The Crusades, the Inquisition, the pogroms against Jews, the holy wars, the witch hunts, the burning of thousands of heretics by the

Catholics, the drowning of thousands of Anabaptists by Protestants, the incredibly retributive penal justice system modelled after church canon law, universal support of the death penalty, the church's blessing both sides of every war in Europe since Constantine, and on and on *ad infinitum.*

"If I just had majority church history to go on, I'd be a raving atheist, too. There has been arguably *no more bloody institution in Western history than the Church since the fourth century!* If this is what Paul meant by 'Christ, the power of God,' then 'the revolt of atheism is pure religion by contrast.' (I heard an American theologian named Walter Wink say that once at Wheaton.)

"Ironically, however, that very revolt is instigated in the first place by biblical revelation. Jesus first elicited the Western atheistic philosophical tradition with his cry from the cross, 'My God, my God, why hast thou forsaken me?' Jürgen Moltmann observes that this is either the end of all religion, and, therefore, the atheists and anarchists are right, or the beginning of a whole new way of understanding 'the executed God.'

"There's a line from a German poem that goes, '*Die Gerechtigkeit der Erde O Herr hat Dich getötet!*' 'The moral righteousness of the Earth, O Lord, has killed You!' The blood spilled on the ground in the name of Christ for nearly two thousand years is by far the strongest counter-evangelistic argument I know. Why should any morally sensitive person want to align with such an insatiably blood-drenched institution? It would be like evangelizing for membership in the Mafia!

"And the violence continues. To this day, missionaries either follow the gunboats as Hudson

Taylor did while evangelizing China or they benefit from the violence of the colonizing powers. One reason that missionaries in this century came to be hated in so much of the Third World was their complete identification with Empire—British or American. Hudson Taylor's 'spiritual secret' was in reality a 'military not-so-strictly-kept secret.' Ivan Illich, a Catholic intellectual, claims 'the corruption of the best is the worst,' that Western civilization can be entirely summarized as the corruption, amongst other things, of the best, *the central peacemaking message of the Gospel*, to the worst, universally sanctioned Western State violence.

"Contrary to all that, if Christ is the foolishness of God in response to the Enlightenment but really God's ultimate wisdom, he is likewise the *weakness of God* in answer to violence and war. But really his is the way of self-giving, non-violent sacrificial love, which is truly God's revolutionary power and ultimate victory over evil. Jesus the (Other) Way, right? A lot of what I'm saying now comes from my paper, which gets quite technical, sometimes, I apologize."

The noise of dishes and pots and pans clanging came from the kitchen. There was also muted conversation.

"How can you appraise the Enlightenment so positively, calling it God-ordained?" Andy asked.

"Yes," Gary added. "I learned at Bible school that the Enlightenment was the real enemy of Christianity today. Yet you paint it as almost from God."

Hans nodded. "The Enlightenment was an understandable reactionary celebration of the brilliance and goodness of man over against a church perceived to exist to glorify violence through its belief in 'god' and a doctrine of 'original sin' that leads directly to a hell of eternal conscious torment and the ultimate degradation of man. 'Wretched worm' theology is handmaiden to a hell of eternal conscious torment. How does the King James go? 'Where their worm dieth not, and the fire is not quenched.'

"The reason the Enlightenment took such root in the first place was the valid revulsion toward the 'god' of the Church, a god who blessed war, bloodshed, and everlasting punishment in Jesus' name on a massive scale. Did you ever read Voltaire's *Candide*?"

"I did—in French," Andy replied.

"Hans, this all sounds not just *neo-orthodox*," Gary snapped, "even *heterodox*! How do you justify all this biblically?"

Hans paused in thought for some time. "Perhaps hear me out a little more and see whether you still think that. I'll summarize a little more of my paper, which, by the way, won the theological prize at Wheaton College last year."

Andy was impressed. Joanne excused herself from the table, saying she'd help Peter and Jean. Couldn't she handle it anymore? Peter had come out at one point to turn on the lights. The entire apartment building was quiet. Not even street sounds invaded.

"In my paper, I suggested that North Americans positively *worship* at an alternative god's shrine, which is Mars, God of Violence. Ironically, while you defeated the Nazis in World War Two, you Americans have become increasingly more like them ever since! 'In God we trust,' I wrote, is a lie. 'In Violence—supremely bombs, bullets, and missiles—We Trust' is the real truth. Bombs built by taking bread from the mouths of the poor. That's what President Eisenhower once claimed. Most Christians worship this god every bit as much as secular people.

"In Germany, there was only a small confessing church that refused to bow the knee to Hitler while the majority of Germany's Christians totally supported the entire Nazi enterprise. Karl Barth, incidentally, was primary author of the *Barmen Declaration* that denounced Hitler. He was forced out of the university he taught at in Germany to Basel, Switzerland. He was one of the few theologians in Germany to oppose Hitler. Another was, of course, Dietrich Bonhoeffer.

"Personally, I think it is somewhat similar in America today. Few of those who refuse to bow the knee to America's devotion to violence and the military are in the Evangelical churches. They are Quakers, Catholics, Mennonites, and others. Not Evangelicals. Not Billy Graham. Not Leighton Ford. Not Bill Bright. And *not* Francis Schaeffer, Andy! Not the rank and file in the pews, either. Ever heard of Dorothy Day? William Stringfellow? Jim Wallis? They all draw blanks, don't they?

"You know the famous statement by Pastor Martin Niemoeller after the War? Probably not. Another name Evangelicals have never heard of. He spent seven years in Dachau Concentration Camp. He said, 'In Germany, the Nazis first came for the Communists, and I didn't speak up because I wasn't a Communist. Then they came for the Jews, and I didn't speak up because I wasn't a Jew. Then they came for the trade unionists, and I didn't speak up because I wasn't a trade unionist. Then they came for the Catholics, but I didn't speak up because I was a Protestant. Then they came for me, and by that time there was no one left to speak for me.'"

Hans paused, looking at each person around the table. Were they getting it? Andy imagined Jesus pausing the same way while teaching his disciples, who were notoriously slow on the uptake.

Andy found this very troubling. He had gone over to Germany convinced of the need to show German Christians their mistaken allegiance to Enlightenment modernist theology. Now, somehow the very Bible he most wanted to defend was being turned against him. This was not right.

"But divine violence is the stuff of the Old Testament," he responded finally. "It's also central to the atonement, God's demand for penal substitution and satisfaction. And the book of Revelation is all about the Lamb who conquers all foes and violently, rules with a rod of iron, and tosses his enemies into the Lake of Fire."

"Andy," Hans came back, "you might read New Testament theologian C. F. D. Moule's article entitled 'Punishment and Retribution: An Attempt to Delimit Their Scope in New Testament Thought.' It is a direct challenge to the violent theories of the atonement. He argues that God never intended the dire consequences that ensue upon sin punitively, retributively. I've also heard American theologian Donald Bloesch argue that the traditional doctrine of hell as eternal conscious torment is not God's final word biblically. Love is. As to the Old Testament, you'd find Vernard Eller's romp through the Scriptures quite entertaining. He says the Hebrew people set out heading north by going south on the issue of violence. It's due out next year and is going to be called *King Jesus' Manual of Arms for the 'Armless': War and Peace from Genesis to Revelation*. Just the thing for all the new Jesus People."

Andy was mystified at how readily all of this was rolling off Hans' tongue. He felt at a loss. He'd never had time to do that kind of study.

"You have a CIA that engages in the same amount of deception, assassination, destabilization, torture,

CHRYSALIS CRUCIBLE

war, and blatantly immoral activities of every kind, just like their counterparts, the KGB," Hans proceeded. "And you have CIA directors who, according to some stories, would make inhabitants of Sodom and Gomorrah blush, their personal lives are so immoral. You are also stockpiling nuclear weapons that are already responsible for incalculable numbers of deaths the world over. The environmental damage to the good Creation by military build-up in which America is the massive front-runner is overwhelming. You are the only country to have actually dropped atomic bombs, not once, but *twice—and* on defenceless civilians, *and* when Japanese surrender was imminent. They claim it was to protect up to a million GI's lives in a potentially protracted land invasion. Just as likely, it was to say to Moscow: 'Watch out! We have the Biggest Guns!' It was doubtless the first salvo of the Cold War. And besides, these were innocent civilians! Do we now justify as well the Aztecs for their human sacrifices of innocents?

"But, 'If it's good for American security, it's good for Evangelicals' is the seeming Evangelical norm. 'America the Beautiful,' right? Just like Israel the Virtuous. In both cases, they can do no wrong, for they are God's Chosen People. Evangelicals throughout America subscribe to such thinking. I've heard the sermons on July Fourth Sunday. I've listened to innumerable prophetic teachings about modern Israel. Hal Lindsay's *The Late Great Planet Earth* is, as you know, an American best seller. With all due respect, *what a piece of garbage!* Eventually, it will be discredited in favour of endlessly shifting theories about contemporary application to world events and figures, as have all others for the last 100 years. But you can bet there will be an endless crop of these, ever best-sellers, since they not only *work* to get people saved, even closer to the American Evangelical and secular dream, *they sell!*"

Andy's mind jumped to an image of Jesus; whip in hand, clearing out moneychangers in the Temple.

Hans continued. "What Evangelical has raised any questions about the CIA—whose top boss is ultimately the President? If the buck for a kind of wickedness—on a level though perhaps not yet the scale of the worst the Nazis ever did—stops with the President of the United States, amongst the main 'money lenders' and advisers to that President are Evangelicals across the nation. They elevate Nation and President to the status of Deity. 'God and Flag,' right? Not 'Jesus and Resurrection,' as Paul preached on Mars Hill so that to some they sounded like two new gods for the Pantheon. Rather, 'God and Flag,' which are American ultimate idols. Evangelicals like Billy Graham have repeatedly been in bed with the President. Evangelicals compare Billy Graham to Daniel. The more valid comparison is to the Whore of Babylon or the Antichrist!"

Hans' nostrils flared. He was really worked up.

Fiona finally exploded. "Billy Graham is a great man of God who has told more people in this century about Jesus than any before him. How *dare* you question his faith?"

Her beauty was only enhanced by her fury. Andy could not miss the rapid rise and fall of her bosom. Norton's Notion came to mind, a midnight skating lesson. His chest heaved, too. He was an enormous fan of Dr. Graham, but he was willing to wait for Hans' response.

"Fiona, let me try to explain what I mean. First though, I'm sorry. I'm not against Billy Graham's faith. I fully affirm it, as far as it goes. I'm just questioning where his and other Evangelicals' faith has taken them—and has not taken them. They tell me every word of the Bible is infallible. But apparently they don't apply that infallibility doctrine to one of Jesus' main teachings, and certainly his premier ethical instruction: 'Love your neighbour and your enemies.'

"Billy Graham published his first book entitled *Peace With God*. But that, according to Jesus, is only half the Gospel. Dr. Graham has yet to publish the sequel, which should not even be such, rather it should have appeared simultaneously with his first publication, namely, *Peace With Man*. Peace with God is a religious sham if it is not demonstrated in peace with man. What were the Apostles' words? I'll quote them from the King James, 'If it be possible, as much as lieth in you, live peaceably with all men.' That's Paul. Then John: 'If a man say, I love God, and hateth his brother, he is a liar: for he that loveth not his brother whom he hath seen, how can he love God whom he hath not seen?' That means the enemy, too, Fiona! And that's why Jesus, when asked for the Greatest Commandment, gave two for the price of one. Peace with God, he said consistently, is a religious *crock* if not demonstrated through peace toward man. It is only half the Gospel and a heresy, baldly put. It is clear everywhere in the New Testament that the litmus test for love of God is love of neighbour. And the litmus test for love of neighbour is love of enemy. *To the extent we fail to love the enemy, precisely to that extent our love for God is phoney—whatever our religious protestations and observances otherwise.*"

Andy had seldom listened to a more lucid or erudite English speaker. And this by someone who had been raised in Germany! His mind was reeling, grasping at anything even remotely familiar.

"Hans, this all sounds so *works-righteousness!* You seem to be adding so much to the simple faith 'once delivered.' Wasn't that Luther's great discovery: *sola fide*—justification by faith alone?"

Hans didn't hesitate in his reply. "And what did James say in his *rechter strörn Epistel*—'right strawy epistle'—so designated by Luther? 'Show me your faith without deeds, and I will show you my faith by what I do,' and 'Faith without deeds is dead.' This just after he says, 'If you really keep the royal law found in Scripture, "Love your neighbour as yourself," you are doing right.' Incidentally, this is what St. Paul said summed up the entire Law and Jesus said was the second greatest command, just like the first to love God."

Andy felt hemmed in. How could Hans keep doing that?

"I'll add some more from my paper, if you wish, to bring the biblical case home. But let me say this: They can talk all they want about Christian revival at the American Army base. If all those good Christian soldiers do afterwards is slaughter the enemy in Vietnam, whatever they are worshipping in their newfound religious zeal is alien to the God of the Bible, an *Anti-Christ!*

"The point of Jesus' critique of the Pharisees in Matthew twenty-three was their spurious faith in God. To win people over to that kind of *half-Gospel* is to make them twice the sons of hell for the effort. That's very interesting arithmetic, and it should be very sobering for your enterprise in West Berlin—not to mention for Billy Graham and thousands of similar evangelists the world over.

"The truth is, Evangelicals in the main don't even see that in their Bibles. So just what are they reading anyway? Doesn't Billy always say, 'The Bible says'? Is he, are Evangelicals, after all, only *liberals in disguise*, picking and choosing from the biblical witness what they will believe? Only they never admit it. Vehemently claim the contrary even. That makes them liars as well as liberals!"

"How can Evangelicals be liberals?" Gary demanded. "That's a contradiction in terms."

Andy chimed in, simply befuddled, "And how can they be liars when they follow Jesus, who is the Truth?"

Hans sat back in his chair. "You tell me, you guys, you tell me."

When he received no response, Hans continued. "As you well know over here, Evangelical military chaplains abound in the armed forces. I know you've met some of them here, not to mention thousands of 'born-again' Christians engaged in blowing their enemies' brains out—and worse—in Vietnam right now. I'm sure there is horrendous human carnage in Vietnam that we know nothing about—yet. Just imagine what we will learn about the effects of Agent Orange alone. Birth defects, I've documented the predictions, will be massive. Even if the North Vietnamese all deserved to suffer from grotesque deformities, does that mean their children do, too?

"You North Americans likewise know so little about the countless atrocities committed by the Allies during both World Wars. For starters, in World War Two, the Allies saturation bombed civilian targets in at least forty-two German cities. Thousands of civilians died or sustained horrendous injuries. War is hell, pure and simple! If American authors and moviemakers afterwards do other than glorify the slaughter, as they mostly did of the first two wars, you can bet

Evangelicals will ban all those books and movies as works of the devil or Communists.

"So where is the Evangelical church right now? Nixon is a 'Christian,' of course. Billy Graham says so—even if he's too busy with affairs of state to attend church. And the Republicans are close to ushering in the Kingdom of God with their longstanding embrace of 'Manifest Destiny' doctrine.

"Meanwhile, Evangelicals go on endlessly about infallibility and the like while ignoring entirely the univocal teachings of Jesus and the rest of the New Testament about how to treat our enemies."

"Hans," Gary said, sounding deflated, "this is coming out of nowhere for me. For all of us, likely. You have to understand how hard it is to follow you, let alone agree! But maybe, to draw this to a close, you could say what your summation of Evangelicals is?"

Hans nodded. "I came back to Germany grateful for the good education I got at Wheaton but deeply troubled about where the Evangelical church was at in America. In my view, it has fallen culturally captive to a longstanding dominant American warmongering spirituality as surely as Jews were led captive to Babylon, or, more analogously, as the ancient Hebrews engaged repeatedly in the idolatrous activities of their neighbours. Tell me if it is not dangerously close to Jesus' idea that we should follow what the Pharisees believed—allegiance to God and Scripture—but *never do what they do*. Their claims about John 3:16 and God's loving the world are rendered pure sacrilege in the jungles or skies of Vietnam."

At that moment, Joanne emerged from the kitchen with a black forest cherry cake ablaze with candles, singing robustly, "Happy Birthday to You!" She had told no one except Jean, but it was Hans' twenty-sixth birthday that very day, May 26th, 1972. That brought an abrupt end to the conversation. The evening finished off in games and celebration. Andy wrote nothing in his diary that night. His mind was churning.

Dear Professor Norton:

Dan told me once that he could deal with the straight-on attacks against the faith fairly easily. Most had to do with starting-point questions, epistemology. It was the fifth-columnist stuff that got to him. Not least for him the question, if Christianity is so true, why is the Church so false?

Well, I have a variation. If Christianity is about Love Incarnate, why is its face to the world through the centuries so often one of Hate Manifest (American "Manifest Destiny," for instance)?

I thought I knew an easy answer. "They're not true Christians in those churches." Besides the sheer arrogance of that, it's a tad more troubling if I listen to Hans Beutler, whom I'm sure you know. Turns out that Christianity's vaunted love ethic—love of God, neighbour, and enemy—isn't quite that way in the Church after all. That contradiction is well disguised under the Church's doctrine of the State. The real bare-bones ethic goes something like this: "Love your enemies, do good to them. But the real *enemies, the ones who actually might kill you, whom you would like to kill, who might do you harm, whom you would love to throttle, does the Church have good news for you! Jesus allows you to turn them over to the State to do an end-run around everything He taught." You see, there's the "personal gospel," and there's the "State gospel." And everything holding you back from evil toward the enemy* personally *is handily available* through the State. *Just a tad more bureaucracy! "Murder" is the State's supreme prerogative, according to Evangelicals. Oh, the word is dressed up in more elegant semantics like "capital punishment" and "just war." But it is all killing. Murder in the first degree—in the worst degree.*

But for most centuries the Church has blessed the State to do its dirty work: premeditated slaughter and savagery, all in the name of "being subject unto the higher powers" (shades of Gothard). Personally, you must overcome evil with good. But as for the "Big Ticket" items, forget about even a whiff of good! FULL THROTTLE EVIL to every Goddamned enemy in sight—and their women and kids, abominations in the eyes of the Lord, like the Amalekites.

"Subject unto the higher powers"? It's really nothing of the sort. For centuries, the Church has directed those higher powers to destroy its enemies. According to its extra-biblical State "gospel," which is anything but Good News to the victims, when Christians may not personally do so, the State is fully authorized to dispatch its enemies through any and every bestial brutality and savagery it can dream up. This is the Great Evangelical End-Run.

For in "giving to Caesar what is Caesar's," it is self-evident that Jesus meant our enemies as sacrifices for the State, as surely as enemy captives were sacrificed to Moloch. And while we quote the text that says God loves the whole world, we really know Jesus only meant the ones we "give to God." Those we evangelize and welcome into our little religious Kingdom. The others we turn over to Caesar in this life and to hell in the hereafter. This is the "binding and loosing" Jesus meant. Hell in the eternal is State punishment and warfare in the temporal. The only difference is, God can sustain life, and consequently suffering ad infinitum, *the State cannot—too bad! Just think what tyrants like Stalin or Hitler (or Churchill or Truman) would have done throughout history with the awesome power of sustaining indefinitely the excruciating pain of, say, burning at the stake or napalming. Why, they'd all be wonderful Liberators like God, I guess. (Or is that the Devil Incarnate—and the difference?) Something's not right here (theo)logically. I'll get it in a minute I'm sure, or an eternity…*

So the Church through the centuries has played this little game called "God is Love," and under that banner has put out the welcoming mat of evangelism, declaring, "Whosoever will, may come." Under its breath, it has, however, whispered wickedly, "God damn our enemies! They are not *welcome, may they rather roast in hell!" And the earthly counterpart to that last consignment is the State. The State may "give 'em hell" as foretaste of what is mere warm-up for the Ultimate Bonfire.*

Well, Professor, this is crazy-making. This wickedly schizophrenic ethic. This two-faced speak-with-forked-tongue Church. This demonic deity Evangelicals worship. Yet that is precisely what you have believed at one time in your life, and for years. Worse, that is exactly what your Evangelical peers and most Christians have subscribed to throughout church history. Sick and obscene beyond imagining!

Professor, I need answers! Now! Hans stirred it all up. But the sediment must be long-since my doing—God's doing? He's shaken the jar, and my mind's going crazy with all the bits of information wildly flying that make Christian ethics utterly impossible if one believes in war; if one believes in hell. But if one does not? Am I an unbeliever or just another kind of believer? Does the Bible force me to a traditional doctrine of hell, of war, or have Christians bought these in spite of the Bible? Is God Ultimate Cosmic Tyrant, Terminal Hater, or in fact Love (as the only text I know of actually says)?

Write when you have the chance, please!

Anguished Andy

41

Hans left for home after lunch on Sunday. Andy was disappointed. He had really wanted to talk with him alone.

B. B. dropped by that same afternoon and asked for some time alone with Peter and Gary. It was a short meeting. At 2:30, the living room doors opened, and B. B. was on her way. Andy asked what she had seemed so urgent about.

"B. B. would like to not only attend our team meetings regularly but is also asking to get together with Gary and me each week. She's suggesting lunch at her place every Sunday. She thought it might be best for Gary and Sharon to start attending *Lichterfelde* regularly as well. Andy took all of this in, one skeptical eyebrow raised.

"She said she feels increasingly the momentous nature of our presence in West Berlin. The *Lichterfelde* youth just loved us, she claimed. She thinks we might just help start a whole missions revival throughout the assemblies. She would like to begin strategic planning for this in our get-togethers.

"What did you guys say?" Janys inquired. She had silently entered the room behind Andy.

Gary swallowed before responding. "I said that we definitely wanted to work cooperatively with her as much as we could, that we accepted there was a close relationship between her and the Centre that we wished to honour, that we could probably look at some kind of arrangement such as she requested."

Gary's eyes darted desperately between Andy and Janys as he looked for a hint of support. "I added that I think it is still important for us to attend

Hohenstauffenstraße like we originally planned. She was quite bothered at that." He shook his head. "Boy, is she ever *pushy!*"

"Why don't we pray about this for a while?" Janys suggested. With that, Gary's tension dissipated.

It was at the second to last team meeting before Joanne's departure that B. B. surfaced again in discussion. B. B. could not attend that meeting, though she had made it to all but two others. "I think B. B. means well," Peter said. "But I grant we have some work to do to get her more in tune with what we're about."

"What's the difference between what B. B. wants and what we're 'about,' as you say, Peter?" Janys asked from her perch in front of the partly open bay window. Sunlight streamed from behind her, silhouetting her face. Janys had taken to sitting there to read. Peter had obligingly found a reading lamp and some cushions.

"I think B. B. is closer to what Peter once intimated," Gary responded, "a bit of a mini-tyrant looking for subjects. Whether the problem is that she is a woman, I doubt. The worst tyrants down through history have been men. But she certainly seems to want us to serve her. There is something off-putting about B. B. I cannot yet put a finger on it. It's not just that she wants to boss us either. There is something more."

"I still think it is simply that women should not be in positions of leadership," Peter responded. "At first, I accepted it, because I thought she was 'under the umbrella of authority,' as we learned from Bill Gothard. I wonder about that now. I don't pick up anything like that from her home assembly in Scotland. Nor do I have a sense of it from the elders at *Lichterfelde*."

"She always mentions one of them," Sharon supplied.

"Herr Schmidt," Peter said, nodding. "Reinhold Schmidt. I think he definitely supports B. B. But I'm not so sure she's under his authority or if it is not the other way around. We met him at her place for supper before you all arrived. He's a widower with two grown kids living in West Germany."

"B. B. is certainly an anomaly," Andy finally spoke up. "I've watched her in action with the youth. There is no doubt that the 'serious-minded' respect her. Amongst the others, she goes over like a lead balloon, I think."

"Of course she does," said Sharon. "Think of how the German youth dress. Pretty fashionable stuff. B. B. is an old prune. I mean, she dresses dowdy, she looks sour, and she cracks a pretty stern whip."

"Man, Sharon," Andy quipped, "and what are her bad points?"

Sharon blushed. Jean jumped in. "Look at how much time we're already spending on her when she's not even here. I predict this will only increase." They all laughed uncomfortably then went on to other things.

Andy and Janys headed out that same evening bicycling. From a brief discussion at the end of lunch, Janys had expressed frustration. Andy suggested a ride to the *Tiergarten* where they could have a good talk.

Bismarckstraße, which became *Straße des 17ten Junis*, was straight as an arrow all the way to its eastern extremity—the Brandenburg Gate—where the Wall divided East and West. On the other side of the Wall, the street was called *Unter den Linden*, "Under the Linden Trees," the name for the full length of the street until the Second World War. Until then it had been the major street of Berlin.

Hitler had the *Siegessäule*—the victory column—

moved from the *Reichstag*, the former German parliament buildings, to a point along the street around which a traffic circle was built. It was Hitler's delight to watch his triumphant armies march through the Brandenburg Gate in panoramic command from his vantage point atop the *Siegessäule*.

The *Tiergarten* surrounded a significant length of *Straße des 17ten Junis*. It was a huge park of trees, spacious lawns, fountains, walkways, and benches. It had all been destroyed during the War, but soon afterwards countries from around the world began sending thousands of saplings to enable a reforestation program, which, twenty-five years later, had greatly restored the "animal park" to something of its former beauty.

Janys and Andy dismounted at a park bench under a large, sprawling elm tree. A vastly different situation, though with a similar setting, was conjured up as he thought of Lorraine and the surprise handful he had grasped at a faraway Toronto commons only a few months earlier. Then he thought of the Great Blizzard and the two hands-full he saw under silken moonlight. In spite of himself, the sensation of bounteous bare boob washed over him.

Janys's voice burst into his imaginings. "Andy, I don't think our team is really headed anywhere right now," she began. "I'm afraid that we've already begun to spin our wheels."

Andy remained silent. It was profoundly peaceful there. A squirrel zigzagged in search of food. Birds flitted and chirped. People some distance off moved about quietly in seeming dutiful deference to the dignity of the surroundings. The receding pleasure of sexual arousal still scented his awareness.

"I don't trust B. B. at all. I had bad vibes the first

time I met her. I think Peter would let her boss him around if he was convinced she was 'under authority.' I think Peter... Quite frankly, I wish he were under authority rather than in authority. That's why I think he'd gladly let B. B. dictate, ironically enough. I suspect she did that from their first meeting.

"Gary is insecure too, though in a different way. I think he's too impressed by a university degree, at least in your case. You know how he always turns to you. Sharon is an enigma. I think she resents Gary's deference. She'd never say anything, but I can see it in her body language. Sometimes I even wonder about their marriage, but I can never put a finger on it.

"Sure, while we've had this language study, we've kept busy. But even then, there's been a lot of goofing around. Jean plays double and triple solitaire with different people all the time. Jack hangs around our place a lot, mainly talking to Fiona, though I don't always see that quite reciprocated. Jean visits with us often, but not Peter, who tends to spend a lot of time alone in his bedroom. Doing what? Sleeping? Reading?

"We've given up talking German at meal times. Maybe that's not a really big thing, since it was always painful for Peter to hear us murder the language—as I'm sure it is for you. But nothing was even said. It just stopped."

At that point, Janys just stopped as well, but Andy could tell she had still more words welling up within her. He was eager to prolong the flow.

"What do you think we need to get us going, Janys?"

Janys responded as if she were reading from a list. "We need specific schedules where we figure out our week in advance, even a whole month, and stick to it.

We need to consider and pursue numerous avenues of evangelism. We need to make good contacts at our churches so we can channel people to them. We need to start attending more youth Bible studies in the churches to get to know the young people. It looks to me like that is the only way of getting accepted in the churches. They've definitely turned a cold shoulder to us otherwise."

"Why don't you raise these things at our next team meeting, Janys?" Andy queried.

Janys shrugged as she stared down at the grass. "I think Peter already believes I say too much at our house about team happenings. Besides, it's you guys who are supposed to lead. Why don't you say something, Andy?"

Just then a park warden walked up and informed them they were in a "no trespassing" zone of the park.

"But there are benches here," Andy replied in his most respectful German.

"You and your girlfriend obviously did not read the signs—even if only in German!" The warden replied in perfect English. "This section of the park is temporarily closed for grass seeding. Where are you two from?"

Janys chimed in before Andy could say anything, a playful look lighting up her face. "My *boyfriend* and I are from Canada, the province of Ontario to be exact. Ever been to Canada?"

He had not, came the reply, but he had studied two years at The London School of Economics, hence the English.

Obligingly, they headed off to another section of the park as the warden continued on his way.

Why did Andy feel chagrined? Yes! The business about "boyfriend and girlfriend." His glance in Janys's direction communicated it had not been lost on her.

She laughed impishly. "I figure that any couple who sleeps together *has* to be at least boyfriend and girlfriend, Andy! Besides, he said it first."

Andy laughed finally as he looked at her suddenly very attractive mirthful countenance. "Janys, have you ever cut your hair?"

"Long hair is a woman's 'glory' and a 'covering,' Andy, don't you know Paul?"

"So what'd Paul think it had to cover, her boobs?" Andy shot back; the words escaping before he quite knew what he was saying. "Sorry, Janys, I'm not usually so crude."

"Well, you did see enough of mine," she said, smiling with equanimity. "Just think if it ever happened again and I didn't have long hair to cover them…" Her face reddened.

"You're blushing, Janys. See! You're more self-conscious than you let on!"

She responded by swinging one arm toward the side of his head, which he deftly fended off. "Watch it, lady! I could have you on the ground in two seconds flat, park warden or no park warden!"

"Oh yeah?" She clobbered him with a left hook right to the chest.

"That's it!" Andy grabbed her small frame, lifted her high, and sprawled her to the ground on her back. He straddled her, arms pinned above her head. The image of Fiona doing this to him strobed Andy's mind. "I warned you!" He shouted into Janys's wildly unrepentant face. He leapt backwards just as quickly, merrily mocking his vanquished prey. "G. E. or no G. E., when a man's very virility is at stake, one has to take drastic measures!"

Janys stood up and dusted herself off. "I'll get you, Mr. Norton! You may have the brawn, but I have the brains! There are ways. Or have you already forgotten your cold shower? And I'm not talking about the night of the big blizzard, though maybe you should have taken one then..." She reddened once more.

Did she think I took my undies off for *that*? He rarely had wet dreams.

There was winding-down silence as both of them sat down on a nearby bench.

"Janys, I want to talk to you rather bluntly about relationships. In a way, that's all we ever talk about, 'cause in a way, that's all there is! I think that's how God made us. Anyway, somehow I feel I need to say—"

"You did not come over here to find a girlfriend. Andy, you've already said that to me in so many words—at the Centre, in case you don't remember. But I agree with you, and for me!"

Just then, a rare thing happened for West Berlin in the early 1970s: a Frisbee banged into the park bench. Andy could not resist. He picked it up and gave a mighty throw, sending two kids scurrying after it for several dozen meters.

"*Erstaunlich!*" He heard one exclaim as he looked back at Andy in awe. They both approached the bench again and diffidently asked him to teach them how to throw like that. Andy's curiosity had been piqued likewise, wondering where they had bought the disc. Apparently, they had found it in the park one day. Andy could imagine American soldiers leaving it behind, but no one else native to Germany, at least Berlin, seemed to know of such a thing.

For the next few minutes, he played with the kids, throwing in a few instructions about stance and propulsion and answering their queries about where he was from and what he was doing in Berlin. Out of the corner of his eye, Andy saw Janys watching intently. When they headed off, Andy thought the earlier conversation might have terminated with the interruption. Not so.

"Andy, you know you're... attractive to members of the opposite sex." Pause. "I hope you don't, well, abuse that power... I mean, girls could easily fall for you... Like, I've got to get this out, like *me*. There, I said it, though I'm probably turning all kinds of crimson shades. I don't care."

Andy was amazed. He had not been fishing for this. There had been no pining or yearning. He really liked Janys, just not *that way*. But there was something else. It bubbled up to arm-twisting self-admission: He *liked* conquering this way. More, he felt greatly tempted to play with such feelings, like a cat might bandy a mouse. Not sexually, except around the edges. Just to *relish* the achievement.

When Andy didn't respond, she continued. "You could end up really hurting someone, Andy, or you could help instead. I don't have this all quite figured out. But everyone needs others to like them, especially those we feel... attracted to. These two years are going to be long and difficult as it is without extra relationship hassles. Though they're bound to come, and you will be at the centre of some of them, I just know it.

"What I'm trying to say is, please don't hive off with any one of us on the team or in the churches. Be a Christian brother to each of us women, show us respect and equal deference. Even make Fiona and me feel... special sometimes, like we had a boyfriend. I think it will be good for you, and best for us."

Andy looked at Janys. She was blushing but determined to get it all out.

"Walk the high road, Andy, no matter how many of

us flutter our eyes at you. Don't commit to any of us—or to anyone else. And I think you can really help us all to grow in general, if not even somewhat in Christ."

With that she stopped. It had been a geyser gush by Janys's standards. As her speech sank in, Andy realized in the most circuitous of routes she had said she was interested in him but wanted it to be on hold for everybody's sake. She wasn't fishing either, he was just as certain. That was not her way.

What to say? Andy was hardly immune to such flattery. His ego could inflate on demand like a helium balloon. He knew since Centre days, though he self-deprecatingly ascribed it to Jack's reflected aura, that lots of Christian girls were drawn to him. Maybe Jack was right: there just weren't enough Christian guys to go around. What did that gender disparity mean?

Somehow the balloon did not expand much that afternoon. He respected Janys too much, perhaps.

"Did it work this evening, Janys?" He asked, finally.

She nodded. "Yes, Andy. It worked. I feel very special."

"Well, it worked for me too, Janys. *I* feel very special. Thank you." He had not anticipated saying that, nor what followed. "Since this is all-around confession time, I know I'm pretty weak, egotistical even, but on this one, I hear you. Proof will be in the pudding. I give you 'henceforth,' just to make it sound a little more official, full permission to hold me to account. Whatever that means. However painful—for us both, possibly! What more can I say?

"I have no idea about nearly everything in God's way in life. Thought I did once—until last month or so! Confused lots of the time without question. Probably a heck of a lot more confusion ahead of me. For all that,

I'll remember this day, just as I'll always remember…"
He didn't have to complete the sentence. He saw her face blush. "Hey! I thought you were 'over that'!"

He took her hand. "Thanks, Janys." It came out very tenderly. His head usually didn't cut his heart much slack.

They rode home together in reflective silence. Funny, Andy thought, I didn't think about sex once throughout that whole exchange, except at the start. Now that's a gift.

That afternoon's conversation also set off a resolve in Andy that if Peter *couldn't*, and Gary *wouldn't*, and even if, technically, Andy *shouldn't*, he would take up the reins, as it were, and get things moving.

"I really think you have a lot to offer us, Andy, *if*…" Janys said as they parted company at the girls' apartment. She failed to complete the thought.

Andy didn't know quite how to complete the sentence either. He did know lots of reasons in his own life for the doubtful conditional. It was Kipling who wrote the "If" poem, ending it with, "And—which is more—you'll be a Man my son!" What would make Andy a man? Kipling wrote, "If you can think—and not make thoughts your aim." That was a tough one.

42

"I don't believe it!" Jack said immediately. "Who cut your hair, Janys? Boy, does it ever look cute! When are you gonna tell your parents?"

Wow, Andy thought. Not a "stunner" like Fiona or Lorraine, but clearly a "looker." Why had he not noticed before? "Designer clothes next, Janys, just like all those sharp-looking German youths?"

She barely missed clobbering him.

"I could do a number on that great mop of yours, Jack Dumont. But it's the style now, I know, even though the Bible teaches, 'it is a shame for a man to have long hair.'" Jean smiled mockingly.

"You're the barber?" Andy asked.

"Hair stylist," Jean said haughtily. She explained that she had actually taken all the training, with apprenticeship, before meeting Peter then had never followed through with finding a job.

Ever since they had arrived in Germany, the "four singles," as they were called at times, determined to go to East Berlin. They were going to be back in time for supper with the other four and Joanne and Hans. Hans had just arrived to take her home. They were leaving the next day, Sunday, June 19th.

"Have a great time," Jean called as they headed through the door. "And Janys, just ignore all those turned heads." She was clearly pleased with her handiwork. Janys reddened. Andy realized he loved that about her.

The four set out by *U-Bahn*. They were excited! At *Checkpoint Charlie* there was not too much of a line-up. They exchanged their requisite five marks at par (an enormous gain to the East Germans), and walked through to East Berlin. There was nothing to it! The only rule was they had to spend all their money in East Berlin.

It was a short walk from there to *Alexanderplatz*, East Berlin's main square and showpiece for all Western visitors. East Germany was the most prosperous of all the Communist bloc countries, but that was difficult to see in East Berlin.

"Man! Everything's still pockmarked from bullet holes and shrapnel," Jack exclaimed. "That's almost thirty years ago."

Jack and Andy had not spent much time together outside of team meetings since their arrival in West Berlin. Andy had never talked to Jack about Fiona either, but Jack's actions toward her were not lost on anyone. Around girls, Jack had always appeared nonchalant. Around Fiona, there was an intensity of interest that only seemed to grow with time.

Joanne, who had been to East Berlin with Hans during his last visit, had told them of a great restaurant right at the square where, for a pittance, they could buy a delicious lunch. Once reconnoitred, they set out to walk along *Unter den Linden*. It was warm and sunny, the sunlight stabbing through the gently swaying trees.

"This is the Unknown Soldier Monument!" Fiona said excitedly as they walked past a church.

"At least there's something eternal in the flame," Jack quipped as they exited a few minutes later. "Maybe that will remind people of what church once meant." He pointed his camera toward the entrance.

"Don't!" Fiona cried, grabbing it. She pointed to two guards in front of the building. Being caught taking photos of soldiers or anything to do with the military could lead to instant confiscation of their photographic equipment, and worse, she warned.

"They're so paranoid," Jack replied. "The same thing at the East German side of *Charlie*. Guards posted everywhere with machine guns like someone might want to steal their country or something. They can have it! It doesn't look like too much of a steal!"

Joanne had also warned them not to draw attention to themselves. Rather hard to do, Andy thought, when a gorgeous blonde and a lithe hunk were amongst a party of obvious Americans. Janys was a head-turner, too. He stole another glance, such a new thought. It felt good to be with Fiona, though he had not ventured so much as a bike ride with her since their arrival. The prohibition had almost turned into a fetish. He made it a religious duty to avoid her, conflicting emotions notwithstanding. She had also been very standoffish since their last days at the Centre.

They strolled along the street, poking around in little shops, snapping a few pictures. The morning went by quickly. They planned to eat lunch, visit the *Pergamon* Museum, and then return home.

Their all-inclusive lunch, including drink, was exactly two marks. They were delighted.

"You know, I don't get it," Jack began, mouth half full of food. "This difference between East and West. I mean, these people all speak German, they look the same, do all kinds of things the same. Go to work. Get married. Have children. Yet, at the drop of a hat, they'd blow each other's brains out. Why?"

"They call it 'ideology,' Jack," Janys responded. "That's what this is all about when you boil it right down."

"Okay, smart lady! I'm in your class. Explain to me what an *ideology* is. I don't think I've ever seen one." Jack laughed.

Janys explained. "You've got Canada, and you've got the United States. Canada believes that hockey rules; America believes that baseball rules. Neither is self-evident. Both are choices elevated to religion. And there you have it: *ideology*. People kill over it. It's utterly irrational, mostly downright *stupid*. How does that saying of Pascal go, Andy?"

Andy almost missed the cue, so intent was he on noticing how much he enjoyed looking at her when she was impassioned. "*Le coeur a ses raisons que la raison ne connaît pas.* 'The heart has its reasons that reason does not know.'"

"Right," Janys said. "Pascal was referring to Christian belief. But it goes for all other kinds, too. Ideology is profoundly irrational, and all the more deadly for that reason. In a world of conflicting ideologies and religions, soon enough people kill for them."

"That's sort of how James puts it, too," Andy said. "'From whence come wars and fightings among you? Come they not hence, even of your lusts that war in your members?' One could argue that the *stupidest* people on the planet are our political leaders and the military who make careers of wars, national defence, nationalism, etc."

"I wouldn't say 'stupidest,'" Janys challenged. "Just plain childish and hopelessly immature. As if they've never awakened to the fact that there are 'wars and rumours of wars' endlessly littering the annals of history. Maybe some country on the planet would just grow up for once and opt out of the pure puerility." Andy watched Janys' vivacious face juxtaposed beside Fiona's. Without question, something had narrowed the gap.

Jack guffawed. "Do they manufacture big words in

Canada, Janys?"

"It means acting like immature little boys, Jack, who all have *fantastic phallus envy syndrome* they never grow out of." She looked at Jack as his mouth opened. "Which means, they build ever bigger and bigger missiles like big *dicks*, Jack, to strut their stuff in the stupidest perennial cock fights known to all history. They're all the same: Russians, Americans, NATO, Israel, the PLO, terrorists, freedom fighters, revolutionaries. All cut from identical cloth. All suffering from enormously retarded human growth *and* egos to make up for it."

All were silent as they took this in—even Andy. He looked out at West Berlin. The restaurant's terrace afforded a view of the city that could make one believe there was really no wall. They were only a few blocks away yet worlds apart in this ideologically alien East Bloc country. Andy thought about the expression "the universe next door." How could people inhabit the same time and space, as did East and West Germans, speak the same language, have been shaped totally by the same history and recent Great War, yet be so utterly different?

Fiona was the first to speak. "My brother was not an *immature little boy*. Timmy was fiercely proud of helping to defend America and the Free World. He'd say, 'Little sis, we live in momentous times. It's an honour to stand up for Jesus and truth wherever. Don't you ever forget it. Don't ever fail to do this.' And he'd be out the door, looking utterly dashing and larger than life in his Air Force uniform." She was near tears. "I'm here because of that. After I saw his great dedication, his untimely death, I vowed to take up a great mission, too."

Andy looked fully at Fiona as she talked, something

he had trained himself not to do. It was not quite like refusing to stare upon the Tree of Knowledge, but akin. If she was Eve in the Garden and he an outside third party, he knew what his sin would be. But he was also aware of Janys, to whom his gaze was directed next as she spoke.

"Fiona, don't you think that is exactly how ideologies work? In the end, your brother was being trained to *deliver death*, and, from thousands of feet up, indiscriminately. Whereas you're over here on a mission to *bring life*.

"When you think of it, aren't evangelism and military activity asymmetrical? One spreads good seed to produce new life everywhere, the other sows bullets and bombs all around to produce death and destruction. With all due respect, I'd take your mission here over your brother's any day. They are diametrically opposed, Fiona." She said the last part very softly, looking directly at Fiona.

Wow, Andy thought, Janys had not held back.

"To produce *freedom*!" Fiona exploded. She caught her mouth as if it had just uttered an expletive. There was no one else on the terrace, not even the waiter. If there were East German spies, they were not in view.

Janys was dogged. "Freedom to do what, Fiona? And for whom, just Americans? Freedom to pursue American vested business interests with impunity around the globe? Spread American values of consumerism and 'enlightened self-interest' everywhere? Impose 'truth, justice, and the American way' unilaterally upon the whole world so there is just one culture called *Americana*? I cannot imagine a sicker, worse, more boring, *wickeder* world."

A waiter came onto the terrace to ask if they wanted anything more. Jack threw down his napkin.

"Hey, let's get going! I've heard we need at least two or three hours to get through the *Pergamon*." Fiona's face had blanched, but she said nothing. They left a substantial tip then headed back out into the sunshine.

The *Pergamon* was massive. It housed priceless treasures from the East. Andy wondered at the political machinations involved in getting items like portions of the gate Nebuchadnezzar literally rode through in biblical times. What kind of plundering had gone on?

The museum was entirely self-interpreting. Andy helped with the translating, though all were having fun trying to figure out the exhibit write-ups. Theirs was not the only interpreting going on. It soon became apparent that the entire museum was one long anachronistic reading of history seen through the lens of Marxist-Leninism. The language of the "proletariat," for instance, was used repeatedly in explaining ancient Babylonian history. Jack guffawed the first time he read it then looked around guiltily. One could not shake the idea that there were thought police everywhere just waiting to pounce. Was this what Janys' world of *Americana* would likewise be, was already like? Andy wondered. Was there, in the end, any difference between imposed capitalism and imposed communism? Were they not both touting freedom and yet delivering the opposite at the barrel of a gun? Democracy? Benevolent state? A plague o' both their houses, Andy thought, quoting Shakespeare.

After wandering for a while, the group sat down on one of the long benches situated throughout the museum. There was no one else around. Andy was completely taken with the bright blue reconstructed tiling of Nebuchadnezzar's wall. "Ideology oozes through every pore here. Makes one wonder how anyone can read history without imposing bias.

Lessing's 'ugly broad ditch' only because of prior philosophical presupposition… Okay, I won't pursue that. Obviously no one can avoid it. But this is utterly blatant! If the Communists are this bald about it, are the Capitalists just as much, only we can't see it, because we were raised in it?"

"Nothing about life or culture is self-evident so much as habituated," Janys replied. "Take a little kid who is raised by a single mom. The dad is not in the picture. Already huge perceptions emerge in this little child just by that father's absence. Stir in that the mom is an active 'women's libber,' very sour on men in general, and the child could be well on her way to turning out lesbian, or at least very anti-men.

"My brother Ted says you have to keep asking, 'Whose rationality? Whose culture? Why these norms? What presuppositions?' He calls it 'biblical realism,' drawing on Kant in ways I never quite follow. He says Karl Barth was that way, too. A robust cynicism about 'the world' is perhaps the greatest biblical legacy."

Andy was intrigued, though Fiona and Jack seemed to be ignoring their admittedly esoteric conversation. "Is that what Paul meant when he said, 'And be not conformed to this world, but be ye transformed by the renewing of your mind'?"

Andy was struck by sudden revelation. "I remember reading Timothy LaHaye berating secularists for denying major biblical truths like the Incarnation, the Virgin Birth, the Resurrection, the Deity of Christ, the Trinity, and *the Free Enterprise System*! He just slipped that last one in, right up there with the Big Leaguers. Now that is cultural conformity, surely!"

Was this the Evangelical norm, at least in American Evangelical orthodoxy? If one stripped it all away, what would American Evangelicals still cling to: God, haunting subject of the Bible, or "In God We Trust"—read "Mammon" or "Guns"? What was the Second American Constitutional Amendment? What was Adam Smith's "enlightened self-interest"? Was Janys, was Ted, infectious? Was Jesus, was the Bible? This was dangerous. Where were the thought police? Andy stopped the questions with effort. Fiona still said nothing. Was she pouting?

Jack finally waded in. "Interesting that this discussion about ideology is between two Americans and two Canadians. I'd say you Canadians are almost pointing a finger at us Americans for being like the Communists or something. Is that what you're saying?"

Fiona blurted out, "Jack, there is anti-Americanism all around the world, because they hate our freedoms, our democracy, our God!" She was wound up. Her silence had merely been a mask for her anger. "My dad used to say that the real cause of the Civil War was how much the North was jealous of us Confederates. Texas has always stood out tall amongst the rest of the states, 'the Lone Star,' for the right. That's what is going on here. Ideology is what the rest of the world suffers from, because they're so jealous of America! We stand for the truth. That is what has made America great. This is the Monroe Doctrine of 1823 and has been America's 'Manifest Destiny' ever since. Just like the Israelites were God's Chosen People to lead the world to Christ, we are the chosen to lead the world to God's Kingdom."

Andy was amazed at the speech. How could he respond? Was this what Fiona really believed? Was this what George Beverley Shea meant every time he sang "America the Beautiful" at a Billy Graham crusade? Was it ever just "God" all in all for Americans? Was it instead invariably "God and Flag"? And when, Andy knew by some intuitive logic, did it end up becoming just "Flag"? Wasn't that the course of Nazism and the *Übermensch*? Had the Americans become the Nazis? Was Billy Graham propagandist for *Amerika Über Alles*, a religious Joseph Goebbels? Where were these questions coming from? What inner wellspring was being tapped? Why could he not stop thinking?

"I'm sorry, Fiona," Janys said, "I did not intend to sound so disrespectful. These are relatively new ideas with me, too. I'm still feeling my way through all this."

With that, they all stood up, as if responsive to a recess bell at school. They wandered through the rest of the museum in fairly short time. There was no further discussion.

43

Shortly after returning to the girls' apartment, Joanne called them to supper. Joanne and Sharon had done the meal together. It was one of Hans' favourites: Bratwurst, sauerkraut, and boiled potatoes. Easy to prepare, they were assured, and delicious.

Unintentionally or not, Jack got the conversation going as supper wound down. The four singles had described their day in some detail, and with enthusiasm. "I learned a new word today," Jack started, "Ideology. It means, if I got it correct, that we all have our ideas about what is true and right, and we end up killing for them."

Hans raised his eyebrows, his mouth still full of Bratwurst.

"Interestingly, Janys accused America of being driven by an ideology of greed rather than goodness toward the rest of the world. I'd like to know, Hans, in light of our last discussion, what are your thoughts on that? Like, for instance, Vietnam. For me it's black and white. Communism is evil. We're fighting evil in Vietnam to make the world safe for democracy. What's your take?"

Hans looked over at Joanne. Joanne looked away and said she'd start clearing the table. Peter got up to help. Jean and Sharon followed.

Hans swallowed his Bratwurst, took a sip of water, and then began. "Let's discuss Billy Graham and ideology, seeing as he trained at Wheaton College, too. Twice, he went behind the lines to preach to the GI's about salvation. I'm sure this was at the expense of the American government. If not, it was obviously done with their full permission. Why? Because Billy Graham was a good propagandist for the ideology of the war America was fighting against the Communists.

"I can guarantee that in no part of Dr. Graham's gospel message was there a call to 'love your enemies.' On the contrary, if soldiers became Christians and proceeded the next day to blow their enemies to bits—for the love of whom Jesus died, too—Reverend Graham would have fully approved. He did, in fact. And that's ideology at work alien to the Gospel. Specifically, that's American anti-Communist ideology triumphing over the Gospel. Or Darkness overcoming the Light, to use biblical language.

"So I ask, how is that in keeping with Jesus' teachings? Did it ever occur to Evangelicals to go to North Vietnam with the message that God loves the Viet Cong, too, and that one should lay down one's life for them rather than take theirs? Apparently not. So when Billy Graham went to the American troops with the 'Gospel,' should not part of his message have been that they should stop the slaughter because God loves the North Vietnamese as much as he does Americans? Or does God *not* love America's enemies?

"My conclusion from simple observation is that Evangelicals routinely practise an under-your-breath ideologized footnote theology that reads repeatedly, 'Except our enemies,' when quoting John 3:16 and all similar New Testament ethical teachings. How could Billy Graham tell the North Vietnamese that God loves them when he fully blessed his own country in displaying the exact opposite feeling—hatred unto death? How could he do this when he was still praying with the President for victory in the War, when he apparently willed the utter inversion of the Gospel regarding treatment of neighbour, enemy, and Creation?

Andy marvelled at how much Hans had to say on the topic, seeing as he'd had no time to prepare.

"Remember James' juxtaposition of 'saying' and 'doing'? Peter, please hand me that Bible behind you. *Moment mal.* 'Yea, a man may *say*, Thou hast faith, and I have works: shew me thy faith without thy works, and I will shew thee my faith *by my works*.' The 'works' of James are found in the Sermon on the Mount, supremely summed up in 'Love your neighbour and your enemies', which is biblical righteousness—justice—in the raw. Without this, Jesus warned the Pharisees, one will never enter the Kingdom! This is what the wise man does, Jesus says in Matthew seven, with reference to the vast background Jesus the Sage brings to Hebrew Wisdom literature.

"This is not the 'works-righteousness' my predecessor, Luther railed against. No, it is righteousness consummated, in the raw, acted out as 'living sacrifice,' as ineluctable corollary to 'justification by faith,' the other side of the two-sided coin of salvation. Salvation embraced, salvation lived. One does not exist without the other. Trouble is, the first exists in American Evangelicalism all too well in utter disregard of the other."

Hans stopped completely at that. Joanne had entered the room. "Hans can go on like this for hours," she warned. "My girlfriend once asked me to consider what would bother me most about Hans. *This is it!*" To Joanne's credit, she had said nothing about Hans' predilection since the last discussion. She was feeling her way now.

Fiona ignored Joanne's remonstrance. She appeared angry, yet tenacious. "But don't we want this war to end soon?"

Hans looked at Joanne. She looked away and

shook her head.

"Yes, Fiona," he said finally with anguished voice. He looked again at Joanne. "Just like the Americans wanted World War Two to end quickly and incinerated over 120,000 Japanese civilians—infants, children, middle-aged, and elderly—to underscore the point. The Americans had held off their obscene napalm bombing of these two cities to await the ultimate laboratory experiment of scientifically (like Nazis in their white coats) observing the effects of not one but two atomic bombs on otherwise unbombed cities. Until the detonations, these civilians were going about their daily lives as normally as anyone else on the planet at that time. Let your mind dwell on that scene. Place yourself in it. Better yet, place any—Place all!—your loved ones in Hiroshima or Nagasaki on August 6th or 9, 1945, scene of the grandest scientific experiment ever imagined. Let your mind imagine the monstrous horror willed upon the Japanese—and your loved ones! And tell me that it is other than homicidal madness, *premeditated mass murder in the first degree!* The Allies also did that repeatedly to over one hundred cities in Germany and Japan, carpet bombed them with napalm to the tune of over two million civilian casualties."

"I make this association in my paper. When the thirteenth-century papal legate in the southern French town of Béziers was asked how to distinguish between Albigensian heretics and 'real Catholics,' he replied: 'Kill them all! God will sort out who are his own.' There is, I believe, an absolute moral equivalency between that medieval inhuman barbarity (they say twenty thousand were put to the sword that day) and America's today. Incidentally, President Roosevelt used the term 'inhuman barbarity' in a memo to all major nations in 1939 with reference to aerial bombing by the Germans of innocent civilians. But America, in sheer numbers, went on under Roosevelt and then Truman to vastly outstrip that body count. Although I do not have the exact figures to prove it, America is arguably responsible for an annual holocaust that since World War Two adds up to that perpetrated against the Jews throughout the time of the Nazi reign of terror. Most of this is kept hidden by the most sophisticated propaganda machine in human history—called American corporate mass media, though such is anything but a 'free press' except for those who own one. It outdoes Joseph Goebbels in spades. One becomes what one hates.

"The sheer wickedness of President Truman's decision, himself an Evangelical Baptist Sunday School teacher, is so utterly beyond imagining, and yet few American Evangelicals today even question the necessity and righteousness of that choice. Those bombs have *cauterized* the American collective conscience into spiritual numbness and induced mass moral blindness. It would be like the Mafia massacring vast numbers of their enemies through a bomb blast, and, because they were all 'godless Communists' anyway, Americans unconscionably elevate the Mafia to hero status! So I ask: Just which 'sacred text' was President Truman reading when he authorized full-scale massacre of Japanese civilians—the *Bible* or America's *Manifest Destiny*? And just what Bible are Evangelicals reading today, when not a question is asked about these horrendous crimes against humanity in Vietnam and elsewhere?"

This was too much for Fiona. "I *believe* in Manifest Destiny for America. I *believe* in righteousness that exalteth a nation, our nation, America the Beautiful. I *believe* in God and Flag!"

"Don't you think you've said enough, Hans?" Joanne asked. She looked pained. Andy quickly surveyed everyone's face listening in. There was tension everywhere. Maybe it would be best to wind down. But this was fascinating for Andy, albeit perilously.

"I want to hear Hans out," Fiona insisted. "I want to prove you wrong, Hans! You obviously were not raised American, despite your American mom. I think you are operating under an *ideology* I can't quite name. But it is alien to America. I think we are the God-given norm, and what you are saying, even when quoting Scripture, is pure ideology. I want to help name it for you and then let you see it, if, like Jesus says, 'you have eyes to see.'"

It was a valiant retaliation. Fiercely "Texan," typical American Empire Loyalist standing up for the "right" against all odds. The only problem for Andy was, so far all the "odds" were with Hans, and all the *ideology* with Fiona.

Ignoring Joanne's request, Hans ploughed ahead. "I grant that by comparison to Stalin and Mao in sheer numbers slaughtered, Truman does indeed look like the Sunday school teacher that he was. But isn't that the point? Sunday School teachers should know better. Much better. Or doesn't the Bible mean a thing even to Evangelicals beyond serving as the central cultural icon of America, all the more, for that honour, to be totally disregarded and trivialized?

"I am not a Marxist-Leninist, if that is what you are alluding to, Fiona. Far from it. I am a committed Christian who has discovered 'the strange new world of the Bible' as Karl Barth called it, and I am trying to find my way through its meaning for today. Of course I'm biased. But I'm trying to make my reading of the Bible challenge my biases, rather than my preconceptions filter the Bible, like I believe American Evangelicals largely do on this issue. That is my conscious ideological commitment. Consequently, in my reading of the Bible, I cannot kill for my ideology nor bless any state that does. I agree with Gandhi who in this case rightly read the Bible, saying, 'It seems everyone but Christians knows Jesus was non-violent.'"

Gary, who had been listening intently, suddenly thought of something. "Wasn't it Christians who not only authorized the atomic bombings, namely President Truman, but also the chaplain who blessed the crew on their mission? Do you claim to know better than millions of believers before you, Hans?"

Hans' eyes narrowed. "Gary, do you really want me to respond?"

"Yes!" Said Fiona and Gary in unison.

Hans took a deep breath. "Father George Zabelka was the Catholic military chaplain who blessed the crew who dropped the first atomic bomb on August 6th, 1945 and the second crew three days later. He has since repented totally and has been telling the world that there is no moral or Christian justification whatsoever for such coldly calculated acts of mass murder. He says the entire Christian church has been utterly brainwashed for almost two millennia to accept war of any description (it always gets called 'just' by Christians), not least the deliberate slaughter of innocents. Ten percent civilian deaths in World War One. Fifty percent civilian deaths in World War Two. Some claim up to eighty percent in Vietnam. You cannot bomb without huge percentages of civilian deaths. And who said 'combatants,' even if that's all you killed, were *Christianly* fair game anyway? Certainly not Jesus—or any other New Testament writer.

"So you say, Fiona, along with High Priest Caiaphas at the Crucifixion of Jesus: 'It is better that one should die than that the whole nation perish.' Or in this case, that 120,000 plus innocent Japanese civilians, or several million North Vietnamese must perish, instead of precious American blood being spilled. Or that multiplied millions of innocents had to have been maimed and slaughtered to stop the Nazis and the Japanese.

"It doesn't matter. That is conventional scapegoat wisdom, as old and ubiquitous as humanity. Of course, sacrificial violence has always made perfect cultural sense and underwrites all rationalizations for immolating scapegoats amongst peoples as diverse as head hunters in New Guinea, cannibals the world over, the ancient Aztecs or Incas of the New World, Nazis in Germany, Whites lynching Blacks in the American South, and Americans slaughtering the Viet Cong in Vietnam. *It is also utter antithesis of all Gospel logic*, though that is emphatically not majority church theory and practice. So much the worse for the Church over against the Bible! The Bible may be the Church's Book, but it has rarely, with reference to State violence, been the Church's Guide.

"Sometime, you must all read an unknown French Catholic author working in America: René Girard. It is doubtful Evangelical theologians will ever appreciate him, since he argues theologically and anthropologically the very inversion of the 'satisfaction theory of the atonement.' Another matter…"

"Hans," Andy interjected, "I read some of Girard in university. What I didn't like about him was his making a theory—scapegoating—fit all, like his own discovery of a revelation. I think life is always more complex than any one meta-theory."

Hans replied slowly. "Andy, I liked Girard, because he corroborated and at times elucidated the Bible's own description and response to violence. Not the other way around. I found Girard supplemental, not revelatory."

"So," Gary quizzed, "my main question since the last time is, are you saying there is *never* a place, according to the Gospel, for killing our enemies? Because if so, not only do I dispute that, but it basically says almost everyone in the Church for two thousand years has been wrong. That is pretty arrogant to say the least! And what about Jesus' cleaning out the Temple with a whip? What about his positive response to soldiers—and John's, without ever telling them killing was wrong? What about the two swords Jesus said were 'enough' when the disciples presented them before his arrest? What about Jesus' depiction of God as a sentencing judge, bringing down the violence of the State? What about a doctrine of hell that is pure violence in the end, ultimate violence?"

The dishes had long since been done. Peter had turned on the lights on the way to his room. Jean, Joanne, and Sharon diffidently had sat down at the table again. Andy felt the vibes from Joanne. Sharon looked, if anything, bored. Jean was just blank, though once again apart from Peter.

Andy remembered his thinking from that very afternoon. He piped up, surprised at his sudden boldness in favour of Hans. "Isn't killing the enemy, Gary, the *exact opposite* of evangelism—what we Evangelicals say all the time is our main mission on earth? How can we warmly underwrite sowing life-giving seed, evangelism to bring life, on the streets of West Berlin while equally supporting strewing cluster bombs—and worse—on the villages of North Vietnam? Is that not evangelism's exact inversion—to bring death—as they once did over Berlin?"

Andy continued to speak as the light within him grew. "Those same people who send us monthly cheques to support inviting Berliners into the Kingdom simultaneously underwrite with their patriotism and taxes and sons and daughters *consignment to hell* of countless Vietnamese, an opposite 'Kingdom Come.' And their parents applauded, participated in, and prayed for the same slaughter of Berliners, parents and grandparents of those we now minister to, barely a generation ago! Isn't that juxtaposition contradictory of all human logic?"

Hans nodded. "Adduce Gospel logic—the only reality test Christians are to employ—and the unfaithfulness of Christian support of war and capital punishment materializes as surely as acid or alkaline solutions are demonstrated in a litmus test.

"So no, Gary, I see no place for ever legitimating killing one's enemies. Not in Gospel logic. And there are responses to the exegetical issues—issues of interpretation—that you raise. I'll ask you: Is there ever a place for extra-marital sex in a marriage? Not in New Testament teaching, no matter how rampant the alternative cultural norm. There are likewise no exceptions to Jesus' call to love neighbour and enemy. On the contrary, see if there is not New Testament consistency that the only way to know you love God is to love your neighbour. And the litmus test for that is loving your enemy."

Gary said nothing, so Hans continued. "Let me add again about Billy Graham, who so classically represents the Evangelical mindset—that's why I single him out. I believe he is a great man of God in his own context, utterly sincere. According to the Gospel as I read it, what

Dr. Graham should be doing in addition to preaching to the American soldiers in Vietnam is going to his own Evangelical churches to challenge them to call for deep nationwide repentance that would end the war. No war since Christ has ever been God's will. The American Evangelical church is worshipping an idol, not God, when it participates in war, sends its children to war, blesses America and others in war. *All wars, past, present, and future, are unreservedly contradictory to the Gospel*, its most complete inversion. War, all war by all sides, is utter transgression and the greatest heresy, according to biblical revelation."

Fiona looked nonplussed. Where could she begin, Andy wondered? "But America stands for truth!" She exclaimed. "The truth that 'shall set one free.' Freedom. Truth and freedom. They are America's birthright and bequeathal to the world. And that's what Vietnam is all about! What do you say to that, Hans? What you are saying is so, is so, *untruth*!"

Janys, Andy suddenly realized, had listened intently to the entire exchange without comment. Was she feeling repentant for having been too hard on Fiona earlier? He looked at her. Her face registered fascination, even contentment. Was she wishing Ted had been there? Was she comparing Ted to Hans? He'd love to have a long talk with her afterwards.

"Well?" Fiona's challenge was almost shrill.

Hans did not look at Joanne. "The first casualty of all war, of all violence, by the State or the individual, is truth. This is what former UN Secretary General U. Thant once said and Cain's religiosity demonstrated. The first casualty of all *religion*, war's first cousin, is also truth, Fiona. And that's why religion and war inevitably intertwine, the one feeding into the other and looping back again. That's why all military chaplaincies are about truth's opposite: *violence*. Their final word is worldly *death,* not Gospel life. I would add, incidentally, all sports chaplaincies too. That's why the worst plague on the planet has ever been religious wars, likewise the ultimate scourge of Western Christendom.

"Now contrast that with Jesus, whom religious people claim to be 'the Truth.' Something has to give. If violence is not truth's casualty, like darkness' dissipation is the sun's supreme handiwork, then all you have left is *Jesus the Untruth*. Jesus the Violent. Jesus the Avenger. Jesus the Cosmic Tyrant. Not Jesus the Truth. Jesus the Life of the World. Jesus the Light of the World. Jesus the Prince of Peace. Then Constantine's *in hoc signo vinces*, "in this sign you will conquer," rings true to Mars the god of war but *utterly false to Jesus the God of love and peace*. The contrasts are utterly stark and irreconcilable.

"But most of us prefer our lies, are addicted as surely as any alcoholic to prevaricating violence. So it is with dominant American Evangelicalism. This is the brilliant point of Hans Christian Andersen's *The Emperor's New Clothes*. As John's Gospel puts it, 'men love darkness—lies and violence—rather than light.' Americans, Westerners, most of us, likewise love lies more than truth. That is why Nazi Germany was so successful in liquidating six million Jews. While truth promises to set us free, we fairly grasp instead after our violent addictions: national security, right to private possessions, nationalism, and the free enterprise system. We thereby negate 'the mind of Christ' that didn't 'grasp after' Christ's own prerogatives as deity. Remember, He could have called ten thousand angels but refrained. Your President calls up ten thousand G. I.'s—hardly angels—to fight in Vietnam, and Billy Graham and the

American Evangelical leadership cheer on the slaughter. Billy even goes to preach in support of them, just like Bob Hope goes to entertain. Same difference. Identical ideology. Both utterly foreign to the Gospel, that's all.

"The truth that sets us, sets nations free is non-violence. In the CIA building is inscribed Jesus' statement: 'You shall know the truth and the truth shall set you free.' The irony is palpable. An organization that is committed to covert violence and secret lies on a massive scale claims freedom as they lie and murder, kidnap and assassinate, and God only knows what else the world over! This is George Orwell's haunting doublespeak. This is Jeremiah's 'peace, peace, when there is no peace.' This is what America's most famous evangelist, and most others, sell to America and to the world as 'beautiful' and God-ordained, blessed, demonstrative of a righteous 'manifest destiny.'"

Fiona was near tears. She was utterly tongue-tied as well. Andy also felt sick but speechless. But Hans still had more to add.

"To resort to violence means to deny God, since we trust in it instead and are bound by the ultimate anti-god, which is the final 'anti-Christ.' 'In Guns we Trust' is America's *de facto* motto, what they really believe. 'One Nation Under the Gun' is the last truth of American social reality played out in American overt and covert interventions the world over. America was born in violent revolution against a lawful state. It proceeded to steal wholesale an entire continent from its rightful occupiers and now acts as Robber Baron to the rest of the world. The CIA, many say, is about to orchestrate a military coup in Chile to overthrow a democratically elected leader, Salvador Allende, because of his socialism! And they almost invaded Cuba because Castro is Communist. And so it goes, all over Latin and South America, Asia—the entire world. But you'll never hear an American Evangelical leader question the righteousness of all this monstrous murder and mayhem. Rare as hen's teeth at least.

"In the end, therefore, as I read Jesus' teaching, evangelism means introducing others to Jesus. But," and he leaned forward to accentuate his words, "Jesus' teaching is, if we cannot find God in the enemy, we will not find God at all! God is most clearly revealed in the face of Jesus. Yes. But that face, as it turns out, is visible first and foremost—and perhaps only—in our enemies!"

Fiona responded, her voice shaky. "Are you telling me that my brother, who loved Jesus but who spent years being educated through the Air Force and in training as a fighter pilot, was wrong?

Hans nodded.

"I can't accept that! My brother was a great man and a wonderful Christian! And I met lots of his fellow trainees, all Bible-believing, born-again, and on fire for the Lord. We've all met lots here at the American Army Base. You can't tell me they're all wrong, millions and millions of them! You can't tell me that standing up for America, for patriotism, for God and flag, is not part of loving Jesus! I've always understood that one leads to the other, and back again. I taught my school kids that in every discussion about the flag we had.

"Your views sound like sheer arrogance over against majority Evangelical and Church teaching for centuries. You say God is against war! How dare you! Have you never read the Old Testament? God repeatedly endorses war there. So who isn't reading their Bible? Who's the liberal? God does not change! 'For I am the Lord, I do not change.'! Malachi 3:6, my life verse."

Fiona's cheeks were flushed, her voice long past quavering. "America was founded by Bible-believing godly men, and God honoured us by making our land rich and powerful, first among the nations, giving us a 'manifest destiny' as some call it. How dare you question all that?"

Jack touched her hand. She wheeled suddenly and ran to her room.

Silence hung like a sticky mist, finally pierced by Gary's quiet voice. "I think we should wind down for tonight. Hans, you have strongly held views, to be sure! Perhaps another time we will hear more of them. If I may say though, for Peter and his family, he's just grateful that the Allies liberated them from the Nazis. Possibly neither he nor any of his family would be here today had it not been for that. Sometimes there is no alternative option to the peace we have grown up with in the West since the last War. Some things you simply have to fight for. One of them is freedom."

The get-together ended on that note. On his way out, Andy quietly asked Hans for a copy of his paper. Hans promised he'd send him one as soon as he got home.

The following day they had an official farewell for Hans and Joanne. Everyone had a great time, and nothing about the previous night's discussion was said. Just like that, Hans and Joanne stepped out of the team's life.

Except the paper. After receiving it in the mail, Andy read it several times, veritably devoured it. He corresponded about it several times with Hans. And though Hans and Joanne had intended it, they never visited the team again. Perhaps just as well, Andy thought.

44

The last Friday in June, Fiona and Jack took off without telling anyone where they were going. Andy, who had stayed up reading, was still awake when Jack crept in after midnight.

"Man, was *Evil Knievel* ever good! Fiona and me got invited to the Outpost Theatre by Gerald—you remember, one of the Army guys. Only fifty cents, Andy. What a riot! The movie was so much fun. I *love* motorcycles *so* much! Fiona tells me her younger brother has just bought a big Harley. I told her I'm gonna ride with him some day."

He paused, his face darkening.

"That was the good part. Now for the bad part."

Andy put his book down.

"Out in the foyer after the movie, Fiona tells me she's going to the bathroom. I watch her head toward the can. All kinds of people milling about. I lose sight of her momentarily. Suddenly, this big bruiser is talking to her.

"Now he's *big*. Much taller than me, Andy. And stocky. I could tell, even from a distance. Suddenly, Fiona turns away, walks straight back to me and says, 'Let's go, Jack, *now*!' She still hasn't used the can.

"She looks like she's seen a ghost. I asked her what the guy said to her. She looks at me shocked but says nothing. Then she says again real urgent, 'Let's go *now* Jack!' Luckily, we had already said thanks and goodnight to Gerald.

"We walk out of the theatre then just about run toward the *U-bahn*, Fiona in the lead. Something about the big guy spooked her, but she won't open up. Not a word all the way back home no matter what I tried.

"This isn't one of the guys who used to hang out with us?" Andy wondered aloud, forgetting momentarily that Jack had just had the most beautiful woman in West Berlin on a date all by himself.

"Naw," came Jack's response. "I towered over all those guys. I wouldn't wanna meet the guy I saw with Fiona in a dark alley. This guy's unknown to us, but obviously not to Fiona. But who'd she know in the Army, Andy, outside of guys we've all met?"

Andy's eyes searched the room while he worked on an answer. Their living room was compact, but nicely set up, thanks to Sharon's artistic eye. There were two comfortable couches and a stuffed reading chair, similar to the "War Room" at the girls' apartment. The conspiratorial glow of the lamp was all that lit their faces as they talked in muted tones.

"Jack, Fiona had a brother who died in an Air Force trainer accident, as she alluded to the other night with Hans." She'd also told Andy the story more intimately, to which Andy did not allude. "Is it possible this guy knows her from there?"

"Bingo!" Jack exclaimed.

"Shhhh." Andy put a finger to his lips.

Jack nodded and spoke in a whisper. "So let's say the guy's in the Air Force and knows Fiona through her brother, Timmy. He's transferred here..."

"I thought that only Army people were at the base."

"No," Jack countered, "the pilot I know is an example..." Jack paused, a new realization occurring. "But Andy, there would not be a lot of Air Force guys, to be sure. And they'd all know each other even if five thousand soldiers would not. You know what that means. It won't take this guy long to figure out where Fiona lives. He knows we couldn't get in to the *Outpost* without someone personally vouching for us. So all he has to do is ask around. It wouldn't take long. Especially if he's a pilot, which gives him instant rank. He could easily know by tomorrow. I think I'll be using the pay phone first thing in the morning."

Sensing Fiona's inchoate danger somehow brought them together. Fiona had also occasioned their rift. Maybe this would change that. Andy hardly felt the Knight in Shining Armour, but he cared greatly for Fiona.

They went off to bed, not a little concerned.

The next morning Jack got through to his pilot friend. He had not heard at all from the only pilot at the base who matched Jack's description: Lieutenant Colonel Todd Braxman. Jack told his friend the reason for asking. The pilot, Scott Cunningham, could not imagine Braxman knowing Fiona. "Just the same," Jack asked, "could you find out if he did any of his training in Texas?"

Cunningham agreed.

That night was a Games Night at the girls' apartment. The Dynamic Duo agreed that Jack would ask fairly nonchalantly about Fiona's sudden exit the night before.

One of the *Wilmersdorf* youth had told them of a game called *Malefiz Spiel*—rendered in English by the manufacturers as *Barricade*. Jean had picked it up and convinced Peter to join with them. There were only four players normally, so they teamed up, mixing marrieds and singles. It was a dice game with some strategy, and became an instant hit.

"Reminds me of all the barricades we've had to overcome so far here in Berlin," Peter quipped. "It's a good game for us. By God's grace, we'll overcome each and every one." Peter did not smile at all as he said this. But at least he had joined in a game, Andy thought. This was a first. And Peter and Fiona even won, to which Peter responded, "Thank the good Lord. I take this as a sign." He said no more. Obviously there was something deep going on that only he, and possibly Jean, was privy to. Andy could tell Jean was loath to see the game come to an end.

Fiona went off to the kitchen to put on some hot chocolate. While the others sat around to talk, Jack saw his chance. When they re-emerged, she did not look happy. Peter even said, "Why the sour face, Fiona? We won!" She smiled wanly. Something was eating at her.

A few moments later in a quick aside, Jack told Andy, "She said this guy was rude to her, that's all. She would not admit to knowing him."

The team retired to the War Room to sip hot chocolate and eat cookies, Sharon's latest experiment. They had dates and chocolate chips together. The plate emptied quickly; the team raved.

"Hey," Sharon protested, "I wanted to take some to church for their break between services. When that plate's done, you're out of luck, *boys*." She looked sternly at Jack and Andy, both of whom were unabashed cookie monsters. They grinned, their mouths too full to respond.

Just then, Andy had an inspiration. He quickly swallowed the remains of his third cookie. "Jack phoned up his pilot buddy Scott Cunningham today. He says he has some goodies to get to us. Jack usually picks them up at the base, but Scott thought he'd drop them by tomorrow afternoon. Can you save enough cookies for afternoon tea with them, Sharon? He said he was bringing by a pilot buddy, someone named Todd Braxman."

Fiona sputtered into her hot chocolate, coughing out cookie bits. She got up and headed straight for the washroom.

Andy saw Jack look at him sharply.

A few minutes later, Fiona returned, her features drawn. "I'm calling it a night, I think."

Peter looked at his watch. "Oh my goodness. It is later than I thought. How time flies when you're having fun. If it's my partner's bedtime, then it must be mine, too."

The evening wound down quickly. Everyone pitched in to clean up. Soon the Duo and Gary and Sharon were walking home. As they went out the door, Janys handed Andy a note.

On the way back, Jack said quietly, "Why did you startle Fiona so? You got your information, but at what expense, Andy? She's clearly freaked by this guy, and she obviously knows him. How are you going to explain your little white lie about that visit tomorrow?"

Sharon picked up Fiona's name in their hushed conversation. "Boy, something was sure weird about Fiona tonight," she ventured. "Or I'm thinking those cookies of mine had an ingredient in them that I didn't know about."

Neither Jack nor Andy rose to the bait. "It was a great evening, Sharon," Andy deflected. "No small thanks to those cookies. And Peter joined in for the first time! This augurs well."

Sharon nodded then she and Gary returned to their own conversation; Andy and Jack to theirs.

When they got to the apartment, the Duo went immediately to their room. "What does the note say?" Jack asked. He had seen Janys pass it to Andy, and they both knew it was from Fiona. Andy opened it and read.

Dear Andy:

Okay, you flushed me out. Jack tried. You pulled it off.

If it's really true that those pilots are planning to come by tomorrow, I need to talk to you right away, before church tomorrow. I'll go out to our phone booth at 8:00 sharp. You can call me there. YOU MUST!

If they are not coming by, I'll wait ten minutes at the booth. Jack and I are going to Wilmersdorf *later as usual.*

I'll say this much: UNDER NO CIRCUMSTANCES ARE THOSE GUYS TO VISIT!

I know you want an explanation. I'm not sure what to think. All I can say is, this is not a game, and I hope you can respect my space.

If we do not talk tomorrow morning and those guys are definitely not coming over, I want to invite you both on a walk after lunch.

That's all I'll say for now.

Fiona

Promptly at eight the next morning, Andy dialled the pay phone number. She answered immediately.

"Fiona, I'm sorry—"

"Andy, are those two guys coming by or not?"

"No," he replied, realizing there was no evading it. "I made that up on the spot."

Fiona was curt. "I'll see Jack shortly for church. You can tell him I won't be talking to him about this at all. We'll go for a walk after lunch. I want you guys to head out on your own, and we'll meet in front of the *Gedächtniskirche*—the old part on the *Ku'damm* side. Let's say at 1:30.

"I don't want anyone else on the team to know about this, Andy. You've forced my hand, and it's not appreciated."

Andy wanted to say they were worried for her safety. To say sorry again. To let her know he cared. But she gave him no chance. The phone clicked abruptly at the other end.

45

Fiona met Jack and Andy in front of the Kaiser Wilhelm Memorial Church—*Gedächtniskirche*—at 1:30, as planned. No one else was to know about the meeting, by her instructions.

She launched right in. "This is really none of your business."

"We just felt concerned for your safety," Jack responded meekly.

Fiona's face told him she was not impressed. She was more upset than Andy had ever seen her. She almost looked like a different person.

"All right," she began, leading them further down the *Ku'damm* away from the church. "I was in a relationship with Todd Braxman before I came here. He was a friend of my brother's…" Her voice trailed off. Andy wished he could be looking at her face-on. She was walking between him and Jack. We must make an interesting sight, Andy thought, tall, lithe bookend hunk, tall, good-looking other bookend, knockout blonde in the middle.

"We met through my brother, actually. They were in training together and in an officers' Bible study group. I never dreamed in a million years that he'd be posted in West Berlin…" There was a long silence. Andy and Jack weren't asking any questions.

As ever, there were all kinds of people on the *Ku'damm,* even more so on this sunny day. But the crowds thinned out the further they got from the church.

"My brother died when I was eighteen. Along comes this big hunk of a guy. He's tender, compassionate, my brother's friend. We hit it off right away. I thought it was mainly as friends. I was grieving big time. Here was someone closely connected to my brother's love, the Air Force, and also a Christian. What better combination?" There was bitterness to her tone.

"He… took advantage of my vulnerability. My guard was down. I'd seen his kind of behaviour before, but I let him get through my defences." She wiped away tears.

"Okay, this is the rough part. We ended up sleeping together, and I got pregnant." She said it all in a rush, as if skimming over it would make it less painful. She convulsed then and had to sit down. They found a small green space with a bench. No one else was around. She sat down and buried her face in her hands, weeping softly.

Then she sat up, her face fierce. "When I came to the Centre, G. E. agreed that this story would never come out…"

Something clicked for Andy like lock tumblers falling into place. He remembered a vague comment by G. E. about Fiona's 'having her problems, too.' So this was why G. E. was so inexplicably hard on Andy about his relationship with Fiona. It all made sense now, though he certainly got the brunt of the vow of silence.

"So you're the first and the only ones to know!" That same ferocity. Andy had never heard that tone before. He could not see her face when she said it, still covered by hands and hair.

"My dad and mom were now grieving the loss of a son *and* a daughter pregnant out of wedlock, all inside of six months.

"They arranged for me to go away to my Aunt Elsie's in Tulsa. She's no prude. She takes me in, no questions. I had a beautiful boy…"

She lost it again. Andy and Jack said nothing, merely waited.

"I named him Timmy. Then, I give him up for adoption, my beautiful baby boy." She sobbed and sobbed. Andy wanted more than anything to put his arms around her and hold her tight. He suspected as much from Jack. But neither did. Two rivals, eh? Andy thought. Only, someone else beat us to the prize…

Andy sat back to process what Fiona had just told them. The green space was tiny. Just one bench, a little walk-through, trees, bushes, and flowers. Thankfully no one else had come around. It was quiet and private.

"Todd, meanwhile," her voice grew fierce again, "went ballistic when my parents wouldn't tell him where I'd gone. My dad is a big man, too, but Todd threatened him physically if he wouldn't tell."

She shook her head. "I gave in, but he still… violated me. Took advantage. Used me *and* my brother's death. He let on he was so caring, such a good friend of Timmy's. Bullshit!" Her shout sent a squirrel scurrying. Both Andy and Jack also recoiled slightly at the ferocity of her tone. "As for Jesus, Todd used him, too. He even used Jesus…"

She was lost for a long while in her own thoughts.

"What happened to Todd?" Andy finally ventured.

"My dad phoned the Base Commander. Not only did he know Timmy, he spoke in glowing terms of his respect for him. When he heard the story about Todd, he said he'd look into it.

"My dad phoned me about a week later. Todd had been transferred. And I never heard from or about him again until I ran into him at the *Outpost* the other night."

All kinds of questions ran through Andy's head. Did she know who got the baby? Did she ever hear about him? How did her assembly handle this? How long did she stay at her aunt's? How have her parents been since? How did it get worked out with G. E. who could be, Andy knew, a pretty stern moralist? Why did she decide to join the team five years later? Andy had many more questions, but he asked none of them. Neither did Jack.

"This is what you forced out by doing your little amateur detective work, Andy. I hope you're both proud!" There was that bitterness again.

"Fiona," Andy began, "I can't possibly think less of you..." Andy was more choked up than he realized. Why was he almost crying, he who never cried?

"What... what might this Todd try to do?"

Fiona grew agitated. "I don't know! I don't know! I need to call my dad right away..."

"Would calling the Base Commander here be worthwhile?" Jack asked.

Fiona winced. "What has Todd done wrong?"

"What did he say to you Friday night?" Jack asked.

"'Hello, Fiona. Fancy meeting you here.' And he smirked big time. That's all. Hardly very incriminating."

Jack's face was pensive. "What might Todd do?"

"I really don't know. I really don't know," came Fiona's reply.

Soon afterwards, they got up and headed back home. Fiona asked that this be kept in the strictest confidence, and that for the time being, nothing be communicated to G. E. She'd talk it over with her dad first.

When Andy got home, he dashed off a brief note to the Professor.

Dear Professor Norton:

Kind of knocks the stuffing out a bit, doesn't it? I mean, she wasn't really raped, though pretty close to it, I'll grant. You just never know. It totally changes what I think of her. Of course. And now I don't know what to think. Of her, of life, of faith.

That's why I'm writing, actually. Not that you've ever been very forthcoming with your answers. But perhaps the answers lie in the questions themselves, like the casing of a nut that gets cracked and reveals the goodies within. Maybe. That's reason enough for writing.

What would you do? What would Jesus do? What will Todd do?

Jack and I talked about all this after leaving Fiona at the girls' apartment. We had no answers. We promised Fiona that we would say nothing. Interesting that the first people she tells her story to are two single guys she knows like her. And it's fair to say, come to think of it, that she was more aggressive with me in initiating a relationship…

Well, I admit, I was instantly smitten, and it showed all over my face, no doubt, even the first time I met her. But why would she not show more caution? Maybe she thinks five years is long enough. Given the brethren rumour mill, I'm amazed some of this story was not already doing the rounds at the Centre.

I'm pretty confused, Professor, pretty confused. Any suggestions of where I go from here?

Andy

46

The first Saturday in July, all the girls, except Sharon, brought water guns when they visited the boys' apartment one evening for a Games Night. Peter did not go, fortunately. They waited until they were inside then pulled out their guns and opened fire.

Hardly the image of sober missionaries, the guys responded accordingly. Jack cornered Fiona, snatched away her pistol, and returned fire. Andy grabbed Janys' and did likewise while Jean popped her guns down the front of her blouse.

Just then, Fiona dove at Andy and grabbed at Janys' firearm. Jean, meanwhile, retrieved her guns and opened fire at Jack as soon as he came to Andy's rescue. Janys deftly snatched Fiona's back from Jack then suddenly found herself flung onto Andy and Fiona wrestling on the ground. For a few frenzied moments, there was a general *mêlée*.

Then they burst apart, laughing and panting hard. By then Gary had retrieved Sharon and Jean's pistols, and Jack and Andy had seized Fiona's and Janys's. Terrible vengeance was threatened until it was agreed the girls would pay full retribution through an exotic dessert evening for the guys.

A week later, at a nearby park, Fiona and Jack began rolling about in the grass, eventually tumbling down a short embankment over some imagined tiff. Janys and Andy cheered their respective gender on.

Andy and Jack finally talked about it after the third time it happened at the girls' apartment the next day, Sunday. Andy wondered whether it was in part release for several deeper dynamics, including anger, frustration, and sexual desire. It permitted lots of physical touching without its ever searing, he said, rather like passing a finger quickly through the flame of a candle. The thrill without the burn. Still, there was some unease with Andy, though Jack had been wrestling girls all his life.

"But Jack," Andy finally said into the dark as he lay on his bunk bed, "you can't tell me you're oblivious to the feel of a woman's boobs."

"I'm only human, Andy. Of course I like the feel, however fleeting. But I like the look, too. And that cannot be helped, or the good Lord would not have given us eyes. In fact, isn't that the point, we're not to 'lust after,' which I take to mean become obsessive about, so that we lose our freedom? That goes for booze, money, possessions, and a raft of other things."

"Okay," Andy shot back, "in our wrestling around, you're aware suddenly that girls' hands are grabbing at your crotch and catching some action there. Just fleeting touch, mind you. Is it still all right?"

"Heck, Andy! You're always so *logical*! The difference is, since it has happened, that we guys can show our arousal so quickly. That lump can become pretty telltale. So no, I don't feel comfortable with that, I admit."

"So because girls don't show it physically, though likely feel it just the same, it's okay?"

"Andy, I give up. You'd argue your mother into the grave. You should have become a lawyer."

"Funny," Andy replied, "that's *exactly* what my mother has told me many times. She never thought I'd become an undertaker…"

"Good night, Andy." With that, they drifted off to sleep.

CHRYSALIS CRUCIBLE

The following Saturday, Janys addressed the issue during an outing with Andy in the *Tiergarten*. He looked forward to such outings with increasing anticipation. He wondered again why there was no vow concerning her. The whole story of G. E.'s restrictions regarding Fiona back at the Centre flooded back with fierce distaste.

"Andy," she began, "I don't want to sound like a prude, but..." She almost clammed up right there. She continued slightly higher pitched and more rapidly. "Don't you think we're a little too free with the wrestling? It seems to be happening more frequently. I know, it's meant innocently enough as good clean fun, but, well, sometimes guys don't know what touch can do to girls..."

Andy knew what she was getting at, knew also that she was essentially right. Only she didn't raise what touch could also do to guys. "Aw, Janys. I'll bet you used to wrestle with all your brothers, right? I think it's just the same thing. You and I did it right in this park just a few weeks ago."

That elicited a winsome smile from her. Andy knew he could easily wrestle her again.

"That was different, Andy, and you know it," she said simply.

"Okay, I grant it. But should guys never touch women until they marry them, and *vice versa?* Is there something inherently wrong about it? If so, what?

"When I... look at a woman's breasts, things register. Their size. Her looks and figure. That happens without conscious thought. I rarely dwell on it, and at times shut it out.

He took a deep breath. "For example, I saw your breasts close-up once, Janys, not a little exposed, remember? I just don't dwell on it." Why was he so emboldened?

"Then why are you blushing, Andy?" Janys's smile was broad.

He was. In spite of himself. He had been caught with her full awareness of what was in his mind's eye.

"I think I just made my case," she said evenly.

Andy was silent for a long time, until his face regained its natural colour. "Then, Janys, why did your 'strip-tease' not bother you more?"

It was Janys's turn to be silent for some time. "Because I trusted you, Andy. Because I knew that had you suddenly caught me even in my all-togethers that night, your hands would not have been all over me—or worse. Because you're honourable, Andy. In Jesus' day, it was not a shame to be naked, only for another to stare at your nakedness possessively. In Jesus' language, Andy, you didn't 'lust after' me."

Andy made no allusion to the rising red in her face.

"Andy, you know better than you are saying, I think. Sometimes… Sometimes I wish I was as bold as you with all your words. But are they at times defence mechanisms or maybe stalling techniques while you patch together your real thoughts?

"Touch, for girls, is really intimate. When you touch us, it had better be for the right reasons! In this culture, far too often it is for the wrong reasons. Even a hug is suspect. We had a high school coach who was fired because he wouldn't stop hugging the girls on the basketball team. They knew he was doing more than congratulating them…

"I don't know how it arouses you guys, but touch is friendly, loving, intimate or sexually aggressive, as far as I have it figured. Friendly if given in empathy, loving if caring is uppermost, intimate where commitment is made, and sexually aggressive far too often.

"My oldest sister Karen is a beauty. Everybody said so from earliest age. So much so, that my parents, I learned years later, asked friends not to talk about it. It went to her head, nonetheless. She became captain of the cheerleading squad and was really popular with guys. She also tried to retain her Christian commitment. Not easy to do when what is most noticeable about a girl/woman is her physical appearance. I watched her struggle.

"A science major at Carlton University determined to become a doctor began to attend our assembly for a work term. He was a few years older than my sister. John was single and good-looking, an apparently sincere Christian, obviously bright, and wanting to serve the Lord on the mission field. He became youth leader the fall he arrived.

"I guess no one was really paying too close attention. But one night my sister came in devastated. John had not driven her home, which usually happened. We were the last house on his drop-off route. I remember I was watching TV, still too young for Young Peoples. She was in tears and went straight to her bedroom. My mom followed, and I could hear sobs and my sister's loud voice at times. It was years later I found out what had happened.

"John and Karen had been cleaning up after Young People's. They were the only two that night. No others had needed a ride home. My sister had picked up a tray of drinking glasses, one tipped, and she spilled juice on the top part of her blouse. John ran to the kitchen, grabbed a dishcloth, and began to wipe the stain. It all happened so fast. Suddenly, his hand was under her blouse, under her bra, caressing. At first she didn't tell him to stop. It felt so good! Then she permitted a lingering kiss. His panting shocked her to her senses, and she pulled away abruptly.

"John asked what was the matter. She said she was going to go home immediately, but not with him!

"His face turned ugly at that point, and she felt very vulnerable and afraid.

"'Fine!' he exclaimed. 'But just remember you wanted it, too. And I'll say that if you ever tell on me!'

"With that he took off. She called one of the elders, who lived near the church, and he drove her home."

"My sister quit Young People's after that. John was never even disciplined by the elders, but he moved away after only one semester. Mom and dad were tight-lipped about the whole experience. My sister felt betrayed. She's seven years older than me, has long since moved away from home, and I only heard this full story from her a year ago when I asked her why she had quit going to church.

"To my knowledge, John never made it to the mission field."

Janys reflected in silence then turned to Andy. "Well, that's my story about touch. It's playing with fire. And I think you know it deep down."

"So what should I do, Janys?"

Janys did not hesitate. "Maybe we're waiting for you to model 'No,' Andy. Something a guy in Christian leadership is supposed to do—unlike John Cooper!"

She said no more. They got up and returned home.

Thanks for spoiling the fun, Janys, he thought to himself later that afternoon. He thought of the six-inch cannons they used to buy at the store until their obvious danger finally filtered through. Those tin cans used to blow twice the height of a house. They were so much fun!

How could Jack do it and he not? Why didn't Janys talk to Jack, too? Was she saying it was safe for Jack but not for Andy? He resented the implication of Janys's talk. He wanted to call her a prude, but he knew it was off the mark. She was not priggish. She had given him high praise.

He wanted to forget about the talk and just let things happen. But now the nail had been driven in, the damage done, the attention drawn. Maybe that was the sword at Garden's edge: conscience activated such that blood was drawn if behaviour continued. Is that what Paul meant when he said, "I would not have known what sin was except through the law. For I would not have known what coveting really was if the law had not said, 'Do not covet'"?

What a paradox this freedom thing! Andy was free to do anything—except what was hurtful. But then was he really free? At least unconstrained. So maybe constraint was a subset of freedom. Maybe constraint was the ticket to freedom. Rules in a card game or hockey were obvious examples. Or what about exiting a building through the wall rather than the door or window? Constraints there, sheer molecular physicality of the wall, if breached, probably meant jail and concomitant loss of freedom, if somebody else's building or house, big repair bills regardless. Exiting an airplane before it landed was an extreme example of constraint—even if undertaken with single-minded commitment to freedom, and unless minimum constraint in the form of a parachute was exercised. In that case, hopefully a few instructions (Still more constraints!) at minimum gleaned, enacted before the jump. Constraints and freedom.

But we're ten years plus into the so-called sexual revolution, Andy thought. What's so wrong with unbridled sexual indulgence? Of all the human appetites, after all, that is far and away the most potent. A woman's body is a surpassing work of art. Why not, like in a painting class, study its exquisite curves to heart's content? Or fondle it freely like a potter's seductive clay?

Sheer fantasizing caused Andy to have an erection. The pure pleasure of that, and further in masturbation to the point of orgasm, were not unknown. Why not a step further to immoderation with a woman as the spirit urged?

I guess it's the text we read, Andy finally concluded. The cultural *con*-text that says, "Yes!" to sexual gratification today whenever and wherever. (Provided it is consensual and age appropriate. Oops! Constraint smuggled into the sexual revolution even.) A faith choice whichever way, in the end. Consciously or not. Then why such railing against sexual constraint? After all, we can't just go out and rob, steal, plunder, and kill at will. So why not constraints to sexual indulgence? And why not biblical ones?

Maybe, thought Andy, because Christians are so judgmental and self-righteous about it all. "Missionary position" to begin and end with. All sexual pleasure be damned! Who said it was wrong to have fun with sex if God invented it and our bodies? Where did that come from? Andy recalled a joke he'd seen recently about a priest at a bar telling the seductively clad waitress he was committed to celibacy like his priest father, and his father's priest father before him…

47

The Americans blockaded North Vietnam the second full week of July. The team heard about it through Scott Cunningham, who dropped over to the boys' apartment for a quick visit Monday afternoon; a case of *Dr Pepper* and a few other goodies in tow. The base was on high alert, he said, knowing how ill favoured toward the war many were in West Berlin. A huge anti-war rally was being planned for the coming Saturday.

Scott also informed Jack that while Todd had not asked him directly about Fiona, he had heard that Todd had made some inquiries. He was pretty sure Todd would find out where the girls' apartment was soon enough, if he didn't already know. But he added, "Todd is in an officers' Bible study group here at the base and thought of pretty highly. So I doubt you should have any concerns."

When Jack and Andy discussed it afterwards, Andy commented, "Todd was also in an officers' Bible study group in Texas when he got Fiona pregnant, Jack. It doesn't exactly wash with me after hearing Fiona's take on it."

Jack agreed. But what else to do? They simply did not know.

Gary and Andy, strictly out of curiosity, attended the huge rally that Saturday.

Several such demonstrations originated at the same place in *Olivaer Platz* on *Pariserstraße*. Despite his discussions with and letters from Hans, Andy still struggled with such demonstrations.

It seemed very well organized. About 1,000 people

showed up, as far as Andy could tell. Gary taped some of the chanting, and he and Andy both took some pictures.

They had copies of a tract they were distributing that spoke of the exciting rise of Jesus People all around the world and of the potential imminent return of Jesus Christ, a topic near to Gary's heart.

They gave one to an interesting guy in his late twenties whom they encountered when the rally finally broke up. Andy led off by saying something to the guy in his best German as he handed him a tract. The man thanked him for it then reached out to shake his hand. Andy reciprocated.

"*Ich heiße Hans*," he said, "*und du?*" Andy responded by introducing himself and then Gary. Then Hans surprised them both by asking, in a perfect American accent, "Where are you guys from?"

Surprised, Andy blurted back: "Where did you learn your English?"

"By hanging around Americans," Hans replied.

"Did you ever live in America?"

"No."

"What about any other English-speaking country?"

"No."

This was too much for Andy. "I can't believe your English," he said finally. "There's hardly any accent, and it's flawless."

"Just a knack," said Hans.

He glanced down at the tract. "So you guys are Jesus People?"

"Not exactly," responded Gary, "But we are Christians over here to tell others about Jesus."

"Shoot!" Hans invited.

A little disconcerted looking, Gary led off. But

he only got a short way into his presentation before Hans interrupted. "You know, I've hung around the Jesus People here in Berlin. And I've met a lot of the Christians on the American Army Base through various contacts. Even attended their Bible studies. One night they showed this movie, *A Thief in the Night*. Everybody got really scared. I didn't. And I started seeing through things then."

"Like what," Gary asked. Andy knew he'd be defensive, since he and others had used the film as the basis for a youth evangelistic outreach through Gary's home church.

"For starters, the film is obviously meant to bring people to faith in Christ. But what induces you to trust people? Their ugliness or their caring? If God is really a God of love, which this film reflects with an example of a teen conversion near the beginning, it just doesn't add up that the real reason for coming to Christ, as I watched the film, is God's *nastiness*. He'll leave you behind to a horrendous fate, quite literally saying, 'To hell with you!' if you don't believe now. This is underscored by that sappy Larry Norman song reprised at various times about being 'left behind.'"

Andy had heard Gary and Sharon perform that very song, "I Wish We'd All Been Ready," numerous times in the coffeehouse back at GO Headquarters. They really liked Larry Norman and had gone with a group of trainees to one of his concerts in Chicago.

"But what if God really is that way?" Gary responded. "If you'll excuse me for saying so, you sound like so many liberals or cult groups I know of who stress the love of God but are really weak on his holiness. God is not only a God of love, He is also a God of vengeance, which, Romans twelve-nineteen assures, he will repay one day. In that way, He's like any parent who must punish to show that He really means business and is in control."

"But does a good parent ever cut off his children?" Hans paused, his eyes looking vacant for a few seconds. "Doesn't a parent punish precisely to bring kids back home? But this movie makes God into some kind of Cosmic Punisher who, once past the cut-off date, never lets anyone home again."

"But Jesus told lots of parables about being too late," Gary replied. "For instance, the people who didn't have oil for their lamps or wedding clothes on. Jesus warns that you've got to be ready *now*!"

"But what about Jesus' answer to Peter about how often we are to forgive? Isn't the implication that you never stop forgiving? If that is what Jesus expects people to do, how come you believe God does something less, in fact, far worse? How come the movie has the little girl scream like she's about to be murdered or something for fear that her parents have suddenly been taken away by Jesus at his Second Coming, leaving her behind? Or how come that guy's wife—the guy who leaves his shaver running because he's been raptured—who desperately wants to get help from God, but the clear message is: 'Sorry, it's too late. The deadline is past. It's over for you now, baby!'"

Gary shook his head. "I don't think the movie is mocking anyone for not believing. But the Bible clearly teaches, 'It is appointed unto men once to die, but after this the judgment.' Jesus also said, 'Ye have omitted the weightier matters of the law, judgment.' That's God's holiness. He is a God of justice, of judgment. He is the Ultimate Judge."

Andy was impressed by Gary's command of Scripture. He was trying to remember the references and guess at the contexts when he heard Hans reply,

"But doesn't the book of James say, 'Mercy triumphs over judgment'? And what about the idea in the book of Revelation about the bad guys throughout, 'the kings of the earth,' who near the end all land in the second death lake of fire, but end up, right after, going into the New Jerusalem coming down from heaven?"

Andy remained silent and watched Gary, who appeared nonplussed. Andy pulled out his New Testament then thought better of it, since it was a bit embarrassing to admit to Hans they weren't quite sure what he was talking about.

"You see, I think you guys have bought into a schizophrenic god. Apparently, Jesus is all about loving enemies. Doesn't the book of Romans say somewhere that the work of Christ (Atonement, right?) is centrally about God's reconciliation with the powerless, ungodly sinners, God's enemies? If that's right, how can you believe that God does the unimaginable to his enemies because they don't believe? Doesn't that make Jesus say and do one thing then God do the opposite? I think that's crazy!"

"God is love, to be sure—" Gary started.

"But," Andy interrupted, "in God there can be no contradiction, so somehow God as our Lover and as our Hanging Judge fit together. For instance, I can imagine that we should not have the right to kill our wife's murderer. That would be revenge. But if God is the great Avenger, then even a human judge can act like God. They do, in fact, act as ordained by God according to Romans 13."

He paused a moment, remembering Hans Buetler's words about this passage, namely that it was not the State's *magna carta* to commit violence through the death penalty and war that Christians had claimed since the fourth century. The perfect 'cake-and-eat-it-too' end run around Jesus' teachings on non-violence. He continued nonetheless. "He is ordained by God according to Romans 13 to do in the courthouse what he would never be permitted to do outside that official role. I don't think that makes God schizophrenic. It has to do with God's right over us by virtue of his having created us." Why did this not seem convincing to Andy even as he said it?

"A bit like a feudal lord of the manor?" Hans asked, "who could order 'satisfaction' from his serfs of any kind for wrongs committed?"

"I guess so," Andy responded.

"But that's my point! I might fear the lord of the manor and give in because of his superior might, but I would hardly trust him, let alone love him, if he acted like that. So why should I trust in the kind of God you're trying to sell me?"

"Besides," he went on, "what about the Prodigal Son story? Isn't the father in the story supposed to be a picture of God? Does the father act like a feudal lord of the manor or like some father so crazy about his kid that no matter what his son does, he is willing to roll out the red carpet as soon as he comes home? There's no hint of a cut-off point in that story. The only punishment I see in it is the self-inflicted sulking of the older brother. In fact, I think the older brother is closer to what you and other Christians, including that awful movie, have been telling me God is like: stern, unbending, bound by the rules, angry, punitive..."

Andy almost lost track of the discussion so taken was he by Hans's biblical knowledge and English fluency. He was staying clued in enough, however, to realize that the discussion was not going well for him or Gary. This guy knew too much Scripture for them to put him in his place but not enough, obviously, to become a believer. Andy felt a mounting resentment that Hans should question God. How dare he?

As they talked, people continued to swirl all around them. Didn't anyone notice the eternal life-and-death issues they were discussing? Wasn't this just the way of the world, so oblivious to spiritual realities just off the corner of their vision?

Andy decided to speak up. "Hans, the problem with Satan in his fall was *hubris*, pride. That is usually what stands in the way of our believing in Jesus. Our pride. You obviously know the Gospel, and the Bible well enough. Is it pride keeping you from trusting him? I challenge you to rethink your rejection of Jesus, what you called, 'seeing through.' C. S. Lewis warned in one of his writings that there is a danger of thinking we can see through so much that we end up really seeing nothing at all. Which in the end is blindness. I think you may be in danger of that."

Having stunned Hans into silence, Andy continued. "The Gospel message is really quite simple. God loves you and has a wonderful plan for your life..." His voice faltered.

Quoting the opening of the *Four Spiritual Laws* made him remember his recent discussion with Hans, who had added the wry comment on that opening line, "But if you don't buy in, God hates you and has a terrible plan for your afterlife." It nagged at Andy's memory that someone else had said that to him once.

He suddenly realized with the force of a hammer blow that both Hans and Hans Beutler were saying essentially the same thing, one as a believer, another as an unbeliever: God as God of love precludes God as God of hate. Or "God" be damned! But Evangelicals proclaim both. He thought all such must hope they catch God on his good day—or rest assured smug that they have already, because they've "bought in," signed the fire insurance policy on the dotted line. And let the rest be damned. Let them burn! He felt such revulsion all of a sudden. Weren't the cults the first to reject the traditional doctrine of hell as eternal conscious torment? Why was he suddenly thinking like the cults?

Sensing Andy's faltering, Gary jumped in. "And so God sent his Son to die on the cross..." and he went on with the Bill Bright presentation that had brought millions to Christ. This was not news to Hans—no Good News either, Andy thought wryly—but he listened patiently enough.

When Gary finished his speech, which he uttered with an eye-fixing intensity reminiscent of the Mormon missionary they had encountered at GO, Hans changed the subject abruptly. "Can you guys loan me some money by any chance? I'm a little down on my luck..."

Just a panhandler, after all, Andy thought with disgust.

"No," Gary said cheerily, this strategy having been discussed back at the Centre, "but we will take you to get a *Bratwurst* or something." There were lots of stands selling such in the downtown area.

Hans agreed, though without great enthusiasm. "I don't even have a place to stay tonight," he said.

First money, now he was inviting himself to stay at our place! Andy felt revolted again. He was surprised to hear Gary saying, "There's me, my wife and two guys all living in an apartment. I guess we could give you our address, and if you're still interested, you could show up tonight. But we won't let you in if you're drunk, and at the most for two nights. Then you'll have to find someplace else."

This was a new one on Andy. What if the guy

showed up with a knife or a gun? What if he was a rapist? He was surprised at Gary's quick invitation, but he agreed that Hans didn't appear too dangerous. They bought Hans a Bratwurst with all the fixings, wished him well, and said they might see him that night.

"I think he's under real conviction, Andy," Gary commented as they made their way back home. "He's obviously resisting the Gospel a lot, but he seems so close, too. Definitely has some weird liberal ideas though. And he knows his Bible! Maybe one day we should write a book about the doctrine of hell, proving how God can be loving and holy at the same time. That seems so central to the Gospel."

After Gary and Andy recounted their experience to Sharon back at the apartment, she shook her head. "You invited Hans to stay at our place, and you don't even know his last name?"

It was true, Andy thought, but who knew if he was telling the truth anyway? "I hope he doesn't show up for supper. I don't have any more meat than just enough for our bunch," she added.

As it turned out, Hans didn't show. They didn't run into him again on the street either. However, Hans kept returning to Andy's mind, uninvited, accusing, questioning. Would he show up in heaven one day, perhaps still questioning, pointing the finger? Does Jesus honour answers more than questions? Andy remembered former American black gang leader turned evangelist Tom Skinner, who would thunder, "If Christ is the answer, what are the questions?" Well, Andy had the questions all right! He wondered if 'Christ the Answer' could be stretched thinly enough to cover them all. No more 'Plastic Jesus,' he agreed. He needed a 'Spandex Jesus.'

48

The letter smacked of intrigue. Scott Cunningham delivered it the day after the rally. That added to the mystery. There were carbon copies for Jack, Janys, and Fiona. It read:

Dear Andy:

As you know, an aspect of our work that we never broadcast too widely is a ministry to the Iron Curtain countries. Others and I make intermittent trips to some countries where we have established Christian contacts.

The purpose is to offer encouragement, primarily in the form of money, which they use to produce Christian literature in their own way.

I am planning a trip in August to coincide with Euro View. Dan is coming, too. I am asking you, Jack, Fiona, and Janys to join me. We will attract less attention as a group.

You needn't come, any of you, if you feel at all hesitant. There could be risks, but they are minimal.

I intend to visit Yugoslavia, Romania, and Hungary.

But please, not a word of this to anyone outside the team until after the mission is over.

God's richest blessings in your work there.

Triumphantly in Christ,

G. E. Moore

P. S. Please store this letter in a safe place.

Their decision to go invigorated the group, particularly the singles. It helped galvanize Andy in other areas as well. He became more assertive in his self-ascribed role as team motivator, if not as team leader. He was relieved that G. E. trusted him enough to be on such a journey with Fiona. He had obviously been checking on his and Fiona's "progress" through Gary and Peter. Euro View was a summer tour of European countries by potential future GOers, culminating with a huge outreach during the Munich Olympics.

A further aspect of his new assumed role was Len Howton's communication with him from Nîce, where he was team leader. Len had also been in France with a team before, but unlike Carl Friesen, the Madrid team leader, he had been with them a year at the Centre. Andy had not had much to do with Len, his wife or their two young kids. But he would periodically bounce his French off Len at the Centre.

"Andy, you should really join our team," Len would say. "What can the Berlin Wall offer that outdoes the Côte D'Azur and the Riviera?" Then he'd add with a twinkle: "You have guard towers watching everybody, we have everybody watching the topless bathers." He was a pretty free spirit.

The letter requested Andy join Len in Munich the week of August 7th. Andy was to make his own travel arrangements and find his way to the Simpson's, American GO contacts in Munich, who were to be conduits for them in getting literature shipped over for the Olympics. The Simpson's were with Baptist Mid-Missions, a Southern Baptist missionary agency. This prospect was a welcome diversion for Andy at a time when he and the other team members were looking for excuses to get away from West Berlin.

There were, it was becoming evident, advantages

to being single, a little older, male, and in reasonable command of the language. Andy found himself keenly anticipating his visit with Len. But there was the immediate reality of team life to adjust to in the meantime.

In the first two weeks of July, team life settled into a pattern, albeit disjointed and disorganized. The members pursued a variety of contacts they had begun to make, with a range of initiatives they undertook themselves and others originating with B. B. Some began helping with the Bread of Life book table on the *Ku'damm* and followed through with visitation.

Others began looking for a location to open a coffeehouse. Some met with Hermann Mainz, a local evangelist quite fluent in English, to discuss ways of helping him, and vice versa. They all undertook to distribute hundreds of *Jesus People* newspapers, purchased from Mainz, which told stories of miraculous conversions. He was excited about their presence in Berlin. The Jesus People Movement in the States had become worldwide news by then.

Mainz had also attracted a fair amount of media attention with public baptisms in the *Wannsee* at a popular mile-long beach area. The cameras did not miss the colour of bikini-clad young girls, fingers jutting upwards, and going down for the count. Hermann was no slouch when it came to delivering a fiery sermon. He had even translated *The Cross and the Switchblade* for David Wilkerson, a book about miraculous conversions in a New York gang. Free copies were distributed by the thousands on Canadian high school campuses when Andy was in school.

Mainz sensed that even bigger things might be about to happen, that the team's presence was a further sign that Joel's prophecy just might be taking place in the midst of Communist Europe. The latter and former rains of God's blessing were, he believed, imminently set to cascade down. Berliners and their satanic minions were perhaps readying for the soggy deluge.

They attended his One Way coffeehouse and were further inspired to start one as well.

Horst Paetkau, the young *Lichterfelde* evangelist, visited them a few times, making Andy wonder if he was not interested in Janys. It did not appear to be reciprocated, Andy noted with satisfaction.

Meanwhile, B. B. met regularly with the married couples on Sunday afternoons. She also attended most team meetings and continued to command an enormous amount of air time.

At the July 17th team meeting, B. B. dropped a bombshell. She was aware that G. E. was going to be in Europe, though he had not, upon her inquiry, planned to visit West Berlin. Instead, he would meet with all three teams during the Munich Olympics. She announced that she had written to George asking him to extend his stay in Europe long enough for a mid-September evangelistic crusade. She had also contacted Hermann Mainz on the team's behalf to ask him to do the translating.

"I know this does not give us a lot of time," she acknowledged. "But George is a powerful preacher, and I think we can capitalize on his presence in Europe. As well, I have written to all the assemblies about this plan, which I knew you would endorse. I have requested a meeting of the *Großbruderstunde* with all of you and George."

The meeting she referred to happened periodically amongst all the assembly leadership on a somewhat *ad hoc* basis, to discuss common concerns. They knew their mission had been run by the eldership at such a meeting.

"I think this would give great exposure to what you are trying to do amongst the assemblies here and possibly kindle a renewed commitment from the elders to support evangelism and city-wide mission." As usual, B. B. said this all with enormous intensity, brow furrowed, breathless.

Andy waited for Peter or Gary to respond. He could wait no longer. "Beartrice," he began, not quite sure where he was going, "can you please think through a little of what you just informed us? You have essentially planned a few fairly major initiatives for us without any consultation! Or have you already run most of this by Gary and Peter?" He looked at them both, then at B. B.

"No, Andy," came her quick reply. "George gave me lots of encouragement to be very creative in involving you in all sorts of evangelistic initiatives. It's been my belief that you would readily join in anything I could bring your way. George more or less commissioned me to keep feeding you opportunities to spread the Gospel, which he assured me you would take. What I've just laid out is so obviously part of George's and GO's goals, how could you refuse?"

Andy felt like saying, "We'll show you how right now!" But he delayed in the hope someone else might say something. He doubted Janys would, more measured than he. The wives of the two leaders would defer to their husbands, who were saying nothing. Jack and Fiona remained silent. Jack was not usually quick off the mark about anything controversial.

"Beatrice," Andy said when no one else jumped in, "the point is you come buzzing into our team meetings and present us with projects that seem huge, needing lots of planning, but are of questionable viability. For you they may be *faits accomplis*, but not for most of us." He paused. Would someone say something now? Apparently not.

"I can't imagine arranging a major evangelistic crusade with G. E. inside of two months, especially when four of us are gone for several weeks in August and early September and all are gone for about two weeks to the huge outreach at the Munich Olympics. It's really out of the question, quite apart from G. E.'s response.

"But more importantly, Beatrice, and I guess I'll be very blunt seeing as no one else is, you are not our team leader. If you want to see us work cooperatively with you, then you must work cooperatively—not unilaterally—with us."

Andy was surprised at his own candour. He had not planned this.

"Second, though I'm not quite sure what this all means, you are a woman 'under authority,' according to Scripture. I don't see that working with you. It looks much more like you are working fairly independently and, furthermore; you want us to be under your authority. I don't think so, biblically, and I don't think so more emphatically in terms of our mandate here. We were not sent to be your team, Beatrice."

There was a long, uneasy silence. Then Peter took a deep breath. "Please excuse Andy's brusqueness, Beatrice. But he does raise a valid concern about how much you presume about us."

Not to be outdone, Gary added, "Andy can be a bit too blunt sometimes. But what he means, Beatrice, is we are feeling our way along in what is best for us to do. As we've said to you at our Sunday meetings, we're happy to consult, pray, and share together. But we need a little space to plan our own activities."

What neither mentioned were the objections Andy had begun to make to B. B.'s presence at all of their meetings. Andy had also begun to question their meeting so frequently with her separately. He was pushing for clarification from G. E. They had agreed to raise this with him when in Europe.

Andy noticed the clock ticking. There was obvious discomfort in the room. B. B.'s eyes were on the floor. "Well, perhaps I have presumed too much. But I am ever mindful of so many dear souls for whom Christ died." She raised her eyes to look at each one in turn. "And when I think of that, I cannot hold back from preaching the Word, being instant in season and out of season, as Paul enjoins. If I think of the multitudes in West Berlin advancing toward a Christless eternity without having the opportunity to be saved, I can hardly contain myself. I thought you dear young people shared the same vision for lost souls, that your earnest prayer was that the Lord of the harvest would send more reapers into the field, that you all had said, 'Here I am, Lord, send me.' Maybe I misunderstood your sense of calling after all."

Something broke in Andy at that point. "Beatrice," he said, eyes funnelled, nostrils flaring, voice quivering, "you are whining 'poor me' and laying on guilt trips. I say *balderdash* to all that! I will not be bossed around by a pushy woman—or by anyone else for that matter. If you are so all-fired uptight about all the German hordes going to hell you'd be out day and night 'rescuing the perishing' until you perished from exhaustion yourself! But didn't you instead just take a holiday late last year in the Austrian Alps at *Schloß Mittersill*?

"All work and no play makes not only our Jack a 'dull boy,' but everyone else! I will not be bullied into doing evangelism, pure and simple. There is still a mandate somewhere to enjoy the good creation. I want to fulfill a mission not be lashed into an evangelism slave ship with you as Captain.

"I'm sorry to be so blunt, but someone has to be. We came over here to do evangelism, yes. But something is wrong if we imagine that everyone who does not confess Jesus Christ as Lord and Saviour by their dying breath will be sentenced to eternal torment and damnation. I don't care what the Reformers taught about double predestination or what J.I. Packer teaches today."

Andy saw a few eyes widen at his last comment, but he continued on. "Something has to give. I sense it is not the Bible. It is an incredibly straight-jacketed interpretation that removes all the joy and leaves us burnt-out death stars not fit for heaven or hell!"

Even Andy felt shocked at his outburst.

Gary jumped in. "Andy, you're obviously worked up. We all know the Scripture, 'It is appointed unto men once to die, but after this the judgment.' We know the Bible teaches everyone goes to a Christless eternity if they fail to accept Jesus this side of death. We cannot change Scripture."

"Gary, what if that 'judgment' is in fact God's mercy that sentences us to 'get it' finally about Jesus, the measure of all truth?," Janys asked, causing several heads to turn. "What if the burning fire of hell is God's agonizing love that makes it all but impossible to reject him? What if God's wrath is God's anguished covenant love crying out like Hosea, 'How shall I give thee up, O Ephraim'? What if the only person we know for sure who went to hell is Jesus, precisely to empty it once and for all, 'bringing captivity captive'?"

Gary just about responded, but B. B. beat him to it. "You know, I think that is the precise difficulty with brethren youth today. They get educated, and all their ideas begin to clash with the plain truth of Scripture.

"If your mission over here is hesitant, like an uncertain sound of the trumpet, then you will fail. God's Word is the only measure of truth. Janys, you and Andy should reconsider your unbelief toward Scripture."

Andy felt his face reddening, not from embarrassment this time. "Beatrice, I have personally spent hours with my uncle studying Scripture. And I have won through the hard way to faith during my four years at university. If Christ is the 'Truth,' we should not fear truth, no matter from what quarter it comes—university or church. Both have been wrong over the centuries. Hard to tell which one has been wrong more often. If you want my opinion, I'd go with the Church."

"I think we have heard enough from you, Andy," Peter said. "I'm inclined to agree with Beatrice and Gary. I'm sure Jack and Fiona would, too." He looked at them. It was hard for Andy to read their thoughts. He knew his own well enough though: Smouldering anger at B. B., Peter, Gary—and Fiona and Jack for not leaping to his side.

"Excuse me," Andy said abruptly. Before anyone said a thing, he opened the French doors and headed toward the washroom.

Inside, he looked at himself in the mirror, thinking his very glance might cloud the mirror's surface, so steamed were his feelings.

By the time he exited, the meeting was breaking up. Andy was in no mood to talk to anyone. He went outside before anyone else. He suddenly found himself hating their mission. He also admitted that he hated—or something akin to it—some of his team mates, too. Great missionary he was turning out to be.

He took a bracing walk before heading off with

Janys an hour later. Janys and Andy had planned to go to the *Aktion in Jedes Haus* office, a German counterpart to the Every Home Crusade. They were to ask for sample literature, since the team planned to do similar door-to-door work after the Olympics initiative.

Midway along their trip by subway and bus, Andy opened up. "I have never felt so frustrated, Janys. Was I misreading the reaction of Gary and Peter or were they not entirely sucking up to B. B.? Give me a break!" He felt his face flush with anger again.

"Andy, you're right, Peter and Gary did wimp out a bit..."

"Not a bit, Janys, *big time*."

"What I was going to say," Janys continued, "is that I think they are not running scared of B. B. so much, though that could be part of it. I think they are afraid that if we break with B. B., what do we have left?

"Put yourself in their shoes, Andy. They are responsible for getting us going in our mission. And frankly, they are not doing too well. Soon G. E. will be in Europe, and will be looking for an accounting. I think they are running scared, because they do not have too much to report. In this sense, B. B. is their major hope. When you begin chipping away at that base, they understandably get nervous."

Janys Thane—psychologist, theologian, all-around Incredible Thinker. She just made so much sense. Andy knew he could take enormously circuitous routes to arrive at similar conclusions. Janys was an intuitive hot knife through butter in response to so much in life. How did she do that?

Her comments already calmed him down some. He knew Peter and Gary were not just being bull-headed or cowardly. There was more to it. If only he could remember that: All behaviour had a reason. Better to understand than judge. How easily that rolled off the tongue…

"So what should we do about B. B., Janys?" Andy asked as they exited the *U-bahn* and walked upstairs to catch their bus.

Janys waited until they had arrived at the bus stop to answer. "I think we give her enough rope to hang herself, Andy. Like you, I do not trust her. There is enormous religious overlay of something smouldering like a volcano underneath. I don't know a thing about her background. But I can tell you, her yen to control arises from enormous pain and hurt.

"The Japanese are not, by and large, big people, as you well know. Yet they produce prodigious Sumo wrestlers weighing in at more than six hundred pounds, men that are utterly anomalous, gargantuan enlargements of the Japanese norm. Andy, *B. B. is a brethren Sumo wrestler*. Perhaps the only good news is, they mostly die off by age forty."

She smirked at her own joke.

"So, Janys, if I take her on?"

"We'll all lose." Janys' response was quick, pointed, decisive. She said no more.

Andy knew that somehow B. B. had to trip herself or they would be stuck with a 600-pound Sumo wrestler as team mascot. It was a terrifying prospect. And B. B. was not yet 40. A brethren anomaly. An anomaly of that anomaly. He went to sleep that night with an uneasy image of being in the same ring as B. B. the Sumo wrestler. It was far more hopeless than if he were up against Jack…

49

Near the end of July, the team received official permission to sell books on the *Ku'damm*. They were also allowed to sing on the *Ku'damm* in front of the *Gedächtniskirche* so as to attract passers-by. This duty was undertaken mainly by Gary and Sharon.

The Kaiser-Wilhelm Memorial Church had been rebuilt since the war, but the bombed-out remains were left next door as reminder of the devastation of the Allied saturation bombing of the Second World War, which had killed and wounded about a million civilians. The only object left standing inside the church was a statue of Christ with vile graffiti scribbled all over.

Perhaps not an unfitting symbol of the sense of irrelevance most in that city felt the Church represented, thought Andy. Especially if Christ and his Church symbolized VIOLENCE. He pictured himself writing vile graffiti all over that Christ, too, such a Christ that had caused the rampant secularization of modern Europe.

When Gary and Sharon sang, the rest of the team carried posters declaring *Jesus Liebt Dich* and *Jesus ist der Weg*, "Jesus Loves You" and "Jesus is the Way." They also passed out colourful Jesus People newspapers to the invariably dozens walking by or simply hanging around. Many were bona fide hippies and did nothing else.

They also conducted an *Umfrage* with B. B.'s language help, modelled after the questionnaire at mission headquarters. They accosted several people that summer, engaging many in discussions. Surprisingly, they were not particularly rebuffed by most. Perhaps it was even out of deference to their general lack of language skills.

The team also began a kid's club, with the permission of the *Wilmersdorf* assembly. It was not really supported by them, but arrangements were made and permission granted for the church building to be used to run a day camp in July and part of August.

Andy drew on his previous year's experience in Kitchener, far away in a different time warp, to contribute lots of creative ideas. He felt fulfilled doing this. They sang songs, told stories (the kids had lots of fun with their German pronunciation) made excursions to the parks, and did crafts. About twenty kids usually attended, and it was gratifying to the team to see several make Christian commitments. Though it nagged at Andy: Then what? Was all they were selling, crassly, just kids' fire insurance?

Three disturbing elements also arose for Andy during this time: First, there was an obvious growing disenchantment exhibited by Peter toward the other team members. He could not handle all the shenanigans, the wrestling matches, the kibitzing. It simply was un-Christian. And he was not around for the half of what often transpired. Peter finally submitted an open letter, which he read aloud at the July 24th team meeting, the week after Andy's challenge to B. B. She was not in attendance for whatever reason that Monday—perhaps at Peter's bidding?

Dear Fellow Team Members:

Why?
This is the question I keep asking as I observe your behaviour from week to week. Why all this frivolous activity? If our primary occupation in heaven is to gaze

on our Saviour's face in complete adoration, then why not start some of that here below?

Why instead do you carry on at your Game Nights, and, I hear rumours, on other occasions when I am not present, with activities that would make... well they make me blush at least. How can you reconcile that behaviour with your walk with Christ? How can you reach out to others with the life-giving message while living something so opposite?

If Paul is to be taken seriously, we have many "principalities and powers" against which we are fighting here in West Berlin. We are invading Satan's strongholds. How? By holding wrestling matches between guys and girls, by playing endless games of Rook, Monopoly, and other card games, and now the new dice game, Barricade?

We are soldiers for Christ, not partiers.

With all the time you spend in frivolous activities, you could be serving the Lord so much more: in evangelism, in studying to make yourselves approved, and in prayer.

I guess I'm saying I'm ashamed. Ashamed to be identified with all that. I won't be. And that's why Jean and I will not be joining with you anymore in any of those activities. Not even in Barricade. We will be doing spiritual exercises instead. We'll be praying for you.

With love in Christ,

Peter

Andy watched Jean's face during the last part of the letter. He did not think she approved; could only imagine the conflict between them over his writing it, let alone reading it aloud at a staff meeting.

Andy also looked at Gary. This letter had not been cleared with him either.

The day had started out cool, even rainy, but it suddenly felt very hot in the War Room. The windows were shut. Andy stood to open them slightly. It was a welcome gesture, accompanied by several slight coughs and clearings of the throat.

Unlike with B. B., Andy showed no eagerness to be the first to respond. He liked Peter, despite his squeaky ways and demeanour, in part for the very reason of the letter at hand. Peter was a straight shooter. And this was his sharpest volley.

Gary spoke up at last. "Thanks, Peter, for the letter. This is not really new, your disenchantment at least. Before we proceed in any way, I think we need to pray."

He led forth in a fervent request for wisdom.

"Heck, Peter!" Jack said right at the end. "Let's face it, I'm the big time offender in all this! Everything you pick up on, I'm the primary instigator. I brought over those games. I even told you about Barricade. Back home, I can't tell you how many wrestling matches I've been in with girls at youth. It was almost a youth activity in its own right some nights."

He paused, choosing his words. "But I just don't get it, Peter. What's so wrong about that? Like, didn't God make our bodies *good*? And didn't He make us for *abundant life* and for *joy*?

"Man! On those streets of gold, I fully expect I'll still be carrying on with all those same girls—only with new bodies. And I want to win the Guinness record up there for Eternity's longest Rook game!

Jack shook his head, smiling but clearly not happy. "Peter, I think you've got this Christianity thing figured out a bit backwards. We're meant to have *fun*—or you can count me out!"

There was steeliness in Jack's last words that made Andy look sharply at him. He thought Janys registered similar surprise.

Sharon delivered the real shocker though. "Peter, I expect to be cooking up there all the time to my heart's content. I hope I'll be publishing all kinds of international cookbooks. And I plan to pursue a music-recording career, too, and win interior design awards for those many mansions.

"The point is, I'm with Jack. I'm looking forward to celebrations and fun all the time."

Gary felt emboldened by his wife's response. "Peter, did you ever read the last chapter of C. S. Lewis's last book in the Narnia series, *The Last Battle*? He pictures heaven as a breathless, tireless, wild race *further up and further in!* Everyone joins in with reckless abandon. It's utterly chaotic. Definitely not a serene Henry Mancini 'Moon River,' rather a wild Scott Joplin pulsating *chaotic* Ragtime tune. Like creation itself. I think that's much more the way God is, and wants us to be, too."

Janys jumped in. "About the only thing for sure about heaven biblically is, it's the stuff dreams are made of. It's the place everyone wishes they could return to like the mother's womb.

"It's not so much *religious* as it is *wish fulfillment*. Walt Disney in conscious rejection of Christianity has kids 'wish upon a star.' Ironically, he's probably closer to the idea of heaven than all the visions of harp playing and Jesus-gazing our pietistic peers and forebears conjured up.

"My brother Ted once quipped, 'If heaven's that kind of place, that's my worst nightmare and another name for hell.' I'm for heaven with upper case F-U-N."

Was Jean wincing? Why was Fiona silent? How was Peter handling all this?

Peter took a deep breath and folded up his letter. "Well, I've said my piece. And Jean and I have made up our minds. I personally think you have a lot to answer to the Lord for. I hope you get it one day."

Jean's eyes were on the floor.

The meeting proceeded listlessly after that. It might have been better had Peter simply left like Andy had the week before.

From that point on, Peter markedly dissociated himself from group socials unless they had to do with "spiritual things." Jean, out of necessary loyalty, remained absent with Peter and thus became gradually cut off from the others too. All future games nights shifted to the boys' apartment.

As a result, Peter's authority began to diminish increasingly. The awkwardness was augmented every time he tried to assert himself over the next few weeks.

Janys especially felt for him and Jean and was clearly distressed at how relationships were changing in this regard.

Another problem was Andy, as he was well aware. It wasn't a conscious decision, but as Peter's leadership role diminished, Andy vied to fill the void. He justified it with a pious sense of mission: someone had to help take the helm and steer the ship toward its appointed goal.

Yet as Andy moved toward the helm, the ship showed it had rudder problems, too. Some, Fiona in particular, and Jack increasingly, were not prepared to let Andy increase his influence.

Invariably, Andy had twice as much to share at team meetings as any other. He argued vigorously for his ideas, including working in closer conjunction with the Jesus People, getting out doing door-to-door work, and regularly leafleting on the *Ku'damm*. The ideas may all have been valid in themselves (the team *had* to busy itself somehow!), but Andy's strident presentation of his ideas created friction.

Janys eventually talked to him, affirming his zeal but questioning his pushiness, especially in light of his previous questions about the validity of their mission. Andy felt hurt and confused. It was one of those rare occasions where *he* clammed up in response.

The third "crack" was Beatrice Boswell herself. B. B. continued to make demands upon the team's availability and invariably laid on a guilt trip whenever she was resisted.

For Andy personally, the most exasperating experience regarding B. B. occurred when he learned from Jack that the *Outpost Theatre* was to show *Butch Cassidy and the Sundance Kid*, starring Robert Redford and Paul Newman. Sharon and Gary had seen it in the States and often sang songs from the soundtrack, which they had loaned to Andy. He especially liked "Raindrops Keep Falling On My Head." He also had a longstanding love for Westerns. One summer he had read every "Duster" in the local library! He was quite thrilled at the prospect of seeing the movie.

Then, two days before the one-time-only showing, B. B. informed Gary that she had appointed him and Andy to lead a special Bible Study session that same night with some new *Lichterfelde* youth, whom she claimed were showing real potential. She had already arranged it and would not hear of rescheduling. (It had been announced in the church the Sunday before.) She was especially scathing in her criticism of changing it so the team could all go to the movies!

"Where is your commitment?" She repeated often enough to Gary that he finally gave in. But his German was not adequate to the task. Peter, B. B. said, would not relate well, so it fell to Andy to go along, too.

Andy did so, angrily.

When they arrived at *Lichterfelde* after wishing everyone else lots of fun at the movies, Andy felt like hitting someone. He knew who it was, and exactly what part of the anatomy the first punch would target.

His target welcomed them at the door. B. B. squeezed Andy's hand. "Andy, I'm thrilled that Horst's older brother, Klaus, is here tonight! He's been off at the University of Bonn studying philosophy. You're perfect for taking him on tonight, I know." Andy knew she'd been impressed by some of his earlier discussions with the regular youth study group there. She had told him so.

So the left hand that itched to plough her on the nose had now been squeezed into service. Maybe the right hand could ignore what the left was doing and still let go a wicked hook? He was fantasizing, but it tasted good. The last thing in the world he felt like doing that night was standing up for the faith delivered once for all to the saints. He was not too high on the "Saintly Scale" just then. He doubted he even registered.

B. B. introduced Andy to Klaus as a "real thinker." All Andy heard was "Raindrops Keep Falling on My Head." All his Christian thinking had turned to mush.

B. B. introduced the evening as an opportunity for anyone to explore the more serious aspects of the faith. She opened with a reading about the "foolishness of the gospel" from 1 Corinthians 1. But this foolishness was God's "wisdom," the text said, as God's weakness was his strength, Andy had read this emphasis in Hans' paper. The inversions, he thought vaguely, suddenly intrigued. Of course! The Church's first great watershed was not when the Enlightenment opened up Lessing's ugly broad ditch. It was when Augustine recruited State violence to achieve justice, State violence in defence of God's justice. Impossible. He remembered the passage from James he had read in his Quiet Time. He suddenly knew, if man's anger did not accomplish God's righteousness, neither did State violence. Of course not. "Vengeance is mine," Paul quotes Yahweh. There was a profound inversion at play here about epistemology and "wisdom" in general, but also about violence.

For the first time, Andy put a word to it: *subversion*. These inversions were profoundly subversive of all received status quo's—philosophical and sociological, likely psychological and theological, too. The Gospel, he remembered G. K. Chesterton in his grade twelve reader, "The Logic of Elfland," invariably turns things upside down for us to see aright. This is the very stuff of *Gospel logic*: ever to challenge one's balance, ever to force one into vertigo so we can see and act aright. Lose life to find it. Deny oneself to discover oneself. Die to oneself to embrace abundant life.

This was not for the softheaded or the faint-hearted—and most definitely not for Pharisees or their contemporary counterparts, Andy realized. And who were the modern-day Pharisees? Had he not "compassed sea and land" to win one proselyte? Would all his efforts just make such converts "twofold more the children of hell"? And he was to convert Klaus to this tonight? He felt sick suddenly. He'd forgotten all about *Butch Cassidy*.

The evening study went well enough. Oddly enough, like Andy, Klaus was stuck on the impossible disjunction between a church proclaiming a God of love and the stark realities of church politics played out over the centuries in unrelenting, massive *Blutlust* and bloodletting, like no other institution known to Western history. "Against which," Hans had quoted Walter Wink, "the revolt of atheism is pure religion." Andy said a hearty "Amen!"

B. B. was not impressed by Andy that night, nor was Gary. On their way home, Gary commented, "Andy, you gave far too much ground to Klaus tonight, I think."

"If Christ is the Truth, Gary, I cannot be afraid of truth from wherever it comes. I have been, because that was part of my Christian formation. Always suppress truth in favour of the Truth. Strange. Hence why I was not to go to university, according to most at Carriage Street Gospel Chapel. The truth at university might challenge the Truth. Ironic, eh? Jesus the Schizoid Truth."

"But doesn't Francis Schaeffer always hold out for the *antithesis*, Andy? You're the one who kept quoting Schaeffer on that at the Centre."

"Sometimes I think Schaeffer *doth protest too much*," Andy replied, not believing his own ears. He stopped to ponder what was happening.

"But," Gary came back, "B. B. rightly called us to Truth. And Truth has no truck with Untruth, Andy."

"Do you want to know what Hans argues the biblical opposite of 'Truth' is, Gary?" Andy replied. "He says it is Violence. He also argues that Original Sin is primordially violence. The sword in the Garden is not so much God's doing as God's acknowledgement of the violent consequences of Original Sin. He also argues that God, therefore, does not undo Original Sin through violence, especially the violence of blood satisfaction at the cross, hence the 'satisfaction theory' of atonement first promulgated by Saint Anselm of Canterbury in the eleventh century. He says that violence of that sort is the inversion of God's will, consequence precisely of a life lived out in *un*faithfulness toward God. Sacrifice, in this case, is not God-initiated but humanity-driven—by the religious as much as by the secular—in denial of the Truth. He draws on René Girard, a French thinker, to present that."

"Andy," Gary shot back, "I still think this all sounds strangely heterodox."

"Or strangely true, Gary?" Andy asked softly. "Or strangely true? What Karl Barth dubs the 'strange new world of the Bible' that is as foreign to most Christians perhaps as to secular people. Especially Evangelicals."

Andy did not know where that last bit came from. Evangelicals had the Truth, didn't they? Or were they, in Jesus' words, rather evangelizing everyone into something twice as hellish as hell itself? He decided to change the topic.

"So, how do you think B. B. reacted tonight, Gary?"

Gary shrugged. "I don't think she was very happy at all. I think she expected you to do a number on Klaus, but instead she heard you mainly agreeing with him!"

"Boy this stuff sure gets complicated, Gary," Andy said, shaking his head. "Before I came here, I had all the answers sewed up. Now, I can barley see the answers for the questions, the forest for the trees…"

Gary stopped. "Andy, I don't like what's happening to you. You were my rock at the Centre. Don't cop out on me over here."

Andy heard the plaintive plea, but he had nothing to say in reply.

Andy went to bed shortly after they returned home. He didn't even ask about the movie.

50

At the July 31st team meeting, again without B. B. in attendance, Gary read a brief letter he had sent to G. E. describing some of their problems with B. B. The letter's final paragraph read:

So G. E., as you can see from these various examples, we, Peter and I, the team, are struggling with our relationship to B. B. I know she's asked you about an evangelistic outreach in September. Even if you were available for that, I'd sooner see you spend a few days with us after the Munich outreach to sort out things with B. B. I think this means a meeting with you, her, and all of us. And it may mean a meeting with the entire Großbruderstunde. *The reality is, for whatever reason, the elders in all the assemblies, with perhaps one exception at* Lichterfelde, *are not supportive of our work here at all. How could this be if they all approved our coming, according to B. B.? This has to be sorted out. Will you spend a few days with us to do that? The bottom-line question: Are we meant to be B. B.'s team or not?*

The team ate a late supper at the girls' apartment that night and continued on into the evening with an impromptu social time around the dining room table. True to form Peter and Jean left for their bedroom. Andy couldn't help but feel sad at this internal displacement, banishment to a bedroom Siberia right under their noses.

At one point, Fiona went outside to make a phone call. Moments later, Peter came out of his bedroom and happened to look out the living room window.

"Does anyone know why a huge man would be talking quite animatedly to Fiona just below our window?"

Jack and Andy ran to the window just in time to see the man suddenly grab Fiona by the arm with one hand and stifle her scream with the other. In seconds, he was muscling her into a BMW parked just in front of the team's car.

"Let's go Andy!" Jack bolted for the door, Andy in immediate pursuit. "Please pray!" Jack called back over his shoulder as he bounded down the stairs.

As they burst through the door, they heard a squeal of BMW tires. Jack leapt over the front end of the team's car, yelling at Andy to hop in, and with a similar squeal of rubber, they were launched.

The BMW headed east along *Günzelstraße* toward *Bundesallee Joachimstraße.* It stopped for the light. Jack pulled up quietly directly behind it in the left-hand turn lane. The driver seemed to be unaware that he was being followed. But Andy was certain that Todd—for they were sure that's who it was—would figure things out soon enough. What match was the their *Deux Chevaux* to his BMW? Andy noticed the distinctive license plate indicating it was from the American Army Base. He asked about the match.

"Forget it!" Jack said. "If he tries to outrun us, he'll leave us in the dust." He looked very grim. "Best thing is not to alert him until we can cut him off or something."

The light turned green. They each turned left. Andy strained to catch a glimpse of what was going on in the car ahead. The windows were tinted. It was dark out. They could see nothing inside.

Andy ventured, "Shouldn't we call the police

or something?"

Jack was all business. "Can you imagine the jurisdictional mess that would create? They'd be figuring out what to do into next week. No, Andy, right now, we're *it!* And we left so fast the rest don't have a clue what's going on. So they're not about to call the cops either."

"What do you have in mind, Jack?"

"I don't know, Andy. I've never done this before. How 'bout you?" There was no fun in Jack's voice at all. Something new in Jack was taking over. Something Andy had never seen before.

"Why don't you pray, Andy?" Janys had asked that same question in Ontario not too long ago. Andy had felt caught then. Was it different now?

He blurted out, surprised by his own passion, "Lord, we don't remotely know what to do right now. We know Fiona's in huge danger and must be petrified. Please calm her fears and give Jack direction as he steers this car toward some kind of encounter with Todd. Lord, we pray for safety all around. Todd is a big bruiser. Amen." It was simple but real, Andy knew. Very real. God had better be, too.

"Todd's a big bruiser all right," Jack echoed. Andy looked over at him. Jack's face was taut. He turned left, still in close pursuit, though one car was now in between them. "Just as well, so long as we don't get stopped by a light," Jack said, not necessarily to Andy. "I think he's heading for *Bismarckstraße*. If he turns left again, I think I know where he's going." A few minutes later, Jack sped left through an amber light. There was now no intervening car. Jack stayed some distance back. "If I remember the map rightly, it's clear sailing all the way to the border."

Andy fumbled with the glove compartment and

pulled out a map. Jack switched on the interior light. "Am I right, Andy?"

Andy followed the route west and agreed: Todd was headed for West Germany via the East German corridor highway.

A light turned before Jack could get through on a yellow. They waited tense moments then sped through when the other light had barely turned yellow. In a few minutes they were gaining on the BMW once again. Suddenly, it picked up speed.

"*Shit!*" The expletive exploded from Jack's lips. "He's seen us. Now it's a race. Well, I've got a few surprises in store, Andy. Is your seat belt on?" There were no speed limit signs, but they must have been doing twice whatever the limit was. Maybe this would alert the cops after all, Andy thought as he buckled up. But whom would they nab first?

They sped across *Stößenseebrücke* and *Freybrücke*. Andy looked at the speedometer. It was hovering at 100 km/hr. Wow! What a whopper of a ticket they would get! Suddenly, the BMW swerved right onto *Pichelsdorferstraße*. Jack followed suit, handling the little Renault like a racecar driver.

"Hang on, Andy!" He was obviously thrilled at the speed of the manoeuvre. Had they turned on two wheels? Then the BMW, hardly braking at all careened sharply to the right and sped toward a darkened park. Jack was right on its heels.

The BMW's brake lights lit up with an enormous screech. Jack barely avoided hammering the rear end, swerved left, and rocketed to a neck-wrenching stop.

The driver's door of the BMW flew open then slammed shut as Todd stepped out. Jack flew out his door. "Andy, get behind the wheel and get Fiona out of here!"

Then he split the night's stillness. "Fiona, if you can, run to our car. Andy'll get you out of here!" There was no response. Todd was closing the gap fast between Jack and himself. Jack raced ahead of the car.

"Jack, he's got a knife!" Andy yelled, catching a gleam of metal in the Renault's headlamps. Rather than hop behind the steering wheel, Andy quietly slipped out his door, leaving it open, as Jack had done with the other. He watched Todd closely then raced to the BMW. He yanked on the door handle and nearly ripped his fingernails off. It was locked, probably electronically by Todd, which meant he had the keys.

Andy knocked frantically, on the window, hoping, praying, pleading, that Fiona would open the door. She did! He grabbed at her violently. "To our car!" he hissed.

"Hey!" Todd yelled. Then Andy heard clashing and clanging. He wheeled toward Todd.

Then there was Jack in steely mocking tones. "Hey yourself, big guy! Looks like the playing field has suddenly been levelled." Had Andy heard not only a knife scraping the pavement but also car keys jangling raucously?

Andy pushed Fiona into the back seat, leaving the passenger side open, then hopped into the driver's seat. Jack and Todd were caught fully in the lights of both cars. They were circling silently. Where was the knife? Where were the keys?

"Andy!" Fiona yelled. "If Todd gets that knife back, we're all goners. Todd was the undefeated heavyweight boxer in the entire Air Force!"

Todd swung at Jack. Like a lithe cat, Jack deftly sidestepped and hammered Todd with an enormous *thwack* to his neck that sent Todd to his knees.

Andy saw the glint then leaped out of the car and

ran to where the knife and keys lay on the pavement, just at the edge of the headlights. He scooped them both up.

"Hop in, Jack! I've got his keys and knife!"

He and Jack leapt into the car. It lurched backwards then forwards and back toward where they had come from, leaving Todd on his knees in the BMW lights, screaming bloody murder.

"We're going straight to my friend Scott!" Jack declared. Then gently as he cast a look in the rear view mirror, "How are you, Fiona?"

She sobbed quietly in the back. "I don't have the foggiest what he was intending to do! I've never been so scared in all my life. Never!" Andy reached back to touch her shoulder. She held his hand. Andy was thrilled but terribly conscious of Jack. When she let go for some *Kleenex*, he retracted his hand.

Jack flew over the streets. Were they the only ones plying the passages of West Berlin that night? Where was Todd? Andy looked to the keys and knife on the floor.

"Don't touch them, Andy. They're evidence," Jack said, intuiting Andy's thoughts. Of course! Where did Jack get such straight thinking? Andy felt in awe of all Jack had pulled off.

"Jack, how did you get these things away from Todd?"

"I kicked them out of his hands. Andy, I never mentioned it, but I hold an advanced Black Belt in *Karate Shotokan*. It is the most powerful form of karate. The kick was thanks to you. You distracted him when you went to get Fiona. Had I not just had running shoes on, I'd have broken his hand.

"The hit I gave to Todd's neck tonight might have killed a lesser man. One thing for sure, he'll have a monstrous bruise there for some time." There was a pause, then, "Come to think of it, so will I! I'm *way* out of practice!" He laughed grimly, massaging his already swollen right hand.

When they reached the Berlin Brigade Compound, it took some time to convince the guard to let them in to see Scott.

Scott's apartment, apparently a bachelor's, was Spartan. What stood out from plaques and a few bookshelves of Bibles and Christian materials was his Christian commitment. His apartment was in a whole row of similar quarters.

Scott agreed this matter was serious enough to place a call to the Base Commander even if it was just after midnight.

Andy and Jack talked quietly as Scott placed the call. Fiona seemed almost catatonic, her motionless form slumped into a soft chair.

"What do you suppose he was going to do… Still might try to do?" Andy wondered.

"I think there's no doubt he was heading for West Germany," Jack replied. "Then what?" He shrugged. "He was an obvious mark in an American army vehicle, even if a BMW. It's anybody's guess."

"There's no way he could have started that car?" Andy said, imagining the gate still sliding open after midnight to let in an enormous man in a BMW.

"Anything's my guess," Jack said simply. He flexed his right hand. It already looked much larger than the other.

Jack noticed Andy's gaze and smirked. "Like I said, I'm out of practice."

They both looked at Fiona just then.

She stared into space.

Scott finally hung up. "Okay," he began. "A

military guard will escort you guys home. That's being ordered right now. Apparently, they will stay on guard outside the girls' apartment the rest of the night. But they will be discreet.

"He, in turn, is contacting the German police, who will be alerted to the possible danger you are in. And he is ordering an investigation immediately. There is no way Lieutenant Colonel Braxman will get into this compound unnoticed."

Scott turned to Fiona. "She's exhausted, isn't she?" He turned back to Jack and Andy, his voice hushed. "The Base Commander also commented on your bravery. He said he would definitely be in touch. So tell me, how did this all play out?"

When Jack—interrupted at times with Andy's additions and Scott's questions—finished the tale some time later, Scott let out a low whistle. He looked over at Fiona's peaceful posture. "Whew. I never dreamed Todd could do such a thing." He held up his hand. "Let me rephrase that. Of course he *could* do it. He can do anything he wants. He's a legend around here—and elsewhere I understand. 'Don't mess with Todd' is written all over him. And he's an outstanding boxer. Never lost a match. Air Force Champion.

"But he's also a born-again Christian. And we just don't *do* those kinds of things." Scott shook his head.

Andy's response came from nowhere. "But Mr. Cunningham, with all due respect, don't Christian soldiers do those sorts of things, far worse, in Vietnam every day? Don't you kill regularly?"

Scott's face registered genuine shock and perplexity. "But that's different. They're the enemy," he replied, catching himself suddenly. "Though I suppose I get your point, Andy. I've just never thought of it that way."

"And when you kill civilians?" Andy wondered at his boldness.

"Necessary part of war, sad to say. But they're kind of enemies, too. I mean, they support the soldiers, harbour them, feed them, hide them."

"Children, too?" Andy barely said audibly. "And isn't that all in Todd then, this enormous capacity to kill the enemy? Does it switch off inside, Jesus in the heart; every time you mow them down? Or do you imagine Jesus right there with you, 'lighting up' the enemy as they say, napalming from on high with the best of 'em, killing, and cheering on killing, the enemy, civilians, and kids?"

Jack coughed uncomfortably.

"I guess I'll have to think about that sometime, son," Scott said. "But right now, we've got a crisis on our hands."

The discussion was definitively over. Scott was not a man in authority for nothing.

The Dynamic Duo, Andy clearly the lesser hero in the night's events, finally crawled into bed just after 3:00 a.m. The guard was posted outside the apartment complex's doors. Andy noted that both men were close to Jack's size. They were also armed.

The next morning, the rest of the team was immensely relieved to welcome Fiona and the Duo home. The question and answer time went on for some time. Fiona was not present for most of it. She had gone back to bed, beyond exhaustion.

The team learned that the West Berlin police were placing the apartment under surveillance for the next month. They even offered to tap the phone—until they found out there was none.

On Friday afternoon, Scott dropped by the boys'

apartment to update them on the case. As they sat down in their living room, Scott looked at Jack's hand, tightly bound in a tensor bandage. "A lot of swelling?" he asked.

Jack nodded.

"They found the car exactly where you said it would be," Scott began. "None of the hospitals reported any American visitors within twenty-four hours of the incident. So whatever damage you did, Jack, it was not treated in any West Berlin hospital, we're quite sure.

"There is a full-scale military investigation, since Todd is officially AWOL. He was scheduled for a flight to the States this week. The military does not treat this lightly, as you can imagine. He has very, very serious charges facing him.

"The Base Commander has taken personal charge of this whole affair. I expect any day he will be asking Jack and Andy to appear before him."

Scott hesitated. "And *son*," he addressed Andy in authoritative tenor, "it's best not to do a Martin Luther King routine on him. He was a highly decorated hero during the Korean War and does not suffer fools gladly."

Andy felt the sting, intentional or not. "So you're saying he has no dreams, just nightmares, Mr. Cunningham?" Andy asked, evoking King's famous speech that began, "I have a dream..." Where did he get the gall?

Scott bristled. "Son, if you were in fact my *son*, I'd whack you for insolence."

Andy did not wish to be disrespectful, but something inside was awakening. "Like Todd was ready to whack Jack, sir?"

"Andy, Scott Cunningham is our friend—my friend. Please show more respect." The voice was

Jack's. He was mad, as was Scott.

Andy nodded. "I am very thankful for what the Base is doing about this incident right now. I'm sorry, Mr. Cunningham, for raising obviously sensitive issues. Until I came over here, I hardly even knew the Vietnam War was on. Not only did meeting so many from the base change that, I have been forced to think biblically through issues of war and peace for the first time.

"I know I am not totally insolent toward the Vietnam War. But from the little I know I have huge questions. And I'm not one to remain silent when I'm working through things."

"Son," Scott was unimpressed and dismissive, "we put your kind in jail in my country. Plain and simple."

"Mr. Cunningham," Andy said, eyeballing him directly, rising anger emboldening, "in my country we warmly welcome my 'kind' when they flee the United States, and we give them refugee status." Andy suddenly realized he was the only Canadian in the room.

Scott's fists tightened. Blood drained from his face. Andy saw it in his eyes and readied himself to duck. Then Scott relaxed his posture. "Maybe we should have taken you way back in the War of 1812. All I can say is, you Canadians don't know what you're guarded against. All those rights and freedoms you so take for granted? They come at a very high price. *And the United States of America picks up most of the tab*! Some of you Canadians need to learn a little respect and gratitude!" He spat out the last words while stepping up right beneath Andy's nose. He was much shorter but stockier than Andy. There would have been no contest.

With that, he turned and strode toward the door. "I'll be in touch," was all he said.

Jack was livid. "What right do you have showing such disrespect after the Army has done so much for us?"

"Jack," Andy retorted, "if it weren't for the Army, Todd wouldn't even be over here, and none of this situation would have happened." He paused, then added, "*And*, if it weren't for the Army, arguably, Todd would not have developed such uninhibited killer instincts. I dare say, they are responsible to clean up their own mess.

"Jack, need I remind you, when these fine Christians get training, it is not in how to 'love their enemies,' it is in how to utterly dehumanize them, how to send them straight to hell!"

"Why don't you just shut your goddamned mouth, Norton, or I'll finish the job Scott almost started!" His face was contorted in utter fury.

Andy glanced at Jack's left hand. Would he use it on him? Andy didn't care. "I'm sorry! Is this what America does every time a nation doesn't kowtow? *Deck them?* According to Hans, that's the story right now throughout South America and much of Asia, including Vietnam.

"He recently wrote to tell me that a guy named John Kerry, a Vietnam War veteran, gave evidence last year before the Senate Foreign Relations Committee. Kerry reported that American soldiers in Vietnam routinely raped, cut off heads, taped wires from portable telephones to human genitals and turned up the power, cut off limbs, blew up bodies, randomly shot at civilians, razed villages, shot cattle and dogs for fun, poisoned food, and generally ravaged the countryside of South Vietnam. This besides the horrific decimation from napalm bombing, Agent Orange, bombies, etc. *And this was not isolated but widespread throughout*

Vietnam! Sounds real pretty, doesn't it, Jack? *Well, goddamn those bastard American G. I.'s whom Billy went over to save!* There, I can swear when riled up, too!

"We've all heard of the My Lai massacre, only one of hundreds, Hans claims. You know the details: women, old men, children, and babies, all brutally tortured, raped, and slaughtered. *In cold blood, Dumont! There's your goddamned, fuckin',' god-fearin,' Jesus-lovin' American G. I.'s in action for democracy and freedom, for God and flag, Lord be praised!*

"It was only stopped at gunpoint by another American commander. With a helicopter crew, he touched down between some fleeing villagers and the American soldiers. He'll never be decorated though, or wait years if so... His name was Hugh Clowers Thomson Jr. You've never heard of him...

"Do you know that Lieutenant William Calley was convicted of murder, though he claimed he was only 'following orders' from his captain, Ernest Medina? This was the commonest defence as well at the Nuremberg trials. In fact, Hans contends, the orders came from the highest levels of US command.

"The man in charge of investigating the slaughter at My Lai, Major Colin Powell, covered up. His report concluded that relations between American soldiers and the Vietnamese people were 'excellent.' Maybe in the brothel, Jack! Otherwise, Powell's report was *pure bogus bullshit!* No one else was ever charged for My Lai.

"Two days after Calley's conviction and sentencing to life imprisonment last year, President Nixon ordered him released. He's currently under house arrest in Fort Benning, Georgia, at the School of the Americas, where reports already indicate instructors like Mr. Calley teach their trainees from right-wing dictatorships the world over how to torture, maim, murder, terrorize, and otherwise suppress all opposition to the rapacious dictatorships their bosses run."

Jack and Gary looked on incredulously. Andy didn't care. He wasn't stopping yet.

"As for Calley, he'll later likely become a senator or run for president someday, and Mr. Powell will doubtless rise through the ranks to be promoted for his 'truth-telling' about the love-in between Vietnamese villagers and American soldiers.

"There's total loyalty in the US Army, of course. Whistleblowers be warned! All truth-tellers be damned! But it is not loyalty to the truth as we mean it, even if it be to 'Jesus' and the entire military becomes 'born-again'!"

"So as you can see, 'The first casualty of war—*and of religion*—is truth. It seems, Jack, that your friend Mr. Cunningham is premier exemplar of that reality on both counts. And that wonderful born-again soldier prides himself in this kind of American army 'nobility'? 'Noble,' perhaps, but only if one means *'noble savages'!* Or is there one law for the Americans, necessary policemen, after all, of the world, and another for the rest of us lesser mortals, Canadians amongst them?"

Jack and Gary merely glowered at Andy.

"Hey, don't shoot the messenger," Andy said, "though Jesus says they always do. But I won't flinch either about telling some of the truth. Or will you guys, will the American Army, will all Americans, like Pilate say cynically, 'What is truth?' then go out and decree 'Crucify him'?

"And America, like Rome, ends up doing what all previous empires have done: kill, rape, and steal, pirates all, and then write the history books so that nice little schoolchildren and pious churchgoers can sing with George Beverley Shea and Billy Graham, 'America! America!/God shed his grace on thee/And crown thy good with brotherhood/From sea to shining sea!'

"It's the stuff of dreams. all right. But they're emphatically *not* those of Martin Luther King or of Kingdom Come. And America's dreams, like Rome's of yesteryear or Britain's most recently and all others in between and before, mean nightmares wherever they come into contact with those unwilling to be Uncle Sam's groupies."

Finally, Andy fell silent. No one stepped in to fill the void. Andy was suddenly overwhelmingly self-conscious. He turned and went to his room, fuming.

What had happened? To them? To him?

51

For the next few days, Fiona hunkered down in her apartment. She would only go out under escort from Jack. She had caught wind of Andy's conflict with Scott and his ensuing tirade to Jack and Gary, and she refused even to talk to Andy. She hardly talked to anyone else. She had made a couple of phone calls home, and her parents were pressuring her to leave West Berlin. There was no further information about Todd Braxman. That worried everyone on the team.

Like Fiona, Andy hardly wanted to talk to any team members. He was still furious at Jack and Gary, at Scott Cunningham, at Todd Braxman, at the United States, at missionary life, at himself, and, ultimately, at God.

Gary and Jack avoided eye contact with Andy for most of the following week. The incident rankled deeply amongst all three, but it slowly began to cauterize. Andy began to let go of his anger. It appeared to be reciprocated.

He finally wrote an unprecedented long letter to G. E. about the team situation. He highlighted problems with Peter, general team inertia, Gary's insecurities, and his own thwarted attempts at "shaping things up." Andy also expressed anticipation of the upcoming "adventure," including seeing Dan again. Andy made no reference to the Todd Braxman affair. That was up to Gary and Peter to report.

On August 6th, Andy headed to Munich to meet up with Len Howton. He would drive Andy back to West Berlin and stay on for a visit with the team.

The next day, Len, Carol, and Andy drove to

downtown Munich. They saw the new subway system built especially for the Olympics and ate at Wimpy's, where Andy had his second cheeseburger and fries since leaving Canada. (He had eaten at one in West Berlin once.)

The Olympic grounds were beyond description, both in terms of size and architectural design. Later in the afternoon, they went inside the famed Munich *Hofbräuhaus,* though they only heard the noise from above, since someone had just vomited all down the stairs, and so disinclined further investigation.

Across from the *Rathaus* in the *Peterhof*, they had *Kaffee und Kuchen*. The cake was exquisite.

That evening, they drove to a Baptist Mid-Missions camp called *Maranatha*, run by a missionary family called the Funston's.

When Euro View, together with the France and Germany teams, were set to converge at the Olympics, *Maranatha Camp* would accommodate everyone. It was beautifully located and appointed in *Bad Heilbrunn*, one of several small towns famous for their mineral springs and *Kurorte*—literally, 'places of healing.' The only drawback to its use was the three-quarter hour drive needed to get to the Olympic site.

It was true Bavarian countryside. Andy thought several times of his grandmother Norton. She grew up in that area before immigrating to Canada. Unknowingly, Andy mused, he might even hand out a tract to one of his relatives at the Olympics!

That evening, plans were put into place for the evangelists to arrive five weeks hence. Andy wrote postcards, had a rousing Monopoly game with the Funston kids, and watched a bit of late-night German TV, something so far never experienced in West Berlin.

The next day, Len and Andy saw Carol off on a

train back to Nîce. Then they headed for West Berlin.

Andy's diary records the rest of the day:

We left the train station this morning at about 8:30 and headed home. It was a beautiful trip the whole way, scenery, sun, and safety (alliteration!). We made it home in about seven hours, after getting lost a little in West Berlin itself. (I never was too good with directions.)

The first thing we did upon arrival was collect junk! There's junk all over the street in our section, since tomorrow is pick-up day. Needless to say, there are junk collectors all over town. Len had some specific furniture needs in mind and thinks he can transport the items on top of or stuffed into his car when he returns to France. It was fun!

Then, tonight, we went into the basement of our neighbour, who happened to overhear Len's enthusiasm for "old things." He showed us thousands of books and magazines, lots predating or published during the War and printed in the old Fraktur *(Gothic) type! Hitler only permitted publications in that unique Germanic type. It was very fascinating. I picked up a copy of Pascal's* Pensées *in German, which the guy said I could keep. I'd love to go back and browse further.*

It is 11:10.

Goodnight.

There was one part of the day to which Andy made no allusion. It was a conversation with Len about some of their evangelistic experiences in Nîce.

"Let's face it," Len began, "we realized soon after our team's arrival in Nîce that the *Promenade des Anglais* and the *Quai des États Unis* was where the action was all summer. As you know, other than Doug, Charles, and myself, our small team consisted in women. After some soul-searching by us three, we proceeded with the decision to sing and pass out tracts at both of those popular places.

"That is to say, we tried it once, but we were a bit overwhelmed by the experience! A crowd of topless bathers came to listen to our performance, a few of whom stayed behind to talk. The agreement was that Doug, Charles, and me would slip out of sight afterwards. Good thing!

"When I was younger, as with many men," Len continued, "I had a real temptation toward pornography. I couldn't easily pass by a *Playboy* or similar magazine without at least taking a second look. And, I confess, sometimes I took more than only one extra look.

"Now, even though I'm married, this experience brought back similar struggles, which I'd thought I'd left behind long since."

"What about Doug and Charles?" Andy queried.

Len grinned. "I guess they turned a few different shades of red, something Jeannie in particular did not miss. (She always was a great kidder.) So they became the butt end of team jokes on this. Some of the girls suggested they should also 'become all things to all men' and be even more effective in their evangelism! I think Doug, somewhat gullible, half believed them for a while.

"Some of the kidding is naïve on their part. They don't realize to what extent bare breasts incite a guy. Funny, because in other cultures, bare breasts are a sign of modesty.

"So our team decided to abandon the outreach as quickly as it began. Thankfully, there are numerous other places where throngs congregate. It's a gorgeous sea resort, Andy."

Afterwards, Andy found himself fantasizing about evangelizing on the beaches in Nîce. He had found the pornography on every downtown street corner in Berlin quite enough and had made a firm decision to ignore its ubiquitous presence. So far, he had been fairly successful.

Len had a night and one day to spend in West Berlin. Andy and the team decided not to talk about Fiona's experience. Andy was still hardly talking to anyone else anyway.

Len's time was spent well. G. E. had encouraged him to do some team building with the group. Accordingly, he held a few long sessions with Gary and Peter, and, during the team meeting, asked several pertinent questions and shared openly about his experiences with both the previous and current France teams.

Janys, Andy noted, also had one good long discussion with Len.

A cheque for $6,300 American funds arrived in the mail for Andy that day, courtesy of G. E. It was to be cashed and then spread out amongst the four singles for their trip behind the Curtain. For Andy, the trip had taken on real dimensions. It also began to look like this would be a crucial diversion for Fiona. For all four!

The night before Len left, the whole team got talking about how they felt they had been spinning their wheels. Len laughed. "Look, you guys, the Spain team hasn't even gotten to the starting-block, by all accounts. And our team, despite the fact that we've known each other for longer than you have, struggles mightily to get going. So don't feel badly. From all accounts, you guys are actually doing the best!"

Andy was delighted to hear the assessment, though it felt just the opposite at the time. He said very little during the discussion. Fiona said nothing. Surprisingly, Janys talked the most. In fact, as Len left the girls' apartment with Andy and Jack, he said, "Now that Janys. We could do with about two of her right now! And she speaks some French, too."

The next day, August 10th, all saw Len off early in the morning. They all felt heartened by his visit.

The four singles spent the rest of the day packing up and making final preparations before catching an early evening train, the first leg of their journey East.

52

Andy, Jack, Fiona, and Janys were to meet G. E. in Belgrade, Yugoslavia, the evening of August 12th. Two days of sightseeing had been planned en route.

Over the previous two weeks, the four smugglers had finalized travel arrangements, and obtained visas for each country they would visit. To accomplish that necessitated two trips into East Berlin. Each country's consulate required a certain amount of marks to be converted into their currency. It was also illegal to leave any Iron Curtain country with their legal tender.

Gary and Sharon said they would hold the fort with Peter and Jean, but all indicated they would take it a bit easy, too. Peter and Jean did not even make it to the train station, since Jean was admitted to the hospital that day for some tests.

As they loaded their bags onto the train, Andy wondered how Fiona would handle the trip. He had hardly even talked to Janys in the last while, and he knew Jack was still quite ticked at him. Jack winced as he tossed his bag into the luggage compartment. Andy noted the swelling on his hand had not gone down fully. What a way to start an intense several days together.

Their first stopover was in Salzburg, where they arrived at 9:35 the next morning. Groggy from a poor sleep, Andy was still amazed by the city's beauty. After settling in to their accommodations, they went on a walking tour of the city. Amongst other things, they toured the Mirabell Gardens and the *Festung Hohensalzburg.*

The Mirabell Gardens were adjacent to a castle, *Schloß Mirabell*. The foursome delighted in indulging their senses of smell and sight repeatedly throughout their meanderings.

The Salzburg fortress was indeed "*hohen*" and dominated the entire city. Viewing the sprawling urban landscape, Andy could only imagine what had happened there and below over the long centuries. Human history and violence were ever inextricably wedded. Andy closed his eyes at one point and listened to the battles rage. When his eyes reopened, he drank in the glorious blue sky that seemed to remember none of the bloodshed. The fortress had never been conquered, dream of every Empire, including Hitler's Thousand Year *Reich*. Andy wondered how long Nixon's would last…

The foursome delighted in their two days spent there. The thermometer held steadily at between 80 and 90 degrees Fahrenheit. No cloud was seen, the azure blue sky their daily accompaniment. Andy recalled having viewed *The Sound of Music* about exactly two years previously, his first movie ever. He had not imagined then that one day he would be standing at the very fountain featured in the movie. He felt wistful and "*rotic*," a term coined by his sister for feelings of romance—"ro*man*tic"—without any "man" in the picture. In this case, it was gender reversed. There was Janys. Fiona was out.

After visiting an information booth, they learned about a place called *Fuschlsee*, outside of Salzburg, where they could swim and rent boats. They rented an electric boat and putted around for two hours. Then they all went for a swim. Andy was astounded by the beauty of the place, the pristine lake with mountains in the background. Then they laid out on the *Liegewiese* until they were completely dried off by a gentle breeze. This was all before lunch, which they ate at a Bratwurst stand.

In the afternoon, they watched a short documentary on the history of the city before wrapping the day up with coffee outside Mozart's tombstone.

At 7:28 that evening, they boarded the train for Belgrade. Andy was amazed as he got on board. It seemed like the entire city was going to Belgrade! The ride lasted until after nine the next morning, but for all the Yugoslavians, it was one wild party the whole night. During the trip, Andy tried several different kinds of liqueurs that were constantly making the rounds. Someone even bought him and his companions some orange pop. The four team members had started the journey standing up in the aisle outside the coach rooms of the incredibly packed train. But before long, they were invited into two different compartments. They spent most of the night there. Sleep was next to impossible. But Andy didn't mind; it was a once-in-a-life-time experience!

When the train finally pulled into the station, their Belgrade contact picked them up and carted them off to the Hotel Metropole. Talk about swank! It was *the* hotel in Belgrade and had just about everything! Andy was delighted to learn that they would get breakfast in their rooms as part of the service. G. E. sure knew how to travel in style.

After a two-hour nap and a quick shower, the group met with G. E. and Dan. Andy was well aware that G. E.'s antennae were scanning for any hint of relationship with Fiona. Andy felt smug knowing he'd held the line and then some. Would G. E. pick up anything between Jack and Fiona? Would G. E. read Andy's changing mind about missions? If he did, what a chaotic jazz piece that would be! Andy had no clue on how to read his own mind.

Then there was Dan. Andy's antennae were

likewise out, probing son and father for hint of their relationship. Could G. E. handle so many days together with Dan? Why had Dan come? Had he travelled willingly, reluctantly, recalcitrantly?

"It's great to see you all," G. E. said as he opened their meeting. "You all look so healthy. You must be eating well!" That was acknowledged readily by all, including raves about both Sharon and Jean's cooking.

"How are you, Dan?" Andy specifically asked in front of them all.

"Just fine," came the friendly response. "I'm looking forward to see the line-up, though."

"Line-up?" Andy asked.

"Of converts! You guys must have dozens by now, or let me tell you, my dad won't be very happy!" Dan was right there sniping. He looked at G. E. "Yup! My dad wants to do an inspection to see how their faith holds up. I've got a few questions. My dad, you see, has all the answers…"

Andy looked at G. E. This was pure baiting. G. E.'s face was inscrutable, as always.

"How's everything looking for Euro View, G. E. ?" Jack changed the subject.

"They've been at it two weeks already," G. E. responded. "We'll meet them first in Switzerland then at *Maranatha*. It's been a great time. Now, how has it been recently with you? Anything new and exciting?"

The Duo's eyes met. Jack launched in as decided with the story of Fiona and Todd. G. E. asked few questions throughout.

Dan whistled at the end. "I guess you can knock Todd off the list of converts. Somehow I don't think I'd like to interview him anyway."

"But," Andy interjected in spite of himself, "Jack never mentioned, he's a 'born-again' Christian. Went to Bible Study regularly. A 'jock for Christ,' and everybody knew it."

G. E. shook his head. "Who would have ever dreamed he'd show up in West Berlin and meet you guys to boot?"

They talked for some time about the implications. G. E. quizzed Fiona about her parents' response, about her own feelings. It was the first time Andy had heard her talk about the incident.

"My dad wants me home. He only agreed to my staying until now because we were doing this trip and I'd be out of harm's way. Though I confess…" She teared up. "I even looked at everyone on the train with suspicion, imagining this hulk of a man lunging toward me and I with nowhere to go." She dabbed at her eyes with a tissue. She tried to speak again then broke into a sob. "I'm sorry. I guess it's all just… right there!"

Jack put an arm on her. It was not rebuffed. It was not missed either. Andy wondered what G. E. was thinking.

"Well, we have quite a trip lined up you guys!" G. E. said abruptly, changing course. He looked at the ceiling and walls and made silent gestures with his mouth and hands, indicating that they should continue their conversation elsewhere because the hotel could be bugged. "Shall we grab supper?"

After supper, they went for a walk in a nearby park. "I've done these trips a few years now," G. E. began, glancing around. "The one thing I've learned is to have all our serious conversations in the open air. I presume, Andy, you have all the travellers' cheques, etc.?"

"Right here at my waist." Andy patted his traveler's wallet.

"Good. Tomorrow we fan out and cash about three thousand dollars in all. I'm looking for our contact right now, whom we will meet at an undisclosed location tomorrow so we can give him the money. Then it's mission accomplished in Yugoslavia.

"They have the least difficulty here. This government is the most open to the West. In fact, its citizens ever are travelling to and from the West on worker visas."

"Don't we know it!" Janys said. She told a little of their wild nocturnal train ride, taking it easy on how many liqueurs they had tasted. Andy noted that she also failed to mention that the two carriages they had been invited into, Jack and Fiona in one, Janys and Andy in the other, were already full to capacity. The Yugoslavs, however, simply waved them in and moved over to make space. He was remembering the rest fondly…

Some of the Yugoslavs spoke German. A few spoke French, too. Andy chatted away in both languages to his heart's content.

Janys whispered in Andy's ear soon after they sat down, "Here we go again, Andy. Another night at close quarters. Though once again, I don't think anything's going to happen." She looked at him coyly, even fluttered her eyelids.

Andy took a deep breath. Okay, the Janys Andy had first met and the Janys he knew now had undergone significant transformation, from caterpillar to butterfly. He had thought about that image regarding himself since he'd arrived in Germany. It was certainly true physically of Janys. If she was not quite the "looker" she said her older sister was, she was well within range.

Andy did not mind, as they squeezed in side by side, that they might be taken for a couple. When he had given his name, she hers, neither mentioned surnames. Had that been intentional? They could also have been boyfriend and girlfriend.

He hadn't minded either the close physical contact, closer by far than that in bed just a few months back! At various points, he had put his arm back of him onto the panelling that surrounded the carriage. This had afforded a little more room, since he could shift sideways. He and Janys were both slightly built, something no one else minded, given especially a few corpulent presences. He thought the other carriage would have more difficulty adjusting. Jack and Fiona just would squeeze all the closer, he knew. And neither would mind that, he also knew. Nor Andy, definitively. Interesting. Rotic indeed for Janys and Fiona. Except, were they happy the respective "man" was now inserted? Andy knew without twinge it was true for Fiona. Okay, he admitted for the first time, true for Janys, too. For Andy? Yes, the tight squeeze felt good.

When he had first shifted sideways, right arm behind and above Janys' shoulders, he knew she had instinctively snuggled in. He remembered once before when that had happened in a Toronto park with Lorraine. He felt an instant wash of pleasure. "Lusting after" indeed had given way to fruit plucked and fondled, even if only momentarily. He knew this wouldn't be happening with Janys that night. But only because there were witnesses? He felt crotch stirrings. God was witness, too...

"So Andy," G. E. was saying, "do you have any questions?" Had his reverie been that obvious?

"Sir," Andy thought fast, scrambling to mask his thoughts, "has there ever been real danger on these trips? I mean, have the cops ever arrested any one of you when you do all this stuff?"

G. E. laughed. "No, Andy. Nowhere close. Our part is pretty safe. It's theirs we don't know the half of. Except some we'll be meeting have already spent time in jail."

"How did you make all these contacts?" Andy asked.

"That's classified information, Andy. For obvious reasons. If ever the unthinkable were to happen, and we're interrogated, the less each of us knows, the better.

"I can say, however, that these contacts were all made primarily through one source. That person shall remain totally nameless."

"Have you met all these people before?" Jack asked.

G. E. shook his head. "No, some of these are new."

"How can you contact them without being monitored?" Fiona asked.

"Everything is done through personal communication inside the Eastern bloc. People come and go all the time, so we communicate openly with our contacts in the West. Then everything in the East is done person-to-person.

"In my case, I carry no notes, no names, no addresses, no phone numbers. I either memorize everything, or on rare occasions, use a code for notes."

"How many trips have you made?" Janys asked.

"This is only my third. But others at the Centre have made a total, with mine, of eight trips. We're somewhat old pros at this now."

G. E. fielded several more questions for the next while. Then they arrived at the park *rendezvous*. They reconnoitred and quickly discovered their contact point.

"It's good to do this tonight," G. E. said. "Andy, can you please ask that guy over there what time it is? Use German or French. Most speak either or both."

Andy did as requested. When he returned, G. E. said, "Thanks, Andy. Now we've established something else—that we talk to nationals. Tomorrow, when we do so again with our contact, he will not stand out as the exception. We need to do this, because foreign visitors are being watched all the time."

This tickled Andy's imagination. They were spies of sorts.

It wasn't long before they returned to the hotel for a much-needed sleep. Before he closed his heavy eyes, Andy jotted down a few notes in his diary, part of which read,

God's creation is beautiful! I've sure learned that on this trip. Okay, I admit it, too: God's creation of Fiona in a bathing suit, modest as it was, is also a thriller! How can some women's bodies and faces be so... You fill in the word, better, words. I felt goose bumps on a hot summer day. Janys was great, too! Where is the line between looking on women like one would vast mountain vistas (Saw plenty of those, too!) and lusting after them? In both cases, the "peaks" are glorious. I guess I won't be indulging fantasies of conquering those Bavarian peaks and moving them into my backyard like Napoleon or Alexander to make them "mine." Is that the difference?

Andy's allusions to the "mission" in his diary were covert. Before leaving Berlin, he had read through the previous months' entries, removing anything that referred to the trip. He was concerned, in cloak-and-dagger fashion, that his entries would fall into the wrong hands and betray the true nature of the mission, and with it, the people to whom they were discreetly distributing money.

The plan of action in each of the three countries visited was simple: Cash the travellers' cheques a few at a time at a variety of locations so as not to attract any undue notice about the large sums of money being actually converted. This was then pooled and handed over to the contact person arranged for by G. E. himself. The identification process involved a little more cloak-and-dagger undertaking.

Andy was delighted to see Dan again. The next day, they grabbed the opportunity for a catch-up conversation while the others went off sightseeing.

"So, what brings you here?" Andy began.

"To see the sights," Dan replied with a smile.

"Then we should have joined with the others," Andy rejoined.

"Naw, it's probably our only real chance to talk for the next while. So how's the 'missionary' doing, Andy? Lots saved?"

Andy wondered whether Dan had read any of his prayer letters. He suddenly felt quite sheepish and hoped he had not. Hard to think of everyone all the time when you write, Andy thought, knowing Dan would have found his piety a bit much. But he'd heard enough of it around the Centre anyway.

"To be honest, Dan, it's been a slow start. We spent our first three months doing nothing but setting up and language study. Now that that's all over, the last month has been further gearing up for this and the Munich Olympics."

"Sounds to me like you're really into the swing of things, Andy!" Dan said. Though evenly said, Andy was sure it was tinged with sarcasm.

"Getting there," was his terse reply.

"Andy, I've decided to go back to university in the New Year," Dan said.

"I thought you couldn't hack that much structure," Andy said.

"I got to thinking. Can't see myself in maintenance type jobs the rest of my life, so thought I'd give studies another go."

"You've sure got the smarts for it. What are you taking?"

"Psychology," Dan said. "Still don't know where it will all lead, but if I manage my money well for the next few years, I shouldn't have to worry too much about that."

"What do your mom and dad think, Dan?"

Dan scrunched up his face in thought. "A bit uptight. But I just tell G. E. that if he can go back to school at his age, so can I at mine. That usually stops the conversation." Dan smiled smugly.

"Are you coming with us to Munich, Dan? And what about Berlin?" Andy tried to shift topics.

"I couldn't hack giving out those Olympic booklets," Dan retorted.

"Why should you, then?" Andy shot back.

"Don't intend to," Dan said, "I have a few tickets to some of the events. And then I'll just hang around."

Their conversation continued on to other matters. Nothing "spiritual" surfaced at all, to Andy's mild disappointment. Soon the others returned, excitedly recounting tales of the sights seen.

The next morning, they boarded a plane for Bucharest. They practically sweated to death waiting for take-off, but it was a good flight once in the air.

That day, they saw a little of the city before meeting up with their contacts. A young woman quizzed them sharply in English. Then she took them into a meeting at a church. It was already in progress and in Romanian, so they could not relate at all. Andy was still impressed by the experience, reflecting later in his diary on how Christ's body was everywhere.

Their contact in Bucharest was another girl about Andy's age named Magdalena, Magda for short. They never heard a last name. Quite likely, Andy knew, they would never see her again after this brief visit. "Two roads diverged in a yellow wood/And sorry I could not travel both," Andy thought of that Robert Frost poem. It went on, "Yet knowing how way leads on to way/I doubted if I should ever come back." It ended: "Two roads diverged in a wood, and I—/I took the one less traveled by/And that has made all the difference."

Andy likewise pondered the chance delightful meeting of a young woman their age with a Christian commitment in an officially atheistic and hostile government environment. What were her childhood years like? Why a Christian commitment when the surrounding culture was so contrary? Did she date? And if so, only Christian guys? What if one was a spy? Did she wish she could travel freely like them? What thoughts were going through her head when she first met them? And by the way, did she think Andy was attractive? He knew she'd shine to Jack. Every girl did! Where did she learn to speak English so well? He was sure they didn't teach it in school. Andy had so many questions but no hope of ever finding the answers. He thought of Frost. Of life. Of roads diverging, roads less travelled.

Most of the afternoon was spent at Magda's place. The girls went off for a walk with her, careful not to raise suspicions from neighbours if English was even heard spoken. She obviously told them lots about her life, and they reciprocated. Andy felt pangs of jealousy. But out of necessity, he carried the conversation that afternoon, held in German—though sometimes it switched to French when either party had difficulty understanding—then Andy would explain to Dan and G. E and Jack (if in French), who would chime in freely in German to mix it all up a bit.

As it turned out, much of what the men talked about in the living room that afternoon (the women were busy preparing snacks and supper) Magda talked over with Janys and Fiona. The conversation centred around the "last days" in which they felt they were living. They took very seriously the prospect that Christian faithfulness could lead to imprisonment or worse. They felt sure that the Antichrist was alive and already living in Eastern Europe somewhere. They couldn't imagine the kind of freedoms they knew the Western world enjoyed.

They expressed concern about moral laxity, raising several matters, including the issue of the shortness of the girls' skirts—a reality in the Western fashion of the early seventies. G. E. had forgotten about that one, he later acknowledged. He had forewarned the girls not to wear slacks when meeting contacts but failed to address the shortness of their skirts. Either way, they were in trouble. Dan found it difficult, Andy sensed, to suppress some laughter, both at his dad's awkward attempt to explain the innocuousness of short skirts and to talk simultaneously about moral laxity generally in the church. G. E. was visibly on edge, perhaps as much from his son's presence and felt cynicism as from the questions posed.

Andy could not help but reflect on the uniqueness of the afternoon. Here were Christians risking their lives to be faithful talking with people who just a few days ago had been basking in the sun near Salzburg or who had gone about their daily lives in America without a hint of curtailed freedom. Further, he had to admit to having appreciated the bikini-clad women at the beach in Salzburg—and Fiona and Janys in their one-piecers!

Pure *anathema* to this group of Christians.

While Andy had his doubts about all the prophetic teachings he'd been subjected to in his upbringing (the interpretations were all over the map), he could agree that they were somehow in the "last days." One afternoon of listening to their stories, even with all the language problems, provided a sense of urgency about things prophetic he had never felt in Canada. That gave him pause.

He was also trying to listen through Dan's ears. He couldn't quite tell, but he felt Dan was at least impressed and a little less cynical at the real danger these believers were in. It had to mean something to him. There surely were some beliefs worth laying one's life down for, beliefs far beyond the immediately tangible world of Dan's little Chicago suburb. Andy wondered whether the best thing that could happen to Dan might be to leave home and encounter the "real world" outside the protection, yes spiritual even, of his current experience at the Centre.

Still, in a world with over five billion people, with a history of at least as many years, against the backdrop of far more than five billion stars, in an endlessly expanding universe, how could this conversation on this particular afternoon, tethered to a specific infinitesimal point of history and geography mean anything anyway? For that matter, how could a birth so long ago, so insignificant, so minuscule by all historical standards, claim a cosmic relevance greater than the incalculable expanses of time and space? Andy almost shivered at the thought.

"Perhaps you could tell us your testimony, young man," he heard one of those present request, in which language, French or German, Andy was only vaguely aware. Andy explained the request to his companions, noting that he would not translate it all into English for their ears but give them a *précis* later.

As Andy began, the thought wormed its way into his consciousness that he was grateful Dan would hear only his summary. He felt he did not have a very "sexy" testimony. He had led an entirely uneventful life, had known no time of real "lostness," had never committed any dramatic sins, and had undergone no commensurate conversion. "Amazing Grace" had never, unlike its composer, appeared all that amazing to Andy. It nagged at him again as he told his story in pointedly pietistic tones that there was something seemingly inauthentic about it. He was real, that afternoon, but his story was not, or something like that. Then again, how could it be otherwise? His story was *his* story after all…

Andy recounted the night his mom had told them about Jesus then invited him to accept Jesus as Saviour. He was four-years-old. He accepted his mother's invitation and prayed a simple prayer. Though doubtless reinforced by his mother's retelling, the event had become fixed in his memory like nothing else from that early age.

By twelve, he was ready for baptism. He remembered that clearly, since he once had been walking home from school with the girl he had the sweets for, Coral Kennedy, and she was amazed that a boy his age would want to get baptized, since "boys usually didn't do those things" at age twelve. She seemed the authority on it then. In any event, he carried through, as did she. He even dated her that winter, skating together at the outdoor rink.

He recounted that when his uncle returned from missionary work in Africa, Andy started attending a Saturday morning Bible Study session with him. This continued for a few years. Andy was faithful about such things as far back as he could remember.

He told of his cousins' grandfather's dire warnings about studying at the university. He was bound to lose his faith soon after going to such a den of iniquity. Andy admitted that his faith was indeed challenged, and den of iniquity it no doubt was, drunkenness being a legendary phenomenon at the University of Waterloo. However, he never got caught up in the lifestyle.

Andy did struggle with unbelieving professors and teaching assistants though. He remembered one such teaching assistant (in history) who used to challenge anyone with a Christian faith to argue the historical truth of the faith. Andy suspected this guy was from a Christian background. He knew there was no one more inclined to be fundamentalist than a convert, in whichever direction. In any event, Andy took him on, based upon some apologetics works he was reading at the time.

Andy shared how the TA was not a little taken aback when confronted with Michael Polanyi's epistemological theories about communities of discourse in the rationalities we subscribe to as given. This explained Lessing's famous "ugly broad ditch" problem between the "accidental truths of history and the necessary truths of reason" in his dispute with the traditional Gospels as "history." As it turns out, those "necessary" truths are not so necessary after all—if one was outside the European Enlightenment community of discourse in which Lessing was immersed. Andy knew this applied to all the changing vicissitudes of the 20th century "historical Jesus questers" as well. Starting points were so crucial. He knew of the dangers of so-called *petitio principii*—arriving by circular fashion back at the conclusions—amazingly!—one had started with as assumptions.

The humanist creed, Andy continued, was truly *Credo ut intelligam*—I believe in order to understand. But wait, Andy said. That was also the basic starting-point Anselm taught for Christian faith, too! He explained it was likewise the beginning of all scientific inquiry, much of which began in solipsism and irrationality before eventually becoming "laundered" into acceptance as new rational truth axioms for the masses. But those changed over time, too, as Thomas Kuhn taught brilliantly in his concept of "paradigm shifts." Such shifts, he explained, repeatedly threw up new plausibility structures for innovative beliefs about reality until subsequent modes of thought took over yet again. To adhere to the scientific method, the ultimate basis of one's epistemology, was, Andy expressed, to die the death of a thousand qualifications as paradigm shifts recurred predictably like faithfully reappearing comets.

Andy had to stretch for some of the German vocabulary during that discourse, switching at times to more accessible French words. However, he stopped soon enough pursuing that part of his testimony when he saw all the blank but polite looks registering. He quickly passed on to his "Summer of Discernment" at the Christian commune and the decision to do short-term missionary work with GO, and hence why he was there that day.

Despite his pedestrian life, he knew his testimony had made an impression when all fell silent for several minutes. Finally, one of the brothers suggested prayer and proceeded with a long, drawn-out rendering worthy of some of the more loquacious "round-the-world" offerings of elders in Andy's home assembly.

By the time it was over, all were summoned to the

dinner table. Another long prayer, this time presumably of thankfulness. Andy sat next to Janys. She whispered to him after the prayer: "She thinks you're cute."

"Who?" Andy whispered, but he knew it had to be Magda. Seeing him blush, Janys poked him. "Not *that* cute!"

Andy was sure from Dan's look of quiet glee that he had heard or intimated everything. As if to confirm Andy's thoughts, Dan mouthed a barely discernible kiss and winked toward Magda. This was too much. Andy feigned a sudden cough and excused himself from the table. In the washroom, he checked for all signs of composure, exiting only when certain he had fully regained his. Upon returning to the table, Dan and Janys sported knowing smiles.

It turned out that Magda was keenly interested in The Jesus People Movement. Was the team part of that? Did they believe, like them, that the "End Times" were almost here?

She also had much more personal concerns: Why did the girls have such short skirts? (Andy had noted that Magda's dress extended as far below the knee as Janys and Fiona's did above.) Why was their hair cut short despite the clear Biblical injunction in 1 Corinthians 11? Was it true that girls in North America dated without a chaperone? Did they have doubts about their faith, and if so, what kind? How did they show interest in boys?

She also had more mundane questions: Had they ever seen the Beatles live? Were any of their books or movies censored? Were the rich in America fabulously rich, living in their protective compounds, and everyone else terribly poor? Were *they* rich or poor?

Magda had learned English while a gymnast abroad. She said little more about that. They understood at one point she had been considered Olympic material. But it did not work out, and that was all many years behind her. She had not only received formal English training as part of that experience she had had opportunity to practice through her travels, too.

Andy was impressed. She did well in languages and would doubtless have cut quite a figure on the balance beam. She was an experienced international traveler, much more than he, likely. She was also a committed Christian. And she found him cute, even. Wow. The complete package.

Before they left Magda's house, the smugglers passed on every piece of English and German language Christian literature they had in their possession. The Romanians would translate each piece then print and circulate them amongst the believers throughout Romania and widely afield. Andy could only imagine how they would be used. Copyrights would be infringed, obviously, but under the circumstances, was not something like that totally justified? A moral dilemma he did not care to pursue, given its implications. ("Tucked away for future consideration," was the terse comment in his diary.)

What he could not help pondering, in spite of himself, was Magda. He imagined her simple upbringing years, her first exposure to the English language, her first competition outside Romania in a free country, her widening world, her inevitable conflicts with her faith. He also imagined her svelte body in a gym suit. How would her parents have felt about her so dressed after she had developed? Were there conflicts over that? What made her stop? Was it lack of ability, time commitments or an emerging tension with the underlying ideology of Communist competitive sports and her faith? Was it any different, he felt himself suddenly ask, in the "free world"?

Finally, he fantasized more than one scenario where he could have stayed longer in Romania and actually dated her. He'd have talked lots about learning languages, about ideas separating East and West, about Christian understandings, about male/female relationships, about life.

In other scenarios imagined over the next few days, he pictured himself asking her for her first kiss, dealing with her very conservative parents, taking her to new places, watching her delight at discoveries in the West: Niagara Falls, the Berlin Wall (from the Western perspective), perhaps a famous museum... This all about a woman he'd never see again, he knew, except through almost miraculous circumstance. Only in heaven. Yes, he'd see her again there. But he had to admit the thought evoked neither romance nor anticipation.

She finds me cute, I find her attractive, Andy reflected. And there the matter ended. Impossible barriers to transcend. "Two roads diverging..." Such is life. Which means what, exactly? That life is a series of unfulfilled encounters where desire, longing, *Sehnsucht*, incite, burn furiously even, then extinguish through lack of existential combustibles? How did God fit into that? How did Andy? Was he just an incurable Romantic for even imagining this way? Or were there, in some far off land, correspondences? What of the hymn, *Jesu, Joy of Man's Desiring*?

They returned to their Intercontinental Hotel—another lavish place—just in time to see the Olympic torch pass through the city. Magda accompanied them to their train that evening. She was loath to see them go. So was Andy, he admitted later in his diary.

The train trip lasted fourteen hours. They were all

in the same compartment, and it was relatively quiet the entire way, which afforded plenty of opportunity for discussion and strategizing. Andy noted how little G. E. and Dan interacted. And when they did, how G. E. always appeared kind of wary, as if he was bracing for a bee sting. He was also struck again by Janys's growing—at least in his eyes—attractiveness. All that, and she was lots of fun.

At one point, conversation turned to the Olympic torch. The encounter with it in Bucharest en route to Munich had been a delight and a surprise. In some way, it seemed to make their anticipated evangelistic convergence upon Munich in just a few weeks a little more real. G. E. noted the juxtaposition of the torch in a Communist country; seeing as the emblem represented cooperation amongst the nations all the way back to Antiquity.

"Such supposed 'cooperation' is mere mythology," Janys said. "In fact, the Games of Antiquity were funeral games, often brutal and 'played' to the death—the full antithesis of cooperation and goodwill." She did not elaborate.

"Kind of makes you wonder about cooperation in the context of such intense competition in the first place," said Dan. "Besides, the competitors are probably all druggies."

G. E. said they were both just too cynical.

The train whistled as it rounded a curve and approached a road crossing. Where did the fault lie? Andy wondered. If the Newtonian law of "for every action there is an equal and opposite reaction" could be applied sociologically, who was to say what was the true cause for the ideological standoff of the Cold War? Still, there was the torch being run through a country where its Christian inhabitants could not be seen openly with Westerners, where distribution of Christian literature was *verboten*, where a government-sponsored ideological overlay dominated like a rigid template, controlling every aspect of public culture. No "naked" Public Square but rather one rigidly adhering to a dress code that was *anathema* and worse to break.

The porter came by to punch their tickets. "*Amerikaner?*" he asked.

"*Kanadier auch,*" Andy replied.

It was a shock to Andy that Dan suggested the only difference between the West and the East was that the latter government openly sponsored a rigid ideology. He contended, in a way that infuriated Fiona, that there was no less a rigid ideology ubiquitous in American culture. He kept saying, "If you don't believe me, read Noam Chomsky," of whom no one else had ever heard. The only difference, Dan claimed, was that the American government didn't sponsor its censorship overtly.

"Like the fundamentalists saying the liberals take scissors and paste to the Bible," Dan explained. "Which is true. Only trouble is, the Fundies do the same thing. They just don't admit it." His eyes scanned the inside of the compartment as he paused to let his words sink in. A look of mirth danced across his face. "Who, upon closer inspection, are caught with their pants down, too, or their fingers in the cookie jar, as much as liberals. Fundies in their undies—Fundies exposed. Only difference is, the liberals own up to it."

How did Dan get away with such blatant rebellion right under his dad's nose? Of course, Andy realized, that was the idea: red flag under the bull's nose.

"Prove it!" Fiona demanded. Her spirit was returning. G. E. sat uncomfortably silent.

Dan was more than up for the challenge.

"Okay. We Fundies make a big deal about the Great Commandment Number One, 'Love God with all your heart,' but fall strangely silent about—take scissors and paste to—Great Commandment Number Two, which Jesus says is just like the first: 'Love your neighbour as yourself.' How far does Jesus take it? All the way to the enemy. He says, 'Love your enemies.' Tell *that* to all the Evangelicals fighting right now in Vietnam or trying to get the death penalty reinstated in America."

"But God ordered killing of enemies in war and for capital offences," Fiona shot back.

"In the Old Testament," came Dan's quick rejoinder. "But doesn't Jesus say, on the contrary, something like 'All the Law and the Prophets hang on these two commandments,' and that 'There is none greater than these'? How can Jesus say that what sums up the Old Testament is doing to others what we'd like done to ourselves then we Christians, who claim to follow Jesus, go out and kill those 'others'? Is that what American Evangelicals want? To be killed? Obviously not.

"So like I say: Fundies/Evangelicals (Evangelicals are just educated Fundies) use scissors and paste on the Bible just as much as the Liberals do, especially on Jesus whom they proclaim the loudest to follow. At least, as I say, the Liberals are up front about it. On top of cutting out some of the clearest statements of Jesus, Evangelicals let on that they believe and act on every word in the Bible. Nonsense.

"Which would you rather: a university prof who declares his worldview openly or one who insidiously injects it into all his teaching but never openly admits it? Evangelicals are two-faced, too, I'm afraid."

He turned to G. E. "You've been awfully silent. What do you think, Dad?"

Andy was sure Dan knew full well what G. E. thought, since this had all doubtless been rehearsed more than once.

"Son, you've heard me say it before: If we can't get Christians on fire about the First Great Commandment, then forget about the Second. It's the chicken and the egg. Most non-Christians of the 'secular humanist' kind think they can pull off the Second Commandment without reference to the first. It just won't work! In the end, no one can be good without God. The Scripture says, 'Without God and without hope.' Likewise 'Without God, without good.'"

"Well, I happen to know a heck of a lot of people who are precisely that: 'good without God'," Dan shot back. "So how can you say it's impossible? Didn't Mark Twain once say, 'Sure I believe in infant baptism. Hell, I've seen it!' Well, I've seen it, too, lots of good in non-Christians—frankly much more than in most self-righteous Christians I've met—present company excluded, of course."

G. E.'s face reddened. "I think you're seeing through filters, son." His voice was menacingly quiet.

"You too, Dad! Fact is, we all do." Dan seemed he had been waiting for the line.

The others had become flies on the wall as the intensity of their exchange increased.

Andy ventured what was to him a novel idea: "I wonder, Dan, if doing good is sustainable without reference to God?" The question seemed to break the spell, at least for G. E., whose posture eased up. "I mean, why should people do good without reference outside of transcendence? If all we are is a collection of random molecules thrown together in chance space-time parameters, and there is nothing *outside* this reality, what difference does it make if I take that pot of tea Janys just boiled and pour it over your head instead of into your cup? It's all just random. On what basis do you posit ethics? What story can be told that gives rise to *goodness*?"

Andy was on a roll. "As I understand it, the Gospels claim to be precisely that story. In Tolkien's language, the Incarnation is the 'eucatastrophe' of human history. That was a word Tolkien made up, meaning the kind of twist in the fairytale that makes everything turn out good in the end. He said further that the Resurrection is the eucatastrophe of the Incarnation. The Christian claim is no other story pulls it off. Certainly there is no other story *not* involving transcendence that can do it—Albert Camus notwithstanding, who would only accept non-transcendent explanations of evil. And of all the world religions, only three claim meaning in an Ultimate Story: Judaism, Christianity, and Islam. Christianity claims to fulfill the Hebrew story and argues with the Muslim claim that Mohammed fulfills the Jewish and Christian story. And, of course, Islam is also derivative from Judaism and Christianity. But the issue is mainly the epistemology of good."

The train whistled again as it entered a long tunnel.

After Dan conceded that Andy had raised a valid point, Fiona piped up and suggested they play some Rook. That effectively shut down serious conversation until they arrived in Budapest. But the tensions of the evening only receded in part, Andy sensed. Both Fiona and G. E. were clearly frustrated with Dan. Dan did not appear all that content either. Andy wished he and Dan could just go off for a good long walk somewhere.

Once in Budapest, it took over two hours to get to their hotel and check in to their rooms in the Hotel Gellert. But what rooms! It was another enormous, majestic hotel. Plush was the only word for it. The rooms were split-level with two washrooms, two beds, a refrigerator, and many other accoutrements. Unlike his Saviour, Andy had a place to comfortably rest his swirling head.

53

After breakfast Tuesday morning, the four singles went swimming. The hotel had two pools; one even had artificial waves. Andy watched Janys and Fiona more carefully. Janys was not Fiona. But her short brown hair, petite figure, ready smile, easy-going personality, and quick wit were a winning combination.

This was further impressed upon Andy at one point when they got into a water fight. Andy scooped Janys high above his head and heaved her into a rushing wave. She screamed with sheer delight, then came flying right back at him, literally throwing her body frontally at his. He flailed backwards, pulling her down with him in an impromptu bear hug. They both burst to the surface gasping, he still hugging her tightly to his chest. She stopped resisting for a long moment then suddenly punched him on both sides with her fists. He howled, catapulting her backwards. She dove under, and suddenly heaved hard with both arms at his legs. It was so violent that he flew backwards, upended, just as a wave crashed over each of them.

Janys and Andy looked at each other and laughed then headed over to join Jack and Fiona on the waterslide. When had he last laughed with such abandon?

After lunch, a dear older brother facilitated a delightful tour of the city. Budapest had 1,000 years of history coiled up inside it, he said, which was unimaginable to them all. This old gentleman, who had travelled extensively in his youth and spoke a passable English, quipped that Europeans consider 100 kilometres a long distance while North Americans think 100 years a long time.

They ate supper on the Hotel Gellert restaurant balcony. It afforded a grand view. Dan was in a rare mood of story and joke telling. Even G. E. laughed at some of them, and there were no particular barbs.

Afterwards, they walked silently down a narrow road and joined an evening service. A couple from Wales, known to that small Christian community, shared some of their work and did some simple Bible teaching.

They got back fairly late. Dan had already gone to bed. G. E. soon followed suit. But the four decided to go out for a walk. This trip was proving so cathartic. The moon was "a ghostly galleon" ("The Highwayman," Alfred Noyes, Andy recalled) with traces of cloud wisping its fulsome features. A scented breeze wafted warmth, precluding need for sweaters.

It seemed the whole city had been magically put to sleep. Some kind of enchantment was at work indeed. Jack and Fiona wanted to wander through a park, but Andy had heard there was a special memorial beyond the park. Janys was game to find it.

They parted company with only a vague idea of where to go looking for the memorial. The streets were dead. They saw no one moving, not even in cars. The cobblestones sparkled with the moon's luminosity. "And who should be waiting there but the landlord's black-eyed daughter, Bess the landlord's daughter, plaiting a dark red love-knot into her long black hair," Andy quoted beneath his breath. Janys's hair, always well kept, exuded a soft nocturnal sheen. Her sleeveless top revealed striking contours, though she was dressed modestly as always.

Andy was about to turn one way, Janys the other, when their hands met and joined, as Janys intuitively led Andy the opposite way to his intended. Their hands remained clasped. He had not planned it. No one else was around. It felt... magical. Neither said anything—afraid to break the spell?

They walked like this in silence for some time, up one, down the next street. How much time passed? Andy did not know. He felt entranced. They just kept walking. Nothing familiar. Nothing interruptive. No destination really. Was Budapest this magical for everyone? Still no words. Andy, veritable fountain of same, was afraid to risk a syllable.

Once, her head brushed close to Andy's, discharging a wonderful waft of freshly scented hair, matching the delicious zephyr breeze. They kept walking. Would it go on forever? Just the two of them, world without end?

The city, and presumably G. E. slept on. G. E. had never forbidden this with Janys. Yet right under his nose. The irony! It was never-never land, a dreamscape from which not to awaken. Could such intimations be portent of heaven? Forget the harps. Something sensuously seductive was happening which was... *heavenly.*

Unlike heaven, it did end eventually. Amazingly, they stumbled across the monument. By that time, the memory of their initial goal had long since faded. It was a memorial column commemorating Hungary's "freedom" after the Russians came with tanks in 1956 to "liberate" them. The phenomenal capacity to make language do inverse service! Shades of *1984!* Like the Americans "liberating" the Vietnamese or the South Americans or... Andy knew well Hans' caustic cynicism about *pax Americana.*

He stepped forward to see if anything on the monument was legible. It was in Hungarian, Russian, and German. His move forward meant hands unjoined.

CHRYSALIS CRUCIBLE

On the short way back, route uncannily intuited by Janys, they walked hands separated. All too soon, they were back at their hotel.

"Janys," Andy began, "what happened tonight..." He did not know how to complete the sentence.

Long pause.

"I hear you, Andy. I think... What are you saying?" Janys said softly.

Andy smiled and shook his head, his eyes on the ground. Then he looked at Janys. "I'm not sure I know. I'd rather not say more, if that's okay. Thanks for tonight. It was *very* special."

Andy was about to turn away when Janys pulled his head down with firm arms, aligned her body against his, and kissed him fully on the lips. Andy was not unresponsive.

Afterwards, they walked quickly into the hotel, up the stairs to their adjacent suites, and hovered outside the doors.

Now it was Andy's turn to initiate a lingering caress. Then they stepped quietly into their respective rooms.

Once inside, Andy took his diary into the washroom and turned on the light. The light did not go out for a long time.

The next morning, there was a note under Andy's bedroom door. Andy looked over at Jack, who was still sleeping soundly, then quickly opened it:

Dear Andy:

Who would have thought it? Well, I for one. And you?

"And not all the King's horses and all the King's men..." so goes the Humpty Dumpty rhyme. I'm writing

to make it easy on you, Andy. The last thing you need – I need – is to be saddled with a relationship over here. So though my heart "bent" last night, no one else will see it. And I hereby give you permission; insist upon it, to ignore me. I don't mean entirely. We are travelling together, after all, and colleagues.

But, well, "ignore me" just the same, in a "bent heart" way. G. E. I know, does not like bent hearts on GO teams. With some good reason! Such just get in the way.

Budapest is indeed the "Paris of the East." There must have been some magic pixie dust released over the city last night. I've never been bold in a relationship with a guy before, Andy. Never. I do not make a habit of kissing guys I really like... Even when they let me. Okay, true confession, I have slept with, well, one of "them"...

I'm not sorry for last night. It was... Beyond delightful. But let's keep it unique that way. Today and tomorrow we have work to do. If you agree with this, whatever happened last night, if real, can go onto a back burner for a while. And we can check under the lid again, say at Christmas or something, to see if it's still simmering.

This is the only way forward, Andy. I'm sure. Otherwise I know I at least have to leave the team.

From a no longer, quietly thrilled, secret admirer.

Janys

When Andy first saw Janys at breakfast that morning, she had changed. She was beautiful. A stunner. Pixie dust indeed. He walked up to her and said, "Agreed." He added, "And sentiments fully reciprocated." She looked up at him and smiled. He added further, "But not easy."

Her smile broadened. "Remember those Cathars," was all she said. Vintage Janys.

There was nothing in Jack or Fiona's demeanour to indicate they had also been under the effects of nocturnal pixie dust. Dan, however, was observing Andy intently. He tried to ignore it.

After breakfast they fanned out to change the rest of their money into Hungarian currency. That took the rest of the morning. Their tasks completed, Jack and Andy were standing about exactly where Andy and Janys had been the night before overlooking the multiply storied Danube that divided "Buda" from "Pest." They watched Janys proceed over the bridge back toward the hotel.

Jack made the observation first. "Look at that guy right behind Janys, Andy." Then he moved fast, Andy right behind him.

They crossed the street in front of the hotel, weaving through busy traffic. When they were on the sidewalk heading toward the bridge, the guy was still right behind Janys, seemingly intent on that trajectory.

As he started over the bridge, Jack said, "I'll bump into him when we get there, Andy. You say, 'Hi Charlotte! Honey, I've been looking all over for you. Why are you headed over this bridge? It's the next one down.' Then take her by the hand and head in the opposite direction. You've got to act like a couple! Keep walking in the other direction, and I'll find you when I think the coast is clear."

Jack hit the guy hard then helped him regain his balance, apologizing profusely. The guy swore just as profusely in Romanian. He kept looking back at Janys as Andy led her away. Cluing in, Janys clasped Andy's hand tightly as they headed the other way.

After his loud speech, Andy whispered in her ear. "Jack said we're supposed to make like a couple, Janys. So sorry, but this has to be convincing!" He bent over and gave her a bracing kiss. She did not resist.

"I hope we were convincing," she said when they resurfaced, "or do we have to try it again for good measure?"

"Just keep moving along, lady!" Andy replied, holding her hand tightly, overjoyed. But he did slacken their pace somewhat, trying to make it appear as if they were just another couple on a leisurely stroll.

"What's going on, exactly?" Janys queried.

Andy explained as they walked. By now they were beyond the bridge, heading past a number of sidewalk stands hawking all kinds of curios and things to eat. The sky was cloudless, the temperature hovering in the low 80s. Andy felt rapturous holding Janys's hand, their scarcely ink-dry covenant notwithstanding.

"Do you think he's a government agent?" Janys asked.

"Haven't the foggiest," Andy returned. "Maybe just a common thief. Or someone who knows a gorgeous brunette when he sees one."

Janys smiled. "You didn't always think that, Andy." She went on before he could respond. "So, if he is an agent…"

"Did you notice anyone when you were changing your money today, Janys?" Andy looked back nonchalantly but saw nothing out of the ordinary.

He directed Janys toward a spreading chestnut tree. He remembered the one at the Centre. The nuts were already falling, though not fully ripe. He stopped, still gripping her hand, and turned them sideways so he could see back down the street.

"Sorry, but this is for the cause," he said. He knew

Jack might have suggested he was overplaying the part a little. But Andy rationalized that he had only learned the skill the night before, so he needed the practice.

Andy liked the exigency of their cause. So did Janys, obviously. They both breathed deeply, breathed again.

"Janys," Andy said, "maybe Jack won't ever come, and we'll have to keep this up indefinitely."

"Andy," Janys responded dreamily, "you're making this *awfully* difficult for afterwards. Our covenant only makes sense—even if this little burp came along."

They stared longingly into each other's eyes. A thousand government agents could have surrounded them, but neither would have known or cared.

After a few moments, they set out walking again. Or were they floating? Was there anyone else around, ahead, behind? They owned the street. The city. The world.

Jack's incessant voice finally registered. "Hey, you guys!" He caught up to them in a few bounds. Andy gently let go of Janys' hand.

"I think the coast is clear. The guy I hit was not a happy camper. But he kept heading over the bridge toward the hotel. I'd really like to have known what he was calling me." Jack laughed. "Why don't you two stop at one of these cafés for lunch? Keep an eye out. Then in about an hour, if the coast is clear, head back to the hotel. I'll let G. E. and the others know." He turned to go. "And make sure you don't show your big wads to anyone." They thanked him, and he was gone.

They had seen an inviting restaurant a block or two back. They made for it, hands clasped once again. "It's for the cause," Andy explained. Janys did not argue. How long would this wonderful cause last? Andy knew they were on borrowed time.

By the time they returned to the hotel, hands dropped before crossing the bridge, they learned that G. E. had tried, unsuccessfully, to move their flights ahead so they could fly out that night instead of the following morning.

"It could just have been an admirer or even nothing at all," G. E. said, playing it down. "Andy and Jack, you guys did the right thing. Great spontaneous action." He smiled at Janys and Andy. "And I understand 'Mr. And Mrs. Norton' performed quite well, too."

Andy smiled back wryly. If G. E. only knew what they had done the first night so designated, and what they had just been doing…

"It was a tough mission, but somebody had to do it," Janys quipped.

Andy noted Dan scrutinizing the interchange.

They had been invited to an evening service at which G. E. was to give a word and Jack to share his testimony. The final cash handover was to take place there as well. After urging extra vigilance by all, G. E. and Jack went off to prepare their talks.

The girls decided to go for a walk. Dan said he was going to take a nap. So Andy went downstairs to the outdoor courtyard to read his Scofield Reference Bible, given to him in Grade nine by A. J. Boswell from his home assembly. It was well read and marked by then. Andy had not been there for long before Dan wandered into the courtyard. Andy guessed rightly he was ready for another talk.

"So what'd you guys do last night?" Dan began brashly. Andy told him, skipping over the moonlit walk in all its essentials. But Dan would not be put off the scent so easily.

"I noticed the bathroom light on for quite some

time, Andy. Good thing we have another one in our apartment…"

Andy was not a little annoyed at being caught out by Dan. He was not about to say more than the minimum. "The four of us went for a walk afterwards. Jack and Fiona went off in one direction, and Janys and I in another. We got lost. But eventually we found what we were looking for, the column erected after the Russian invasion of 1956. It was disgusting, Dan. The monument makes it sound like the Russians were the Hungarians' liberators, when just the opposite was the reality." Then more quietly, "I guess we had better not be talking too loudly. It was a gorgeous night though. The moon was perfectly round, and it was so deliciously warm!"

Dan looked askance at Andy but mercifully let the subject rest. "So, were you surprised I came?"

"Yes and no. You'd talked about such a trip back at the Centre. So in that respect I'm not surprised. But I also knew it would not be easy between you and your dad. How has it been, exactly?" Andy was thankful for the opportunity to shift subjects.

"Dad's kind of eased off the past few months," Dan began. "I know he really wishes he could shape my life, but there have been no heavies so far at all. He knows I won't interfere with what he's here for. I won't embarrass him or anything like that. And he seems content to give me some space." He smiled sardonically at Andy. "No doubt he hopes that all your good influence will rub off on me, like at the Centre. He was thrilled, though tried not to show it, that I was going to visit you guys in West Berlin, too. Dad really respects you, Andy. He thinks you're good for me."

Andy couldn't deny the inner glow Dan's words elicited.

"I just can't figure him out. He's so driven. I know all of this is real to him. He's not a phoney. Neither are you, Andy, though I think lots are. But, like that discussion the other day, he gets so doggone defensive when I critique Christians, especially his kind. Why doesn't he admit to seeing what I see? I know he's been hurt badly a few times.

"When he was younger than me, he was a promising leader in an assembly in Scotland. Then one of the elders got on his high horse about some big youth event he had planned, and suddenly Dad is hauled up on the carpet in front of the elders' board. I don't know all the details, but after that experience he moved to the States. He was hurt real bad by that, Andy. It's a wonder he didn't simply turf it all then, seeing as he converted from outside that faith upbringing."

Dan toed the grass then squinted up at the sun. "At least he's not bitter. But that's what I don't get." Dan turned to face Andy. "In most ways, he's bigger than the brethren. But he restricts himself to them and some of their weird hang-ups. I know he's been invited a few times to join forces with Operation Mobilization. He's good buddies with what's his name, George Verwer, the founder. But Dad always stays faithful to the brethren. In his off-guard moments, he has a real critique of their exclusiveness. All their nonsense about the *New Testament pattern*. My dad would often say, 'Sure not the New Testament I read. Find only *one* pattern on anything in the Book of Acts, and you just aren't reading the right book.' But outwardly, he toes all the party lines. I don't get it."

"Maybe he's working to bring change from within. Can't be done too easily when you're an outside critic," Andy suggested.

Dan shrugged. "Maybe. So why do you stay

brethren, Andy?"

The question took Andy off guard. He'd not really given it much thought. "Guess that's the way I've been raised," he responded finally.

"So why not change?" Dan retorted.

"I can ask just as readily back: Why change?" Andy quipped.

"Fair enough. But don't you wonder, Andy? I mean, it's immense out there. How can this minuscule sect, not unlike any 'cult' in its outward trappings, possibly think it has *the* corner on truth?"

Andy studied Dan's face. It was an earnest question. "Well, it's easy to ask that, but what you mean is, how can any group claim to have the corner on truth? Right?"

Dan nodded.

"Take a step back. It's not all that unusual for 'truth' to be an overwhelming minority. Think of Copernicus or Galileo or virtually all scientific breakthroughs. Or Jesus, of course. Truth is not established nor discovered by majority vote. Nor at the end of a gun, for all the revolutionaries and dictators throughout history who have thought so.

"You know the story of the little girl who lost a coin and searched for it in vain under a street lamp? When someone came to help her find it, she indicated that she had actually lost it somewhere in the dark part of the street, but was looking for it under the streetlamp, since there was more light there! Moral of the story? Truth is not always found where the light burns brightest!"

Dan smiled slightly, nodding.

Andy continued. "Like Albert Camus, as I mentioned the other day, who was open to truth from any source except those claiming transcendence. Kind of limits the field just a tad, doesn't it? As if we can control the conditions for discovering truth. If we think so, we're already doomed to failure. It was the grand *faux pas* of the Enlightenment. So, on principle, I would not dismiss the brethren because they are a tiny minority."

"Then, to quote Pilate, 'What is truth?'" Dan responded.

Andy thought for a moment. "If Jesus said he was 'the Truth,' I conclude two things. One, there is such a thing. Two, it is above all relational and personal, supremely respectful and non-violent, since Jesus is that before all else."

"If that's what you believe, then why are you such a Francis Schaeffer fan?" Dan asked, again catching Andy off-guard.

"What do you mean?"

"During all of our talks, you keep emphasizing the rational, propositional nature of truth, which is anything but relational, about its opposite, seems to me," Dan observed.

Andy felt stung as the truth of Dan's remark sank in. Schaeffer, along with his Fundamentalist/Evangelical peers, spoke of truth in largely rationalistic, propositional categories: objectively analyzable, out there, accessible through rational, logical thought. It occurred to him that this was the distinguishing mark of the Enlightenment, too. But where did one read any propositional statements in the Gospels? And where, for that matter, did he find much of that even in Paul? Andy did not like where this was taking him. "Fair enough," Andy heard himself reply. "I need to think about that more."

Dan shook his head and reached down to adjust his shoe. "I don't know, Andy, I could never do what you're doing, trying to talk people into believing in Jesus."

CHRYSALIS CRUCIBLE 523

"You sound just like my sister, Susan," Andy replied. "That's her sentiment, too. I guess I don't find it all that hard. At least so far." But it sounded hollow to Andy even as he said it. He knew with a shock of guilt he was feeling more like Dan than he wanted to admit.

"But what do you intend on *doing* with them once you get them saved, Andy?" Dan was genuinely perplexed.

"Do with them?" Andy repeated.

Dan gestured with his arms. "I mean, do you just land them like a fish then let them flop all around in the boat? You're only over here for a short time. So you get a few converts. What happens to them after you leave?"

Andy paused some time, doubtful. "I guess we introduce them to some of the local churches in hopes they will look after them."

"Are the churches in Berlin that way?" Dan asked. "Would new believers feel safe there?"

Andy shrugged. "I honestly don't know. We're just getting to know about them." Andy knew that wasn't completely true, but he let it stand. The questions were uncomfortable.

"So you've come all the way over here to win new converts, and you don't even know what the churches are like?" Dan asked. He shook his head. "I'll tell you one thing, Andy, if they're at all like the one I grew up in, forget it! The rules and legalism are thick, the genuine warm welcome paper-thin. Didn't Jesus say you can win converts and make them 'twice the sons of hell'? That's the 'brethren', if you ask me, and lots of other Evangelicals besides.

"Take this evangelistic thing you're doing at the Munich Olympics. As I understand it, you're joining with all kinds of other groups, including all the European literature crusade teams, to blitz the spectators with the Gospel. I've seen the glitzy booklet ready for shipment over here. Now what happens to them after they decide for Christ? They could be from anywhere. You won't be linking them up to any churches. What about them, Andy?"

"I guess we have to leave some of that to God," Andy ventured.

"I see. Get them their fire insurance, then let them fend for themselves." Dan's cynicism was back in full force.

Andy wanted to say the fire insurance was surely good enough. But he was confused about the nature of a God who would light such a fire in the first place, especially for eternity, only as punishment, then offer to "save" humanity from himself. He dared not express any of this to Dan though. Wasn't it Nero who fiddled while Rome burned, then blamed the Christians – though he himself was the arson? Was God like that? "Not ideally," Andy said weakly, "But I guess it's better than nothing. What else can we do?"

"Maybe not go to all the trouble in the first place," Dan said quietly, very quietly. Just as he made the remark, G. E. came into the courtyard to call them to supper.

Andy found himself seated opposite Janys. He wondered what if anything she had said to Fiona about the previous night or their "acting" that morning. Had they kidded her about being out so late? What time had they gotten in themselves? Nothing showed on Janys's face. She seemed, if anything, a bit preoccupied. Andy, for his part, was still back in the conversation with Dan. Neither he nor Janys said much over the supper hour. They said so little, in fact, that at one point Jack remarked, "Are you two having a monk's supper?" Andy mumbled something about trying to practise talking less.

The evening meeting they attended was the most cloak-and-dagger event of their entire trip. One of those present had been arrested and released from a jail term only the year before for illegally printing and distributing Christian literature. To be caught with Westerners now would be immediately suspect. Nevertheless, he was still producing literature. Even Dan, who had tagged along, had to admire his courage and determination.

They were led a few at a time in a roundabout way to the house where the meeting was held and sworn to silence until they entered. The procedure was reversed upon their leaving.

By Andy's estimation, both G. E. and Jack did well that night. Jack spoke through an interpreter who knew English well but wasn't quite up on the colourful American *argot* with which he was confronted. Andy was sure that some things went entirely missing in the translation. But what needed no translation was Jack's wholehearted enthusiasm, commitment, and compassion. What a great guy, Andy thought again, for all their recent differences. Jack had such a combination of strengths all wrapped up in an uncomplicated love for Jesus. He made living the Christian faith seem so easy and fun. Why couldn't Dan find it that way? Why couldn't Andy?

G. E. said little about prophecy that night, a kind of departure for him. Instead, he emphasized the assurance of Jesus' presence in all we do. In the "doing," he really emphasized the call to love the neighbour, even the

Communist oppressor, he was bold enough to say at one point. Consciously or not, he was showing he had been listening to Dan. Andy glanced at Dan several times during G. E.'s talk. His face showed nothing, but Andy hoped it was sinking in.

Despite their fears, there was no incident that night. No secret police bursting through the doors. Whoever that guy had been in the morning, nothing had come of it. The rest of the money was passed on. In six days, $10,000 had been dispersed. That was the last of their formal meetings. The next day was their own entirely. Mission accomplished.

54

The next afternoon, the Euro View Team, which included the Nîce and Berlin teams, descended upon Hotel Rosat, nestled into the side of the mountains in Chateau D'Oex, Switzerland. All had flown into Zurich that morning then taken the train out. It was a joyous reunion. The only ones missing were Peter and Jean, who had stayed back because of Jean's continuing medical concerns.

Colleen Townsend, who was from Andy's home assembly, accompanied the Euro View Team. They had a great talk that first day.

"Andy, what's the most important thing you've learned so far?" She asked excitedly. They were standing just outside the hotel, sheer shards of Alps thrusting upwards all around.

Andy smiled wistfully. "Colleen, I studied a sixteenth-century French writer named Michel de Montaigne, a great essayist and sceptic. His lifelong question was, '*Que sais-je?*' What do I know? That's what I've mostly learned since being over here."

Colleen raised one eyebrow.

Andy laughed. "I came over with all the answers. But so far, I've been snowed under with endless questions. I didn't know the universe could throw up so many, like an eternal rapid-fire skeet shoot. Problem is, I see them fly but don't have a hope of shooting down even a fraction of them."

Andy's smile faded. "What have I most learned? Easy. A little bit of intellectual humility.

"That's why I can't wait to get to L'Abri. I'm hoping for the chance to go over one afternoon, stay over supper and join in the evening question period with Dr. Schaeffer himself. Do I have a few questions in mind! In fact that's what I've most thought of – with one exception – since we got out of Eastern Europe!"

Colleen looked up sharply, but Andy said no more. "And what if he's not so good at skeet-shooting either?" Her question jolted Andy like a sledge hammer blow.

They talked for a while afterwards about home, her question ringing constantly. Andy caught her up a bit on team life, leaving out all the boy-girl stuff and playing down the Todd Braxman affair.

Colleen, who was about ten years older than Andy and single, stopped him at a certain point and smiled, saying, "Andy, you've changed."

He did not ask her why she thought so but took it as a compliment.

Near the end of their conversation, Janys came out of the hotel. Colleen did a complete double take. "You look… gorgeous!" She said it as only women can compliment women without nuances.

Janys smiled and coquettishly touched at the back of her hair, Marilyn Monroe style. "Yes, dawling, I've had to fight off my share of admirers." She looked fully at Andy as she said so. Andy winced. During their conversation, Colleen had mentioned Janys sufficiently that she might as well have asked straight out if there had been "any developments." She had told Andy once that Janys was a girl to watch. Andy gave no quarter. The moment passed. Had Colleen missed the exchange? Andy doubted it. As Colleen and Janys started to chat, Andy seized the opportunity to excuse himself.

They had a robust singsong that first night. It brought back positive memories of their Centre experience. Then G. E. outlined the week's schedule and the challenges ahead. At his talk's close, he said, "In Munich we will have the opportunity to pass out thousands of booklets that tell the message of salvation very simply. It is the occasion of a vast evangelistic effort, of which we are only one part. Numerous missionary organizations are joining together to reach all Olympics-goers for Christ." He turned toward Andy. "The Berlin team will be busiest afterwards. For months to come, they will process all the responses to requests for a free book and follow-up. Peter and Jean's address is printed on the booklet. The free book is by Dr. Richard Harlow. Help me out here guys, it is entitled *Die Bibel Sagt*."

All the German team guffawed. G. E. made it sound like "Die Bible Sagged." Andy pictured an old woman with drooping boobs who was about to expire. What many took religion to mean, he thought wryly. Andy enlightened G. E. on his pronunciation.

"Now that I stand duly corrected, let me continue." Andy detected a tinge of annoyance. "We intend that this week be primarily one of 'gearing up,' putting on God's full armour, as we prepare ourselves for battle."

G. E. had lined up numerous speakers and outings, but had also scheduled in free time. He really was quite masterful in all these respects. In the course of the week, the gathering listened to Eugene Getz of Dallas Seminary, Dr. Robert Evans of Greater European Mission, Jim Cox of Swiss L'Abri, and others. Some of these shared frequently and led discussions and workshops, too. For Andy, it was very rich.

Interspersed was a visit to a summer camp, conducted by Dr. Brian Tatford, a brethren evangelist active in France; and a tour of the Chateau de Chillon, where François Bonivard was chained to a pillar from 1530 to 1536 for his Reformation faith, about whom

Lord Byron wrote the famous poem, "The Prisoner of Chillon" including the lines, "And the whole world would henceforth be/A wider prison unto me." They also had a wonderful visit to the quaint city of Gruyères, including a tour of its world-famous cheese factory.

Then the opportunity came to go to L'Abri, along with Jack, Gary and Janys, who offered to take Jim Cox back in the *Deux Chevaux* instead of his returning with the bus after his presentation in the morning. Andy did not mind squeezing in beside Janys and him in the back, while Jack and Gary sat in front. Andy peppered Jim with questions about the entire set-up there. He had enjoyed Jim's presentation.

After the spectacular alpine drive, they first simply toured around the little village of Huémoz with Jim as guide, then got out of their car and walked the trails. Andy reluctantly held in his desire to get directly to the L'Abri library in the main chalet. He had heard about the tape room where hours of Francis Schaeffer's lectures and others were stored. He so yearned to spend the afternoon with earphones on, and browsing the library, but was aware of Janys and the others.

The views all around Huémoz were magnificent. Andy mused writing home about that would be a bit like informing his folks Swiss cheese had holes.

They arrived at the chalet in time for High Tea, and gratefully joined in. Andy took a quick peek at the library with its stacks of tapes and books. He felt enchanted. He caught sight of Francis and Edith Schaeffer decked out in Swiss garb in animated discussion at one of the tables. Schaeffer had chiselled features and a distinctive grey goatee. Edith sported long hair done up in a bun.

There was a short break after the light supper, then announcement that evening discussion would soon begin. They moved to the adjoining Chapel with windows all around. It must be magnificent Andy thought on a bright sunny day, light streaming in, voices of worship raised.

Francis Schaeffer strode to the front with a short three-legged chair he squarely planted himself onto. He was medium-height and very European-looking with his Swiss knickers.

Schaeffer announced there were to be questions that night on Os Guinness' book, *The Dust of Death*. Andy felt a little excluded, since he had not yet read the book (written by a young English intellectual, one of Schaeffer's star pupils). Guinness was away just then, so Schaeffer would field questions for him. Andy felt keenly excited since these were cutting-edge issues: the Evangelical believer surrounded by the death of modern culture.

Schaeffer began by giving a synopsis of the book, then opened it up for questions. The questions by some in the audience, and the answers by Schaeffer, resonated a lot with Andy. It was a kind of relief for his mind to let someone else do his thinking. He had questions formulating, but not quite ready to pose.

During coffee break, Andy tried with Janys and Gary at his side to get a chance to talk with Schaeffer directly. They could not break in to the group already surrounding him. Jack wandered off sipping coffee. Gary enthused, "This was so energizing! I could come stay a month!" Andy said nothing. He knew he should be agreeing with Gary, wanted to, yet… Had all the niggling doubts about Schaeffer's approach to faith been working on him more than he knew?

Janys said, "Gary, do you really think that faith can be so neatly tied up and expressed with words and propositions? 'Honest answers to honest questions,' what Schaeffer and L'Abri stand for, has always made me wonder how a question can be 'dishonest'. As to answers, I find they are always less theoretical for my mind. I guess I mainly want to *see* answers more and more, not just *hear* them.

"What I really like about L'Abri, I find, is hearing from Jim how much the Schaeffer's really care for the people who come – and have been doing so for twenty years! They open their doors, make themselves vulnerable, reach out with love and care to everybody who crosses their doorstep. Now that's convincing Christianity to me!"

Gary started to respond when people were called back for the final hour of discussion.

When Schaeffer invited more questions, a voice at the back began: "Dr. Schaeffer. You speak lots of the death of modern Western culture. I'd like to ask you what you think of the death of another culture going on as we speak. Only the death of this culture is fully blessed by your kind. I'm referring to the North Vietnamese culture and mass killings of its people brought on by slaughter on the ground of hundreds of thousands of innocent Vietnamese, and from the air of vast ecological destruction of pristine jungle by Agent Orange and napalming, including a "secret" war in Cambodia and multiplied millions of cluster bombs dropped by Americans throughout Cambodia, parts of Laos, and Vietnam that destroy thousands more civilian lives. Do you have anything to say to that kind of 'death of a culture': one brought on and sanctioned by your American government and by millions of American Evangelicals?"

Francis Schaeffer bristled. But there was the question, dangling in front of his face, though far removed from Guinness' book.

Another voice responded before Schaeffer. "You can't bring politics into this! We're talking a far remove from the Vietnam War. 'You and your kind' endlessly protest but never give solutions! If America did not stand up against Communism in Vietnam right now, in another generation, godless Communism would rule the world. This is Russia's intent, and no doubt China's. I say, the Free World says, 'God bless America for standing up against this ultimate threat to Western culture!'"

There was rousing clapping, someone leapt to his feet, and there was standing ovation in the small chapel. When Andy's eyes returned to Francis Schaeffer, he was standing too. After everyone sat down, Schaeffer responded, "I could not have stated it better." Cheers and handclapping again erupted. The questioner at the back waited seemingly for more, which was not forthcoming. Francis Schaeffer called for further questions, issue apparently closed.

Andy found it hard to focus after that. He looked at Janys who returned his gaze. Was she reading or reflecting his mind or both? The hour dragged.

At the end, Andy and Janys sought out the questioner about Vietnam, telling Jack and Gary they wouldn't take long. Gary and Jack said they'd join in. A few others gathered around the guy, whose name was Thomas. "Saint Thomas" someone supplied.

Andy thanked him for his courageous question, and for taking the flack of a crowd mainly opposed to the point. "Did you feel you got an honest answer?"

Thomas laughed. "No," and did not elaborate.

"So what should Evangelicals be doing about the War in Vietnam?" Andy asked straight out.

Thomas paused a seeming long time. "They should follow Jesus," he responded quietly. "Just follow Jesus."

They left shortly after that, again thanking Jim Cox for L'Abri's hospitality.

Gary began the conversation on the way home, "I suppose, Andy, you liked that Thomas guy's question?"

Andy replied, "I liked his final answer better, Gary. 'Just follow Jesus'. Can you imagine Jesus dressed up as an American G.I.? I can't! Can you imagine Jesus dropping Agent Orange or napalm onto his own beautiful creation? I can't. Can you imagine Jesus at the controls of a Huey helicopter while his buddies spew out death below? I can't. Can you imagine Jesus in command crying out, 'Kill them all! They're godless Commies anyway. Viet Cong, villagers, old people working the fields, little kids blown away, Commies and enemies, scum of the earth, vermin all! *I can't!*"

There was a shrill anger in the final two punctuated words.

Gary said, "I can't imagine Jesus getting angry…" then changed slightly, "I can't imagine Jesus being so judgmental that way," then finally, "Andy, this stuff is hard! This isn't what I came to Germany to do, to get all confused about our mission, about evangelism, about the Gospel!"

Gary sounded almost plaintive. Jack piped up, "Why don't you guys feel free to grab a nap? I've had enough thinking for one day! I'm wide awake, and will do just fine driving the rest of the way back."

They did. Andy thrilled to holding Janys' hand and to her head and body snuggling into his. He did not easily slide into sleep, but kept his eyes closed, churning on "honest answers to honest questions," doubting he'd answer to "Francis" any longer.

Two German girls visited a few times later that week. All rejoiced when one of them made a commitment to the Lord. The other seemed so close, too. Andy had a direct hand in the witnessing. It helped that they were both nubile young women from a nearby horse-riding camp. Andy knew the girl who made the decision for Christ liked him. She was fascinated with Canada and asked lots of questions. The day the girls returned home, he promised to stay in touch, a little doubtful about what that might mean. He genuinely blushed when each hugged then kissed him upon their departure. His reaction was not lost on Janys.

During the week, Andy also caught up with further news from Gary and Sharon. They had been active on the doors with Peter, when Peter wasn't with Jean, that is. There had even been some fruit. Sharon talked in particular of Petra Delitz, whom Andy and Jack just had to meet! She grinned knowingly like when she had kidded Andy about Sieglinde.

Peter and Gary had met Petra, who was a nurse-in-training, while going door-to-door. She responded very favourably to Peter and Gary's witnessing but had yet to make a commitment. The whole team prayed together a few times for Petra and for Jean. It felt like things were actually happening at last, pushing Andy's doubts back a bit further. It was not hard at all to "lift up eyes to the hills" and know "whence cometh mine help" in the awesome setting the late summer Alps afforded.

Gary had also brought along the team's mail. Amongst the letters was one from Lorraine, concealed in an envelope from Susan. As soon as he could, Andy found a private place to read it.

August 12, 1972

Dear Andy,

I guess that as I write you will soon be somewhere behind the Iron Curtain. Susan has kept me up on things. Must be exciting visiting such incredibly faraway places.

I got a letter yesterday from the University of Toronto. I begin my Masters studies September 5th. It will take me two years at least, since I have to do a lot of make-up for having just a general B.A., and I have to write a thesis. Sounds like a long road, but I think it's worth it. So when you get back, I'll still be slugging away at the books. I'll continue working part-time, too.

I haven't been getting to church too regularly lately. I've really liked Little T in some ways, though in the last while, it's left me a bit cold. Besides, I've been away with friends some of those weekends. I know you like all that intellectual stuff. But I find Little T kind of long on the esoteric side of faith, and short on the practical. Like I told your sister, their evening discussion group would appeal to you, but it doesn't to me. I'm not critiquing them or you, just telling you like it is. That's surely okay?

I've been going through some major changes, Andy. Nothing new about my dad. The police take forever on these things, though claim they are still conducting an "investigation."

I'm not so sure about lots of things anymore, not least religion. I guess reaction to my dad is finally setting in. When I told one of my friends about my "used-to-be" boyfriend (that's you, Andy), she just couldn't imagine anyone being so "fanatical" about religion. Don't worry; I assured her you weren't a fanatic. But what would you call yourself, Andy?

Right now I just feel really confused about what I believe. What I know for sure is, you and I seem to be heading in totally different directions. Still, I miss you terribly (I hate even admitting that), and cry, then dream of the hugs and kisses we shared last summer. (Is it already more than a year ago? Seems like forever!) Like I said in that long-ago card: "All I really want for Christmas is... you!" Not just for Christmas either, Andy...

There's no hope now at all of me getting over for a visit. The money I'm making in childcare will all be ploughed back into my studies. Two years seems so long! And you're barely even at the halfway point of the first. Please write, though I understand you're not supposed to. And I know a little about you and rules...

Like you more than a friend.

Lorraine.

Part of Andy, the hopeless romantic, yearned to scoop her up in his arms and deliver an utterly passionate kiss, say he loved her, and wanted to spend the rest of his life with her. But that was precisely his dilemma. He balked at the prospect of "the rest of his life" with any woman. Was that what love finally meant: commitment to lifelong partnership? Probably. If so, then he knew he didn't "love" Lorraine in that way. But what was it then? He was physically aroused at the mere sight of her. Her photo tucked away in his Bible was evidence of that. Her wry sense of humour, yes, her cynicism, too, also appealed. She was talented (a great pianist), intelligent, passionate in expression of her views, and lots of fun to be around. How was it that all the individual ingredients did not add up to elicit "love" from him?

If he wasn't prepared to love in that way, why did he take the initiative to date her from the get-go? Wasn't it just a big set-up for exploiting her: the physical gratification from the relationship, (sheepishly) the surprise handful one romantic evening, the hugs and kisses, the thrill of discovering he was attractive to the opposite sex? He couldn't deny that was in part what the relationship became. But, he argued back, that wasn't his intent! Then what was his intent? He didn't know.

Andy reflected on how the allure to women was so similar to his attraction to God. Both tapped the same emotional wellsprings, facilitated a kind of transcendence that looped back to his own gratification. Was that bad? Or was it just the human condition? If so, why was he so fickle? Why was he ready, metaphorically, to jump into bed with every pretty face and shapely figure that came his way? No doubt, that was the vain side of the equation. He *liked* being romantic. There was intense pleasure, he knew, intertwined with sexual arousal, in the very pursuit of an attractive woman when she reciprocated.

Perhaps that was the nub. In the end, his quest for the pleasure of romance for its own sake worked against a willingness to commit seriously. Once so committed, one was suddenly out of the race. The sheer delight of imbibing infatuation like some heady elixir precluded commitment. Was that his problem? Possibly, he concluded. So what had just happened from his side with Janys?

He slept fitfully that night, his thoughts a-twirl.

55

Maranatha Camp was a Baptist Mid-missions ministry operated by the Funston's, who had been on site for several years. It was to be Euro View's home for almost two weeks. It consisted of a main building that slept up to sixty people and also served as a meeting place for main gatherings and meals. It was all done up beautifully in Bavarian style. Flowers burst forth everywhere.

Allan Funston, the father, fairly murdered the language despite years of practicing it. His ancestors were partially German, but there must have been linguistic short-circuitry somewhere. Ruth, his wife, though not of German provenance, had nonetheless mastered the language in every respect. Allan told them how his wife had aspired to become a doctor until he had swept her off to Germany as a missionary's wife. This latter detail was told with a co-incident twinkle. There still seemed to be some far-off wistfulness in her response. Their children all spoke German fluently, a proficiency Andy envied openly.

The only potential drawback of this otherwise unmatched facility was its location. It was forty kilometres south of Munich in a small village called *Bad Heilbrunn*, which meant "Healing Springs Bath," one of several noted local hot springs areas. But no one, as it turned out, complained about the daily requisite drive.

After a quick introduction, Len and Andy in one car and Jack and Fiona in another drove off to the Simpson's, the Baptist Mid-missions folk Andy had met on his previous visit to Munich. They were to pick up the 160,000 Olympic booklets ready for distribution over the next two weeks.

The Simpson's had actually phoned to Hotel Rosat earlier in the week with an urgent message that prayer was needed to raise 120,000 DM ($30,000 US) for a surcharge Customs wished to slap on the books before clearing the shipment. That such a thing had happened at the very last minute was no surprise. German bureaucracy was legendary for such stunts. Intense prayer took place over the next few days, and suddenly, for reasons just as arbitrary, Customs cleared the lot with not an extra *Pfennig* being paid out. On the eve of the *Evangelisation* planned for Munich, it was just the kind of dramatic sign all were excited to receive to reassure them that God was truly in the enterprise.

They only managed to load up half the books on this trip. They would have to come back again for the rest. But the first installment would keep them going for several days.

En route back to Maranatha, Len opened up. "Andy, the time we just had in Switzerland and now this outreach here had better amount to a *big* shot-in-the-arm for our team or I'm afraid we're really in trouble."

"Why?" Andy asked, surprised.

"G. E. had a long talk with me in Switzerland. He said things simply are not gelling on the team. Apparently, he has received correspondence from some members who are not telling me all. He wouldn't say whom, but I can guess at who they are. He called one major session for us all at the end of the week. That's why we couldn't join in the last football game, but we were not free to say so at the time." He shook his head. "I don't know, I just don't know where we're going to go this fall..." He fell silent a few minutes.

"Why do you think you're experiencing such inertia?" Andy asked.

"I really don't know! Maybe G. E.'s right in noticing some burnout in me. It's true that this is our second time around without a real break in between. It's definitely been harder here right from the start. Clearly for us, the enthusiasm's just not the same.

"I'd also say the 'material' on this team is somehow less promising. The only person really on the ball, in our opinion, is Cathy Somerville."

Andy tried to encourage Len by recounting the Berlin Team's woes. He was careful not to assign direct blame to Peter's inability to take up the torch of leadership or Gary's fear of same. He did speak in some detail about Todd Braxman, but nothing of his and Fiona's relationship.

Andy expressed the irony: Here they were, poised to distribute a booklet that told of Jesus' love, of the great happiness and joy there was in following him, and yet both teams were feeling anything but.

"None of it would be phoney," Len allowed, "but it wouldn't exactly be true, either. Following Jesus most emphatically *is not* just a fairy tale romance: 'And they all lived happily ever after.' So why does almost all evangelism claim it is that way?"

Andy nodded, asking further, "Why do I hear endlessly quoted Romans eight, verse twenty-eight? 'And we know that all things work together for good to them that love God, to them who are the called according to his purpose'? Why do I quote it to myself often enough? I remember a sentence from a friend's letter: 'That *all things work together for good* line seems to mock me right now, and if I dwell on it, even haunts.'"

Andy fell into a reverie. From the same passage in Romans eight there was another telling claim: "Nay, in all these things we are more than conquerors through him that loved us." "More than conquerors"? Andy mused. The more he heard about team woes in Nîce and Spain and the more he knew of their own, the more he thought that "less than conquerors" would be a more apt description. Far less.

Andy remembered as a kid going to a cottage at Ipperwash Beach on Lake Huron. It was a beautiful spot. He recalled quite distinctly thinking it so strange that water was poured down the pump at the kitchen sink so that water would come out the other way, what he learned was called "priming the pump." If not enough water was poured down; the pump simply would not work.

It made him think of Jesus' promise that if anyone came to him, wellsprings of water would gurgle up from his or her innermost being. Is that what the faith enterprise was really all about, "priming the pump" in the hope that Living Water would start flowing? If so, it occurred to Andy with a cold stab of fear and despair that maybe some people never get the pump working. Maybe that was his problem and that of most on this evangelistic gig. They believed in the pump. They knew what it could do. They had poured the water of faith down the drain repeatedly to get the thing working, but somehow, unaccountably, the pump was not delivering. Maybe, even worse, just maybe the pump really didn't work after all! Maybe emerging from the cocoon was this: Living with a pump that was either not working or nonexistent and nonetheless getting on with life.

Andy didn't like where this train of thought took him. But he failed to see an exit ramp. There was no pat answer. He thought of Blaise Pascal's famous *Pari* and wondered: What if all Christians believe in a wager on which they think they'll collect but it doesn't, after all, deliver? What if, indeed, we are "of all men most miserable," to quote Paul about the issue, "If Christ be not risen," because the pump is not working and perhaps does not exist? Or is it our failure? Perhaps it hasn't been primed enough. If so, how much faith was needed to produce faith? Andy had no idea. Had wellsprings of faith ever flowed from his innermost being?

He looked over at Len, lost in thought as he drove. Andy wasn't about to blurt his thoughts out then and there. He didn't know Len well enough. Besides, they were almost back at Maranatha, where all were eagerly awaiting their arrival. This was their first opportunity to see the booklet. It had been written entirely by G. E. then translated and printed in the U. S.

"Thanks for a listening ear, Andy," Len said as they turned into the driveway.

"Sorry I couldn't help much," Andy said.

"Just listening was enough."

Andy thought he'd file that away as admonition.

Inside the chapel at Maranatha, with chairs all in a circle, G. E. opened one box of booklets, and everyone scooped up a copy. Andy proceeded to translate, with a little help from his friends. It was Thursday night, August 24th. The Olympics officially opened in two days. G. E. had actually secured tickets for the entire group to attend the opening ceremonies. They were all thrilled. Besides that, each participant had tickets to two events.

Andy had barely looked at the booklet when errors began to leap out at him. "G. E., there's no *umlaut*—two little dots—over *Güntzelstraße*. And the word for publication, *Publikation*, should be capitalized (an Anglicism too). This glares right on the back page." He turned a few pages. "And when I open up to the middle, the same mistaken spelling of the girls' apartment address appears each time. This is not good for the fastidious Germans."

By the time Andy had pointed out the third error, G. E. barked, "Okay, so the production is less than perfect. Let's get on with the translation!"

Andy thought to shoot back that he should have had the German team act as proofreaders. Instead, he proceeded to translate without further commentary.

Despite the errors, just about everyone had an exuberant comment about the book upon first being taken through it. The booklet looked sharp. It was not long-winded, and it drew people in. "Way to sock it to 'em, G. E.!" A chorus of "Amens" followed Jack's comment.

"If this doesn't hit them right between the eyes, what will?" Gary asked. "Man's need, and the plan of salvation are so plainly laid out."

In fact, there was nary a contrary word, except for Andy's few brief barbs.

The long-anticipated piece left Andy unsettled nonetheless as he went through the booklet again in detail before retiring for the night.

G. E. was a propagandist, Andy knew. A cursory glance at the booklet demonstrated that. He had worked with a professional graphics artist to come up with the eight-page, multi-coloured handout. The centrefold was a full-page graphic of stylized runners caught seconds into a 100-meter race. An attractive tear out section yielded two postcard-sized mailers with the words:

"**Book Offer.** Send in this card *today*, and you will receive *at no cost* and without obligation a book."

To the casual recipient, certainly to any child, the implication, if the rest of the booklet was not read in its entirety, was that some kind of Olympics publication

CHRYSALIS CRUCIBLE   545

would be arriving in the mail, free of charge.

Andy was appalled. This was so deceptive! He looked again at the free book being offered, picked it up, and imagined a ten-year old eagerly opening the mailing with an approving mother watching. Against stark red and white colours, a most unappealing book cover worthy of the worst of Jehovah's Witnesses publications would suddenly tumble out, entitled, *Die Bibel Sagt*, "The Bible Says." Obviously not an Olympics publication. The handout had by this time been lost or discarded, so the little boy would be left holding a 111-page book with the concluding words: "*Ihm aber sei alle Ehre!*" "To him, however, be all the Glory!" What a letdown. What a dishonour to God!

Two thousand copies of Dr. Harlow's book, summarizing succinctly as many years of church doctrine, into a pocket size publication had been ordered and were already in the hands of Peter back in West Berlin, awaiting the beginning of an expected flood of requests for the book.

Andy thought back to an incident two weeks before leaving West Berlin for the eastern tour. While going door-to-door, Andy had met a former theologian, Jörg Salaquarda, who had, he said, lost his faith. Andy found out later he was already a noted published thinker, especially on Friedrich Nietzsche. He had been quite a Barthian scholar at one point. Thankfully, Andy had known of Barth through Francis Schaeffer's negative depiction of his theology as "neo-orthodox."

On a whim, Dr. Salaquarda invited Andy into his study. There, occupying several bookshelves, was the multi-volume, unfinished project Barth had entitled *Kirchliche Dogmatik*, "Church Dogmatics." Andy stood in awe of the over 10,000 pages of theological writing Barth had generated in his lifetime on that theme. He had written more theology by far than most Christians, certainly most Evangelicals, would ever read in a lifetime.

Upon Dr. Salaquarda's urging, Andy thumbed through one volume and noticed the three different font sizes on each page, each following a specific line of interactive theological inquiry, one on the biblical text, another of Barth's own theological musings, and a third interaction with myriad other voices, as explained by his host. "Wow!" was all Andy could say. "This is a scholar beyond imagining."

"As we used to refer to him affectionately, 'a veritable theological Mount Everest,'" came the response.

Dr. Salaquarda went on to describe in some detail a little of Barth's long life and enormous theological output. "In sum, *Herr* Norton, he was engaged with the world around him like few contemporaries, religious or not."

Dr. Salaquarda slipped the book back onto the shelf, his tone and demeanour changing as he did so. "Now, against that backdrop you come over from America to tell us what to believe about Jesus, the universe, and all else in between. All summarized in a little tract about 'four spiritual laws.'

"If you will excuse me, I think any fair-minded member of the human race might think this just a tad impertinent. If you do not, I question your fair-mindedness at the least."

Andy's face flushed again in memory of the scorn delivered ever so politely by a man of education and culture way beyond Andy's ken and years.

Andy reflected again on Karl Barth's lifelong and yet unfinished attempt to depict what "*die Bibel sagt,*" thousands of published pages that interacted with obscure and noted theological publications in several major European languages, both ancient and modern. Perhaps only at that point did the monstrous arrogance of their evangelistic outreach at the Olympics begin to truly dawn on him.

What helped rescue him from the staggering gall of GO was the story Hans had told Andy in a recent letter. It concerned Karl Barth's only visit to America. A seminary student asked Dr. Barth to state his greatest theological insight. Barth paused a moment, then responded, "Jesus loves me, this I know, for the Bible tells me so." So if "*die Bibel sagt*" is such a simple profundity that the youngest child intellect could grasp it and a brilliant, expansive theological mind could cite it as his greatest insight, then their book offer might still have some merit, Andy allowed.

He picked up the booklet again. In large red print, the front cover read, "Munich 1972" then in smaller print below, "FREE: This booklet is not for sale." The "almost" Olympics symbol appeared above, a patterned spiralling circle with vertical lines enclosing both to complete the look. Legally, they could not use the actual Olympics logo.

The first inside page yielded a stylized blue-tinted photo of hurdlers in full flight, with a quiz below asking, "What do you know about the Olympics?" Several interesting facts and figures were adduced on that page.

Seemed indeed like an official Olympics publication, Andy thought wryly.

The next page, with a green-tinted stylized swim meet photo in the lower half, told the story of "How the Olympics Began."

The third page was entitled "The 20th Olympic Games in Munich, 1972," with a text that praised the site, architecture, planning, and ingenuity of human creativity by the German hosts. Below the text were several striking photographic images, including one of a very pretty, nice-figured, mini-skirted teenager holding up some glass panelling for the spectacular ceiling of the main stadium.

The following page was a tinted green photo of runners just off the mark, reprised from the "Book Offer" tear-out cards in the middle of the page, with the same symbols and wording as the front cover. By this point, one had the undeniable impression that a free book about the Olympics was being offered. And judging from the graphics, one would anticipate something at least up to the standard of the booklet itself. Hence the incredible disappointment of the ten-year-old upon receiving R. E. Harlow's, plain-Jane Reader's Digest version of the secrets of the universe.

The following page depicted three different activities taking place, all in blue tint. The clearest, non-stylized photo, right-to-centre, was of Neal Steinhauer putting shot. Steinhauer was a non-Olympic record holder, but the caption beneath read: "Some Olympic Records." Here another error was evident, one Andy had missed reporting. The adjectival form of "Olympics" was missing the requisite "n" at the end of the word.

The succeeding page met the reader with a close-up of Neal Steinhauer in a more stylized reprise of the full-length photo on the previous page. The caption read: "An Olympic Champion Speaks about Sports and Life." This was the longest piece of writing so far. It told the story of how Steinhauer had been preparing for the 1968 Olympics, when, just five months before, he had a sudden stabbing pain in his back while lifting a 136 kilograms weight in training.

After three months of pain, he contemplated undergoing an operation but held off a few more days. In that time, the pain suddenly vanished! He returned immediately to training camp.

Three days before he was to compete in his event, he tripped in the weight pit, fell off a platform, and sprained his ankle. That definitively eliminated his bid to compete. The story continued that it took him two years to recover from that injury. During that time, he found himself asking, "Why God, why?"

He found the answer, he informed the reader, on June 23rd, 1970 when he attended a conference of 300 athletes. He listened to Brian Sternberg, the 1963 world record holder in the pole vault. Sternberg shared from a wheelchair that he would sooner be as he was for the rest of his life and know that Jesus Christ is with him than win another Gold Medal.

Neal found himself scarcely able to imagine this but decided to accept this greatest offer ever made to man, namely, to accept Jesus Christ into his life as Friend and Redeemer. Then he quoted from Matthew's Gospel, where Jesus said that anyone who loses his life for his sake will find it, and that it is otherwise useless to gain the whole world and lose one's own soul.

The testimony ended with: "*Ich sagte ja zu Jesus!*" "I said yes to Jesus!" Andy could not help but associate this with a *Brylcream* ad he used to see on TV that ended with similar words, "I said yes to *Brylcream!*" Jesus and *Brylcream*. "Jesus, just a little dab will do ya," he could hear the jingle. "Just the right amount and the girls will all pursue ya."

The final page featured a reprise, this time in blue, of the runners from the middle Book Offer section. The caption read: "Life is like a running race." It also had a lot of text.

A pitch followed it: "You can have joy, true joy, if you really want it. You can even find out what the secret of happiness is. The race of life can be exciting, if one permits Jesus to run alongside. Neal Steinhauer found the answer to his problems when he invited Jesus to become his personal Saviour."

The text continued by denying that this meant, "getting religion." No, it centred entirely upon Jesus. Many, it indicated, were approaching life's finish line. "The Bible says that it is appointed unto man once to die, and after this, the judgment. There are many who have no fear of that day. Why? Because they have been competing in the race of life according to Jesus' rules, one of which assures that if one hears his word, and believes the one who sent him, he will have eternal life, and will not come under judgment but is already passed from death to life. For such, there will be no condemnation, rather heaven's glory, and a reward more desirable than an Olympic Gold Medal."

"But," came the dire warning, "those who have not accepted God's plan of salvation, and obeyed him, will be declared one day to be unfit, and will undergo suffering, grief, and pain in the eternal darkness of hell."

The text concluded by indicating that Jesus Christ died on the cross for man's sins so that one could finish life's race with joy. Any reader need only do the following: invite Jesus into his or her life as Saviour and Lord, and mean it. If one did this with all one's heart, he or she could be certain that God would uphold His promise. He would fill the person's life with much blessing and provide a glorious hope for the future.

The reader was finally invited to send in the enclosed card or simply to write to the address for further information about this most important topic.

The whole booklet ended off saying, "We would be happy, and consider it a great honour, to be able to help you discover the secret of a full, happy life. We will gladly send you *free* and without obligation a book."

Andy reread one part of the text, and translated out loud: "Those who have not received God's plan of salvation, and obeyed him, will be said one day to be unfit, and will experience suffering, grief, and pain in the eternal darkness of hell."

During a coffeehouse evening the previous summer, Andy had gotten into a long discussion with someone who could not understand why he should become a believer. Andy finally told him there was a "dark side" to the Good News he should consider. He proceeded to indicate the biblical teaching that there is everlasting conscious torment for everyone who fails to bow the knee to Jesus.

The guy was a thoughtful senior philosophy student. After Andy finished, he responded quietly, barely above the din of the evening's activities. "If that is really what you believe, Andy, then all I can say is, your God is worse than the worst human tyrant who has ever lived. Whereas what human tyrants can only undertake to do on a temporal finite scale to their enemies, the God you believe in will do on a cosmic scale *without end!*" At that, he glanced again at *The Four Spiritual Laws* booklet Andy had pulled out at one point in the conversation. "What was that First Law you said?"

"God loves you, and has a wonderful plan for your life," Andy replied.

"There's a part missing there, according to you," said his dialogue partner.

"What's that?" Andy queried, taken aback.

"Well, the next part, the corollary about hell,

sounds like you're saying just the opposite about God. I think that is closer to what I always thought Satan was supposed to be according to you Christians..."

Andy was utterly shocked about how his own sharing about hell had been turned back against him. Imagine, his God a cosmic hateful tyrant on a par with Satan! Andy was speechless. He told the guy he would really need to do some more thinking on that, but that somehow God's love and God's holiness in the end were not incompatible, he was certain. The guy thanked him for their talk, not a little disdainfully, and shortly afterwards left. Andy felt a horrible failure.

That conversation, as well as his more recent one with Hans in West Berlin, flooded his thoughts. God, the Ultimate Cosmic Tyrant?

Andy imagined what it would mean to be the son of a feudal lord in some ancient time who fell madly in love with the beautiful daughter of a serf. The lord of the manor would finally approach the daughter's father at the repeated bidding of his son. "My son would have your daughter's hand in marriage," he would declare, and proceed with an announcement of all the arrangements to be made.

He imagined if, when the father presented this to his daughter, she refused the son's intentions.

"But you must understand," the lord of the manor would declare to the father, with his son present, "my son does love her greatly, and has a marvellous plan for her life that he cannot wait to unfold for her. *But*," his tone would turn menacing, "if she refuses my son's hand, then hear this: After a fixed time, which I forthwith decree as two months, if your daughter will not have my son's hand in marriage, then we have together agreed that she shall be subject to the most abject tortures and mutilations for three days, after which she shall be fully dismembered and thrown to the wild dogs."

Then the lord and the son would withdraw to await the daughter's decision.

Could it be truly said that the son ever loved the daughter if he could contemplate such retributive vengeance for not taking his hand in marriage? Could it ever be said that God truly loves us if He was perfectly prepared to exact everlasting conscious punishment upon us for failure to make a decision for Christ? "Once to die, and after this judgment." Could such love and hatred abide together in the same bosom? Did God love the whole world—except those, of course, He consigned to hell, whom he "loved" with a pure hatred?

Andy felt miserable for thinking such thoughts. But could he not? Or did faith just mean looking the other way? The lustre of God's love in Andy's life, a love that, though not unproblematic, had always been fairly axiomatic for as long as he could remember, was suddenly tarnished that day. And this on the eve of the largest evangelistic crusade in which Andy had ever participated.

Was there anyone he could talk to? Was there anyone he dared talk to? He thought of Janys.

56

The opening ceremonies at the Olympic Stadium were absolutely spectacular. Günter Zahn, a West German athlete, lit the Olympic torch. There were multiplied thousands in attendance. It was thrilling beyond Andy's wildest expectations. He sat with Janys and Dan. Both Andy and Janys were on their best behaviour under Dan's watchful eye.

One hundred and twenty-one nations had produced 7,134 athletes to compete in 195 events over the next two weeks. This Olympics was the largest ever, setting records in all categories. Twenty-two-year-old Mark Spitz of the United States did similarly. He competed in seven swimming events, won gold in every one, *and* set a new world record all seven times! Get him saved, Andy remembered thinking as the Olympics unfolded, and you'd have the Ultimate Witness for Christ, including biblical symbol-laden perfection of the number seven. That he might become a "Jew for Jesus" seemed too much to hope for. It was. They would have to settle for Neal Steinhauer.

Sunday morning was the first distribution of the booklets. G. E. had planned for all to do so in front of the main entrance to the Olympic Park.

The weather was beautiful, a fresh breeze was invigorating, and all were evidently pumped. Except Andy.

He dutifully began distributing the booklets. His mind churned as he did. He imagined himself recipient of one, casually leafing through it, becoming suddenly aware of the religious agenda. He could barely look people in the eye. What if someone really wanted to talk with him? What would he say?

The hours dragged by. No one asked any questions. He handed out hundreds. He got through the day, his mind leaden.

They arrived home in time for clean-up before supper.

There was a pleasant path from Maranatha leading down to a stream that Andy had walked during his earlier visit. He and Janys followed that after supper. Andy had told Janys he wanted to talk to her about hell. A little taken aback, she was nonetheless game. He dutifully refrained from holding her hand.

The evening was still full of light and warmth, but Andy hardly took note, so intent was he on the issue before him. After summarizing his recent ruminations, he finally stopped and turned to face her. "As I see it, Janys, if the doctrine of final damnation is ultimately brought on by God, then the final reality of God is not, as the Bible says, *love*, but *hate*, is it not?"

Janys took a moment to ponder this.

"I mean," Andy went on, "Christians have done horrible things to others through the ages. Isn't it just a short step from believing God intends hell for the infidel to believing Christians can give anyone '(temporal) hell' they deem deserving? Isn't that what the Church has done or willed for two thousand years?"

Janys still didn't say anything.

Andy took a breath. "I borrowed a concordance from the church library and looked up all New Testament references to hell. Unless I missed something, and I don't believe I did, only once, in Revelation twenty-twenty, is there a clear reference to hell as a place of intentional torment. But that is all highly symbolic language, and besides, no humans are so tormented according to that passage.

"Further, if God really does torment, as is claimed, for ever, then God must be the one to sustain their lives for such torture. Otherwise it would be impossible for anyone to live through it. So God must somehow keep them alive to continue punishing them. And forever, Janys! Just imagine the worst electric shock torture, only you never die, never lose consciousness, just keep on getting zapped, screaming in abject pain. For ever and ever Amen!"

"Maybe it doesn't mean eternal conscious *physical* punishment, Andy."

Andy thought for a moment. "But pain is still pain, whether emotional or physical. I know that too well—so do you! And in that case, shouldn't such emotional pain be designed to lead to remorse and repentance? If so, how could it be eternal? Or do we believe in a God who, despite our repentance, still punishes us on and on?"

Janys held up her hand. "What about that story of King Saul's disobedience? Weren't he and his whole future bloodline punished for just one act of disobedience? He lost the kingship and begged Samuel and God to forgive him. But God refused."

"In that story," Andy said, "didn't God also order Saul to wipe out every man, woman, child, infant, and every other living thing? And then destroy everything else? Today we'd call that 'genocide' and 'scorched earth.'

"One of my dad's most quoted Scriptures is from there, First Samuel fifteen, verse twenty-two: 'Behold, to obey is better than sacrifice, and to hearken than the fat of rams.' As I used to say to Dad, after my sister first pointed this out, what Saul failed to obey was doing to people what Hitler did against the Jews, Stalin to fellow Russians, Mao against loyalist Chinese, and the absolute violation of every human and property right we hold dear today. The more I thought about it, the more I realized how it blatantly, fully, abjectly contradicts Jesus' command to 'Love your enemies.'

"In that story, you may also recall that King Agag is brought back alive, and Samuel, speaking for God, bawls out Saul for that, too. Then Samuel turns to Agag, who says surely the time for killing is past, but Samuel says something like, 'Just as you have made many mothers in Israel weep, so today I shall make your mother weep.' Then Samuel hacks King Agag into little pieces—before the Lord, according to the text—which means with God's full approval. Did you ever see that TV clip of a Viet Cong being summarily executed, gun held to his head one minute, next minute blood spurting out, lifeless body dropped to the ground? That's God-fearing Samuel—only worse in that Samuel had no quick trigger to pull. He probably had to hack away for some time to get the job done. Imagine the gore! And God looked on and smiled?

"The whole story is really about God seeking revenge on the Amalekites for waylaying the Israelite ancestors centuries before. What a way to picture God, nursing a hateful grudge toward the Amalekites for hundreds of years until he finally gets one of His servants to slaughter them all!

"When I challenged Dad on this, all he would ever say back was, 'God's ways are not our ways.' But can God arbitrarily make black white and not cause the whole concept of morality simply to implode inwards?"

He paused to allow Janys to respond, but she remained silent.

"So can God really conquer all evil, finally, when

hell, *which is ultimate evil* by definition, exists? And why? Why would God sustain a tortured person's existence for ever and ever? Just to bring him pleasure, He who takes no pleasure in the death of the wicked (so it says in Ezekiel) and who does not willingly afflict or grieve anyone (that's Lamentations) who is love according to First John? Isn't such a notion precisely the kind one can well imagine a Hitler or a Mussolini wanting, *or a totally sick psycho?* But God—who 'loves us and has a wonderful plan for our life'—and afterlife, unless we don't buy in, then it's torture BIG TIME for ever and ever? Isn't hell, in the end, in the way we have traditionally believed it, *sheer gratuitous evil of the most abominable kind?*"

Andy waited. Still no answer. They started to walk again, both silent for several minutes.

"Then why do evangelism?" Janys asked, finally.

Andy thought about it for a moment. "My uncle used to say that you could come alongside any child at camp and get them to pray the sinner's prayer, especially when hell was mentioned. He really disagreed with the scare tactics of some of the preachers, especially when directed toward children. He called it 'spiritual child abuse.'

"If God is so scary that He banishes us to hell for not believing, then it's just as well not to introduce people to that kind of 'god' anyway, in my opinion. I feel sick about all this, Janys, and I don't know where to turn. I have felt God all my life. I've always accepted the idea of hell, even raised it in various discussions. But lately I just don't know."

Andy stopped again. "The thing that really bugs me is, how come no one else seems bothered by this? How come everyone just accepts this thing and asks no questions? I don't get it. Does no one else *think* about these things? What Evangelical can I ask about this without getting into trouble?"

They started walking again. "I guess the bottom line is, I know God as one who loves me. If heaven is there for me because of that love, then I can't fit hell in as 'the other side' of that love. Whatever hell or punishment is, it has to be part of God's love or God is the ultimate schizophrenic Tyrant, and I want no part of his 'love' anyway. For, in that case, God's heaven is hell, since hell finally contradicts, swallows up, heaven. If God wills hell as some kind of ultimate punishment, then that's who God is in the end: a hateful being that I want nothing to do with. Trust in such a "god"? Not in a million eternities!

"So where does that leave me tomorrow when I hand out this booklet to likely hundreds again, Janys? What do I do?"

They stopped on a bridge that passed over the stream and stared down at the water.

"Sometimes I think you think too much, Andy! If Evangelicals mainly don't *think* but *feel*, just want to *feel* good about God and themselves, and their *thinkers* just think enough to make the *feelers feel* good about not thinking, about their selfish little self-righteous lives, like an inoculation, you *think* way too much!

"I look back over all the discussions we have had, and I could get a headache just thinking about all that thinking you've done. I do a lot of thinking, and I know you find me an intelligent person, but I just am not always *thinking* like you are. Sometimes it's good to just take a deep breath and smell the roses."

This was not quite the response Andy was looking for, but he digested it all the same.

"I guess I've accepted the teaching about hell I was raised with, because that's just the way things are:

punishments and rewards are with us in every aspect of life. So why not after death, too? Why can't God be God and we just accept what the Bible teaches? Isn't that what you always say?"

Andy pondered this for a time. "Janys," he began, "what would be one time of total contentment for you in your life? Think about that. I'm guessing one such is beyond memory, when you were a newborn child totally surrounded by your mother's warmth, love, and nurture. Think about the image of a newborn baby, Janys, of a mother's total care of and love for her. Then imagine God in that role. That fits what we know and say about God. Remember, Jesus wanted to gather the people of Jerusalem to himself like a mother hen gathers her chicks. Remember all those biblical images of God nurturing his people like a mother?

"Then switch your imagination to a torture room in Central America, where that same little baby, now grown to mature adult, is stretched out on a cold mattress, is viciously raped and undergoes routine indignities beyond imagination. She cries out for the release of death, but that does not come. And the pain and torture is endless.

"Now, can you honestly imagine the same mother in both roles, arranging for and superintending the second reality, no matter what the rationalization? Yet that is precisely what teaching you and I have been led to believe, that the same "god" who created us out of an enormous free act of love—who loved us so desperately that He gave 'His only begotten Son' to birth us a second time—somehow just as determinedly plans the most malicious eternal outcome imaginable if we do not *believe* in him. In that case, Jesus dies *above all to save us from God!* That's crazy! It boggles my mind, Janys, that this has been taught for two thousand years! If this is the only way we can think about God according to the Bible, I'm checking out. It is sick beyond all human imagining! But the reason I say this now, Janys, *is precisely because I read my Bible!*

"Meanwhile, I have to hand out an evangelistic tract, as do you, about God's love for us that forewarns, at the same time, that any who reject Christ's offer *werden Schmerzen, Kummer und Pein erleiden in der ewigen Dunkelheit der Hölle.* That's what it says, Janys, in just about those exact words. That if we reject Christ we will experience everything that woman tortured in Central America experienced *in the eternal darkness of Hell.* And Dr. Harlow's book says the same thing: that if we reject Christ we will experience *Furcht, Trauer und Zorn*. Fear, sadness, and wrath, Janys. He quotes several passages from Matthew to prove it. That's what we're saying God is planning for each person who rejects him! Do you really believe that? I don't. I can't. I won't!"

Janys had no answer, certainly nothing remotely satisfactory for Andy. Andy knew she knew that. They both felt trapped by the awareness.

Andy walked over to a nearby bench and sat down. Janys followed. The stream gurgled beside them. Birds sang. Butterflies fluttered through the trees. It was "Edenic," Andy thought. Suddenly, Andy snapped to the realization that he was all alone in glorious nature with the most remarkable woman he had ever met. Yes, he had finally admitted that on this trip. He felt the fool for having taken nearly a year to acknowledge it and was suddenly overwhelmed that she was actually attracted to *him*.

"Andy, you make my head spin sometimes with what you say," Janys responded. She smiled. "I like your *lips* better than your *quips*, I guess."

Andy looked at her. There had been some vague talk of covenant in distant memory, existentially displaced by such immediately accessible presence. He did not know whose lips moved forwards first, but he did know sudden exquisite delight. Whatever hell might be, in that moment Andy was experiencing its polar opposite.

They pulled apart tenderly, self-conscious that others could be walking the path. They stood to continue the loop. Neither said anything about their covenant, but neither did they hold hands.

"Andy," Janys said softly, "I've never met a guy like you. You think hard; you're honest, gutsy, tender, and respectful. Okay, you have an ego. But so do we all. And your thinking at times really does scare me. Not because it's off the wall, but because it makes so much biblical and common sense!

"I don't like your questions about hell, because I have no answers, and they are so biblically rational. It bothers me that you would be thinking this way when we've already had enough problems getting started on our evangelism. What a time to be having second thoughts about our core mission!

"On the other hand, these questions arise from your personal faith journey, which I think is full of integrity. If you're thinking these thoughts, surely others are, too. How could you suppress them and remain honest about the very faith you claim to be 'the Truth'?

"Andy, why not do a session on the issue with all of us here? I know it would upset some, but still, wouldn't it be just posing honest questions, which G. E. has always taught us never to shrink from? And isn't that Francis Schaeffer's trademark, 'honest answers to honest questions'?

"Besides, there are several leaders here who have

attended Bible School and have sat under Christian teaching for years. They must have thought through this issue and come up with satisfying answers. Why not arrange something?"

Why not indeed? Andy thought.

They had almost done an entire loop, back to where their walk had begun.

"Janys, you know what scares me even more than all this stuff about hell and evangelism? That I have missed something for almost an entire year… That the most exquisite gem I have ever seen in my whole life should have glittered under my nose, and I did not even notice. I feel I owe you an apology. Then again, maybe it was just as well when we ended up sleeping together early on. Can you imagine the challenge of that stormy night now—Cathars notwithstanding?"

Janys said nothing, though a ghost of a smile played across her lips. Luscious lips, Andy thought.

"So many years of blindness about violence, hell and what else? It's scary. There *must* be lots more to which I've also been blind. Maybe life consists in 'catching sight' just off the corner of our vision of what's *really* going on all the time. Like seeing those elusive Irish leprechauns or fairies who seem to dematerialize just as we glance their way. Enter faith, right. Or Jesus' 'eyes to see, ears to hear.'"

"An art, not a science," Janys said quietly as they entered the dining hall for supper. She added quietly, "Andy, you do not owe me an apology. You have no idea…"

He looked down. Her eyes were glistening. He knew that sentence was not going to be completed. Neither did it need to be.

57

Andy was steaming. They had finished another, for Andy, disturbing distribution day at the Olympics. Andy had asked to talk to G. E. after supper. They went to the "Quiet Corner," a mini-chapel modeled after some of the local Catholic *Kapellen*. A few benches were arranged in a covered enclosure with several candles kept burning all the time. Up front was a table with the "elements" of bread and wine on it. Someone looked after the chapel daily.

Andy took no time to launch in with his struggles about hell. It was probably too much too fast.

Finally, G. E. held up his hands. "Whoa! Whoa! Andy, you have just subjected me to such a torrent of words, how could I ever hope to follow?

"But, as I gather, you are increasingly questioning the traditional doctrine of hell as a place of 'eternal torment.' You know our booklet threatens this in response to unbelief, and you'd like to see an open forum discussion for everyone at Maranatha. Does that about sum it up?"

Andy nodded.

"Son, let's go for a walk."

That set Andy off. The last person to use "son" in discussion with Andy was Scott Cunningham. But Andy pushed the words, if not the feelings back down.

They headed down the same path Janys and he had been on the day before. It was much the same ambience, warm sun, bubbling brook, ordered nature.

"Andy," G. E. began, "you remind me in so many ways of my son. Not surprising that you two have hit it off.

"But sometimes you need to take a step back from the incessant question, 'Hath God said?' like the serpent in the Garden, and just accept that God hath said, and we acquiesce."

Andy drew a breath.

"Let me continue, son. There is a 'time for everything,' and youth is the time for questions. True enough. But you also need to grow out of that stage, for it is a stage, Andy, on the way to spiritual maturity. Questions must give way to Jesus' definitive, 'It is written!' To answers. To certainty. That is what we offer the world, Andy. Faith's certainties.

"Hell is one of those issues on the way to Christian maturity. No one likes to think of God as a tyrant like Hitler, as the Great Cosmic Avenger. Problem is, *that's exactly how God is depicted biblically!* I'll go one better: God *does* look like a Dictator worse than Hitler or any feudal lord. That *is* the biblical picture of God in the end—the final Lake of Fire the book of Revelation depicts. And it is for everyone rebellious, disobedient, and unbelieving, toward God.

"Ask all the questions you will, Andy. They break apart utterly against the granite rock of biblical truth that God has ordained some to eternal bliss, others to everlasting damnation."

G. E. had taken them in another direction from where Andy and Janys had gone the previous night. Andy noted it was darker and more overgrown, a path nonetheless. He wondered what G. E. would have done had he come across Andy and Janys in passionate embrace.

As if the previous discussion were already over, G. E. asked, "What happened between you and Fiona, Andy?"

"Nothing," Andy said, not wanting to get into it.

"And what do you think of Jack and Fiona?" G. E. asked, gesturing for Andy to sit down beside him on a bench.

"Not much to think, sir," Andy replied.

"Is it right?" G. E. pushed.

"I guess I hadn't given that a thought," Andy replied honestly.

"And yet," G. E. rejoined, "you question God's truth about hell so readily, a mere gnat of an issue given the clear teaching of Scripture, while allowing the whole 'camel' of aberrant sexuality escape you.

"See what I mean about growing in maturity, Andy? 'Rightly dividing the word of truth' is not child's play. Part of the 'youthful lusts' we are beholden by Paul to flee is playing fast and loose with biblical interpretation. Like all the cults." He paused, "So what exactly is going on between Fiona and Jack?"

Andy almost said it was none of G. E.'s business. He chose to throw it back at G. E. instead. "Sir, you watched them for a whole week. Surely you have drawn your own conclusions?"

Before G. E. could respond, Andy added with sudden inspiration, "You remind me so much of Bill Gothard's approach to Scripture. It's a 'tail-wag-the-dog' approach. Gothard tells us repeatedly what to think about God, the world, life, then proceeds to find a biblical proof text somewhere to back it up."

Andy took a deep breath then plunged headlong. "With all due respect, G. E. it is *precisely* my biblical understanding of God—not my 'youthful lusts'—that precludes a hell of eternal conscious torment. I could, by the same account, accuse you of Pharisaic overlay of Scripture as Jesus warned vehemently against in Matthew twenty-three, not least going across the ocean to win converts, and turning them into twice the sons of hell for all your effort."

Suddenly, G. E. grabbed hold of Andy's hands and began to pray imploringly. "Lord, you are here right now listening to our every word. I pray for my dear brother Andy, so desirous of serving you, so confused about your Word. Intervene in his life today, right now! Challenge him to seek the 'better way,' namely, to spend time adoringly at your knees and fall rapturously in love…"

G. E.'s prayer went on and on like some old preacher in his home assembly, Andy thought. Some brethren habits didn't die easily. He became conscious of their surroundings as G. E. droned on. How had they gotten here, exactly? It didn't look like people came this way very often. Certainly not that evening.

Andy had to sneeze. He withdrew his hands in a violent bid to stave off the explosion.

G. E. waited a moment, wordless, then took hold of Andy's hands again as if to continue praying! This was too much. Andy pulled them back.

"Amen, G. E.!" He stood up and walked back toward Maranatha.

Andy was fuming. Why had he even wasted his breath on G. E. about hell? Who was wrongly dividing the word of truth, twisting it entirely to suit his fancy? He strode on at a quickened pace, not caring if G. E. followed, mindful only of his smouldering fury toward him, toward all his kind. He'd had it!

"Andy!" It was G. E. Andy stopped but refused to turn around. "Andy, you'll see. All this questioning is not good. I'm still wrestling for your soul, Andy!" G. E. stopped for breath, panting from exertion.

Andy started walking again. Then came the corker, "And I hope nothing got started between you and Janys. I realized there were real risks in having all four of you along on this recent mission. I've kept my eye on you. I hope I'm right, Andy. Am I?"

Andy did not look back; did not respond. For all he cared right then, G. E. could *go* to hell. His anger felt good. Suddenly, he laughed and thought no more of the irony.

58

Andy used to chuckle at the Jesus People bumper sticker: "Read your Bible. It will scare the hell out of you!" No longer. If that's all the Bible was designed to do, then Andy was done with it.

No more "Just sign on the dotted line and get your fire insurance free." How could one beat such a deal? A dab of belief, and one's entire hereafter was secured against all odds.

Andy remembered Dietrich Bonhoeffer's expression, "cheap grace." Cheap like borscht, like *Brylcream*, like G. E., and like Neal Steinhauer's Jesus. He pondered the consequent question of whether the Gospel they were spreading was the real McCoy or some sick inversion of the same, designed, however unintentionally, only to bind people faster to hell than they were already.

There was a telling ring to those two words, "cheap grace," that seemed to point a "Thou art the man!" finger at Andy and the sort of Evangelical Christianity he had embraced all his years. No matter how he tried to duck it, it found its mark repeatedly. It established a dybbuk of doubt in Andy's evangelistic impulses that nothing could shake or remove. Its constant return to his consciousness, like an unpredictable comet, unnerved him beyond his rational ability to control.

Despite these thoughts, Andy participated in the literature distribution routine each day. But he became increasingly detached. He watched the eagerness of many others plying the same waters, pressing the flesh for converts. He admired their zeal. But he could no longer buy into the mission. Not that way. He disliked the booklet. He disliked its author. Worst and above all, he intensely disliked its "god." He glared at G. E. Just who was the "god" of this mission after all?

Andy also wrestled with the sheer sea of humanity he encountered daily at the Olympics. He remembered a similar struggling during Expo '67 in Montréal. He had taken training the previous winter as a Grade 13 student through Campus Crusade for Christ. It had centred entirely on *The Four Spiritual Laws.* The little booklet was for all intents elevated to Holy Scripture status. The trainees, Andy amongst them, memorized its every word, had it drilled into them not to vary one iota from its time-honoured, field-tested, worldwide cross-cultural success. "Do this and ye shall get them saved," was the Third Greatest Commandment message of the Campus Crusade trainers.

The dam burst one day when, emerging from his shift at the "Sermons from Science" pavilion, he was struck by the bald impossibility of the evangelistic task. How could God ever establish a personal relationship through Christ with the sheer masses of visitors that streamed around him, much less everyone else in the world? Similar thoughts flooded his consciousness several times at the Olympics.

Yet, Andy countered in his mind, "the fields are white unto harvest." And they were surely labourers who had responded to the call. He remembered a recent talk from Dr. Evans as part of their training in Switzerland. He had said there were three classic filters in Christian history that prevented people from taking the Bible seriously: *experience*, *tradition*, and *reason*. Evangelicals were supposedly they who set aside all those filters in their faith or repositioned each not to filter but to refract Scripture's light as in a prism. Surely this "experience" of the huge numbers who likely did not know Christ, and never would, was one such filter. How could he turn it into a prism instead? It bothered him, but he finally decided to let it remain an unresolved, and possibly irresolvable, issue in his faith journey.

A few days into the campaign, the police accosted Andy. They took exception to the sheer volume of green booklets that were being discarded everywhere. It was becoming a genuine litter problem. If they were still in good shape, the evangelists agreed to recycle them. Nonetheless, one plainclothes official said they could not even give the literature out in Munich without a city permit. But he was suddenly called away, acting like a member of the Secret Service. Andy never saw him again nor met that same response.

Even so, it became evident from their two weeks at the Olympics that the world was full of petty tyrants who delighted in throwing their lighter-than-air weight around in a bid to establish miniscule petty fiefdoms. Bureaucrats of every description seemed especially prone to this, from Andy's experience. He suspected that most of humanity felt an amazing lightness of being, like billions of helium-filled balloons dotting earth's crust. Perhaps we attempt to anchor ourselves, as it were, to this existence through wilful acts of petty tyranny. Else we all fear floating away into the great nothingness of space and non-being. Faith as anchor, faith as "weight of glory," took on new meaning in that context. "Aim for earth and you'll get nothing," C. S. Lewis had observed. "Aim for heaven, and you'll get heaven with earth thrown in." Faith, a paperweight on earth, weight of anti-gravity glory in heaven.

On Saturday, September 2nd, several took time

out from their evangelistic work to tour Dachau Concentration Camp, a short drive northwest of Munich. The camp had been preserved in perpetuity as a Museum of Horrors by an association of concentration camp survivors.

As Andy walked through the gate, he recalled Martin Niemoeller, an outspoken pastor who criticized the Church after the war for their failure to oppose Nazism, had been jailed there seven long years.

"Dachau was the first and arguably the worst of the Nazi camps," their museum tour guide, a dour woman in her mid-thirties, told them. "Heinrich Himmler established it in March 1933. Under Theodor Eicke, the first camp commandant and later inspector of all the camps, Dachau became the model for a whole new level of mass brutality. It was also 'murder school' for the infamous SS."

Andy was amazed at the guide's outspokenness. Perhaps one of her family members had been interned there.

"The first prisoners were political opponents of the National Socialists," she continued. "Communists, social democrats, and trade unionists. Eventually Jews, homosexuals, Gypsies, Jehovah's Witnesses, and some clergy landed there due mainly to their political beliefs. Then after the November 1938 'Crystal Night' anti-Jewish pogroms, over ten thousand Jews were sent to Dachau. Eventually, up to two hundred thousand prisoners from thirty countries were imprisoned there. Thousands became involved in the production of armaments in huge underground factories at subsidiary camps.

She pointed to some horrific pictures on the wall. "Unknown thousands were also transported to Dachau for execution. Some of these were used for medical experiments, as you can see here, dying under horrific conditions. Starvation, sickness, exhaustion, degradation, beating, and torture claimed further untold lives."

She moved on to a scale model of the camp, pointing to the various buildings as she talked. "A gas chamber was built in 1942 but never used on a mass scale. However, a crematorium with four ovens was kept busy processing the enormous number of bodies the camp produced. Once lit, the fires never went out under Nazi rule."

Andy recalled Hans' paper. To get to that point of liberation, in Germany alone more than one million civilians became casualties of American and Allied carpet-bombing campaigns in forty-four German cities. Three months before Dachau was freed, the Allies killed between 30,000 and 300,000 civilians in Dresden alone – depending on who did the estimates. This may have surpassed the total number of civilian victims liquidated by the Nazis in all twelve years of Dachau's operation, Andy realized.

Later, Dan, Andy, and Janys again found themselves walking through the compound together, each lost in reverie.

Andy felt so overwhelmed with revulsion that he took absolutely no photos. It seemed like an act of historical voyeurism to indulge his tourist instincts. Besides, one had to *experience* the place, not see it vicariously on slides. Still, Andy knew that the narrow dimensionality of that encounter was exponentially removed from actually living it. His whole being shivered involuntarily, though it was a perfect summer day. The mind's celluloid alone would record the event, and he knew he would never return for fear that the revulsion would be blunted through familiarity.

He suddenly saw all the post-War movies and TV programs in that light: pro-mass slaughter propaganda campaigns to sanitize the unspeakable. "It was a dirty job, but golly gee, somebody had to do it!"

Ordinary citizens just following orders, who at workday's end embraced their kids and took in a Beethoven Concert or other enriching cultural events. "The origins of all human cultures are a founding murder," René Girard taught, whom Andy had read a smidgeon of in a university anthropology class.

Andy realized the Allies were not all that different from the camp guards. The guards were not necessarily monsters, nor were they unduly sadistic. For them, torturing and killing was all in a day's work, like delivering milk. It made good rational sense. The cancerous cells were being removed from the body politic. The scientific men in white coats at the end of the train lines told them to do so. Just as priests and countless religious leaders throughout human history had ever blessed human sacrifices—and still did!

Andy shuddered again as the full weight of the moral equivalency sank in. His mind was pulled back to a single woman in her sixties and her elderly mother that the team had gotten to know that summer. They attended *Hohenstaufenstraße* assembly. Both sparkled with mischievousness at times and were very encouraging of the team's efforts. A rare exception amongst church folk.

Once, after they had treated the whole team to a delicious meal of *Rouladen mit Rotkohl,* Andy asked a straightforward conversation stopper. "Yes, but didn't you surely *know*?" Elderly Frau Luzie responded simply, "Nein." But her troubled eyes said, "Yes." So did those of her daughter.

How could it have been otherwise? Jewish families

disappearing from neighbourhoods all over Germany, Jewish businesses boarded up, Stars of Bethlehem as forced apparel. It was known all right, and by everyone!

Yet, in another way, the matriarch was not lying. The average citizen didn't know the true extent of the horror. Then, with a shock of insight, *because they didn't want to know!* Because that knowledge would demand commitment or induce moral dissolution. Because such knowledge, "a little learning," is ever a dangerous thing, as Alexander Pope pointed out.

Was it any different today? Were they, in the comfortable bubble of the West, likewise knowingly ignorant, deliberately uninformed? Until recently, Andy had been wilfully ignorant about Vietnam. What else was going on in the world that benefited him at his end of the market continuum but was sheer terror at the other? Had it ever been any different? Frankly, in that moment *he didn't want to know!*

He was struck by another bolt of sickening insight: Why was the Allied Holocaust never taught in school just like the Nazi one? The answer came with a similar dreadfulness of understanding: Because Holocaust is okay as long as the "Good Guys" perpetrate it. He imagined all those brave Allied airmen embracing their wives and kids after returning from a day's bombing. The moral equivalency was exact. "You have defeated us Nazis. But the spirit of Nazism has arisen like a phoenix amongst you," so said one of the Nazi war criminals, Andy could not remember who. Why had no one ever taught *that* in all his schooling? He felt angry. Why did his mind make such associations?

His mind turning to the Vietnam War, Andy recalled how Ho Chi Minh initially believed the United States would back North Vietnam's bid for "freedom," because they were simply aspiring to the same stirrings for freedom that had motivated Americans in their War of Independence. They couldn't have been more wrong.

Andy recalled what he had read in Hans's essay about the Bay of Tonkin ruse that launched the Vietnam War in 1964. The claimed attack by the North Vietnamese was complete American fabrication. The first casualty of war is truth. Millions of others, on all sides, are civilians. Andy wondered about Pearl Harbour and what else the American Empire might fabricate in the future to fight a "just war" for Manifest Destiny to… What? Rule the world? Andy thought of the verse in Job that his dad often quoted: "Yet man is born unto trouble, as the sparks fly upward." If "violence" were inserted for "trouble," it would be just as true, he was sure.

Janys and Dan had not waited for Andy. He moved on alone into the crematorium with the four ovens and gas chamber. The door to each oven stood ajar. He read the specifications: the actual size of each oven, the number of bodies incinerated at one time, the total number of bodies consumed by the four Molochs. Andy closed his eyes, as at Salzburg, and heard the noises, gagged at the reek. As he did, he recalled that the crews of the last American bombers over Tokyo had to be fitted with gas masks, because the stench of burning flesh was so overwhelming even at great height.

In his mind, Andy followed the oven-stokers home. Saw them with their wives and kids, accompanied them to family barbecues. A great time was had by all! He flew back to the base with the B-29 bombers, took in the evening movie with them, watched them write love letters to their wives and girlfriends, felt the tenderness of missing their kids, leaders all of next generation America…

Then a realization blasted into his consciousness like the imagined sudden blistering heat of those ovens at full burn: *Dachau is Christendom's most perfect human picture of hell!*

The parallels overwhelmed. *God is Hitler. The ovens are God's specially built chambers of eternal conscious torment*, to which human victims by the billions are fed because they refused to take the hand of the feudal lord's son in marriage. Jesus the Jilted Lover, whose cry of wrath echoed throughout the Corrupted Cosmos. Only unlike Daniel and his companions in Nebuchadnezzar's fiery furnace, these victims would experience the full suffering of the oven for ever and ever, God be praised, amen! For there even the worm "dieth not." This was Christendom's "god." This was Evangelical's hell. This was what Billy Graham warned his listeners about, what G. E. holds onto in his evangelistic vision of deity. This was the deep dark open secret about Neal Steinhauer's, Bill Bright's, Evangelicals' "God who loves you and has a wonderful plan for your life."

"*Nein!*" Christendom, Evangelicals, Christians, and Billy declared. But their eyes betrayed them. Deep down, they all said, "Yes!" This was the fundamental, fundamentalist, Evangelical footnote theology of John 3:16. This was the truth about their god: God is the Ultimate Sadist of the Universe, whom tomorrow, with a smile, they would invite Olympic-goers to meet through a personal relationship with Christ.

"Open House at Adolf Hitler's from 1:00-3:00 today. Come get to know him, whom to know is to love," the personal invitations all read, with Neal Steinhauer's signature at the bottom. The small print read, "But we're constrained to say: If you turn down the invitation today, tomorrow it's into the ovens.

Sorry. 'His mercy lasts for a moment (two hours to be exact), but his wrath is everlasting.' Have a nice day and a bright forever—though it may not be quite the kind of 'brightness' you imagined..."

Andy was startled from his reverie by Dan Moore's voice. "I suppose they're really all on a continuum...."

"What?" replied Andy, shaken by where his train of thought had taken him.

"War, concentration camps, armies, prisons, police," Dan said.

"What do you mean, Dan?" Andy asked.

Jack and Fiona happened to walk up to them at the same time, barely acknowledged by either Andy or Dan.

"I mean, isn't something like this really just a question of degree? Sure, we all deplore it. But what was the Six-Day War, if not a mini-Holocaust, with all the Christians cheering on the Israelis, figuring Jesus was coming right behind? Does what happened here make it right for Jews to do the same thing to the Palestinians? We all deplore others' violence, but *never* our own."

No comment from the others or from Andy. He thought of that ambiguous passage where Jesus said the Pharisees erected monuments to prophets in the past, letting on *they* would never have treated them as their ancestors had.

"There are two images I cannot put together," Dan continued, "God telling the Old Testament Jews it's all-out genocide at times, and Jesus and Paul saying not to resist evil with evil.

"I read that the early Christian Church was largely pacifist until Emperor Constantine gave 'em a huge embrace by declaring Christian worship legal and hiring Christians to lower court postings. Pretty soon, word got out that to be a Christian was good for your career, and eventually, the only path to success. Thousands of opportunists flooded the churches to get baptized. But who really baptized whom?

"'Do you betray me with a kiss?' takes on new meaning when Constantine arguably won over the Church to the exact opposite morality of Jesus. Without a shot fired or a spear thrust, he turned the Church inside out on all moral levels: love of enemy, the weightier matters of the law, justice, mercy, faithfulness, forgiveness toward all, especially 'the least of these'…

"So, argues this one guy I read, the Church quickly moved to 'do unto others as had been done unto them,' baptizing violence against all outsiders—including Jews and pagans, just as they had been violated by these groups not so long before. So Jews and pagans began to experience the same kind of alienation and persecution at the hands of the Christians as the early Christians had at the hands of the pagans, as Jesus at the hands of the Jews as… Violence endlessly recycled! This was formalized centuries later into the Inquisition, which demonized the Church's domestic enemies as 'religious heretics,' and the Crusades, which set out to convert or kill the accursed 'infidel,' the Church's foreign enemies."

"But they were not all real Christians," Fiona spoke up.

"Unlike the Evangelicals in Texas, Fiona?" Dan shot back, scorn tainting his voice.

Jack leapt to her defence, as usual. "Evangelicals would be totally against this sort of thing," he said, waving his arms to take in the ovens.

"So," Dan took a breath, "these 'Christians' weren't the real thing? Did you know that it is precisely conservative Evangelicals in America who most support nuclear armaments and harsh punishments, including the death penalty? In spite of Jesus' constant emphasis upon 'love of neighbour' and 'love of enemies,' Evangelicals prove to be the *least* loving of all identifiable religious or secular groups in society.

"Last century, when one converted to Christianity, one understood that 'loving God' automatically threw one into some kind of social action on behalf of others, to take up causes such as abolition of slavery, rights for women, and prison reform. Though even then conservatives quoted their Bibles loud and long to prove the God-given superiority of whites and men.

"Evangelicals bless the current wholesale slaughter of the Viet Cong; napalming entire villages of men, women and children; the enormous destruction of the environment through the use of Agent Orange on countless acres of lush jungle; the dropping of multiplied millions of land mines that destroy or maim anyone stepping on them. But, of course, we must 'contain the Communist threat,' and 'God and country' as ever soar to the top of the charts. With all due respect: BULLSHIT!"

Andy recoiled at the vehemence, then remembered his own.

"I wish, Dan, you'd be more respectful of Fiona," Jack said, his words edged with steel.

Dan snorted and wandered off on his own.

"There's something eating Dan," Jack said.

"And there shouldn't be?" Andy replied, as much to Fiona as to Jack. Just then he saw Janys and called her over.

"Have you seen enough?" He asked. She had, so all four wandered back toward the entrance even though Andy had not completed the tour.

Something else felt finished though.

59

Finally, the end of the "Munich Ordeal," as Andy had come to call it, arrived. Andy was delighted. Not only had he and Janys quietly arranged to attend the same Olympic events together, they had also been able to obtain tickets to a third event. Andy was amazed that no one, least of all G. E. seemed to notice how they had slipped in a day-long date together. It was their last day in Munich. They were leaving for Berlin in the morning.

After being dropped off at the gates, Janys could scarcely contain her excitement. She looked so sharp: fresh jeans, matching denim top, bright scarf around her neck, beautiful auburn hair teased and full of delicious bounce, all topped off with a scintillating smile. It was all Andy could do to keep his hands off her. But they had a covenant, and they had to be wary of spies. All they allowed was one side-swiping hug as they walked together toward the gates.

Janys had done a major Grade 13 history essay on the Olympics. As they walked toward their first event, Track and Field, she talked a little about it. "The ancient Games were celebrations of death in origin, hardly the noble symbols of international peace and cooperation we'd like to believe. They were in no way 'celebrations of humanity.'

"There were actually four ancient Games, some occurring every four, others every two, years: the Olympian, Pythian, Nemean, and Isthmian Games. They commemorated the deaths of mythic mortals or monsters.

"They also evoked death. Especially the heavy

combat sports like boxing and the *pankration*, a combination boxing and wrestling match that was often fought to the death. In ancient Greece, this kind of competition was the ticket to immortality, the only one in a culture without belief in heaven or hell.

"Ferocious competition was the norm throughout Greek culture. Its epitome were the funeral games, including the Olympics. They were directly connected to war and the battlefield. Arguably, they arose to allow for individual acts of heroism to be displayed, as warfare became more communitarian, ironically enough. At the various Games, there was a dominant 'all-or-nothing' mentality lifted right out of the battlefield."

"Then where did the notion of the modern Olympics as gentlemanly cooperation arise?" Andy asked. "I know that the modern founder, Baron Pierre de Coubertin, held such high ideals, and definitely staked them in the Ancient Games. But you're saying the bottom-line of the Olympics is something like 'Victory or Death.'"

"Exactly," Janys responded.

"So the Olympics today are really just sanitized warfare? What about football, I wonder, and all the professional competitive sports? Hockey? Chess?"

Janys laughed. Chess as an international blood sport. Then again, Bobby Fischer had just defeated Russian Boris Spassky, the first American ever to become World Champion, thereby breaking Russian domination of chess at the height of the Cold War. Hmm…

"Hey," Andy suddenly said, "did I ever tell you about my prowess in Grades 12 and 13 in Track and Field?" They had arrived at the huge stadium where the opening ceremonies had been. "Remind me sometime…"

Janys laughed, "I'm sure I'll hear about it, like it or not. You do have an ego, Andrew Norton. One I can see I'll have to work on."

"Hey!" Andy said, feigning wounded pride. He dishevelled her hair with relish as they entered the cavernous structure, delighting in the silken feel. He remembered the locks to her waist on a howling night in December...

The morning went by quickly. They exited the stands for some lunch then set out in search of the cycling venue. They found it with some time to spare.

"Come with me young lady," Andy said officiously. He led her toward a small wooded area just over the brow of a hill. When they got there, few people were around.

"Care for a stroll, *Mademoiselle*?" said Andy, offering his arm. No one was in the stand of trees at all. They walked down toward a small lake surrounded by trees. They sat down on a bench in the shade.

As Andy looked at Janys, for the first time he thought he could see his way clear to a lifelong commitment.

Janys broke the spell, "Andy, we better get our seats. They'll be starting soon. One thing everyone's said is, the Germans sure have been punctual!"

"Naw," came Andy's dreamy reply, " I think I'm just going to hold you like this right here for good. This is life at its most perfect, Janys. Just exactly the way I want it to last forever."

Janys laughed, "You'd eventually have to pee!" Janys, ever the practical one.

The cycling gave way to Bratwurst enjoyed together on a grassy knoll overlooking the entire Olympic grounds, then soccer in the evening. The US team lost 7—0. That felt gratifying to Andy somehow, though he said nothing of that sentiment to Janys.

When Janys and Andy met with the others that evening at the vans, they looked at each other and smiled. It had been a nearly perfect time. Was it not all right to wish such a day to last forever?

60

A light fog shrouded the valley when Andy awoke early for Quiet Time. What an idyllic beginning to the day of their departure, he thought. He knew the fog would burn off by mid-morning followed by a crisp, perfectly clear fall day he wished could be replayed at will frame by frame.

Andy first caught wind of the news at breakfast. Everyone was astir. At about 4:30 a.m., five Arabs climbed the fence surrounding the Olympic Village, weapons hidden in athletic bags. They knocked on the door of Israeli wrestling coach Moshe Weinberg then gunned him down and weightlifter Joseph Romano. Nine Israeli athletes were taken as hostages.

The terrorists were Palestinians, members of the PLO's "Black September" faction. They demanded immediate release of 200 Arab prisoners and safe passage out of Germany.

At breakfast, G. E. proclaimed soberly, "We should really be praying. This could be the beginning of the End. The entire world is looking at the Middle East today, site of the final battle of Armageddon. And the revived Roman Empire, where the Olympics are taking place, could also arise from this conflict.

"So much seems to be lining up. Praise God! With the whole world watching, it is just possible that we have all just participated in the most historic declaration of the Good News the world has seen, this side of the Rapture. Jesus is Coming!"

If anyone hadn't been awake before, this news and the responsive shouts by all certainly brought the adrenalin to full dose.

"Let's take a moment to pray for the Jews." There was an instant holy hush as G. E. lifted up a long petition to the Almighty for God's protection over his Chosen People. He prayed for the safety of every hostage, of all the other Jewish athletes, of Mark Spitz, who hours before had just achieved his seventh Gold and World Record.

He prayed for a great outpouring of God's Spirit upon the whole world as it held its breath that day. May they be motivated to look unto Jesus for the moment, and for all eternity. His prayer was followed by dozens of hearty "Amens."

Andy's voice was not amongst them. He thought of the juxtaposition of Nazi Germany with the Israeli State and the denial to Palestinians of an agreed-upon homeland. Were the Jews in Israel any different to the Palestinians than the Nazis had been to them? *We always become what we hate*, he thought.

Andy could not bring himself to gloat over tragic world events as those unfolding, gleeful that at the last moment he and a great throng of the Elect would be snatched out of harm's way and afforded the most incredible VIP seats at the Heavenly Olympics Stadium to watch "all hell break loose" on earth. He was sickened at the image, sickened at G. E. and the arrogance of his Evangelical certainty. A passion for the lost? Andy suddenly got it. *Not really*. A passion to prove through one's proselytizing one is in the right. Much closer to reality. And twice the sons of hell, each convert, to that kind of self-centred, selfish, self-serving, self-righteous Christianity. Was Evangelicalism of this sort simply a contemporary name for Pharisaism?

Andy also thought on that day's tragedy *qua* tragedy itself. No talk about the doubtless devastating effect upon all the families impacted. No mention about how Christians could possibly encourage peacemaking between the two factions, potentially ushering in another kind of "end" not unlike the lion and the lamb, the Arab and Israeli, peacefully coexisting...

Dan had once told Andy a possibly apocryphal story of a senator near the end of the Civil War encouraging President Lincoln to order the total crushing of the Southerners now that they had been defeated. Lincoln is said to have responded, "Mr. Senator, do we not also *destroy* our enemies by making them our friends?"

Andy found himself wondering why, in all his upbringing, after six months of missionary training, and now several months into evangelistic work in Germany, he had never been exposed to any Christian thought or action that might understand the Gospel as having to do with human relationships and how people live together.

He shared in the endless pursuit of his fellow believers for a more spiritual life. What, however, if the "more" was simply in learning to love the neighbour and enemy as much as Jesus? Is that what Jesus meant by saying he was always to be found "in the least of these"? If so, a wild thought hit Andy: Is that *only* where Jesus is to be found? What if Jesus was not in Church at all, for all our religious protestations, unless we first glimpsed him, however minimally, in our caring response to the other, especially that most alien other, the enemy? Let Billy Graham suggest *that* to the American troops in Vietnam! The penny dropped: This was *exactly* what Hans had argued, a leavening at work in Andy ever since.

Janys sat down across from him. Andy turned to her, dare he?

"Janys, I'm feeling horror-struck at the juxtaposition of what G. E. said and where my faith is taking me.

Just the opposite direction, in fact. G. E., Billy Graham, Evangelicals, are extremely one-sided.

Andy glanced around to ensure no one was listening then leaned across the table, his voice muted. "The first great North American evangelist was Jonathan Edwards, who made sinners shudder at the prospect of falling into the hands of an angry God. According to Dan, 'technique' evangelism has been around for only two centuries, trying to work up spiritual fervour from below—multiple verses of "Just As I Am" sung softly while an appeal wooingly whispers from the pulpit, some kind of real or symbolic "sawdust trail" with time-calibrated movements of seekers ushered step-by-step through the rooms until ushered back outside "saved"; the Gospel reduced to an undemanding 'Four Spiritual Laws,' *believism* kept simple so as to make 'getting God' like getting laid—not too onerous or painful but rather quite pleasurable."

Janys said nothing, just kept eating her oatmeal.

Andy continued, on a roll once again. "I can just hear contemporary Richard the Young Ruler exclaim: 'I don't have to give up anything after all? Just pledge allegiance to God and Flag, pay my dues, and get Heaven, Fire Insurance, and Pie in the Sky when I die?'

"'Yep, that's about it,' say the four dominant evangelists of the past two centuries to varying degrees and their myriad lesser imitators: C. G. Finney, D. L. Moody, Billy Sunday, and Billy Graham. Technique and KISS are in. Don't make the Gospel offensive or onerous. Don't place too many demands. Make Jesus attractive—a sugarcoated pill to heal your every ill. Except for hell. Use that only as a last resort warning to scare 'em *straight*—straight into heaven!"

Janys laughed. "Andy, your caricatures are so right

CHRYSALIS CRUCIBLE

on. But you're scaring me. And not about hellfire."

"What then?" Andy asked.

"You're taking away all my props and incentives to do evangelism."

"Am I? Remember Bonhoeffer's words? 'When Jesus calls someone to follow him, he bids him come and die.' That idea is not found in any of Campus Crusade's teaching. Nor at GO Headquarters. Nor with the Billy Graham Evangelistic Association. Am I right?"

Janys nodded.

"So let me ask, Janys," inspiration suddenly flashing, "did Jesus consciously turn away more would-be followers than he ever attracted to believe in him? If so, what does *that* say to modern-day North American evangelism?"

He sat back triumphantly. "And what did Jesus mean when he said, 'Not everyone who calls me 'Lord, Lord,' will enter the Kingdom of heaven,' and when he taught that the difference between the saved sheep and unsaved goats had nothing to do with belief in 'four spiritual laws' or any other kind of pietistic faith but everything to do with how one finds Jesus in the alienated, the enemy, the 'least of these'?"

Andy was stricken silent for a moment as a thought hit him. "Janys, is it possible to *do evangelism without the Gospel?* I wonder if that's not what we've been doing all along in West Berlin, and now in Munich! What most Evangelicals do most of the time…"

Andy glanced around. They were the only two left at their table. A few others were still lingering over coffee. G. E. was engrossed in conversation with Len on the other side of the room. He turned back to Janys. "You know, sometimes I wonder when we do outreaches like this, are we inoculating more people against the Gospel than we attract to it? I remember one guy I led to the Lord at our coffeehouse back at the Training Centre. Seems like ages ago, now. He was so thrilled that night. But, due to his school and part-time work schedules, we only rarely got together after that. He never got involved in a church. Will he be more open or closed the next time? I don't know.

"Dan told me about a place in upper New York State that was so frequently evangelized last century it became known as the 'burnt-over' district. He also told me of studies done on past major evangelists, including Billy Graham, where only a tiny percentage of those who streamed forward to 'make a decision' ever followed through with regular church attendance or any other kind of outward faithful commitment.

"So I don't know. It seems this Gospel thing is incredibly slow in propagating, if it's even real. I know how slow it's been in me, and I've been at it since I was four."

"But don't you think," Janys interrupted finally, "that it's God's business how people turn out, who make decisions for Christ?"

"I agree," Andy responded. "This whole thing is finally God's business. But as I have reread the booklet we just handed out by the thousands, I feel it borders on the deceptive. Further, I feel that somehow it invites people to such a 'lowest common denominator' decision for Christ that I honestly wonder what it really means. And I have no use for trying to scare people into the Kingdom with the threat of hell-fire, which the booklet also does. So, I don't know..."

He smiled then and turned to Janys. "*Que sais-je?*"

"Pardon?" Janys replied.

"I thought you knew French," Andy said, still grinning. Then he finished up his breakfast, saying nothing more but wishing he could have a good talk with Michel de Montaigne and Alexander Pope.

61

Some of the team members, including Dan and G. E. took the train back to West Berlin. Andy, Janys, Jack, and Fiona drove in the Renault. They listened to regular updates about the hostage drama. Apparently, the German government was working on getting the hostages to the NATO air base at Firstenfeldbrück. Beyond that, there were no new developments.

It was only the next day that the awful news reached the world: the nine hostages had been killed. Five of the eight terrorists and one policeman were killed in the subsequent shootout. Israel followed up by launching a massive retaliation against Syria and Lebanon.

A short while later, on October 29th, terrorists hijacked a Lufthansa jet and demanded the release of the three captured Arabs. Eventually, Germany capitulated.

Through the news, Andy learned that an Israeli assassination squad subsequently tracked down and killed the released terrorists, along with others involved. But the self-proclaimed mastermind, Abu Daoud, remained at large.

"Violence begets violence," Andy had read in Hans's paper. There was also no new violence, just boundlessly boring, utterly unoriginal, ridiculously retaliatory, violence. Little children all, terrorists and democratic world leaders alike, freedom fighters and Allied/NATO soldiers, and everyone in between, caught forever in the time warp primitivism and endless scapegoating cycles of William Golding's *Lord of the Flies*. Grand irony that a British *gun*boat should rescue the children…

The massacre of the eleven Israelis was not grounds for cancelling the rest of the Olympics. Jim Murray of the *Los Angeles Times* wrote, "Incredibly, they're going on with it. It's almost like having a dance at Dachau."

Of course, Andy knew. Violence was the very ethos, elixir, of our human existence from time immemorial, world without beginning. Humans had not even *begun to grow up*. Andy had seen in his dad's military effects the motto, "*onni soit qui mal y pense,*" "May he be despised who thinks badly of the military." Andy felt revolted by such nonsense and would take any amount of scorn for saying so.

The chorus "Oh, when will they ever learn? Oh, when will they ever learn?" from Pete Seeger's song, "Where Have all the Flowers Gone?" captured the folly and the pathos hauntingly. The oldest profession known to man, prostitution, Andy mused, matched by the oldest dance, the abominable dance of war. Madness and stupidity all, yet the very stuff of human history with its ubiquitous horrors. Was genocide humanity's most consistent legacy?

Upon their return, Peter and Jean greeted everyone warmly. Jean had been discharged from the hospital a few days earlier. She still wasn't well, and they were giving serious consideration to returning home.

A stack of mail and a newly installed phone (At last!) awaited Andy and the others in their apartments.

Dan was slated to visit for the next week, G. E. for only three days. A meeting with B. B., G. E., and the entire team was booked for Friday, September 8th.

In a way, it felt like summer holidays were over and school was about to begin. That was always a time of serious foreboding for Andy. He had no less that sense this time as he returned to an uncertain fall routine.

Their first night back, Peter and Jean invited over their star convert, Petra, to meet the team. She entered the girls' apartment laughing infectiously at something Peter had just said. He and Jean had gone to pick her up at her mom's. They all heard her joyous laugh before setting eyes on her.

Andy had heard she was vivacious, but nothing prepared him for the reality. She had long flowing black hair, a quick smile, gorgeous dimples, and tinted glasses that perfectly matched her complexion. She wore bright red lipstick that coordinated with her outfit. She dressed stylishly, was tall, slim, and liberally endowed.

All stood as if on command as she walked into the War Room, introducing themselves and shaking her hand. She did not hesitate to try out her somewhat halting English. Her great ambition, she said, was to go the United States and become a fluent American. Andy could think of nobler aspirations.

Over supper, Petra recounted a little of how she had first met Peter and Jean and then subsequently made a decision for Christ. Peter chimed in several times to help out her English. Andy jumped in, too, though unnecessarily. Was he trying to impress her? Pretty normal for any man to want to.

Dan excused himself right after supper. He had planned to see the sights on his own, he said, given his short period of stay. "Do you want me to show you around tonight, Dan? I'm available," Petra said. She glanced at the others. "That is, provided there is nothing else planned for us tonight?"

Peter said there were no plans, that if Petra wanted to head off with Dan, that would be fine. Did any others like to go too? No one else volunteered.

"How about you, Andy?" Dan asked. Andy sensed he was looking for a bail out.

"I've got some catch-up letter-writing to do," he said, glancing at Janys. What would she think if he took off with Dan and this sexy new babe? This was a new consideration for Andy…

A few minutes later, Petra and Dan thanked them for the delicious meal and were out the door.

The night of their encounter with B. B. finally arrived. Andy was concerned that they hadn't taken time beforehand to discuss strategy. He had raised a few issues with Gary while away, but there had been no serious discussion.

Interestingly, G. E. seemed more nervous than anyone when they sat down at about 7:30 in the War Room. Andy wondered if it had to do with their encounter at Maranatha. Petra and Dan had gone off again, which felt good to Andy. Dan was obviously enjoying himself, and quite comfortable with Petra, who was loving all the English practice—and being with a single American guy. Strange that G. E. acted unconcerned.

G. E. started their meeting with a short prayer then launched right in. "I know there have been some issues. I'm leaving tomorrow, so I hope we can resolve them tonight.

"I guess the main one as I see it is the question of your relationship to the team, Beatrice." Andy appreciated G. E.'s cutting to the quick. "As you know, before the team left for Germany, we commissioned Gary and Peter to be team leaders. That commissioning holds.

"But you and I still had an understanding that the team would work with you as they deemed fit…"

"George, if I may interrupt you right there."

B. B. did the very thing she asked permission for. "You made it quite clear to me from our discussions before the team came that for all intents, the team was coming as an extension of my ministry."

Bingo! Andy was pleased this had been flushed out at the outset. She couldn't have been more emphatic.

"Excuse me. Beatrice," G. E. said, without feigning request for permission, "there is obviously some misunderstanding here. When you took the request to the Inter-assembly Elders Gathering two years ago, what did they say? I think this has some bearing on this."

G. E.'s question evidently set her back on her heels. "You have to understand, George, that I didn't take the request to them, it was brother Paetkau."

Andy had heard that defensive tone before.

"I do understand that, Beatrice. The Elders Meeting is for men. But what did they say to brother Paetkau?"

Everyone leaned forward to hear her response.

"Well, George," she cleared her throat, "I don't have an exact transcript before me…"

"Beatrice, that's not the question. Can you please just summarize what was said to brother Paetkau?"

B. B.'s face looked like she'd just been caught with her hand in the cookie jar.

"Well, George… You see. Brother Paetkau didn't exactly get the answer he, we, were looking for. So he raised the question slightly differently. He asked if they would be open to a team coming sometime, provided they could meet with you. They said yes.

"Then almost right after I read about thoughts of sending over a Munich team in time for the Olympics. I thought this could be our chance. So I contacted brother Paetkau. He said there would be no way to expect another Elders' Meeting for at least two years.

So brother Paetkau… authorized me to inform you that there was elder support for a West Berlin Team, which there was—his. And he is a member of the larger council. That's why I wanted you to meet them this time. It's really quite unfortunate, George. They actually meet Tuesday night. It's too bad you can't stay. I'm sure once they met you…"

G. E. spoke in a calm, deliberate tone, but his face betrayed him. "I think the word, the nice word, is 'subterfuge,' Beatrice. There is a stronger word. I will not state it.

"The short of it is, our entire team is here in West Berlin on false pretences. This is why the team has noticed such a negative reaction toward them from all the assemblies. Your actions probably set the team back a long time; yet that did not seem to matter provided you got 'your team' to rally around your projects.

"Beatrice, please tell me it is not so. Please tell me you did not lie to me about the openness of the Elders for our team to be here at all."

B. B. positively cringed. Andy felt sorry for her.

"Well, George…" She used that same mollifying expression a third time.

G. E. sighed. "I am on an open ticket. Tomorrow I will try to move my departure ahead to Wednesday. You may try to get me a slot at the meeting." He sat back in his chair. "This meeting, however, is now over. We'll all be in prayer."

A few moments later Andy witnessed a phenomenon, he had never seen before, B. B. with her tail between her legs being led out the door.

As it turned out, G. E. could not change his ticket. He departed without giving clear instructions on what to do with B. B., and they were also not forthcoming upon his return home. Out of sight, out of mind?

However, he did hint at possibly returning in a few weeks. The team took some consolation in that.

62

"You've been staring at that spot on the wall for so long it's a wonder you haven't burned a hole right through it!" It was Dan.

Andy turned toward him. "Good morning, Dan. We were so intent on our discussion with your dad last night I never even asked how your day was yesterday."

Dan told Andy he had spent the entire day in East Berlin. He raved about the *Museum der Deutschen Geschichte*, wishing someone had been there to translate. "Imagine, the very gates King Nebuchadnezzar used to ride through, and you could almost walk through them yourself!" He told Andy that would be an absolute "must-see" again before they left Germany. Andy agreed. Then he talked about another good time with Petra the evening previous. "We sure got noticed everywhere we went!" he commented, but said nothing further. Andy asked no more questions.

"So what were you thinking about so intently?" Dan asked.

"Sex," came the unabashed reply.

"That'll keep you going all right," Dan replied.

"Hey Dan," Andy suggested, "I'm sure I could free up today with a little arranging. Interested in climbing Bismarck's *Siegessäule*? Afterwards, we can buy some lunch and eat in the *Tiergarten*. The Victory Column, as it's called in English—"

"—is what Bismarck built and reviewed his triumphant troops from during the Franco-Prussian War," Dan interrupted. "Hitler relocated it to march his troops past it."

Andy smiled. "Right. In any event, I hear it's quite a view from up top."

Dan was game, so after a few brief preparations, they were off.

Some late summer days unfold like a carefully crafted piece of music. Theirs was just such a day. As they emerged from the apartment, a gentle breeze picked up, almost on cue. Traffic proved light as they biked across *Olivaer Platz* and headed toward *Unter den Linden*, then turned right toward the Victory Column and the Brandenburg Gate, which was also part of the Berlin Wall. There was an indefinable deliciousness in the air, a sense that the sky was a notch bluer, the sun definitely brighter, the birds jollier, and the day in general beneficiary of an invisible make-over artist.

They locked their bikes at one of the yawning entrances to the Victory Column. It was situated in the middle of a huge traffic circle. Underground walkways from all sides of the huge street led to the spiral staircase. Until the Wall, it had been Berlin's main thoroughfare, a spacious showcase of European grandeur with its chic shops and magnificent straight lines.

"So how are things with your dad these days?" Andy asked as they headed underground.

"All right I guess, if you discount Dad's world-conquering evangelistic zeal and optimistic public Christian spirituality that makes him sign off everything he writes with 'Joyfully in Christ.' One thing I vow never to do for as long as I live is put on a phoney front. I don't understand it. He has such a yen to always appear happy, enthusiastic, 'more than conquerors,' as Paul would put it."

"And he's not that way all the time?" Andy asked.

"That's an understatement, Andy! Sometimes I watch him go from his private *persona* at home, where he's just argued with Mom about 'one more unanticipated night away from home,' to that joyful bravado he cultivates so carefully in public. He's not alone in it, of course. What Evangelical leader doesn't do the same? Or politician? And why? Everybody has up and down times. Everybody's life is full of sorrows. Even Jesus was called a 'man of sorrows.' So why this need to appear what one is not rather than just being what one is? It's all about image, and, well, *lies*."

"But at times it's honest, too, Dan. I do believe that Jesus brings joy." Andy's tone sounded a little too defensive to his own ears.

"There you go, Andy, sounding just like Dad. Why do you always have to defend being what you're not? I'm not just talking about my dad but about Christians in general, and you guys right now. I see how you all scurry around, so intent on doing your evangelism, but there's a kind of general *malaise* about you all that it doesn't take a Ph.D. psychologist to discern."

Andy felt stung by the words, but it was quintessential Dan Moore: forthright, no mincing.

By this time, they had arrived at the first level. They each took in the majestic view in every direction silently. Andy regretted not having brought a camera. The traffic noises below were already muted. The breeze was brisk but delightful as it wreaked havoc, especially with Dan's long hair.

"Shall we continue?" Dan asked at last.

"What exactly do you pick up from us, Dan?" Andy asked as they continued up the staircase, not quite winded but breathing heavily.

"I see obligation more than compassion motivating you to go out to 'witness.' I see a kind of 'oughtness' that in my view drives Christians to *do* far more than just to *be*. But what else could one expect? You came over to do a job that by nature is driven, and kind of doomed.

"I'll be blunt. I think you're a dysfunctional community waiting to come unglued. All the ingredients are there. You just need a bit of stirring. You're a bunch of strangers thrown together with no community skills learned, or being learned, or likely to be learned. Certainly not from back at Headquarters. They're all as individualistic as they come. And no impetus here.

"But again, what else would one expect? Go all the way back to the Reformation, and you find a long legacy of commitment to individualism in Protestantism that is the very inversion of Christian community. What was the central legacy of the Reformation? Summed up in one word: *schism*. And that has entered the collective bloodstream of Protestantism like nothing else before.

"As Shakespeare would put it: *The lady doth protest too much, methinks!* And true enough, we are *Protest*ants! Protestantism's logical extension is violence and mayhem. And kill they did! Both in words and in deed. Massively. You have to read only a little bit about what the Calvinists did to the Anabaptists in the sixteenth century to get the pattern for the entire Reformation. They accommodated the Anabaptists' belief in rebaptism by drowning thousands of them in the local rivers and lakes. Great Christian legacy! And Calvin himself oversaw the burning at the stake of his arch-rival Servetus when he stupidly travelled to Geneva and showed up in Calvin's church one day. After the barbecue, Calvin chortled, "He squealed like a Spaniard!"

"And yet the likes of Francis Schaeffer, J. I. Packer

and thousands of other Protestant apologists point to Calvin and his ilk as model Christians. Truth is, they were killers, butchers all. But according to Protestant/Evangelical hagiography, they formulated the ideal cultural expression of true, Bible-believing Christianity. The sixteenth century is praised to the heavens as the Golden Age of 'true spirituality'—to use a book title by Schaeffer. One you own, right, Andy?"

Dan paused to catch his breath. They had reached the top of the Column. As they took in the view, Andy pondered Dan's words. He readily admitted he knew nothing about community-building. Yet, as Dan pointed out and as Andy was becoming convinced, that was the Gospel's heart. How could they possibly be *doing the Gospel* when they had no church base, were at odds amongst themselves, and were incredibly private, individualistic, and ultimately violent about what salvation meant? Why, at the top of a victory column, was he feeling so non-victorious? How many steps to victory? He had neglected to count.

"Extraordinary!" Andy exclaimed as he scanned the city below, his words reflecting nothing of his inner turmoil. Sun, breeze, warmth, and crystal clear skies conspired to vivify all vistas. And unlike Toronto, the city did not disappoint. It was vast, even grandiose, like a Wagnerian Opera. It overloaded Andy's optical senses data with pleasurable impulses in every line of sight.

Even Dan was limited to a monosyllabic "Wow!" They were the only two at the top that day, though other structures thrust higher.

The minutes stretched into the better part of an hour before they had their fill. Even then, there was a reluctance to begin the descent. The thought struck: Was that all Andy had been doing since his arrival in West Berlin, descending? How many steps before bottoming out? What would that look like?

"That was definitely worth it!" Dan exclaimed as they headed back down the staircase. They stood to the side to allow a young couple to pass.

"Was I too hard on you?" Dan asked as they resumed their descent.

"No. You've never been too hard on me, Dan.," came Andy's reply. "But that doesn't mean our conversations don't lead to some hard thinking on my part. To put it mildly!"

"I guess one way of stating it, Andy," Dan said, "is Evangelicals don't *think* very much. That's not their tradition. They're pietists for the most part who mainly *feel*. Evangelicals are also, at least in popular expression, *ahistorical*. They live out their faith as though they can lift off from the New Testament directly and simply ignore two thousand years of intervening history. Not unlike Protestantism as a whole. Kinda crazy. And thoroughly dangerous. 'For they who do not learn from history are destined to repeat its mistakes.' I think that was Winston Churchill. Not only do Evangelicals not learn from history, they act as though there isn't such! Yet they ardently believe in a real *historical* Resurrection." Dan shook his head at the paradox.

At the bottom, Andy realized he'd totally forgotten to count the number of steps. He wished he knew. He was grasping for reassurances.

During their picnic in the *Tiergarten*, Andy was silent for some time, processing. Dan did not try to strike up conversation.

After lunch, they threw around a Frisbee. It made Andy think of Janys.

They took a break under the shade of a tree that had been sent, the plaque indicated, from Argentina.

"Dan, at times I think you're too harsh on

Evangelicals," Andy began.

Dan replied readily, "Jesus said, 'by the measure we use to judge others, we will be judged.' I think Evangelicals set the stage themselves.

"Do you want to know why I finally began reading the New Testament seriously about a year ago? My dad. He was always quoting Scripture so freely that I decided to sit down and read the Bible, too. Maybe a bit like W. C. Fields looking for the loopholes. And then I got drawn into other kinds of reading, including systematic theology and church history. All books on Dad's shelves at the Centre. And, don't tell anyone, I've even borrowed a few from Chicago Divinity School through our local library.

"As I read, I was amazed repeatedly at the disjuncture between the sayings of Jesus and what Evangelicals teach. What became clear to me is, on the particular issue of how to treat the neighbour and enemy—as you have obviously also been discovering—Evangelicals are as unbelieving, as *unfaithful*, as liberals are about the Resurrection."

He sat back and chewed on a piece of grass. "I recently wrote to Billy Graham about it, actually. Well, to his Evangelistic Association. I even mentioned that my dad headed up an international evangelistic organization, thinking that might assure a response from Mr. Graham, himself." He spit out the grass and shook his head. "No such luck."

"The point I raised was, how, in the name of the Jesus Billy is forever preaching about could he and most Evangelicals bless the war in Vietnam, and, for that matter, all other military interventions by the United States since World War Two? How, I simply asked, was this possible when Jesus' straightforward, repeated teaching was, 'Love your enemies'? How, when virtually the rest of the New Testament is univocal on the same issue? How could Billy Graham claim allegiance to Jesus and to the absolutely clear teaching about violence and non-violence in the New Testament if he ignored and, in fact, outright contradicted such plain teaching? I suggested in my letter that the teaching was as straightforward as Billy's own 'plain teaching' account of salvation. 'The Bible says!' he is ever thundering. Like the booklet you handed out at the Olympics."

Dan picked another piece of grass and chewed it as he stared out at the park. "The response I got was that Dr. Graham was too busy to answer such personal mail. But there is, I was told, much difference of opinion on this matter amongst Christian believers. Then I was referred to a few books on the subject, which I'd already read, and was thanked for my letter. I also was assured that I was welcome to write at any time about any matter of concern to Christian believers.

"So, on the crucial issue that is the core of the Gospel, *interpersonal reconciliation with both neighbour and enemy* (Paul wrote this summed up the entire law), this is, according to the Billy Graham Evangelistic Association, an allowably negotiable issue, about which different opinions are fine, and one may remain agnostic, though by default pro-violence. In the end, ostensibly, according to Dr. Graham, there is only one 'Greatest Command.' And that leads to 'Peace With God,' title of his first and best-selling book. But what about peace with man, Andy? And on the matter of personal salvation, Billy Graham's pet doctrine in Evangelical trappings, there is no quarter: *Turn or burn!*"

All Andy could do was shake his head. It was like Dan was reading his mind.

"Though I'm a nobody alongside Billy Graham," Dan continued, "I beg to differ. Evangelicals, on the issue of violence toward others, have 'gone a-whoring after other gods,' to use the harsh prophetic designation. In this case, it is the god of war, the god of retaliation, the god of nationalism, the god of punishment, *the god of violence*. Evangelicals fornicate with many gods, all leading to violence toward the neighbour. But I ask you this: How can Evangelicals love God, whom they have not seen, if they cannot love their enemy, whom they have seen?"

Andy let the question hang.

"So no, to answer your question, Andy, I don't think this is some minor Evangelical blind spot. It has to do with fundamental faithfulness to the Gospel. Evangelicals are *massively unfaithful* on this issue. I cannot see it any differently."

As Andy pondered Dan's words, he wanted to tell Dan he was wrong, to play Devil's Advocate. But that was exactly the problem: *That's what Evangelicals had been playing all along, Devil's Advocate!* What had Jesus said about the Pharisees being sons and daughters of the devil, a murderer and a liar from the beginning? And Evangelicals were the contemporary Pharisees…

"Dan, you first got me thinking on these issues back at the Centre," Andy heard himself say. "Since then, I've had a thought or two of my own. So let me ask you again, Are you a Christian, Dan?"

Dan smiled. "Guess."

Andy studied his face. He had not changed. Or had he? The smile had warmth, peace.

The ride back was quite uneventful. When they arrived at the apartment, there was an invitation for them to join everyone at the girls' place. They were all heading off to the Outpost Theatre to take in a movie. Even Fiona was going.

For Andy, it was a relief to do something completely mindless, and also to extricate himself from further intense one-on-one conversation with Dan. He needed time to think, lots of it.

That night, Andy's diary read:

Intense, fascinating conversation with Dan today. Boy, does he ever have some contrary—convincing!—opinions. Why is Christianity so confusing? Why is life so confusing?

It is 12:10 p.m.

Good night

P. S. Dan told me to 'guess' when I asked him if he was a Christian. I guess he is—but would be the last to reveal that to G. E.! Life's ironies.

63

Dan announced at breakfast the next morning that he would try to fly out the following day. He had phoned a few days before, and apparently standby flights were readily available. Andy was sad to see him go. But perhaps the discussion they'd had the day previous, together with the fun at the movies that same night, signalled to Dan that it was time to move on. Dan definitely marched to the beat of his own drummer. But despite the harshness of his criticisms of Evangelicalism, there was an increased softness in his demeanour. Something was at work in Dan, whether his dad recognized it or not.

While the Collins' headed off for a farewell lunch with Dan, Andy retired to his room. A letter from Lorraine had arrived while Andy and Dan were out sightseeing, and he wanted to read it.

Dear Andy:

Your letter to me at the end of your time in Munich arrived. I'm responding immediately.

You say in it how much you really like me. But at the same time, you say you are committed to keeping me at arms' length (not your expression—mine—but accurate reading) until you return from Germany a little less than two years from now! How convenient. You thereby keep me dangling in a no-man's land (pun intended) of expectation while you keep doing your thing.

What if I simply didn't want to wait that long? What if I told you I had met some really nice guy (not necessarily even a "Christian" by your definition), and he and I had been dating the last while? What would you think of that? Especially if I told you he never lectures me, just accepts me as I am, warts and all. And what if I told you that he doesn't talk a blue streak about the things he believes in, leaving me no time to discuss—with far less words—what I believe? Which I grant, I can't say with nearly the same dogmatism or certainty as a certain Mr. Norton! And what if I told you that he never tries to psychoanalyze me or my family but just lets me be the "me" I am?

Okay, there really is no such guy... except in my fantasies. Even then, every time I try to imagine such a man, he always looks and sounds like you. Am I a fool for being so hooked? You basically made me fall in love with you last summer, then you disappeared for the next two and a half years. Who do you think I am? Who do you think you are? And worst, who do you think God is? You keep on blaming this on "seeking God's will"! I'm not so sure anymore what kind of a mission you're on over there, other than trying to convince people to become like you. Well, I would not wish at least one part of you on anyone. And that's your religious side that is so dogmatic and self-assured. Or so you seem. I wonder, even suspect, that your very self-certainty hides a pretty deep-seated self-doubt.

Oh Andy, I just wish for even one good hour to talk out so many things with you! Why are you so far away? Why can't you hold me in your arms like you did in the summer, and we simply forget everything that has come in between us since then?

She went on to tell him about her schooling, but then came the big shocker:

Anyway, like it or not, I'm thinking again of visiting you by spring of next year. How do you think all the single girls on your team will handle that? No, I wouldn't plan on going door-to-door with you or distributing tracts on the Ku'damm! I don't care what you say. God hasn't called me to that. But I would go for long romantic walks with you. I would snuggle up close to you and just enjoy your presence. I would let you see that I can relate to God in a meaningful way, too, though different from yours. And we would talk, Andy, about us. About our future.

I can't wait two years, Andy! I just can't! So, no matter what you say, I just may be coming. Be prepared! I'll keep you posted.

And don't start preaching at me again like your last letter. I just won't listen!

With hurting love,

Lorraine.

P. S. If you do share this with one of the girls there, just don't tell me about it, okay? You're altogether too transparent as it is. Some things I'd rather not know. And if you ever go for a romantic walk with any of the girls, or anyone else, keep it to yourself. I couldn't abide finding out.

P. P. S. I guess I'm still really confused. I'm sorry for sounding so harsh. I guess I'm discovering some pretty deep-seated anger in me about religion.

Andy felt guilty after reading it. Had he really been that judgmental toward Lorraine? And just why had he come to Germany anyway?

He picked up the recently arrived copy of *Scatterers* and looked at the reflection piece he had published there, that he'd read at his church's send-off, entitled, "*Yes, Lord, But....*"

"But seek ye first the kingdom of God, and His righteousness; and all these things shall be added unto you." (Matthew 6:33)

"Yes, Lord, but... I have an education to get. And after all, you can't get very far any more in this world without one. And besides, just think what a B.A. or an M.A. or a Ph.D. can do for your cause."

"But seek ye first..."

"Yes, Lord, but... You're only young once, and if I don't take in the world now, I'll never be in the condition to do so later on. And didn't Paul say that you have given us 'all things richly to enjoy'? I just want to revel in your beautiful creation—that's all, Lord."

"But seek ye first..."

"Yes, Lord, but... There's this girl, Lord. And if I don't move now, I might lose her. Didn't you say that 'it is not good that the man should be alone'? I agree with your Word, Lord."

"But seek ye first..."

"Yes, Lord, but... You don't really know what you're asking. There's a big world out there, and precious few are even aware you exist, let alone live by faith in you. And just look at your own people, Lord. How many of them live as loose to the world as you're telling me to? One in a hundred maybe? It's scary to step out like that. Couldn't I have one of those ninety-nine other jobs?"

"But made himself of no reputation, and took upon him the form of a servant, and was made in the

CHRYSALIS CRUCIBLE 613

likeness of men: And being found in fashion as a man, he humbled himself, and became obedient unto death, even the death of the cross." (Philippians 2:7-8)
But... Yes Lord!

Andy gagged now at the sentiments. He had meant every word of it then. In fact, when he had sent a copy home after first having read it at church, even Susan commented on how much it had impacted her.

So his motivation was not that superficial. Still, Lorraine's words stung him. Her critique was too on target.

The phone rang. It was Janys. She had some things to talk about, *immediately*. Andy said he'd be right over.

When Andy got there, Janys was outside waiting for him. She was not Lorraine, not Fiona, and certainly not Petra. Yet she still managed to outshine all three. What was it about her? He loved her hair, her face, her trim figure, but there was something else…

With a quick glance to ensure no one else was around, Andy gave her a quick kiss and an embrace. "Surely that much is allowed," he said.

She smiled and kissed him again, slowly. "Yes," she said when it was over, "it's allowed. Can we go for a walk?" There was urgency in her voice.

She didn't wait for them to arrive at their destination before opening up. "For the third time this week, just now, I picked up the phone, Andy, only to hear someone breathing at the other end. I didn't waste any time hanging up. But it's totally unnerving. I'm not alarmist, Andy. But you've guessed who I think it is."

Andy didn't have to say the name. "Would he really go to such lengths? He knows he's in enormous trouble. Why would he take such a chance?" Andy asked these questions in quick succession.

"Men do crazy things, Andy. Desperate things. Like kidnapping women to…"

"Okay, Janys, let's head over to our place. Better, do you have any money? We'll use a pay phone."

In his best German, Andy explained the situation to the police. Surprisingly, he talked to an inspector almost immediately, one familiar with the case. Must be the American influence, Andy conjectured. The inspector asked Andy if they had any time that morning. They agreed to meet at Andy's apartment in a half hour. As soon as he hung up, Andy and Janys walked over there.

The inspector was in plain clothes and all business. He spoke passable English. "I have seen a few pictures of *Herr* Braxman," he said. "He is to be taken very seriously. Where is *Fräulein* Sanchez right now?"

"In our apartment. Jack is there, too. You know the story of the car chase?"

"Yes," the inspector replied, nodding. He pulled out his notebook.

"Can you please give me the girls' apartment number? I should like to use your phone, please. His name is Jack, you say?"

"Yes," Andy responded. "Jack Dumont."

In moments, the inspector had arranged to meet Jack at the girls' apartment. He asked if there was more than one way into the place. Janys told him there was a second entrance from inside the courtyard.

"I want you two to stay here," the inspector said, and then he left.

With Gary and Sharon off with Dan and Jack at the girls' apartment, Janys and Andy had the place to themselves for the next while.

They went into the living room, sat down and

CHRYSALIS CRUCIBLE

embraced. Andy's thoughts raced immediately to a moonlit night under the covers just before Christmas.

"Andy," Janys finally broke the silence, "I've never known such… pleasure, joy, bliss. Whatever. I never dreamed this could be so good…"

Andy watched her brown eyes intently. They were so calm, so full, so… They embraced again, this time coming up for air, panting.

"Janys," his voice grated huskily, "here we are, right now, alone, indulging joy, giving each other great pleasure. Mine is through the roof. We both know there's more… I mean…" His voice trailed off.

She looked at him fully, longingly. He saw pure desire in her eyes. He tasted it. What covenant? What inhibitions?

Janys closed the gap again with a caressing kiss. Then she spoke, no less hoarsely. "Every fibre of my being wants to give myself wholly, utterly, in reckless love, to you, Andy." She paused, selecting words carefully. "I've fantasized about it, lots. That night under the blankets. My whole being wanted to seduce, arouse. But I hesitated. So did you. Why?"

To Andy, she was the apotheosis of Desire, the Ultimate Fruit there for the joy of plucking. The stillness of the apartment, the street, the universe, impinged. She was the only other person in the Cosmos. They were primordial Adam and Eve. Not yet naked. Why not?

He shifted her onto his waist and embraced her more fully. Every point of contact, lips, chest, groin, arms, hands, sent out shards of sensation sufficient to blow his circuitry.

"I so could do it!" He said panting.

"I so could let you!" She responded as rapturously.

He thought of Lorraine again. Of Coral read out of the assembly. Of the youth leader running his hand over Janys's sister's boobs. He thought of unopened Christmas presents…

She was his, every piece of her being. Totally. Pure gift. His for the taking.

He pulled back. "Janys, I can't. I know we could both give ourselves fully, freely right now. That I could have every part of your body, you mine, for pure pleasure. I know. I…" Janys kissed him tenderly again.

"This is agonizing, Janys. But I can't, I won't… take off the wrappings yet! I'd like to say, right now, 'Will you marry me Janys?' But I can't even say that. Not here. Not with prior commitments."

There was a long silence. He held her tightly. Their breathing began to return to normal.

64

About a half hour later, Dan and the Collins returned from lunch. They were surprised to find Janys and Andy alone there then immediately learned why.

"What do you suppose the inspector is up to?" Gary asked. No one ventured a guess. Gary and Sharon decided to take a nap. Dan was headed off for a walk and asked if Andy and Janys wanted to join him. They declined, saying they'd grab the phone should anyone call.

They played double solitaire quietly at the dining room table for the next hour. Janys roundly trounced Andy.

The phone rang. It was Jack with great excitement in his voice. "Andy! You've got to come over! They got him!"

"Braxman?"

"Yes! Come on over, bring Gary and Sharon, and we'll tell you all what happened."

In no time the four were heading over to the girls' apartment. They left a note telling Dan to join them as soon as he came in.

Jack and Peter met them at the door and ushered them into the War Room, where Jack and Fiona recounted the story.

The inspector had called in two unmarked cars. Four burly men converged on the address of the Great Olympics Book Offer.

The inspector quickly described the sting operation to Jack. Fiona would be put in some danger, so she need not take the risk if she would rather not, he explained, acknowledging that Todd could be armed.

Surprisingly, Fiona accepted the challenge, perhaps tired of living in fear.

"What about me?" Jack asked.

"With all due respect *Herr* Dumont, but we cannot allow you to participate," the inspector said. "You've already done more than your duty."

Shortly after 3:00, Fiona had exited the apartment building at ground level, alone, and headed toward a bakery two blocks away. The four undercover cops headed casually in the same direction across the street.

Just then, a car with German license plates came out of nowhere, literally driving onto the sidewalk in front of Fiona. Todd jumped out and lunged toward Fiona. She screamed and ran.

The four men streaked across the street and tackled Todd before he could touch Fiona. They found a small revolver. Then they cuffed him and led him away to a waiting police wagon. Braxman swore a blue streak at Fiona.

"I just looked at him blankly," Fiona added. "I kept saying, 'I'm sorry, Todd. I'm sorry.'"

Her lower lip quivered. Jack put an arm around her. "It's over," he said gently. "It's over." He turned back to the group. "We spent the rest of the afternoon giving our statements. I called you as soon as they left."

"So what's next?" Gary asked.

"I asked that question, too," Peter said, talking as if out of breath. "They said he faced criminal charges under both German law and US military law. They said it could take months."

Fiona burst into tears. "I just want to go home, Jack. I just want to go home!" She leaned into Jack's strong arms.

"You will, Fiona."

He led her gently to her bedroom.

Gary stood up. "I think we'll bow out and give Fiona some space. Anyone who wishes is welcome over at our apartment after supper."

Jack stayed with Fiona that evening, as did Peter and Jean. The other four, plus Dan, had a fun evening of games and light discussion. There were piles more questions, but they could wait for another day.

As he fell asleep that night, Andy thought of Todd Braxman. And then the eleven murdered Israelis. What kind of vengeance would the Israelis wreak? The endless cycles of violence and retaliation, crying out "Next!" like the tired whores of Amsterdam. World without end…

65

Andy awoke early the next morning and worked on a draft of his third prayer letter. He knew most of the people on the distribution list, but Gospel Outreach had added some supporters who gave monthly designated donations for Andy. He had never met them, so he was careful not to reveal much of what was really going on.

He summarized recent events, including their trip behind the Iron Curtain, their training period in Switzerland, and the Munich outreach. He noted that they had passed out 160,000 booklets and to date had received nearly 3,000 requests for more information. He was also careful to mention that they were not at the Olympics on the day of the massacre, but that he could well imagine the horror. He concluded with an obligatory request for prayer, but it was totally sincere.

There was no further opportunity to have a private talk with Dan. Before going through security at the airport, he had pulled Andy aside and said, "Boy, Gary sure is dogmatic!" But that was all.

On the way back from the airport, Gary wasted no time in expressing his concern about Dan. "I think we need to really pray for Dan, and G. E. in relation to him. Dan has drifted dangerously, in my view, into Neo-orthodoxy and the Social Gospel."

"What makes you think that, Gary?" Andy stared at the buildings streaming past his window.

Gary explained that Dan was not sounding at all like an Evangelical when he talked about Scripture, about church mission, or things like the free enterprise system, which, Gary said, was probably the most biblically justified of any. "And, when I asked him explicitly about his views on homosexuality, he waffled! He did so similarly when we talked about hell. He really has problems with the clear biblical witness that it is a place of eternal conscious torment prepared by God, first for the devil and his angels but also for all unbelievers.

"I know he is widely read, and frankly, he alluded to more than one theologian whom I had never heard of. But they all seemed to be in the Neo-orthodox or liberal camp, which really made me wonder what kind of influence G. E. has on him."

"He is twenty-two-years-old, Gary."

Gary continued, undaunted by Andy's response. "I received a letter this week from Jim Billings in Spain. He warned in some detail about the folly of Marxist thought coming into Evangelicalism through various avenues. At times you'd think he was describing Hans Beutler!

"Have you ever heard of the Post-American community in Chicago? I suspect now that Hans visited them a lot while at Wheaton. I guess you could call them Evangelicals. In fact, their leader, a guy named Jim Wallis, is a former plymouth brethren. But they are spouting all kinds of leftist, radical ideas on a whole range of social issues. First, it seems they are elevating the Social Gospel above evangelism. Second, they are condemning America for defending the Free World, and in particular, free enterprise. Third, they say that salvation is not so much *belief* in Jesus as *doing* things like in the Sermon on the Mount.

"It is, according to Jim, dangerous stuff. Jim explained in the letter that his mother was an avid leftist in Canada, supporting all kinds of social causes. She's not a Christian, so she couldn't be into evangelism. But she was a staunch supporter all his growing-up years of the 'New Socialist Party,' I think he called it."

"The New Democratic Party—N. D. P." Andy interjected.

"Maybe that was it," Gary replied. "In any event, it's strongly socialist and anti-Christian. So Jim goes on to explain that, when he became a Christian in Vancouver while essentially a hippie, it was people like Ward Gasque at Regent College who helped set him straight on some of these issues. He's since done some of his own studies and reading, 'cause they are facing a lot of that kind of stuff amongst some of what he calls 'radicalized Catholic mobsters.' Jim is nothing if he is not picturesque! Apparently there are emerging 'base communities' of Catholics and their converts who are pursuing what they call 'God's preferential option for the poor.' Jim dubs it 'man's abominable obsession with Josef,' meaning Stalin and Communism.

"You need to read his letter, Andy. It certainly is pertinent to what we have already encountered here, especially at the universities. It's insidious, like heresy always is, because it contains some truth. But Jim really helps cut through the crap and exposes the underlying Marxist analysis, about which I know nothing.

"Despite our earlier discussions, Andy, the more I've thought about it, saying America does not have the right to defend itself and its vested interests abroad is ludicrous! How can we question that when God uses ultimate violence in hell and throughout the Old Testament, not to mention in the Book of Revelation? I have believed, have always believed, I think rightly, that God raises up in every generation a people or a nation to defend his Truth and to model righteousness to the nations. I firmly believe that is what America has been, at least since World War Two."

"So, Gary, do you believe the Vietnam War is just?" Andy queried.

Gary nodded vigorously as he rounded a corner. "Yes. I know what Hans said a few months ago, and some of what you've said! I'll borrow his paper from you sometime, perhaps. But I also know that Billy Graham has personally prayed with the President on this matter several times. And he, at Pentagon request and expense, travelled to Vietnam to preach God's Word to the G.I.'s. Hans wasn't too thrilled about that. But I go with Billy. Besides a clear call to get saved, he strongly endorsed America's raising such a standard of righteousness against the evil hordes of Communism."

"Gary," Andy responded, "Billy Graham apparently supported the bombing of the dykes in North Vietnam, though it might have meant the deaths of hundreds of thousands of North Vietnamese. Doesn't God hate the sin of Communism, yet love the sinners, the Communists? You can't evangelize the dead, Gary—unless you're Jesus 'leading captivity captive.'"

"Yes," Gary said, "and that's why we evangelize Communists at the universities and gladly introduce them to Christ."

"So, we evangelize *here*, but pulverize *there*?" Andy asked. "Are those Communists in North Vietnam loved less by God than these here?"

"But they have now fallen under God's wrath, Andy," Gary said, striking the steering wheel. "That's the difference. They're ripe for judgment."

"Why?" Andy demanded.

"Because God has given them up to wrath as a

consequence of their perverse ways—Romans one."

"For believing in the wrong ideology, Gary? Really?"

Gary would not let go. "That's what God did repeatedly in the Old Testament, Andy."

"But we're *New Testament* people, Gary."

"So then, you're saying the Bible contradicts itself?" Gary's voice rose. "I can't believe that from you, Andy! Of all people, you have most defended the Bible as the ultimate truth."

"I'm not so sure the Bible contradicts itself," Andy said, "as it shows some kind of progressive movement toward Jesus, who finally says, 'You have heard that it was said... But I say, Love your enemies.' I think that statement by Jesus, whom we *claim* to believe in and follow, trumps whatever is in the Old Testament. Maybe 'trumps' is a good paraphrase for Jesus' contention that he came to fulfill the law, not destroy it. Don't both John chapter one and Hebrews chapter one teach that there was something ultimate and final about Jesus, through whom we are to view the rest of the Old Testament and human history? Doesn't it say that the pre-existent Christ predates Genesis and Old Testament ethics?"

When Gary didn't answer, Andy continued. "Doesn't Jesus indicate that the entire sweep of Old Testament ethics is summed up in—hangs on—two 'Greatest Commandments': love of God and love of neighbour? That the essence of the New Covenant is 'mercy, not sacrifice,' sacrifice that 'once for all,' according to Hebrews, is fulfilled in Christ, and, therefore, never again on the battlefield or at the gallows? That the summation of the entire Law, of all Hebrew ethics according to Paul in Romans thirteen—interestingly right after Paul talks about the State—is 'love that does no harm to the neighbour'? That state killing in warfare, in capital punishment, is reintroduction of sacrifice into Christian ethics, *anathema* to Jesus the Way, at total variance with the ethical summation of the entire Old Testament revelation, high water mark of which is Micah six-eight? 'What does the Lord require of you? To do justice, love mercy, and walk humbly with God.' Exactly what we Evangelicals fail to do according to Matthew 23?"

Gary was speechless, out of disappointment in not finding an ally in Andy or intimidation, Andy did not know—or care, at this point. "One of the things Dan claims is Evangelicals *teach* high allegiance to Christ in theory but *practise* non-allegiance to Jesus in reality: Jesus the innocuous icon, devoid of any real content. So let me ask, Gary, did you ever hear a sermon in your assemblies experience that actually taught that the Sermon on the Mount is to be lived out *today* by Christians? I never did. So James says, 'You show me your faith by what you *say;* I'll show you it by what I *do.*' To the contrary, the Sermon is so often relegated to a future time after Christ's return, or declared an impossible ethic in the *Realpolitik* of human existence. Whatever happened to the teaching of Jesus and Paul that the Kingdom is God's Reign and Ultimate Reality *now,* even if not yet fully come?"

Andy didn't know quite how to stop himself. "Likewise, did you ever hear the story of the Good Samaritan interpreted as something we should be doing to our neighbours and enemies now? I never did. It was always seen as an allegory of the sinner going down into sin, being waylaid by the devil, then rescued by Jesus and being kept safe for two millennia by the Church (that's what the two *denarii* paid to the innkeeper signified), until Jesus' return. Why did we never hear it as a story about a Palestinian reaching out in compassion to a hated Jew, like God in the Incarnation, '*while we were God's enemies,*' Paul writes, modelling our response to all our State enemies?

"Furthermore, Gary, did you ever hear a sermon preached about Lazarus and the rich man, where the emphasis was placed upon God's care, indeed 'preferential option,' for the poor? Instead, at least in my upbringing, the passage was always upheld as the ultimate detailed warning by Jesus about hell! I'm not so sure it had anything to do with telling us about hell, except the hell of our own making when we refuse to show love to the needy neighbour."

"Whoa, Andy!" Gary exclaimed finally, reminiscent of G. E. "I think you've had your say. You're sounding just like Dan or Hans. What's gotten into you?

"Well, I'll tell you, the primary mission for Christians is saving people from hell. As D. L. Moody used to say, 'When the boat is sinking, you don't waste time polishing the brass, you get busy rescuing the perishing!' And that's what we're about here, isn't it? Isn't it?"

It was Andy's turn to fall silent.

Gary pressed on. "Something's coming over you, Andy. You've been a great defender of salvation truths and the Bible. Don't go soft over here, Andy!" His voice sounded plaintive.

Andy still said nothing.

Suddenly, Gary was parking the car in front of the apartment. They climbed the stairs together in silence.

Andy went straight into his bedroom, claiming he needed a nap. Jack was at the girls' apartment, as usual. Andy flung himself onto the lower bunk. Sleeping was unthinkable!

Maybe, Mr. Moody, Andy thought, one could take

a stab at stopping the leaks! Though it probably would have made no difference when the *Titanic* was going down. So what should one do in such situations? Help the dying do so with dignity, as Mother Teresa was doing? But what if, the moment after their dignified death, their soul was snatched away to hell, as Gary and most Christians believed? What an awful juxtaposition! Christian compassion to the point of death trumped by God's holiness and retribution!

A thought struck Andy. Was such a rendition of hell really about God's holiness or man's yen for cosmic exoneration, revenge? Would hell, after all, really stand up to Christian analysis, or was it one of these surface doctrines that fitted man's longstanding commitment to violence and vengeance, with God like the Rook card, ultimate Christian revenge trump to get everybody in the end?

Andy recalled numerous instances of wretched church history: the Crusades and the so-called "Inquisition," which left thousands of victims dead. He thought about the "Smite, slay, and kill" letter of Martin Luther to the German Nobility that saw tens of thousands of peasants butchered, though he was of peasant stock. He thought of the Anabaptists drowned by the thousands or burned at the stake, about the Saint Bartholomew's Day Massacre when more died in one day and night of terror at Christian hands than were killed by the atheistic French Revolution "Reign of Terror" two centuries later. He thought of the Thirty Year War fought entirely over religious differences and the consequent massive decimation of the German population. He thought of the blessing of every war since Christ by Christians of all stripes, the Church's maintenance of the death penalty for social and religious heretics. State violence was *ubiquitously* blessed throughout Christian history, *quintessentially* entrenched in Christian theological justification for centuries, and *profoundly*, he was increasingly feeling convinced, *anti-Christian*.

Certainly the doctrine of hell was welcome bedfellow to that line-up of Christian "holiness," under which guise it was invariably cast. It did give one pause. *Major pause*, Andy reflected. Despite such thoughts, he finally drifted off to sleep.

66

Petra more or less adopted the team in September. She spent several evenings a week at their apartments and issued a few invitations to her mom's. She sparkled all over the gatherings.

She was also very sincere in her faith. It amazed Andy how she talked so simply about her love for Jesus. There was a correspondence between her word and deed that was so refreshing it jolted him. Maybe that's what he was lacking, *authenticity*. Her faith seemed so natural, so childlike.

Petra was especially taken with apologetics. Peter and Gary had primed her about Andy's knowledge and arguments, so she spent hours talking with Andy about such things. Andy did not mention to anyone all the times Petra dropped over, phoned or invited Andy over. He wondered how she fitted in her nurse's studies. She was highly intelligent, he knew. That was a real appeal. Janys seemed oblivious so far. Was she?

Petra also supported their street and university evangelism with her characteristic enthusiasm. She even accompanied Andy, at her request, door-to-door a few times. Sometimes it was a relief to have her speak up fluently, if naïvely…

On the last Thursday of September, the team stopped by Petra's mom's for lunch before taking her out for an outreach event. Midway through the meal, she launched into a discussion of B. B. "So what if her style, even her motives, are bad," she exclaimed. This was all in German, with her unbelieving mother listening in. It also meant that Andy and Peter effectively carried the conversation, though Gary often chimed in, and some of the others on occasion. "What about that place in the Bible—Andy you'll know—where the Apostle Paul gets talking about people preaching the Gospel even out of spite toward him personally? But he still thinks it's great that the Gospel gets preached.

"Don't you get it? We're all pretty flawed people. If we refused to serve Christ because of that, waiting until we were perfect, none of you would ever have made it to Germany!"

"Speak for yourself, Petra," Gary said with a bit of a nervous laugh.

"But I was here already," she shot back. "It's you guys who aren't perfect enough to be missionaries…" She caught herself for a moment but continued. "I mean, really. I've been around you a lot. I know about some of the squabbles, I know about, well, let's just say I know things about you. Even things you haven't talked to me about.

A few nervous glances were exchanged.

"My mother always said I could read her mind. I guess I pick up things. But that's okay. *I ain't perfect either, baby!"* This last line was enunciated in perfect American drawl. She sounded like Jimmy Stewart.

Andy felt slightly offended. Others sat silent. No one was looking around.

"More soup, anyone?" Petra's mother said. That broke the silence. Fifteen minutes later, the team was out the door.

Andy's mind churned on Petra's words as they went door-to-door that afternoon. So much so that Janys alerted Andy to her awareness of his moroseness. "It's nothing," he said unconvincingly.

It bothered him greatly that Petra had been, in his mind, a disciple. But suddenly her stature had changed. She was no longer a disciple but a prophet, and he felt the brunt of her accusing gaze.

If Petra still was working on any of the sentiments expressed at lunch that afternoon, she gave no sign. She was unusually bubbly, in fact.

Almost as soon as they were in the car for the ride home, Petra announced that she and Andy had the most marvellous conversation with a guy at one of the doors. "He really listened! He even invited us in, which we turned down, of course. But he went through our materials with real interest. He asked a lot of questions."

Andy looked over at Janys in time to catch a faint roll of the eyes.

Petra continued to tell in some detail about the conversation. The guy was a psychology student at the *Freie Universität*. He also had an interest in theology, but he was a Marxist now. Petra asked him to say what being a Marxist meant. She found she agreed with much of his philosophy. "Only," she added, "for him, the change (he said revolution) coming is as inevitable as history. Whereas we believe it comes only through Jesus."

She continued: "He said he'd be willing to talk again, sometime. Of course I didn't give him my number. But I took his and said I'd call. I think he might be really close..."

Andy asked Janys about her rolled eyes after supper that evening as they sat in the War Room.

"Petra's a little naïve around men, Andy. Don't you think?"

Andy detected nothing like jealousy in Janys' comment, though she knew Petra's natural sex appeal.

"Who knows, though? People have come to Christ out of less pure motives," Janys conceded.

"How can we help Petra?" Andy asked. "She's young and impressionable, but she has a lot to offer."

Janys paused a long time. Too long for Andy's impatient spirit. Finally, she spoke. "Perhaps the most important thing for her is time. She has a good grounding. She obviously loves Jesus. Her mother, though not a Christian, supports her in her faith, or certainly does not oppose her. Why not just wait for her to grow, Andy? 'Wait and see the salvation of the Lord.'"

"But shouldn't we—you, others—take her aside to warn her about guys like that student? Petra can't see anything wrong with sleeping with a boyfriend. And, well, I guess there's so much she needs to learn."

"Doesn't that apply to all of us, Andy?" Janys asked.

"Yeah, but…" Andy did not know how to finish.

They decided to go for a walk. Outside, there was an evident touch of fall in the air. So far the dark reds of an Ontario fall had not been evident, possibly were nonexistent, Andy suspected. Winter was milder here, hence seasonal transitions subtler.

Janys picked up on their last thought. "Ted used to tell me that Evangelicals just about have it reversed. He says we're long on talk and advice but short on silence and listening. He says we're so activist-oriented we probably wouldn't know a vision from God if one hit us over the head. He told me of this quote from another Francis, Francis of Assisi—who was about the exact opposite of your Francis. 'Preach the Gospel everywhere you go. Sometimes, if necessary, even use words.'"

"According to Ted," she continued, "Evangelicals want to have everything so sewed up and cubby-holed they're like the Pharisees, whom Jesus said we should do what they *say*, because they did know 'right' doctrinal truth, but not do what they *do*. Ted says it's so ironic that rationalism is seen to be such an enemy of the faith and yet Evangelicals are amongst the most rationalistic there are when it comes to their spirituality and in defending and promulgating their faith. It's all words, so seldom deeds."

"What does your brother say we're supposed to do then, Janys?" Andy asked, his voice carrying a hint of despairing perplexity.

"He says Evangelicals should simply learn to be *evangelical*. To take Jesus and the Gospel seriously for once.

"He keeps reminding me how much of the Bible is really about waiting and patience. That is really God's game. The idea behind a day being like a thousand years is precisely that: God patiently superintends his creation, like a gardener. He teases out his will from the groaning creation rather than superimposing it. So should we. And that's why I think the best we can do in discipling Petra is to be like a good gardener."

They had sat down at a bench on the *Ku'damm*. The noise of traffic mixed with other street sounds dusted the borders of Andy's consciousness. But it was, again, just they alone. He placed his arm around her.

"How come I'm so incredibly lucky, Janys? The luckiest guy on earth, I reckon," Andy asked quietly.

Janys let the question hang.

"Did you ever imagine this back at the Centre?" he asked.

"Yes," was her soft reply. "Long before you ever did, Andrew Norton. Okay. I'll be honest. I imagined this from the very first time we talked together. But you likely do not even recall that moment."

Andy said nothing.

"The next time I fell in love with you—which you will remember—was the night of the blizzard. In those initially awkward moments, you were a perfect gentleman. That showed above all when you caught me full blaze in my undies. After that, if you had wanted, I could have crawled into bed totally naked with you. I even fantasized about it, falling asleep that way, your arms wrapped around me—except I'd have had a slight problem with my period… Yes, I thought more than once of those Cathars. Maybe they were onto something."

She smiled at the memory. "Another occasion where I knew I loved you was our public skating performance. I fell in love with you again that night, Andy, because you were not vain about that or Norton's Notion. Because I saw through your ego to a guy who, deep down, was really trying to be human, with or without an overlay of religion.

"The most recent time I fell in love with you was the other afternoon when we almost had sex. I might have gone all the way, Andy. But you did what our culture says the girl's supposed to do—then blames her when she otherwise gets pregnant!"

Andy had become oblivious of passers-by, of the steady stream of cars, of the gathering dusk. Janys shuddered. He drew her closer, kissed her ever so gently.

"Janys," Andy said, barely above a whisper, "I don't know how long we can keep this up. Not for two years, that's for sure.

"I also don't know how long I can keep up this 'Gospel Charade.' All this world-conquering yen to evangelize the masses? Evangelicals don't love the masses any more than Hitler did. If there is a Great Awakening sweeping the world, such as the Jesus People Movement, it is religion without *Gospel essence*. And that's a double dose of hell, to paraphrase Jesus." Andy paused, realizing he was drifting off topic. "Where do we go with our love affair, Janys? Where do I go with my disenchantment affair with Evangelicals?"

Janys did not respond. They got up and held hands almost all the way home.

The following Saturday morning, the phone rang in the boy's apartment. Andy picked it up. It was Petra. She said she was hoping that Andy might come over, because she had some serious questions to discuss with him. Her mom was away visiting with an aunt for the weekend, so it would be a perfect time to discuss some of her deeper questions in whichever language he preferred.

Gary and Sharon were out on errands, and Jack was already at the girls' place, so Andy phoned Peter to say he would be busy with Petra that morning.

"Andy, this is of the Lord," Peter said. "Petra seems to be working through a lot of stuff right now, and it's been obvious over the past while that she really respects the kinds of answers you've been giving. We'll pray for you."

Petra's apartment was five levels up, so Andy was a little breathless when he reached her door. He felt even more so when she opened it. She wore dark, tight-fitting slacks and a thin sweater on top. There was obviously no bra beneath.

He followed her into the living room, unable to deny her allure: evocative curves, full bust, shimmering hair cascading to her waist.

She had been speaking the entire time, but Andy only keyed into that fact when she offered him a drink. Was she bothered he turned down a beer?

"Andy, I have been studying about the Evangelical faith for some time as you know. I am *really* attracted to it. But I have some lingering doubts. I have written all of my questions out at the table and have a Bible sitting there, even an English language concordance. Are you able to spend about an hour going over my questions with me?"

Andy nodded. They sat down side by side at the table.

Andy felt dazzled by perfume, hair, body shape, arresting good looks, and pure propinquity. The stark, sinewy sensuality of the experience overwhelmed. He felt he should run like Joseph, but wanted to stay like Samson.

"Andy, what I seem to least understand," Andy was barely aware of Petra's voice. "is John one-one and one-fourteen. As you know, Jehovah's Witnesses deny the full deity of Christ, that he really was God-become-man. I dabbled in that a bit before. I really accept now what Peter told me, that this passage nonetheless teaches this profound truth. But can you please help me understand it better?"

Andy told himself to keep his eyes on hers. He tried not to breathe too deeply. She was undeniably desirable. Why was all this happening to him? Had he harboured some deep, unbidden yearning to be aroused? Was God testing him? Had he not just been told by Janys how honourably he'd passed a few tests? His mind worked simultaneously on several fronts, only one of which was valiantly trying to engage Petra's questions.

When Andy finally responded, his voice was unexpectedly husky, making him clear his throat.

"Petra, I think you are dealing with a central passage to the Christian understanding of life. In Goethe's *Faust*, as you may know, Mephistopheles took delight in playing with this Scripture, saying, *Am Anfang war die Tat*, making the deed prior to the Word. So what is it you are wondering about exactly?"

"If Jesus is really God's Incarnate Word to us, spoken in the form of a human life lived out for all to see, hear, and follow, what is it exactly about Jesus that we are to *imitate*? He was, for starters, male. That I can never imitate."

She paused. Andy looked at her fully, and agreed heartily.

"He was also single and celibate," she continued, "and he died really young. He hardly ever travelled any distance and lived a rather unique rabbinical lifestyle that few even back then could have imitated, let alone now. So what is it about God-become-man that we are to copy? What is the core?"

Andy did not respond immediately. At the best of times, he always had more than one track playing in his mind, but right then he was registering a multi-track sensual overload. He was still working on focusing entirely on what Petra had just said. For while speaking, she had tossed her head to one side, occasioning a beautiful surge of iridescent black hair, which she took up in both hands and threw over the back of her chair, chest slightly thrust forward.

"In one word, Petra, *love*." Did he almost let slip out, "sex"? The insight caught his breath away. "The imitation of Christ boils down to that. Jesus taught that there are two 'others' on whom this love is to be fixed: God and neighbour. And the Apostle Paul said that three things in life are of the essence: faith, hope, and love. But the greatest one is *love*. *One, two, three* – like that Billy Wilder movie with James Cagney set right here in West Berlin just a few years ago. Only a tad more spiritual," he added, remembering the movie's shapely blonde German secretary in spite of himself.

Andy did not quite know where that little summation came from. It seemed to have been long since forming in some subconscious way and just flowed out. He liked what he heard himself saying. It somehow made salvation more immediate and urgent, at minimum *more active,* than so much of what he had always stood for and understood. God's will also suddenly became immensely simple: *Life is love*. He remembered that was Paul's admonition in Ephesians 5, "Live a life of love." That summed it all up. What did the Lord require of us? That was the ultimate question of the Prophets. The Christian answer was: "Live a life of love," not unlike "Do justice, love mercy, and walk humbly with your God." A new awareness welled up within Andy—it all centred on the neighbour in tandem with God.

Andy took up the *Strong's* concordance. "Petra, I'm going to go over what the New Testament says about 'law.' What is the core of the law? What is the essence of life?"

For the next few minutes, Andy became intent upon his concordance search. It proved fascinating and commanded his full attention. Andy wrote down brief phrases from the various passages he looked up in the New Testament, as they appeared in sequential order. Then, after a few minutes, he turned to Petra and summarized:

"How had Jesus come to 'fulfill' the law? By demonstrating *love* to neighbour. What is the 'righteousness greater than that of the Pharisees'? *Love* of neighbour—about which the whole Sermon on the Mount engages, and against which there is, ironically, 'no law'! What 'sums up the Law and the Prophets' according to Jesus? Doing to others what one would have done to oneself. That is *love*! That is the two Greatest Commandments.

"And what is the 'Greatest Commandment' in the Law? *Love* your God. But the second—'*Love* your neighbour'—defines the first. It is the test of the first. And what defines 'neighbour love'? What is its test? *Love* of enemy. So, *no enemy love means no neighbour love means no God love—just God talk,* which is, in Bonhoeffer's term, 'cheap grace,' crassly '*bullshit*', the kind about which James would say, 'Show me your faith without deeds of *love*, and I will show you my faith by what I do through deeds of *love* toward my neighbour and enemy.'

"What are the 'more important matters of the law' the Pharisees missed? Justice, mercy, faithfulness. Sounds like Micah six. In a phrase, '*love* of neighbour.' What 'flows from Moses' law through Jesus as a kind of continuity yet juxtaposition? Grace and truth toward the neighbour. What is the 'righteousness revealed apart from the law,' to which the Law and the Prophets point? *Love* of neighbour. How does one 'fulfill the law' according to Jesus? Through *loving* one's fellow. What is the 'fulfillment of the law' in Romans? *Love* of neighbour. How is the 'entire law summed up in a single command'? *Love* your neighbour as yourself. How can we 'fulfill the law of Christ'? Carry each other's burdens. What is the 'royal law'? *Love* of neighbour. Who 'demeans the law?' The one who slanders a brother or sister.

"What then is New Testament love? An endless bid to nurture relationship through concrete actions taken toward two 'others': God and neighbour. With the enemy included."

As Andy talked, he was vaguely aware that Petra had stood up at one point to look over his shoulder at the concordance, hands resting on the back of Andy's chair and hair falling over his neck as she leaned closer.

"Andy, you are so smart and good looking," she said softly into his ear. He barely heard, exclaiming, "Now this is breathtaking, Petra! You know that passage in Matthew 25 about the sheep and the goats? This is 'salvation' for Jesus! It all turns on how we treat the other: with or without *love!* So, how do we 'imitate Christ'? By showing love to our neighbours and enemies; this, in turn, is our only way of showing love toward God. Grab a seat again and read it, starting right here." He turned to look back at her, and his face collided into her chest precipitously. He recoiled backwards, lost his balance, and cracked his head sharply against the table's edge.

He came to to a sensation of a hand running through his hair, then was aware that Petra was holding his right hand and stroking it. His head rested on a pillow. "I knew you were alright, Andy. Just a big bump on the head – in English a '*goose egg*' right?... You have really nice hands, Andy." He held her eyes steadily, unsure of what to say, certainly knowing where *not* to look.

"Oh, I have a snack and more drinks in the kitchen – just what you need!" she said, and stood up, letting go of Andy's hand in a soft, sliding motion. Over her shoulder she said, "I like the biblical emphasis on *love*, Andy. You made it come alive for me."

When Petra returned, Andy stood up shakily, took a drink of the proffered apple juice, and said with resolve, "Petra, I need to go back now! We'll continue this sometime at the *girls'* apartment. I have to dash. *Es tut mir leid*!"

And he was out the door, taking deep breaths yet

again as he bounded down the stairs two at a time.

At a quiet breakfast eaten alone the next morning, he sat and pondered sex. He had been raised with only one sister, Susan, who was the object of not inconsiderable attention throughout high school—even back into grade school. Andy had paid little attention to all that, however, since it had not seemed a big deal to her. Even now that she was a working girl, she was dating no one steadily and really not even dating regularly.

He remembered only one long talk with her about guys and, well, sort of, sex. As far as she was concerned, she wanted to keep her twenties as free as possible. No guy was going to get in the way of her interest in travelling, in particular. So far she had done none but had lots of intentions. But there had been no guys either.

At one point Andy asked whether she ever fantasized about sex. She hadn't particularly. Not that she was unaware of the male anatomy. Her anatomy classes and nursing presented her with all the awareness she might have wanted. It was just not a big deal with her.

He wished she wasn't such a poor letter writer or else he'd be consulting her. What would she say?

Andy was quite similar to Susan on this matter, actually. Sure, he'd seen his sister in her undies several times, something her mom often scolded her about, as she got older. And just once he had gone into the bathroom by accident as she was getting out of the tub. But she was less embarrassed than bothered he hadn't knocked on an obviously closed door, and he really had had no desire to look closely. She was his sister, after all!

And yes, he had on occasion perused the girlie magazines. But with no great incentive. He had felt it was wrong to do so, and for the most part had not indulged, even though a lot of his friends in high school had.

His uncle's perspective came back to him now as more than insightful. Andy remembered his uncle continuing with stories of experiences in Africa that relativized the great North American male preoccupation with women's breasts. "Why, in some African cultures, to cover one's breasts is a sign of a loose woman! Topless women were the morally upright."

Andy also thought of his first experience at a German Bible Study, when everyone smoked and drank beer even though such activities were utterly *anathema* to his Christian upbringing.

No wonder Petra was trying to get at the *core* of imitating Christ, Andy thought. After her brief stint with the J.W.'s, she was probably totally confused.

Desires are natural, he thought further. The stuff of life. In university, he had read parts of René Girard's *Deceit, Desire, and the Novel* and sensed he had crossed a great frontier (like C. S. Lewis had in discovering George MacDonald). Some day, he'd return to learn more. For Girard, *desire qua desire* was the very building block of our social-spiritual being. It's how we are socialized, how we learn language. Something Girard called "mimetic desire."

It was interesting, Andy mused, that the Hebrew word for "desire" was found right in the opening texts of Scripture. And for good reason, he realized. That meant desire was not necessarily wrong, but it often went askew. Then it was really wrong, not in terms of some arbitrary Christian morality or religiosity but rather in terms of human freedom.

In dissecting his desire toward Petra, it was pretty evident: He wanted her body in a straightforward, skimming-off-the-top sort of a way. But there were deeper layers. He had an interest in her spiritual well being. And he found her interesting.

The first desire was simply ruled out, he knew. Old-fashioned lust, or as the King James quaintly put it, *concupiscence*. It is the most binding. Indulge it and literally all hell breaks loose—like cancer cells released into the bloodstream—if hell is the downward spiral of human self-centredness. Or, as he remembered Georges Bernanos having the priest say in *Diary of A Country Priest,* "Hell, Madame, is to love no longer." In this case, hell would surely be to indulge his lust and spread the cancer throughout his system.

He knew he had done the right thing in following the tracks of Joseph with Potiphar's wife. He'd gotten "the hell" out of there, he thought wryly. But could he deny the pleasure of the temptation? Should he? "With a little bit of luck," sang Elisa Doolittle's father in *My Fair Lady*, "a man can duck!" When? "When the Lord is throwing goodness at you" in response to his imminent marriage "in the morning," while "there are drinks and girls all over London" still to be sought out and indulged the night before. The "goodness" of the Lord is abstinence and freedom, to which the song light-heartedly says, "No thanks!"

Of course, that was inversion of Christian asceticism. But probably with good reason, Andy thought further. For ever since Augustine, he had read in an essay by Krister Stendahl that Ted had sent Janys, the West had an uneasy conscience about sex. But sex was not the issue in Christian abstention. Faithfulness and addiction were. Andy knew that anyone could score "holes in one" repeatedly, like legendary Wilt the Stilt, a. k. a. Wilt the Stud. But not just anyone could muster up the guts and determination, not to mention willpower, to say no to the drinks and girls all over London.

Newton's Law, "For every action, there is an equal and opposite reaction," surely applied to sexual indulgence. Like endless ripples from a pebble thrown into a still pond, the repercussions of illicit sexual gratification went in every direction, Andy thought, setting up new chain reactions that led endlessly to grief, though intermixed with enormous pleasure. Why? Because the end of the matter was self-gratification—the polar opposite of what led to nobility and freedom in humans. Certainly opposite to Jesus' ideal for humans.

What had Jesus said? "You shall know the truth, and the truth shall make you *free*." Surely in this area of sexuality, the "truth" was faithfulness, which is ultimate liberation. Andy thought of the reprobate priest in one of Graeme Greene's novels. After a life of debauchery, he said, "In the end, everyone wants to be a saint." And in the end, Andy knew, the sad little priest was right. It was for freedom, for *saintliness*, that Christ had set us free, Andy remembered Paul's wild cry in the book of Galatians.

He remembered the "lip-smacking" in the eyes of one guy he'd met while handing out tracts on the *Ku'damm*: "Boy, the hookers are sure good in Amsterdam, aren't they?" Andy saved his embarrassment at not knowing for sure what "hooker" meant by saying he'd never been to Amsterdam. But he knew intuitively what the word signified. It was all over the guy's face. And there was no hope, it seemed, of getting through to him.

"Sold under sin" was the quaint King James version of Paul's words. Primarily in matters of sex and violence did desire so overwhelm and imprison, Andy surmised, conjoining them for the first time.

He further recalled his discussion with Len Howton, leader of the Nîce Team. For their own good, the guys had to stop evangelizing at the topless beaches. "A tad too distracting," Len had said wryly. Andy also remembered hearing at the Centre about the huge struggle with lust that one of the Spain Team members had experienced on a past mission. It had all begun with his taking in a strip show and watching one of the performers do nude cartwheels across the stage, big boobs bouncing so enticingly. He got hooked. The next ten years, during which he married, were pure hell, even though he knew in some areas of his ministry he had really matured.

Andy decided to write the Professor.

September 1972

Dear Professor Norton:

You are not a dumb man. You probably anticipated this letter to you. I've got to sort out some more things about faith and sex.

I'll start with the easy one—for you. Sex. By this time, I presume the whole physical side is "old hat," as I indicated in an earlier letter. But what, at your distance in time, do you make of the whole affair with Petra? I presume she has long-since dropped out of your life. When did you even last think of her? Sorry to revive memories if they have been laid to rest.

Sometimes, faith presents as a grand, transcendental temptation, a mirage even, one I wish I had never given in to pursuing. Life would have been much simpler, surely! It's difficult enough negotiating all the vicissitudes of life on this planet without a complicating metaphysical overlay constantly impinging upon and at times wreaking intellectual and moral havoc.

Dan's cynicism, Lorraine's rebellion, Susan's indifference, Hans's questions, and my own agonies of self-analysis and doubt. Why should I not, like Job's wife, simply curse God and be done with it? Why hang on to a faith that so often seems to get in the way of life rather than enable it, let alone enhance it? Why this incredible yen to believe in Jesus?

I know that even raising these questions is part of the biblical "revelation" (can I ever escape it?), that the origins of Western cultural scepticism and atheism are embedded in the Good Book itself. Just try the lamentations throughout the Psalms for starters, or the book by that name, or the prophets. "Why do bad things happen to good people?" They ask the question endlessly. The wicked always prosper, and thereby throw into question the second fundamental biblical assertion about God, namely, that he is good.

What about Jesus' cry of dereliction from the cross. "My God, my God, why have you abandoned me?" A powerful atheistic cry if ever there was one! The first fundamental biblical assertion about God is not so much that he exists but that he is present, even accessible to us, in all the wild vagaries of life's journey. Who has a consistent belief in that without some pretty serious and often despairing—even desperate—wrestling?

Dan's, Lorraine's, my sister's, Hans's, my own struggles testify abundantly to that, as does life after life, including that of Jesus, ultimately pointing to such profound questioning of God's presence. "God is There and is Not Silent" (Francis Schaeffer) indeed! A tad too quickly affirmed...

My faith is changing even as I write. Is it always that way, you who now have twice my life experience under your belt? Or does faith plateau at some point, providing for smooth sailing for the rest of one's life? Somehow I doubt that.

Where will I come out in the end? At your age? And then what? And then? Like the Huxley short story about the little boy who desperately wanted to turn the next page of his living book, only to discover that his very drivenness to know expelled him from the "Garden."

But the Garden is not all mystical delight. These days it is mostly struggle and doubt. Is it the Garden of Eden after all? Does expulsion mean liberation, transformation, celebration? Sometimes that Tree of Knowledge looks very tempting indeed! Maybe I'm going through an inverse rebirth—at least by the standards of my religious upbringing.

Well, Professor Norton, I presume by now you have this all figured out! And if not, what's the matter with you, anyway? At least you know what will become of me by the end of my time here. I wish I did. Is it Kafka's Verwandlung *into a new dimension of existence, utterly terrifying and alien? Or is it rather a Halleluiah chorus? Or more of the same, whatever that is? I wish you were telling…*

Back to sex. I have to. If God created it good, why did he create it so compelling, too? How did he ever expect that most males would keep that little poker out of the receptacles delectably designed for it? I mean, just curiosity alone about all kinds of variations on mountain peaks with their triangular verdant valleys surely would guarantee a lot of exploring! And once hiked, those valley and mountain trails would become awfully appealing to try out again, especially different *peaks and valleys, given the "monotony factor" in human experience. And men would be wanting to "raise the flag" in a lot of those new terrains. It only makes sense.*

So along comes God, who made the mountains and valleys so achingly beautiful, who capped those volcanic thrusts with irresistible bite-sized nipples, who made man's sex drive so dominant. Along he comes and puts up "No Trespassing" signs on all but one of those valleys and twin peaks. Hiking is allowed only on one mountain "range" once it is staked out.

It seems unfair, unreasonable. Further, his Son comes along only to jack up the prohibition by saying you may not even scan the other mountains with any view to conquering them. So he creates all that impossible beauty, then he snatches it away just as the eyes turn toward it, as the hand reaches out for a touch. Not unlike the Tree in the Garden, I guess.

But why? Why especially if those mountains are indeed invitingly beautiful, every one, and declared "good"?

Is sin (sexual anyway) just arbitrary after all? Paul's saying he would not have known sinful desire had the law not so pegged it? Give me a break! Why couldn't God just let us sort it all out as we grow into puberty and maturity? We indulge that appetite, repeatedly until we all find our own kind of sexual level, libido, as it were, and like most things in life, it settles down, we settle down, and life goes on. Isn't that just what is happening anyway since the sexual revolution? Well, let's face it, since time immemorial?

So what if Marilyn Monroe steps up to the mike in stunning dress, every curvaceous contour of her body literally sewn into place, and sings a throaty, sexually evocative "Happy Birthday" to President Kennedy with all of her astounding nubility blowing the circuits of every male who even hears about it, let alone Kennedy who must have, in the moment, been going mad with desire? Why not indulge the craving fully, repeatedly, until, well, one is ready to move on to other things? (Mind you, I know, President Kennedy never really did move on, possibly challenging Wilt the Stilt amongst American notables as Ultimate Philanderer.) So much for truth-telling in the "I do." But then, as I am realizing, since when did American leaders—or any world leaders—ever value or honour truth?

Sure, of course that could get messy. He's ready to say "Next!" and she is not. And I know Jacqueline was in the picture, too, not to mention the kids and Marilyn's longsuffering Joe DiMaggio...

I remember Jim Billings telling of his hippie days

in Vancouver. One girl in his commune would yell out at times, "Does anyone want to lay me?" And she'd always get willing takers! What's the harm in that? Presumably, she was an attractive female piece of flesh (being crude I know) with no boyfriend or anything. The obliging guys were just doing what came natural— God-endowed, in fact. If it was dark, she wouldn't even have to be good-looking—just good feeling—and she presumably was not too picky about the guys herself! So the deed was done, mutual pleasure was exchanged, and people moved on. Aren't one-night stands beautiful that way? No obligations, no regrets, no consequences (hopefully). Just incredible gratification!

But what happens after that? Two people flip over each other, and there are no restraints. Just "what feels good." The ride is wild and intense. But soon enough, the desire plays out, as it always must. She farts. He belches. They both sweat. And their bodies aren't quite the "10" they each imagined. Then what? NEXT?

So it starts all over again. Like Dr. Zhivago. *Maybe it lasts a few months, even years, but no larger framework informs the affairs, no overriding commitment, no form to the freedom. So why not exit the building through the wall, if one is so inclined, so resourced, sledgehammer in hand. On to the next one again, and again, and again...* ad infinitum, ad nauseum. Sartre's La Nausée *and concomitant "spleen" (Baudelaire) of such a surface existence.* À La Recherche du Temps Perdu, *indeed, for Proust in his voluminous masterpiece.* Lost Time Sought *but never found. Relationships discarded like clothing so fast and furious that time indeed is lost, possibly never found. Suddenly one wakes up old and transformed, not unlike Kafka's character awakens metamorphosed into a despicable (to all he holds dear) insect. "What was that all about?" becomes the searing question of a life misspent in pursuit of wanton Desire that never satisfies.*

I've heard the preachers and read the Bible a thousand times on this one: "Say unto wisdom, Thou art my sister; and call understanding thy kinswoman: that they may keep thee from the strange woman, from the stranger which flattereth with her words. For at the window of my house I looked through my casement, and beheld among the simple ones, I discerned among the youths, a young man void of understanding, passing through the street near her corner; and he went the way to her house, in the twilight, in the evening, in the black and dark night: and, behold, there met him a woman with the attire of an harlot, and subtle of heart. (She is loud and stubborn; her feet abide not in her house: now is she without, now in the streets, and lieth in wait at every corner.)"

I can accept that.

I don't want sex with just anyone. I have no interest in serial monogamy. I really want sex in context of commitment and transcendence of pure desire.

I'll never fail, I'm sure, to notice with winsome wince the excruciating enticement of a woman's body. Close to the surface will ever be libido in response to the double sensual triangle of effulgent bosom, preternatural peaks protruding (Near mystical desire!) and mid-corporal dark triangle. But I don't want just triangles squared, however enthralling, like so much sexual meat one might purchase at the third world market, full of flies and feces!

I know it will only satisfy if framed appropriately, properly contained. Rivers, oceans, and fires are surpassingly wondrous within boundaries, wantonly destructive if such confines are breached.

Well, you've heard my case, Professor. I presume I

know most of your response—if you are still professing the Christian faith, that is. Apart from the potential dangers of VD and unwanted pregnancies, you would talk about the psychological impact of two becoming one flesh, even for just one night, and the emotional scars left on all. You'd suggest the "Happy Hooker" was perhaps not so happy after all, rather compulsive and needy, that 007 was modelled on a happily married man, and that Ian Fleming's secret agent fantasy would likely have long since contracted syphilis and died raving mad like Nietzsche. You'd propose that hiking well-known trails repeatedly, even "'til death do us part," is perhaps not so bad after all. Fewer nasty surprises for sure! The view and the flag raising could vary infinitely, even if always in the same valley! And you'd say overall, perhaps God knows best, which presumes there is a God and that He's written a book…

And since you're not answering just now (you've been consistent in that resolve), I'll sign off. 'Til next time.

Sincerely

Andy

67

Andy joined B. B. at *Lichterfelde* for another youth Bible study the second last Friday of September. Gary had also been asked to come along. They had quite a discussion that evening on biblical authority. B. B. became very impatient with some of the soft views being expressed. Andy was more amenable, looking beyond the immediate argument to the reason behind it. Invariably, it was out of anger with the church.

"What these youth need is someone to speak the *Truth* to them!" B. B. exclaimed as the three washed dishes in the church kitchen afterwards.

"But B. B., the Bible says, 'Speak the truth *in love*,'" Andy responded.

"Where does it say that?" Came the pugilistic response.

"I'm not sure. It's one of Paul's letters, I think Ephesians. But it's in there, I know." Andy grabbed a Bible and quickly found the reference. "It's in Ephesians four-fifteen: *"But speaking the truth in love, may grow up into him in all things, which is the head, even Christ."*

This silenced B. B. for a moment, allowing Gary to chime in. "Warning people about hell is obviously an example, and it makes sense. Paul always warned people to 'flee the wrath to come' out of love for their souls. Likewise here. These youth need the Truth given them in the most unambiguous of terms, considering how easily they can be influenced away in this surrounding pagan culture."

"I've never seen the like, Andy," B. B. added. "Everywhere you go, pornography. And from what I hear the kids tell, the movies are no different. Blatantly sexual. They need the truth of the Word, and of course it is for love of their dear souls. A Christless eternity awaits them otherwise. Even the promising kids get sidetracked into social action or forms of Marxism or other kinds of diversions from the faith. They need the *Truth*!"

B. B.'s eyes showed fire. But it appeared cold fire. Andy contemplated Jesus' claim that one would know the truth, which would *set one free.* What else, other than love, he wondered, would affect that kind of liberation? Not gushy pious sentimental love but self-giving love, which by definition transcended self in initiatives toward God and others such that freedom was the outcome, indeed the concomitant. That kind of "truth-in-love" meant that in reality, truth *is* love—as God is love—Andy realized. All the arguments about the truth of the Bible, the Virgin Birth, the Resurrection, the Deity of Christ paled into insignificance alongside simple gestures of loving care and compassion toward others. The cup of cold water. The visiting of prisoners. Feeding the hungry. Clothing the naked.

Andy's mind whirred so quickly that he felt taken aback. Had Dan, had Hans, really influenced him that much? But he knew the negation in the very asking. No, it had simply been ongoing life experience that had forced him, ineluctably, toward a reconsideration of core faith commitments. He knew therein the inherent dangers. The three classic alternative authorities to biblical revelation were *reason, tradition,* and *experience.* The last was what was influencing his faith reformulation.

He knew the naïveté of the first. There was no disinterested reason, there were no Kantian *categorical imperatives* lying around on the surface of life to be gathered up like gold nuggets. There was only reason as shaped by a prior community of dialogue. Step outside those communal conventions, the first move of genuine anthropology, and the "logic of Elfland," as G. K. Chesterton put it, might just as readily apply as any other.

As to *tradition*, it was becoming increasingly clear that mere protestation in disclaiming such, which plymouth brethren leadership did in spades ("We are not a denomination!"), was surest sign of captivity to that so vehemently denied.

It was all too confusing for Andy. He did not like where his mind kept on taking him. Gary's words pierced him. Had he lost, was he losing, his faith? Or was he still *faithful* but emerging from some kind of straightjacketing of that faith? Like a butterfly from its cocoon? The image captured Andy's imagination. A beautiful Monarch triumphantly taking flight under resplendent blue skies and sparkling sunlight. Was he similarly on a trajectory of rebirth? But wasn't he already "born again"? And just what might this renaissance mean—if not disenfranchisement from his "born again" status and community? That seemed chillingly unsettling to Andy, yet somehow simultaneously energizing and liberating.

"Well, Andy, I guess the cat got your tongue," he heard B. B. say.

Andy looked at B. B., saw someone trying a losing game of foisting certain religious truths upon an unwilling group of youth, a missionary troupe, churches, an entire city. He wondered what kept her going. How lonely must she feel? Had he ever seen her smile? Who was her "god," really?

He looked at Gary; saw in his face all that Andy only a short time before was so eager to do in West Berlin.

"B. B., sometimes I wonder about preaching the 'Gospel' that is not *Gospel*," Andy said, "I also wonder about holding up Jesus Christ as a religious straw man, a holy icon we never meet in the Gospels, only in pious churches, whose 'lordship' is our self-righteous projection. About putting abstract rationalistic belief, doctrine, *ideas* so high on the list of what is important that we lose sight of following or imitating the only One who counts.

"Freud used to observe from his counselling that if Christ is Saviour, why did so many Christians he counselled not appear more 'saved'?

"I shudder sometimes at what we're selling, B. B. We want a mindless formula, *Four Spiritual Laws* swallowed hook, line, and sinker. We urge others to follow Jesus and then look so often like we are on a funeral march. We accept divine forgiveness but deny it to everybody else, from Communists to homosexuals to criminals to the person in the pew next to us.

"We think the world will come beating a path to our doors because we look so… What? Pious? Holy? Sanctimonious? There's a path to our doors all right, but that's because many with integrity are heading in the opposite direction."

"Andy," Gary said, "you sound so cynical! What's happening to you?"

"Maybe," Andy said with feeling, "I'm just beginning to see truth for the first time. Maybe it's not primarily about *believing* a certain roster of propositions about God but rather *living* a certain Way. Deeds not words. 'Live a life of love,' Paul said, Jesus taught, they both exemplified."

"How shall they hear without a preacher, Andy? We need words," Gary shot back.

"I agree," Andy replied. "But what did Saint

Francis say? 'Preach the Gospel wherever you go. Sometimes even use words.'" Andy repeated the words Janys had shared with him just days earlier. "Karl Barth wrote over ten thousand pages of words about God, about theology, but he did actions all along. He was passionately caught up in concern for the well being of the entire creation, including the socio-political order of things. Maybe faith is far, far less about me and my words than about the *other* and embracing actions of neighbour near, enemy afar, the entire created order, the cosmos."

Gary threw down his towel. "Andy, the Social Gospellers are always making it social, never personal. As Schaeffer says, however, we relate to a personal-infinite God who is there and is not silent. Who is a very present help in danger. Who loves us and has a wonderful plan for our lives. 'If any man is in Christ,' Paul wrote, 'he is a new creature.'"

"That's not how the verse goes," Andy said, "It reads, 'If anyone is in Christ, *there is a new creation.*' Everything in creation changes consequently: our relationship to God to be sure, *theologically,* to ourselves, no less, *psychologically*. Those are the personal elements. But it means also to others, *sociologically*, and to all creation, *ecologically* and *cosmologically*. Those are the socio-political aspects. On all fronts, in all areas of brokenness, we are to live *now* what the world is intended to be *then*.

"*And that means Social Gospel, Gary, social and personal holiness!* That means marching with Martin Luther King in Selma, Alabama and with the anti-Vietnam War protesters right near where we live. That means a 'heart strangely warmed' like John Wesley in first encountering Christ, but also King's heartfelt passionate cry, 'I have a dream!' That means peace with God through personal reconciliation, but also 'peace on earth' through global peacemaking and calling down nations that work against that like Russia *and* the United States of America—and mimicking little dictatorships the world over.

"Did you know that a year exactly before King was gunned down, he made a speech against his own country, America, saying *it was the most violent nation on earth?* Even more so than Russia! Did you know that at precisely the same time, Billy Graham was calling on President Nixon to bomb the North Vietnamese dykes, thereby drowning a million innocent citizens if need be to end the War?"

"I don't believe that!" Gary exclaimed. Andy could tell he was really upset. He saw the arched back, the incredulous look, the shooting eyes. B. B. looked likewise dark and ominous.

Andy shrugged. "Believe what you want. Dr. Graham, the world's ultimate evangelist, has prayed with every President since the fifties each time America has intervened militarily around the globe. That same logic authorized born-again President Truman to instantaneously liquidate with two bombs 120,000 men, women, and children for whom Christ died every bit as much as those today in West Berlin we say we're so interested in evangelizing."

"Billy Graham is the greatest man of God on the planet today, Andy," B. B. hissed, "You don't *dare* question him!"

Andy was unrelenting. "A short time ago, Allied Christians were saying 'Praise God and drop the bombs' on the parents and grandparents of the very youth we want to evangelize right here in Berlin. Maybe when we sing 'Great is Thy Faithfulness' for once we won't just sing it with *unto me* at the centre, hallmark too often of Evangelicalism. Maybe when Paul promises that 'all things work together for good,' for once we won't claim consequent, personalized, divine VIP treatment.

"Andy," B. B. protested, "we are all about loving the lost…"

Andy kept on talking, ignoring her intrusion. "Maybe we find God precisely when we enter into suffering—the suffering of the entire creation groaning like a mother in birth pangs. Maybe Ananias got it right in welcoming Paul into the fold, saying how much he must *suffer*. Maybe Paul got it right about making up in his own body *what was lacking in Christ's sufferings*. Maybe Hebrews was onto something in saying that Christ learned *through suffering*, implying that we must, too. Maybe the ancient Greek saying, *mathein pathein*, '*to learn is to suffer*,' is the only spiritual Way. Maybe Bonhoeffer was right that when Jesus bids someone follow him, *He bids him come and die*. Maybe Jesus was right in saying that "unless a corn of wheat fall into the ground and die, there will be no life.

"The problem is, B. B., none of this sounds very much like 'Good News' for me when *I* am Subject of the Evangelical Gospel, of *the Gospel according to What God Can Do For Me*. Believe it or not, *God* is Subject of the Bible and Gospel. 'Liberals' classically exchange God for *man,* but too often Evangelicals displace God with *me*. What always gets promised by Billy, by us, by you, by thousands of American evangelists, smacks of the American way not *the Gospel Way,* not *Jesus the Way*. The American way is personal success *in* life through winning over others. The Jesus Way is personal loss *of* life through service to others. They are polar opposites.

"Maybe we should replace 'country' for 'God' in President Kennedy's famous line, 'Ask not what your country can do for you, but what you can do for your country.' Maybe we need to embrace, 'Ask not what God can do for you, but what you can do for God, neighbour, enemy, all creation.' That would revolutionize us overnight."

"Andy," Gary exclaimed, "why are you painting everyone with the same brush? Aren't there all kinds of people in the Movement who have laid down their lives for their friends? The same can be said for soldiers who do amazing acts of selfless bravery, giving up their lives on the battlefield.

"And Billy Graham. I've heard you and Hans rail against him. I'm sorry. Who refused to allow the Jim Crow laws at his crusades in the south? Who arguably did as much for integration in the south as Dr. King himself? Who inspires missionaries to go to the far corners of the earth in selfless service? Dr. Graham—and a host of other evangelists.

"Who heads up some of the greatest humanitarian aid initiatives and programs in the world? Evangelicals. Just by virtue of being there out of love for Jesus. Who were leaders in the past century in the anti-slavery movement, the suffragette movement, the prison reform movement? Evangelicals.

"You are altogether too negative. You only see the bad. You caricature Evangelical theology. My dear brother, first cast out the plank in your own eye before even noticing the mote in the Evangelical eye."

Gary shook his head. "Andy, what's come over you? This is not the same Andy who so impressed me with his theology and thinking back at the Centre."

Andy was dogged. "You give some good counter-examples, Gary. So life is complex. I honour the *sacrifice* of a soldier for his comrades, his country, but not the *slaughter* done by that same soldier of his enemies, the aliens, of innocent civilians. It all boils down to this: I contend, above all, that Evangelicals need to learn to be just one thing—*evangelical!*"

B. B. exploded. "I've heard more than enough of this liberal nonsense! They once said of Christians in the early church, 'Behold, how they love one another.' It's the same today. You will not find a more loving group anywhere! Billy Graham is the picture of love as he willingly takes his crusades to anywhere on the globe.

"You have an enormous amount of repentance to do, my brother. I don't want you back in these studies until you work this through with God!" Both her voice and lower lip quivered. Andy had never seen her so emotional. Was she unusually emboldened with Gary present?

She turned to Gary. "I'm writing a letter to George about Andy. You heard him today. I don't know how Andy can pull together in the same plough with the rest of you given his display of anti-Evangelical prejudice. 'Can two walk together unless they be agreed?' Gary, I think you have a serious problem on your hands." She glowered at Andy.

With that, Andy turned and walked stiffly out the door. He did not look back. He was walking away from something else, too, he knew. He did not care. It was about time.

Andy remembered Hans' claim that Evangelicals were themselves *liberals*. Jesus appeared to be almost a complete stranger to Evangelicals—despite their constant call and claim to follow him—at least the Jesus who did more than come into the world through a Virgin Birth and exit through a justification-by-faith death and resurrection. "The Evangelical *essential*," belief in Jesus' death on the cross for salvation, was on the contrary "the Evangelical *heresy*," since it left out the intervening works and words of Jesus after his birth and before his death and those of his followers. It relegated Jesus' Kingdom teaching to the entirely *not yet*, making a mockery of living out the *already*—"living a life of love," Paul put it.

Andy was beginning to get the picture from Hans, Dan, Jesus, and the New Testament in general, that a tight bond existed between the call of Jesus to "repent and be saved" and performing necessary concomitant good works, "working out one's own salvation," showing faith by what one did by way of justice toward the neighbour. Not salvation through works, to be sure, but works of justice toward others, nonetheless, as the *only* way of legitimately claiming salvation. Not *displacing* love of God, the Greatest Commandment, but *demonstrating* it through offering oneself a living sacrifice of reasonable service and societal nonconformity on behalf of one's neighbour and enemy. "Owe no man anything, but to love one another: for he that loveth another hath fulfilled the law." There was the nub.

Therefore, Andy extrapolated, not mission as evangelism only but mission as justice-making, so as to demonstrate a righteousness greater than the Pharisees, so as to actually be the wise man who not only heard Jesus' words and believed but heard them and *put them into practice*, which included everything in the Sermon on the Mount. He reflected that, to his knowledge, he had never in his entire upbringing heard a sermon on the Sermon. Nor had he ever heard that one's salvation was demonstrated *only* through acts of justice to the "least of these," the poor, the hungry, the naked, the destitute, *the enemy!*

Anyone could claim to love God, whom he or she

had not seen, of a Sunday morning. But how did that translate to the one in the next pew, not to mention to one's business associates, competitors, customers, and rivals, on Monday morning? How did one look "saved" toward them? By the hymns sung Sunday morning, the prayers prayed Wednesday nights, the tracts passed out on the weekend or the special evangelistic and prophetic teaching services organized? Or by simple attention paid to the neighbour near in need—and more difficult—the enemy afar.

Andy remembered Joe Bailey's *The Gospel Blimp* story, and felt he was getting at some of the same stuff in that. In the story, a whole enterprise grows up around getting people evangelized through use of an annoying "Gospel Blimp" that shatters city quiet, showers Gospel litter like geese droppings on resistant lawns, and only tells of God's love through anti-Incarnational, arms-length evangelism, such that real-life relationships with neighbour and enemy—the reason why the whole idea "took off" in the first place—wither and die. And the evangelists turn into ogres and worse. Evangelicalism, the Ultimate Gospel Blimp?

Almost a week later, Andy was seething at B. B. again. She had to be out of town suddenly, and for all her fiery response the week earlier, she had booked Andy to lead a Thursday night Bible study discussion with a group of inquiring youth from their recent *Evangelisation*. It just so happened it was the final game of the hockey match of the century between Canada and the Russians!

Peter was philosophical about Andy's frustration. He suggested it was likely the Lord teaching him something about priorities. Andy usually liked Peter, but he found himself consequently seething at Peter too. He was so put out that he awoke on Thursday morning depressed and sullen. He felt in no shape to discuss faith issues with anyone. Others commiserated with him perhaps, but he, alone, bore the pain.

Then guilt set in, that greatest cultural motivator, learned from a Master, Saint Augustine, who taught the entire Christian and non-Christian West to have a guilty conscience about merely *existing*, not to mention one's sexuality. If he was only more spiritual, he knew, he would be rejoicing in this opportunity to make a clear moral choice between a frivolous piece of entertainment that would mean nothing in the light of eternity and the privilege of nurturing some along on a new walk of faith.

If only it could be another night! But even more guilt arose, since he knew his faith was changing hue as inexorably as the autumn leaves. Would his own beliefs, he wondered, turn similar colour, wither, even die? The image of the Vineyard Dresser removing dead branches leapt to mind. Was he destined to become a pruned branch thrown into the fire? The thought proved disconcerting.

Andy felt wretched no matter what direction his mind took during Thursday morning devotions. He yearned for an outlet. The phone rang. It was Janys. An answer to prayer? She wanted to talk. He said he had something to talk over, too!

They met and headed off for a walk. The first thing he asked her was to record the night's game while he was off at the "stupid" Bible study.

Each time he saw her, she looked more desirable. She wore denim pants and shirt. No scarf around her neck this time. She had on a matching fall jacket. No German youth outdid that smartness.

"Is your hair growing longer?" Andy asked.

Commenting on her physical presence often primed the pump. She smiled. Her greatest asset. The world was all right when Janys smiled.

"Yes," she replied simply.

"Do you want to know what your brother's last words were to me at the airport, Janys?" When was that? Another time. Another galaxy. "He said that there was more going on under that tangled mop than most realized, or something like that. He was right, a thousand times over, of course. I mean, that you had a tangled mop then." He smiled at his cuteness.

"Very funny!" She punched him playfully.

"What he failed to say," Andy stopped walking and gently turned Janys toward him, taking her hands, "was how much more there was going on, *on* the surface as well. You're beautiful, Janys Thane. You're beautiful beyond words. And it took me nearly a whole year to see that. I wonder how long it will take me to see all the other beautiful things I don't have eyes to see right now." He paused: "Maybe about Evangelicalism too!"

He lifted her off her feet in uninhibited embrace.

As they resumed walking, she replied, *"Quidquid recipitur per modum recipientis recipitur.* 'Whatever is received is received only according to the capacity of the one receiving it.'"

"How do you know that saying, Janys?" Andy exclaimed. It was he not she who had studied Latin.

"Ted."

Andy nodded. Of course.

"Andy," Janys continued as they wended their way along the *Ku'damm*, faintly astir from its previous late night carousing, "what are we going to do about B. B.? Gary and Peter both seem at a loss. You've just been *shanghaied* again. I warn you, she could still simply take over. Everything about her tells me that is a danger. And, whatever my brother tells me to the contrary about women's liberation, there is nothing worse than a battleaxe woman for a boss. I know. I worked for one back home once. It was awful!" She paused, obviously reminiscing about the experience.

"You know new winds are blowing in Evangelicalism about women's roles in the church, the home, and society in general. My mom, and yours, grew up with the traditional "women-silent-in-the-churches-and-under-the-authority-of-the-man" syndrome. Yet my mom was in many ways more suited for leadership than my dad. She was better educated, far nimbler of mind, and competently directed home life, though technically dad laid down the law.

"And it worked. At home, mom was really the authority figure. But in church, that was a different story. Suddenly, she became this subservient little mouse of a thing, so much so that, as we kids got older, we found it painful to behold."

Andy nodded. "My mom is the gifted one in our family, too. Dad is acquiescent to mom, despite his public *persona*, even happily so. Mom types out all dad's sermons, does quite liberal editing in the process. So much for not 'suffering a woman to teach.' If they only knew. Mom has always ruled the roost at home. In every way intellectually and in natural leadership, mom shapes our family life far more than dad. Very similar."

Janys smiled. "When I was a teenager, Mom once said to me, 'Of course we know how to get our way with the men!' She winked knowingly at me. My mom is striking looking. I said, 'Mother!' and we both laughed and laughed."

Janys continued. "Ted tells me that there are fresh winds blowing. It's not that Evangelicals are taking the Bible less seriously, more that its traditional interpretations about women and violence are being reappraised.

She turned to Andy. "Ever heard of a woman named Letha Scanzoni? She claims that the Bible, rightly interpreted, makes no distinction between genders, and that our roles in church, home, and society are predicated not on gender differences but on giftedness. She quotes Paul, who says that in Christ there is neither Jew nor Gentile, slave nor free, *neither male nor female*. You know how he says in Second Corinthians five that we no longer view anyone after the flesh? Scanzoni applies that to male-female relationships, too."

"But coming back to what you and Ted are saying. What about clear biblical statements that women should keep silent in the churches, wear head coverings, and not usurp authority over men? They all seem fairly straightforward to me in their implications, whatever Paul meant by 'neither male nor female.' What does your brother, or Scanzetti say to that?"

"*Scanzoni*, Andy. I don't know all the arguments. But Ted says that everyone *interprets* Scripture. No one just lifts off from the text to a crystal clear understanding and application. How many different ways can you see the mountains—and I don't mean mine!" Janys punched Andy playfully as his gaze drifted in that direction.

"For starters," she continued, "every Bible translation is already an interpretation. Just like the translating you've been doing already in both directions between German and English. It's never a one-on-one word swap. The fancy word is *hermeneutics*. Already feminized, take note!

"Ted tells me that one can be faithful to the biblical text and also be a feminist. However, he also says he won't be preaching that from any brethren pulpit for the next while. He values his life. Or at least his brethren connections."

"Your brother is obviously someone I'd really enjoy having a long talk with sometime, Janys. He makes me jealous doing that kind of studying. Maybe one day," Andy added wistfully.

"I want to get back to B. B.," Janys said. "She is not the liberated feminist Scanzoni is talking about. She is really a traditionalist with a controlling impulse that seems to know no bounds away from Scottish soil. She's dangerous, Andy. And the sooner we distance ourselves from her, the better. Otherwise, I predict we will be in for endless conflict with her as she slowly entrenches her stranglehold on Gary and Peter and takes over the team entirely."

"Wow. You really do have it in for her with those dire predictions, Janys. I know she said some bad things about me—to me—last week, and that I'm really peeved at her right now about the Bible study I have to lead tonight. But is she really that bad?"

Janys nodded quietly. Then she squeezed his hand and pulled him toward a department store that had just opened. "I need to pick up a few things. Are you game?"

"Sure," Andy said.

She released his hand as they entered the store.

"When we come back out, I'll tell you about Petra," Andy said.

Andy had never shopped in the lingerie section before. A couple of times Janys held up some skimpy black number to ask him how he thought this would look. He was the one with all the "look." Embarrassed. She was enjoying herself.

"Which colour do you prefer?" She asked about two bras.

"Neither," Andy replied. "I prefer *au naturel*." He was catching on. She looked a feigned scandalized.

When they came back out, Andy turned to Janys. "Game to find a bench somewhere?" They watched in silence from where they sat.

"Janys," Andy said quietly. "Even if we weren't…" He hesitated at his choice of words.

"What?" Janys met his eyes evenly. "What are we, Andy?"

Then, in pure capitulation, "*Lovers*, Janys. We're lovers like over the top of anything that has ever happened in the whole world before! We're impossible, crazy, zany, wild, *wonderful* lovers!"

Was it an eternity of staring into each other's eyes?

The embrace was slow, utterly self-conscious, delectable beyond all words, worlds. The quiet panting lasted a long time, two heads and bodies dreamily, closely contiguous as the rest of West Berlin, the East, all Germany, Europe, the world, receded into oblivion.

"Janys, I never dreamed of saying this over here, but what's left?" Pause. Deep breath. "Will you marry me?"

Where had that come from? Budapest pixie dust? Andy had not ever formulated the question to himself. Was it taking her an eternity to answer?

"Yes!" She exploded so passionately he jumped. "Yes, a thousand times yes, Andy!" Suddenly, it felt like they were whisked upwards on a magic carpet that looped every which way across the sky, the universe, the cosmos to the wild jazz music of Scott Joplin. Then it deposited them back at the girls' apartment. How else did they otherwise get there?

68

When Andy returned from the Bible study that night, he found a tape in his room with a note on it from Jack that said, "Yeah Russians!" It was a recording of the final hockey game between Canada and Russia. It had finished about two hours earlier, but Janys had recorded it for him. Andy popped it into his tape player right away and lay back to listen.

With only thirty-four seconds left to play, Andy literally leaped off his bed when Paul Henderson scored the game-winning goal—his third winning goal in a row! It was the most exciting game he had ever listened to in his life. Canada was number one in the world!

Only later did Andy learn that the Russians scored another goal that Ken Dryden, the lawyer goalie, totally missed. But he managed to snatch the puck out of the goal before the referee saw it, and the point was not attributed to the Russians.

He sat in the dim light of the living room afterwards reflecting on the game, hockey, life. Henderson had his moments of glory. How many seconds of worldwide recognition? Then oblivion. Or at least Andy wondered how many details anyone would remember by say, 2000. How ephemeral is such glory, though a personal epitome for Henderson no doubt, and for Canada in that era of the Cold War. Like Mark Spitz. It showed up the West as the "good guys" once again, a mythology perpetuated by every conquering nation or people known to human history.

Andy pictured the victory dance Henderson no doubt did seconds after dumping the puck into the net.

Stick flying high, and the other arm up too, just like the Jesus People—minus the one-way finger—teammates swarming in to congratulate. It was a moment of triumph to savour for the rest of one's life.

A great moment while happening but forgotten relatively soon thereafter. What about other moments of great achievement by athletes, such as in the history of the Olympics? Great personal achievement, sometimes against all odds. The glory of the victory wreath, one's name in all the media. Temporal immortality. Was there a single name any modern Olympics-goer could give of any past gold medallist in any of ancient Greece's four recurring games?

Would the next generation of Canadians know anything about Paul Henderson? Would there still be a Cold War in 2000? A Wall? Andy could not imagine the city otherwise. And even the current generation moved on so quickly to the next sports thrill. To the next sex thrill. "Next!" If only the crowning moment could really be captured to endure, Andy thought. It was the same dilemma again. The old order changeth!

What did it really matter, in light of the past, and even the future, that Canada won the first ever Canada-Soviet grudge match? Did it mean that the "free world" was vindicated, at least in hockey prowess? What did that matter in light of eternity? Yet, there it was, an event that electrified a whole nation, that sent his heart pounding as the final minute of play began, and that similarly caused the Soviets immense shame and embarrassment. Were people in Russia even shot over the loss?

What infused events with meaning—or denied them significance? How could such meaning and significance be measured? By how many people knew about it? Andy couldn't help but think of a birth in an obscure part of the then-known world, in a cattle barn, that only a rag-tag group of shepherds seemed to find out about. And that baby's eventual death, when a grown man, was no less obscure: on a garbage heap outside Jerusalem with other criminals. Only a group of nondescript women and three men stayed behind. All the no-account men fled.

Yet those two events, with the work and words of the person in between, have impacted world history to a vastly greater extent than any other similar set of events. Overwhelmingly more. And further, it is claimed that those same events even have ultimate retroactive and proactive dynamism, such that all human history, even the cosmos, are transformed.

So maybe there was simply no way of knowing the full significance of any event, let alone its impact backwards or forwards. The slightest movement of our human choices made, and the rock has been thrown into a still pond whose ripples are the stuff of history with real meaning, not just "one damn thing happening after another," as one jaded historian once put it.

Andy reflected that for the second time, B. B. had forced him to do something so contrary to what he had planned—even if in neither case was the alternative a "spiritual" exercise. The ripple effects were anger and resentment.

Well, this time, Andy would create some waves, too! Though just how, he was unsure. For starters, he could write to G. E. Maybe his and B. B.'s letters would arrive together.

So much for women's liberation if it led to this kind of pendulum swing, Andy thought. Then he remembered Janys' comment that B. B. was not a model of liberated womanhood but rather traditionalism with a twist. But if women began to take over leadership positions in the church, would they prove to be just as domineering as men? Wasn't that like rearranging the chairs on the deck but doing nothing about the sinking vessel? Like every revolution known to humanity that only has changed the names of those in power, the deposed would be sent off to prison or executed but the reality of the power game itself never changed. Andy wished he had an "Andy" to talk to. No one else could talk at his level, though Gary showed signs of beginning to think. The Professor never wrote back. Janys was several blocks away.

Then he scolded himself for such arrogance, and changed the topic in spite of himself. He fell asleep thinking about the recent "Yes" he had elicited from Janys, and where to go from there. He heard the word echo in his dreams. Echoes and ripples, world without end…

He knew no ancient Greek athlete's name.

69

In October, the team added to its activities a boys' club, having received again permission from the *Wilmersdorf* assembly to use their facility. Still no offers of help from any of the churches to which they connected.

Despite Braxman's arrest, Fiona remained melancholy. She went through the motions of team life, but the lustre had gone. It even showed in her complexion and hair. Jack understandably cursed Braxman. There were phone calls going back and forth between Fiona and her parents, Fiona and G. E., and Jack and G. E. The phone bills, Peter's domain, must have been significant. But so far, nothing had been resolved.

Meanwhile, Jean's health remained constant. So for the time being, everyone was holding.

On occasion, the guys' apartment took in "strays" met on the *Ku'damm* during open-air *Evangelisationen*. One night in mid-October, a guy named Mannfred stayed with them. He had become "saved" through a local Jesus People group known as the *Children of God*. He spoke not a word of English but strangely claimed comprehension of the English-language through Christian magazines he perused in their apartment, believing the Holy Spirit somehow supplied spontaneous comprehension. Andy felt tempted to press him on the content, but other than obliquely so as not to embarrass him, and to satisfy his cynicism, refrained.

Mannfred only stayed one night then rather mysteriously disappeared with not a word of thanks. A few others disappeared with a little more. The first found the change purse and absconded with it. Thankfully, there was little in it. The next disappeared with one of Andy's Schaeffer books. He was less chagrined about that. He knew he was changing...

Gary mentioned some of this petty theft in a letter to G. E. A clear directive arrived shortly thereafter: STOP TAKING IN THE HOMELESS! G. E. went on to say that they had gone to Germany to preach and teach the Gospel. This, he explained, would engage them in Bible studies, door-to-door and open-air work, and many similar kinds of activities. But it was too risky to take in street people. Especially with Sharon, not at all unattractive, living in the apartment. *What is the Gospel?* Andy wondered again.

On the last Friday of October, Jack booked yet another visit to Scott Cunningham at the Army Base. He was going weekly now, working out with him and hanging out. Jack never said much about the visits. Todd Braxman was apparently being held at the Base now. He had suffered a broken collarbone the night of the abduction. No one quite knew how he had survived in the intervening weeks. New German charges were pending for several break and enters, however.

Jack asked Andy if he wanted to join with him for the ride that afternoon. It seemed like he wanted to talk. They agreed that he would not meet with Scott. Andy had no interest, and Cunningham had said as much in stronger terms to Jack. Andy said he'd be glad to go along and take the car to a nearby park for an hour or so while Jack worked out.

The daytime drive to the Base, Andy's first since Fiona's kidnapping, brought back memories of their wild drive there that frightening night.

"You know, Jack, I can imagine the terror of those

Israeli athletes at the Olympics. Look what it's done to Fiona weeks later, even with the guy caught.

"She's a mess, Andy," Jack acknowledged. "You know what she's been talking about most? Her son, Timmy."

"So where's this all going to end up, Jack?"

"Almost for sure G. E.'s comin' out in early November. One of the things I'm gonna talk to Scott today about is whether there may be any kind of psychiatric help for Fiona. They have a responsibility we both think. It's a real bummer. Her parents want her home. I think that's best." He paused and glanced at Andy. "I'm thinking of leaving, too."

Andy said nothing, just processed the implications. Was the whole team tottering?

When they had parked outside the base, Andy got out and stretched. "I've got my own key. I think I'm just going to stroll around. Take as long you need."

Jack waved and headed toward the gates.

"Hey Jack!" Andy said, a novel idea striking him. Jack turned to face him. "What if you were to ask, maybe even with Fiona, to actually see Braxman in jail."

"Whatever for, Andy?" Jack looked incredulous.

"I don't know... What if you could actually win him over? That would sure set Fiona at ease."

Jack shook his head and strode toward the electronic gate. Soon, he was ushered inside, leaving Andy to wander along the *Allee*.

It was like an Indian summer fall day back home, though on the cool side. Andy remembered that soon it would be Hallowe'en. On which planet again? It all seemed frightfully far away. He was glad Janys had not joined him. He had some serious thinking to do: about Jack and Fiona, about the team, about life. The sight of

CHRYSALIS CRUCIBLE

the Base, indicative of American power flung to the far corners of the world, was serendipitous inspiration. But not to sing *The Star-Spangled Banner*.

Andy's mind turned first to G. E.'s forceful missive about only "preaching the Gospel." He thought immediately of the Matthew 25 passage. Once again, he was overwhelmed by the salvation message of the passage. It all turned upon good works performed in this lifetime. And yet he had been raised all his life to believe "*not by works, lest any man should boast*," Paul's teaching, which was all after-death oriented. So did Paul simply contradict Jesus? Did a choice have to be made of that sort? Or was James, in echoing Jesus with, "Show me your faith without deeds, and I will show you my faith by what I do," simply out to lunch, author indeed of a "right strawy epistle," unaware that salvation was freely offered without good works?

Were James and Jesus somehow heretics in their teachings? Even though Jesus the icon saved us through his blood? But not through his words lived out? Then Andy remembered the startling discovery in Matthew's Gospel that the "wise man" was not the one who believed, and the "foolish man" not the unbeliever destined for hellfire. Rather, the wise man was "everyone who hears these words of mine and *puts them into practice*." And what was the immediate context for Jesus' "words" to discern that practice? The Sermon on the Mount, which was chock-a-block full of the call to treat the neighbour and enemy with justice, mercy, and compassion. That was the purview of the wise man. That was the concrete actualization of salvation that is "today." How had Andy—the entire Evangelical tradition—misread such evident biblical teaching?

As he walked alongside the Base, Andy turned

to the immense human capacity to inflict suffering upon one's fellow. The American Army was the most capacitated in the entire world to do precisely that! Images of Agent Orange defoliating multiplied hundreds of thousands of hectares of pristine jungle and doubtless deforming thousands of unborn children for a whole next generation competed with images of gas ovens; massive bombings; scientific excising of "cancer" from the body politic; cluster bombs scattered by the millions; jungle torture; maiming and slaughter of soldiers, villagers, and anyone else caught in the crossfire; napalm sending an eight-year-old girl naked down the road, the searing pain all over her face, captured for the world by a happenstance photographer. He wondered at the enormous human capacity and lust for perpetrating overwhelming misery against others.

He realized this had to be the ultimate inversion of evangelism, when bombs and bullets, Agent Orange, and God only knows what else in word and deed, not "the good seed," were scattered indiscriminately upon the earth. Pain, death, and devastation followed. Massively.

Then the terrifying reminder that, with few exceptions, Evangelicals *en masse* blessed all that! The ultimate world evangelist gave routine assent to such mass carnage and murder as surely as Saul and those stoning Stephen persecuted the early Christians. What utter perversion of the Good News. What Gospel travesty. What complete inversion of evangelism. By the world's greatest evangelist and the world's most virulent religion propagators.

How could this be? How could a man, not to mention an entire faith tradition, so endorse and defend pure, unadulterated *evil* perpetrated against God's good creation and his image-bearers, for whom, additionally, Christ suffered a painful victim's death by "legitimate" State decree? Andy's mind recoiled at the emerging sense of horror over what he and his fellows accepted as nonchalantly as going out for a Sunday school picnic: mass slaughter of enemies of the State. This was in company with dominant Western Christian tradition since Constantine. It was also in lockstep with Machiavelli, Napoleon, Bismarck, the German Kaiser, Lenin, Stalin, Hitler, Mussolini, the Japanese Emperor, Mao, to name only relatively recent mainly Western tyrants.

His horror turned to terror that his entire life he had worshipped God and had been formed in all his core beliefs in company with such sycophants of mass murder and mayhem. As if he had been born into a Mafia family, where killing and slaughter were simply routine, justified as what was needed to "get the job done," to enable "normal" life to go on. "Just War" theory, as Christians had always enunciated it, Andy suddenly understood, was equally the prerogative of the Mob and every vile tyrant known to humanity. No doubt Christians were more sophisticated than what a Mafia family godfather or dictator might articulate, but in the end, it all boiled down to exactly the same thing: *terror and slaughter*. People destroyed, the earth raped and pillaged, all for a "just" cause. How could he have been so duped and not have seen the true face of Christendom viciously "red in tooth and claw"?

He crossed over the *Allee* at a light and walked toward the Base from the other side. As he looked at the Base, he imagined all the keen Christians wanting to propagate their faith while they gleefully slaughtered their enemies in Vietnam. The juxtaposition was stark.

He thought of past Christian support of the slave trade. Thousands of people were stolen, brutalized, raped, terrorized, and discarded at the behest of those whose unquestioned (until politician William Wilberforce) participation in "Christian" genteel society was as grotesque as Nazi concentration camp guards 150 years later or Allied bombers or majority Christian supporters of the death penalty and warfare throughout church history. The entire edifice of Western civilization built upon a gargantuan garbage dump of Christianly justified "holy" terror. *Corruptio optimi quae est pessima*, "the corruption of the best is the worst" indeed.

There was a bench at the edge of the sidewalk. The sun was warm. Andy sat and looked at the expanse of the entire Base.

Again he realized, like awakening from a terror-filled nightmare, that this kind of *justification* was dominant Evangelical Christian reality. Not "justification by faith" putatively productive of a "life of love," which seemed largely a formidable Christian fraud, a ferocious legal fiction, but *justification of every imaginable form of harm and destruction wreaked upon humanity and nature*—in the name of Jesus. Andy wondered what kind of powerful sorcerer had incanted such a pervasively potent spell, that so much of Evangelical tradition, including millions upon millions of ostensibly Bible-believing, Jesus-following, God-fearing souls, accepted such indescribably sick justifications as Gospel truth? Was there ever any hope of breaking such a spell when the Bible, God, and Jesus, according to most mainline leadership past and present, queued eagerly in unequivocal endorsement?

His mind moved inexorably to justification of every war fought in the entire history of the church. All had been blessed by the Church on both sides of the conflict. Andy knew that over 100 million had been slaughtered in the twentieth century so far alone, mostly with the blessing of the Church from every side. He knew from Hans the terrible recitation of mass butchery by Western Allies. These hundreds of thousands of immolated innocents just happened to be living in the wrong place at the wrong time, like the infants under age two that Herod had destroyed to wipe out the Christ child.

Just like that! And they were still murdering the Christ child! What was that Christian World War Two slogan? "Praise God and pass the bombs!" Sick and designedly destructive of the Christ child in every last one of "the least of these"! Herod's decree became marching orders ever since for virtually all Christendom, world without end, world brought to a horrible end possibly in nuclear nightmare! All enemies for sure consigned to a God-forsaken end, Amen and Amen, intoned by every military chaplain in the history of Christendom.

Why was such an obvious biblical association so out of step with virtually everyone else living in the West? Incredible! Astounding! The power of monstrous myth-making to perpetrate the Ultimate Lie: "*Might is right. Violence is holy.*" Isn't that exactly what he was looking at? One clarion symbol of that very mythmaking? A two-millennia religious phenomenon, Christendom, including right up to its most vehement contemporary defenders, Evangelicals, utterly at odds with the most straightforward, most pervasive, most undeniably central Gospel ethical truth: *Love your neighbour; love your enemies*. The Core of the Gospel: *all-inclusive reconciliation.* The Core of Christendom: *mass violence.* Each in diametrically opposed juxtaposition.

Who did Andy think he was to see things so

differently? Who did Hans think he was? Dan? Jesus? The questions thudded home like a sledgehammer. Andy recoiled physically, held onto the bench as if falling. Then he wondered: If we're not following Jesus, who are we following? What had Gandhi said when asked what he thought of Western civilization? "I think it would be a *great* idea!" Andy knew the prevaricating ironies: Freedom of the Western press for those who own one. Freedom from violence for those who possessed the biggest guns. Stupid white men facing each other down on Main Street at High Noon. Little kids all, puerile, utter fools every last one.

Gandhi might have similarly responded to, "What do you think of Western Christianity?" with, "I think it would be a great idea… *Why don't they start by following Jesus?*" What a novel thought. And for different reasons, but in the end with identical outcome, both believer and non-believer respond, "So what?" The lowly private in Vietnam, latest evangelistic convert stroking his New Testament like a good luck charm while proceeding to engage in routine acts that were utterly *anti-Christ*: blowing, not welcoming, the enemy to Kingdom Come! "Kingdom Come" all right, when all is said and done, at the point of the gun, the discharge of the bomb, the launch of the missile. Praise God and drop those bombs, toss those grenades, spew death from the automatic weaponry, fire those missiles. That's God's true Kingdom Come on earth for Western Christianity. All enemies be damned, God be praised forevermore.

Andy knew that most of his peers did not see war that way. They invariably intoned that war was a tragic, unavoidable necessity so that people could live in freedom and peace. Which people? The hundreds of thousands who "are the dead, though short days ago they lived" whether or not "poppies grow in Flanders fields"? They were to be accorded only the peace of the graveyard while most of Christendom cheered, saying indeed, "Praise the Lord, and pass the bombs." Sick and desperately evil. What a monstrous lie Christendom had believed and perpetrated for centuries. And with ubiquitous, iniquitous, world-conquering outcome.

Andy could not stop his mind's stream of consciousness. What an abject, calculated rejection of the one who taught and lived, "Love your neighbour, especially your enemies." He wondered, as in the story of the Rich Man and Lazarus, what emissary from hell might be sent to lift the veil of abject evil from Christians' eyes so that they could see? Or would they rather be as Jesus warned, "seeing, yet they do not see; though hearing, they do not hear or understand?" They already had Moses and the Prophets and Jesus and the Apostles. If they didn't "get it" by reading them, what hope were one even to rise from the dead? Did not Billy Graham and "a great cloud of witnesses" preach "Jesus Christ, Risen Again, Mighty to Save, Able to Keep"? Didn't Andy's home assembly boldly announce the same thing, visible above the pulpit for all comers? The iconic Bible wide open in Billy's and millions of preachers' hands as they thundered their evangelistic message *without the Gospel*—Jesus denied and crucified in blessing of mass victims everywhere. Jesus the Salvation Icon, but not Jesus the Exemplar. Horrors no! *Horrors yes, upon multiplied terrors*.

Andy's mind reeled but had nowhere to turn. He was under no illusion that Evangelicals believed in Billy Graham, for all intents the Pope of Evangelicalism, far more than they believed in Jesus. If Billy prayed with every President for victory in whatever war America was fighting, then *Billy must be right and Jesus be damned*! Was it as blatant as that?

And who would be thanked for saying, "But the Emperor has no clothes"?

"Crucify him!" Andy suddenly heard the religious hordes crescendo in response, as robustly as the mob in front of Pilate 2,000 years before, or as the soldiers doing Herod's bidding to the two-and-under toddlers in Bethlehem so long ago. Why did Andy's mind think this way? What was the matter with him? What had seized his troubled mind to arrive at conclusions that would get *him* crucified and blacklisted by most Evangelical leaders in the world? Who did he think he was?

He wondered about Scott Cunningham, who wanted Christ and American Empire, to have his cake and eat it, too. God and Guns. He and Jack were obviously having a good discussion. There was no sign of him yet. Andy felt okay about that. The sun was warm on his face. He still had some ways to go in sorting some of this out.

Had he somehow misunderstood? Did Evangelicals really take Jesus seriously after all? He thought of all the "born-again" military personnel right in front of him. A real revival, the team had been told. He remembered what Hans Beutler had said, recalled his discussions with Dan, and reviewed his own awareness of church history. No. He was not wrong. The vast majority of Christians throughout history and of his contemporaries, best represented by Billy Graham at the White House in his constant blessing of U.S. military interventions, had always underwritten mass slaughter of enemies worldwide. Whenever it served their interests.

There was always justification for Western Holocaust. The "other justification," like Paul's "other gospel," was pure symmetrical inversion of biblical "justification by faith." Was it Evangelicals' primary gospel, foremost kind of "justification"? Was the Gospel of Jesus Christ, of the Bible, unknown or secondary? Andy concluded that there was no difference between Christian doctrine and Mafia belief in the end. Regrettably or not, in cold blood, or with a glimmer of conscience, *people must die, the good earth be wasted!* Whatever it took to get the job done. It was the logic of High Priest Caiaphas, who said of Jesus that it was better that one man should die than the whole nation perish. Evangelicals, all of Christendom, had simply repeated that scapegoating anti-Gospel dogma throughout their long, sick, and desperately evil history. The dynamics that had killed the Prince of Peace were identical to those theologized, endorsed, and perpetuated by *most* of Christendom throughout *most* of history, by *most* everyone. Andy's mind echoed with the words of Jeremiah, "The heart is deceitful above all things, and desperately wicked, who can know it?"

And there was Andy door-to-door at the Centre, on the streets of Berlin, with the evangelistic throngs at the Munich Olympics, preaching the "anti-Gospel," representing reversed "Good News."

He stood up then sat down again; feeling like he might throw up, oust some kind of forbidden food. But he knew it was far too late. He had long-since swallowed such belief, which included, like King Herod, perpetual endorsement of mass slaughter of innocents. Most Christian believers were King Herod's foot soldiers when it came to war and capital punishment.

So what about all the Germans, Japanese, Koreans, and Vietnamese—enemies all within the past thirty-five years—murdered on a grand scale by the "Good Guys" and blessed by all Christendom, except "enemy"

Christendom, who, most likely, called down God's blessing on the slaughter of the "Good Guys"? Had God not made them in his image, too? Had Christ not died for them? Were they not equally entitled to hear the Good News? Did "love" mean, in the end, what the papal legate said centuries before and majority Christians explicitly follow in the present day, "Kill them all, God will sort out who are his own"?

Andy wished Jack would hurry up. He needed to put a stop to the impossible build-up of thoughts somehow. There had been very little traffic on the *Allee*. He felt tempted to get up and walk again. His mind roared on.

What kind of utter perversion, inversion, of biblical "love" had Christendom embraced, to permit the wholesale slaughter throughout the centuries of domestic and foreign enemies, who were neighbours, who were "God," at least God's image-bearers, in whom, "the least of these," Jesus was to be found? Why had seemingly so few in the history of the Church from within screamed out, "*The Emperor has no clothes!*"?

In consideration of the overwhelming unrighteousness of Christian belief and action for centuries, was not the era of the Enlightenment a supreme gift from God to the Church? To the world? Were its proponents not the "stones" made to cry out by God after the Church had endorsed and committed endless atrocious adulteries with the State for centuries? Was not the revolt of atheism over against the church's horrendous unfaithfulness *pure religion* of the sort James spoke of? Were not Unitarians in their pacifism far more faithful even when throwing out the baby, Jesus' Incarnation, with the bathwater? Was not Gandhi "right on" in his rejection of the missionaries' Christ?

Was not Martin Luther tragically misguided in *only* trying to find justification before a holy God, yet never likewise before God's image-bearers, not least God's chosen, the Jews? Had not Luther instructed the German nobility, "Smite, slay and kill!" the peasant hordes and committed to writing some of the most vituperative anti-Semitic hate literature known to humanity? (Which the Lutheran church officially rejected only *after* the Nazis, steeped in Martin Luther's German Christianity, had slaughtered six million Jewish innocents.)

Contrary to mainstream Protestant understandings, was not the *only* way to find a holy God *through loving embrace of neighbour and enemy*? How had Evangelicals, so adamant about following Jesus, sucked him utterly dry of all true content when it came to his central teachings and example about love of neighbour and enemy?

Andy's mind had built up such momentum that nothing was able to stop the ineluctable questions he was posing to himself. He felt immobilized, like a terrified mouse before the proverbial snake. Yet somehow the serpent, unlike in the Primordial Garden, *rightly* was about to swallow its prey. Wasn't the Church, in light of its long and terrifying history of violence, *one of the most evil scourges on humanity the world had known?* Possibly *the most evil?* He remembered a line from a German poem, *Die Gerechtigkeit der Erde, O Herr, hat Dich getötet*—"the righteousness of the earth, O Lord, has killed you." Only Andy would change *O Herr* to *O Kirche*. The Church had self-imploded in light of all human standards of righteousness, which were far more vaunted than the Church's. Or were they? Had the secular world simply imbibed the Church's biblical teaching despite Christendom's contrary example— the corruption of the best—and was now holding the Church to account when it had so quickly and so long since turned faithless to its founding texts?

Andy didn't know where to turn. Who had written on this stuff? Why didn't he know of it? When in Church history, if at all, did at least a few lonely voices cry out about the Emperor's, Christendom's, Evangelicalism's stark and shameful, vile and unconscionably evil, nakedness; its unrepentant and endlessly repeated whoredoms? Were there at least 7,000 in the long history of the Church who had not bowed the knee? Would he have to leave the Church to find God? Would he have to turn to the secular thinkers and philosophers to discover true biblical religion? Was the Church, in the end, the ultimate evil?

A car honked. For a split second, Andy actually thought someone was acknowledging his question. He decided he would get up to walk some more. His mind plunged forward headlong.

Andy wished he could tear out that part of his brain that was causing so much offence, like Jesus had said one should do with an eye or a hand. But wasn't the Church, in fact, *the primary offender*? He recalled a saying he had read by Simone Weil: "The church is that great totalitarian beast with an irreducible kernel of truth." Weil refused to join it throughout her lifetime. No wonder. Hadn't she also said the most fundamental act of forgiveness humans needed to undertake is toward God? Wasn't she right? Might it have been better had Jesus never been born, had the word "God" never first been uttered long ago amongst Semitic nomads, given how the Church and its precursors had desecrated so violently its content?

Andy felt wretched. It seemed like he was being thrust inside an Alfred Hitchcock horror movie, when all perspectives and norms were rendered kaleidoscopic. Where could he turn when everything normal had convulsed into a thousand distortions? He had come over to Germany to propagate faith and instead had found his faith buffeted and sent topsy-turvy, not by contrary intellectual argument from others—he had braced for that—but from his own experience and rethinking within the faith. He was his own fifth columnist, his own desperate traitor. Self-betrayed! How distressing! He had unwittingly been lying in wait to ambush his easy-believism, cheap-grace Evangelical faith, so proud and cocky about having "the Truth" that he didn't know that he was the hunted, not the hunter.

The tables had been turned. The shoe was on the other foot. *He* needed to be evangelized. *He* was that Emperor without any clothes. This was *his* moment of truth. Would he repent and turn? But from what? Faith? Or would he, like the Emperor, thrust his head a little higher and strut stark naked to the beat of Christendom's droning blood-drenched drums? He knew the sycophants who would cheer him on. Out of the frying pan, into the fire. Was he, in his evangelistic zeal, only guilty of traversing the ocean to make his converts *twice the sons of hell* for his efforts? Was this the indictment of most missionary and evangelistic efforts worldwide, of every Billy Graham evangelistic crusade he had so unthinkingly prayed for? How dare he think such thoughts? Wasn't this ultimate heresy? *Who did he think he was?*

"O wretched man that I am!" He cried out suddenly He glanced. No one had heard. God perhaps?

Around the corner there was a horrific thundering as Army vehicle upon Army vehicle rolled down *Clayallee* to enter the Base compound. There must have been twenty or more—tanks, armoured cars, and a fleet of others he could not identify. They must have been on some kind of training exercise. He was wrong, therefore. All the Christians were not at the Base. Some at least were training once again to kill. He felt like launching a rocket to wipe them all out, and then felt even more wretched at how easily his mind had slipped into such a vindictive mode.

Jack came out after the last vehicle had turned in to the Compound. For the first time since leaving Jack, Andy remembered that Jack and Fiona might be leaving the team, so engrossed his ruminations had become.

When Jack saw Andy, he said it looked like Andy had seen a ghost. Andy said he *had*, millions of them. But nowhere the Holy Ghost.

Jack did not even try to understand. "Let's head back. I'll tell you about the visit on the way," he said.

Andy looked again at the Base for the Holy Ghost, maybe Jesus. He saw neither.

70

Scott had informed Jack that there was really nothing the Base would do to help Fiona. He also had told him they would be shipping Braxman back to the US to face a court martial. In that case, the German criminal charges would be dropped, meaning no one would have to testify. That was a relief.

Andy asked Jack why he was thinking of leaving.

"Andy," Jack replied, "Me and Fiona are in love. I'm sure after G. E. gets here that he'll agree she has to go home. If she does, I'm going with her. Besides, you know Centre policy on pairing off. We can't last here as a couple anyway.

"I've asked Gary and Peter to let Fiona take some time off right now. Trouble is, she has no place to go on her own, except home. We thought we'd let her take a break until G. E. arrives, then see. He's catching a plane for sure Sunday night, October 29th. We all agreed we'd try to hang in until then. It's tough though."

Andy let out a low whistle. "Boy, Jack. You and Fiona are talking of going home, Peter and Jean might leave at any time if her pregnancy gets worse. That decimates our team, which just this summer in Munich was looking pretty fine."

"Shit happens, Andy," Jack replied.

Despite Jack's revelation, Andy decided to say nothing about him and Janys. He was amazed at how well kept their secret had remained, given their overt demonstrations of affection at times. No one close had seen them yet. The earlier covenant was now a dead letter. Andy took Jack and Fiona's predicament seriously, however, *vis à vis* Centre policy. Andy was not entirely sure how clear that policy was, though he could understand how complicated such pairing could make things.

The hugest rally ever planned to protest the War was scheduled to take place Saturday, October 28th. B. B. had proposed, and the team had agreed, to permit some of the *Lichterfelde* youth to distribute a Gospel pamphlet to the thousands of expected protesters.

Gary suggested they write and distribute a pamphlet about the War from a Christian perspective. He offered to write it if Andy and Peter would help with the German and all on the team critique its content.

Over the months there, they had distributed a variety of tracts and pamphlets, many from *Aktion in Jedes Haus*—Every Home Crusade. But they pulled in a variety of material from an eclectic number of sources, including Emmaus Bible Correspondence School, the Billy Graham Evangelistic Association, and other German evangelistic agencies. Recently, the team had acquired a *Gestetner* duplicating machine, something Andy had pursued. They were now producing some of their own materials with it, including this leaflet.

The production for the protest rally showed a rudimentary dove and an olive branch with the arresting title: *STOP DEN KRIEG!*—STOP THE WAR! It began with the line, VIETNAM: THE GREATEST PROBLEM… OR? It continued with a litany of conflicts and wars the world over and other kinds of scourges, manmade or otherwise: poverty, pollution, famine, earthquakes, sickness, and hatred. Then it juxtaposed these with church people singing praises to a God who seemingly did nothing about it all. It went on to tell of Jesus Christ, asking whether He had any relevance for people today. It emphatically stated that history had proven Jesus had lived, died, and risen from the dead. It drew on C. S. Lewis' famous three options about Jesus, that he was either a charlatan, a madman or God incarnate. If he was the last, then his contemporary meaning became clear, it was claimed.

Yes, the last paragraph affirmed, we have fighting in Northern Ireland and war in Vietnam. But there is also a universal human inner warfare—one between God and Man. And Man repeatedly chooses to go his own way. That is rebellion against God, in other words, sin. So man is separated from God. But God still loves Man, and always will. For that reason, Jesus came, so that through his sacrifice we might have a relationship with a living personal God. It's our choice. We must decide! And then the kicker: *Our world can never find real peace until we have inner peace with God.* People were invited to contact the team by mail or telephone. Gary had spent hours writing it and presented it at their October 23rd team meeting.

"Gary, I just don't buy the dichotomy anymore," Andy began.

Gary sucked in his breath.

Andy continued regardless. "Inner peace with God and peace on earth are all the same in God's intention for the cosmos. You make a simplistic dichotomy between the two that does not ring true biblically nor in experience. There is no divide between the private/personal and social/political. It's all the same call to holiness in the Scriptures."

"That sounds like Liberalism," Gary countered. "There is no hope whatsoever for world peace until Man is right with God."

"Gary," Andy responded, "where in the U. S. would one go, right now to find the worst racism, greatest intolerance, and shrillest war-mongering with blind patriotism for whatever America does to its enemies? In other words, the exact opposite of peace with neighbours?"

Gary felt the trap: "I don't need to answer that, Andy. We're to look to Christ and the Bible, not others claiming to be Christians."

"America's 'Bible Belt' in the South, Gary," Andy continued, as if Gary had not answered. "If it is true that peace with God inexorably leads to peace with Man, why is it not empirically so? In other words, Gary, peace with God is a crock if it is not concomitantly shown in relation to one's fellow man."

Gary bristled. "Then you're saying, Andy, to get this right, that good works *do* save us?"

"What I'm saying," Andy shot back, "is salvation, justification by faith, is a legal fiction if it does not show up in good works, our lifestyles, how we treat the other—neighbour near, enemy afar."

"So it is our works that save us?" Came Gary's insistent riposte.

"No, but only our works demonstrate we are saved!" Andy said.

Janys chimed in, in an obvious bid to defuse the discussion. "I think you're both saying the same thing, really. Andy, you're not denying the need for faith—peace with God, and Gary, you're not denying the need for deeds—peace with our fellow man. You're just saying, Gary, it has to start with faith. And Andy, you're saying faith has to complete with deeds.

"To put both of your claims together, it seems to me you're saying there is a tight bond that exists between faith in Jesus Christ as personal Saviour that leads to peace with God, and commitment to follow Jesus Christ as Lord and Examplar that leads to peace with Man. They are really two sides of the same coin. Neither can exist on its own. Peace with Man is unsustainable without peace with God. On its own, peace with Man, the Second 'Greatest Commandment,' is the ultimate Liberal heresy. On its own, peace with God, the First 'Greatest Commandment,' is the ultimate Evangelical heresy."

Janys' perceptive commentary stopped Gary and Andy in full flight. Her creative summary was so symmetrically tight and succinct that neither could immediately critique it, though each felt uncomfortable with how she had stated it. Especially the idea of "heresy."

Janys just smiled. Andy loved her smile.

Peter chose that moment of silence to change the topic: the need for a name for their group. If people were going to write them after such leaflet distributions, they needed more than an address. They weren't a church, and they couldn't even identify with any church given churches' general standoffishness. So they needed a name.

Many ideas were bandied about, before they hit upon *Die Neue Richtung*—The New Direction.

Peter's intervention proved successful. It sufficiently diverted the discussion away from the argumentative ugliness between Gary and Andy. But it left both parties sullen and strangely quiet. As though they had each suffered some kind of diminution of prestige or status.

As the team meeting continued, Andy thought hard about the first time he had begun to wonder about missions, evangelism, God even. To be truthful, he couldn't remember a time when he hadn't. But he had usually buried such misgivings or covered them with various slogans and clichés. He thought of his Campus Crusade training in preparation for *Expo '67* in Montréal.

Key to the entire commitment was memorization of *The Four Spiritual Laws* booklet, which began with the memorable line, "God loves you, and has a wonderful plan for your life." Andy eagerly committed the entire booklet to memory. It provided something clean and sharp, without nuances, unlike his mind's labyrinthine ways. He'd already embraced C. S. Lewis for similar reasons: Lewis provided unambiguous argumentation for the existence of God, the truth of Christianity, and the certainty of faith. As long as he was reading such books, later Francis Schaeffer's writings, and others, he had a firm foundation of belief.

The problem was, his certainty tended to leak a bit around the edges, or sometimes quite bled away when the books' influences began to wear off, like Novocain after a visit to the dentist. It bothered him that it was so. So something as succinct and digestible as *The Four Spiritual Laws* was helpfully anchoring.

The downside was, it was hopelessly incomplete, and, therefore, terribly misleading. It made evangelism into a technique, jostling with myriad others. This sense of *technique*, leading to mass production, was only heightened when Andy spent three troubling weeks at *Sermons from Science*.

The crowds filled the auditorium at the front end of the building and watched a *Moody Science Film*, produced by Moody Bible Institute. The films were unusually creative, given their fundamentalist origin. Andy's favourite was *The City of the Bees*, which he had also seen in school a few times—minus its evangelistic pitch at film's end. That was the pattern of them all. To entertain and inform with facts from science and then connect the themes to Jesus. Sometimes the application presented as quite arbitrary.

Once the film was over, the viewers were directed

CHRYSALIS CRUCIBLE

to exit one way to leave the pavilion, another if they cared to talk more about the message just encountered. In that case, Andy and others laid in wait, like cattle ropers at a rodeo. The window of opportunity for the unsuspecting steer was about eight minutes. During that brief time, one had to wrestle the prey to the ground through use of *The Four Spiritual Laws*, and don't miss a word! Hog tie them next through a triplicate form filled out with all pertinent information needed for follow-up, and finally release them with a prayer of hope and challenge for the new Christian's future journey, first step of which was out into the bright sunlight of a Montréal summer day. And that was it! Salvation by the assembly line. Yet one more rescued, snatched from the burning fire to which otherwise destined. Then it was on to the next unwary game.

Andy saw many "saved" during his three weeks at the pavilion then promptly forgot all their names by summer's end. Whether it was a genuine new spiritual awakening or inoculation against further attempts, Andy would never know. But he began to suspect the latter. Yet it didn't matter to the organizers, a consortium of Evangelical churches in Québec. The higher the numbers of decisions recorded, so much greater was the rejoicing and reporting! For Andy, the much-vaunted thrill of "leading a soul to Christ" proved vacuous, like intercourse attempt without the ejaculation.

The team meeting droned on. He sat there seething. Most obviously at Gary. But it was far deeper. He continued with his thoughts while Jack shared about his and Fiona's situation. That took some time.

In grade thirteen, Andy had studied Heinrich Böll's collection of short stories, *Dr. Murkes Gesammeltes Schweigen*. Böll was an award-winning author who wrote ironic commentary on contemporary German society. In one story, *Die Neue Brücke*, "The New Bridge," a war amputee was assigned a "wonderful" new job of counting the pedestrian traffic over a new bridge the city had just built. The politicians and bureaucrats were immensely proud of not only the bridge but of simultaneously providing meaningful employment for a war amputee.

So the pedestrian counting began. And overall, the amputee was fairly dutiful—with a significant daily exception. At about the same time mornings and late afternoons, a certain shapely young female unfailingly walked across the bridge. Then all else blurred into inchoate shapes like background figures in a close-up photograph. He had eyes only for her figure progressing across the walkway. At those two times of the day, time itself stood still, as well all others might have. She alone was in sight, like an entrancing desert mirage, his gaze utterly captivated. The world might end catastrophically even, and he would be oblivious of it in deference to the daily beatific vision of *her*.

But not to worry, our amputee storyteller cheerfully assured, for he simply *inflated* the numbers utilizing the bridge during those glorious apparitions. Then the revealing line, *Je höher die Zahl, um so mehr strahlen sie!* "The greater the number, they just beam all the more!" The supreme twentieth century preoccupation, finally, is not with violence or even with sex. It is, in the end, all about *numbers and statistics*! Andy had felt it most of his life. To which the tired bureaucrat, ultimate master of Western humanity's destiny, vacuously cried, "Next!"

As in Montréal. So in Berlin. Not coins dropping into the indulgence coffers, but much the same thing: converts falling prey to the evangelistic Chamberlainesque enticements of "peace with God for our time." A questionable peace, however, no more substantial than Prime Minster Chamberlain's promised on the eve of the outbreak of World War Two. For it assured instantaneous "God," in eight minutes, like some kind of instant soup, so that one would be ever afterwards, potentially inoculated against "neighbour." And possibly for many, against mainstream evangelism and God. Andy was now caught up precisely in its machinery. He felt great unease, alienation, quite simply a phoney. All he was doing, he acknowledged with a shiver, was crying, "Next!" And that kind of spiritual prostitution was Christian mission?

He suddenly wondered whether Jeremiah's statement, "The heart is deceitful above all things, and desperately wicked, who can know it?" might not apply most to religious groups like Evangelicals, who seemed to believe that, on the contrary, they had the truth all sewn up. What if it was just the opposite?

Andy felt a new resolve, and he acted on it the moment it was his turn to share. He spoke calmly. "I will not be participating in the pamphlet distribution at the protest this Saturday. I do, however, plan to be there. I will be carrying a sign that reads, '*STOP DEN KRIEG! JESUS LIEBT ALLE FEINDE. WIR SOLLEN GLEICHFALLS.* STOP THE WAR! JESUS LOVES ALL ENEMIES. WE SHOULD, TOO.'

"I will also be informing B. B. that from this time on, I will have nothing more to do with her and a 'gospel' that appears the opposite of the Gospel according to Jesus. This means no more Bible studies at *Lichterfelde,* no more tract distribution with her or anyone, unless it contains the Gospel of reconciliation between God and Man, Man and Man, and Man and all Creation. Anything less, I am no longer part of. That is final."

Andy stood up. "My sharing is done. I'm leaving now for a long breath of fresh air—perhaps the first I'll have taken since I signed up for a mission I now understand as hell-bent *to do evangelism without the Gospel*. I would like to invite my *fiancée*, Janys, to join with me."

As he held out his hand, there were audible gasps. Janys looked caught out momentarily then got up and followed him out of the room.

71

"Andy!" Janys hissed, "Slow down! I can barely keep up!" It was true. He had taken the stairs two at a time.

He stopped at the bottom. "Sorry, Janys. I guess I just lost it. I had to get out of there or go *bananas*."

They exited into an overcast fall day.

"Game to go to the *Ku'damm*?" Andy asked.

"Sure," came the reply.

"Janys," he said along the way, "I'm sorry. This was not how it should have been. Almost like forcing you into having sex. It wasn't fair at all for me to blurt out to the team *as we're leaving* that we're getting married. I really wrecked it…"

In spite of himself, he sped up more.

"Andy, you're going too fast again," came Janys's patient response. "And apology accepted. It was about time, anyway. Let them have their fun processing it, and we'll still enjoy their responses later."

He stopped then and swept her up in a hug. "You're amazing, you really are! You should be blasting me." He paused to give her a warm, lingering kiss. "I love you, Janys. What is contained in those words entrances my entire being."

They held hands in silence until they got to the *Ku'damm*.

"Where do we go from here?" Janys asked.

"Let's head toward the *Gedächtniskirche*," Andy suggested.

"I meant I think we both kind of burned bridges at today's meeting. I don't know how we can go on with the team mission after what you said today. And I can't imagine G. E. allowing us to stay on the team once he finds out we're in love." She paused. "We're in love, Andy! I still feel like pinching myself every time I say it! The remotest thing from my mind was finding a mate when I signed up to come here. I was more thinking of maybe finding a bit of myself. What's that C. S. Lewis line about 'aiming for heaven' versus earth? You got thrown in, Andy, beyond my wildest dreams. I love you."

They stopped and embraced again.

The street was typically alive, even with the biting fall air. It felt so good to walk down the street not thinking of distributing tracts or trying to catch the unwary out with a religious questionnaire or feeling the need to "witness" all the time so that a plastic look of contentment was ever pasted on one's face. It felt good to be real for a change, like he was human again.

Andy and Janys did participate in the march that Saturday. It felt good. They carried the sign he said he would: *STOP DEN KRIEG! JESUS LIEBT ALLE FEINDE. WIR SOLLEN GLEICHFALLS.*

They encountered the other team members, minus Fiona, together with B. B. and several German young people handing out their "*STOP DEN KRIEG!*" tracts. Several were shocked at seeing them. Did they look like traitors?

Suddenly, Andy thundered in both languages, "If Christians will not stop the slaughter in Vietnam *right now* and refuse to kill *from now on*, then Christians have *no Good News to declare* here in West Berlin or anywhere else on the planet!" He smiled broadly as he held the sign high.

B. B. looked furious, but she said nothing. Andy had not phoned her. He thought this action was message enough.

72

The next day after church, Andy told Janys he was heading off to the *Ku'damm* to put some thoughts to paper so he would have a letter prepared for their team meeting the next day. G. E. would be present, if a little jet-lagged. "This letter ought to wake him up," Andy told Janys, smiling.

The meeting was set a little later the next afternoon to accommodate G. E. They would continue on through supper, a light *Abendbrot*, and into the evening.

When it came Andy's turn to share, he took a deep breath, looked at Janys, and said, "I have a long letter to read to everyone. May I ask that you all take a bathroom break first so that I can do this without interruption? That is my request. Please permit me to read it through without interruption. For that reason, I will not even look up until I'm done. I think you'll understand why as soon as I launch into it."

G. E. looked very uneasy at the prospect. He had been hearing intimations. But all agreed, and a few moments later reassembled in the War Room for the ordeal. Andy began:

October 30, 1972

Dear Berlin Team:

Throughout my life there has been a strong evangelistic impulse. But there is, I contend, a wider understanding of mission that has been overlooked by GO and my upbringing. In the Sheep and Goats passage in Matthew 25, what did Jesus mean by the mission mandate "to the least of these," if juxtaposed with the much more frequently quoted passage about the "Great Commission" in Matthew 28, "Go ye therefore, and teach all nations, baptizing them in the name of the Father, and of the Son, and of the Holy Ghost"? Yet even in the Matthew 28 passage, surely the "Teaching them to observe all things whatsoever I have commanded you" references back to Matthew 5—7, "whosoever heareth these sayings of mine, and doeth them," the central early church catechism that calls for a consistent and persistent justice done to the neighbour.

Then there is the Great Commission in John 20 that said Jesus was sending out his disciples as the Father had sent him out to (according to Luke 4) "preach the gospel to the poor... to heal the brokenhearted, to preach deliverance to the captives, and recovery of sight to the blind, to set at liberty them that are bruised, to preach the acceptable year of the Lord." That all sounds very socially oriented, though doubtless with a spiritual dimension, too. As does Mary's Song in Luke 1, which includes, "He has performed mighty deeds with his arm; he has scattered those who are proud in their inmost thoughts. He has brought down rulers from their thrones, and Presidents from their Snow White House, but has lifted up the humble. He has filled the hungry with good things but has sent the rich away empty."

There is also the understanding of the two "Greatest Commandments," not just one when Jesus was asked for only one, which sum up the entire sweep of Old Testament ethical revelation, according to Jesus. Yet whenever this double commandment is referred to in the rest of the New Testament, it is always only the Second mentioned. Which is all about the social, all about "politics." This is also what the great love chapter in 1 Corinthians 13 turns on, what the work of Christ calls us to model in Ephesians 5:1: "Live a life of love." So is there not a non-negotiable neighbour-love mission call coursing through the New Testament, impossible of denial once discerned? Did not the writer of 1 John ask how can we love God whom we have not seen if we do not love our brother whom we have seen? Is not the extreme case of "neighbour love" enemy love?

So doesn't the litmus test for authentic Christianity go something like this: "To love God means to love the neighbour, which means to love the enemy"? To whatever extent we fail to find God in the enemy, to that extent we fail to find God anywhere else on the continuum. God-talk without enemy-love is plain hypocrisy—"sounding brass and tinkling cymbal."

How that squares with a wider Christianity, that this century alone has endorsed participation in warfare occasioning over 100 million killings, is God's business to judge. It is our business, however, to repent. This is not to mention at least a millennium of Christian teaching that has blessed the State in the wholesale slaughter of religious and social heretics within, State enemies without.

Just because the Church has been massively unfaithful to the neighbour/enemy love mission mandate throughout most of its centuries is no reason to go on with business as usual. Surely! Someone must cry out. For there is another Gospel mandate besides winning converts to believe in Jesus. And it is no less valid and compelling as the call to invite people to personal faith in Christ. And it is Paul, himself, who tells us at every instance of power-relations in the New Testament to enduo *the Lord Jesus Christ: to "clothe oneself" with the Prince of Peace.*

I appeal to you, G. E., to all of you on our Berlin mission, to test out the truth of these claims against the teachings of Jesus in the Gospels, Paul's and other writers' instructions in the rest of the New Testament, and what has transpired, on the contrary, throughout church history.

Now consider the longstanding "Christian" doctrine of hell as "eternal conscious punishment" for the unbeliever. I know this has been a prime motivator for evangelism in general and for the first GO team in particular. But is it biblical after all? I now think not.

First, is not the doctrine of hell ominously close to the church's longstanding embrace of destroying the enemy, despite Jesus' explicit teaching to the contrary? Is God not contradicting his own teaching by relegating his enemies to eternal conscious torment?

Second, whom did Jesus threaten with hell? As I have read and re-read the Gospels, I come up with one consistent answer, no exceptions: the self-righteous religious believer is the only one ever warned about hell.

Third, isn't Jesus' definition of hell the downward spiral of an inward-turned self destined for self-destruction? Isn't hell, by definition, the incapacity of a person to see beyond him or herself to God or neighbour? Isn't hell ultimately man's choice not God's sentence? Isn't C. S. Lewis right in observing that in the end, there are only two kinds of humanity: those who say to God, "Thy will be done," and those to whom God says with profound sadness, "Thy will be done"?

I appeal to your sense of biblical commitment to see the truth in what I am saying. I challenge you not to just go along with Evangelical tradition, however hoary in its contrary reading of Scripture.

I came over here with a whole bunch of answers to questions I found people were not even asking. Then, through a variety of experiences, discussions, and the sheer weight of living, I found that my *answers didn't remotely relate to* my *real questions! And the questions I was asking were not giving way to ready answers the way I was raised.*

I find it impossible now to remain one-sided about mission. As you know, we have been doing evangelism. But while doing it, we have encountered all kinds of basic human needs. And we started meeting them as best we could. Until you, G. E. reminded us we were here to do evangelism not social work! So we've been limited to telling *people about Jesus but not* showing *them by our actions what Jesus means. That's evangelism without the Gospel. The irony is immense. Evangelical practice ubiquitous.*

I also met several people who challenged me about what "mission" means. I have been changed as a result. I still believe in telling people about Jesus. But I'm much more interested in the showing than I used to be. Or at least it has grown on me, this idea that there are two fundamental Christian callings, both related to the Two Great Commandments according to Jesus. One is to draw people into a love of God that is liberating, not binding. The other is to encourage Christians to love the neighbour and the enemy like they love God. They're inextricably interconnected.

On the second one, Christians throughout history have not just allowed, they have dictated and endorsed massive exceptions. The love of enemies, despite Jesus' specific test case use of this to illustrate neighbour love, has been generally inverted to mean that any state may do whatever is needed to destroy its domestic and international enemies. For overriding love of neighbour and enemy, and demonstrably, therefore, love of God, is an allegiance to and idolatry of the State that seemingly knows no bounds. This is so supremely in America, land of "In God We Trust"! The lady doth protest too much, methinks. *Whether that be the Statue of Liberty or "Aunt" Sam, Americans are overwhelming idolaters. Life's extreme ironies.*

This is certainly the case with C. S. Lewis (British I know) and Billy Graham, the two most representative Evangelicals of the 20th century. Likewise, the vast majority of Christians of every stripe in Germany supported the Nazis both passively by doing nothing to resist them and actively by supporting the huge war effort wherein between 35-60 million, half of them civilians, died worldwide by war's end. At the same time, in the pre-War and War years, multiplied thousands were also guillotined and sent to places like Dachau.

Then there was the Holocaust, which saw at least six million Jews slaughtered, not to mention an estimated equal number of undesirables liquidated through no crime except being a despised minority. And somehow that was all justified because the "State" is ordained by God? If the State in Nazi Germany wasn't the Beast of the Book of Revelation, I don't know what was. I wonder the same about contemporary America and its Pax Americana *worldwide, especially right now in Vietnam.*

Lest we think Western Christendom is otherwise exempt, what the Allies alone did during the last War is utterly bone-chilling: routine bombing of residential areas in over forty cities throughout Germany with unnumbered civilian casualties; Dresden, overflowing with refugees, almost entirely levelled; incendiary bombings of more than sixty Japanese cities, again with almost 100 percent civilian deaths. In one night of terror alone that would make Robespierre of the French Revolution's "Reign of Terror" look like a pious Sunday School teacher or the Catholic killers of thousands of Huguenots on St. Bartholomew's Day in 17th-century France feel utterly outdone. Or even make Hitler feel jealous at the massive killing efficiency of the Allies, American bombers slaughtered 100,000 innocents in Tokyo a night of unmitigated terror, burning the whole mass of them: men, women, children, babies—to death! Then they dropped two atomic bombs a few months later. And 120,000 more men, women, and children were instantly incinerated. Not to mention the thousands more who died slow, agonizing deaths subsequently, the multiplied thousands maimed for life, the horrendous ecological destruction...

What amazes me, now that I really let my mind dwell on it, is how utterly devoid of guilt the West, including the Christian West, is about all this incalculable obscenity of terror. Did any of us ever catch a hint in school or church that this kind of mass murder was wrong? Did you even know what the Allies did in Germany? Do you think most Western Caucasian Christians know about more than the atomic bombs in Japan? (Which are always justified, by the way). The State, no less the Western democratic state supported fully by virtually all Evangelical Christians, in every instance is a monstrous idol spewing doublespeak, declaring wrong right, fundamentally inverting the Gospel call to love of enemies. It has to be the ultimate fallen power, given its massive destructive impact upon lives for whom Christ died. Its pouring out of death this century alone is well past 100 million.

So for centuries the Christian West has been front

row in helping produce the major mass murderers of the twentieth century: Stalin, Hitler, Mussolini, Churchill, Roosevelt, Truman, Eisenhower, McKenzie King, Nixon, etc., etc., etc. Where will it end, this succession of mass killers whom we good citizens, most Christians, wildly cheer on? But don't dare even to whisper this contrary perception around. One would be an irreligious traitor deserving of the same fate! Jim Billings on the Spain team intimated such desert in a letter I received recently, written in response to my own expression of consternation.

I guess it comes down to this: When the West has participated equally in upwards of 100 million victims slaughtered so far in international conflict this century, our ethical sensors, even if attuned, must simply shut down from (im)moral overload. We are forced to resist or justify the mass murders. Evangelicals have always chosen the latter. We either choose to opt out of the kind of society that would sanction this kind of unconscionable grand scale murder or we justify it by our very refusal to even think about it—except on Remembrance Day each year, when we glorify it. And then there are the endless death hucksters in books and movies who actually soothe everyone's sensibilities so that we may step with clean consciences over the ubiquitous corpses littering the entire Western scapegoating cultural landscape in order that we may get on with living. "In State Violence We Trust" has always been most Christians' ultimate creed—at least since the Middle Ages. A creed more final than allegiance to the true and living God.

Being in the West is like growing up in a Mafia family of murderers who oppose killing of their own kind, until they are reminded that others might feel similar opposition to their rampant carnages.

As I understand it, just try living in Ireland or the Middle East. Both sides to the conflicts excoriate violence—then commit it cold-bloodedly in the name of retaliatory vengeance. And the rest of the West condemns it, constantly calling the killers to peace. But guess what! There are multiplied millions of skeletons rattling in our own closets, belying such unbelievable hypocrisy.

And yet, incredibly, no one gets it! No one will blink in this centuries-long game of deadly chicken and say: I guess, across the board, the real enemy is State violence itself!

So where does this leave me? Not a little disillusioned with Christianity, mission, evangelism, and Western values, so informed by Christendom for two millennia. The massive unfaithfulness to Jesus' delineation of Two Great Commandments, not least of which as subcategory is, "Love Your Enemies," and the cold-blooded inability of most of the Christian and secular West to "get it," not least of whom are Evangelicals, leaves me not a little jaded.

But right now, I don't quite know where to go with that. I can't just opt out of the world—like the Apostle Paul would say. I want to shout at the top of my lungs, "But the Emperor has no clothes!" Yet the theological and philosophical dupes and sycophants have been strutting otherwise for nearly 2,000 weary years. How can one (or a few) lonely voice drown out that long history of murderous cacophony?

I have kept my mouth shut for as long as possible. But it finally showed. I had quite a sharp disagreement with you, Gary, recently. If you only knew how deeply I'm offended by your cheap-grace rapacious, murderous Evangelicalism. It terrifies me. What terrifies me even more is, until not long ago, I bought into all that, too.

In sum, if I had one appeal to make to Evangelicals, to Christians of all stripes, it would be: be evangelical! *Really do take seriously, for once in two millennia, Jesus and the Bible!*

Thanks for hearing me out.

Andy

To Andy's amazement, everyone sat through the entire letter, right through to the bitter end!

G. E. was the first to break the lingering silence that followed. "Son, you are nothing, if not articulate, I'll grant you that. What you just presented should be read in a seminary ethics class. We're just a lowly missions agency trying to get on with being faithful to… Well, that's the problem," G. E. shook his head. "You deny what we are doing is the Gospel. I'm honestly at a loss." He looked it, hardly joyful or triumphant as in his letters. He appeared, rather, haggard and travel-weary, but much more deeply troubled. Andy saw it in his eyes.

Andy stood up. "Mr. Moore, I'm going to make it really easy for you." He walked over to Janys, took her hand to get her out of her chair. In front of them all, he placed a warm, tender, lingering kiss onto her lips.

Jack hooted. "That kiss is about as long as the sermon we just had to sit through—but a heck of a lot more interesting!"

There were a few titters.

"Mr. Moore," Andy said, finally breaking away from Janys, "we have fallen in love and wish to get married. It is time for us to go home."

G. E.'s jaw, Andy noticed, had dropped to the floor.

"S*trange world we live in*," Andy began in his

diary entry that night.

I've been feeling not a little overwhelmed by my changing mind these past weeks and months. It certainly is impacting how I think of mission. Where once I thought the most important issue for me was to defend the Bible at all costs, I am now learning that the Bible is the chief interpreter of what is instead the most important: the Christ event itself. And if Jesus is the supreme way, the Bible does not have to be so rigidly defended as in the past.

Further, I've been reading, thanks to Janys's brother, that the "satisfaction theory" of the atonement originated against the backdrop of a feudal society where the lord of the manor could demand "satisfaction" from the serf who offended against him by laying on a beating or any other punishment, up to death. (How Ted Thane found a copy of C. F. D. Moule's article entitled "Punishment and Retribution" in a Swedish theological journal, I do not know. It's fascinating, though. I must read more by Moule. I think Hans Beutler mentioned him once, too.) When I read this in conjunction with some of Girard's insights, I was blown away. Though I still do not understand how to relate this all to the Hebrew sacrificial system. Whatever else, Jesus cries out, "I desire mercy, not sacrifice," challenge of the later prophets to what all sacrifice points.

And this theory of the meaning of the event of Christ—"why God became man," as Saint Anselm put it—has dominated the Christian West ever since. For the satisfaction demanded by Anselm's "god" was blood. It is not surprising then that the satisfaction theory, which grew out of feudalistic endorsement of ultimate violence, should, now with God's stamp of approval, all the more underwrite an entire State culture of violence for centuries, right up to the modern era. No wonder the history of the West, relative to the State, so thoroughly permeated by the Church's blood satisfaction view of the Christ event, should be so horribly violent!

Surely there is no parallel irony so massive in human history than Jesus Christ, the Prince of Peace, being made over so completely into Mars, the State god of war! And by the Church no less, ever since Emperor Constantine embraced it! That had to be the ultimate Western re-enactment of the Judas kiss—and it has persisted ever since! So my question is: Can one be a State functionary at any level and not thereby participate in the apparatus of death, so long as the State promulgates war and/or practises capital punishment? More ominously, can one even be a State citizen, pay taxes, and not thereby contribute to the State culture of death? How does one escape it? How do Tibetan monks not step on their ancestors by virtue of just walking the earth?

So what do I do with all that? That's the unbearable question. It simply will not be ignored any longer, nor go away. THE EMPEROR HAS NO CLOTHES! And few are listening—or wish to hear! Hardly any are saying it. "Because straight is the gate, and narrow is the way, which leadeth unto life, and few there be that find it." So we have on the one hand religion unto death, on the other Jesus' Way unto life. And n'er the twain shall meet. O wretched man that I am. But for different reasons, now...

It is 11:45 p.m.

Goodnight.

73

G. E. spent most of the next morning with Jack and Fiona. It was obviously very intense. They broke just before noon in time to make a few phone calls in the privacy of the War Room.

Right after lunch, at G. E.'s request, Andy and Janys sat down with him to discuss their future. G. E. still looked drawn and worn. He also looked fearful. Had Andy said "Boo!" how might he have reacted?

There was no discussion at all of Andy's paper from the day before. G. E. accepted as *fait accompli* that they were leaving as soon as they could arrange flights home. Andy felt sorry for the resignation on G. E.'s face.

After their brief meeting, during which G. E. had looked at his watch several times, he said he needed some fresh air. Andy and Janys headed towards the *Ku'damm* shortly afterwards.

"Isn't that G. E. just ahead?," Janys suddenly said.

"I wonder where he's headed at such a pace," Andy confirmed.

G. E. crossed *Bregenzerstraße,* and headed across *Olivaer Platz* toward the *Ku'damm*. Andy and Janys followed at a respectful distance. G. E. seemed intent upon his course, and never looked behind.

The *Ku'damm* was teeming as usual. There was such a vibrancy to the street at almost any hour. Things were always happening there, even if just at the corner of one's perception. One might never quite catch it, like trying to jump onto one's shadow or snatch a moonbeam or spot a leprechaun.

G. E. proceeded across the street at a controlled

corner. The two missed the light, waited impatiently, fearing they'd lost him. Andy really wanted to follow. But just as it changed, they saw him headed down the street right ahead. They followed until G. E. disappeared suddenly. One moment, they had seen him moving on ahead at a slower pace, the next, he wasn't there. Gone. Into thin air. They perplexed as they surveyed a 360 degree radius of sight.

There was an underground bathroom.

Andy told Janys to wait while he descended. As his eyes adjusted to the dim lighting, he saw three men at the urinals. They all eyed him with furtive glances. None was G. E. But there was one stall with the door closed. Andy walked past it and glanced down. He recognized G. E.'s distinctly brown suede Hush Puppies. Most troubling, however, was the fact that there were not two shoes in the stall but four. Both sets were filled with upright legs. There were shuffling motions...

Andy recoiled instinctively and turned to head upstairs. He promptly collided with another guy who looked like he was about to burst! Andy muttered an apology and bounded up the stairs, two at a time, without another look back.

"Was he down there?" Janys asked.

Andy grabbed her hand and said, "Let's go!" Then a pause, "Yes, he was down there. Something was going on I don't have any inkling of – but got the idea soon as I looked."

Andy suddenly gulped for fresh air, waves of nausea engulfing him. Had he not just seen with his very eyes and heard the most revolting thing he could possibly imagine? He and Janys started heading along the street in the same direction from which they had come, Andy filling her in.

Was this what G. E. had been doing on all his private walks when he went to other cities? Was this also the "seed" G. E. had been interested in scattering around Berlin and other evangelistic sites? Andy shuddered in complete revulsion.

B. B. needed the Gospel big time. G. E. however, his one-time hero, mentor, conscience, motivator and judge… He needed so much more… Where to even begin?

They arrived back at the girls' apartment and were able to book flights together on Friday, November 3, only a few days away.

They went out for a walk afterwards, holding hands the entire way. There were no more secrets. They missed G. E.'s return to the girls' apartment later that afternoon.

Janys went back inside, but Andy decided to walk around the block, as it turned out, a few times.

What was he to do? Talk to G. E.? He could begin straightforwardly, "I observe, brother, that you have been engaging in repeated acts of sodomy with… unknown lovers." How did G. E. meet the man? What did they do together, if anything, outside the bathroom stalls? Why wouldn't they "do it" in privacy somewhere? Andy knew the obvious answer for G. E.

"Do you mind if I bring my homosexual lover to the team meeting?" Andy could imagine G. E. asking nonchalantly. Right away, all the girls would ask, "What does he look like? Is he handsome? Is he friendly? When did you meet? Do you think it might lead to a permanent relationship: wife and kids back home, lover or lovers here, perhaps in every port? How exciting!"

Andy knew the chemistry at time of conception was utterly gratuitous. The creature created male or female then was only slightly nuanced differentiation into male or female streams. If so, why the huge fuss years later?

"Because the Apostle Paul condemns it in the most uncompromising of terms!" He'd once read Anita Bryant, famous singer and born again homophobe activist, declare such. It was perhaps the purest of all sins, she continued, since it threatened to tear apart the fabric of America by destroying America's building block, the family. Problem was, her own "building block" fell apart in the course of her activism, she whose own sex appeal was not unnoticed in Miss Oklahoma and Miss America pageants, and on TV. But that didn't seem to matter. She was on a mission for God, and she had to speak out—even if to the destruction of her own marriage and family.

So were G. E.'s other lovers married and perhaps not free to bring him home? Had G. E. been cruising the gay bars while in West Berlin, and wherever else his globetrotting meanderings took him? Had he picked up his contacts that way? Had he shared his activities with anyone else? How did he justify to others, to himself, such activity? Did he even try to or think about it? Was he just addicted? How did all this square with his stern reining in of Andy? Suddenly, Andy remembered his hands. G. E. loved holding Andy's hands! Andy's mind swept over all those vibrant prayers with G. E.'s hands holding his. Andy wiped them involuntarily with a shudder. He remembered a counselling session with Ken Kincaide in a car in the GO parking lot on a cold night, and shuddered again.

His mind reeled out of control. Not for the first time. He whose yen was ever to put into ordered understanding a universe that made sense with God central in it, seemed ever destined to lurch madly instead at the barest inkling of God's presence in a world endlessly tilting sideways to all his perceptions and explanations. There was little congruity between lived experience and theory. At least it had begun to disintegrate, this sense of proportionality, since he had first gone to university. He'd been forewarned! His cousin's grandpa had told him bluntly it would destroy his faith. Andy couldn't help but think it wasn't university that had challenged him in his faith; it was life itself! Just the sheer effort of living had repeatedly made him wonder at God's place in it all at just about every turn. Didn't Grandpa Martin sense that kind of existential angst, too? The sheer hard realities of life repeatedly squeezed God into the cracks! Or did it make one see an ever-present God differently? Was he the only one "listening" to his life?

Now this, G. E., caught in a behaviour that seemed a direct denial of faith. Yet there he was, witnessing to faith. Was it all a complete sham? Or did G. E. still believe but struggle?

"G. E. I'd like to talk to you tomorrow morning for a while," were Andy's opening words as they got up from supper at the girls' apartment. G. E. agreed they could talk after lunch instead.

They sat on one of the benches down the street from their apartment at the little park on *Olivaer Platz*. Andy noticed a plane coming in for a landing at the airport and marvelled again at the time of the *Luftbrücke* crisis when all supplies had to be airlifted to West Berlin. What a massive undertaking by the Americans and Allies! In 1963, on West Berlin soil, the year of his assassination, President Kennedy had spoken likely his only words in German, *"Ich bin ein Berliner!"* and was forever loved for it. Though the joke was, he really said he was a "jelly-filled doughnut." *Berliner* can mean doughnut, though not necessarily jelly-filled. He should have said, "*Ich bin ein Courmacher!*" I'm a philanderer. Andy wondered idly who were the willing German *Mädchen* his Secret Service rounded up for him in West Berlin as the President called out eagerly, "Next!" He might better have made his confession to a Catholic priest…

It was a crisp autumn day. Leaves had changed hues, but not into so vibrant colours as the spectacular red Maples back home. Still, autumn was a welcome season in Andy's life. It spoke of change and slowing down, which were good things at times.

As they chatted for a few moments, Andy wondered if G. E. had an inkling of what he hoped to talk to him about. Almost certainly not or G. E. would likely be showing much more guard.

Andy finally decided to launch into it. "G. E., Janys and I followed you on a whim yesterday down the *Ku'damm*."

For a brief moment, G. E. was uncomprehending. Then Andy saw a flash of awareness flicker across G. E.'s face. He bristled.

"I'll confess," Andy continued, "to being rather overwhelmed with what I discovered. What do I do? As you might guess, I have been all over the map in my mind for an answer."

Andy paused. G. E. said nothing.

"In the end, the only sure thing I decided to do was talk to you. I'm doing it. What do you suggest, G. E.?" Memories of long sessions in G. E.'s office flooded Andy's mind. He was churning inside, but his voice sounded unhurried, even flat.

G. E. paused for a long time. Then, "I figured this day would come sooner or later…"

"Let me ask," Andy said, "how long have you been

doing homosexual acts?" Andy was surprised his tone was so evenly unemotional.

G. E. hesitated but replied soon enough. "I guess for some time. I resisted it at first. But, well, you must know what it's like, Andy. Can you keep from looking every time you pass by the magazines on a street corner?"

Andy acknowledged there had been more than just a few furtive glances. Andy found the contemplation of the subject matter highly disgusting, disturbing, alien, and just downright uninteresting. His libido, he knew, was not nearly so aggressive as G. E.'s. He thought back to the apartment scene with Petra. Two gorgeous fulsome breasts hovering above him, a body that oozed sexuality, and he refused to bite—literally and metaphorically. Why? Why the difference between him and G. E.? He had once actually felt Lorraine's bare breast. But that had determined him more than ever to wait until "Christmas Day." He had gone to bed with a half-naked Janys. Was it different here? What could G. E. legitimately await in a Christian community opposed to homosexual love? Especially when he had a wife and family!

"G. E. what would your wife and kids think, not to mention people impacted by this ministry around the globe?" Andy asked. "Do you know of the book, *The Returns of Love* by Alex Davidson? I read that in my fourth year of university. Back then, it was just theoretical. But it was an eye-opener about how a guy could be a committed Christian and a struggling homosexual. That's what it's all about, in fact, coming to terms with his homosexual orientation while a committed Christian. That isn't his real name, by the way. He couldn't be so bold in the wider Christian community. You'd find it helpful, G. E., I'm sure. It was news to me that people could even have struggles like that. Shows how protected my world has been. I don't know what to call you in this case though, given you have a family."

"'Bisexual' is the term, Andy." G. E.'s voice was lead.

Andy barely heard. He was too amazed at his own non-judgemental attitude toward G. E. A year ago, would he have discussed such a revelation so calmly? Not on your life! Had he become that dreaded word, "Liberal"?

"I guess you'll have to reveal this to your wife and to your community somehow. I suspect it will be devastating for everyone concerned." He said it without an accusatory tinge, thinking of Dan.

Andy realized he felt great pity for G. E. at that moment. Inside, he wondered whether all sexual sins related to the issue of freedom. What permitted us to live uncluttered, free lives? Love of God and neighbour. Simple. Profound. Impossible. All of the above. But also consistent with a Creator who would have us live out lives designed to make us most fully human. Maybe this gets us away from just religious notions of sin and, well, life itself. But just maybe it made sense to obey God not out of religiosity but for freedom to most demonstrably erupt in our lives.

Andy stood up, causing a flock of pigeons to leap up around him. Andy felt a rush of freedom.

"Are you going to tell anyone?" G. E. asked, his voice barely audible.

"No. That's your business, G. E. Between you and God, I think—and your family and community. Janys knows of course, but she will say nothing."

G. E. nodded then got up and walked off in the vague direction of the girls' apartment. Andy sat down again on the bench, pondering, wondering. Did he even catch himself praying?

November 1, 1972

Dear Professor Norton:

The big news is, though I think you know, Janys Thane and I are getting married! I want to shout it from the rooftops. This is Good News like nothing else since I came over here. Though our parents don't know yet, nor Lorraine…

Now I'd like to add, "And they lived happily ever after," but I cannot. You, Dr. Norton, however, know about the next twenty-five years…

What was Macbeth's soliloquy?

*Tomorrow, and tomorrow, and tomorrow,
Creeps in this petty pace from day to day
To the last syllable of recorded time,
And all our yesterdays have lighted fools
The way to dusty death. Out, out, brief candle!
Life's but a walking shadow, a poor player
That struts and frets his hour upon the stage
And then is heard no more: it is a tale
Told by an idiot, full of sound and fury,
Signifying nothing.*

How does the Wisdom of Solomon *put it? "Our life shall pass away as the trace of a cloud, and come to nought as the mist that is driven away with the beams of the sun. For our time is as a shadow that passeth away and after our end there is no returning."*

Maybe before it passes away you'll write a book to commemorate a thing or two? How does it go in Hamlet? "The play's the thing/Wherein I'll catch the conscience of the King," right? Maybe "catch the conscience" of an Evangelical or two? Or of a good "secular humanist." Hold "the mirror up to nature"? You might consider it Herr Professor... *"The lady doth protest too much, methinks," Queen Gertrude's own words catching her in the very act, to which Nathan need only reply, "Thou art the man!"*

Last night I had a dream:
Jack and Fiona get married and produce a lot of kids. They renew relationships with her firstborn, and live a life of joy centred around their first loves: teaching kids, big trucks, fast bikes, and cars.

Todd Braxman faces the music of his aggression toward Fiona. But he is offered and accepts the chance to make things right. He delivers a heartfelt apology for his terrifying behaviour. In ways that only Fiona knows, this is satisfying to her. He follows through with all the amends-making he promised. Jack and he discover they have a mutual interest in motors and kids. "Uncle Todd" hangs around their place a lot, a kind of godfather to the kids. He eventually marries well and produces a bevy of his own, with all kinds of familial exchanges. All the boys become great boxers, and the girls perform masterfully in martial arts. Some of the kids eventually intermarry.

Gary and Sharon work on their marriage that suffered in the crucible of GO West Berlin. It emerges stronger for the experience. Gary pursues his interest in theology and philosophy, becoming a professor, which suits him perfectly. She becomes an interior decorator of national repute. Whenever I visit, she puts on a Rouladen mit Rotkohl *meal, topping it off with* Schwarzwälderkirschtorte. *They have lots of kids who work on modifying their dad's blunter edges, especially in theology. He discovers after all that "Hell Madame, is to love no longer" (Georges Bernanos), and consequently becomes the very picture of* agape *love.*

Peter and Jean go on to have their totally healthy son. Peter discovers an "inner child" and becomes known as the "life of the party." So much so that at times Jean pleads with him to take all the wild partying a little slower. But she loves it and him, too. They find that, after all, they hold just about everything in common, except Peter always retains an aversion to blaring rock at 3:00 a. m., a recurring problem with their hip teenaged son.

G. E. returns home and confesses tearfully to his wife, his kids, his church, and his worldwide constituency that he has sinned before God and Man and is no longer worthy to be called husband or father or church leader. But he is embraced at every point of brokenness, and though it is long, the day comes when he is fully restored to fellowship with all he has broken. This includes each of his sexual partners, whom he tracks down one-by-one and apologizes to, consequently receiving forgiveness and reconciliation. This forgiveness is extended to all of their families as well. The healing is an enormous undertaking, but the ripples eventually reach the most distant shores.

Dan Moore reconciles with his dad big time. When it comes down to it, Dan works hard at forgiving his dad and God. For his part, G. E. demonstrates true repentance toward Dan. Not least around his profligate bisexuality. Dan goes back to school and becomes world renowned (now Dr. Daniel Moore) for breaking new ground philosophically and theologically. He reinterprets Friedrich Nietzsche, meets Jörg Salaquarda along the way, and wins him back to faith when he demonstrates that Nietzsche's venom toward Christianity was just a heart cry for love. That revolutionizes Nietzschean studies, more so Salaquarda's life. He, in turn, reconciles with Karl Barth post mortem *and writes the definitive study on his life and times.*

During G. E.'s rehabilitation, George Myers learns to have a mind of his own and actually supplies creative independent leadership to GO. He still never publishes my apologetics paper (small loss), but he moves GO so dramatically toward love of neighbour and enemy the organization breaks initially with Evangelicalism so contrary, joining forces with Dorothy Day's Catholic Worker Movement and Jim Wallis' incipient Post-American community. When he dresses up as Amos in the future, which he continues to do at their huge Congresses, he no longer chortles about the horrors to be visited on earth's teeming billions, praising God for the imminent rescue of them the believing—and oh, so self-righteous—remnant; rather thunders from the pulpit, "But let judgment run down as water, and righteousness as a mighty stream," meaning let the whole cosmos be awash in God's healing river of justice and mercy!

Ken Kincaide discovers the joy of being wrong in further going on with his study of the Bible. He discovers nuance and learns to forgive himself, his wife, his kids, and God. Above all, he forgives his dad who drove him in the first place by reaction to such overweening heights of perfection. He discovers the only way we are to be "perfect" is in love of God and neighbour. And that love is the only entity on the planet that you give to get. Though even there, it doesn't work. You must give without thinking of the getting or you're not giving love in the first place anyway!

CHRYSALIS CRUCIBLE 727

Ken finally breaks with Bill Gothard on all this, Gothard, who continues to find proof texts in the Bible to back all his pet ideas about life, sex, religion, etc., etc., etc., ad nauseum. Trouble is, the biblical jigsaw puzzle he continues to put together doesn't come close to matching the picture on the box. He goes on with the charade anyway, like the Emperor's courtiers. There is little hope, sadly, for Gothard. He eventually takes all his marbles, as have so many Evangelical and other Christian leaders, and starts up a new game somewhere else. There are always willing dupes. Ken eventually heads up a charitable society like World Vision devoid of any exploiting the predicament of the poor, and uses his not inconsiderable skills to spread peace and love worldwide.

Susan Norton falls for a free-spirited guy who has little use for religion, as is the case for Susan. But in the loss of their first child to stillbirth she, then he, rediscovers the comfort of a transcendent Father and makes her peace. She goes on to head a society that works with moms recovering from trauma around all kinds of pregnancy and birthing issues, including offering alternatives to thousands of pregnant moms whose only hope is the terminal violence of abortion. They also care for parents in the crucial zero to five years, helping them toward pro-social formation and peaceful living.

Joanne and Hans have an idyllic marriage, especially after Joanne helps Hans see there is more to life than the intellectual. It helps that he takes up a practice for several years amongst the poor of an inner city ghetto in India. He makes little money but great strides toward becoming human. He also writes, publishing the definitive theological work on "just peacemaking" wanted for all God's creatures the world over, no exceptions, Martin Luther King Jr.'s dream furthered and expanded.

Uncle Joe gets it at last about the brethrenism he has been steeped in all his years. As does Dad. They reconcile between themselves first, since Dad never forgave Uncle Joe for being a non-combatant during World War Two. But they also grasp at last just how high the walls of denominationalism are in brethrenism, that most self-proclaimed non-denominational and non-traditionalist of all restorationist church denominations and traditions.

Aunt Sarah never beats her breast cancer but gets over a far worse malignancy, that of cluck-cluck legalism around every private and personal aspect of Christian existence. She discovers that, like the State, pious Christian moralism has no business in the bedrooms of the congregants, the "missionary position" notwithstanding. Before she succumbs to cancer, she throws off all restraint and takes up jazz dancing of the kind God's good Creation jives to, and dies with a smile on her face on the dance floor with Uncle Joe, capering to the wildest Scott Joplin early jazz piece written. Uncle Joe is devastated, but at her funeral he celebrates that final fling and smile that portends pure Kingdom Come!

Beatrice Boswell, B. B., learns that Christianity is all about grace on the one hand and justice to the neighbour on the other. With her passion and discipline, she helps lead the Christian movement worldwide in a newly discovered campaign of great energy to bring justice to "the least of these." She becomes a household name for Christian compassion and mercy.

Petra Delitz learns to redirect her wonderful sexuality into appropriate channels (pun), such that she becomes moderator of a top-rated American TV talk show that addresses all kinds of contemporary issues. She speaks fluent American after marrying a soldier and moving to the U. S. But he quits the Army upon seeing the utter discontinuity between faith and slaughter, her input no small factor. She never preaches the Gospel with words but rather demonstrates its riveting power wherever she goes. She bares her boobs only to her husband, who takes no small delight in them!

And Lorraine? Her dad is found guilty of the horror of parental love gone tragically, horribly askew. And her dad consequently sets out on a long healing journey, no small cause of which is her utter persistence and insistence that he own then transcend his perversions. One day, she finally hugs him and says, "Dad, I love you." And though he is ever after vigilant, she carefully wary, the reconciliation and his new chastity hold.

And all the other trainees at the Centre, wider brethrenism and Evangelicalism, all Christendom? The majority gets it for the first time in 2,000 years (!!!) about the inviolability of the tight bond between love of God and love of neighbour/enemy; between justification by faith and demonstration by deeds of charity, ever two sides of the same coin. They consequently beat all their swords into ploughshares and witness to the State to do the same, since there is only one ethic for the cosmos, which, when a second is claimed, smuggles violence and brokenness through the back door of "just war"— an utter abomination. And the Church universal for once becomes in real time *what the universe is destined to be* beyond time: *a place where they will cease their violence utterly. Like the text in Isaiah: "They shall not hurt nor destroy in all my holy mountain: for the earth shall be full of the knowledge of the LORD, as the waters cover the sea."*

This is the cosmic destiny for which every fibre in our being yearns. God pulls off a most amazing thing: He sets a force in motion that retroactively flushes the entire sweep of cosmic history clean. And all humanity so washed streams into the New City, which is the Old Eden, which is Kingdom Come.

I'm finally that little precocious boy, Lionel Wallace, in H.G. Wells' short story, "The Door in the Wall." I'm introduced to all this wonder of retroactive, pro-active universal peacemaking, and my happiness is off the charts. Now I'm looking at my life, in all its wondrous twists and turns, in a living storybook that contains all my realities. I, like young Lionel, turn each page avidly until I am hovering outside our apartment, waiting to bid farewell to G. E. whom Jack is driving to the airport.

I cry out, not like those tired whores in Amsterdam, but like Lionel, with exuberant anticipation, "And next?" And again, "Next?" Then I suddenly remember. There is no "next" without the daily choice to remain in the Garden. Lionel forced the "next," and was haunted the rest of his life by expulsion from the only true joy of his existence, plummeting to his death finally in a mistaken quest to re-enter the idyllic garden. I pull back just in time—and eternity.

Lionel was looking ever in the wrong place. The entry is here and now, is it not, Professor Norton? And the door is ever visible when needed for those with eyes to see. Isn't it, Professor?

Isn't it?

Andy

74

The team chose to go bowling together the last night Andy and Janys were in West Berlin. G. E. had left the day before. His tail was distinctly between his legs. In spite of himself, Andy could not help think his tail wouldn't have been there in the first place had something else between his legs been held in check. If the tongue, as Saint Paul wrote, is a "little member" yet an "unruly evil, full of deadly poison," so must it be likewise with that little "third leg" unbridled.

The bowling was great fun. As it turned out, Jack and Andy emerged with the highest collective scores. The "Dynamic Duo," the "Jack and Andy Show" for the last time, it was pointed out. That night, whatever else was happening on the planet, it was somehow good to be associated with Gospel Outreach in West Berlin.

Later at the girls' apartment, the party was as festive as it could be considering the circumstances. Andy and Janys had declined having over any of their German contacts since. They had spent most of the last couple of days visiting them personally or on the phone.

During the evening, Andy found himself turning with keen anticipation to seeing his mom and dad again, his sister, other friends he'd been missing this last while.

Near the end of the farewell, all were sitting in the War Room sipping hot chocolate, coffee or tea and reminiscing. Fiona had perked up somewhat. She and Jack were to go home next, the following week, in fact. Quite possibly, Peter and Jean would leave after that. The future of GO Team Berlin looked bleak. But no one discussed that that night.

"Andy, what are your regrets?" Peter asked.

Andy answered after some reflection. "I have no real regrets about the past year and a half with GO. Well, I guess I do, but it would do no good mourning losses anyway…"

"What about you, Janys?" Jean asked.

Janys shook her head and smiled. "I have so much to sort out about faith and life. I wish I'd done more. Now, however, Andy and I will thankfully be working on it together." She looked at him evenly then said, "I think we're in for a ride." She smiled. The universe stood still.

"You guys should write a book!" Jack said.

"What was your most memorable experience, Andy?" Gary asked.

"I can think of a lot," Andy replied immediately. "But likely it was an incident with Petra Delitz that I'll tell you all about sometime—maybe in our book." He was pleased at his untroubled equanimity.

Gary turned to Janys. "And you?"

Janys answered immediately as well. "A howling snowstorm." She gave no further details when prodded except, "Maybe in our book."

Sharon raised the evening's stopper question: "Andy, what have you most learned about God since coming to West Berlin?"

Andy paused long enough that everyone *had* to comment that Sharon had done what few others in history had achieved: render Andrew Joseph Norton momentarily speechless. He remained silent until the kidding had died down.

Then he said quietly, "Jesus loves me this I know, for the Bible tells me so."

About the Author

Wayne Northey is Co-director of Man-to-Man/Woman-to-Woman Restorative Christian Ministries (M2/W2) in Abbotsford, British Columbia, Canada. He has been a keen promoter of restorative justice since 1974. Wayne has written widely on these and many other topics. His work has been published in numerous magazines, journals, and books, including *The Catholic New Times, Contemporary Justice Review,* and *Stricken by God?* Wayne and his wife Esther live in Langley, BC.